LONG DISTANCE

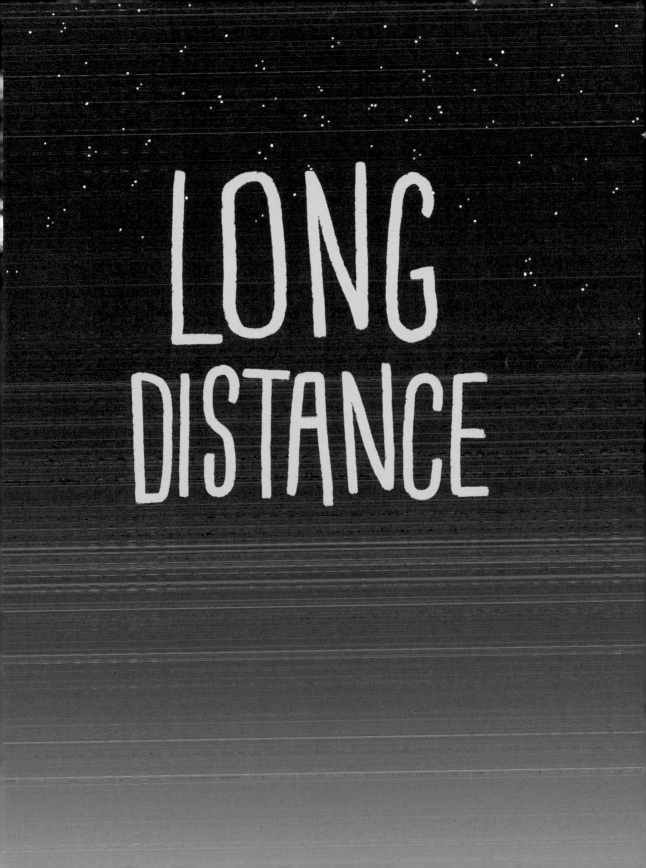

Also by Whitney Gardner

Fake Blood

Becoming RBG

LONG DISTANCE

WHITNEY GARDNER

SIMON & SCHUSTER BOOKS FOR YOUNG READERS

NEW YORK   LONDON   TORONTO   SYDNEY   NEW DELHI

SIMON & SCHUSTER BOOKS FOR YOUNG READERS

An imprint of Simon & Schuster Children's Publishing Division

1230 Avenue of the Americas, New York, New York 10020

SIMON & SCHUSTER BOOKS FOR YOUNG READERS

and related marks are trademarks of Simon & Schuster, Inc.

For information about special discounts for bulk purchases, please contact Simon & Schuster Special Sales at 1-866-506-1949 or business@simonandschuster.com.

The Simon & Schuster Speakers Bureau can bring authors to your live event. For more information or to book an event, contact the Simon & Schuster Speakers Bureau at 1-866-248-3049 or visit our website at www.simonspeakers.com.

Also available in a Simon & Schuster Books for Young Readers paperback edition

Interior design by Tom Daly

The text for this book was set in Minion, WGH2, and WGH3.

The illustrations for this book were rendered digitally.

Manufactured in China

0421 SCP

First Simon & Schuster Books for Young Readers hardcover edition June 2021

2 4 6 8 10 9 7 5 3 1

Library of Congress Cataloging-in-Publication Data

Names: Gardner, Whitney, author, illustrator.

Title: Long distance / Whitney Gardner.

Description: First edition. | New York : Simon & Schuster Books for Young Readers, [2021] | Audience: Ages 10 up. | Audience: Grades 4–6. | Summary: After moving to Seattle, Vega's dads send her to the very strange Camp Best Friend, where she discovers that one can make new friends without forgetting old ones.

Identifiers: LCCN 2020010343 (print) | LCCN 2020010344 (eBook) | ISBN 9781534455665 (hardcover) | ISBN 9781534455658 (paperback) | ISBN 9781534455672 (eBook)

Subjects: CYAC: Friendship—Fiction. | Camps—Fiction. | Moving, Household—Fiction. | Family life—Fiction. | Gay fathers—Fiction. | Science fiction.

Classification: LCC PZ7.1.G373 Lon 2021 (print) | LCC PZ7.1.G373 (eBook) | DDC [Fic]—dc23

LC record available at https://lccn.loc.gov/2020010343

LC ebook record available at https://lccn.loc.gov/2020010344

To all my friends both
near and far, far away

CHAPTER 1

Start small with people you know.

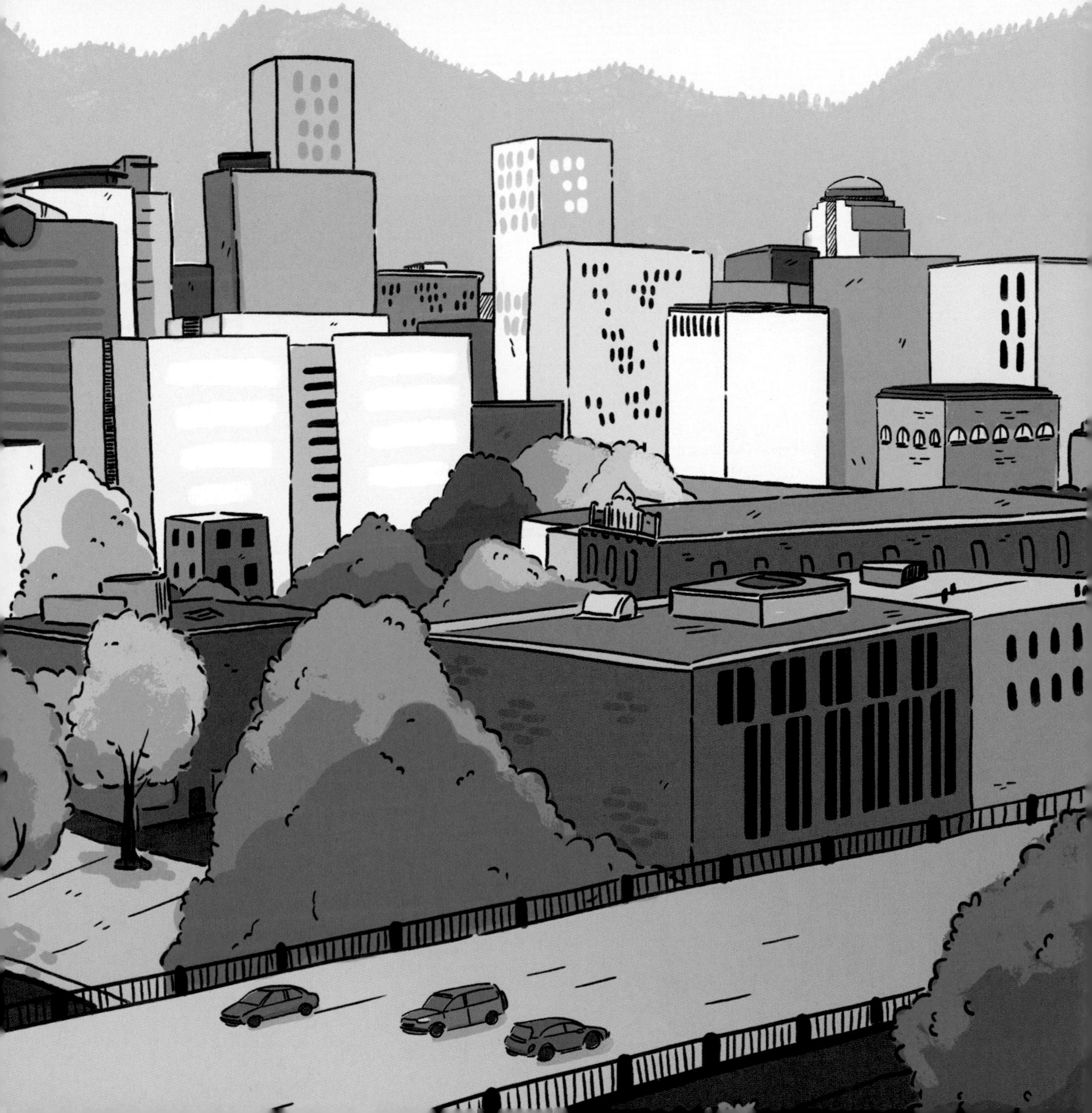

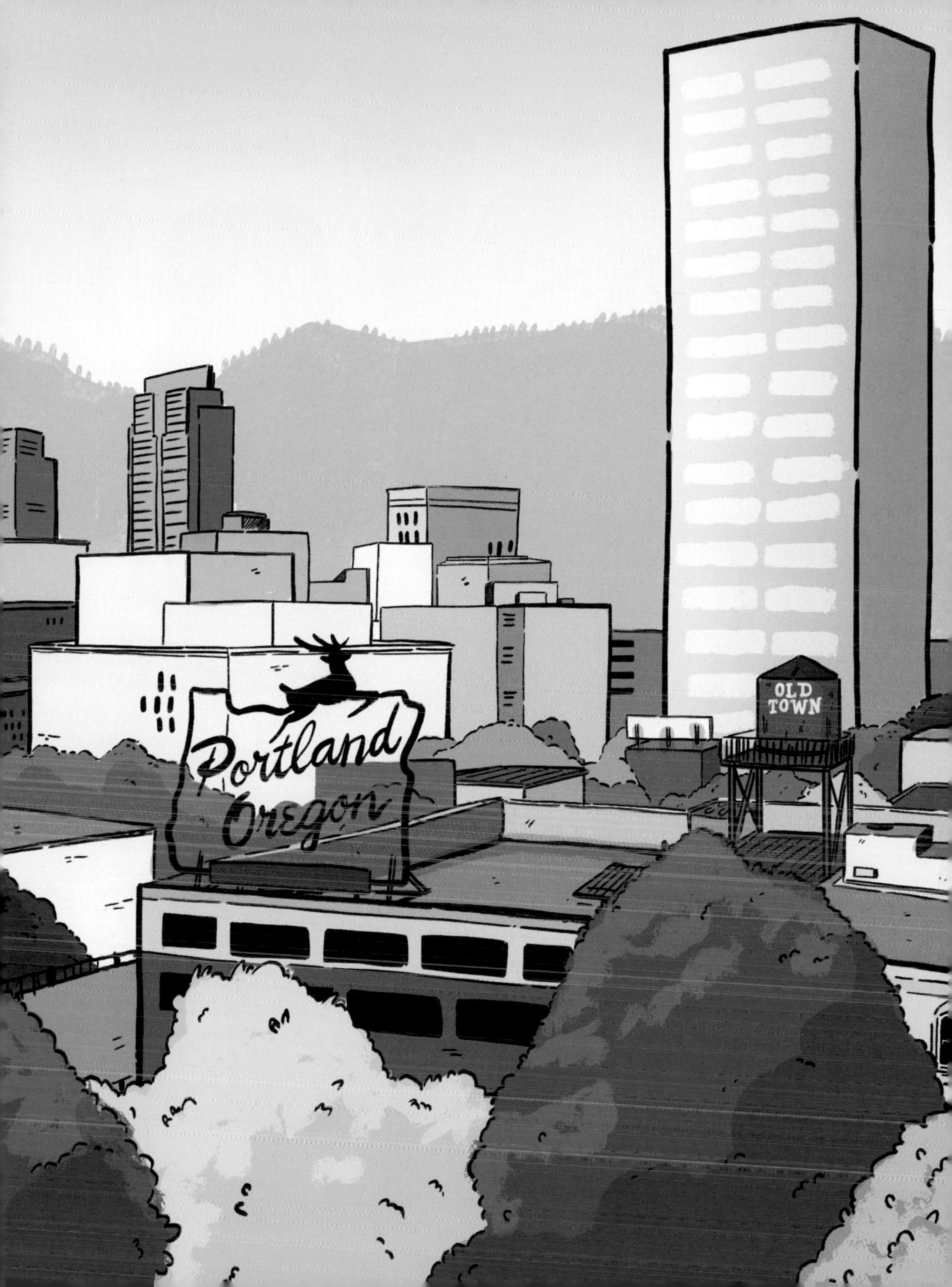
Portland
Oregon
OLD
TOWN

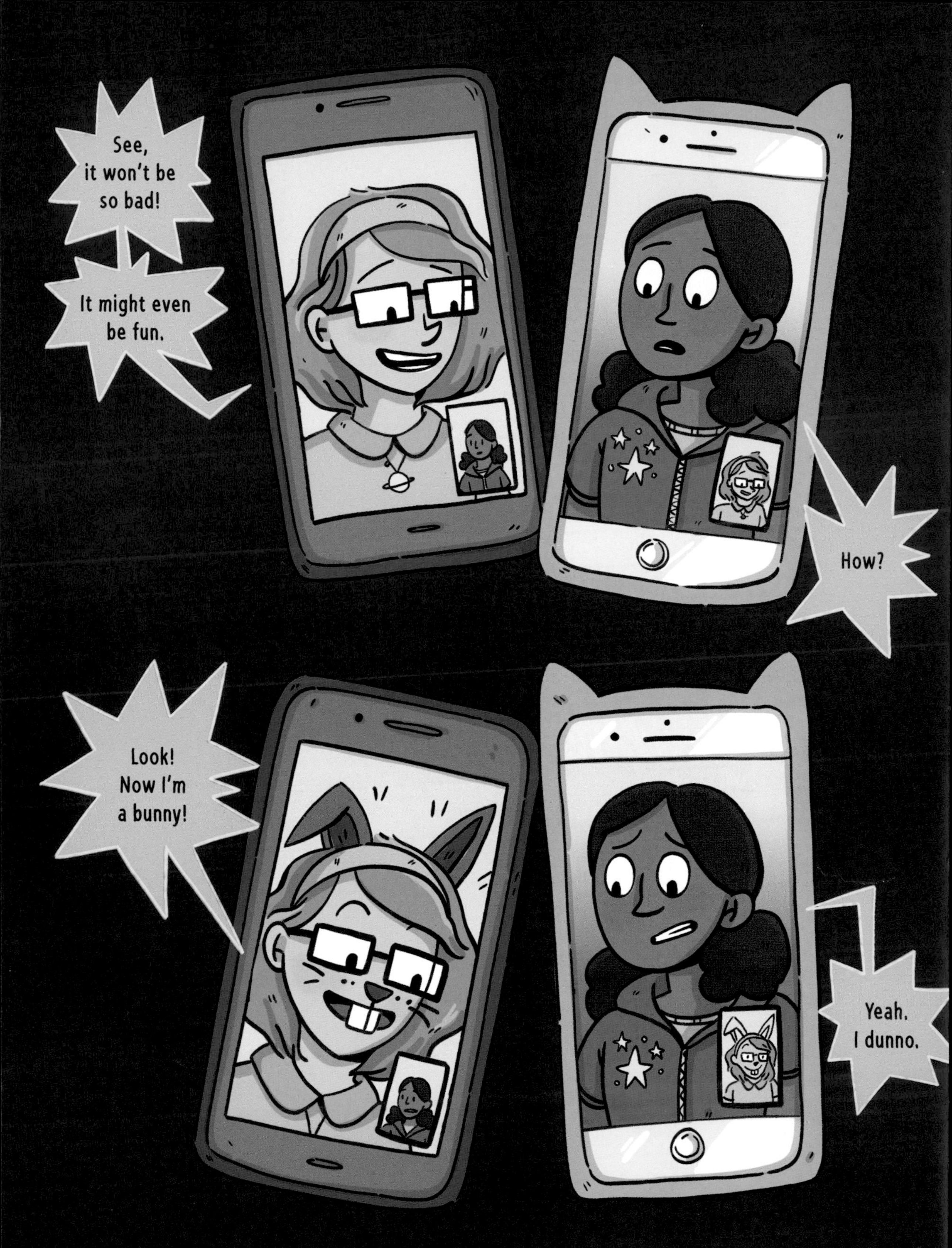
See, it won't be so bad!
It might even be fun.
How?
Look! Now I'm a bunny!
Yeah. I dunno.

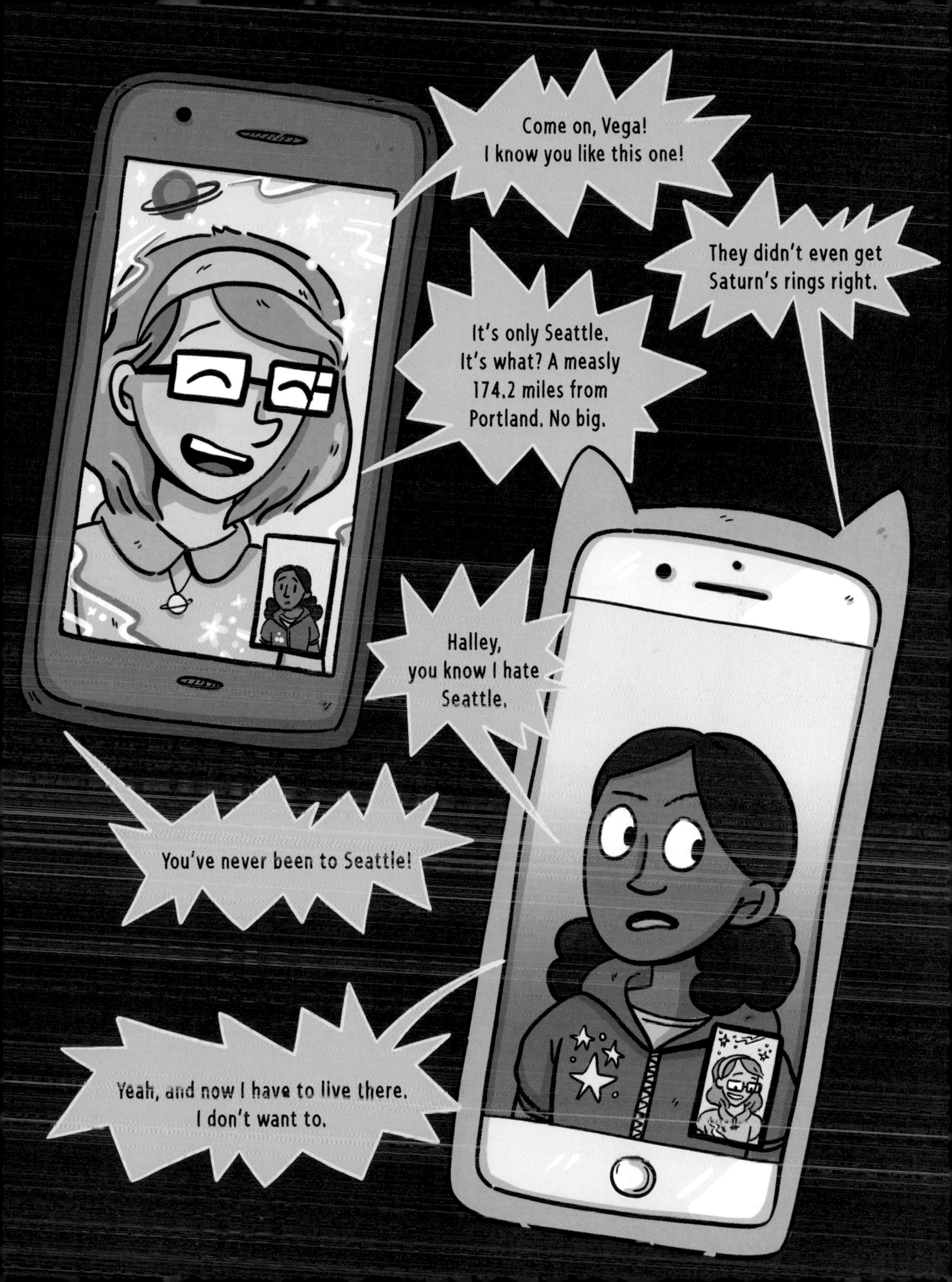
Come on, Vega! I know you like this one!
They didn't even get Saturn's rings right.
It's only Seattle. It's what? A measly 174.2 miles from Portland. No big.
Halley, you know I hate Seattle.
You've never been to Seattle!
Yeah, and now I have to live there. I don't want to.

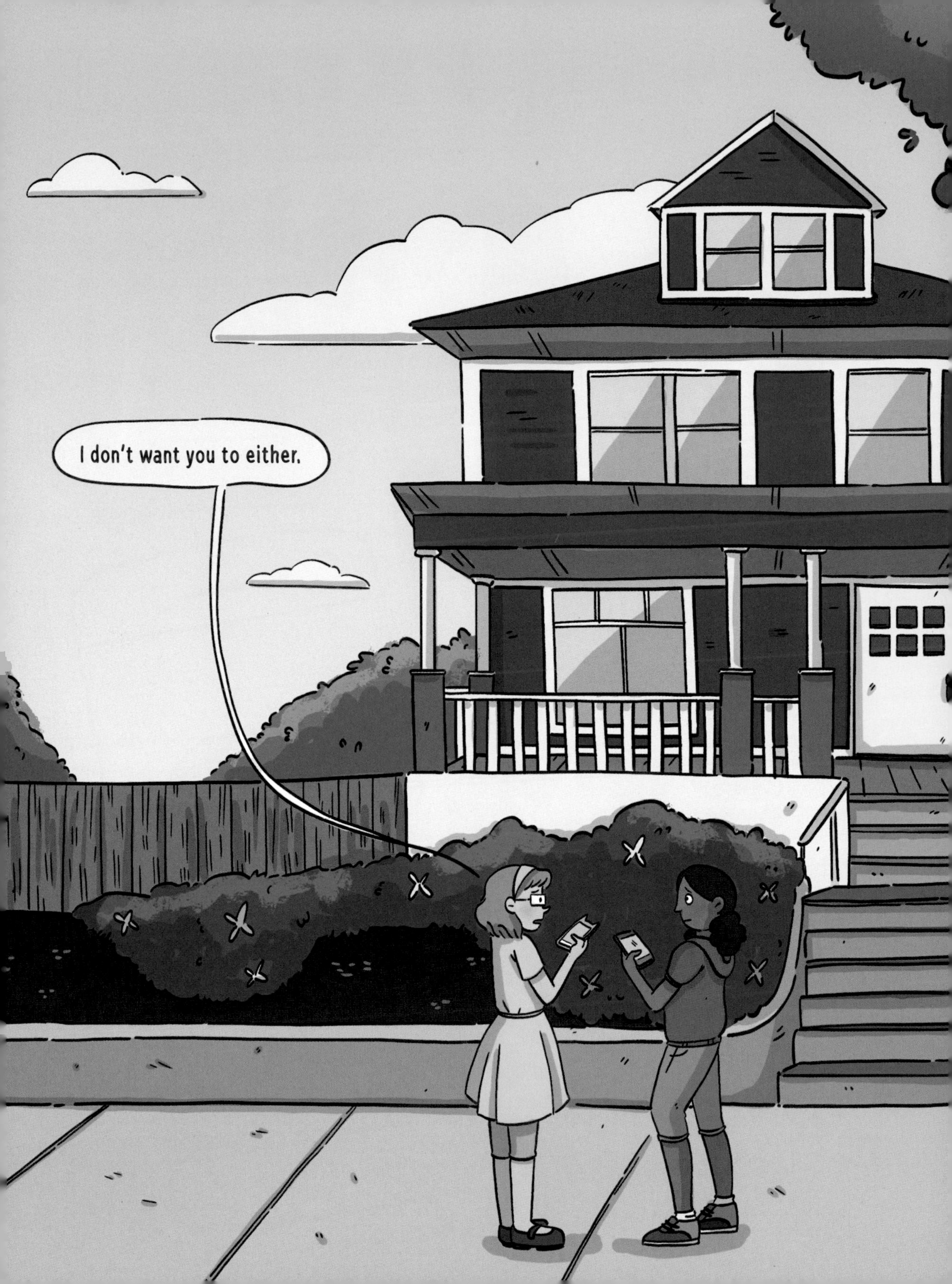
I don't want you to either.

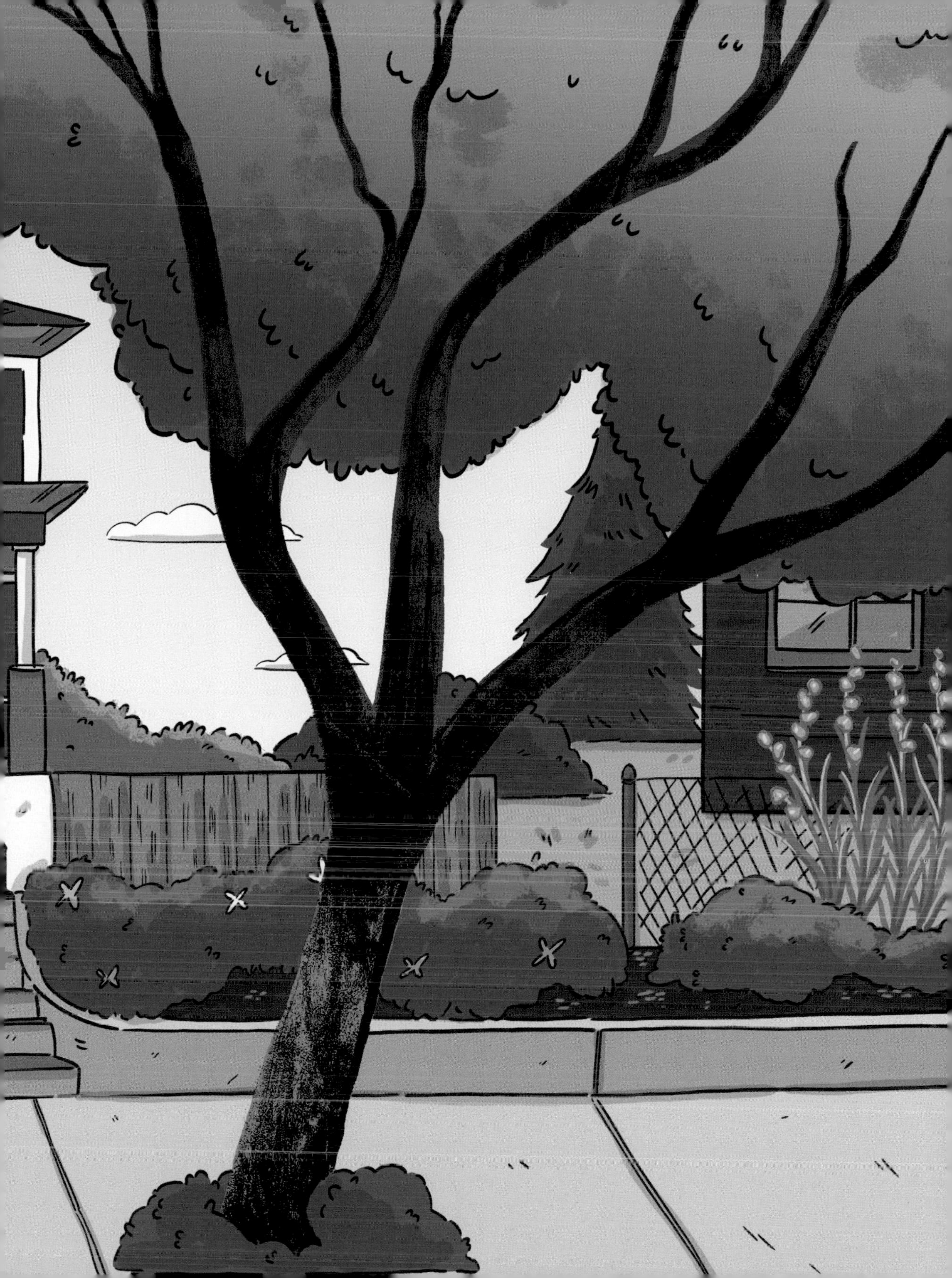

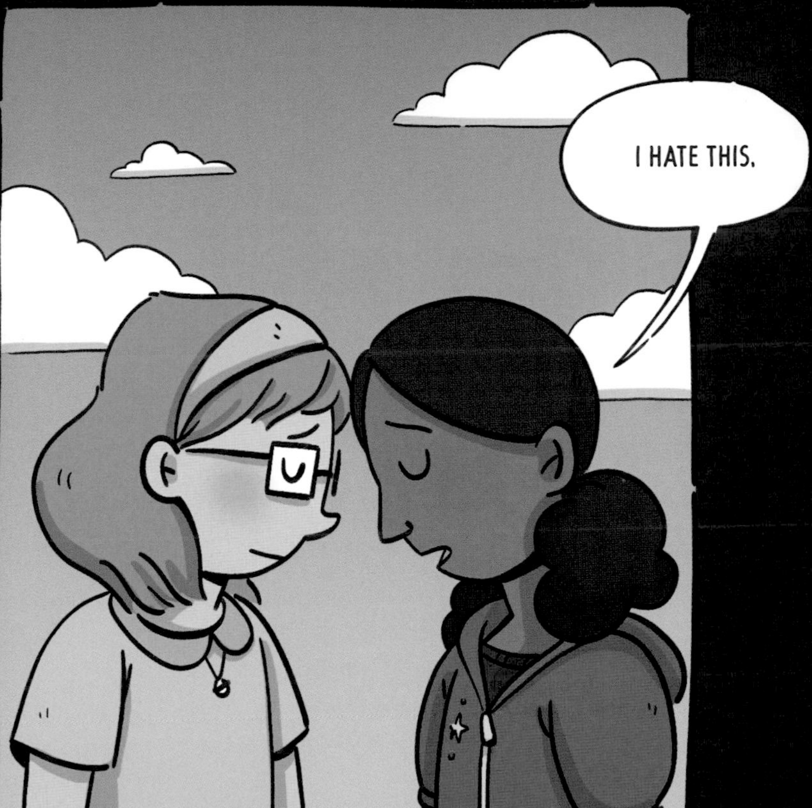
I HATE THIS.

LONG DISTANCE

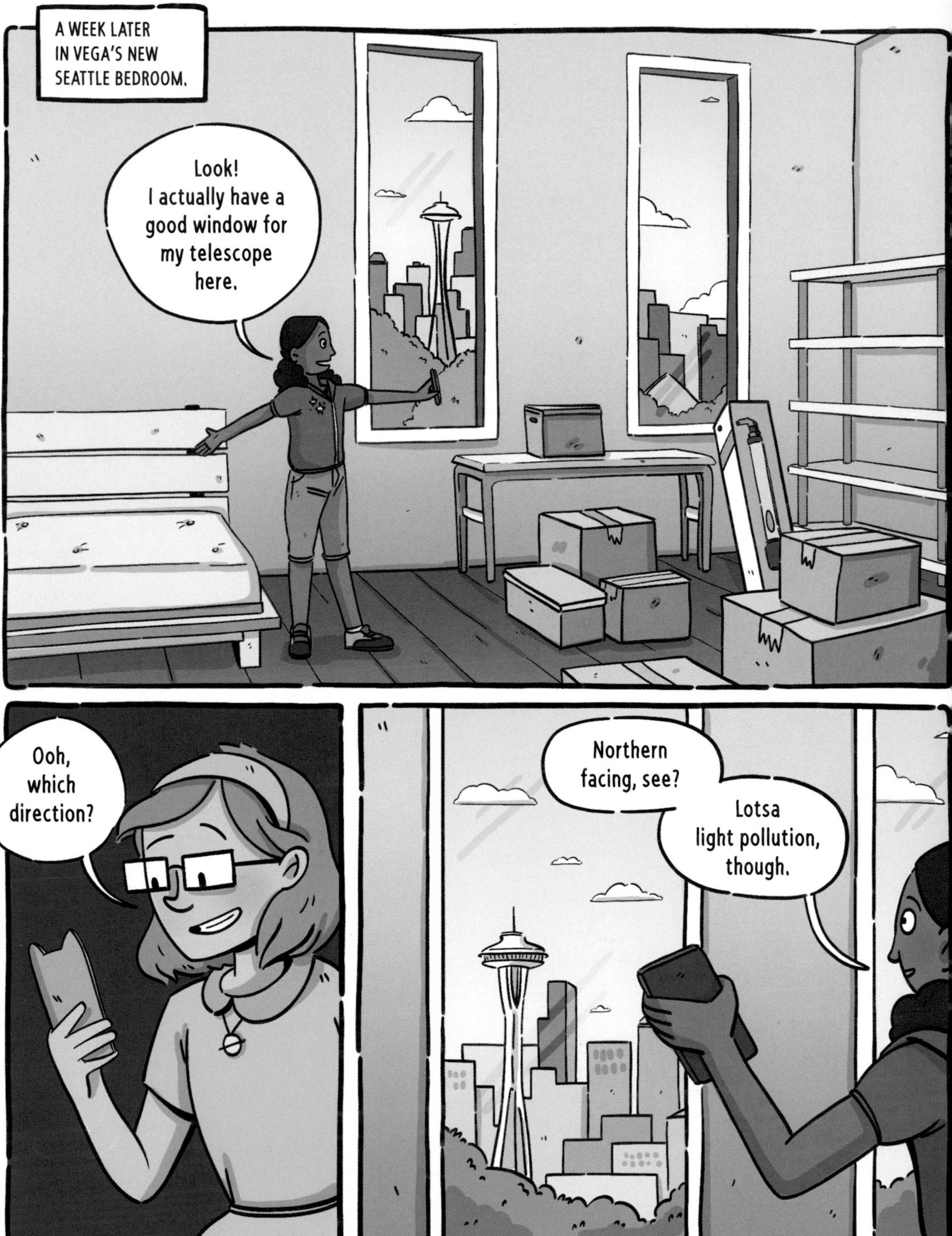
A WEEK LATER IN VEGA'S NEW SEATTLE BEDROOM.
Look! I actually have a good window for my telescope here.
Ooh, which direction?
Northern facing, see?
Lotsa light pollution, though.

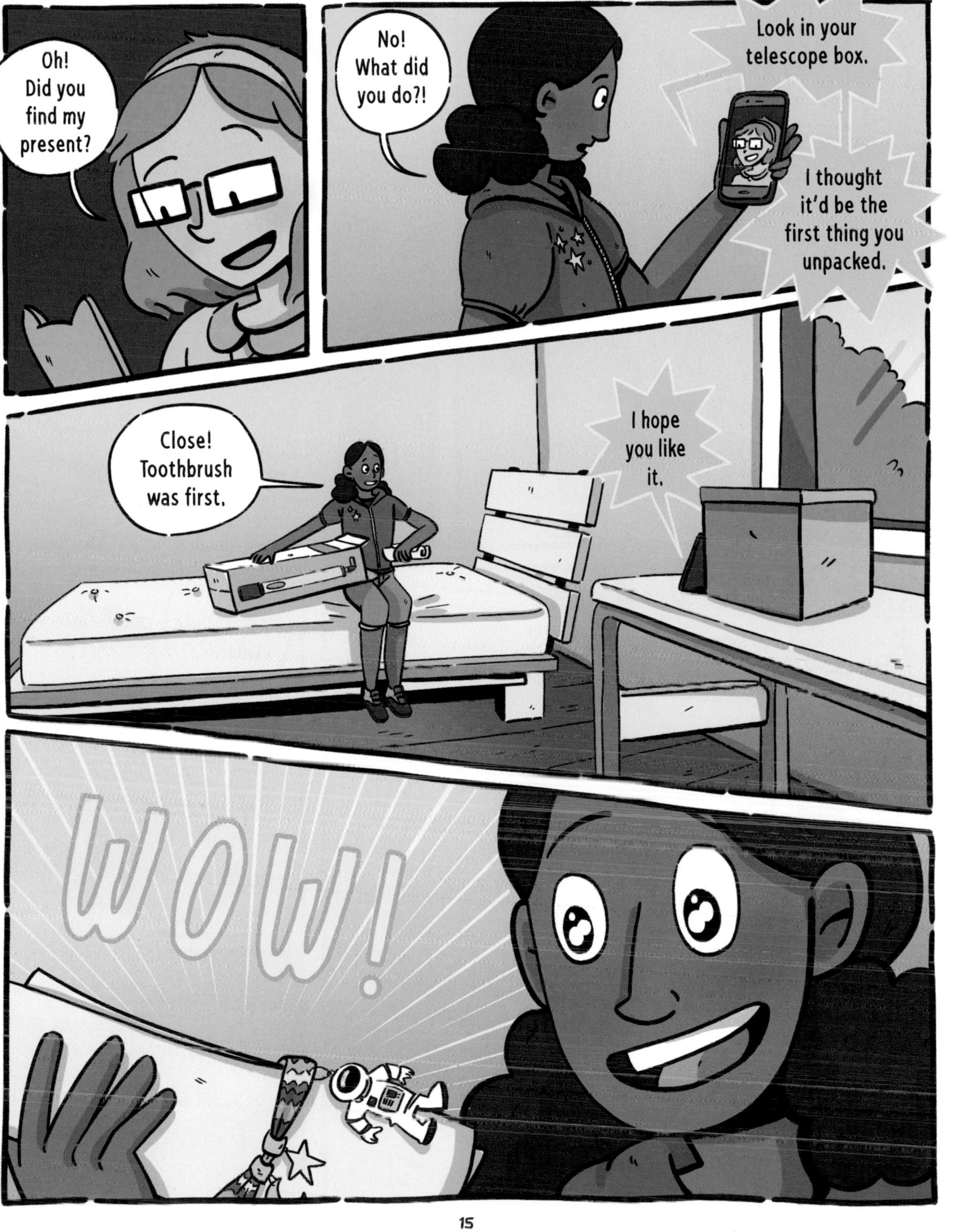
Oh!
Did you find my present?
No!
What did you do?!
Look in your telescope box.
I thought it'd be the first thing you unpacked.
Close!
Toothbrush was first.
I hope you like it.
WOW!

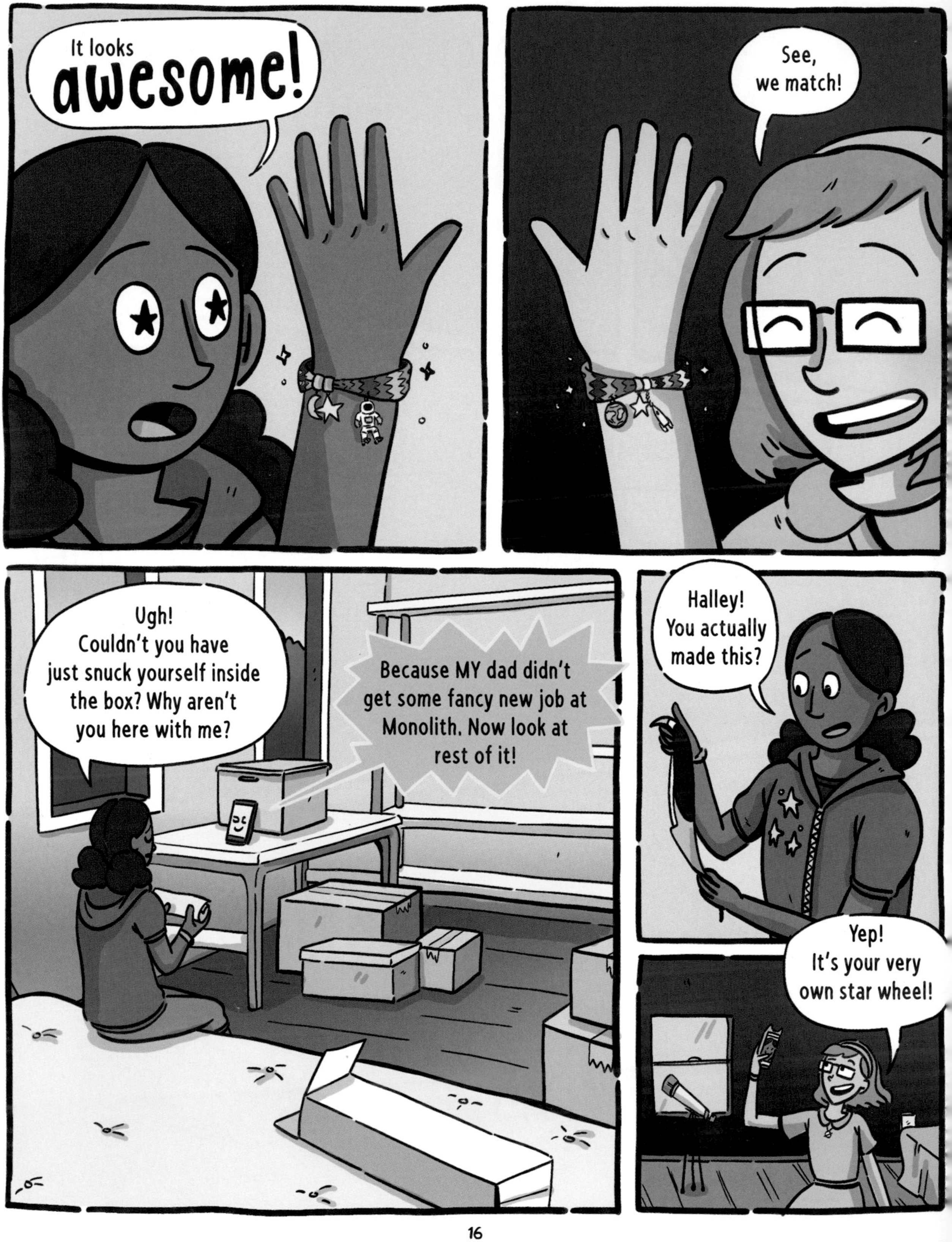
It looks awesome!
See, we match!
Ugh! Couldn't you have just snuck yourself inside the box? Why aren't you here with me?
Because MY dad didn't get some fancy new job at Monolith. Now look at rest of it!
Halley! You actually made this?
Yep! It's your very own star wheel!

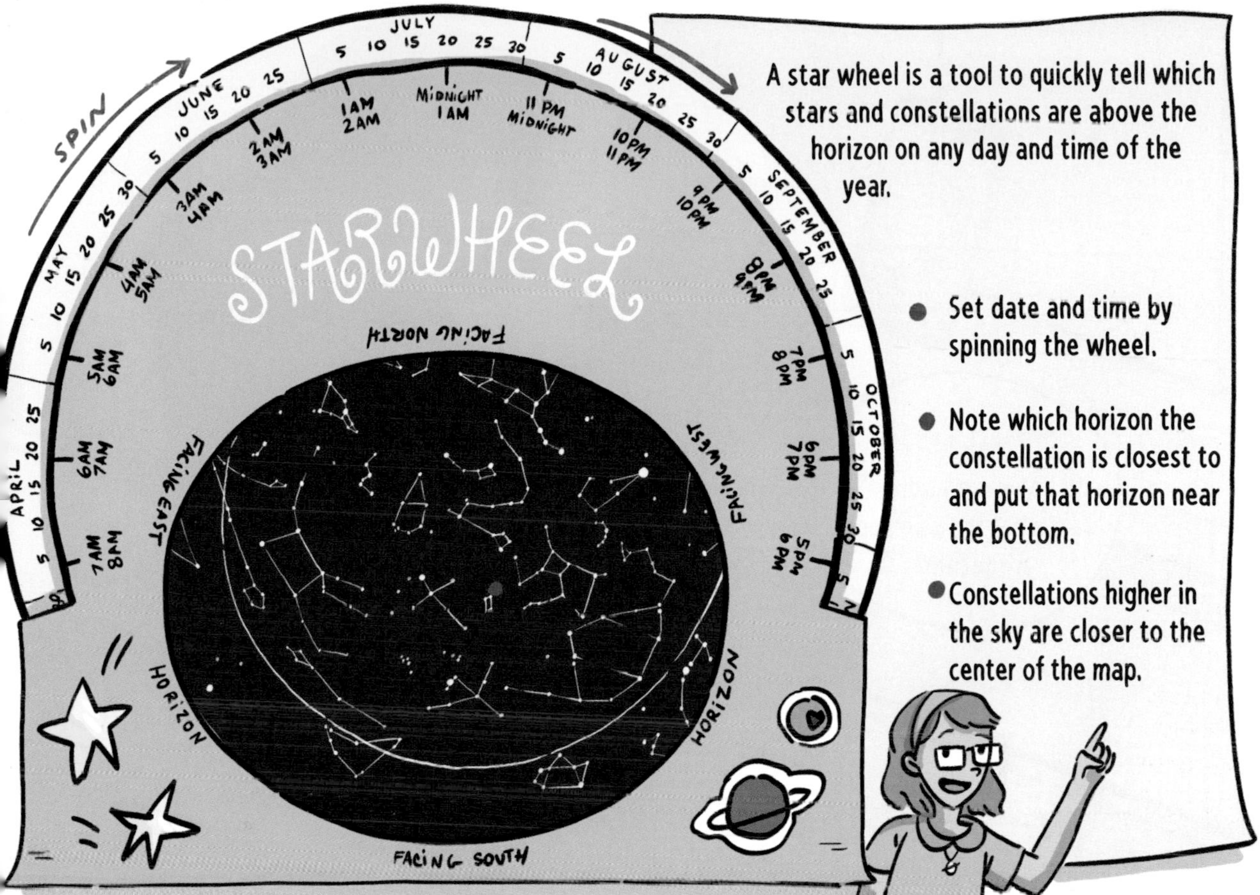
A star wheel is a tool to quickly tell which stars and constellations are above the horizon on any day and time of the year.
Set date and time by spinning the wheel.
Note which horizon the constellation is closest to and put that horizon near the bottom.
Constellations higher in the sky are closer to the center of the map.
SPIN
STARWHEEL
FACING NORTH
FACING EAST
FACING WEST
FACING SOUTH
HORIZON
HORIZON
APRIL
MAY
JUNE
JULY
AUGUST
SEPTEMBER
OCTOBER
MIDNIGHT 1AM
11 PM MIDNIGHT

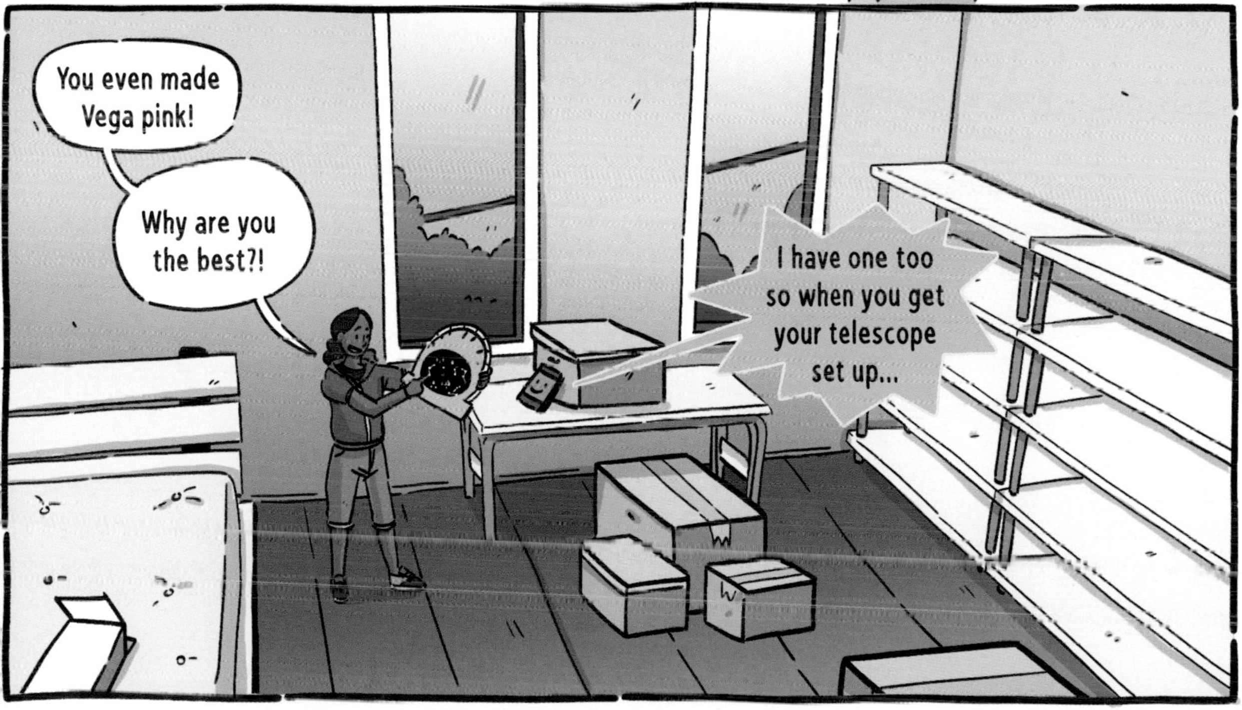
You even made Vega pink!
Why are you the best?!
I have one too so when you get your telescope set up...

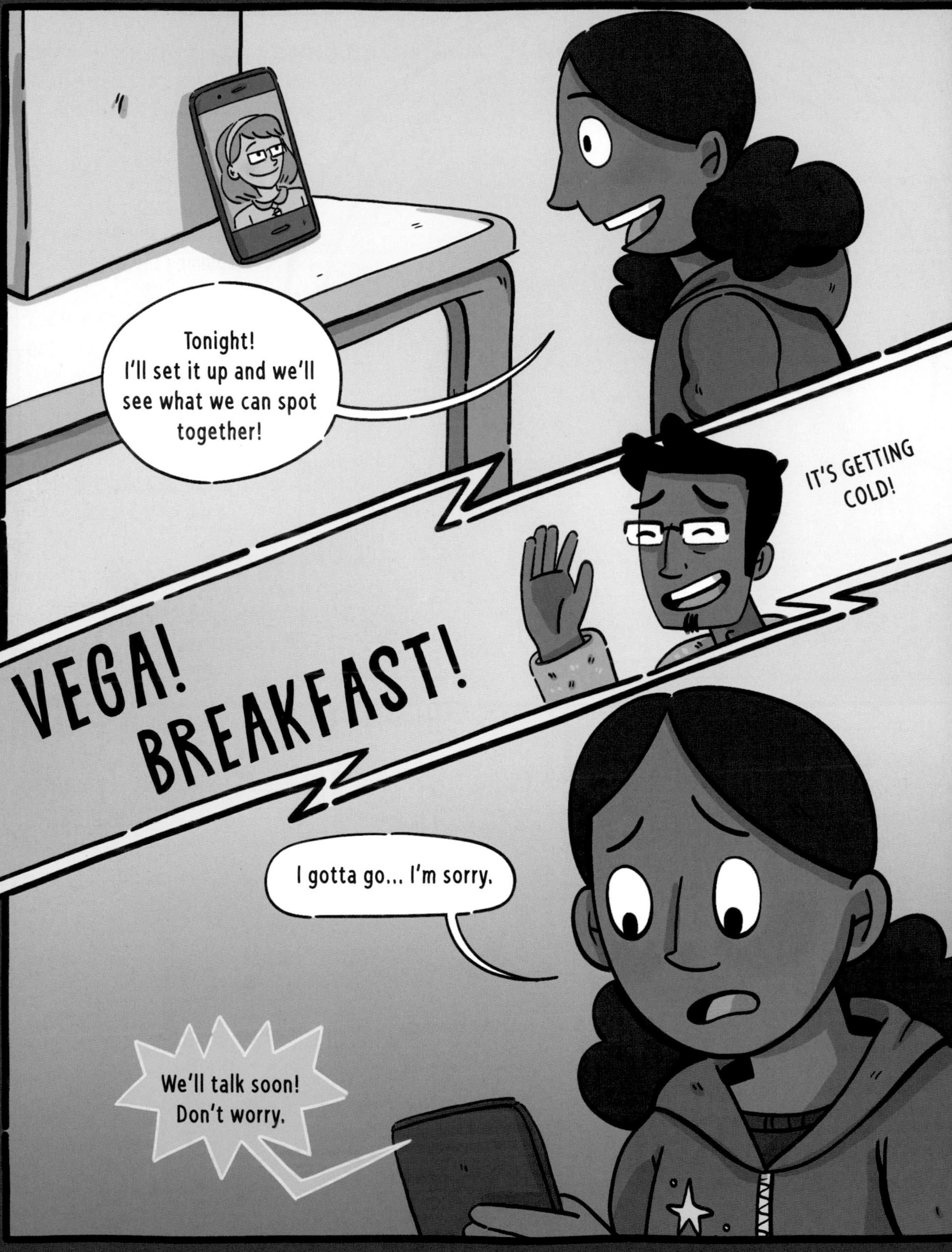
Tonight! I'll set it up and we'll see what we can spot together!
VEGA! BREAKFAST!
IT'S GETTING COLD!
I gotta go... I'm sorry.
We'll talk soon! Don't worry.

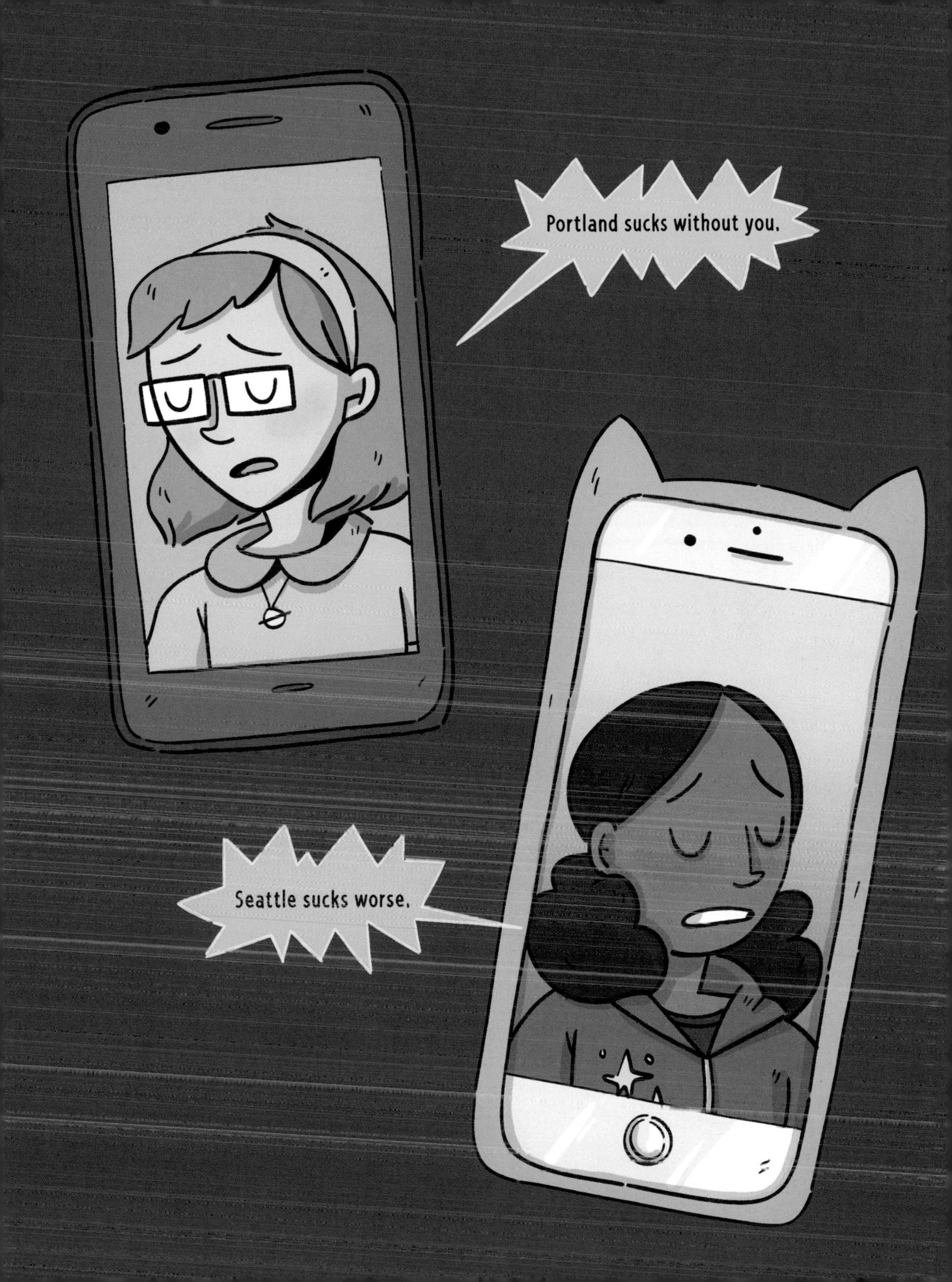
Portland sucks without you.
Seattle sucks worse.

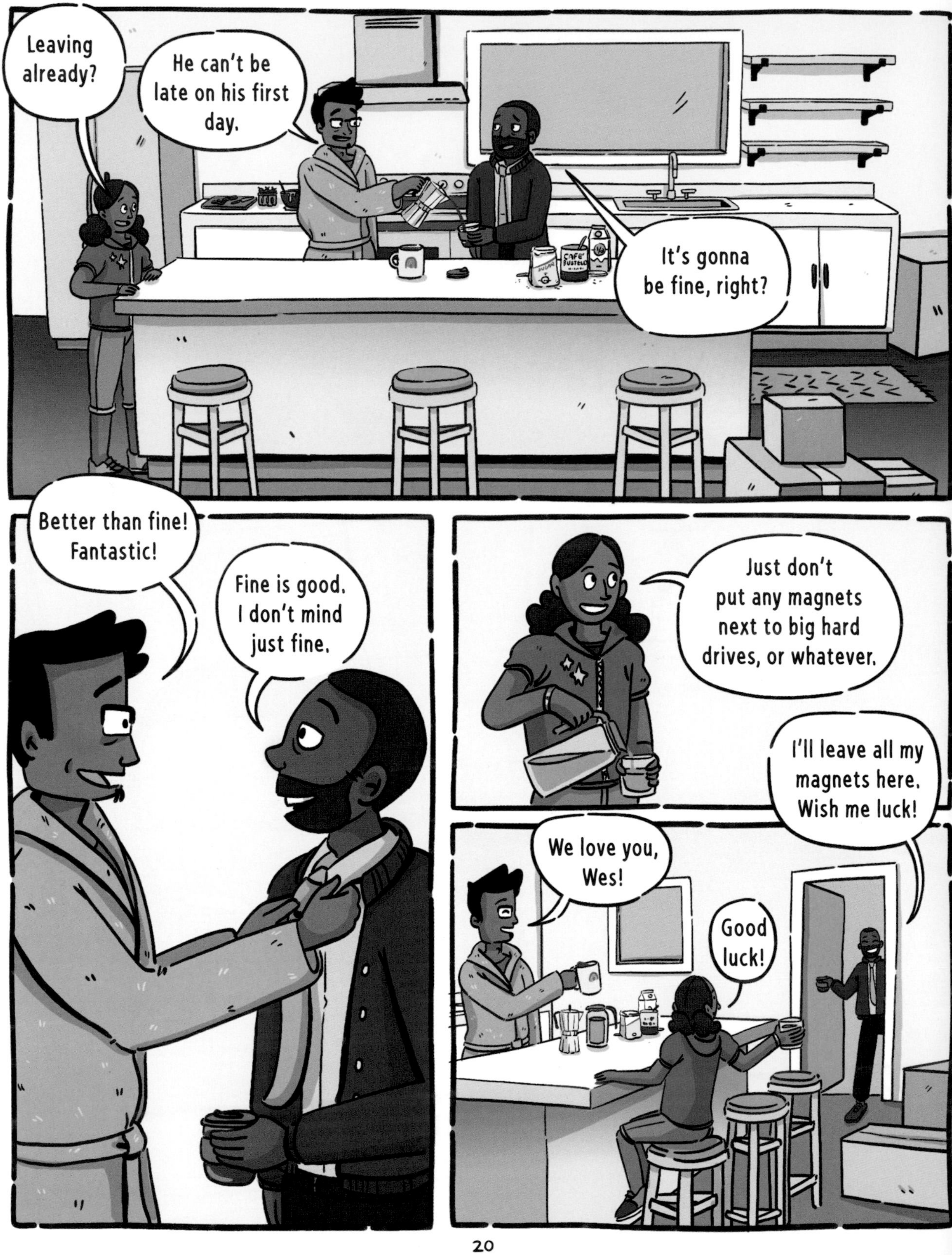

Leaving already?
He can't be late on his first day.
It's gonna be fine, right?
Better than fine! Fantastic!
Fine is good. I don't mind just fine.
Just don't put any magnets next to big hard drives, or whatever.
I'll leave all my magnets here. Wish me luck!
We love you, Wes!
Good luck!

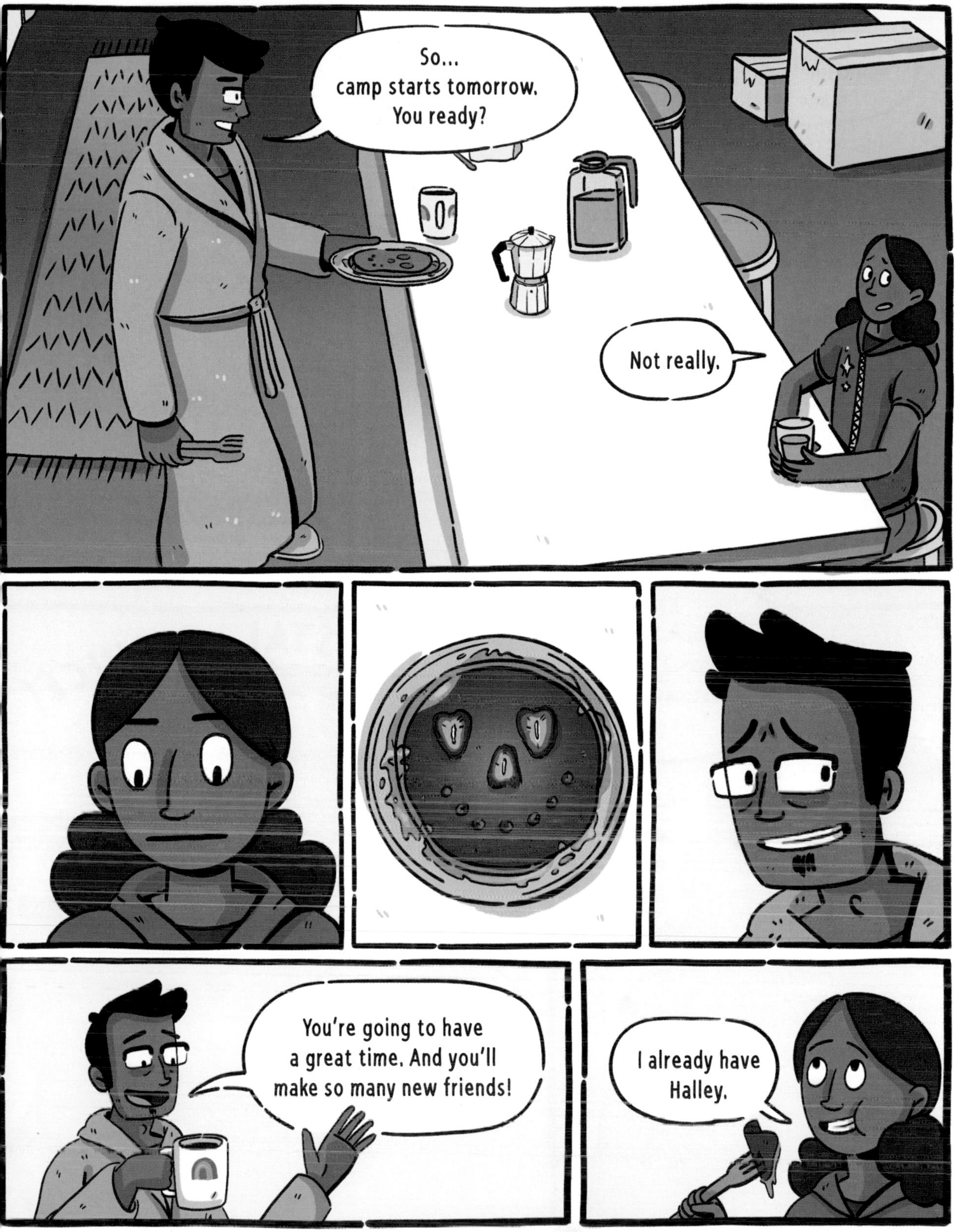
So... camp starts tomorrow. You ready?
Not really.
You're going to have a great time. And you'll make so many new friends!
I already have Halley.

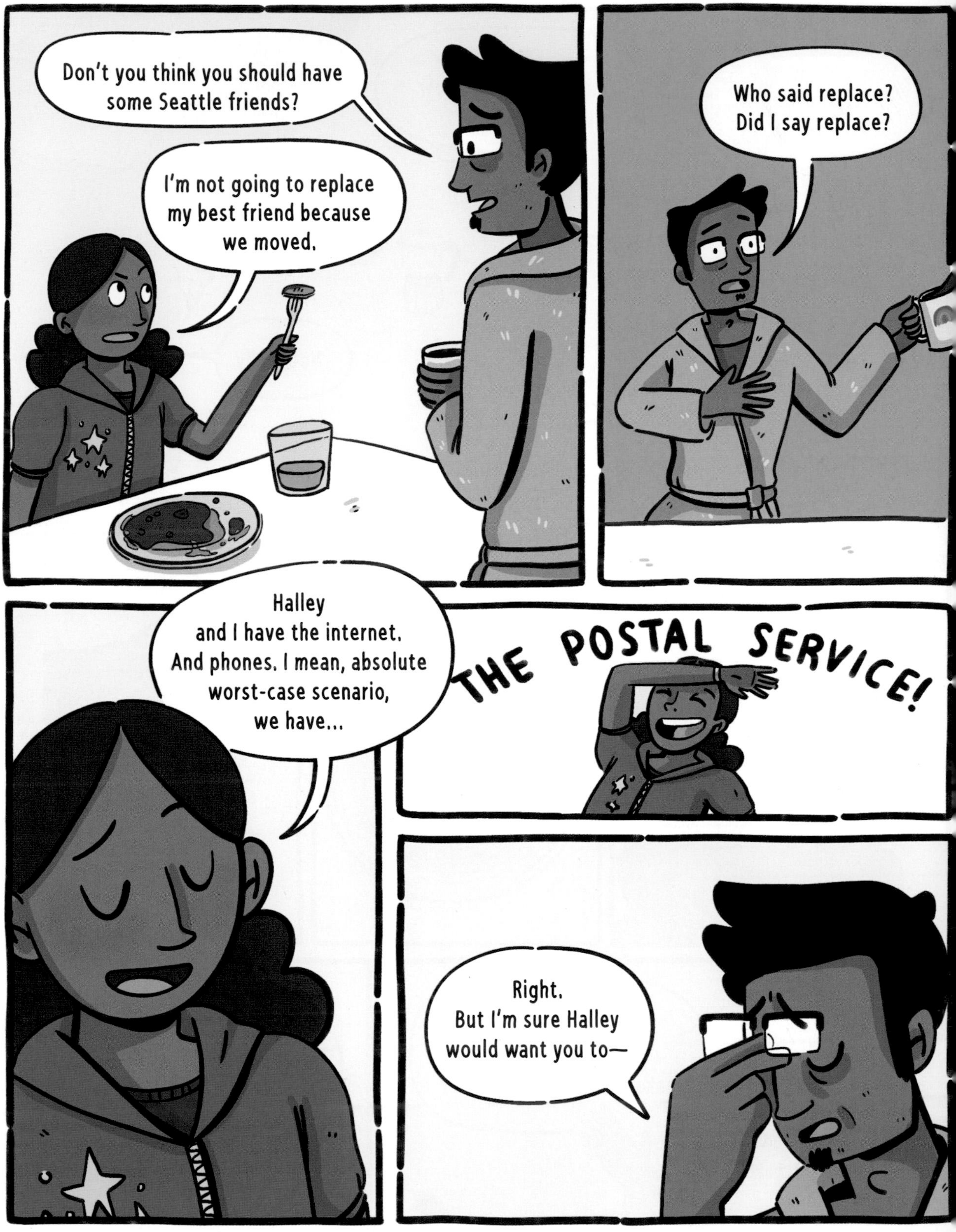
Don't you think you should have some Seattle friends?
I'm not going to replace my best friend because we moved.
Who said replace? Did I say replace?
Halley and I have the internet. And phones. I mean, absolute worst-case scenario, we have...
THE POSTAL SERVICE!
Right. But I'm sure Halley would want you to—

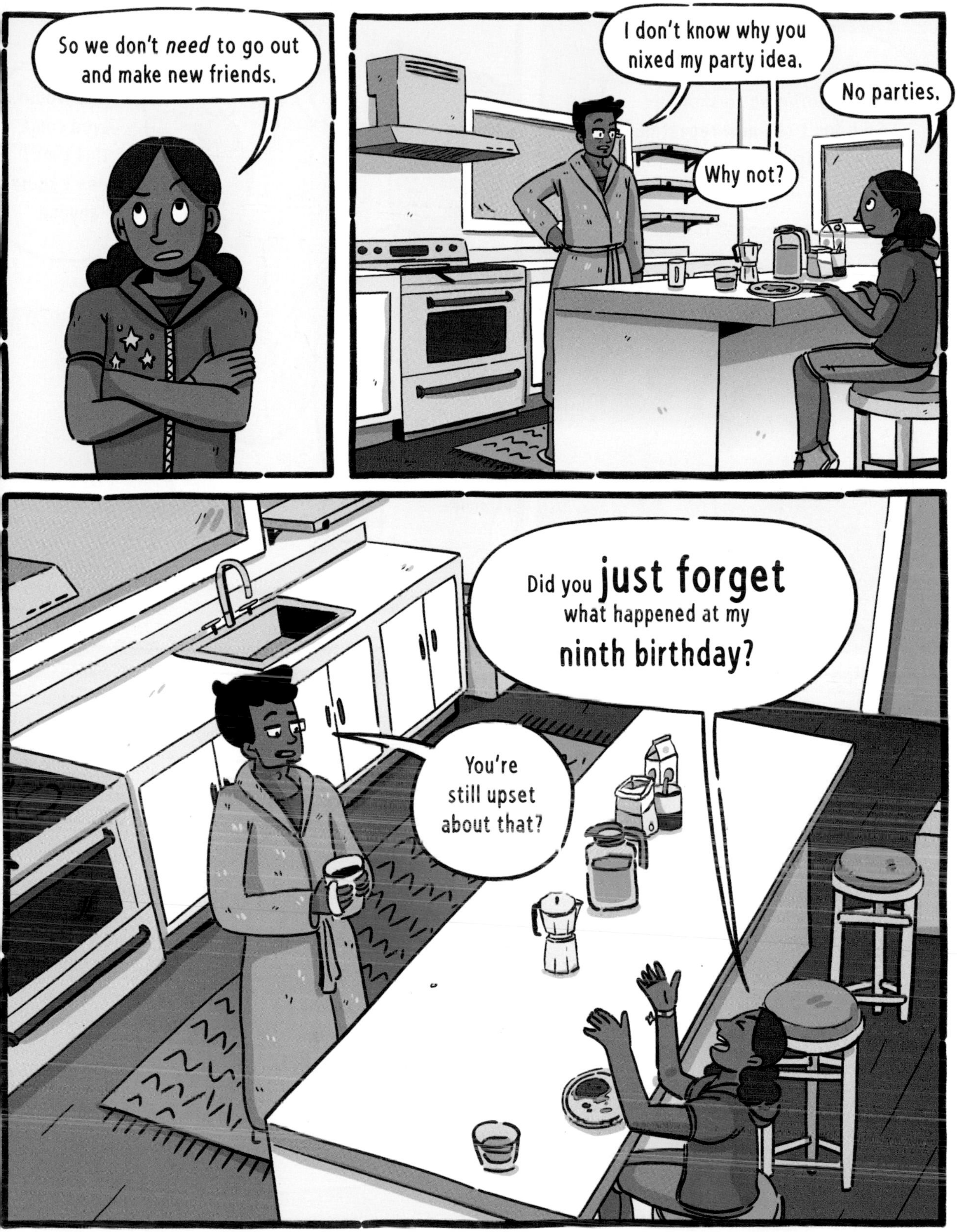
So we don't *need* to go out and make new friends.
I don't know why you nixed my party idea.
No parties.
Why not?
Did you **just forget** what happened at my **ninth birthday?**
You're still upset about that?

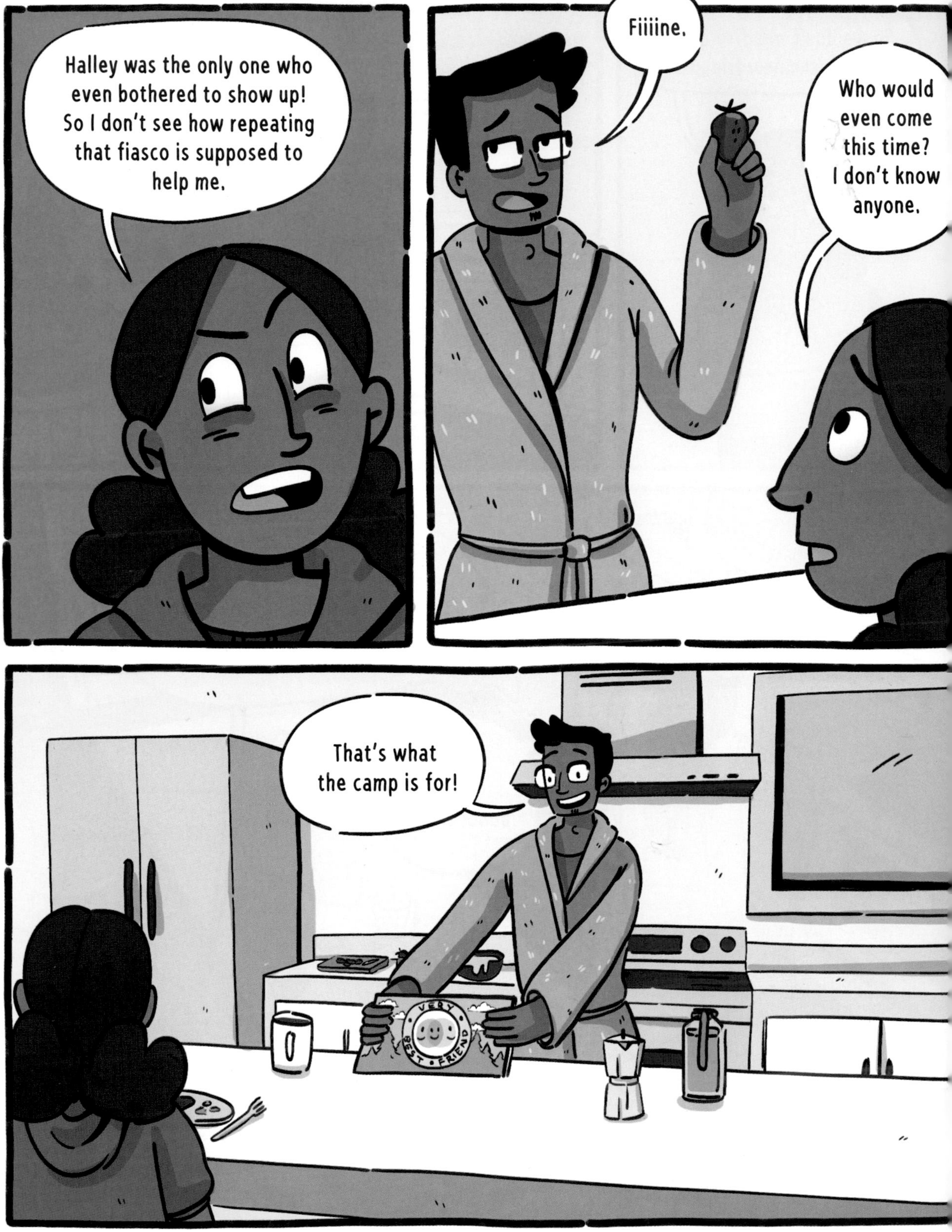
Halley was the only one who even bothered to show up! So I don't see how repeating that fiasco is supposed to help me.
Fiiiine.
Who would even come this time? I don't know anyone.
That's what the camp is for!
VERY BEST • FRIEND

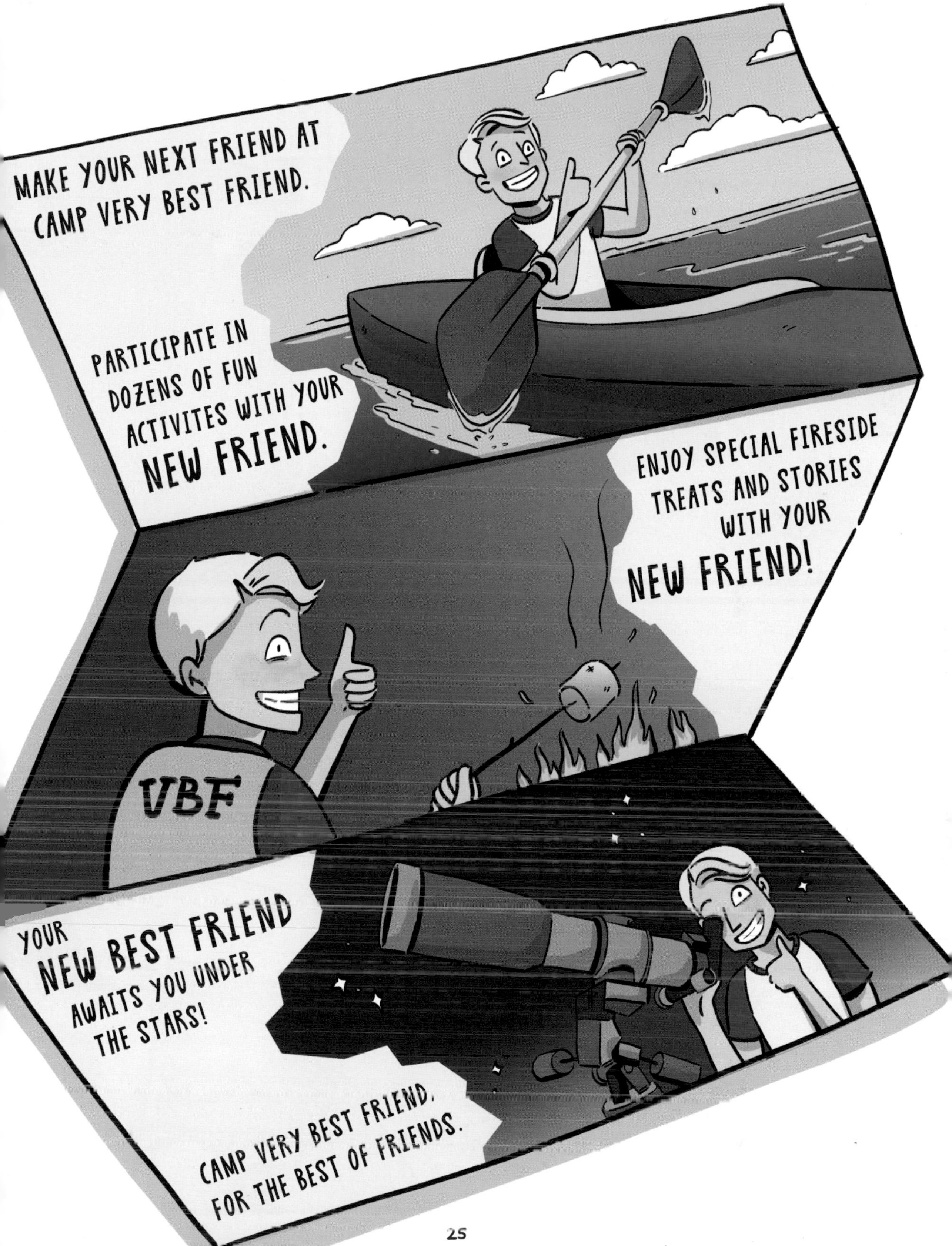
MAKE YOUR NEXT FRIEND AT CAMP VERY BEST FRIEND.
PARTICIPATE IN DOZENS OF FUN ACTIVITES WITH YOUR NEW FRIEND.
ENJOY SPECIAL FIRESIDE TREATS AND STORIES WITH YOUR NEW FRIEND!
VBF
YOUR NEW BEST FRIEND AWAITS YOU UNDER THE STARS!
CAMP VERY BEST FRIEND. FOR THE BEST OF FRIENDS.

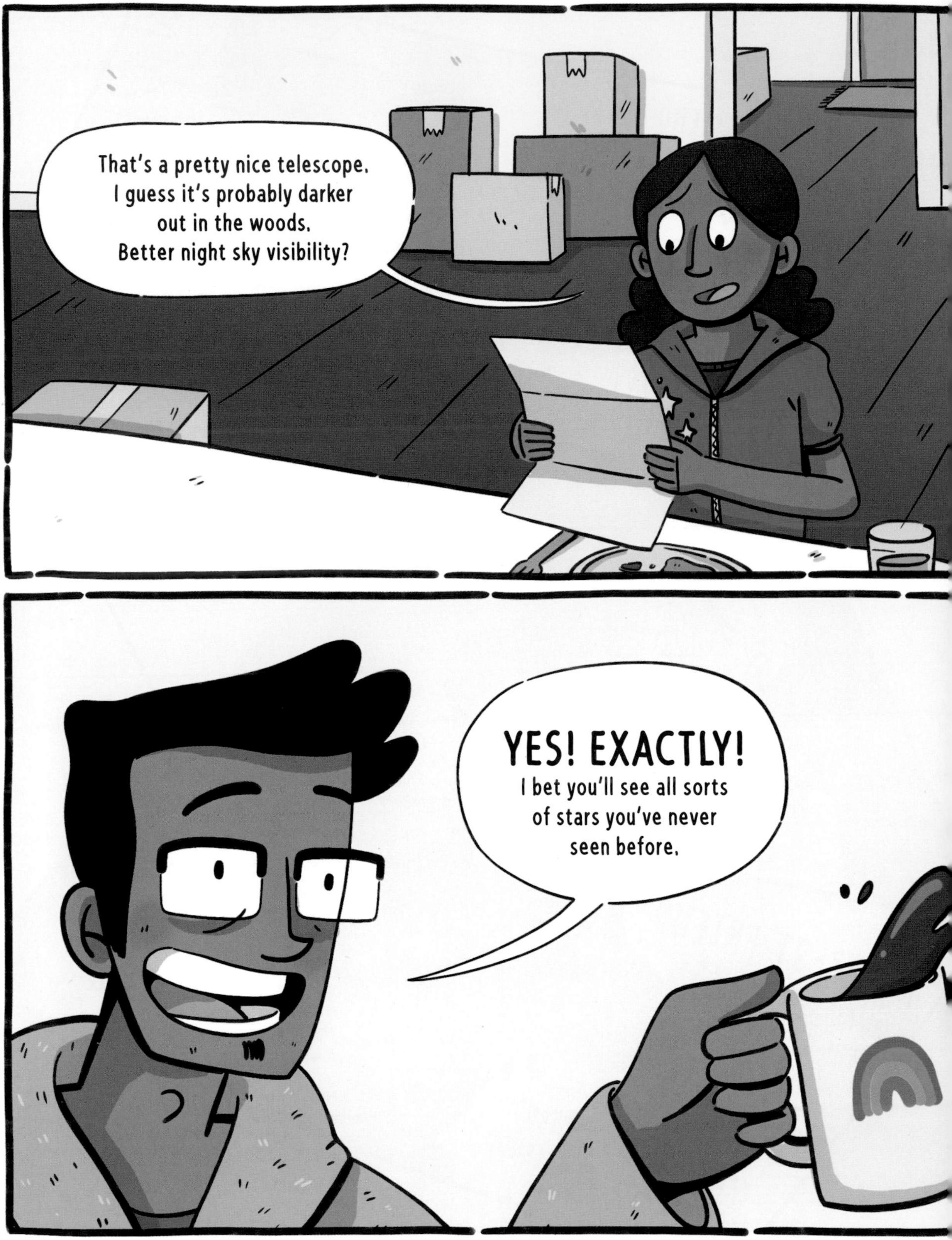
That's a pretty nice telescope. I guess it's probably darker out in the woods. Better night sky visibility?
YES! EXACTLY! I bet you'll see all sorts of stars you've never seen before.

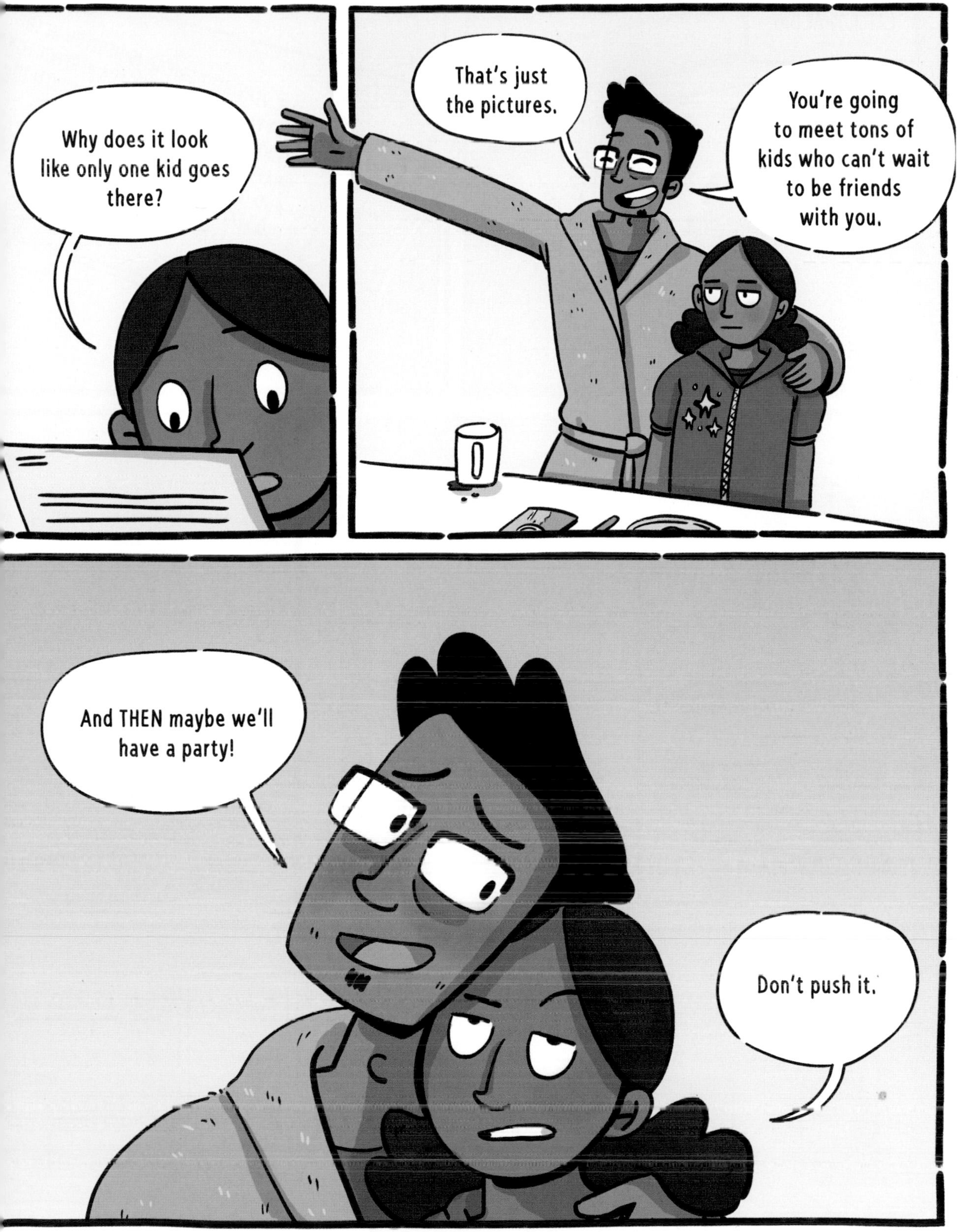
Why does it look like only one kid goes there?
That's just the pictures.
You're going to meet tons of kids who can't wait to be friends with you.
And THEN maybe we'll have a party!
Don't push it.

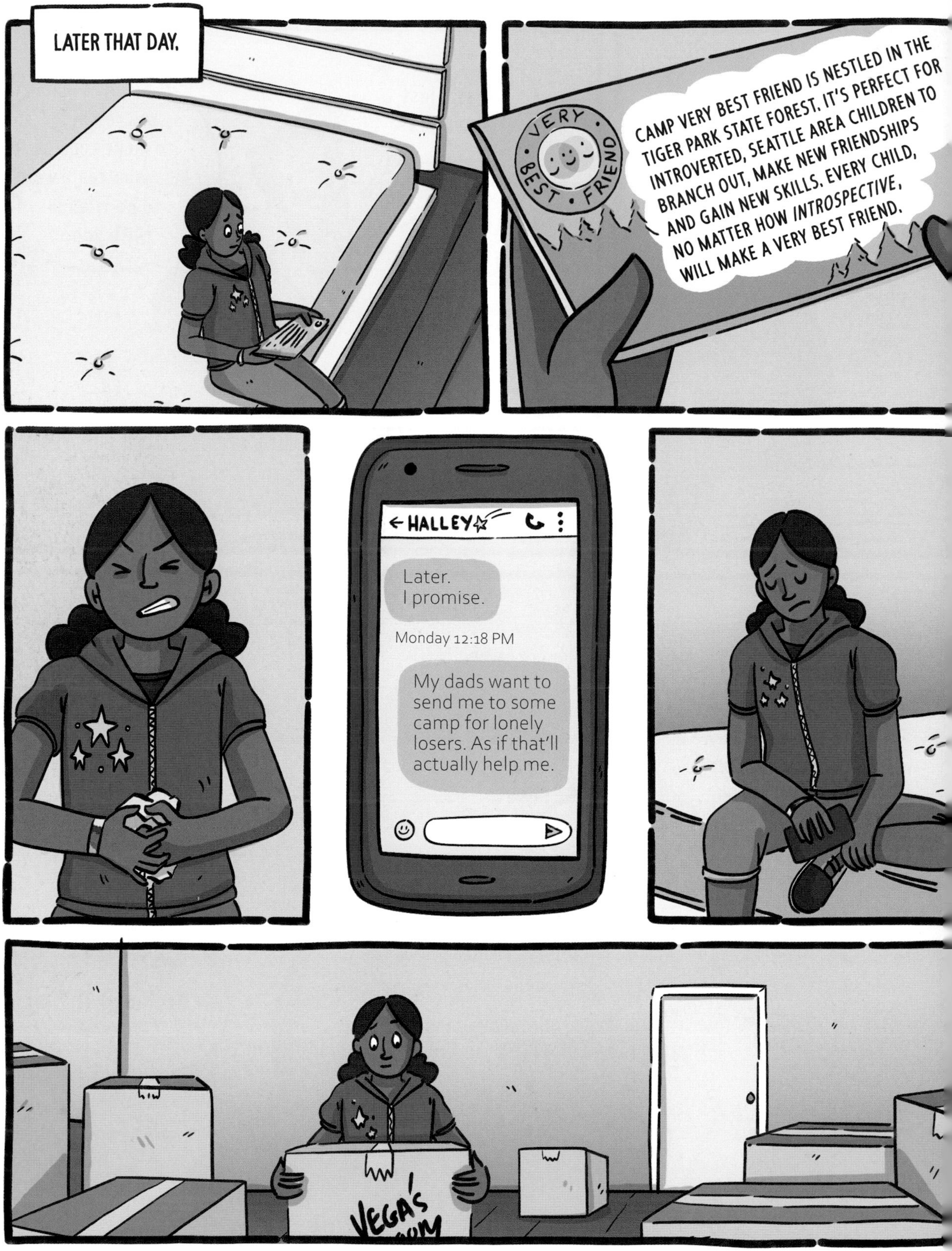

LATER THAT DAY.
VERY BEST FRIEND
CAMP VERY BEST FRIEND IS NESTLED IN THE TIGER PARK STATE FOREST. IT'S PERFECT FOR INTROVERTED, SEATTLE AREA CHILDREN TO BRANCH OUT, MAKE NEW FRIENDSHIPS AND GAIN NEW SKILLS. EVERY CHILD, NO MATTER HOW *INTROSPECTIVE*, WILL MAKE A VERY BEST FRIEND.
← HALLEY
Later.
I promise.
Monday 12:18 PM
My dads want to send me to some camp for lonely losers. As if that'll actually help me.
VEGA'S

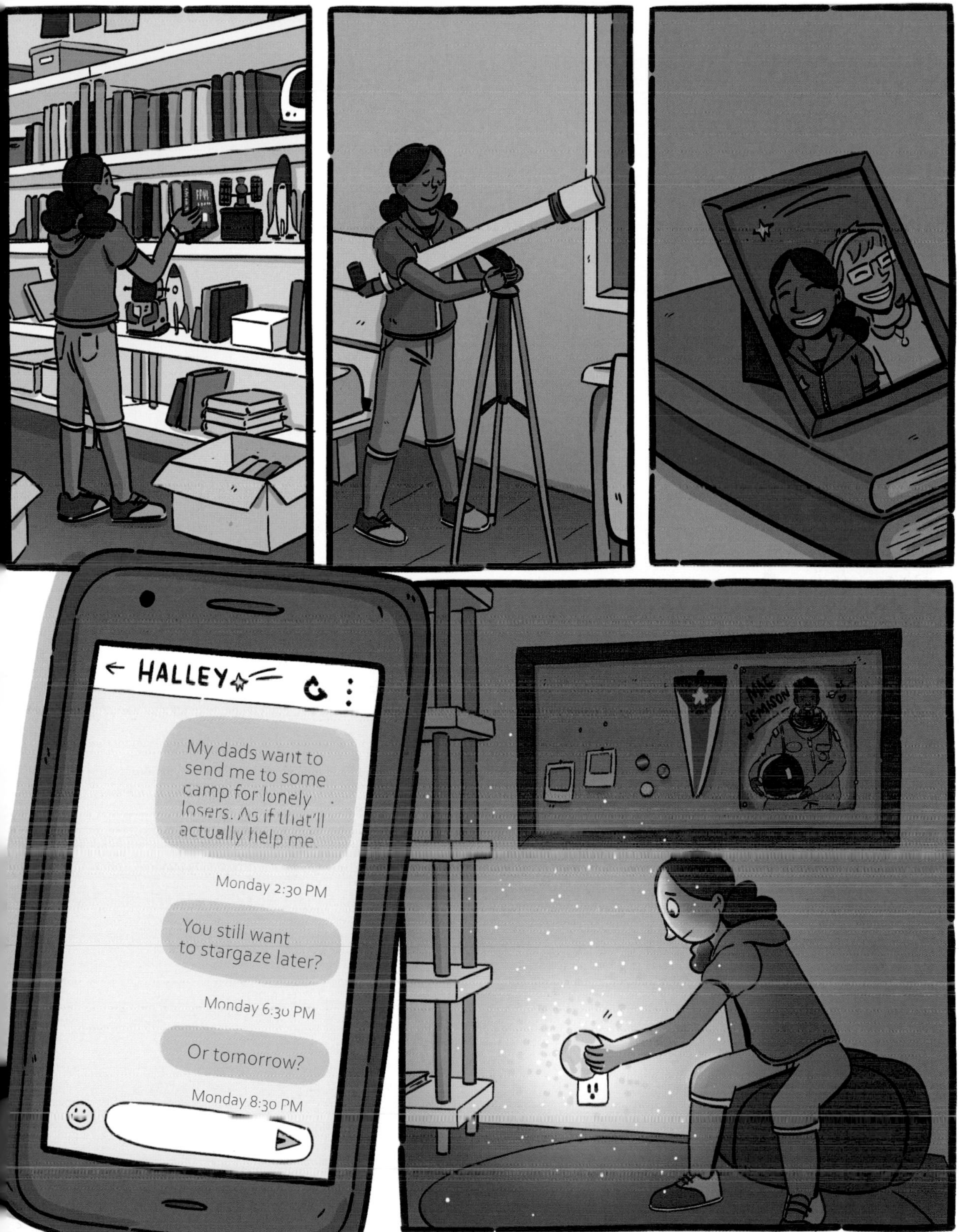

← HALLEY
My dads want to send me to some camp for lonely losers. As if that'll actually help me.
Monday 2:30 PM
You still want to stargaze later?
Monday 6:30 PM
Or tomorrow?
Monday 8:30 PM
MAE JEMISON

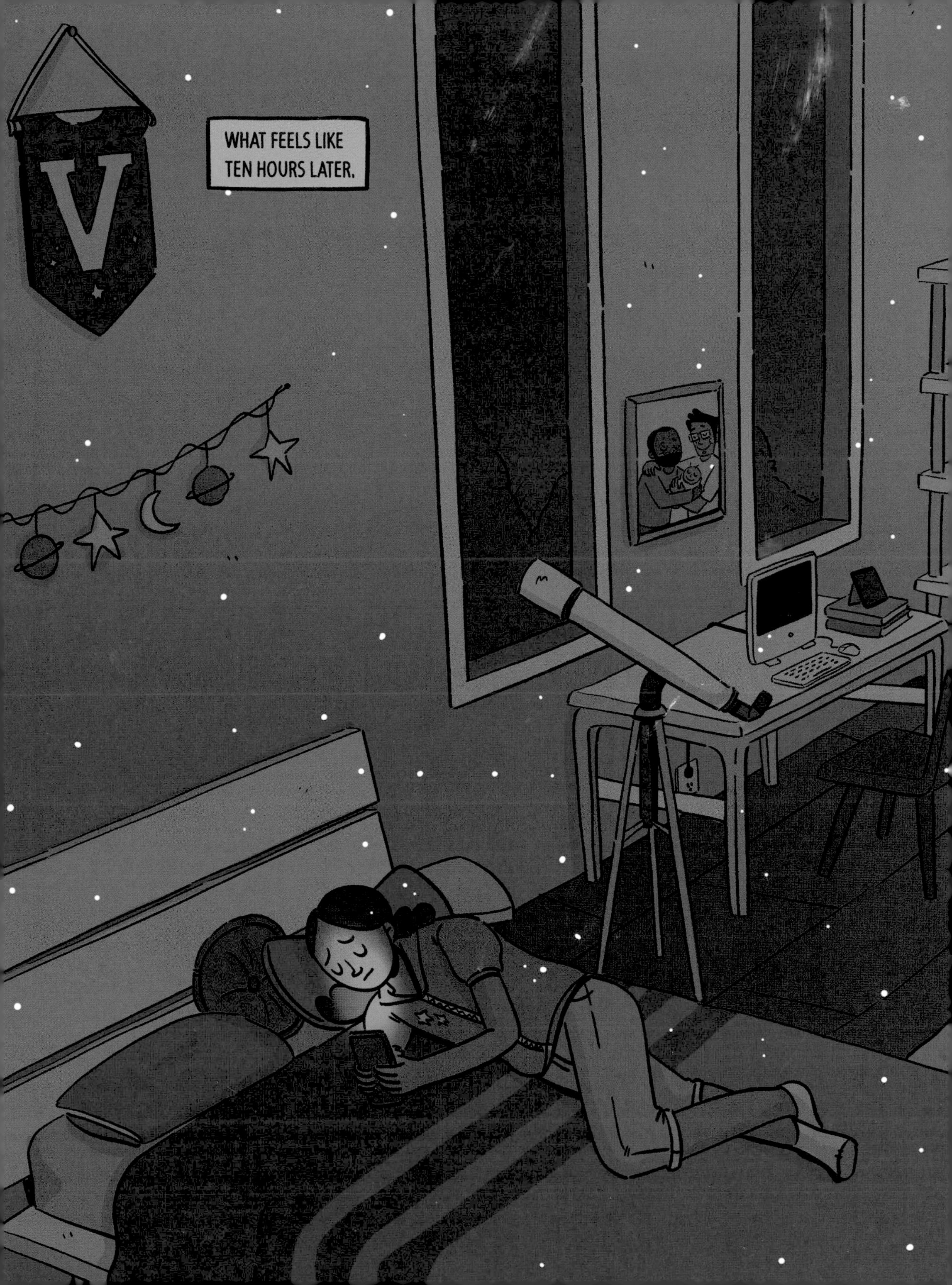
WHAT FEELS LIKE TEN HOURS LATER.

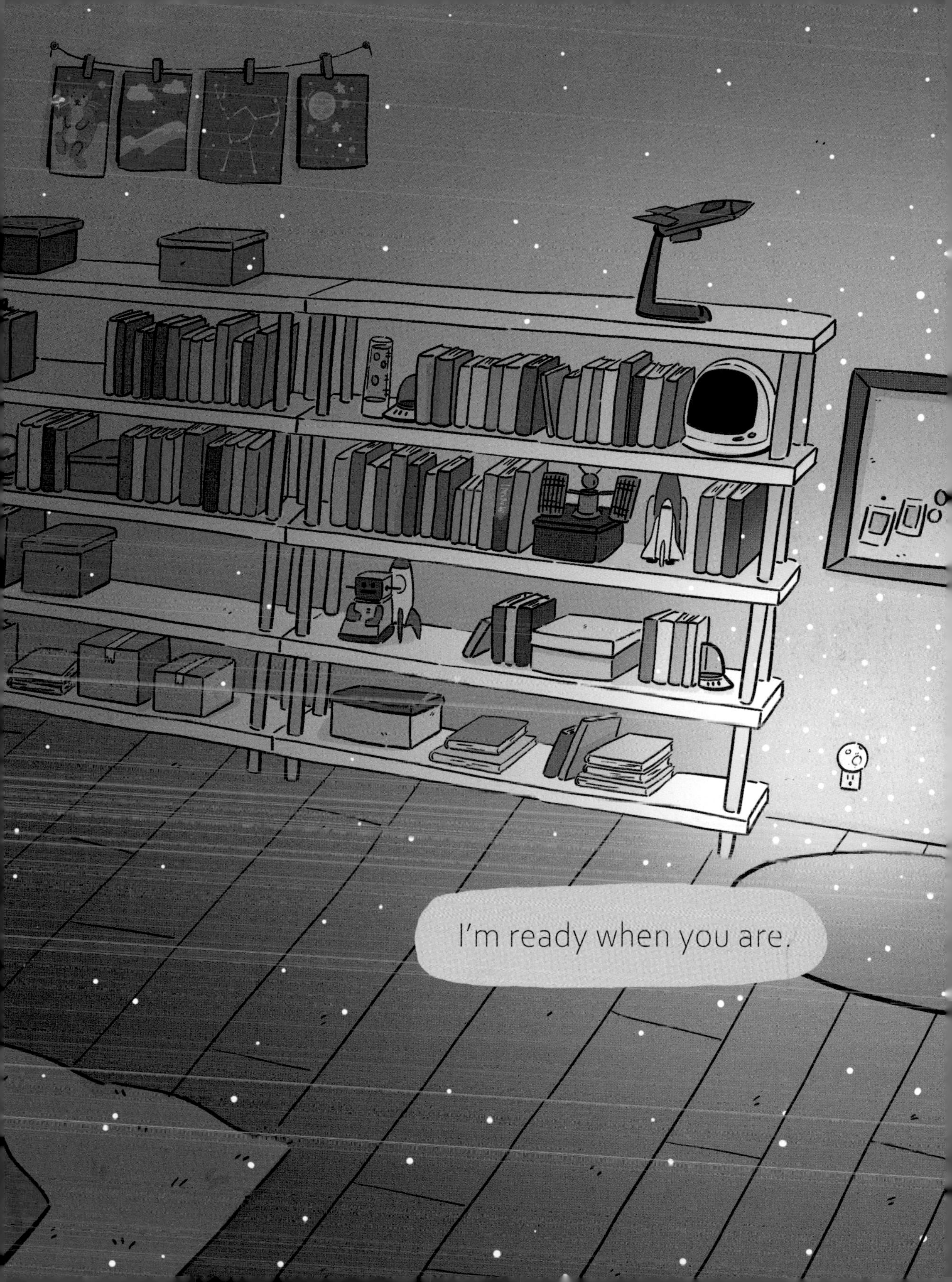
I'm ready when you are.

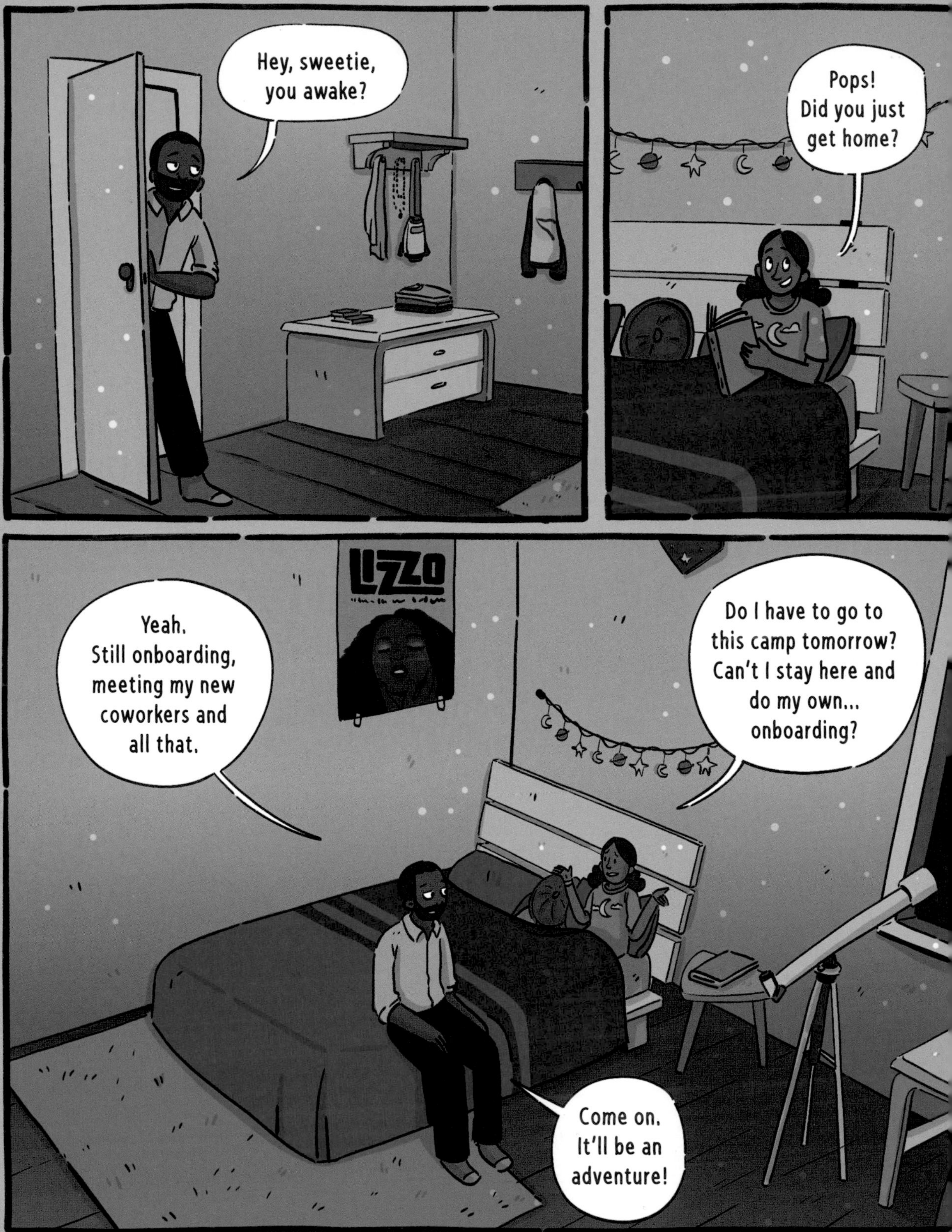
Hey, sweetie, you awake?
Pops! Did you just get home?
LIZZO
Yeah. Still onboarding, meeting my new coworkers and all that.
Do I have to go to this camp tomorrow? Can't I stay here and do my own... onboarding?
Come on. It'll be an adventure!

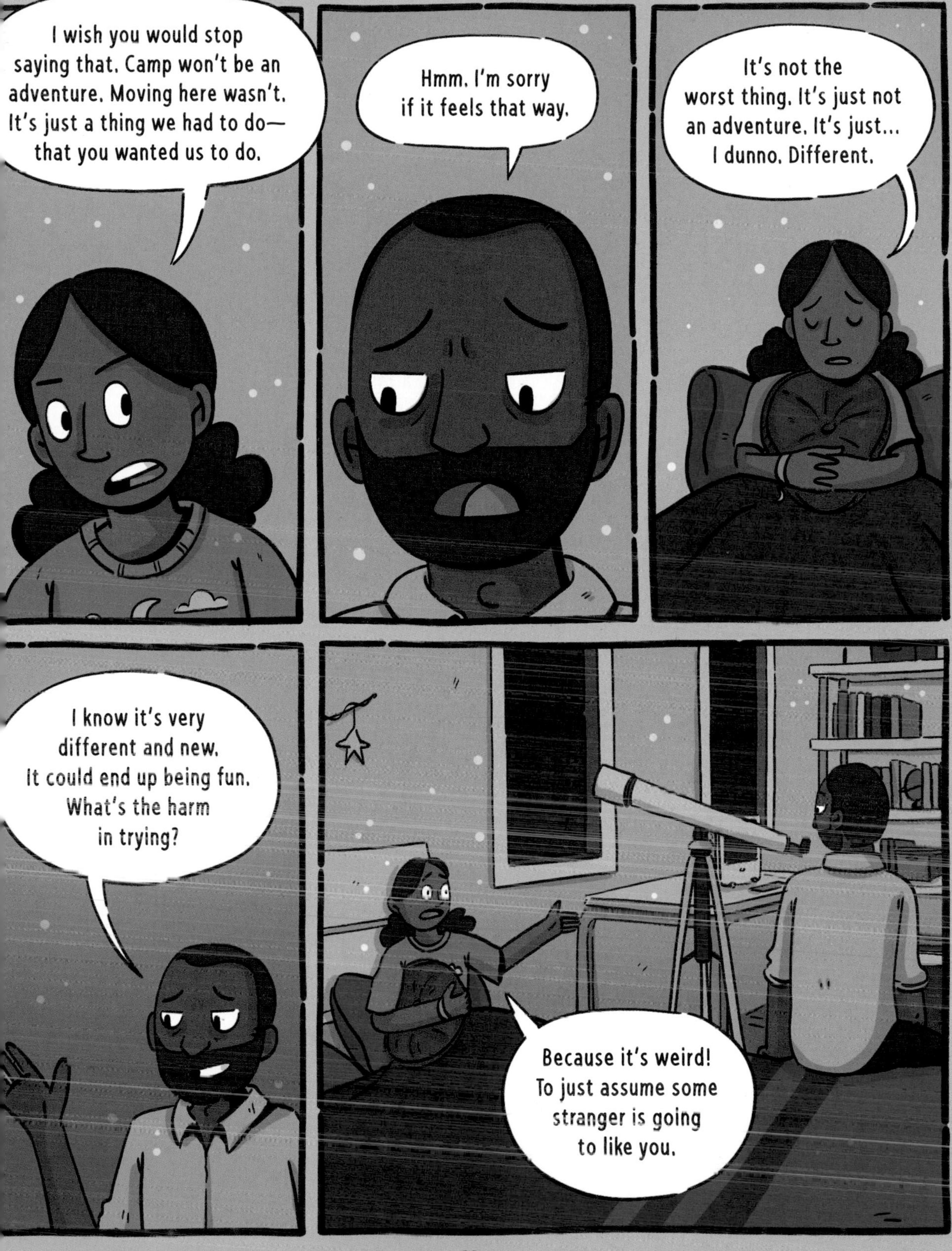
I wish you would stop saying that. Camp won't be an adventure. Moving here wasn't. It's just a thing we had to do—that you wanted us to do.
Hmm. I'm sorry if it feels that way.
It's not the worst thing. It's just not an adventure. It's just... I dunno. Different.
I know it's very different and new. It could end up being fun. What's the harm in trying?
Because it's weird! To just assume some stranger is going to like you.

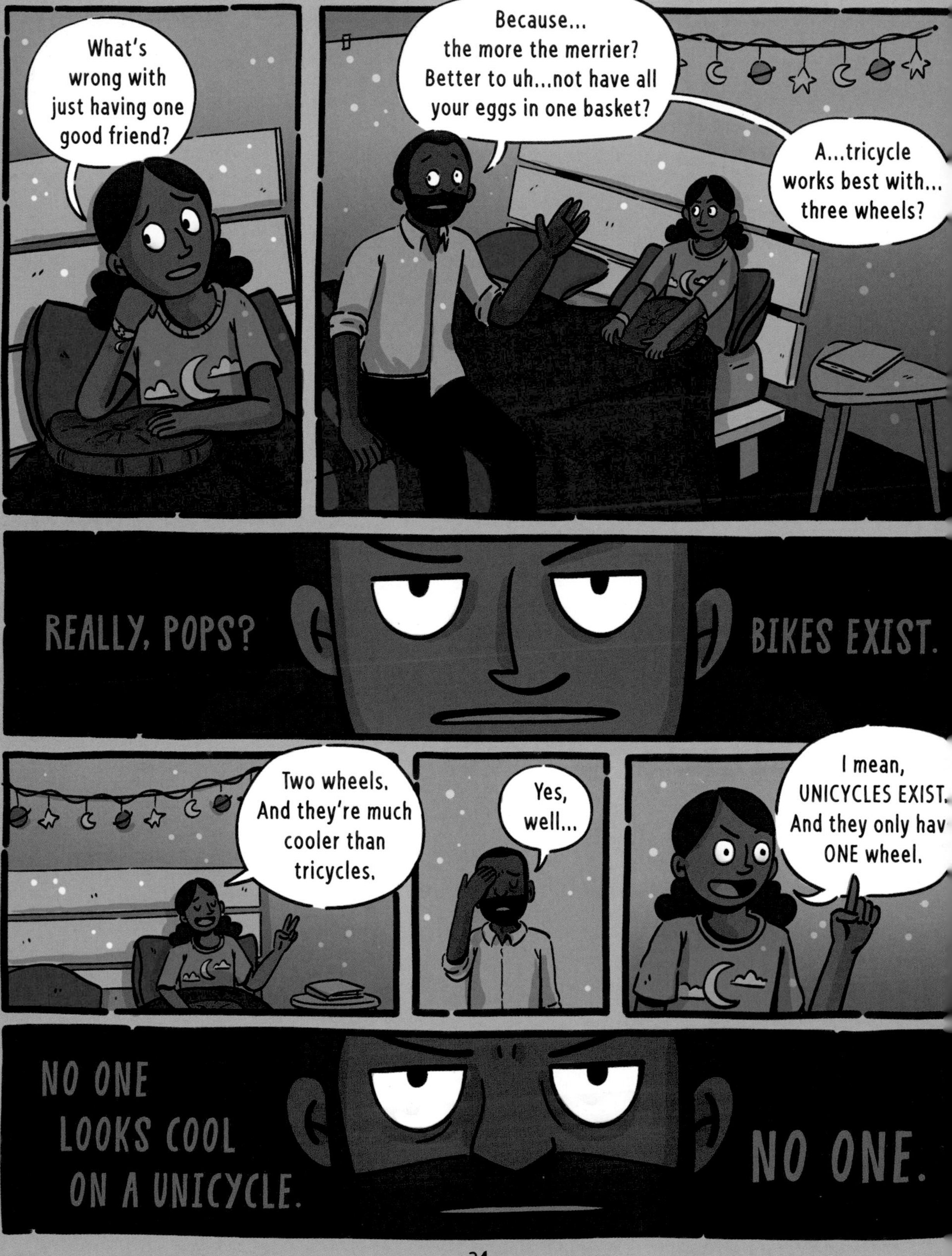
What's wrong with just having one good friend?
Because... the more the merrier? Better to uh...not have all your eggs in one basket?
A...tricycle works best with... three wheels?
REALLY, POPS?
BIKES EXIST.
Two wheels. And they're much cooler than tricycles.
Yes, well...
I mean, UNICYCLES EXIST. And they only hav ONE wheel.
NO ONE LOOKS COOL ON A UNICYCLE.
NO ONE.

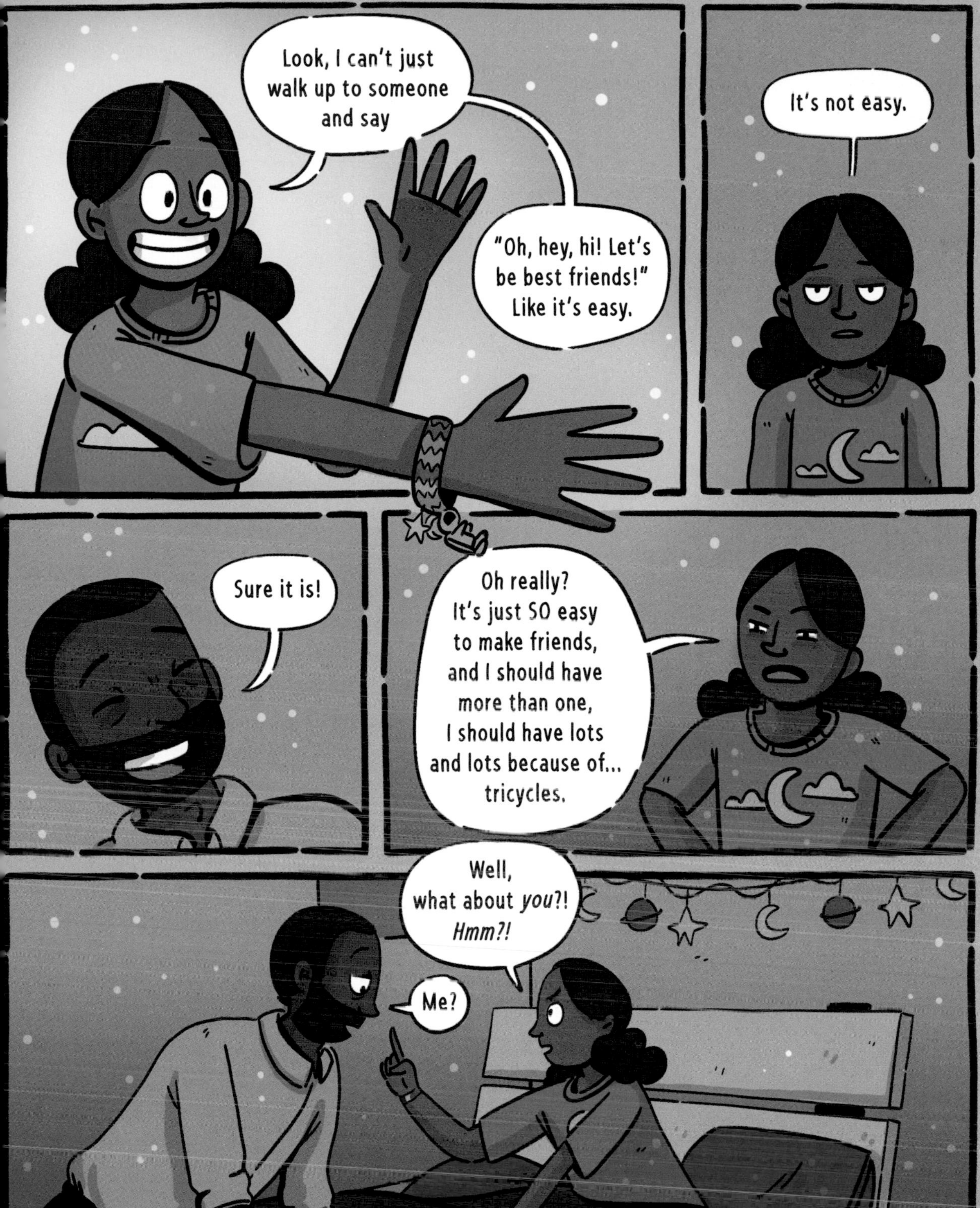
Look, I can't just walk up to someone and say
"Oh, hey, hi! Let's be best friends!" Like it's easy.
It's not easy.
Sure it is!
Oh really? It's just SO easy to make friends, and I should have more than one, I should have lots and lots because of... tricycles.
Well, what about *you*?! *Hmm?!*
Me?

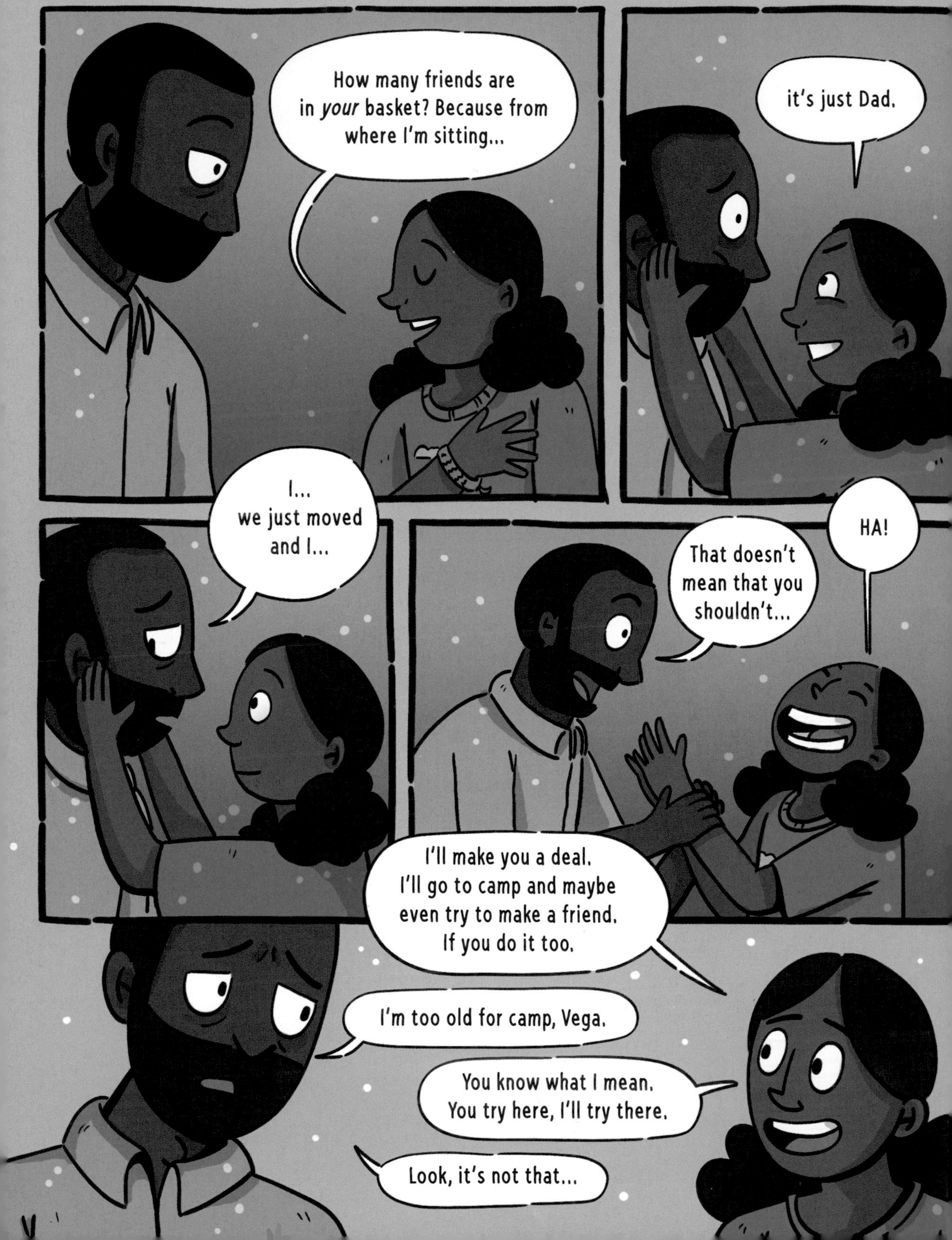
How many friends are in *your* basket? Because from where I'm sitting...
it's just Dad.
I... we just moved and I...
That doesn't mean that you shouldn't...
HA!
I'll make you a deal. I'll go to camp and maybe even try to make a friend. If you do it too.
I'm too old for camp, Vega.
You know what I mean. You try here, I'll try there.
Look, it's not that...

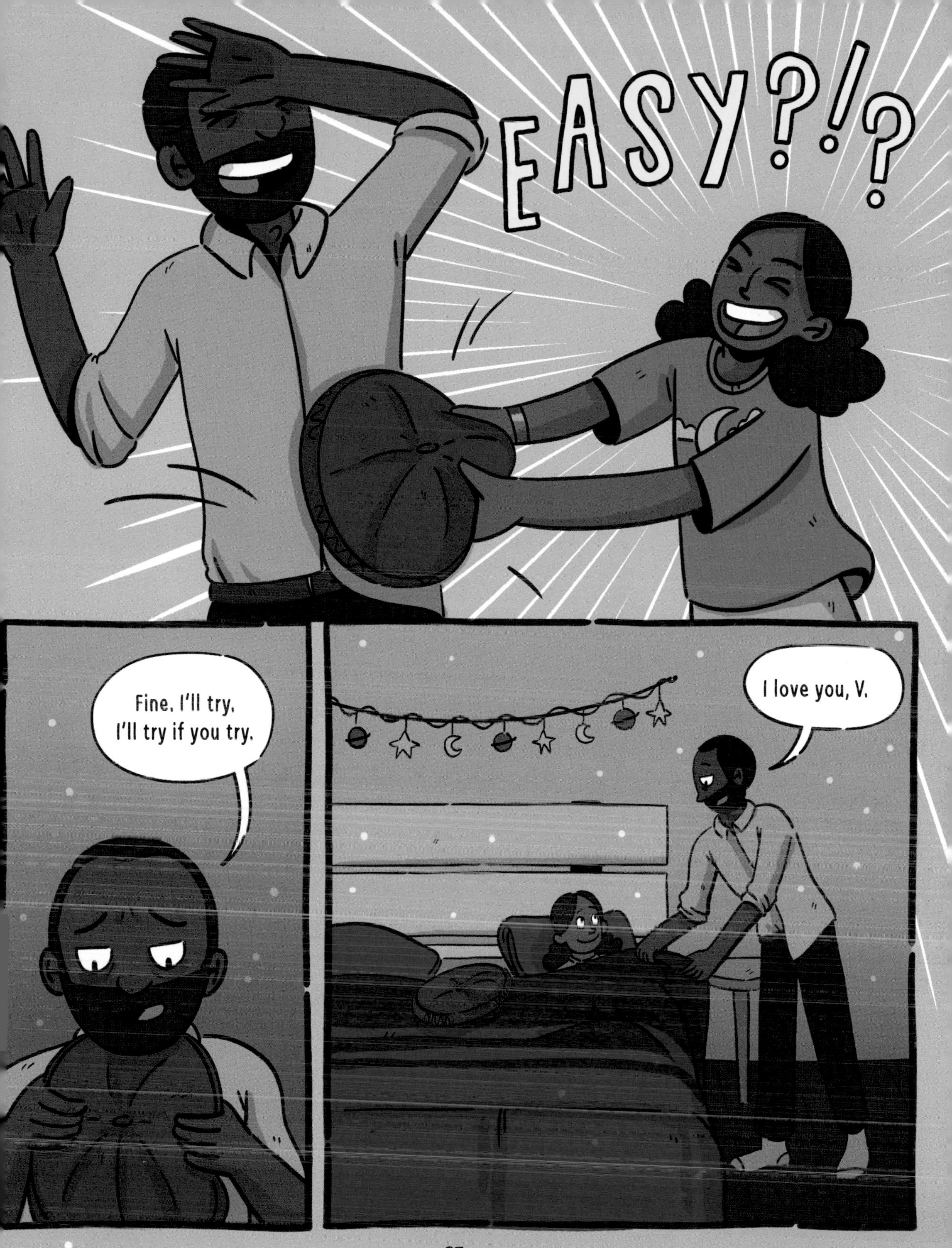
EASY?!?
Fine, I'll try. I'll try if you try.
I love you, V.

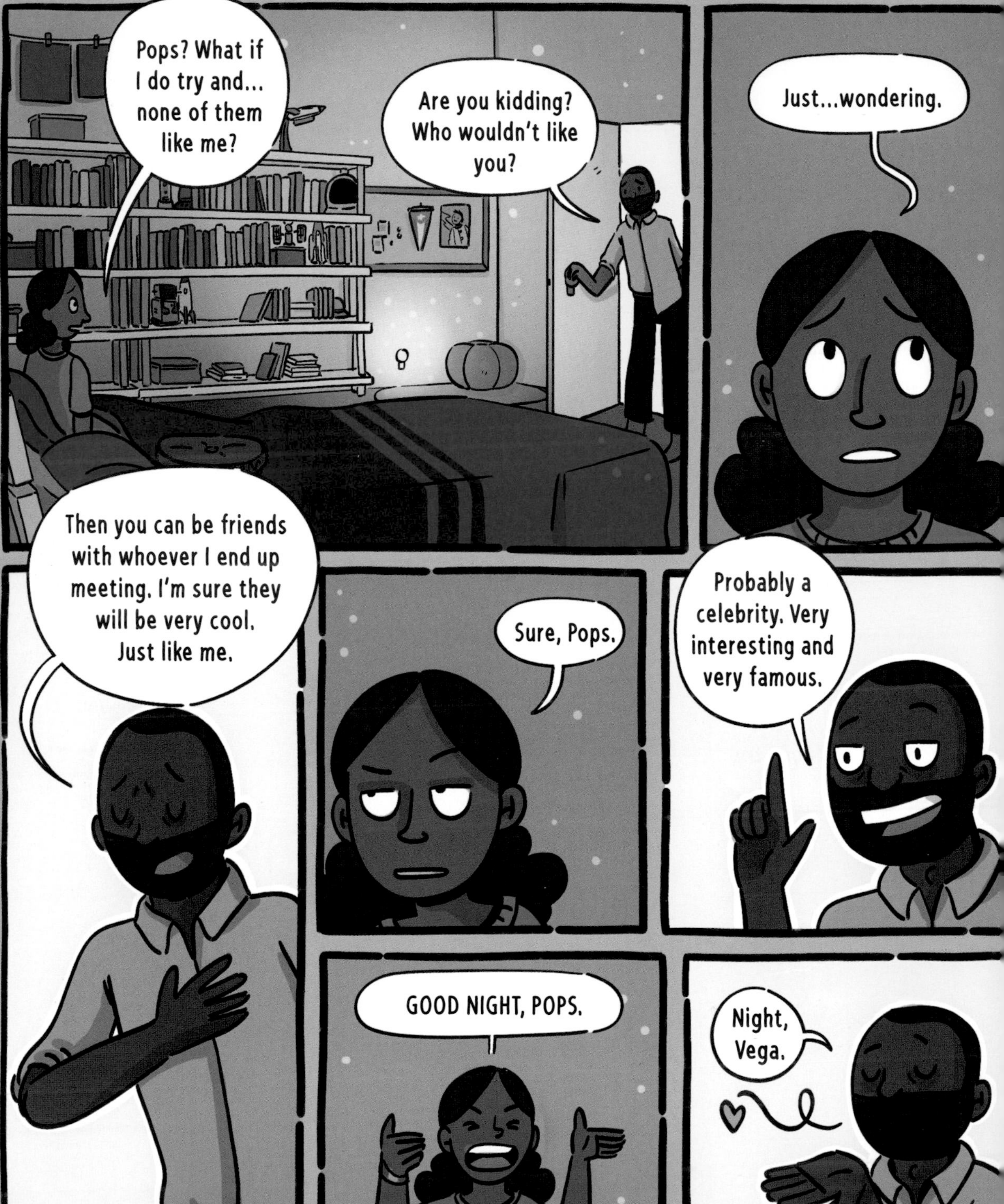
Pops? What if I do try and... none of them like me?
Are you kidding? Who wouldn't like you?
Just...wondering.
Then you can be friends with whoever I end up meeting. I'm sure they will be very cool. Just like me.
Sure, Pops.
Probably a celebrity. Very interesting and very famous.
GOOD NIGHT, POPS.
Night, Vega.

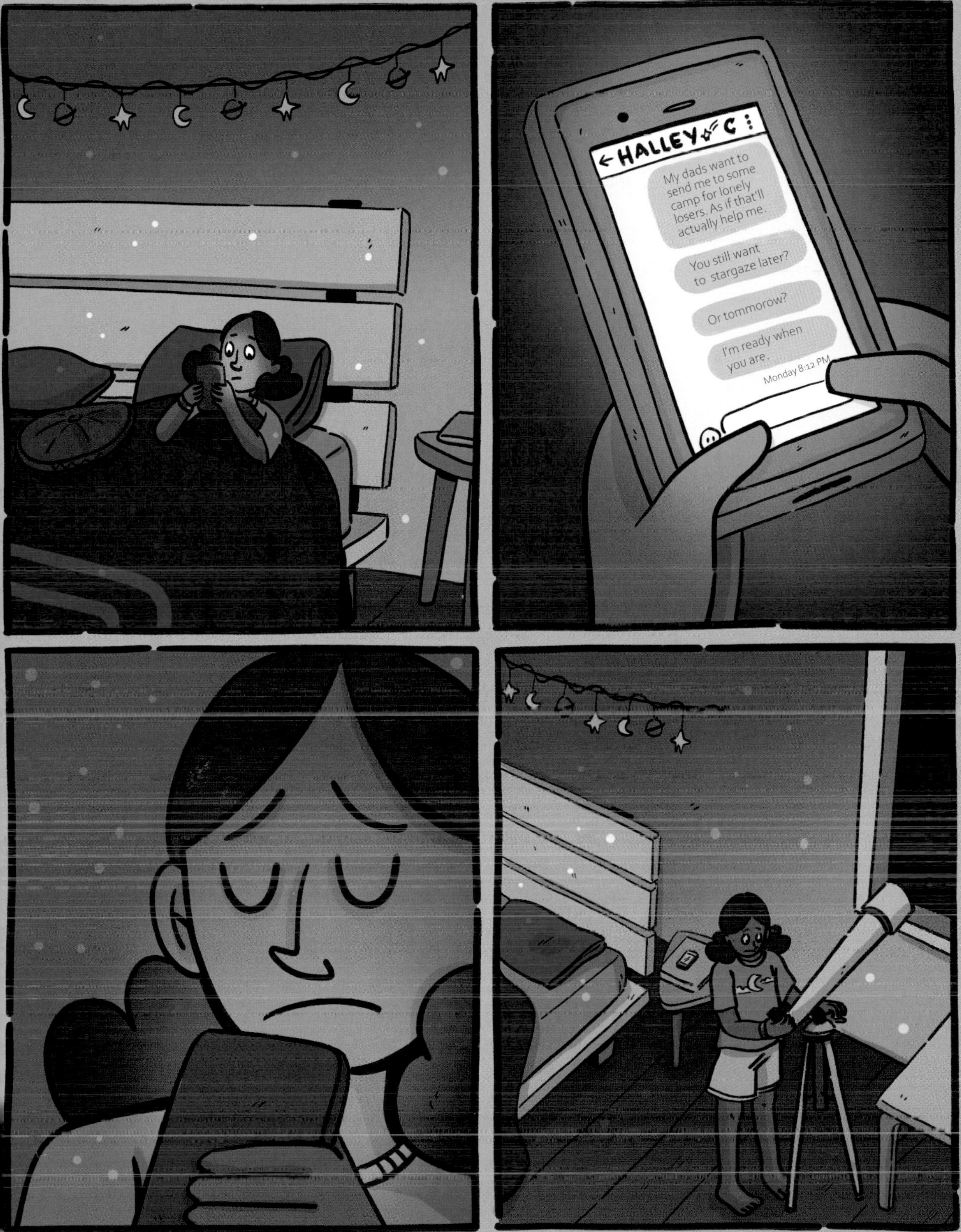
HALLEY
My dads want to send me to some camp for lonely losers. As if that'll actually help me.
You still want to stargaze later?
Or tommorow?
I'm ready when you are.
Monday 8:12 PM

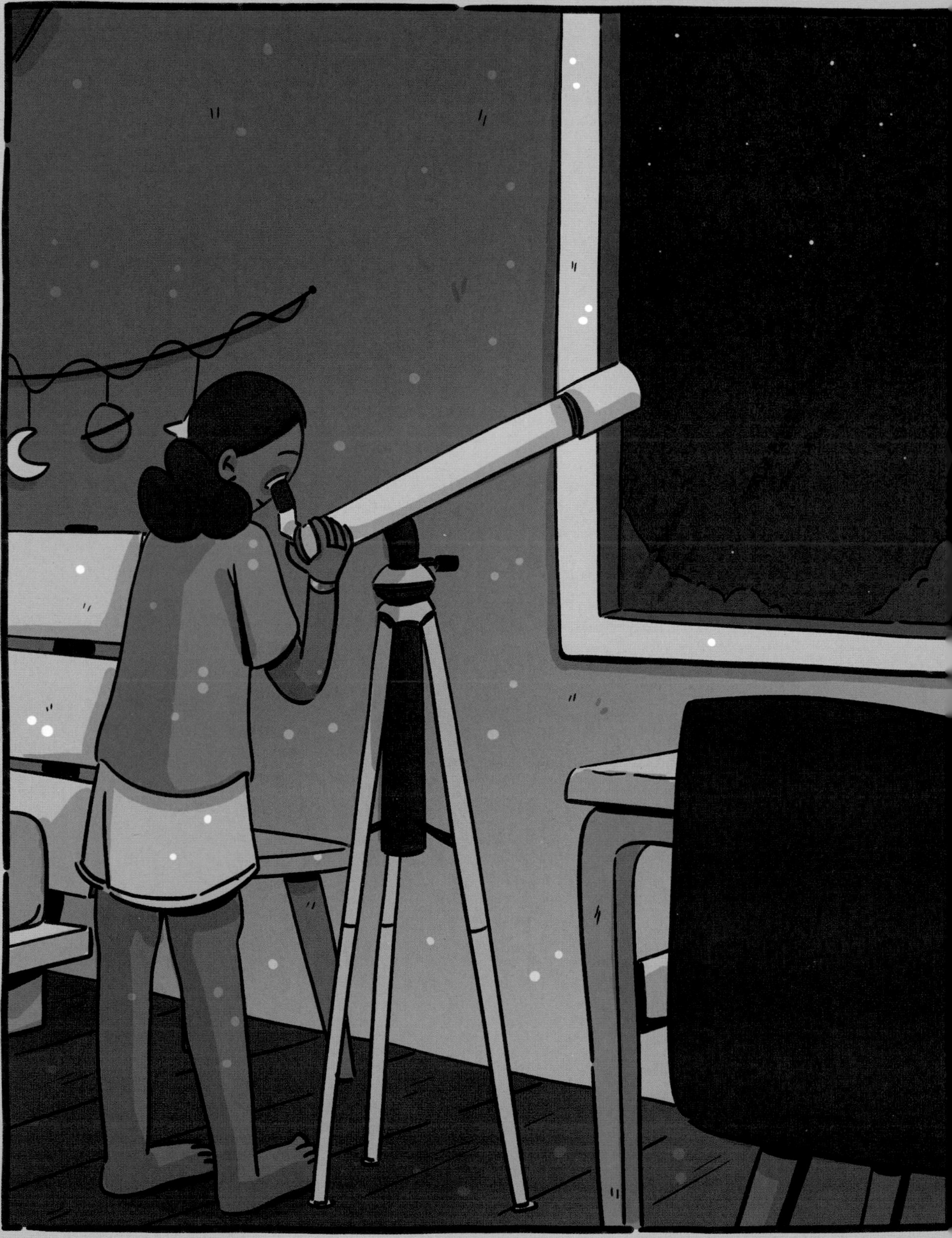

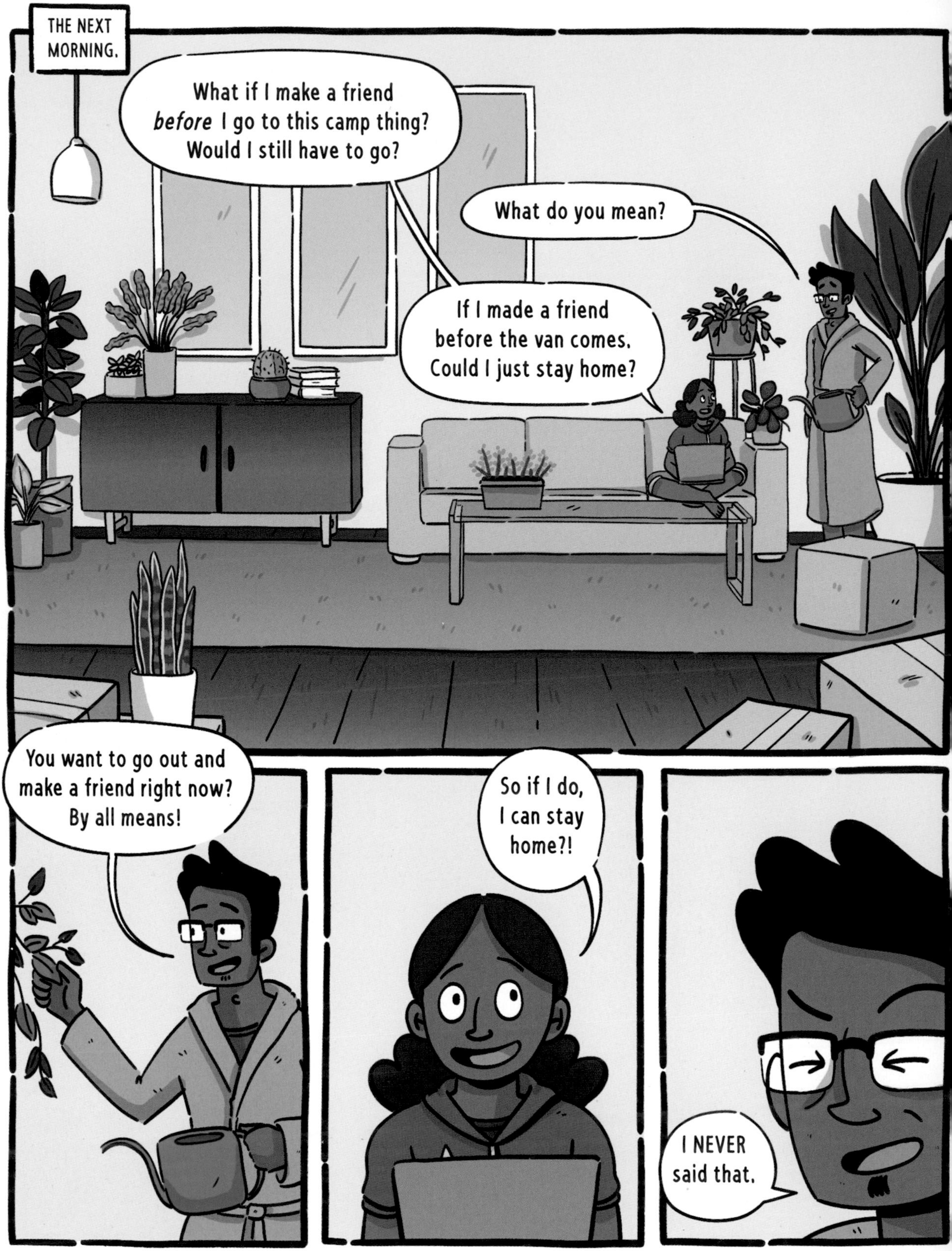

THE NEXT MORNING.
What if I make a friend *before* I go to this camp thing? Would I still have to go?
What do you mean?
If I made a friend before the van comes. Could I just stay home?
You want to go out and make a friend right now? By all means!
So if I do, I can stay home?!
I NEVER said that.

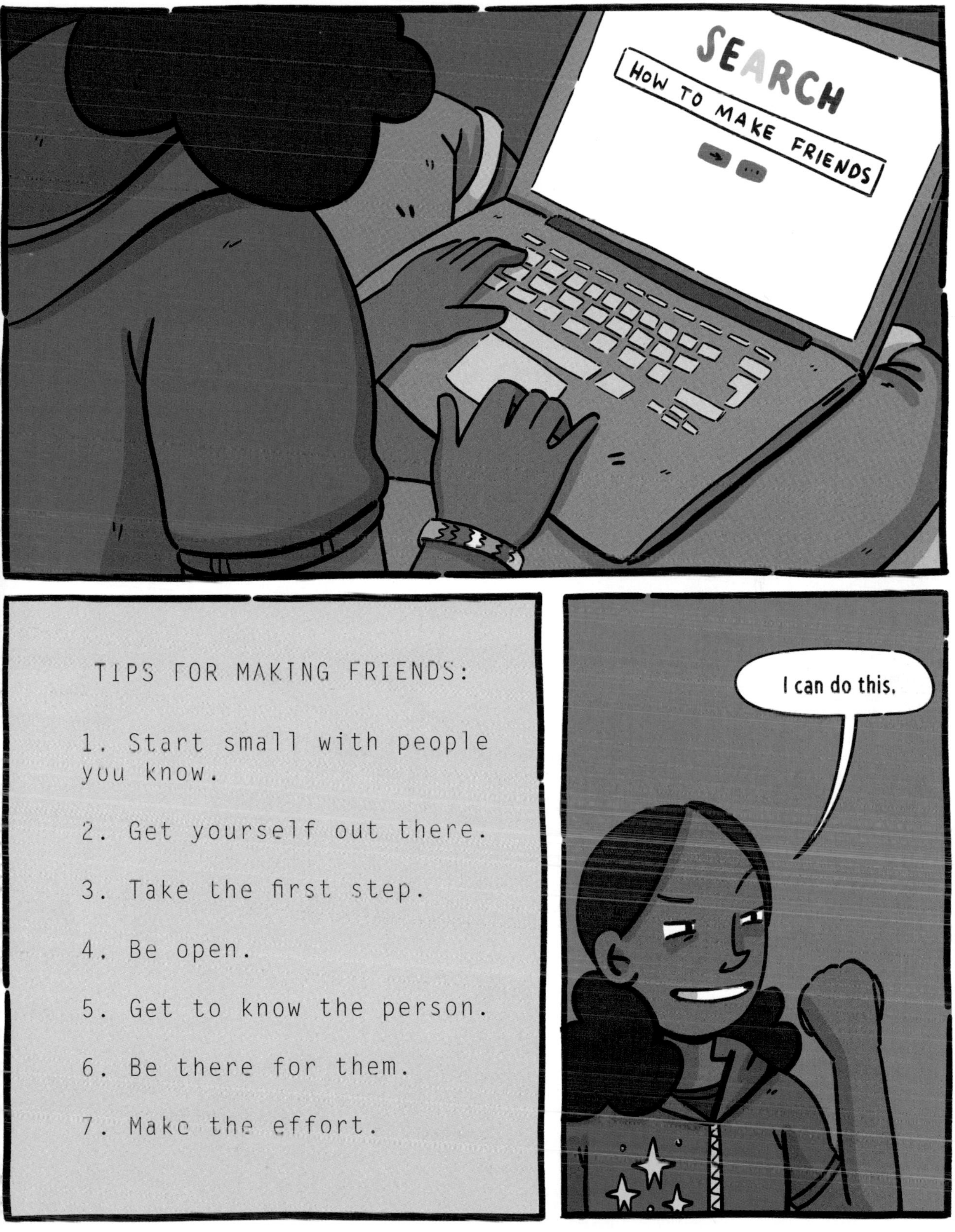
SEARCH
HOW TO MAKE FRIENDS
TIPS FOR MAKING FRIENDS:
1. Start small with people you know.
2. Get yourself out there.
3. Take the first step.
4. Be open.
5. Get to know the person.
6. Be there for them.
7. Make the effort.
I can do this.

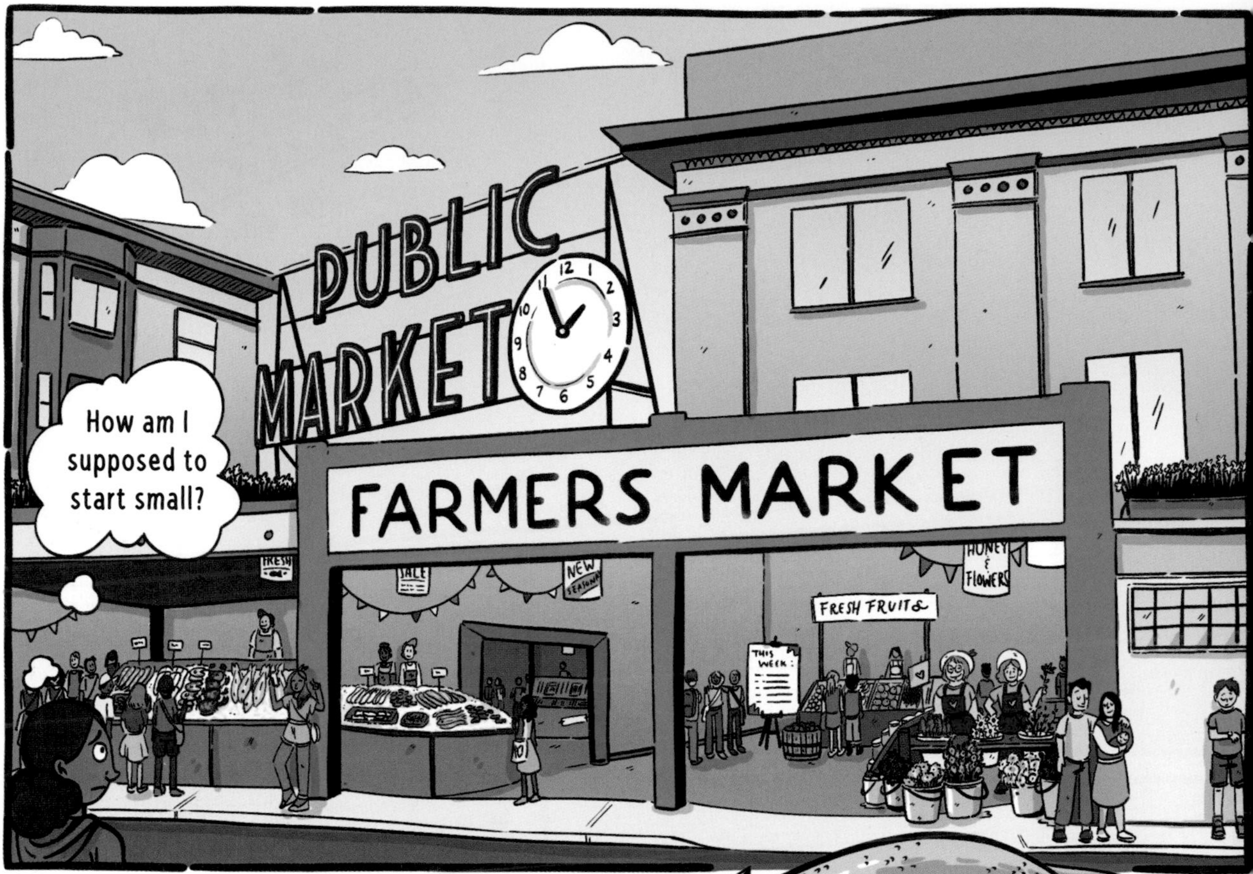
PUBLIC MARKET
FARMERS MARKET
How am I supposed to start small?
FRESH
SALE
NEW SEASON
HONEY & FLOWERS
FRESH FRUITS
THIS WEEK:

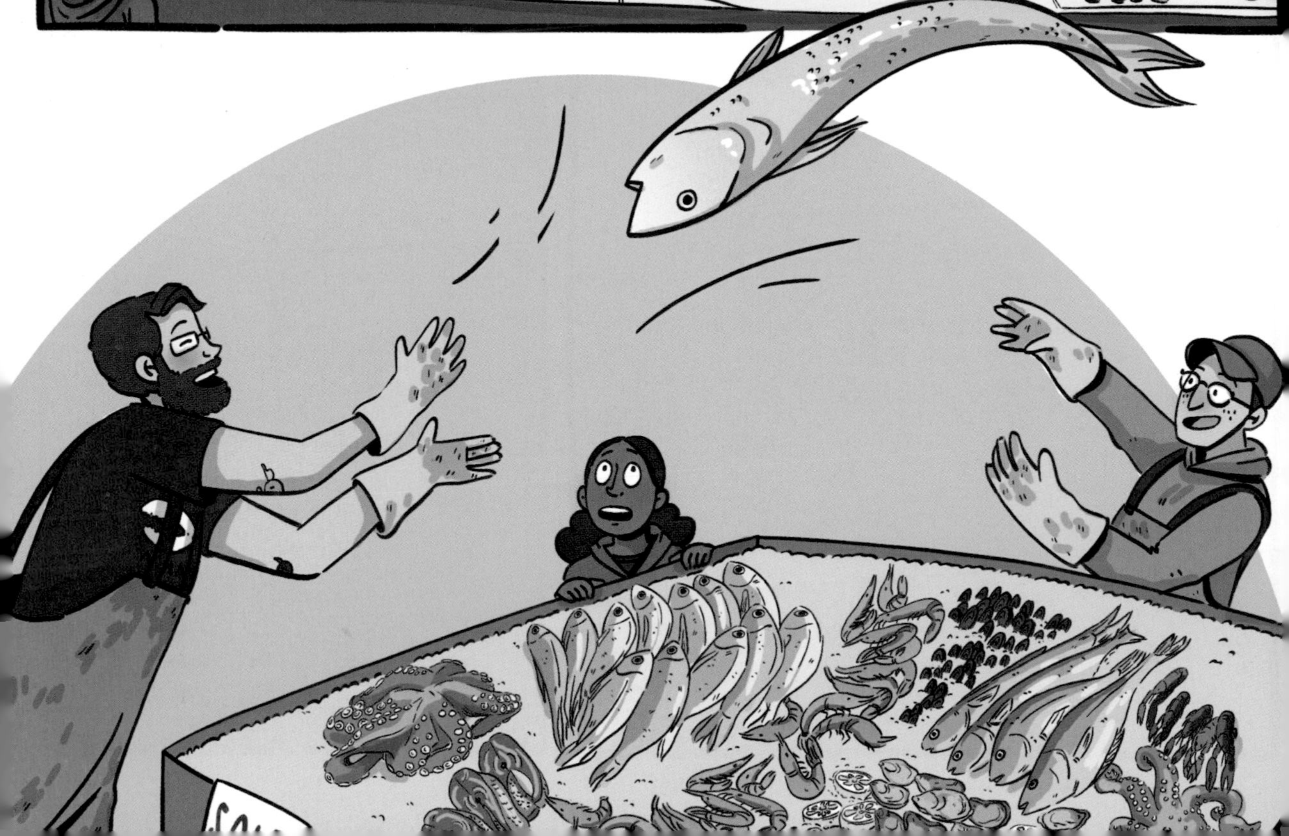

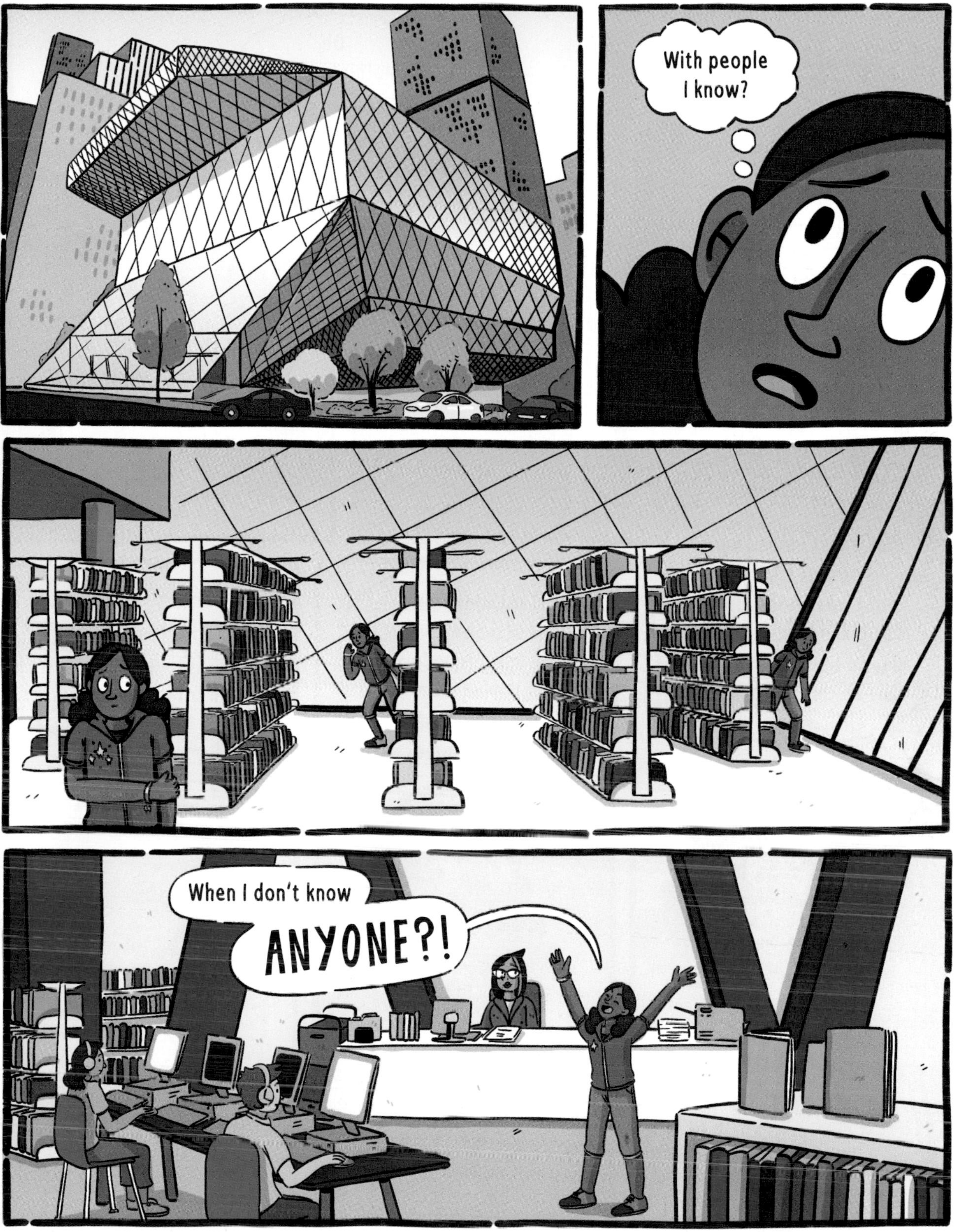

With people I know?
When I don't know
ANYONE?!

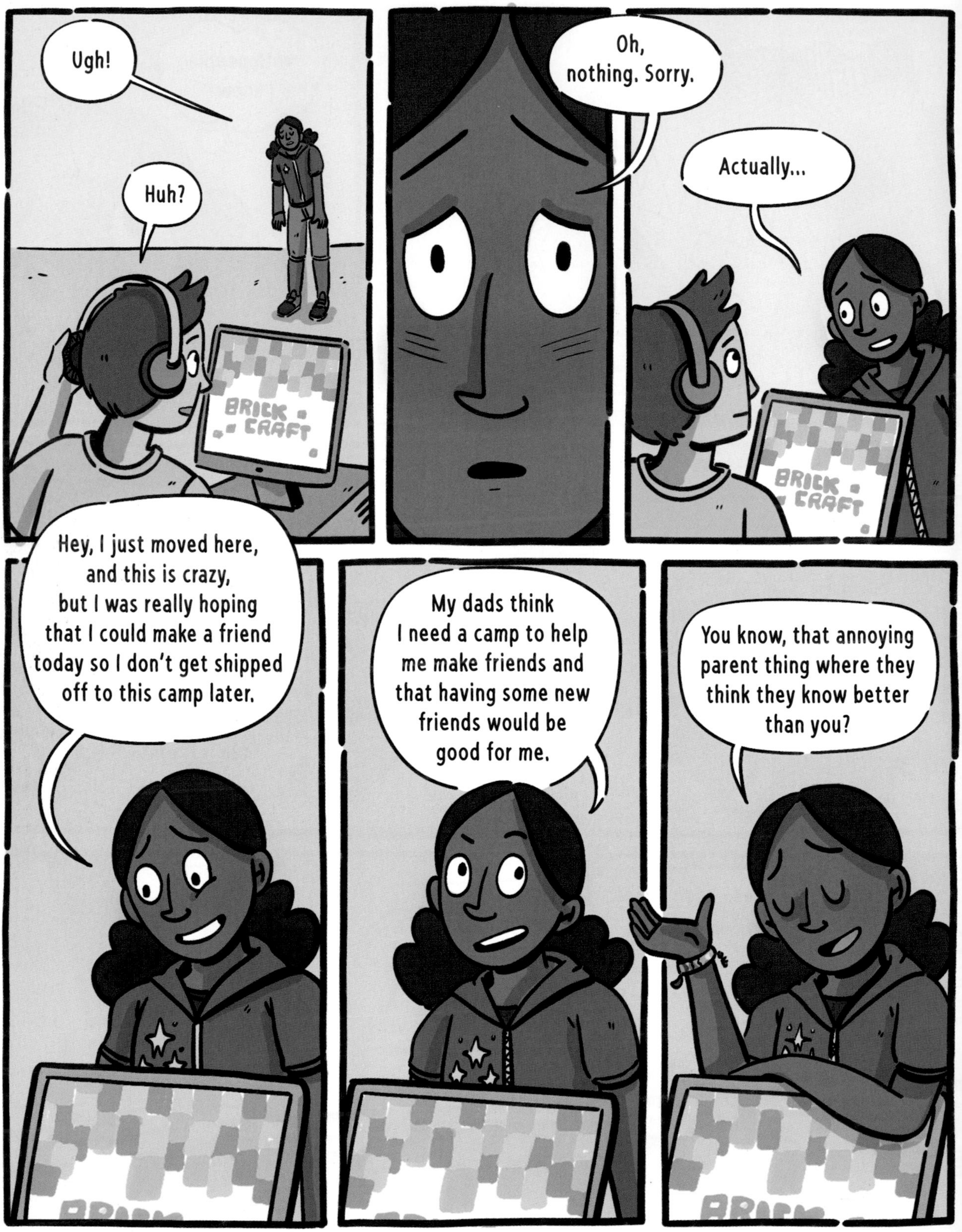
Ugh!
Huh?
BRICK CRAFT
Oh, nothing. Sorry.
Actually...
BRICK CRAFT
Hey, I just moved here, and this is crazy, but I was really hoping that I could make a friend today so I don't get shipped off to this camp later.
My dads think I need a camp to help me make friends and that having some new friends would be good for me.
You know, that annoying parent thing where they think they know better than you?

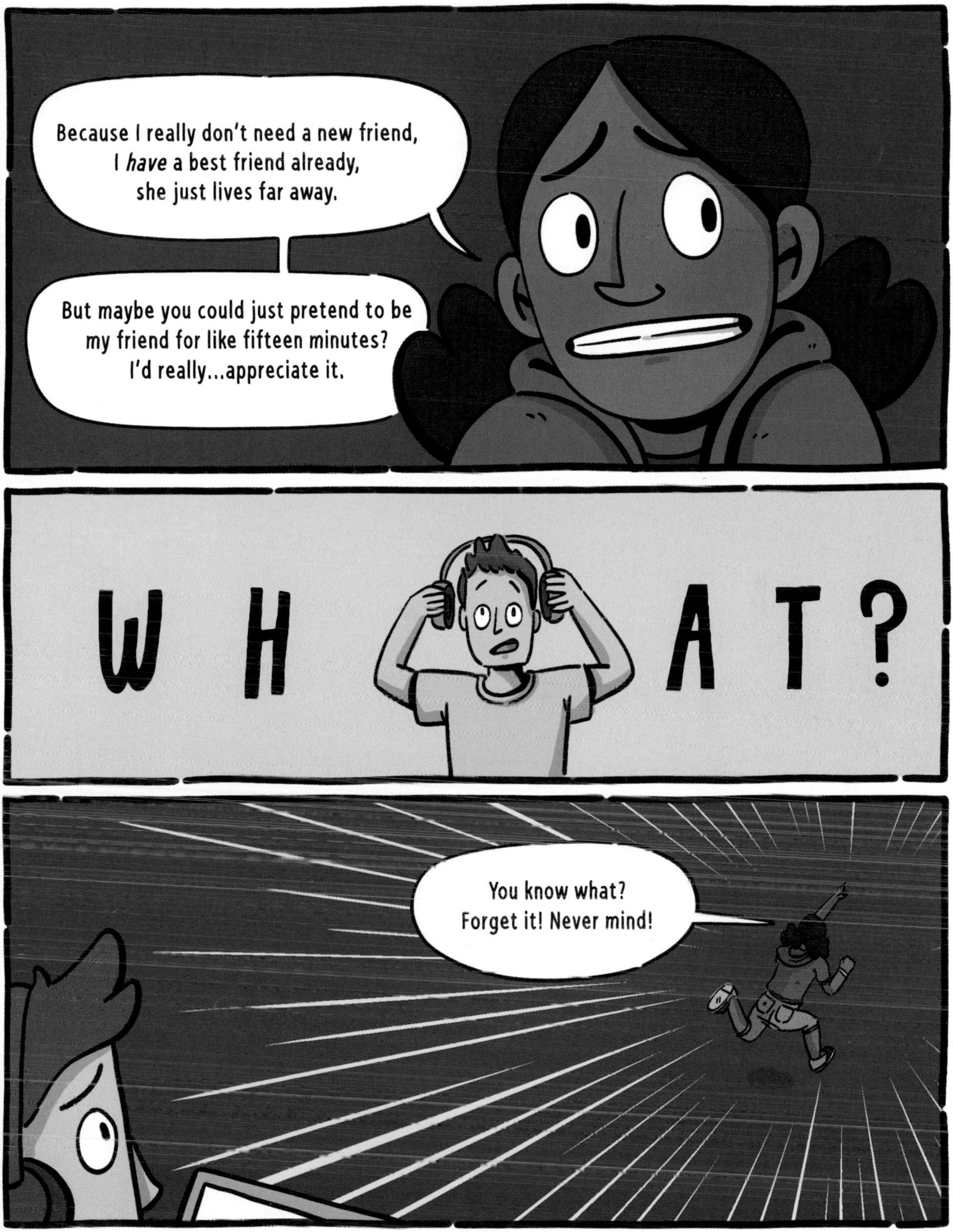
Because I really don't need a new friend, I *have* a best friend already, she just lives far away.
But maybe you could just pretend to be my friend for like fifteen minutes? I'd really...appreciate it.
WHAT?
You know what? Forget it! Never mind!

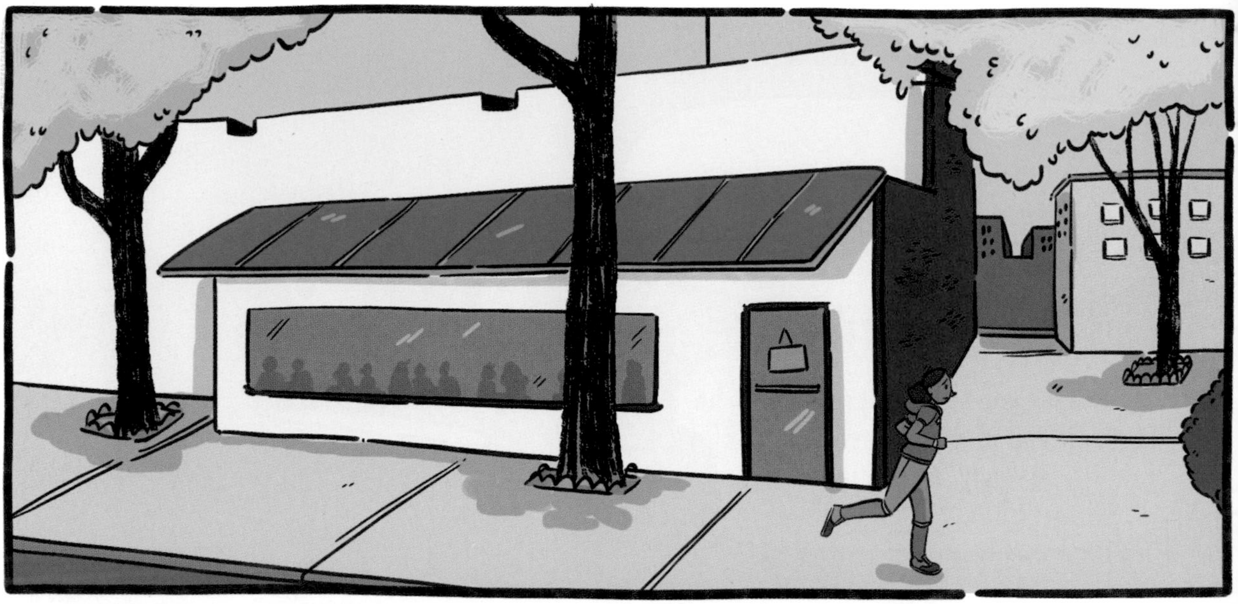

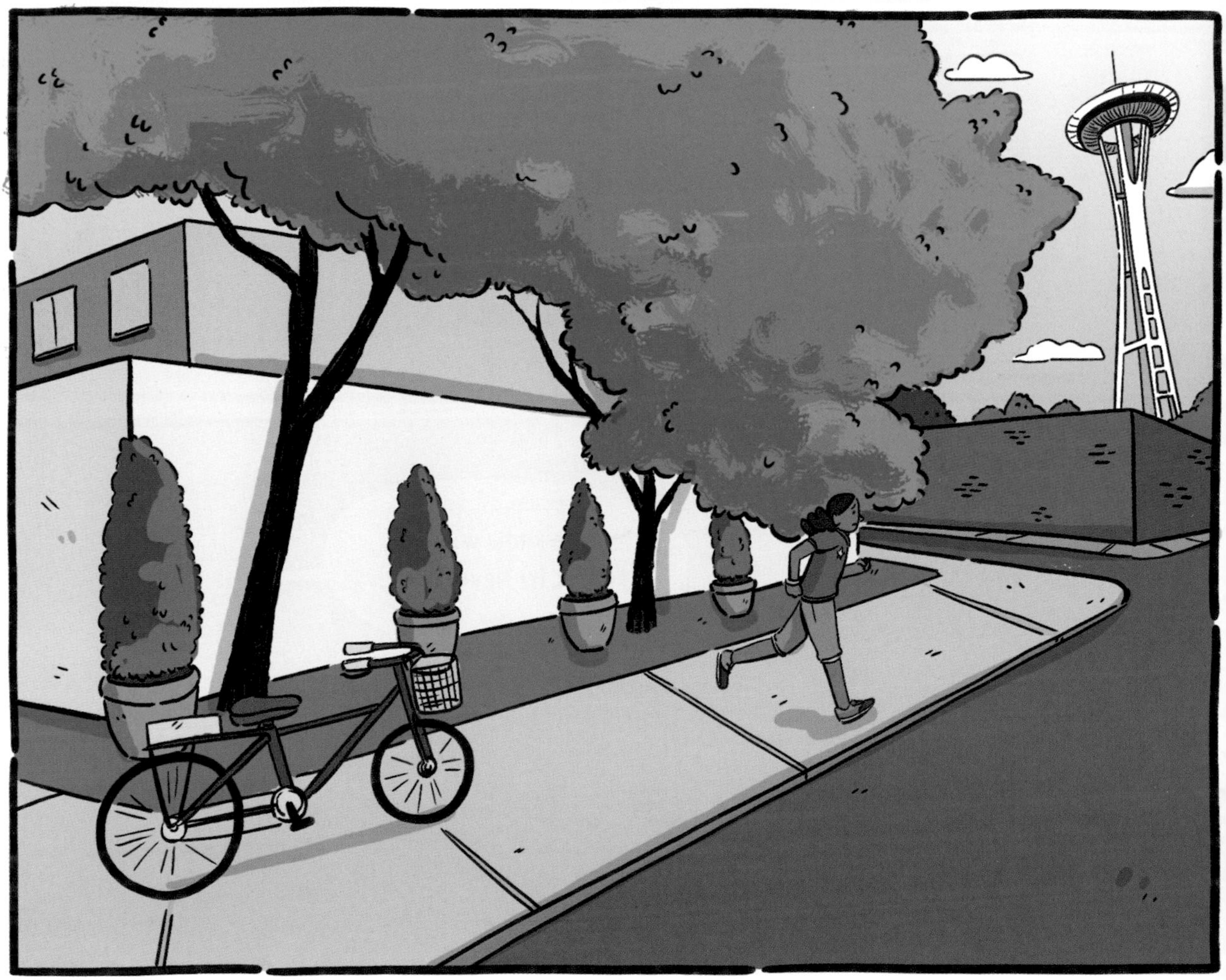

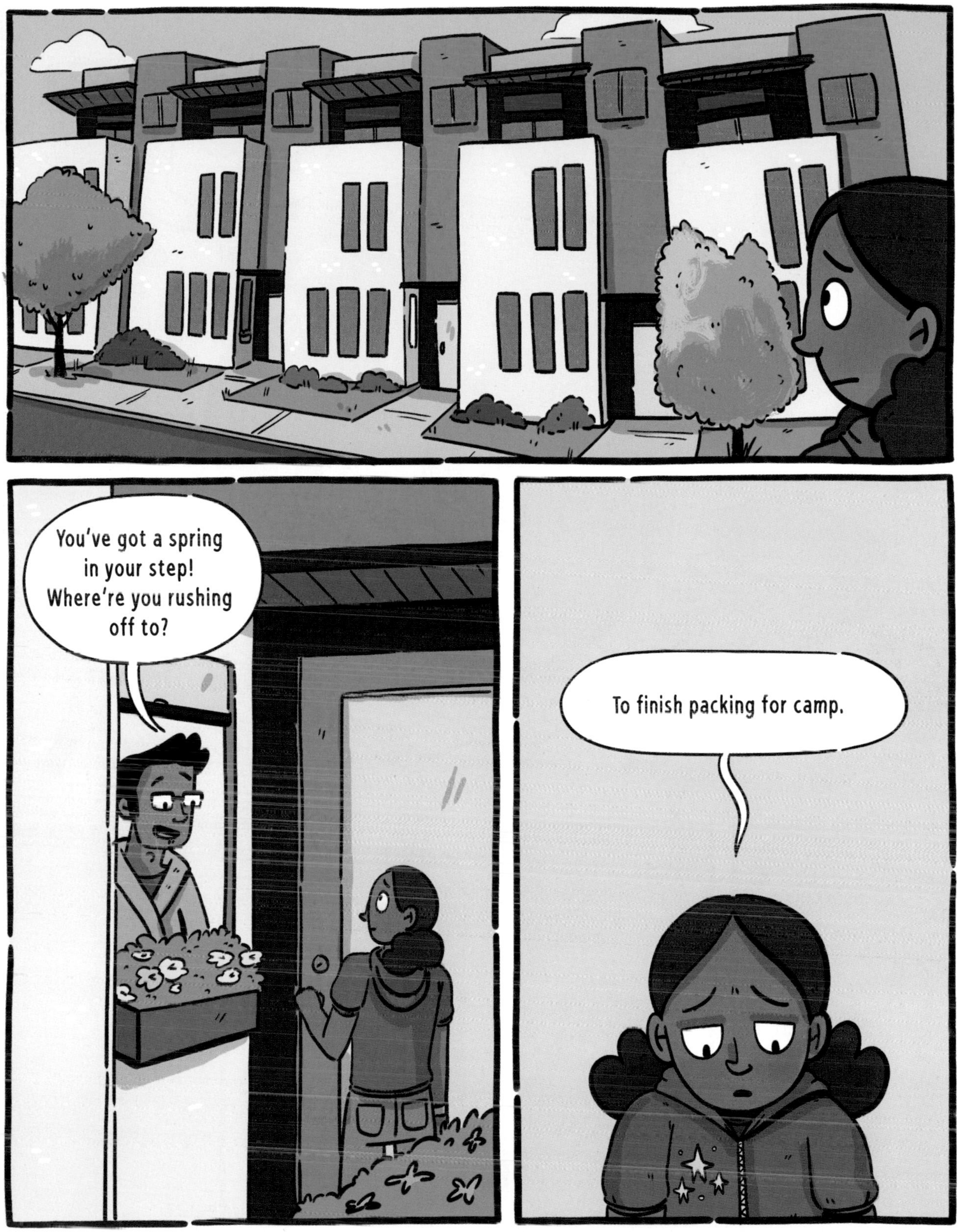
You've got a spring in your step! Where're you rushing off to?
To finish packing for camp.

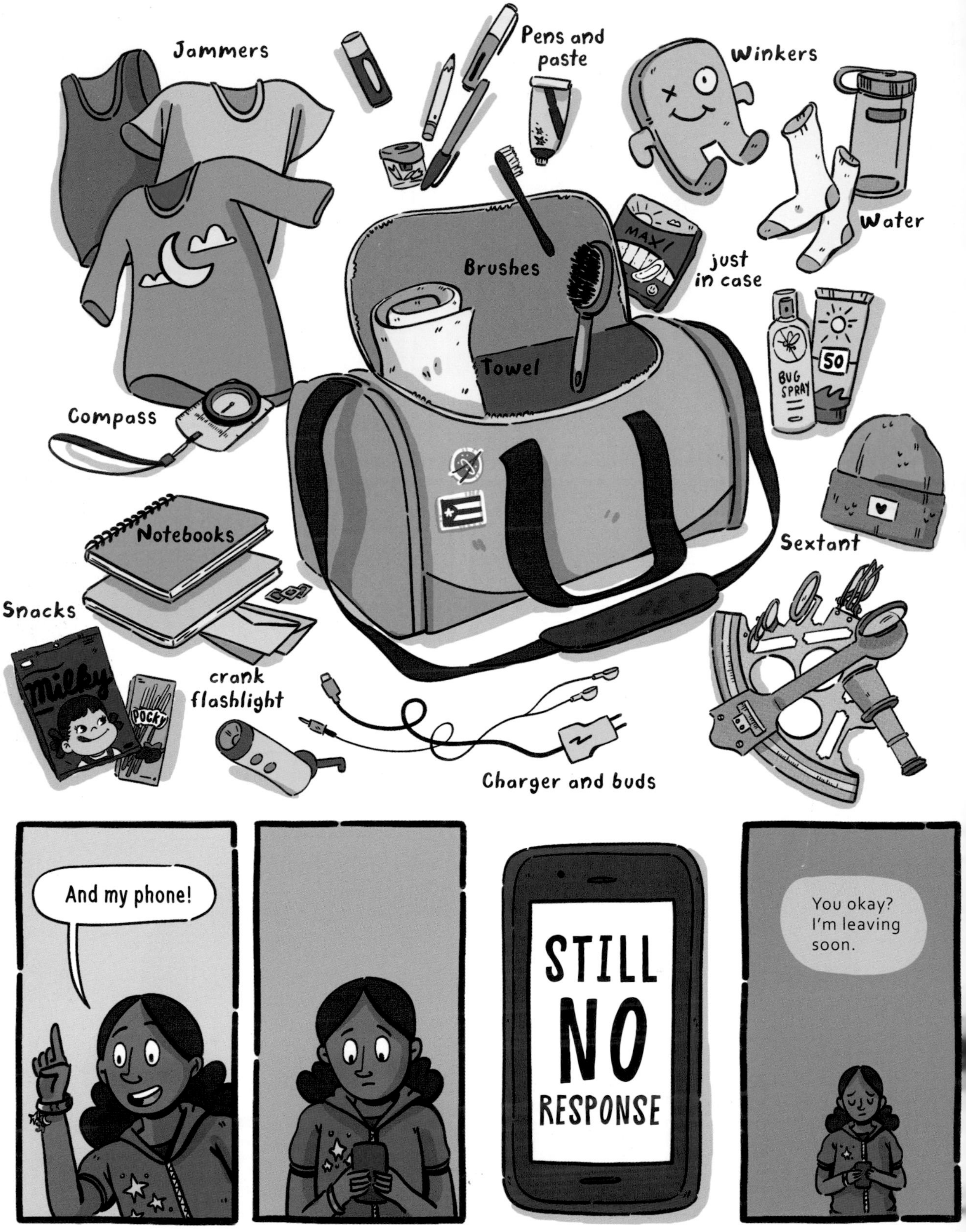

Jammers
Pens and paste
Winkers
Water
Brushes
MAXI
just in case
Towel
BUG SPRAY
50
Compass
Notebooks
Sextant
Snacks
milky
POCKY
crank flashlight
Charger and buds
And my phone!
STILL NO RESPONSE
You okay? I'm leaving soon.

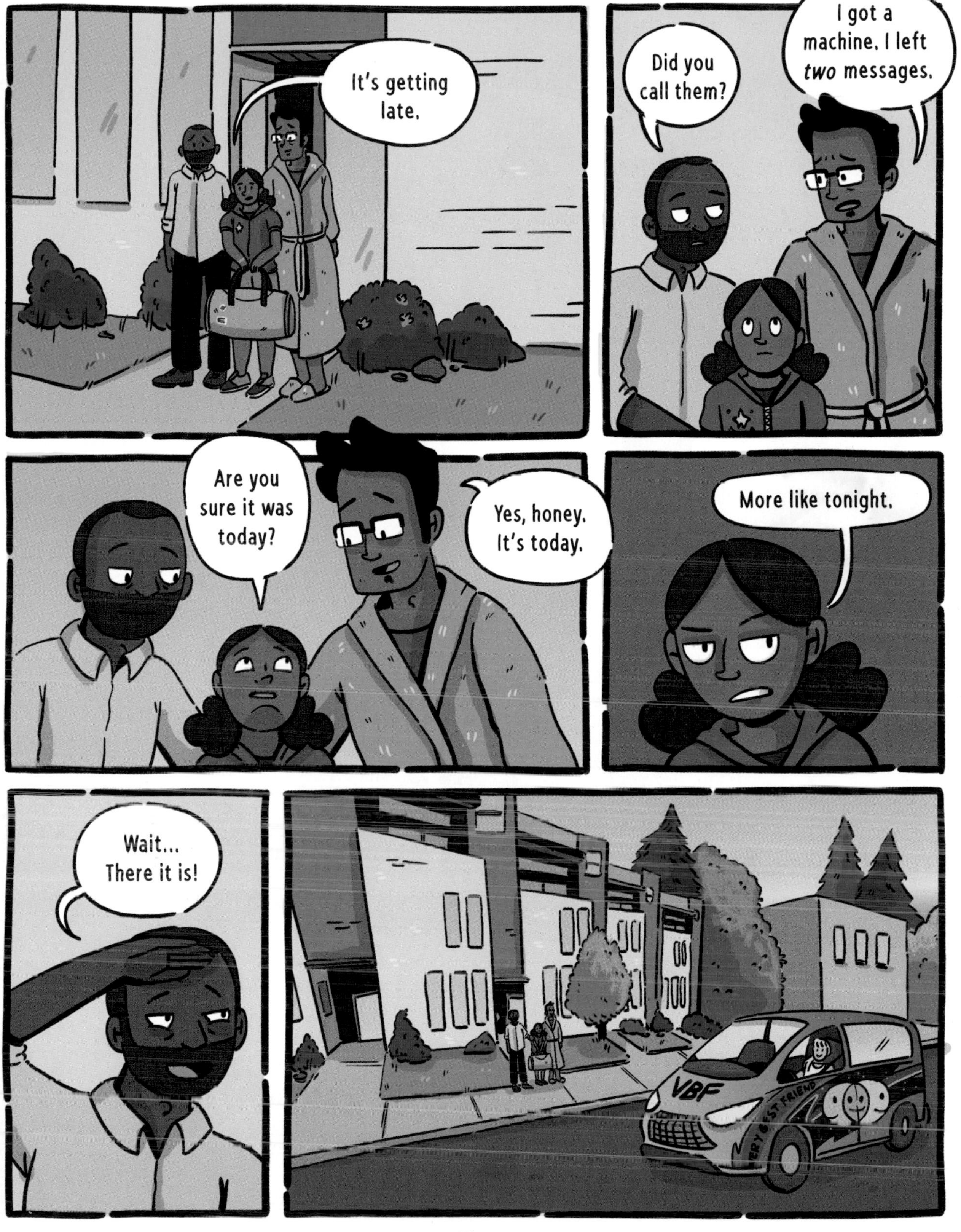
It's getting late.
Did you call them?
I got a machine. I left *two* messages.
Are you sure it was today?
Yes, honey. It's today.
More like tonight.
Wait... There it is!
VBF
VERY BEST FRIEND

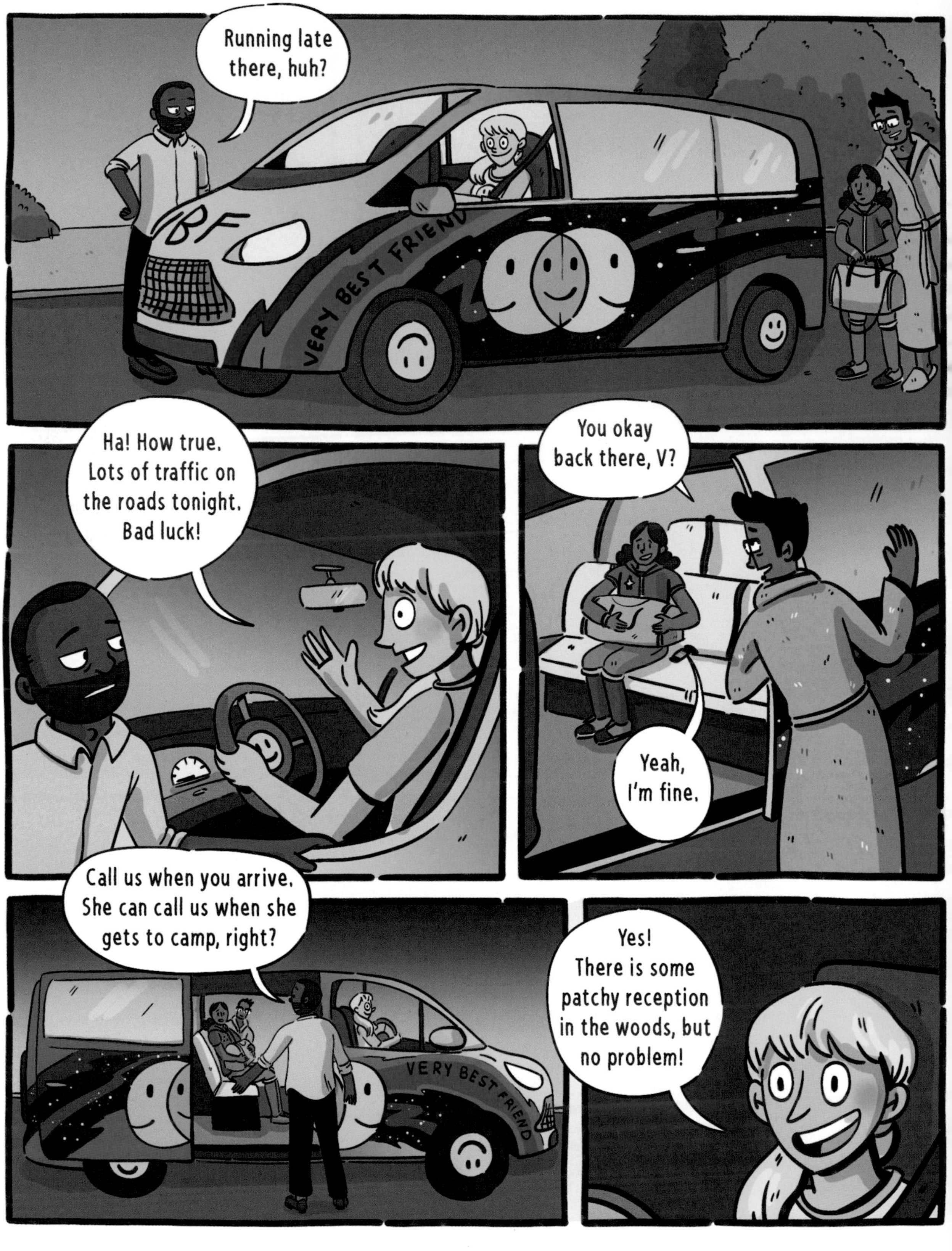
Running late there, huh?
VBF
VERY BEST FRIEND
Ha! How true. Lots of traffic on the roads tonight. Bad luck!
You okay back there, V?
Yeah, I'm fine.
Call us when you arrive. She can call us when she gets to camp, right?
VERY BEST FRIEND
Yes! There is some patchy reception in the woods, but no problem!

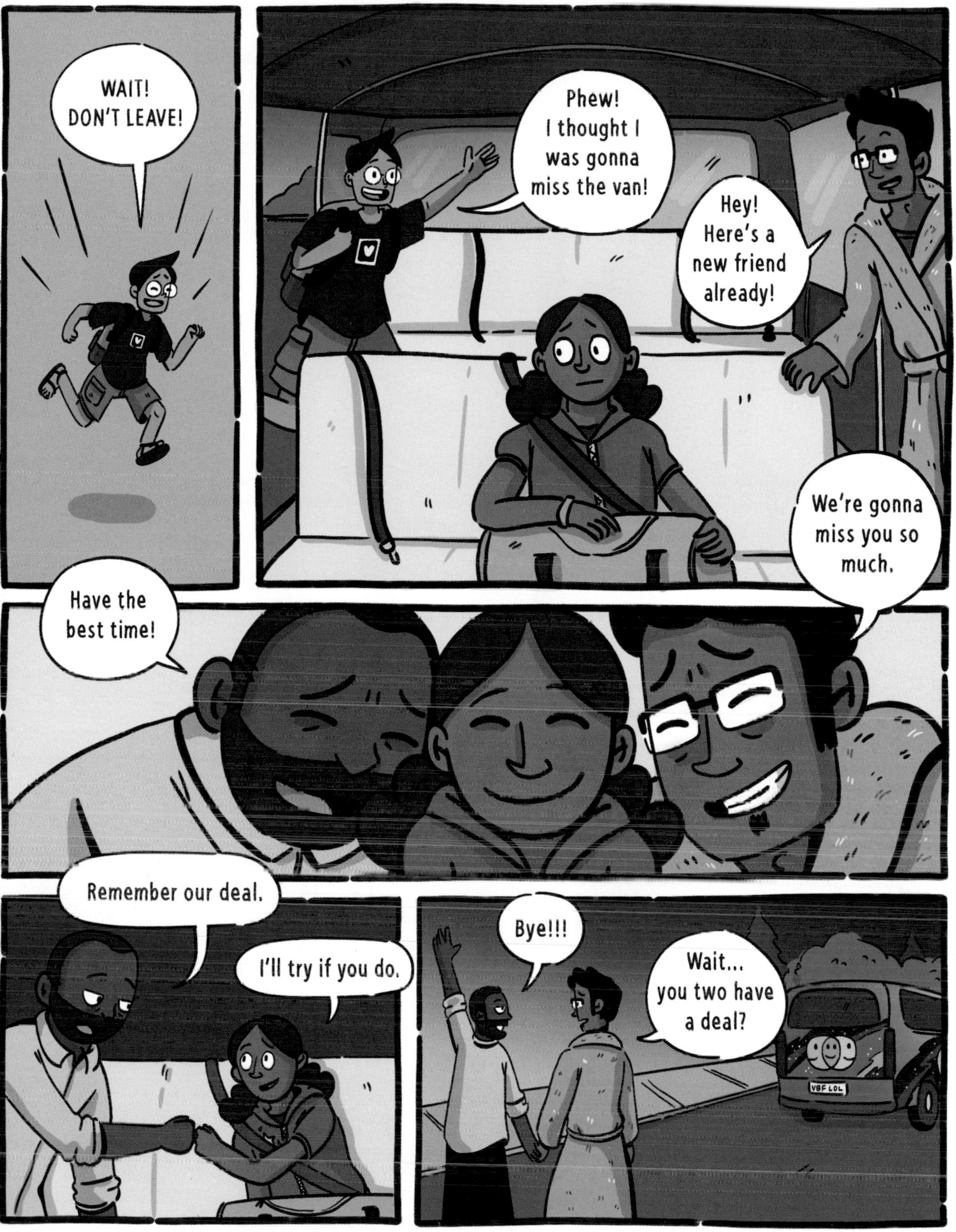
WAIT! DON'T LEAVE!
Phew! I thought I was gonna miss the van!
Hey! Here's a new friend already!
Have the best time!
We're gonna miss you so much.
Remember our deal.
I'll try if you do.
Bye!!!
Wait... you two have a deal?
VBF LOL

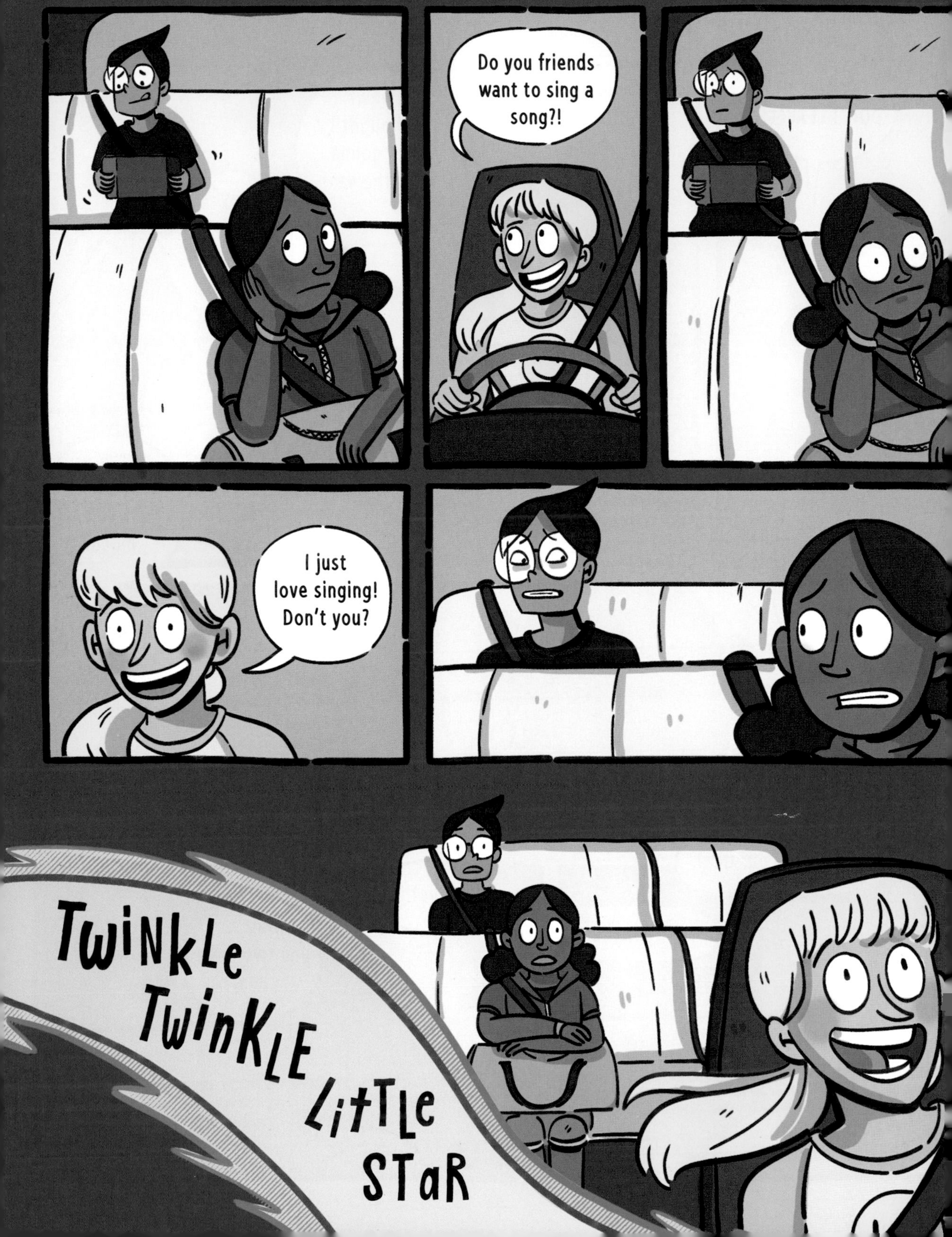
Do you friends want to sing a song?!
I just love singing! Don't you?
TWINKLE TWINKLE LITTLE STAR

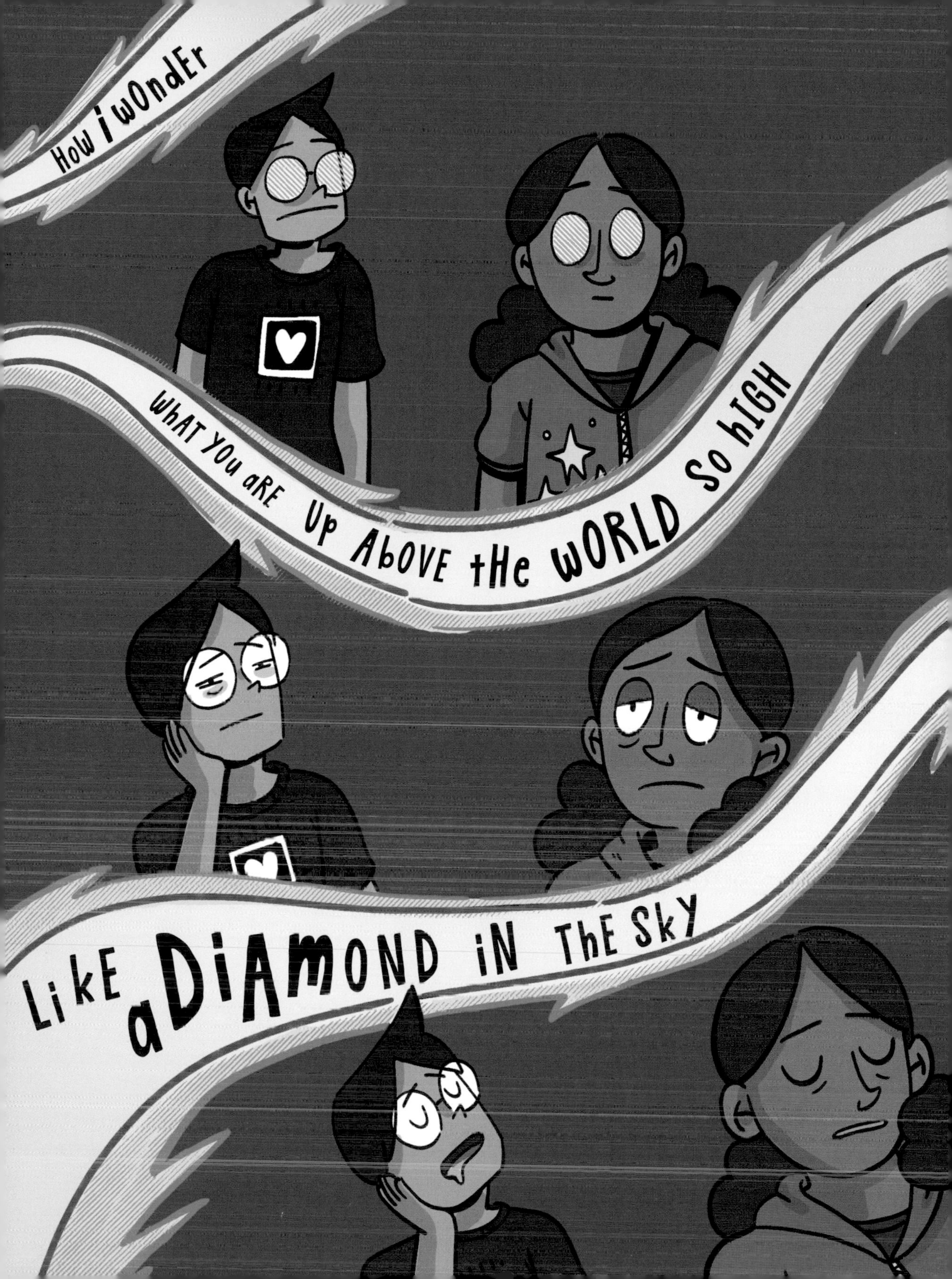
HOW I WONDER
WHAT YOU ARE UP ABOVE THE WORLD SO HIGH
LIKE A DIAMOND IN THE SKY

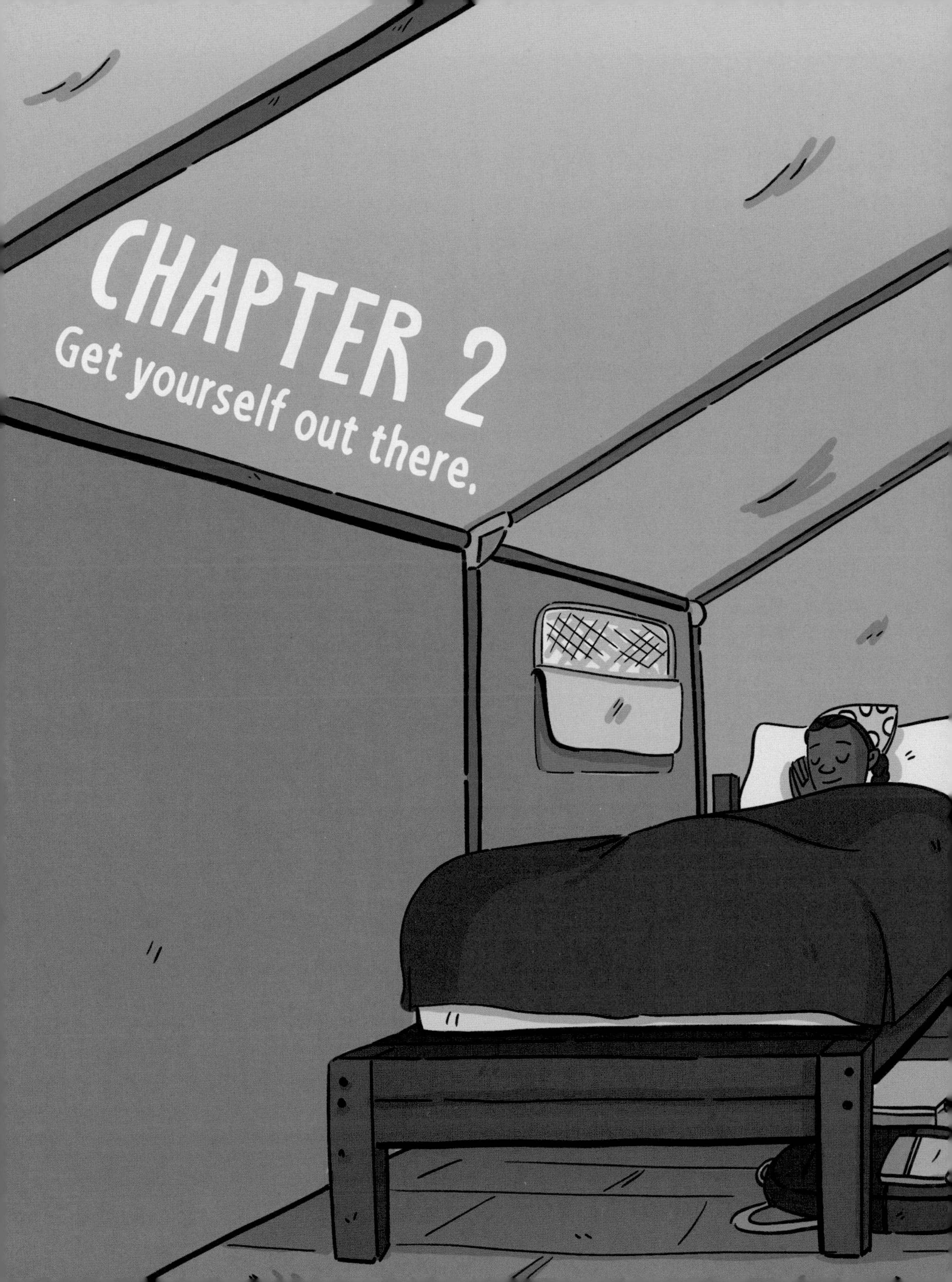
CHAPTER 2
Get yourself out there.

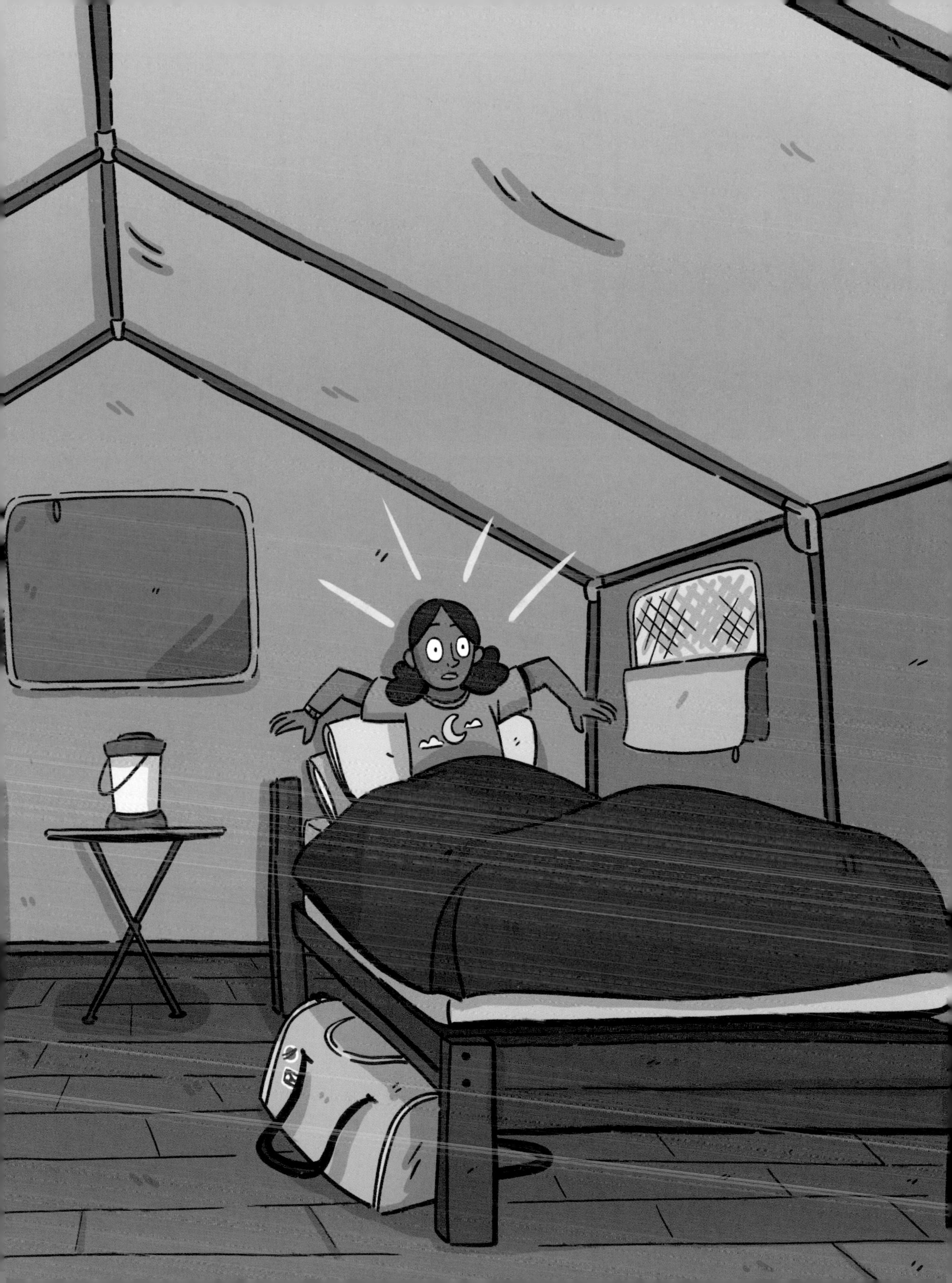

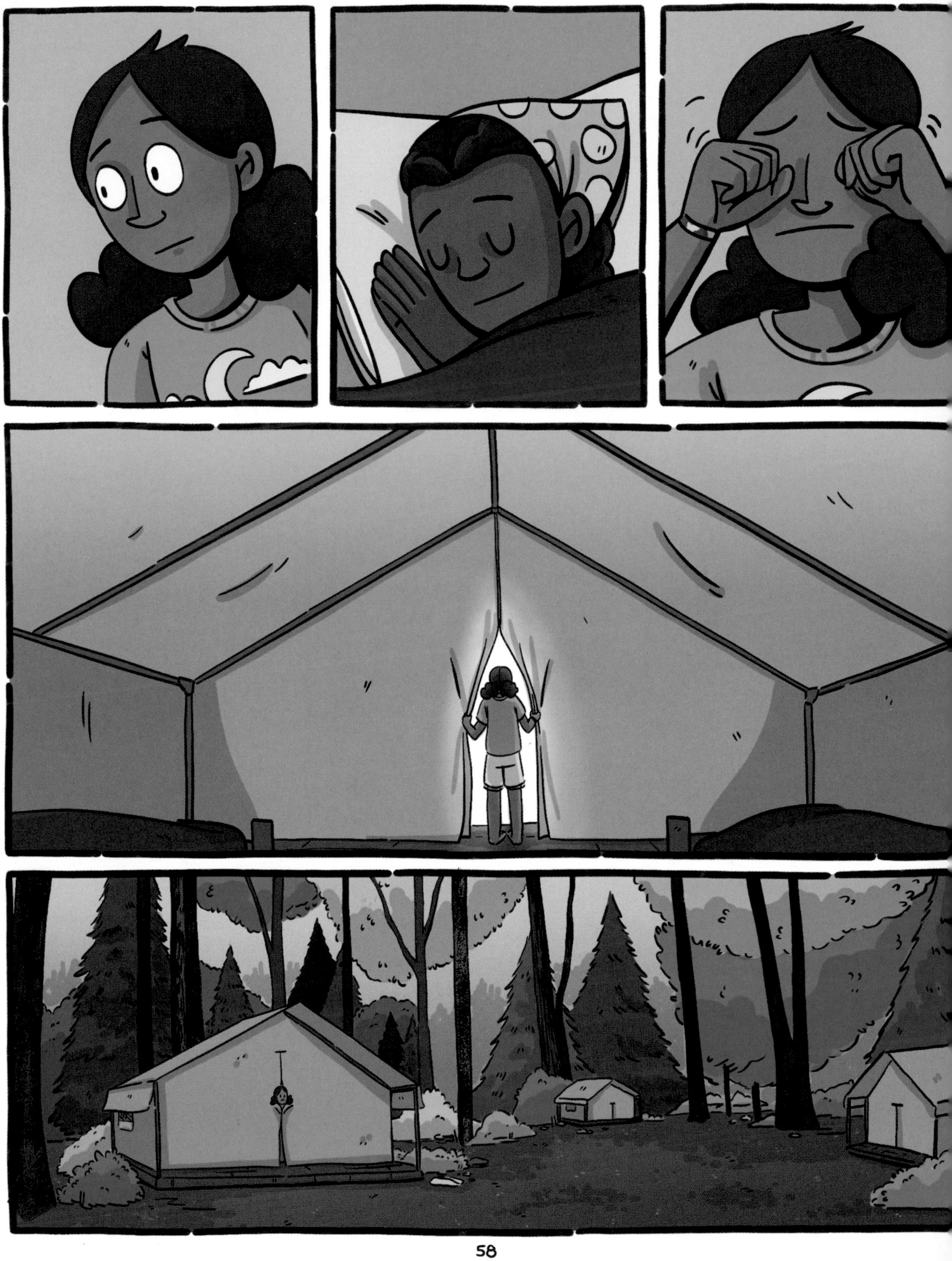

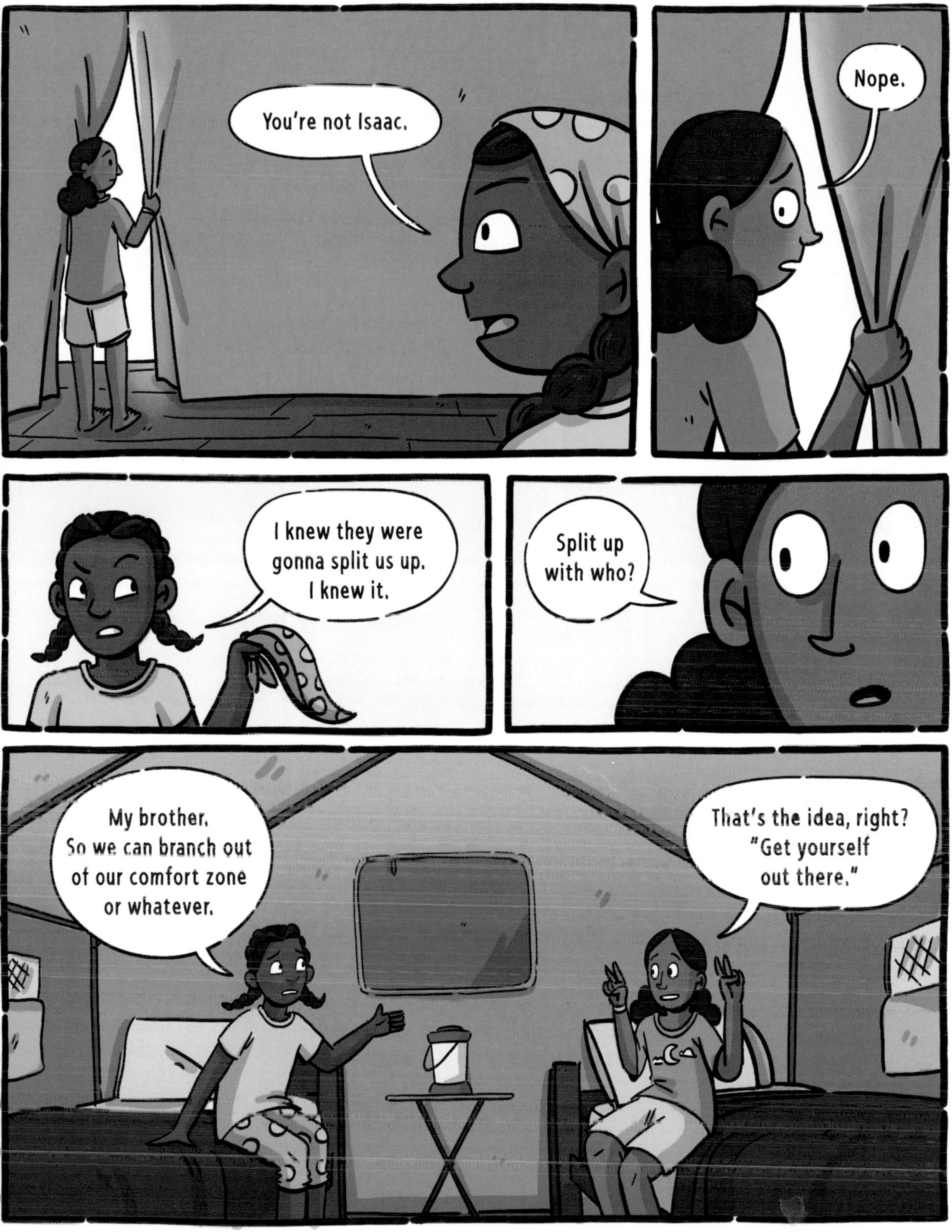
You're not Isaac.
Nope.
I knew they were gonna split us up. I knew it.
Split up with who?
My brother. So we can branch out of our comfort zone or whatever.
That's the idea, right? "Get yourself out there."

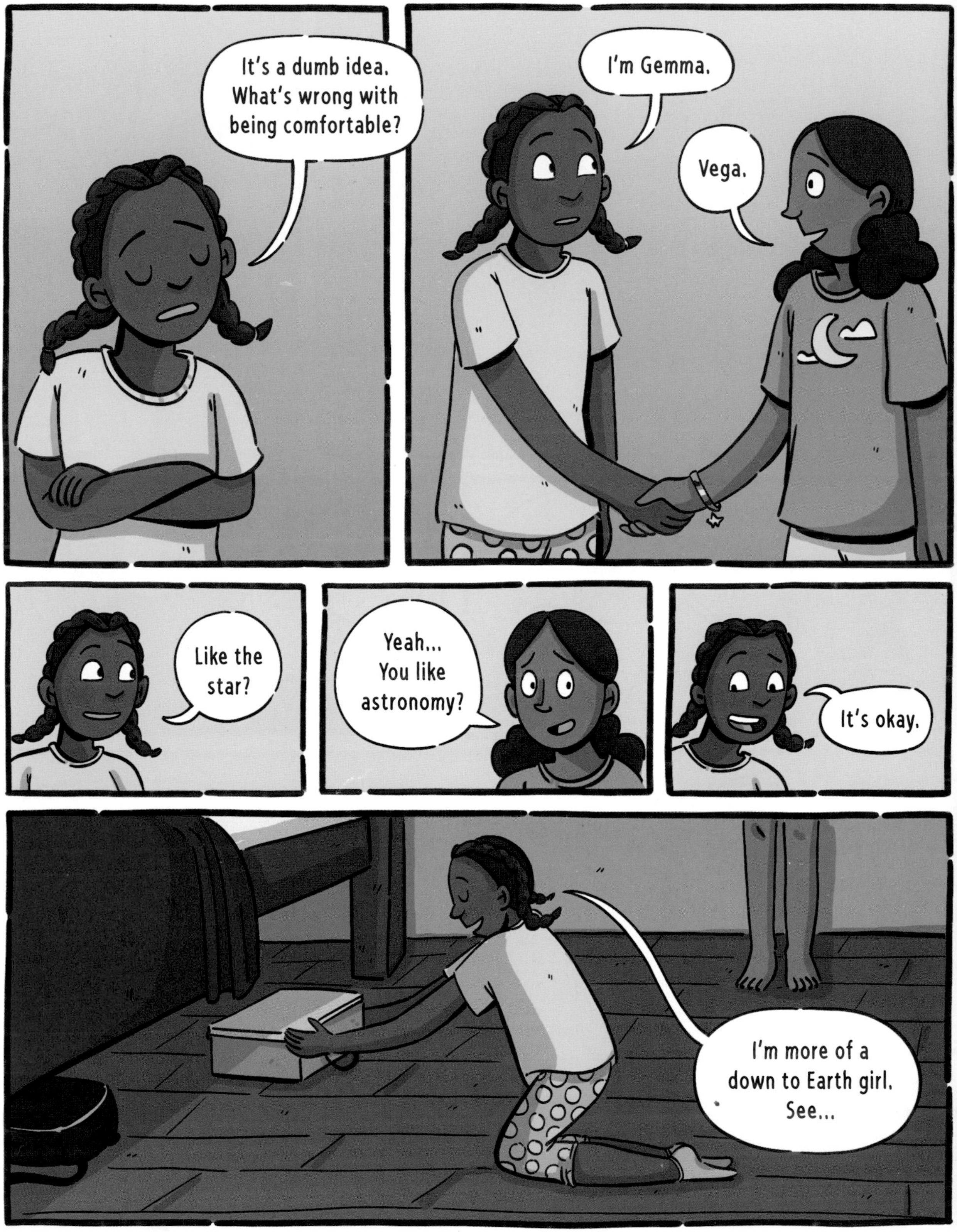
It's a dumb idea. What's wrong with being comfortable?
I'm Gemma.
Vega.
Like the star?
Yeah... You like astronomy?
It's okay.
I'm more of a down to Earth girl. See...

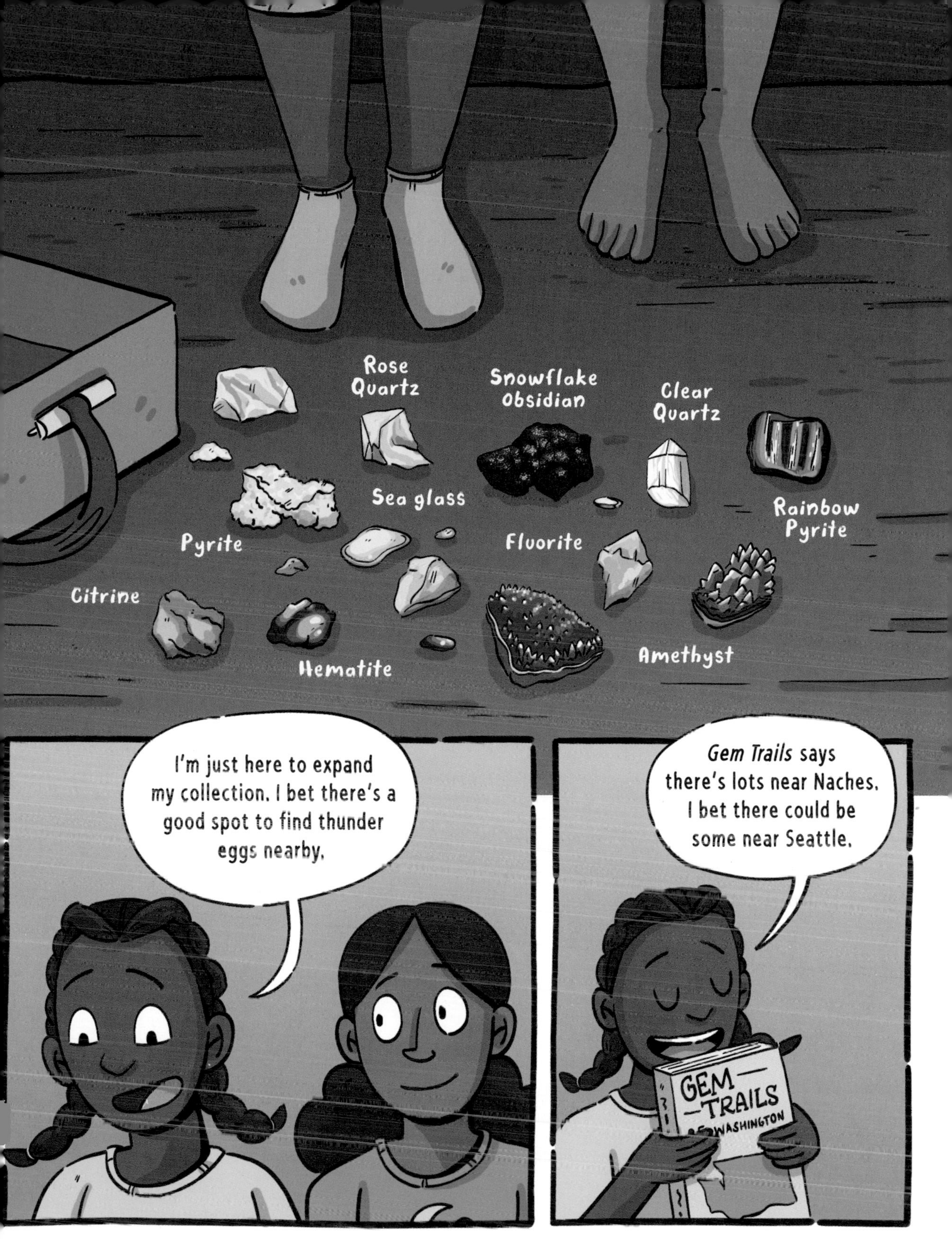
Rose Quartz
Snowflake Obsidian
Clear Quartz
Sea glass
Rainbow Pyrite
Pyrite
Fluorite
Citrine
Hematite
Amethyst
I'm just here to expand my collection. I bet there's a good spot to find thunder eggs nearby.
Gem Trails says there's lots near Naches. I bet there could be some near Seattle.
GEM TRAILS OF WASHINGTON

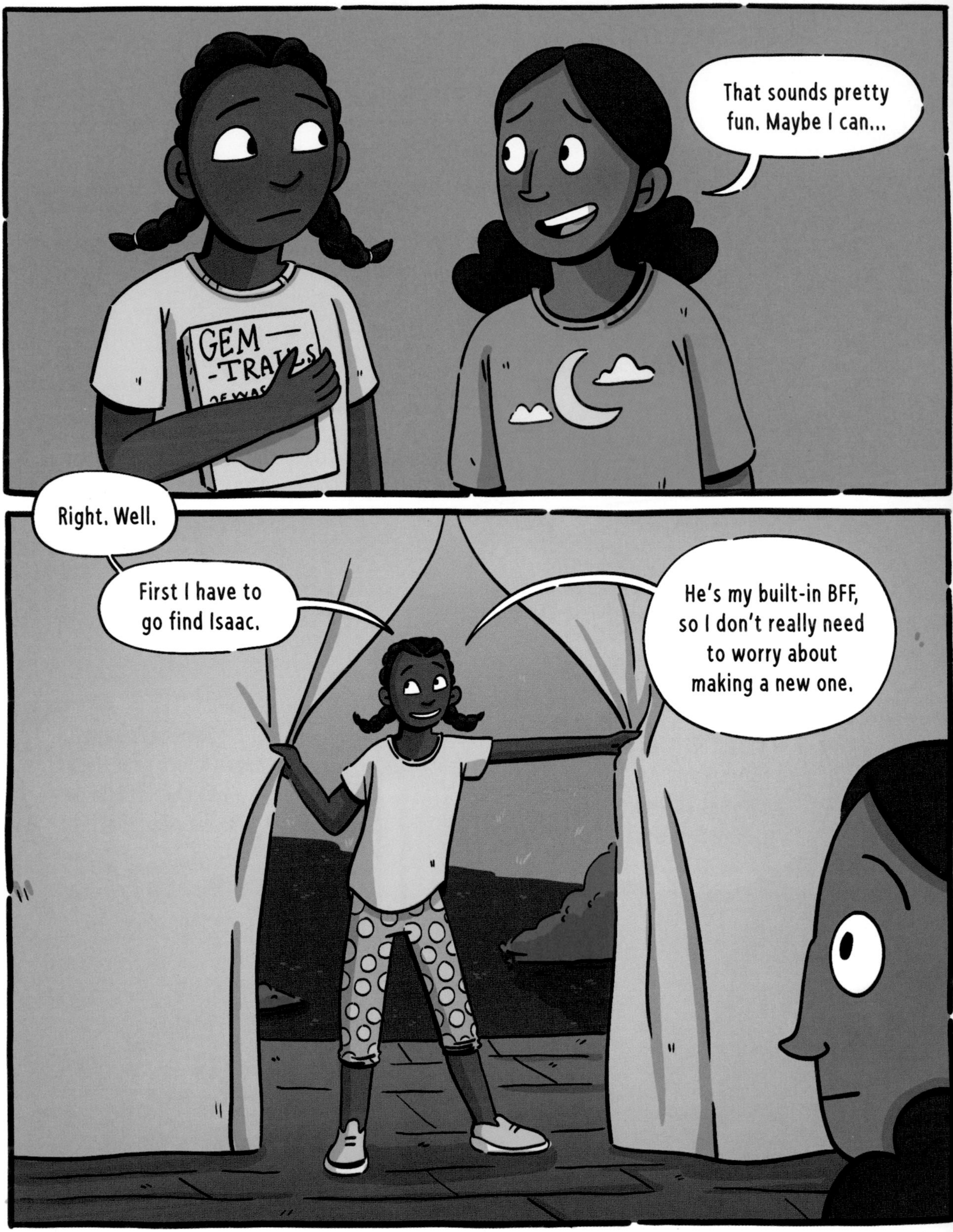

That sounds pretty fun. Maybe I can...
GEM-TRAILS
Right. Well.
First I have to go find Isaac.
He's my built-in BFF, so I don't really need to worry about making a new one.

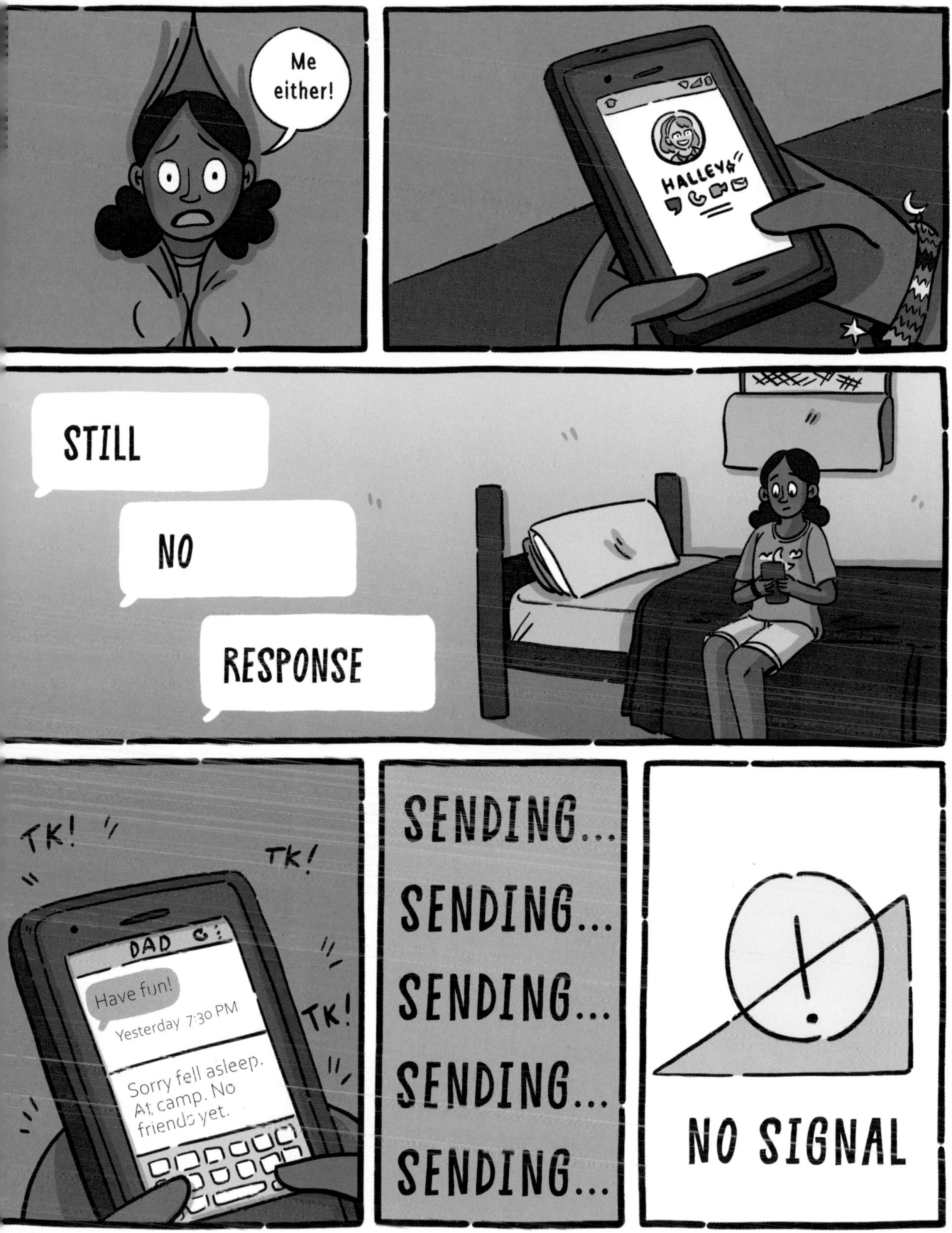
Me either!
HALLEY
STILL
NO
RESPONSE
TK!
TK!
DAD
Have fun!
Yesterday 7:30 PM
Sorry fell asleep. At camp. No friends yet.
TK!
SENDING...
SENDING...
SENDING...
SENDING...
SENDING...
NO SIGNAL

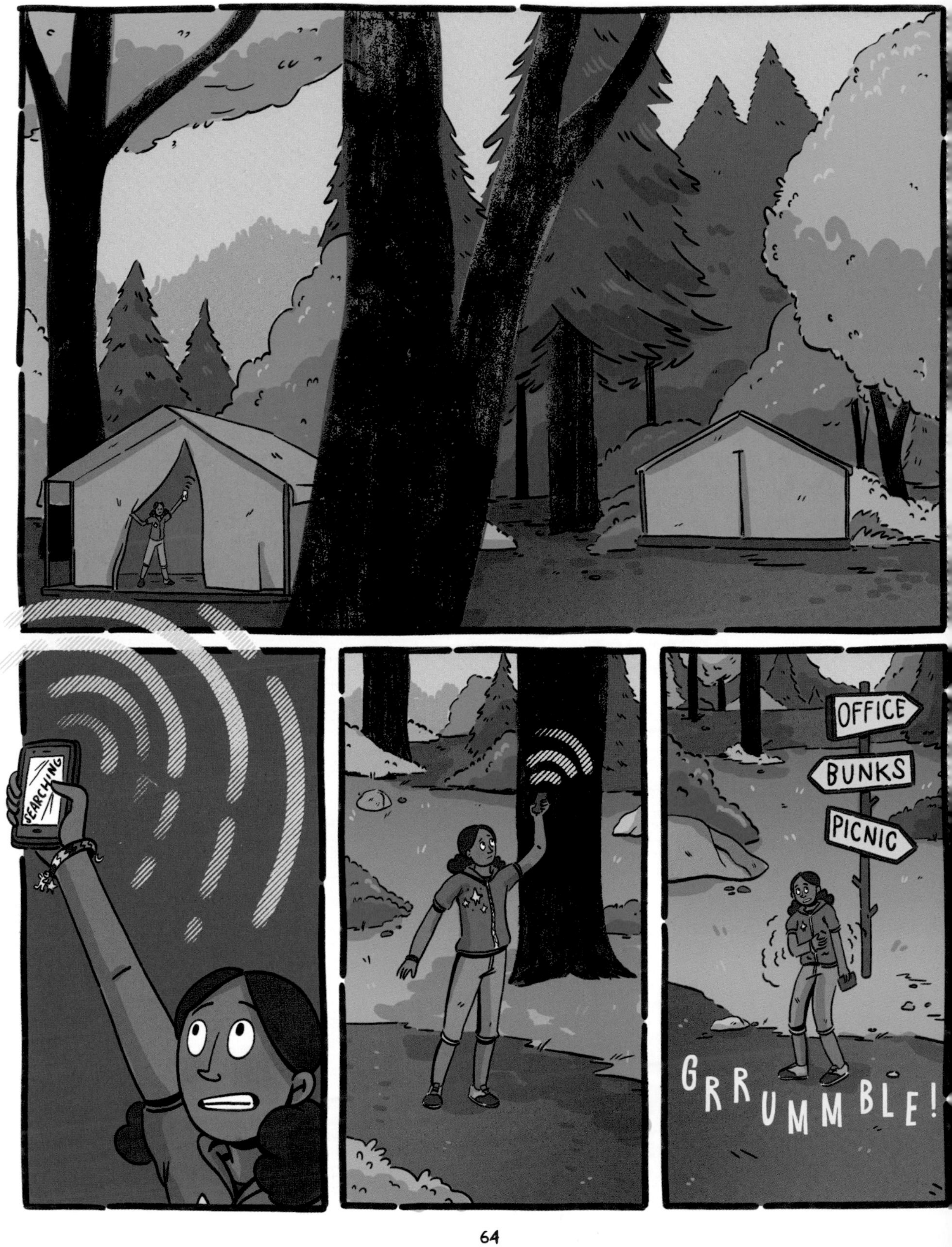
SEARCHING
OFFICE
BUNKS
PICNIC
GRRUMMBLE!

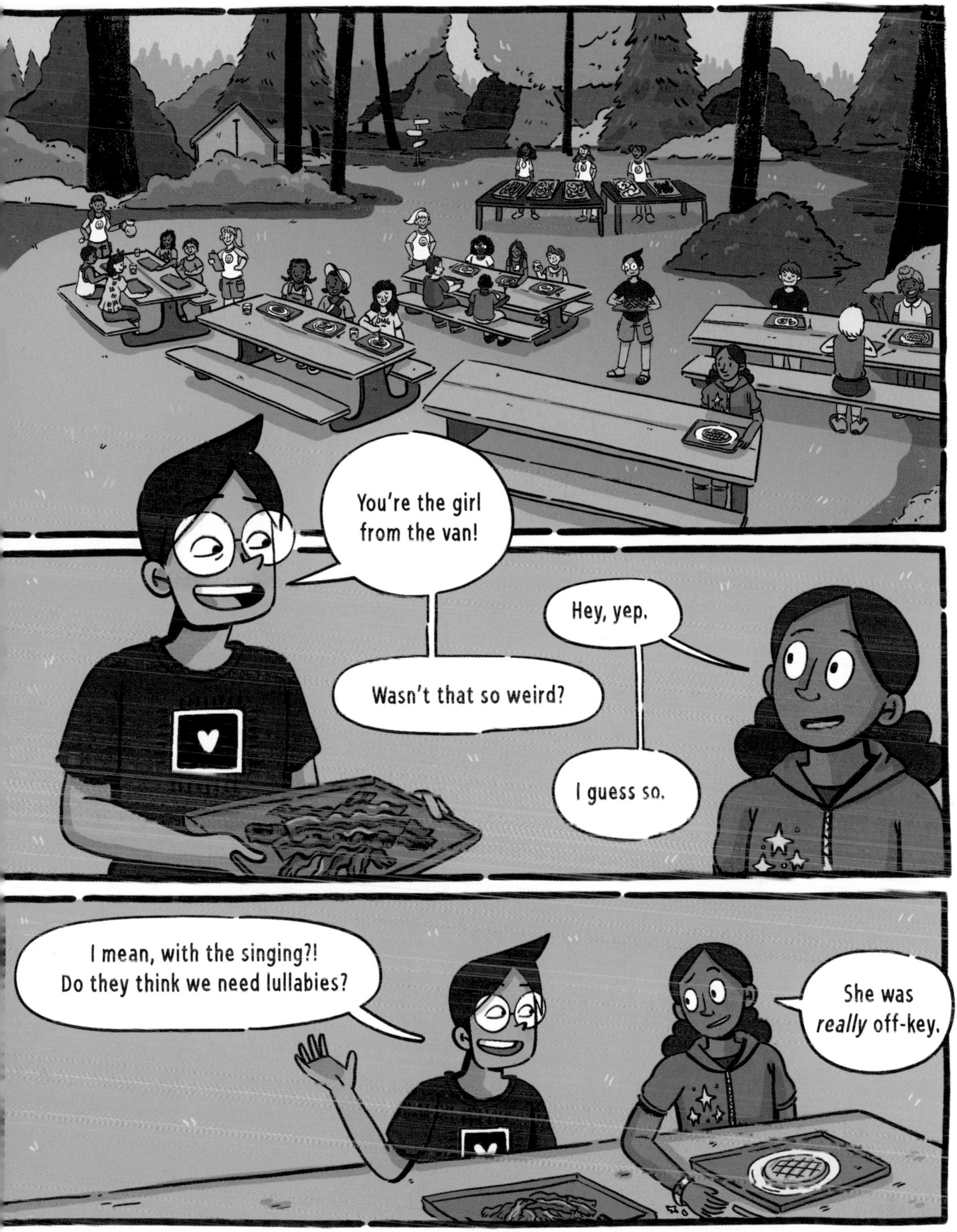
You're the girl from the van!
Wasn't that so weird?
Hey, yep.
I guess so.
I mean, with the singing?! Do they think we need lullabies?
She was *really* off-key.

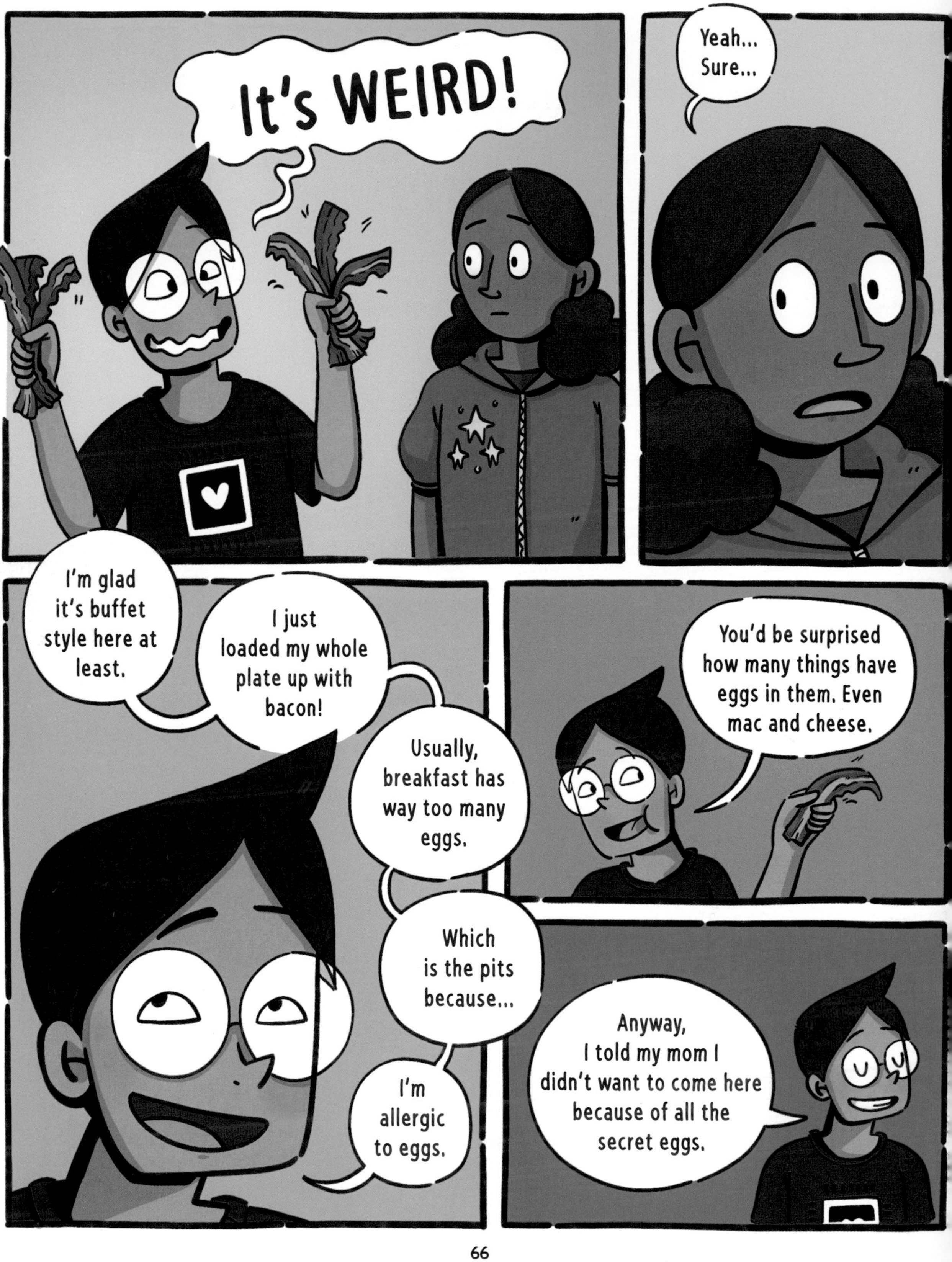
It's WEIRD!
Yeah... Sure...
I'm glad it's buffet style here at least.
I just loaded my whole plate up with bacon!
Usually, breakfast has way too many eggs.
Which is the pits because...
I'm allergic to eggs.
You'd be surprised how many things have eggs in them. Even mac and cheese.
Anyway, I told my mom I didn't want to come here because of all the secret eggs.

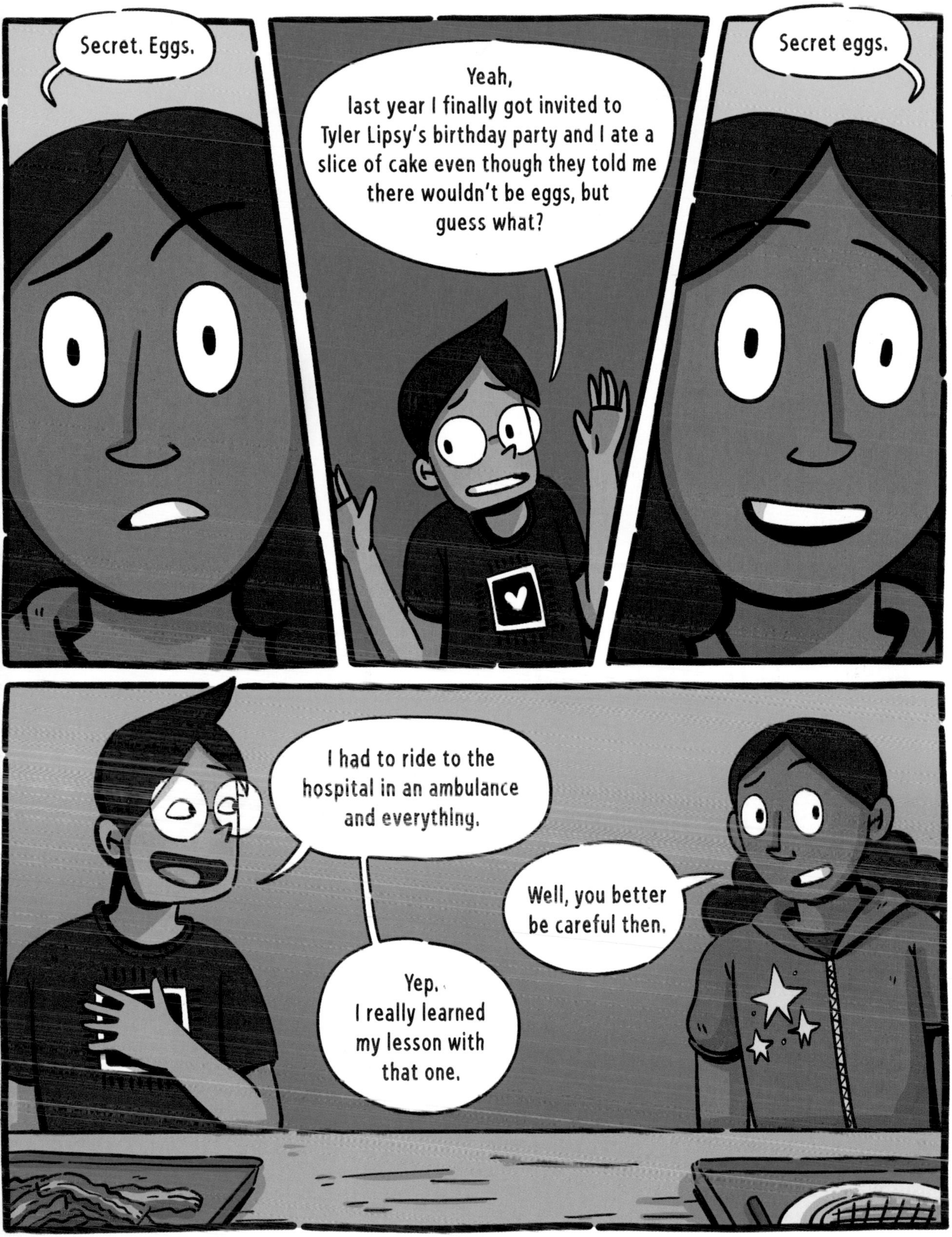
Secret. Eggs.
Yeah, last year I finally got invited to Tyler Lipsy's birthday party and I ate a slice of cake even though they told me there wouldn't be eggs, but guess what?
Secret eggs.
I had to ride to the hospital in an ambulance and everything.
Yep. I really learned my lesson with that one.
Well, you better be careful then.

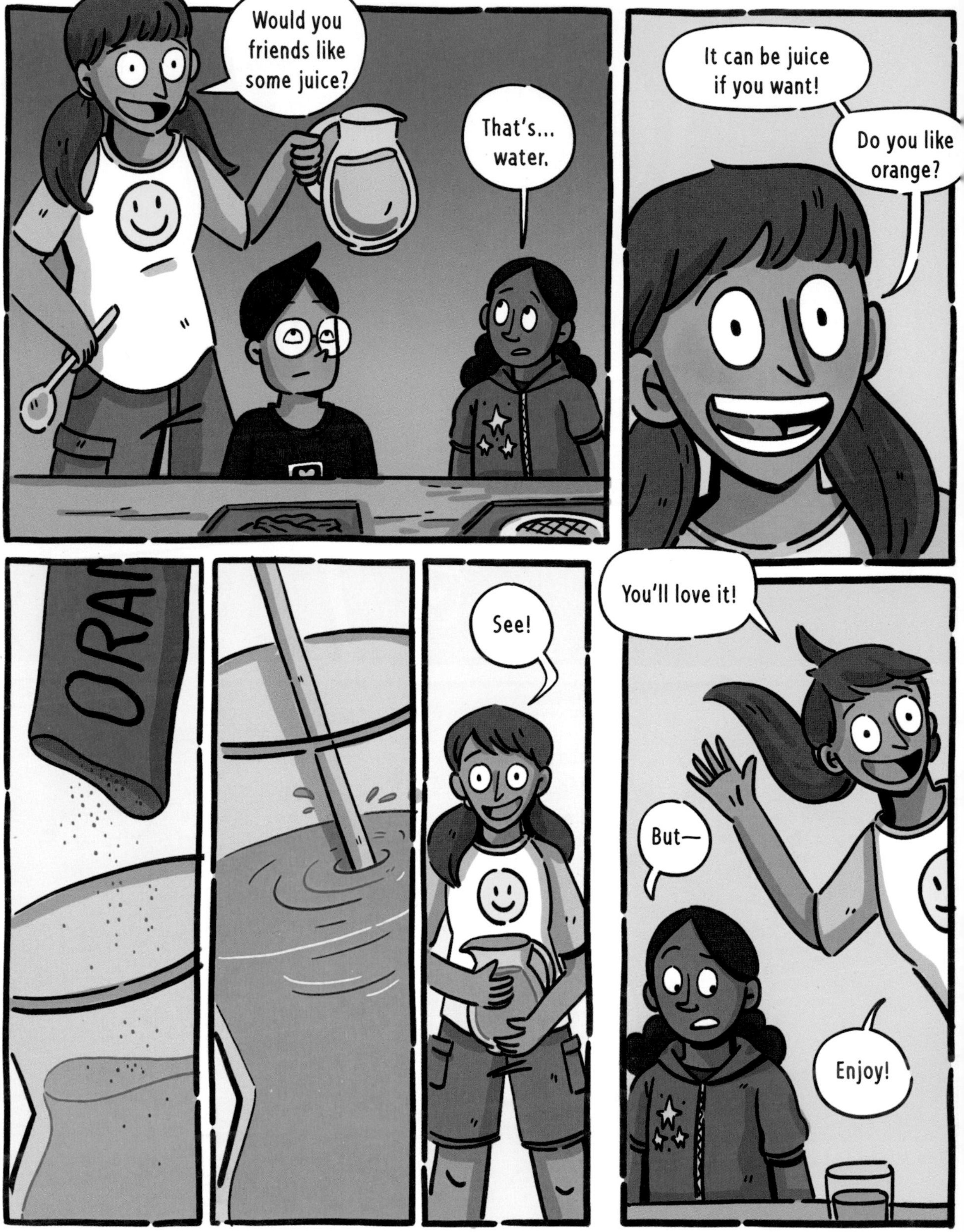
Would you friends like some juice?
That's... water.
It can be juice if you want!
Do you like orange?
ORAN
See!
You'll love it!
But—
Enjoy!

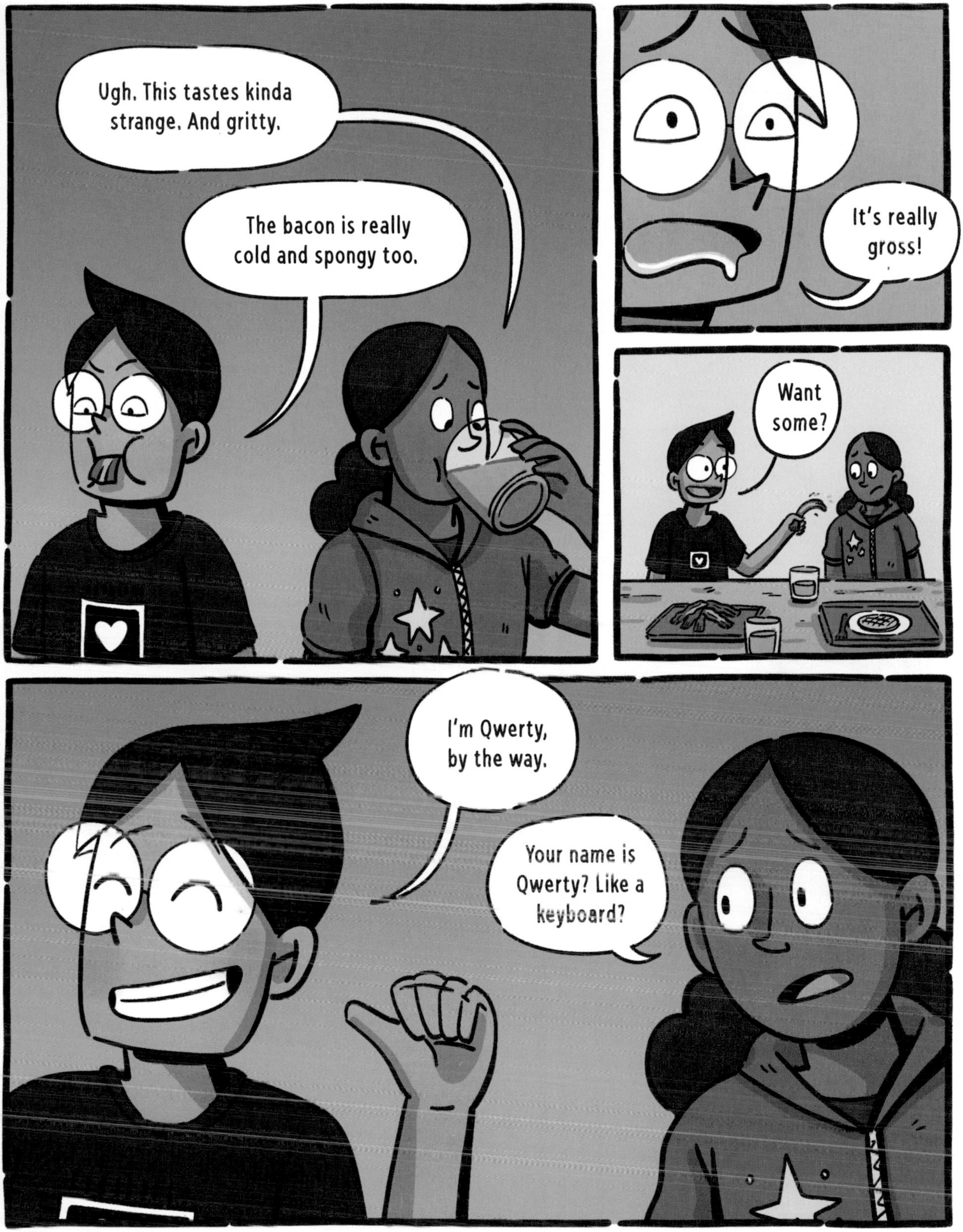
Ugh. This tastes kinda strange. And gritty.
The bacon is really cold and spongy too.
It's really gross!
Want some?
I'm Qwerty, by the way.
Your name is Qwerty? Like a keyboard?

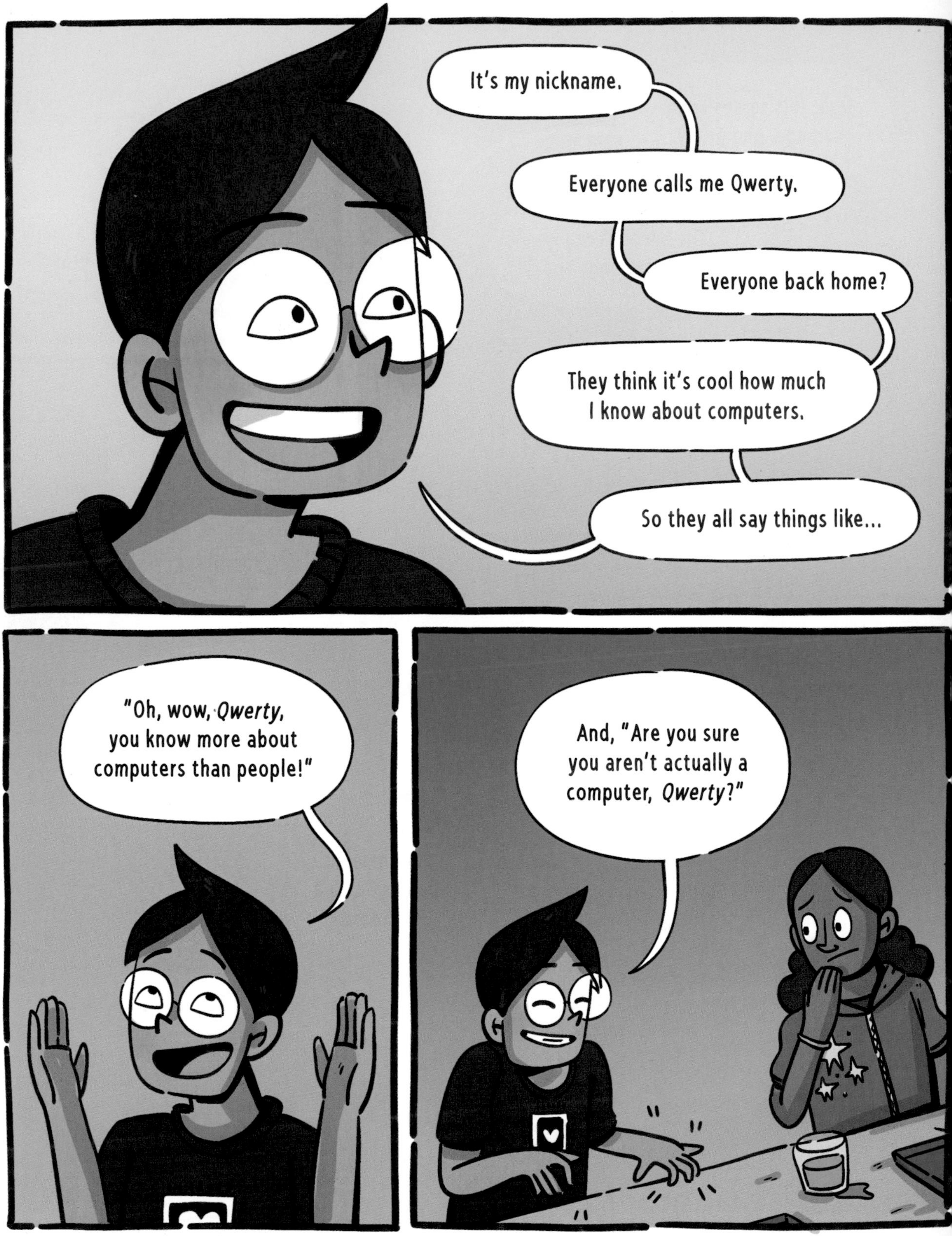
It's my nickname.
Everyone calls me Qwerty.
Everyone back home?
They think it's cool how much I know about computers.
So they all say things like...
"Oh, wow, *Qwerty*, you know more about computers than people!"
And, "Are you sure you aren't actually a computer, *Qwerty*?"

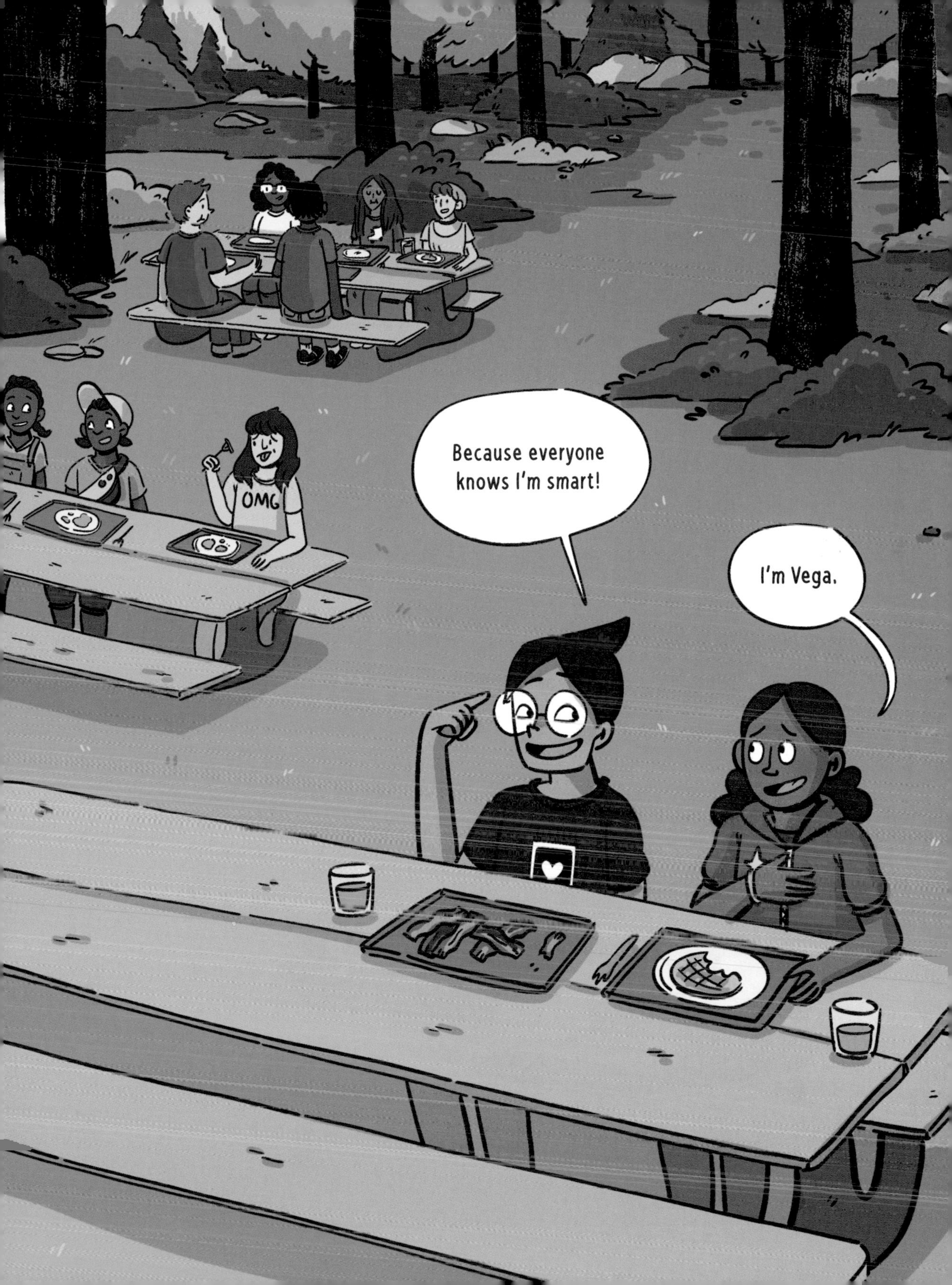
OMG
Because everyone knows I'm smart!
I'm Vega.

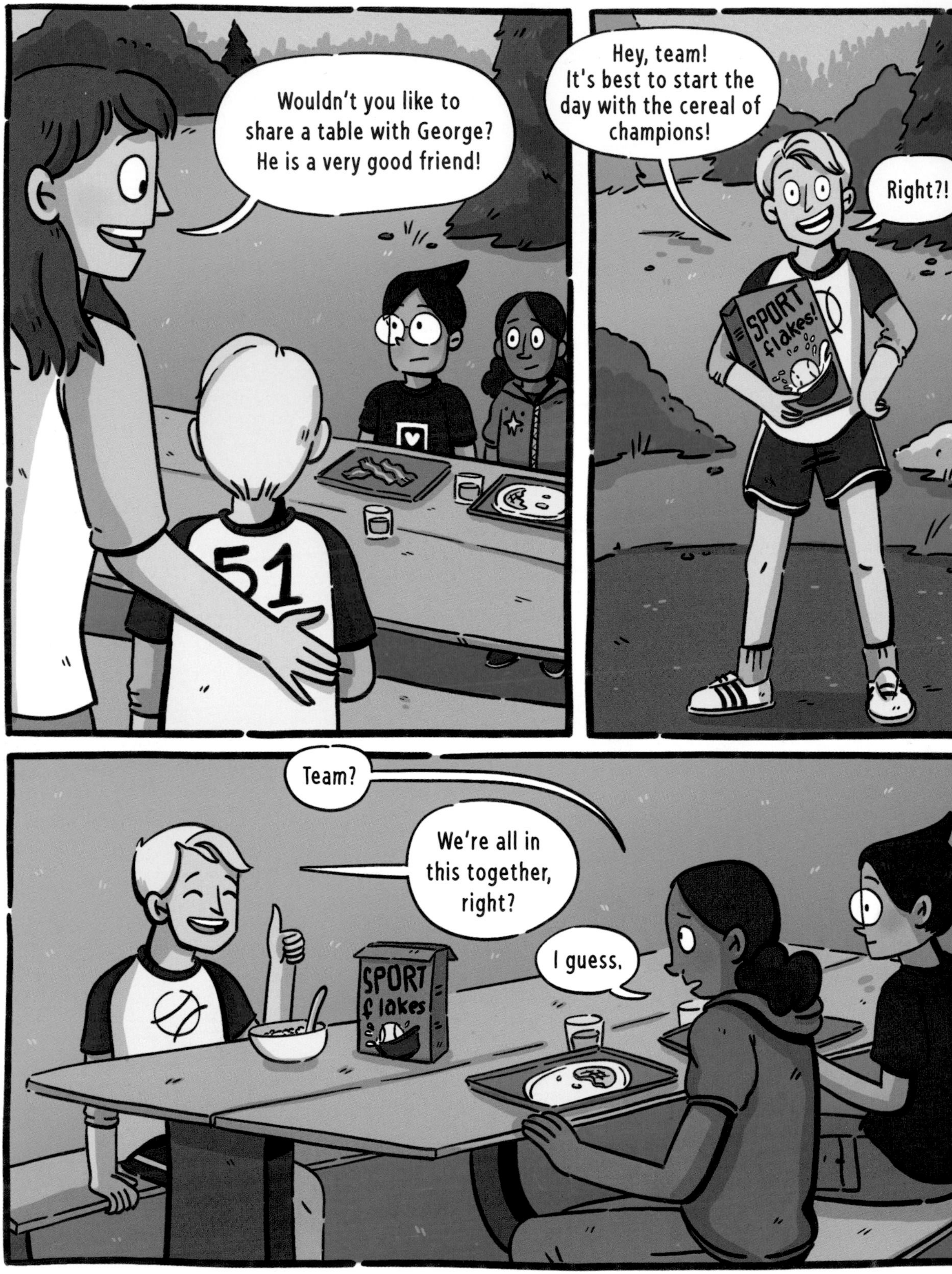
Wouldn't you like to share a table with George? He is a very good friend!
51
Hey, team! It's best to start the day with the cereal of champions!
Right?!
SPORT flakes!
Team?
We're all in this together, right?
SPORT flakes
I guess.

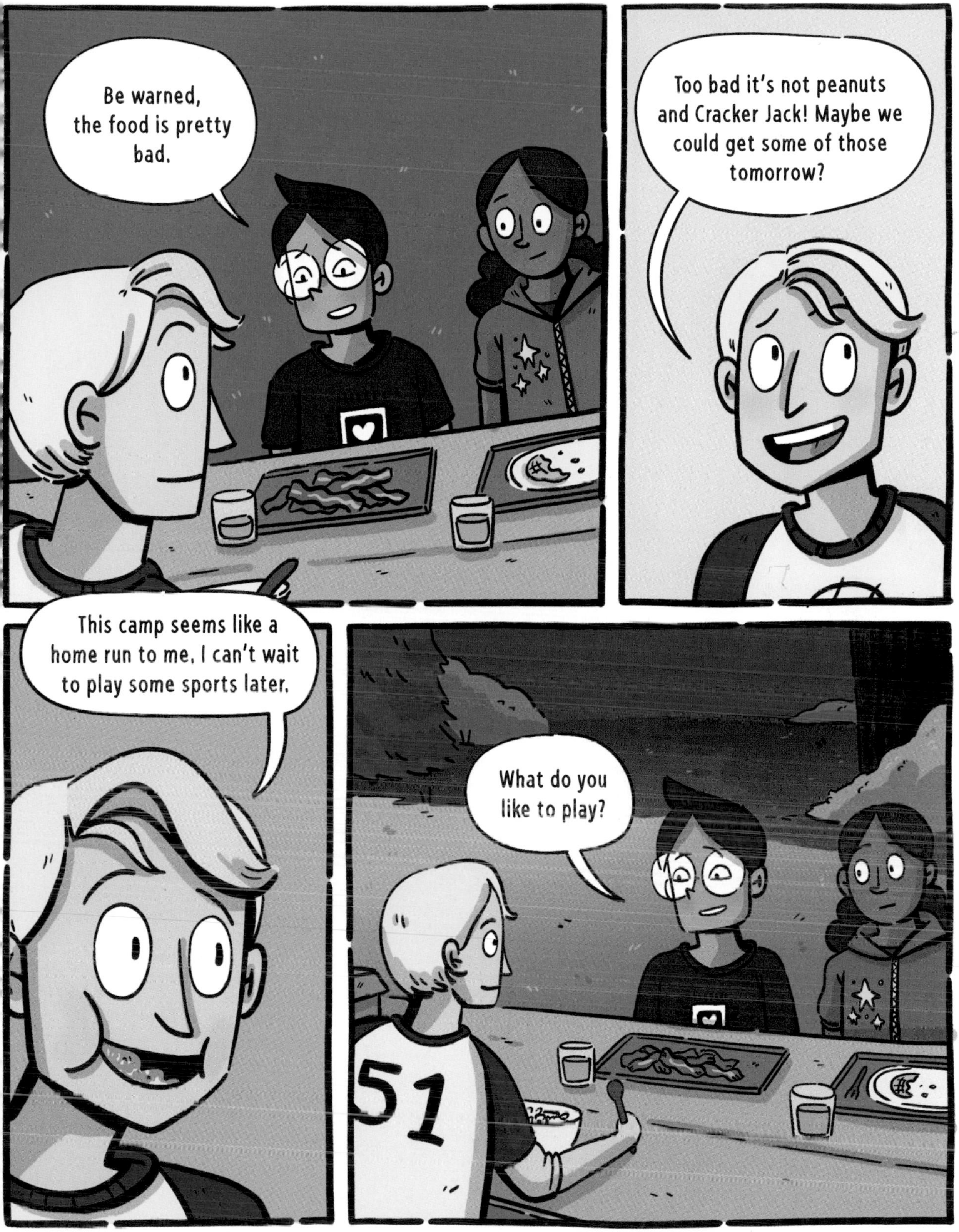
Be warned, the food is pretty bad.
Too bad it's not peanuts and Cracker Jack! Maybe we could get some of those tomorrow?
This camp seems like a home run to me. I can't wait to play some sports later.
What do you like to play?
51

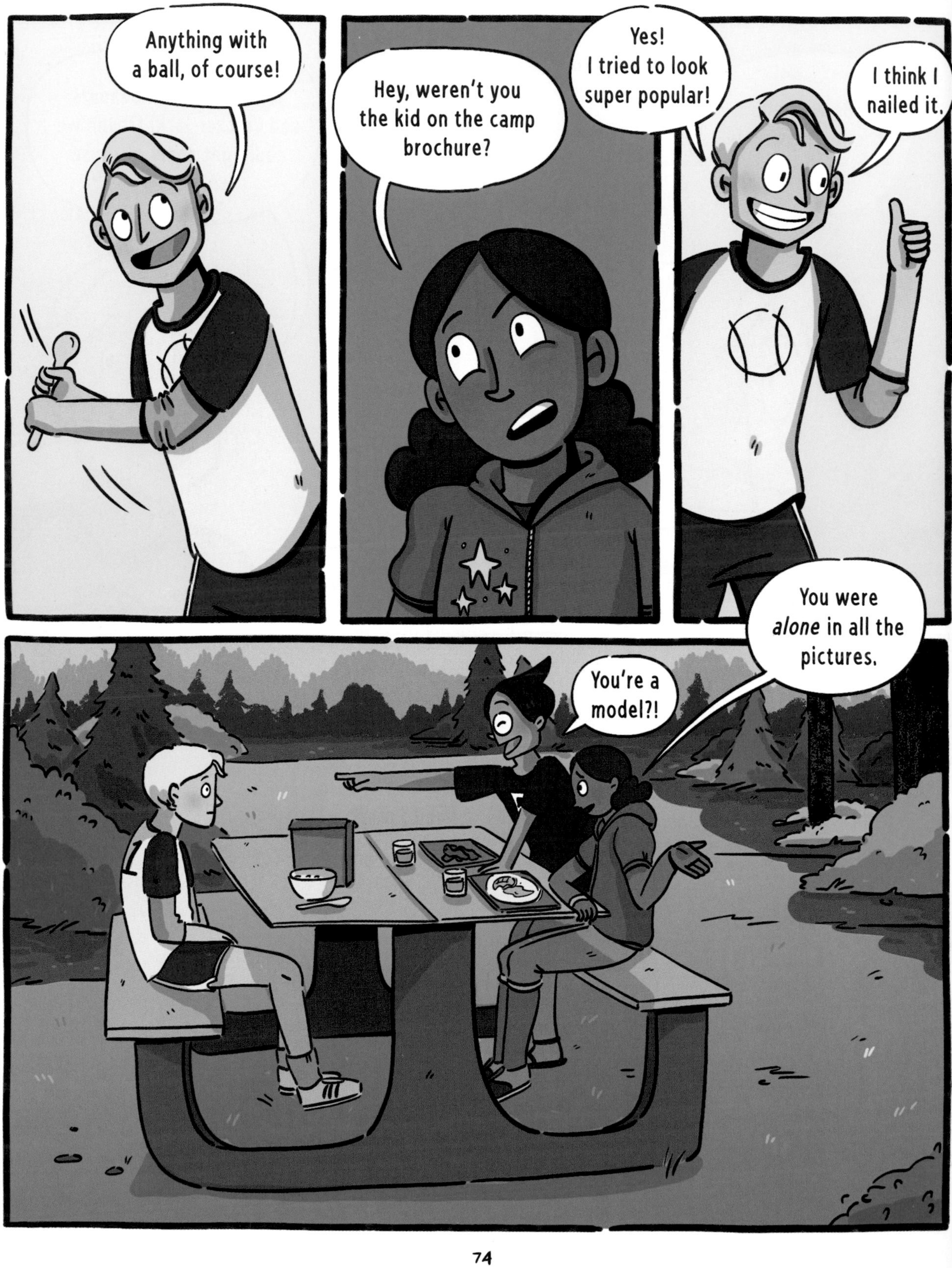
Anything with a ball, of course!
Hey, weren't you the kid on the camp brochure?
Yes! I tried to look super popular!
I think I nailed it.
You're a model?!
You were *alone* in all the pictures.

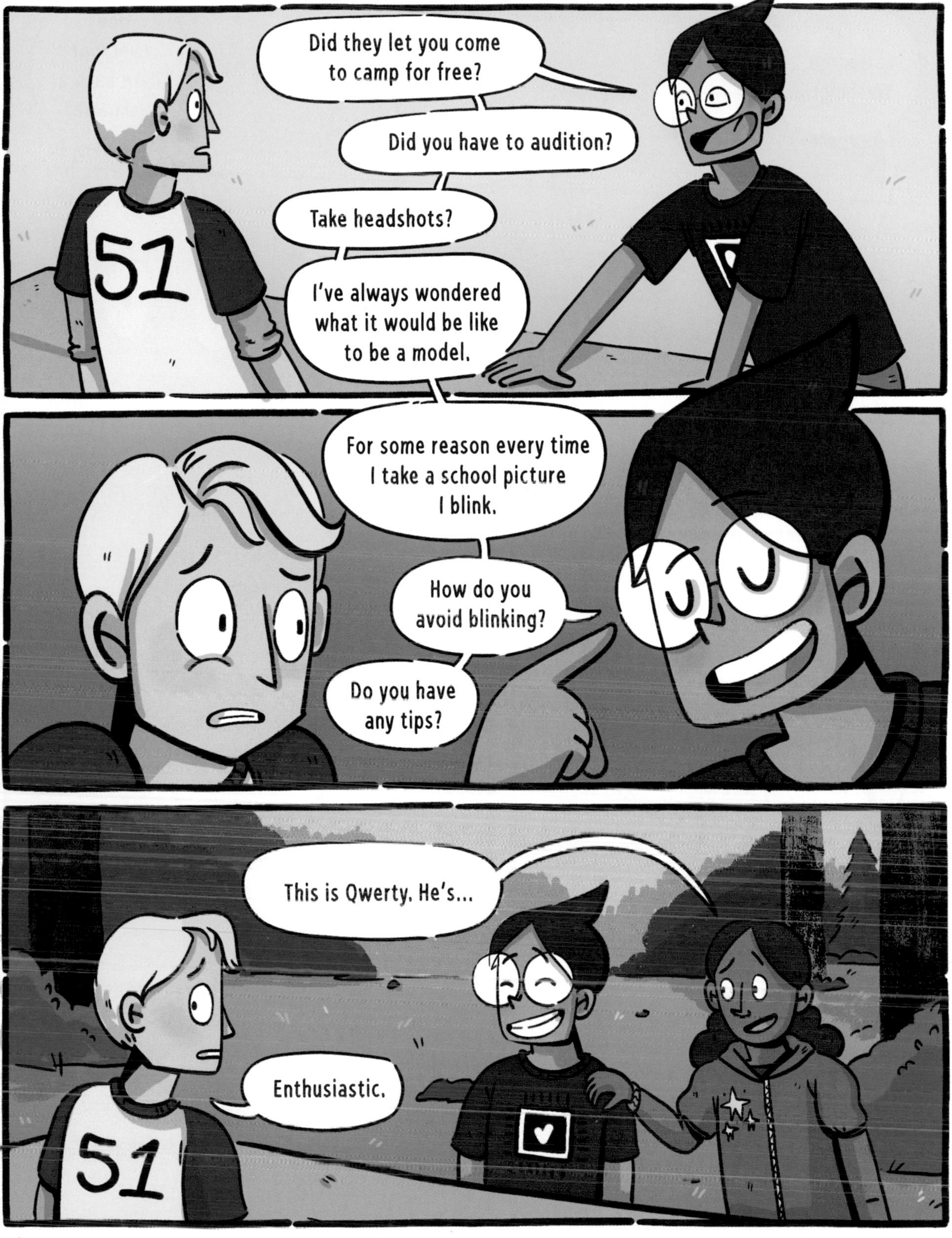
Did they let you come to camp for free?
Did you have to audition?
Take headshots?
I've always wondered what it would be like to be a model.
For some reason every time I take a school picture I blink.
How do you avoid blinking?
Do you have any tips?
This is Qwerty. He's...
Enthusiastic.

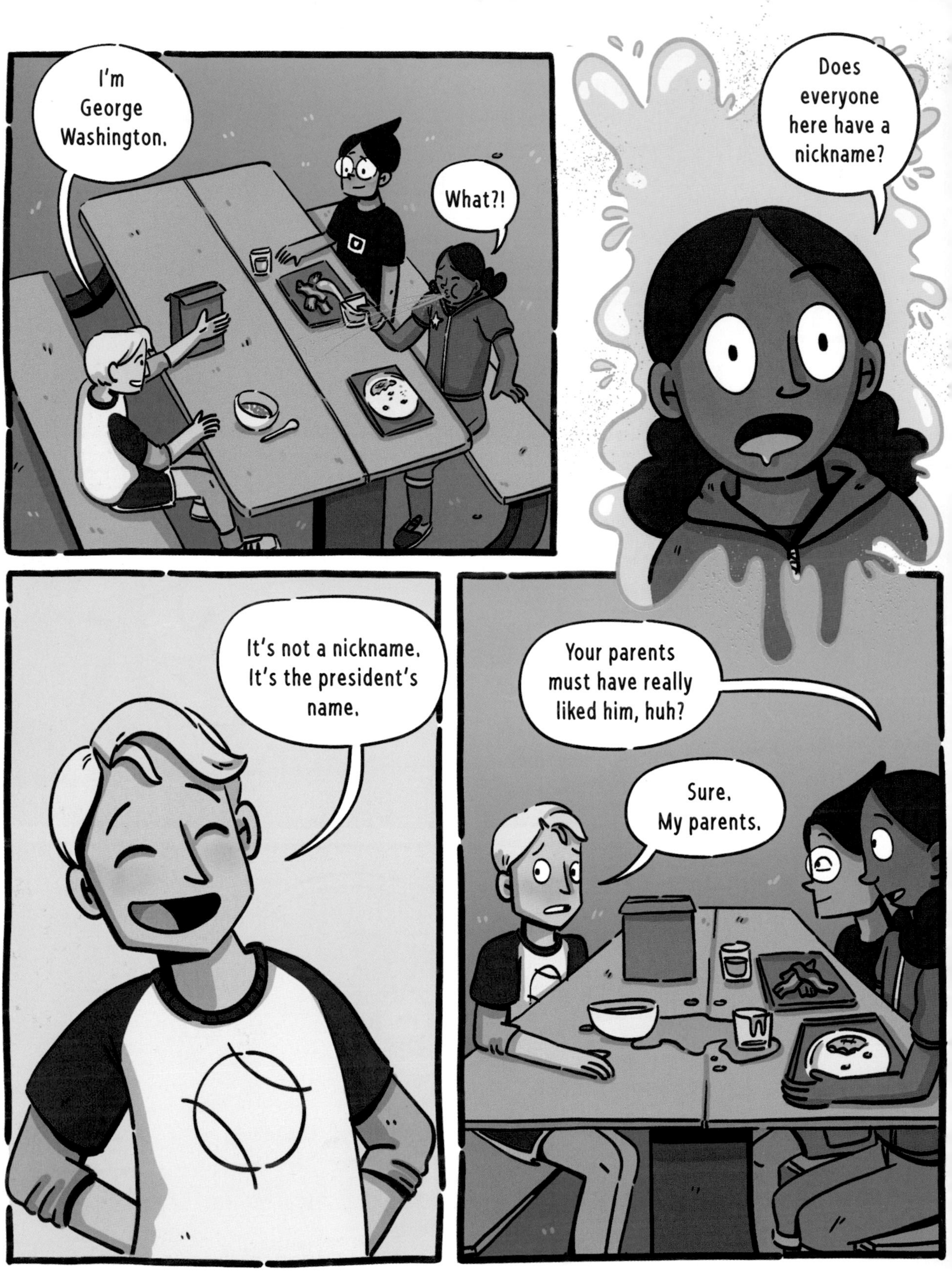
I'm George Washington.
What?!
Does everyone here have a nickname?
It's not a nickname. It's the president's name.
Your parents must have really liked him, huh?
Sure. My parents.

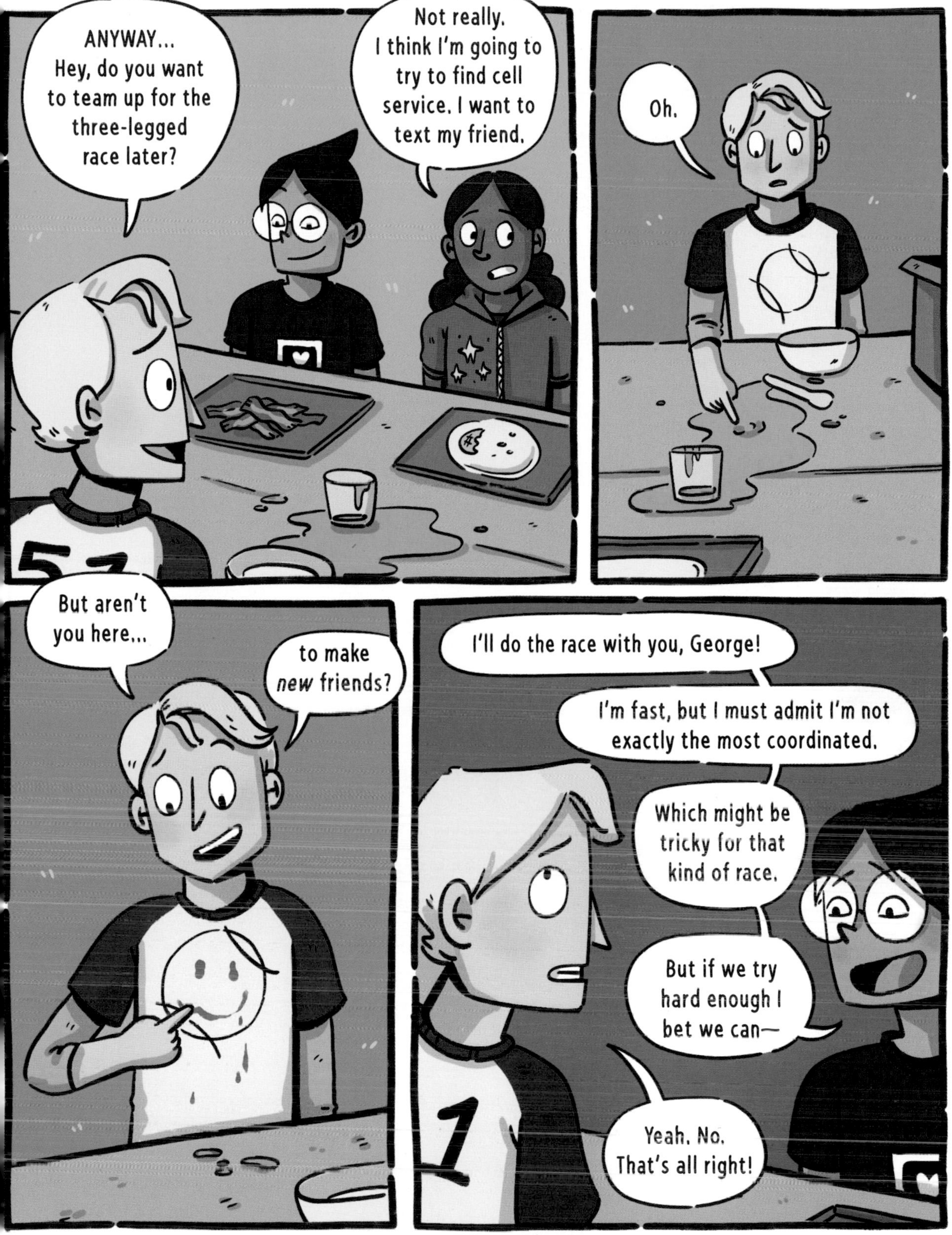
ANYWAY...
Hey, do you want to team up for the three-legged race later?
Not really.
I think I'm going to try to find cell service. I want to text my friend.
Oh.
But aren't you here...
to make *new* friends?
I'll do the race with you, George!
I'm fast, but I must admit I'm not exactly the most coordinated.
Which might be tricky for that kind of race.
But if we try hard enough I bet we can—
Yeah. No. That's all right!

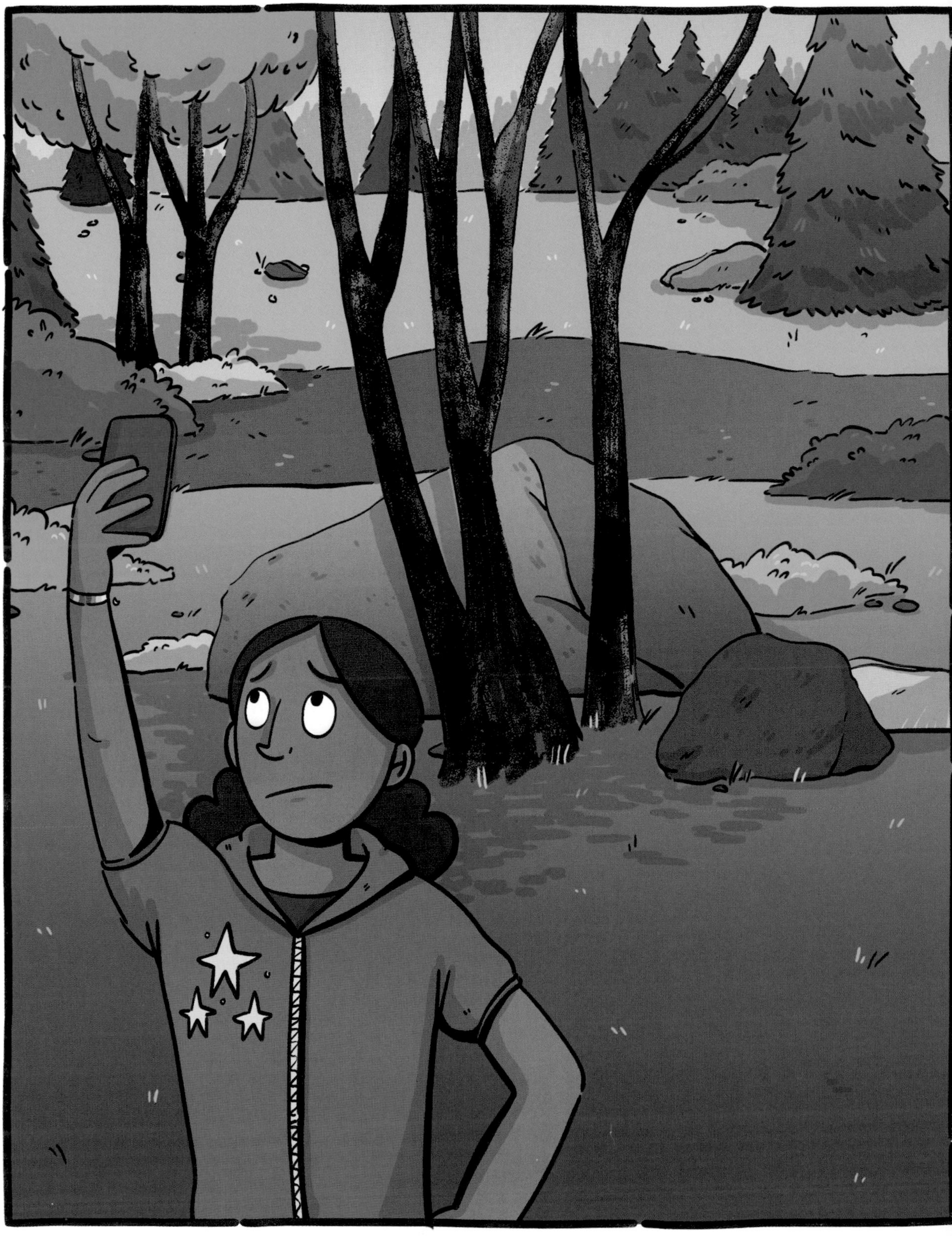

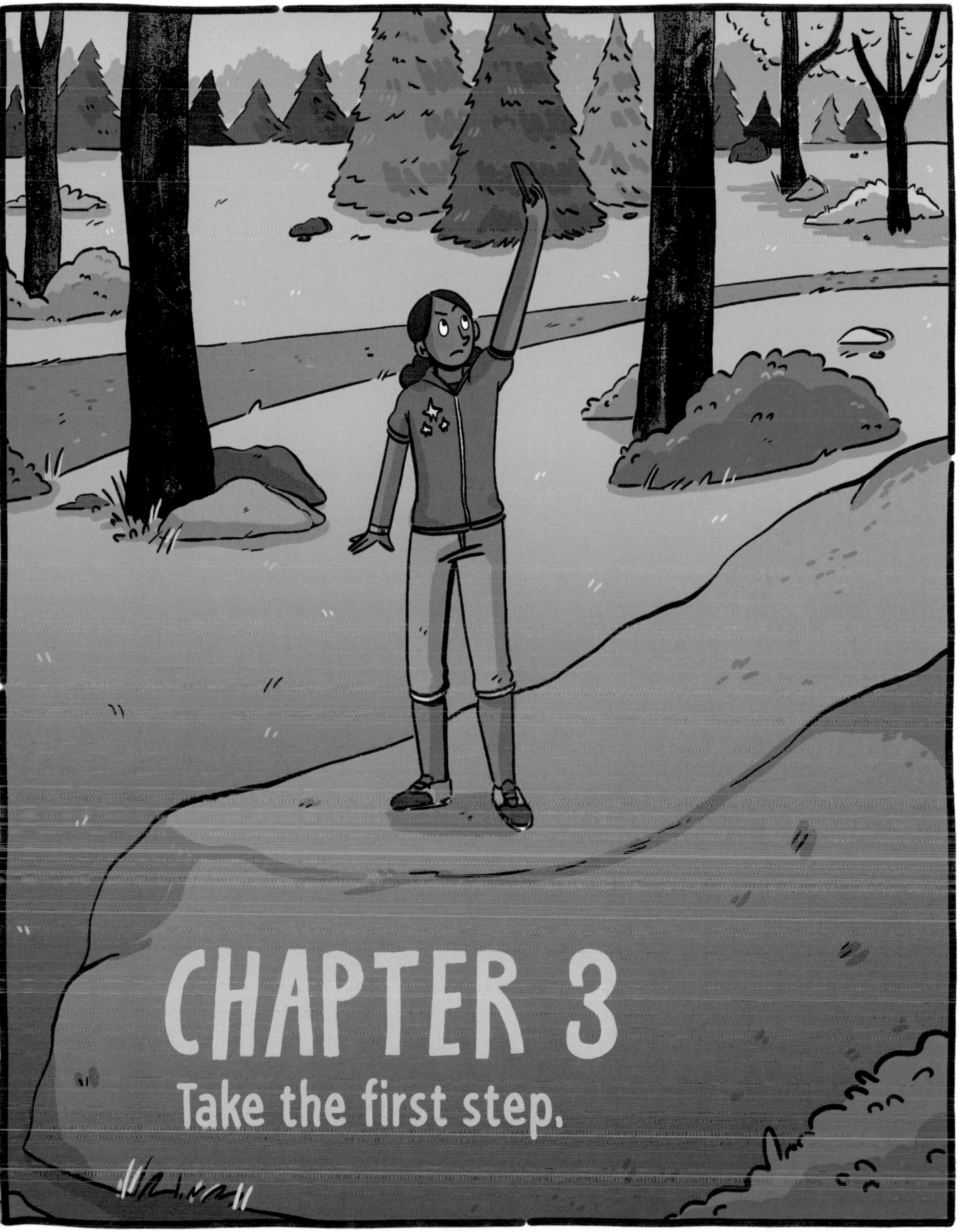
CHAPTER 3
Take the first step.

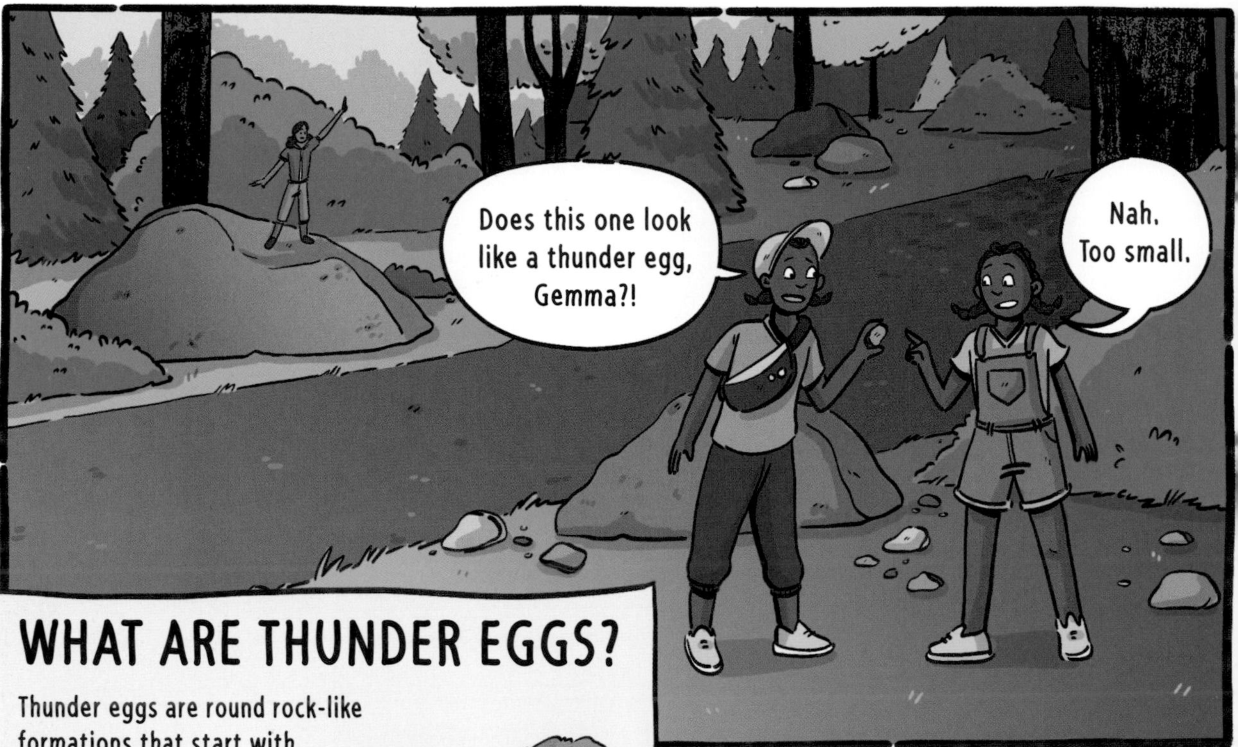
Does this one look like a thunder egg, Gemma?!
Nah. Too small.

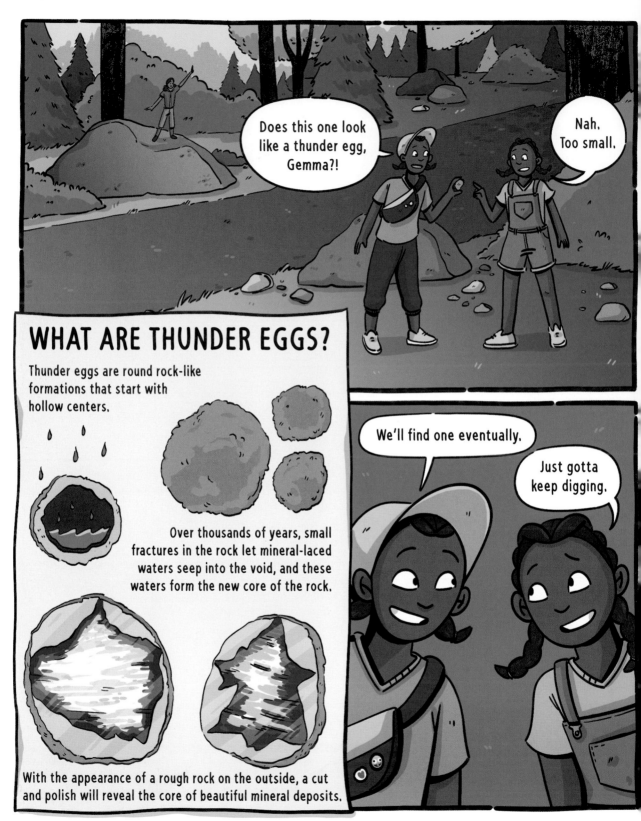

WHAT ARE THUNDER EGGS?

Thunder eggs are round rock-like formations that start with hollow centers.

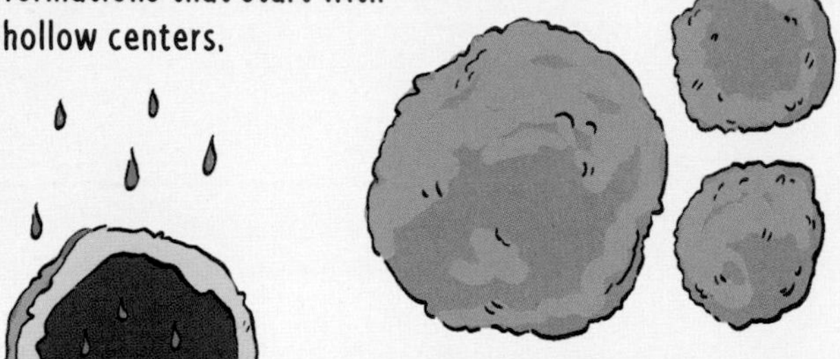

Over thousands of years, small fractures in the rock let mineral-laced waters seep into the void, and these waters form the new core of the rock.

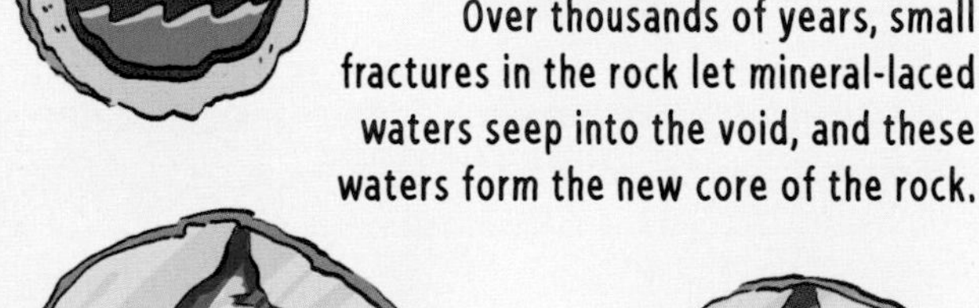

With the appearance of a rough rock on the outside, a cut and polish will reveal the core of beautiful mineral deposits.

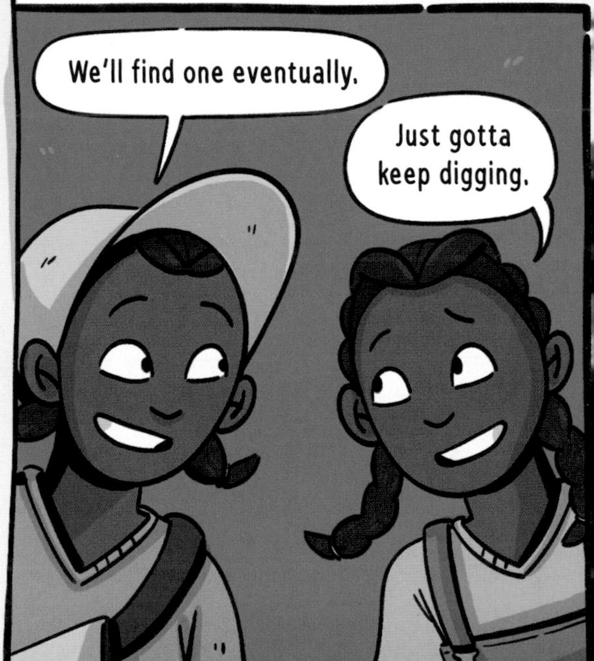
We'll find one eventually.
Just gotta keep digging.

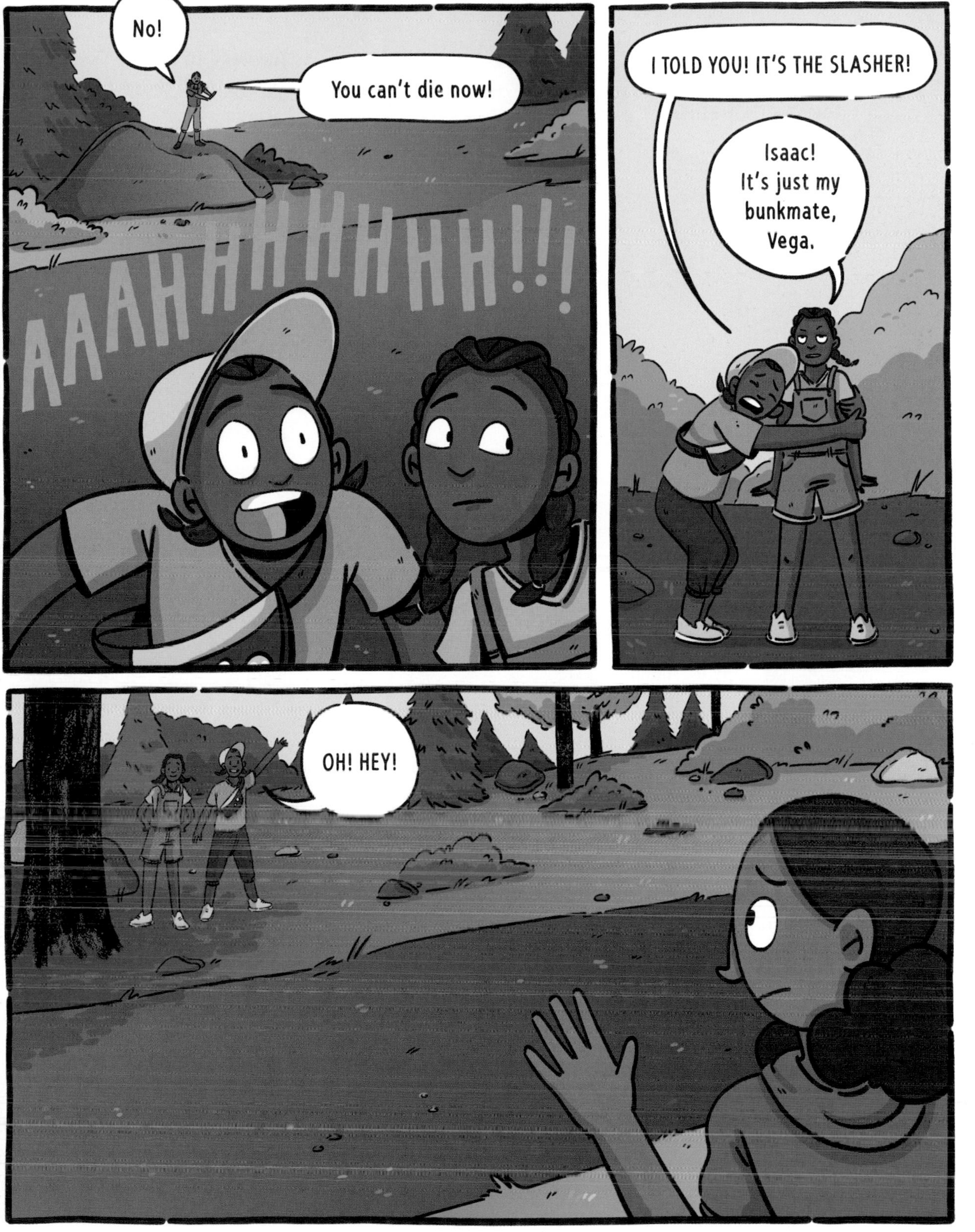
No!
You can't die now!
AAAHHHHHHH!!!
I TOLD YOU! IT'S THE SLASHER!
Isaac!
It's just my
bunkmate,
Vega.
OH! HEY!

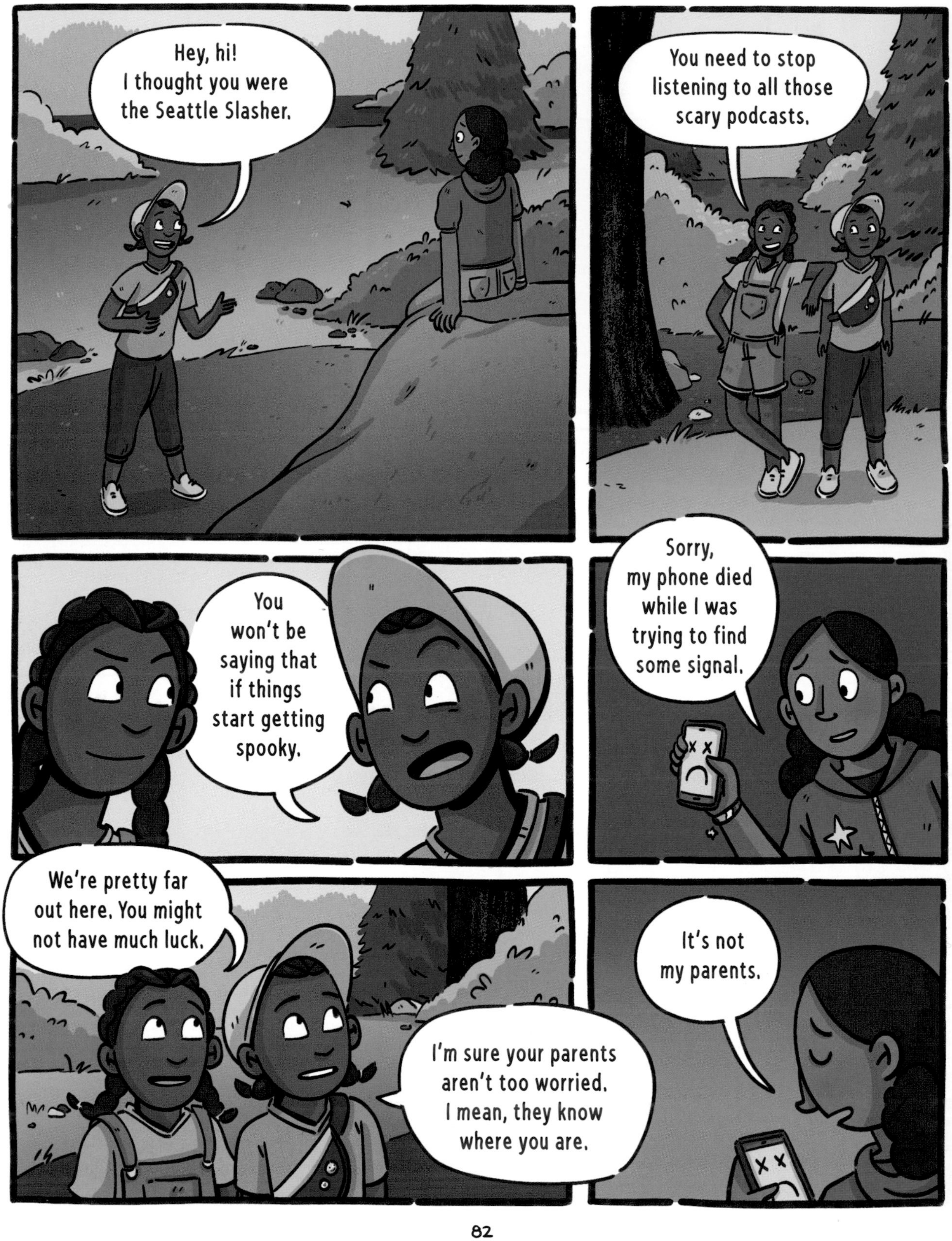
Hey, hi!
I thought you were the Seattle Slasher.
You need to stop listening to all those scary podcasts.
You won't be saying that if things start getting spooky.
Sorry, my phone died while I was trying to find some signal.
We're pretty far out here. You might not have much luck.
I'm sure your parents aren't too worried. I mean, they know where you are.
It's not my parents.

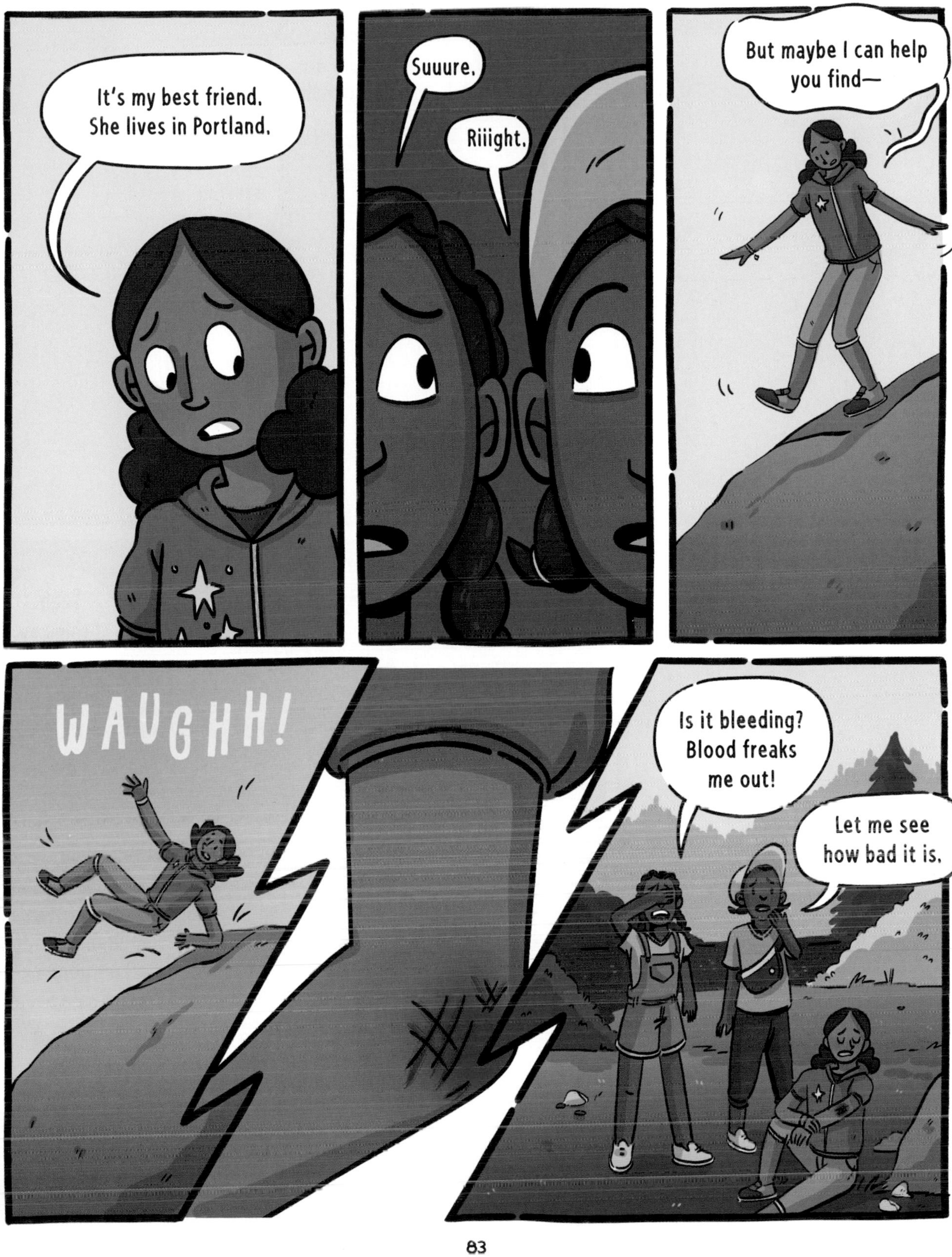
It's my best friend. She lives in Portland.
Suuure.
Riiight.
But maybe I can help you find—
WAUGHH!
Is it bleeding? Blood freaks me out!
Let me see how bad it is.

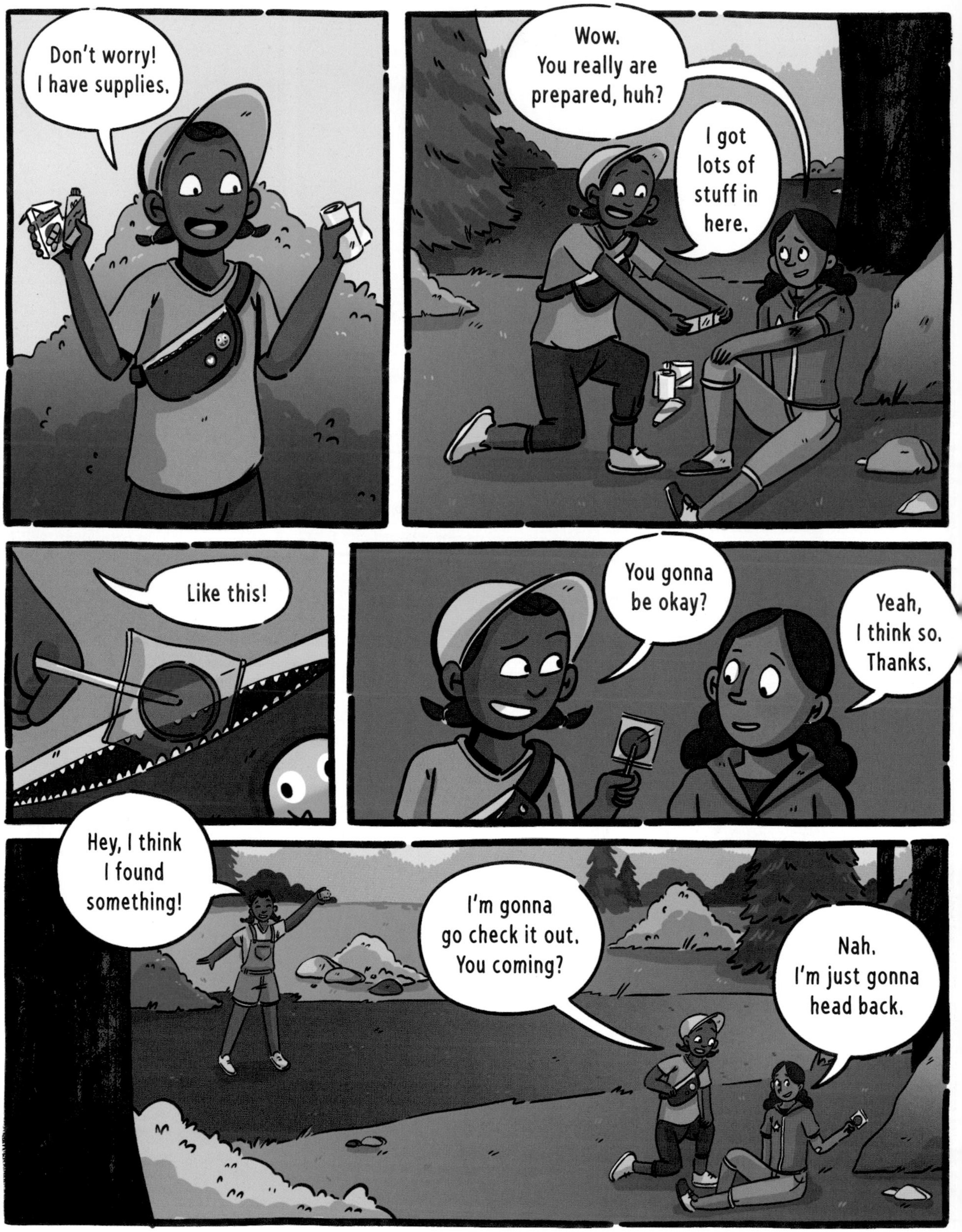
Don't worry!
I have supplies.
Wow.
You really are
prepared, huh?
I got
lots of
stuff in
here.
Like this!
You gonna
be okay?
Yeah,
I think so.
Thanks.
Hey, I think
I found
something!
I'm gonna
go check it out.
You coming?
Nah.
I'm just gonna
head back.

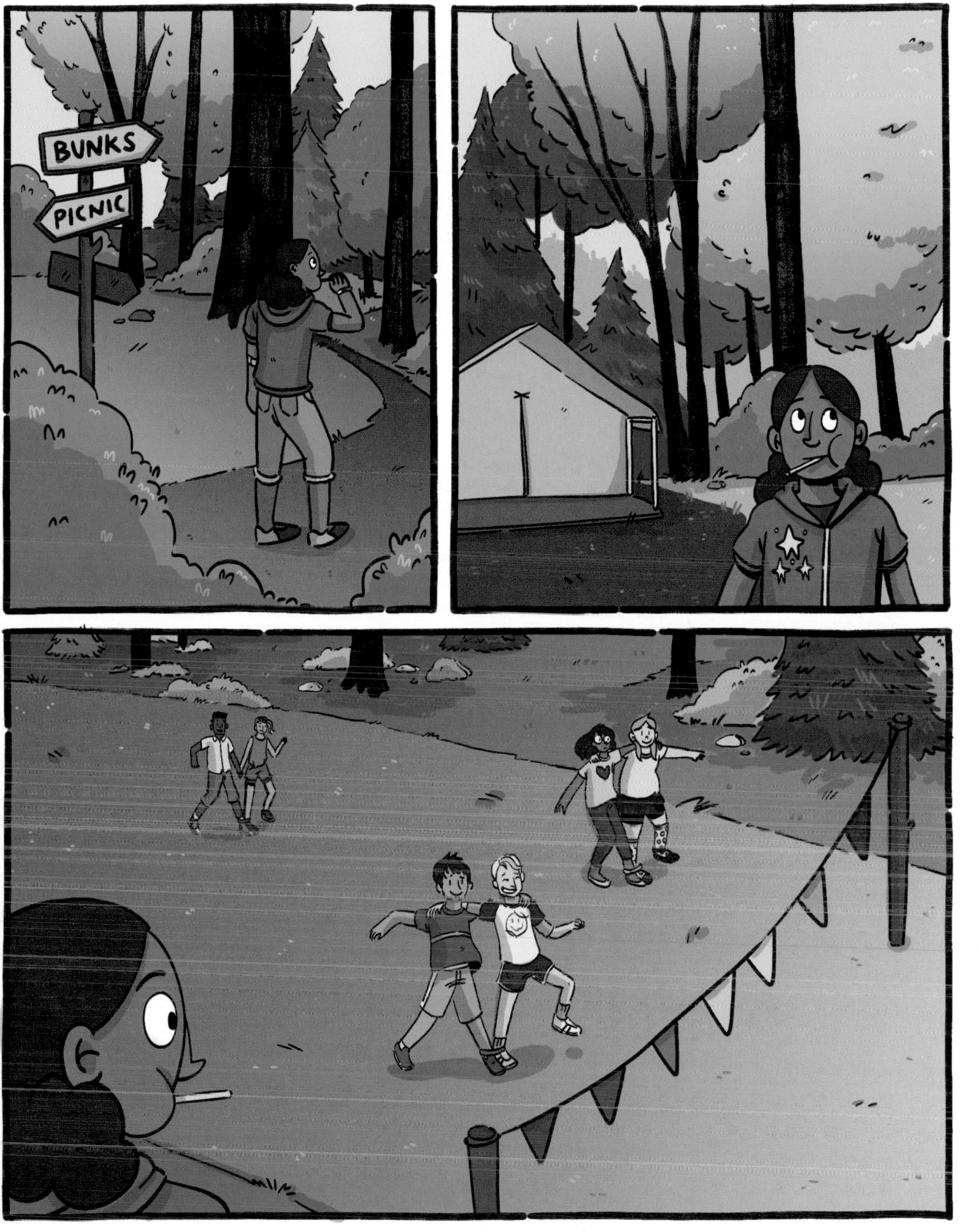
BUNKS
PICNIC

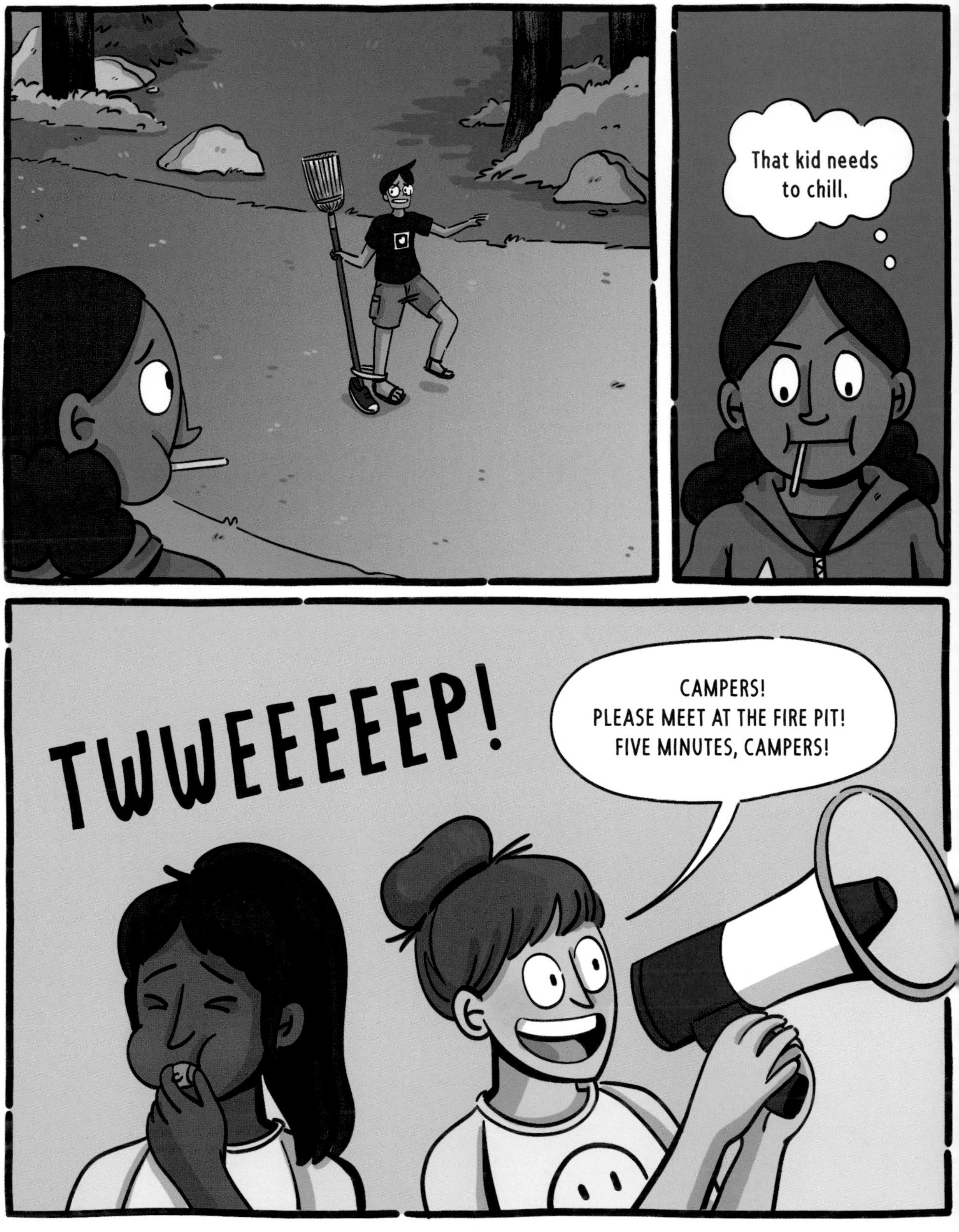
That kid needs to chill.
TWWEEEEEP!
CAMPERS!
PLEASE MEET AT THE FIRE PIT!
FIVE MINUTES, CAMPERS!

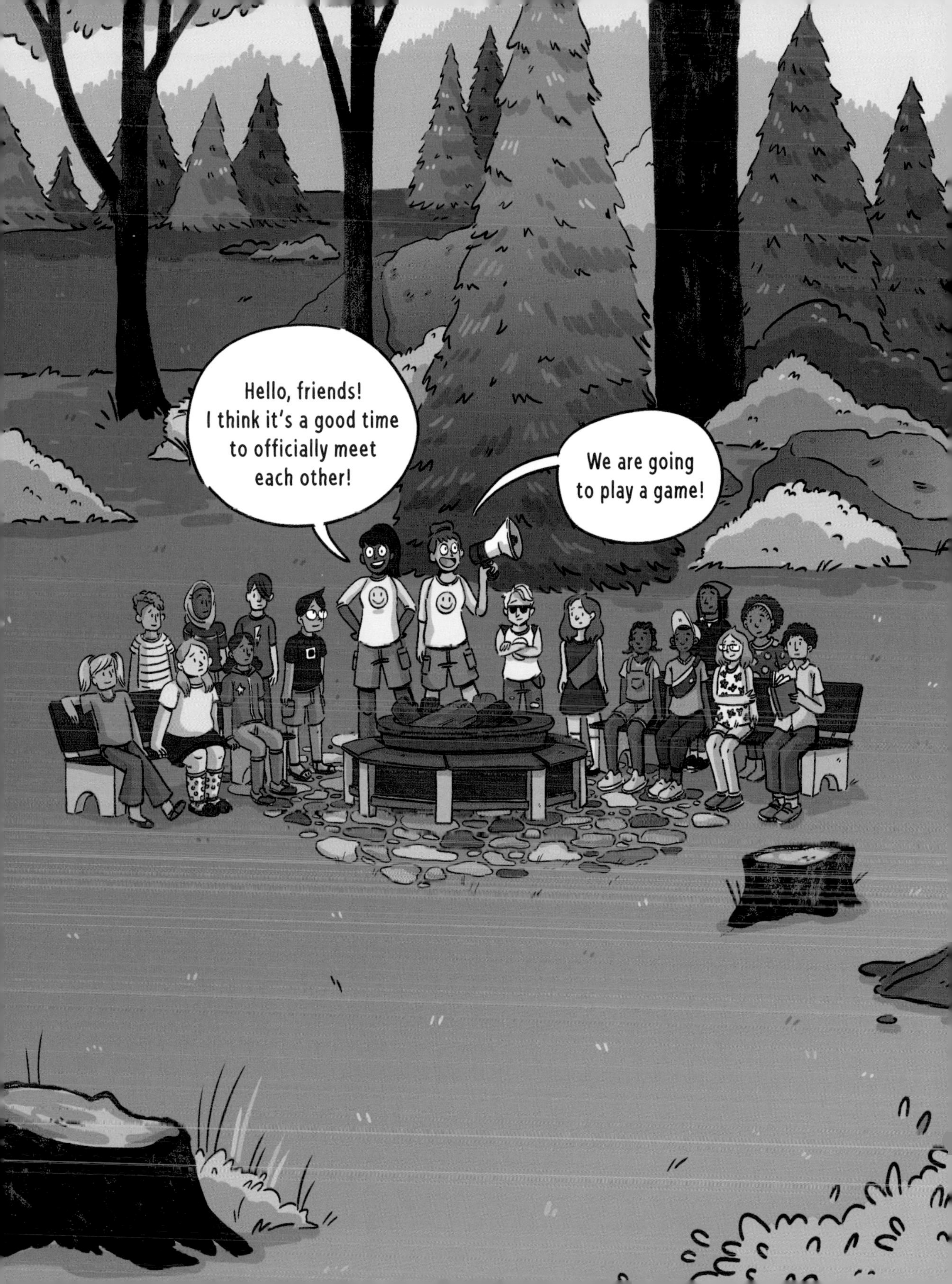
Hello, friends! I think it's a good time to officially meet each other!
We are going to play a game!

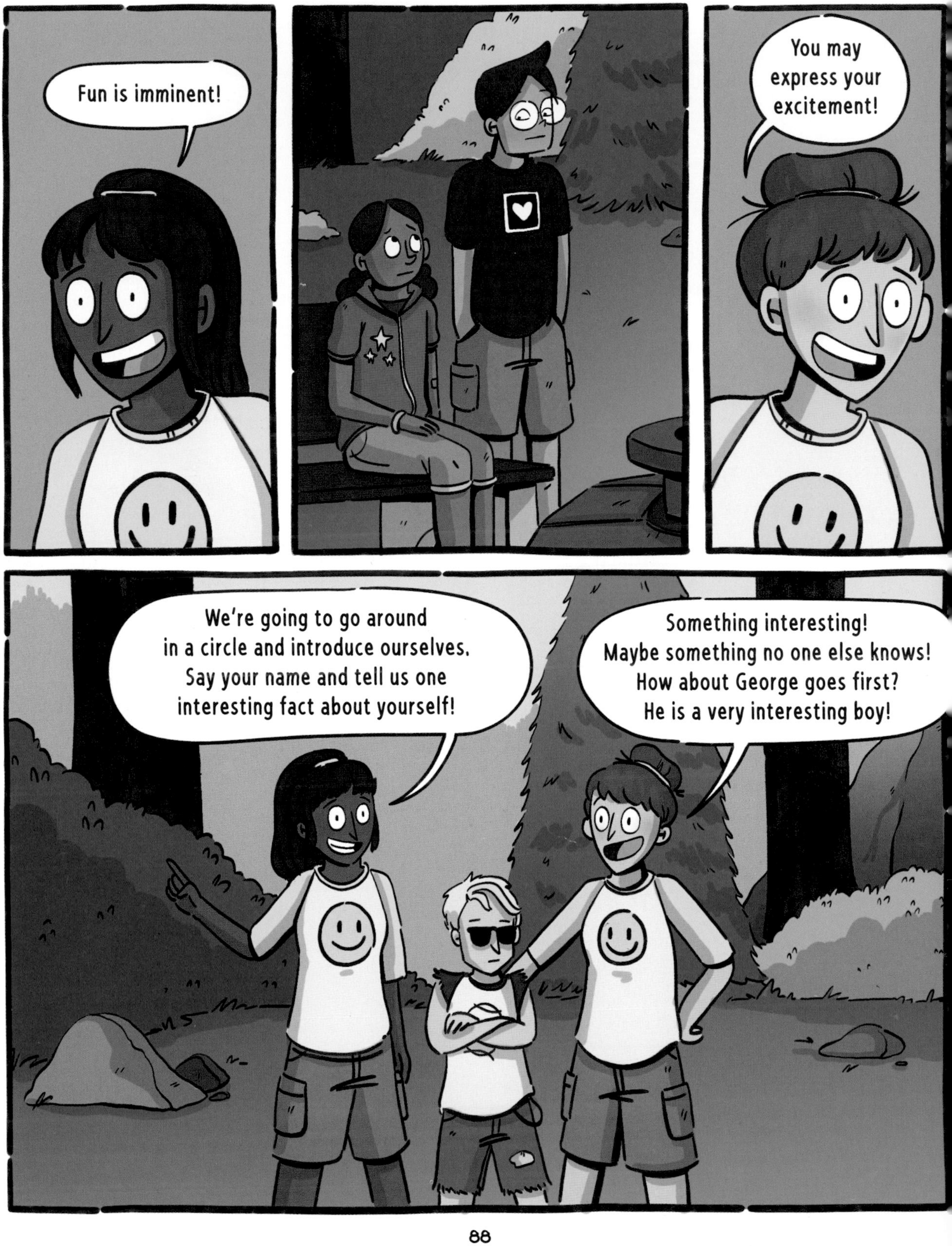
Fun is imminent!
You may express your excitement!
We're going to go around in a circle and introduce ourselves. Say your name and tell us one interesting fact about yourself!
Something interesting! Maybe something no one else knows! How about George goes first? He is a very interesting boy!

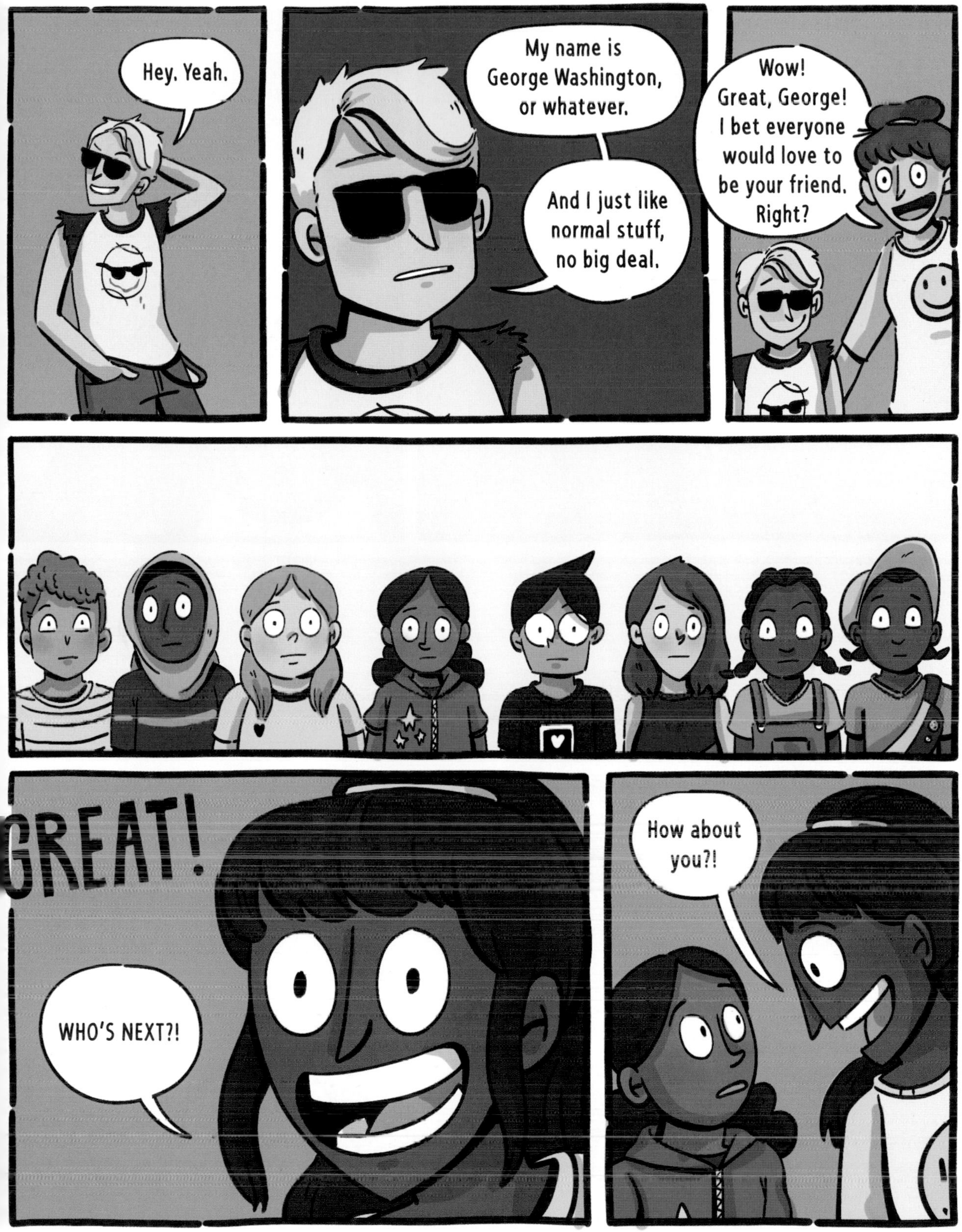
Hey. Yeah.
My name is George Washington, or whatever.
And I just like normal stuff, no big deal.
Wow! Great, George! I bet everyone would love to be your friend. Right?
GREAT!
WHO'S NEXT?!
How about you?!

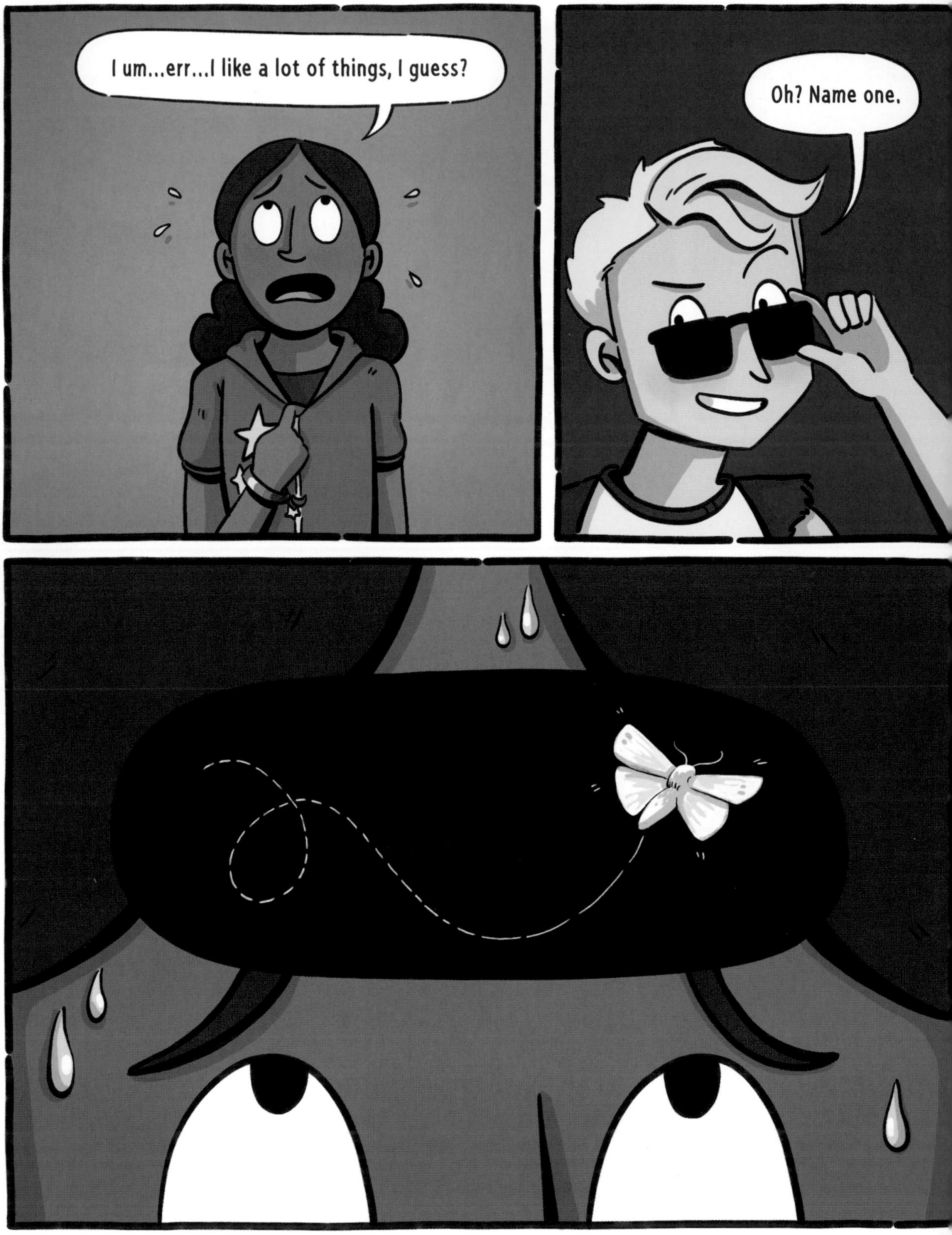
I um...err...I like a lot of things, I guess?
Oh? Name one.

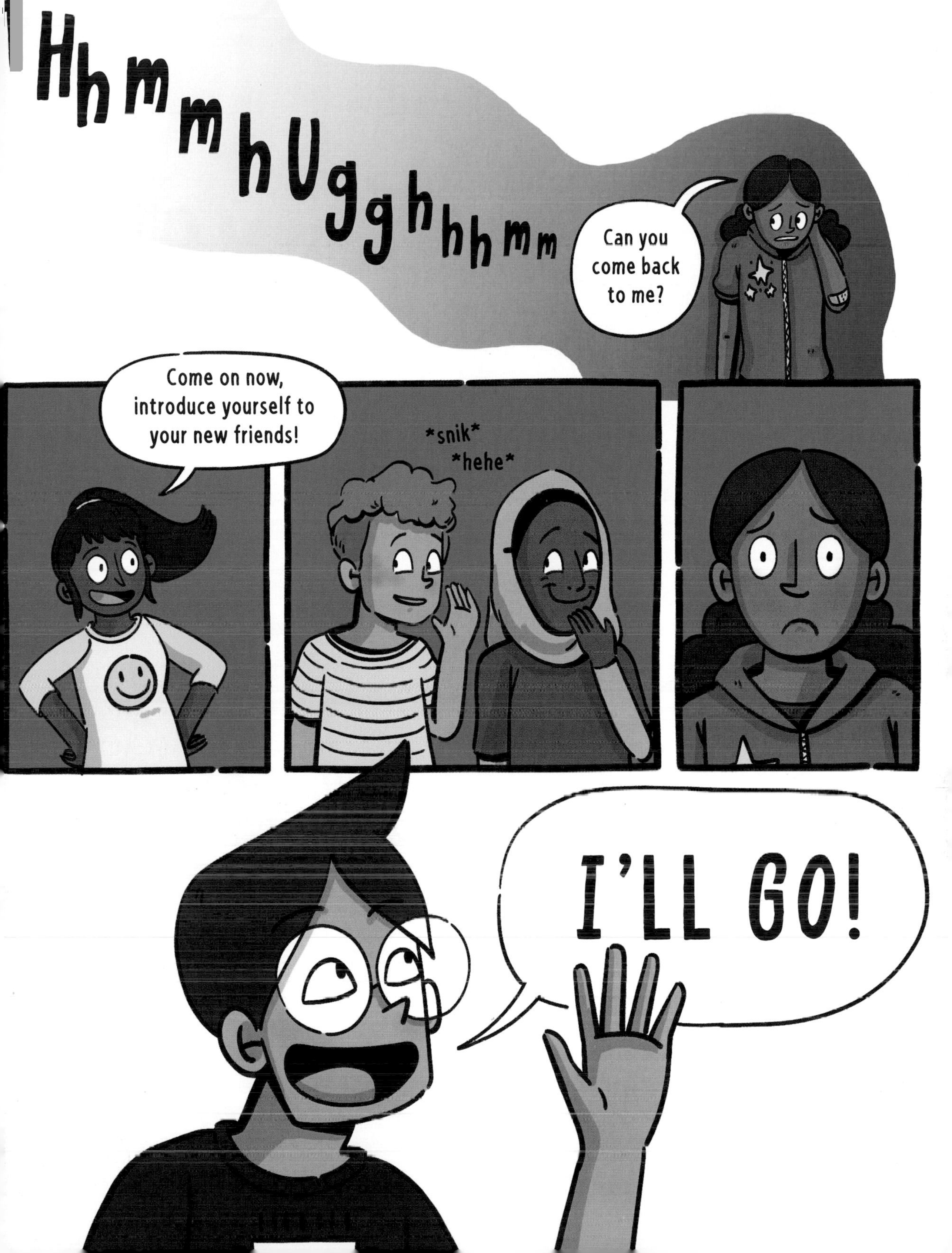

HhmmmhUgghhhmm
Can you come back to me?
Come on now, introduce yourself to your new friends!
snik
hehe
I'LL GO!

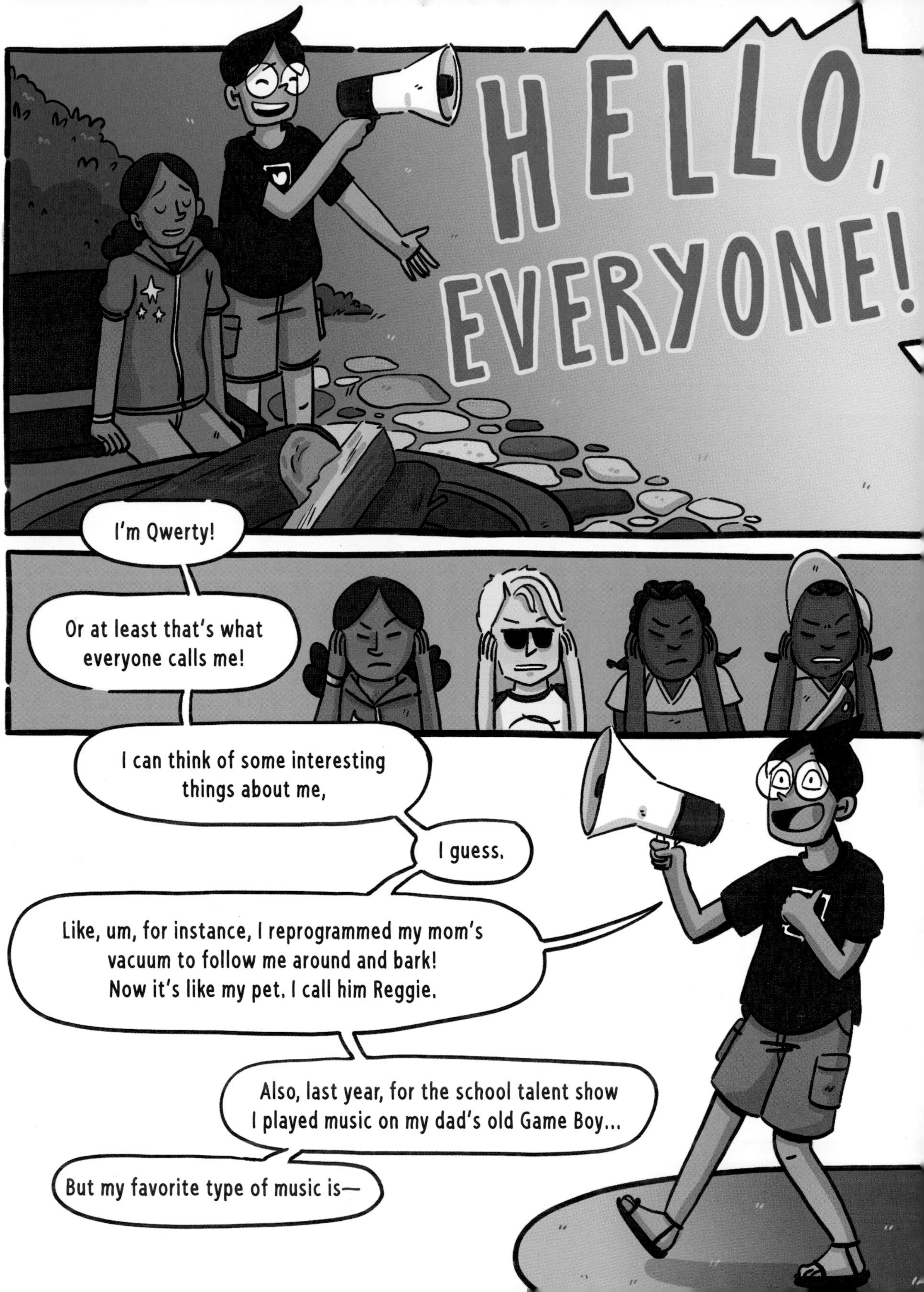
HELLO, EVERYONE!
I'm Qwerty!
Or at least that's what everyone calls me!
I can think of some interesting things about me,
I guess.
Like, um, for instance, I reprogrammed my mom's vacuum to follow me around and bark! Now it's like my pet. I call him Reggie.
Also, last year, for the school talent show I played music on my dad's old Game Boy...
But my favorite type of music is—

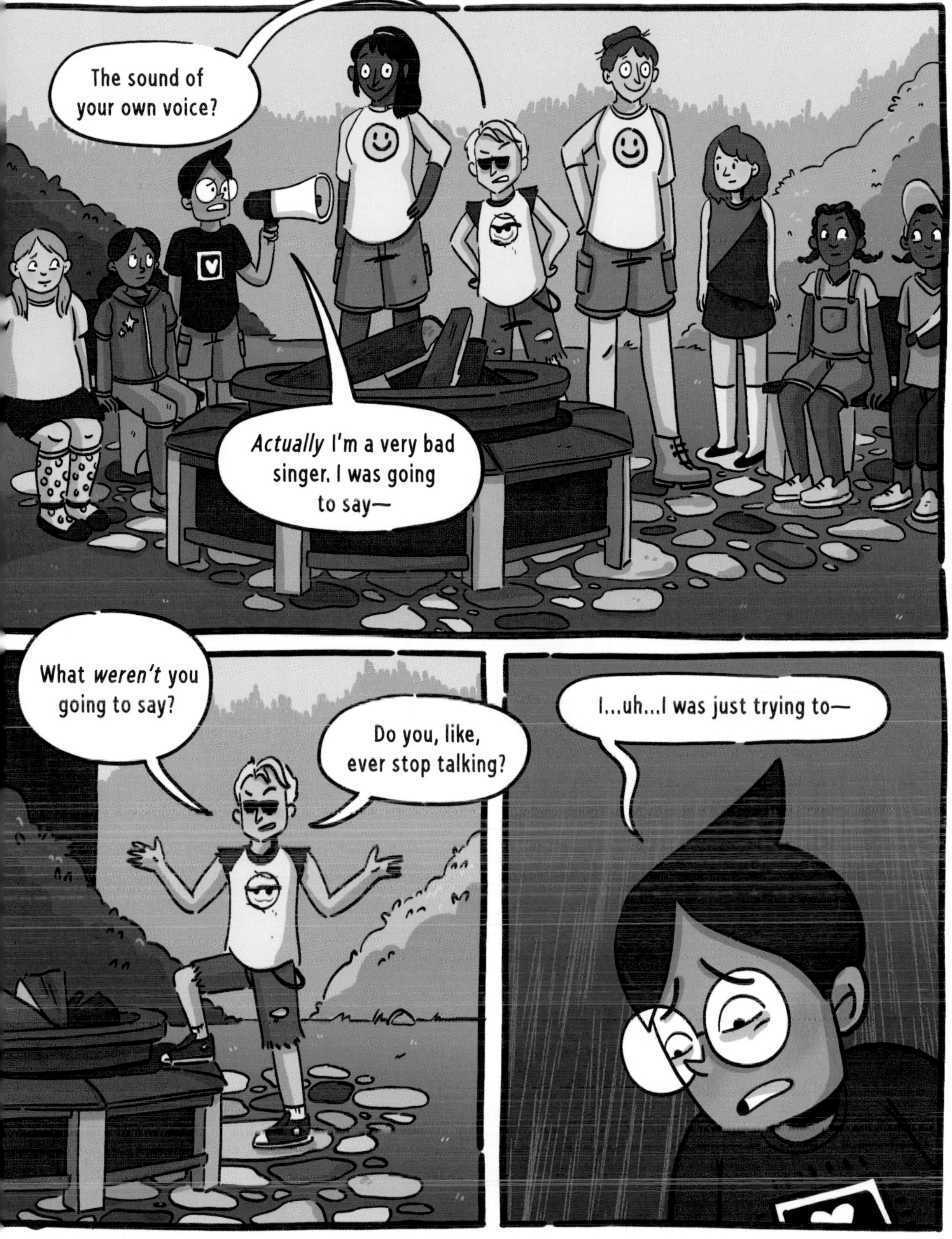

The sound of your own voice?
Actually I'm a very bad singer. I was going to say—
What *weren't* you going to say?
Do you, like, ever stop talking?
I...uh...I was just trying to—

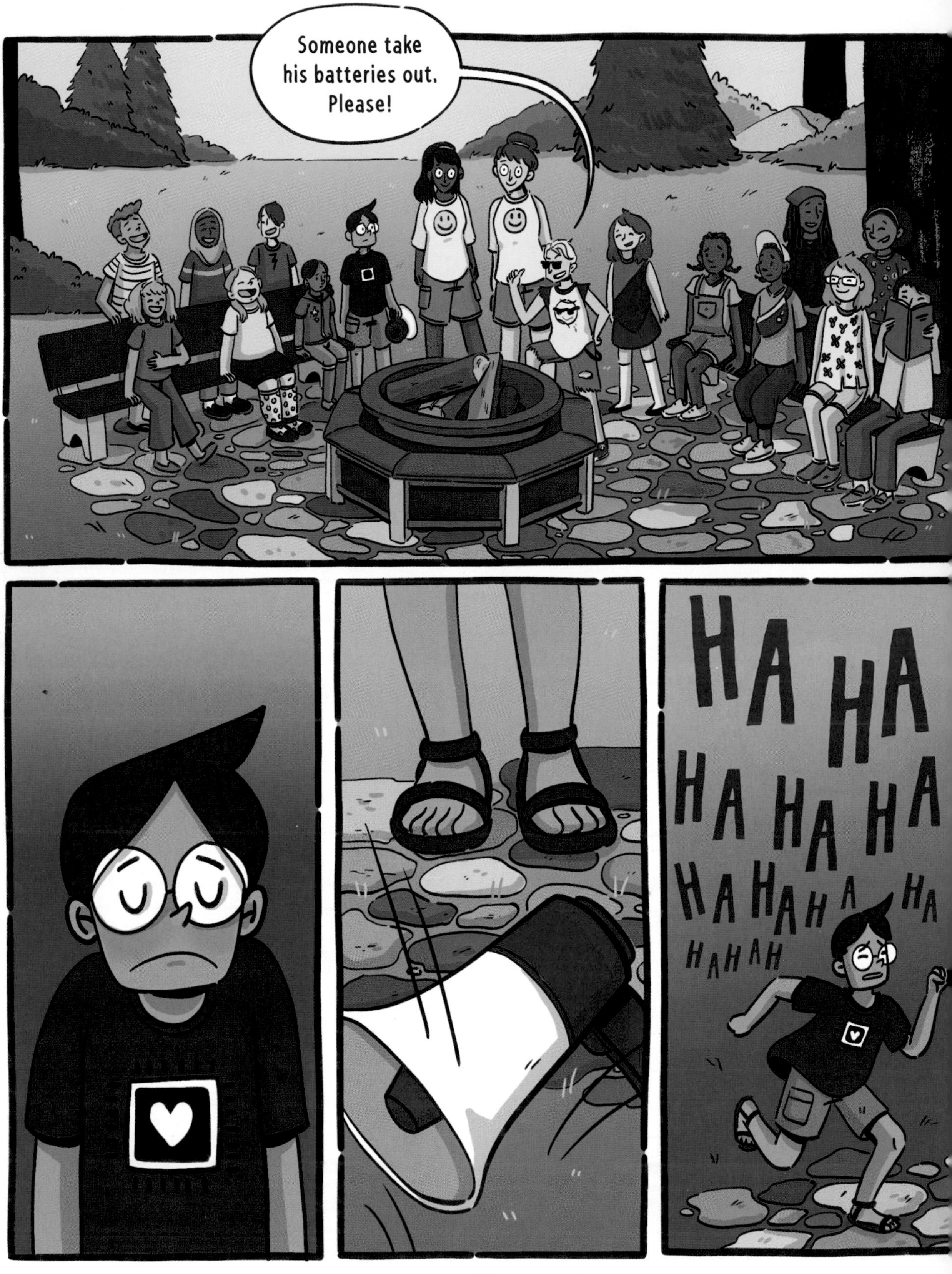
Someone take his batteries out. Please!
HA HA HA HA HA HA HA HA HA HA HA HA HA HAHAH

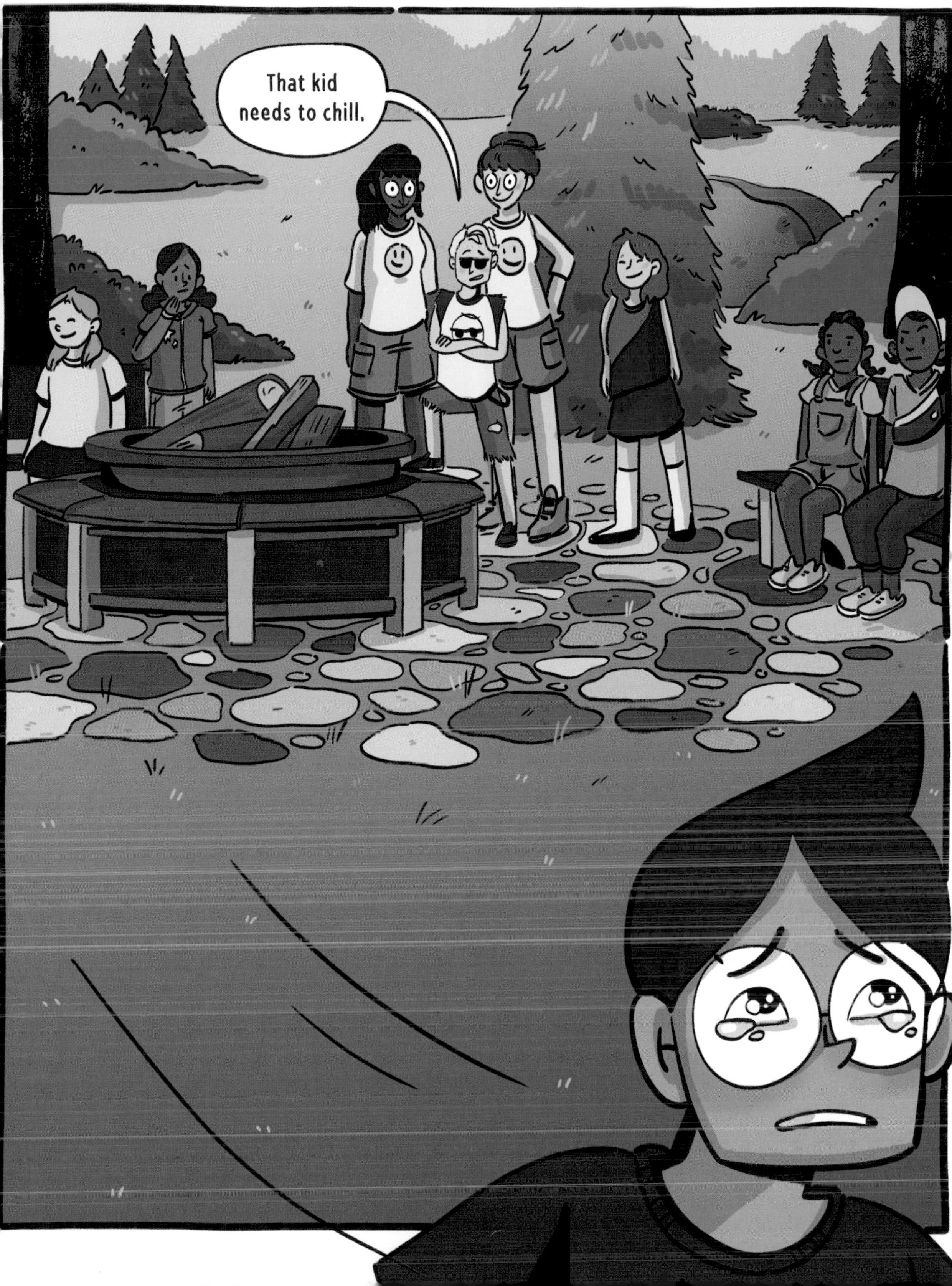
That kid needs to chill.

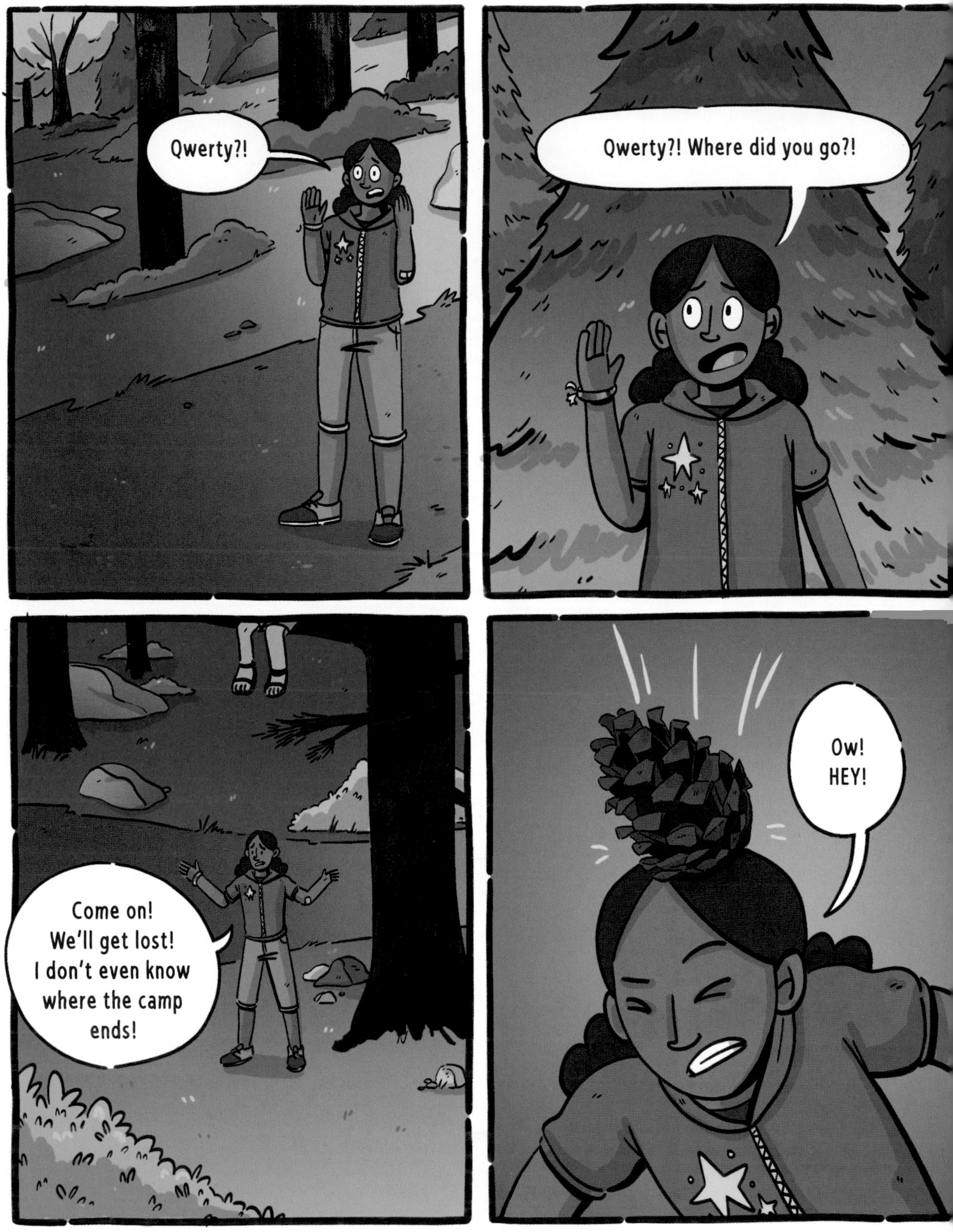
Qwerty?!
Qwerty?! Where did you go?!
Come on! We'll get lost! I don't even know where the camp ends!
Ow! HEY!

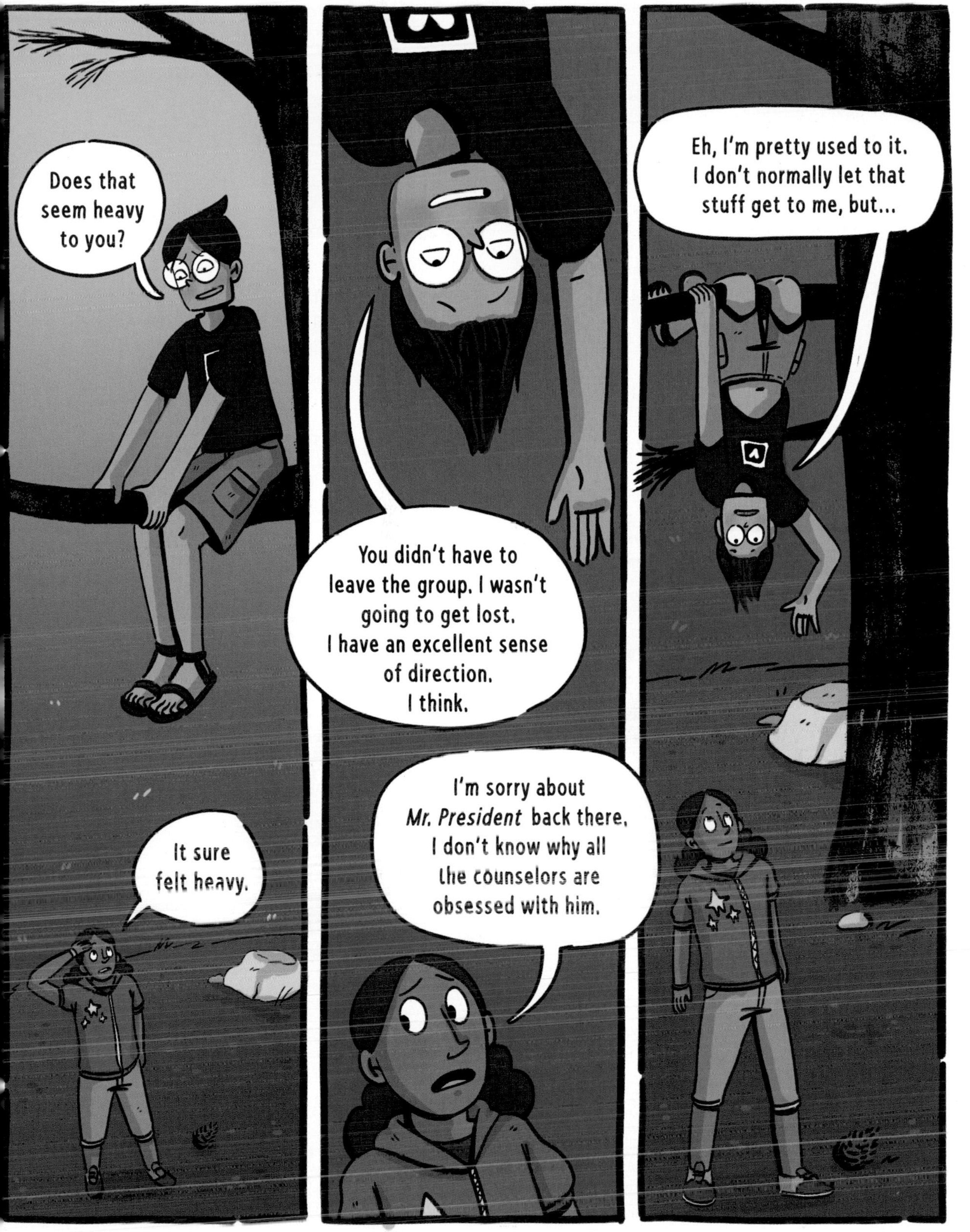
Does that seem heavy to you?
It sure felt heavy.
You didn't have to leave the group. I wasn't going to get lost. I have an excellent sense of direction. I think.
I'm sorry about *Mr. President* back there. I don't know why all the counselors are obsessed with him.
Eh, I'm pretty used to it. I don't normally let that stuff get to me, but...

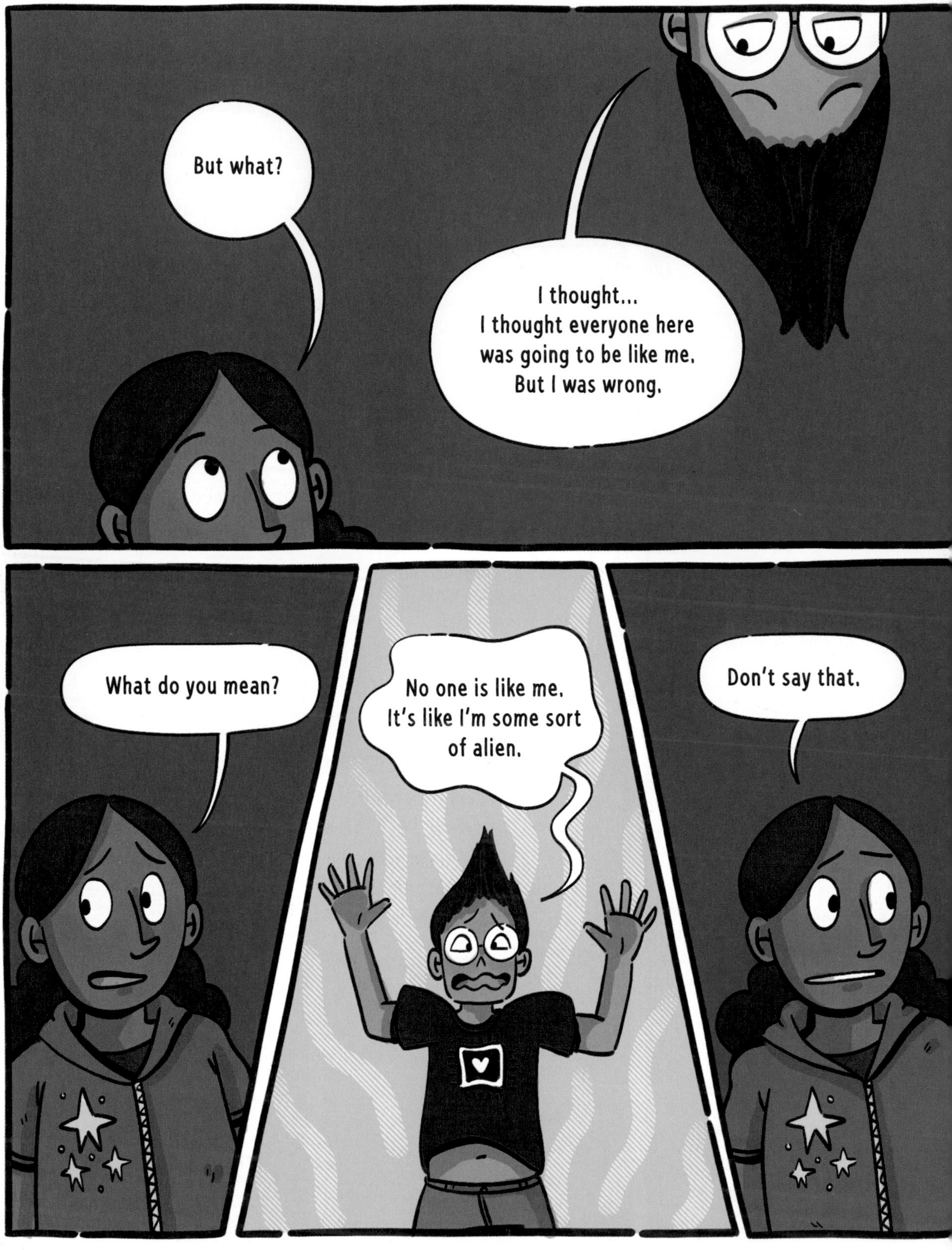

But what?
I thought... I thought everyone here was going to be like me. But I was wrong.
What do you mean?
No one is like me. It's like I'm some sort of alien.
Don't say that.

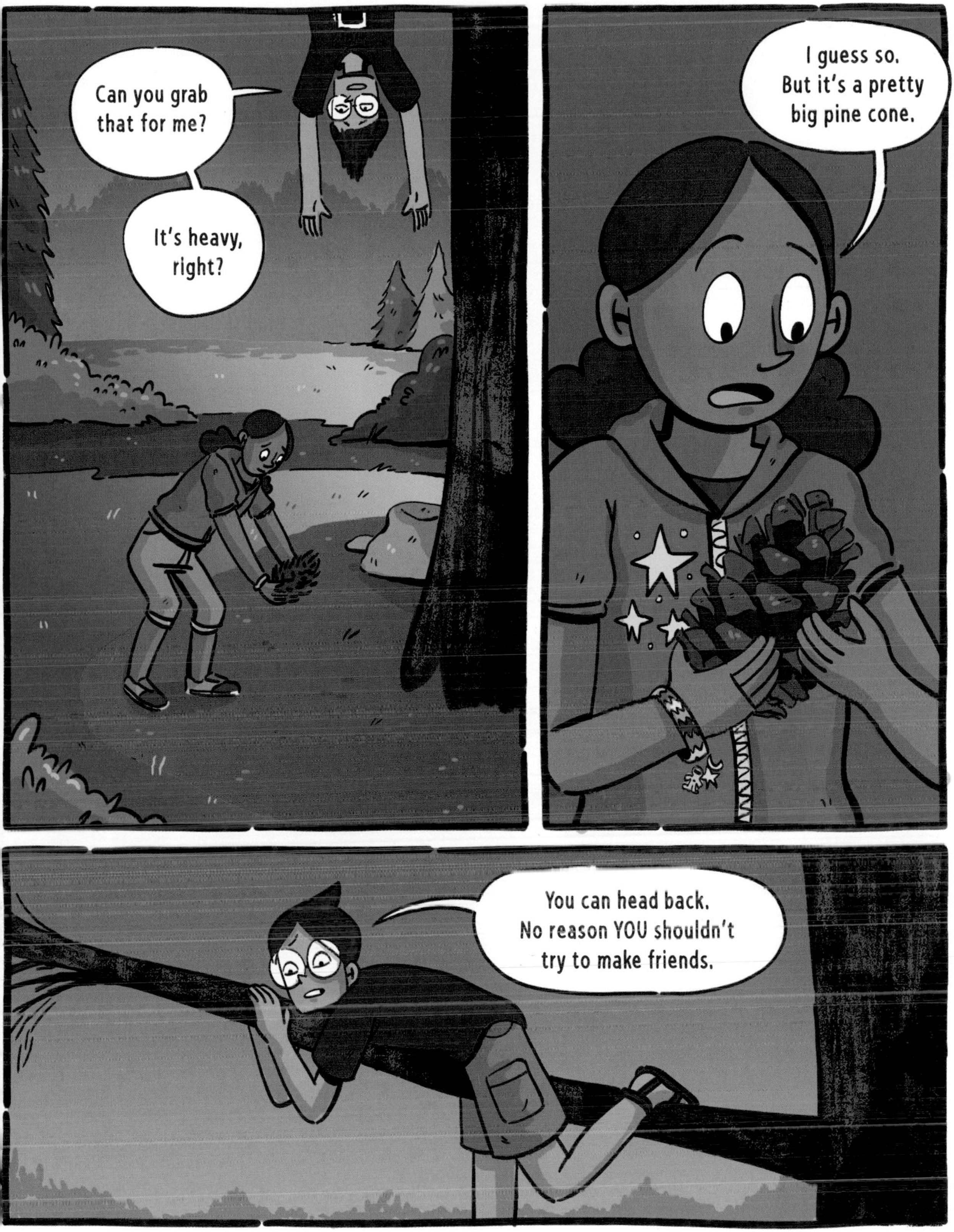
Can you grab that for me?
It's heavy, right?
I guess so. But it's a pretty big pine cone.
You can head back. No reason YOU shouldn't try to make friends.

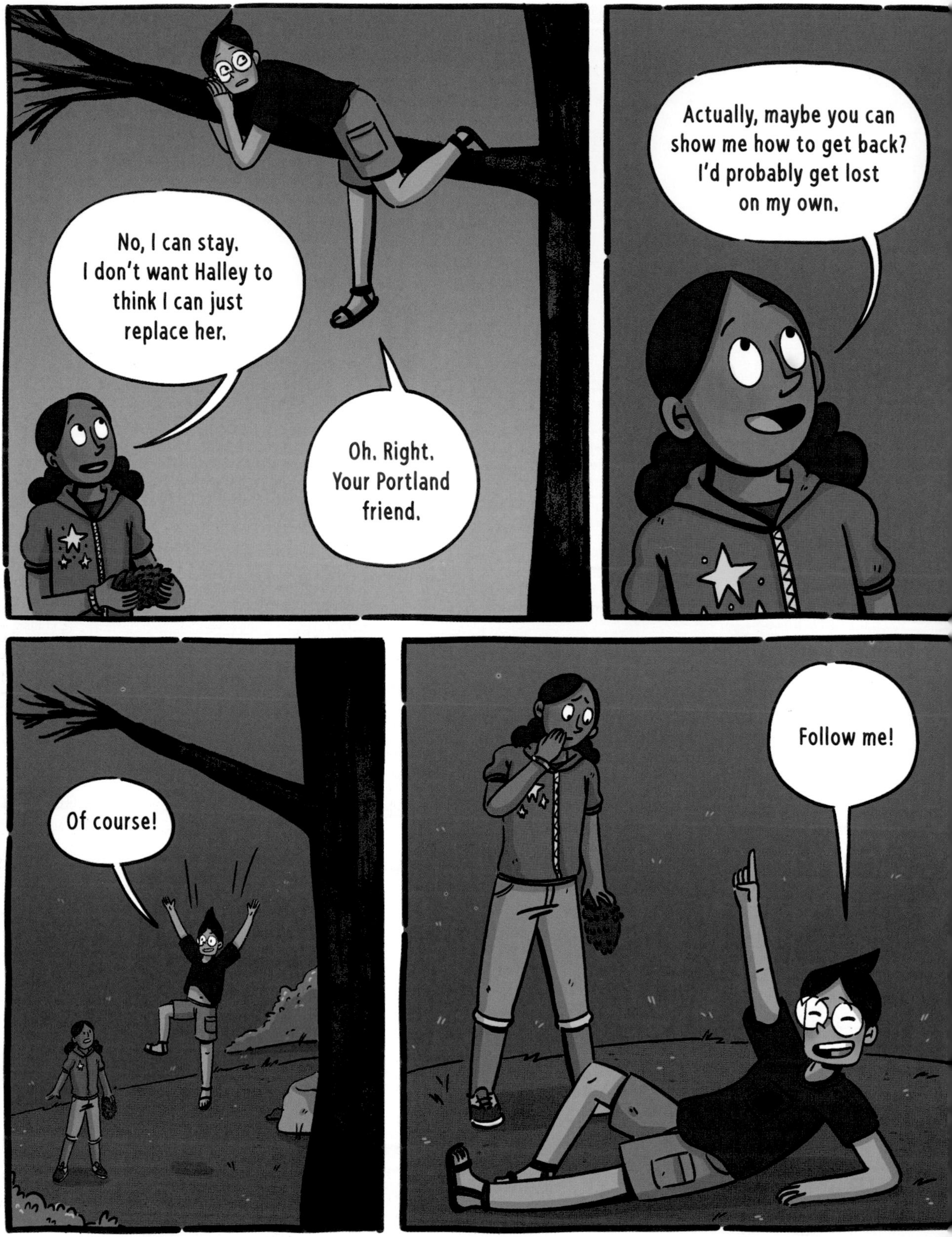
No, I can stay.
I don't want Halley to think I can just replace her.
Oh. Right. Your Portland friend.
Actually, maybe you can show me how to get back? I'd probably get lost on my own.
Of course!
Follow me!

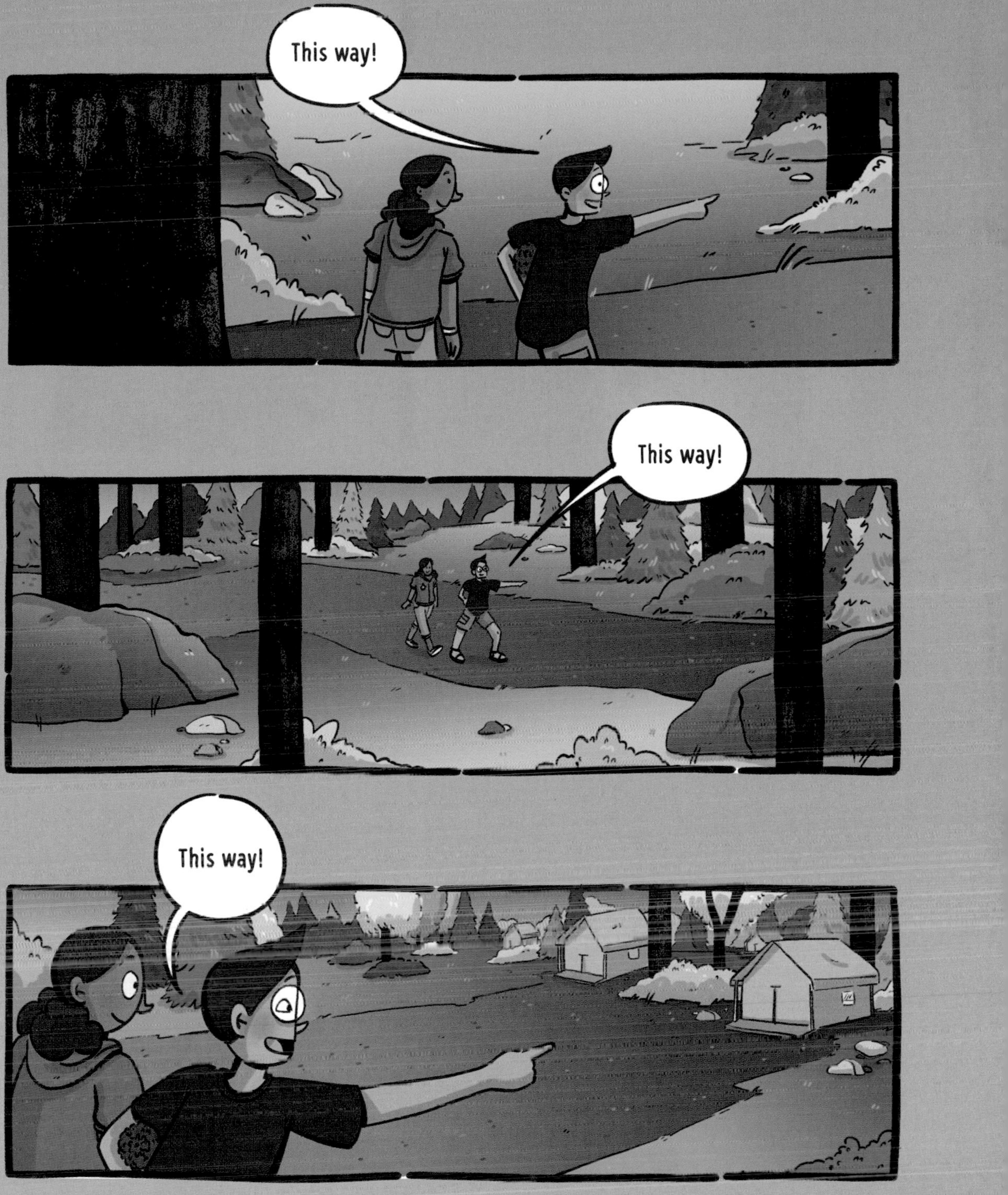
This way!
This way!
This way!

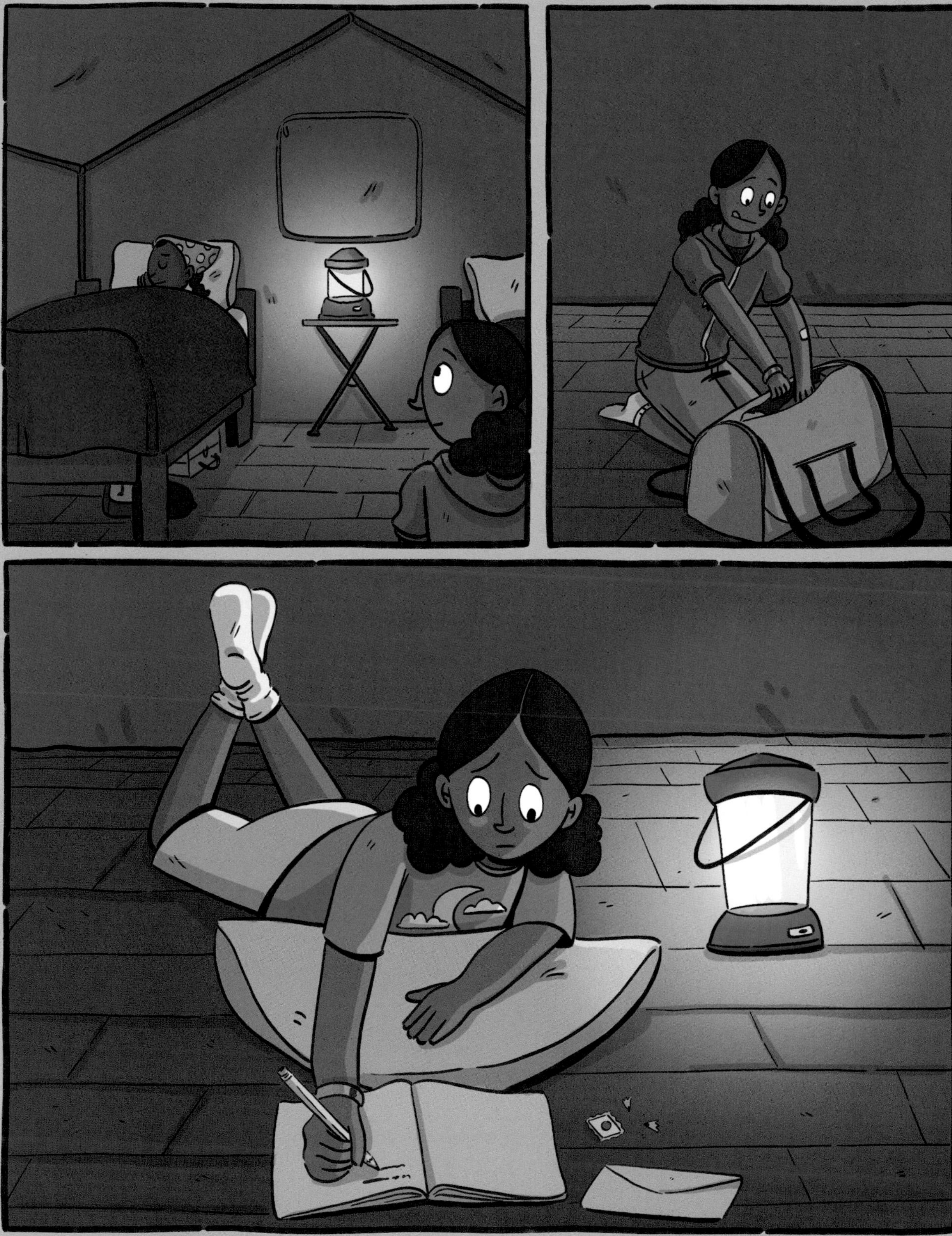

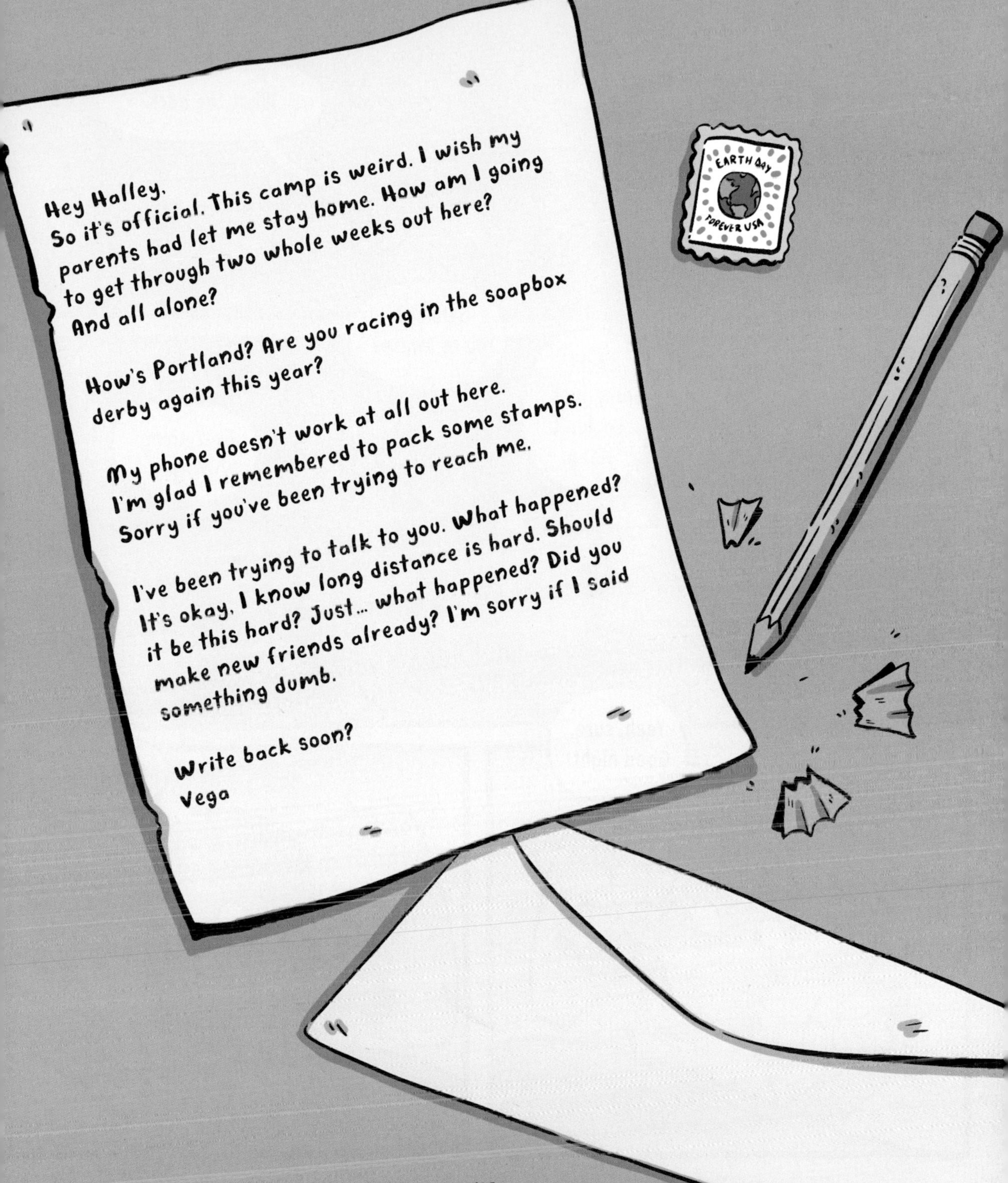
Hey Halley,
So it's official. This camp is weird. I wish my parents had let me stay home. How am I going to get through two whole weeks out here? And all alone?
How's Portland? Are you racing in the soapbox derby again this year?
My phone doesn't work at all out here. I'm glad I remembered to pack some stamps. Sorry if you've been trying to reach me.
I've been trying to talk to you. What happened? It's okay, I know long distance is hard. Should it be this hard? Just... what happened? Did you make new friends already? I'm sorry if I said something dumb.
Write back soon?
Vega
EARTH DAY
FOREVER USA

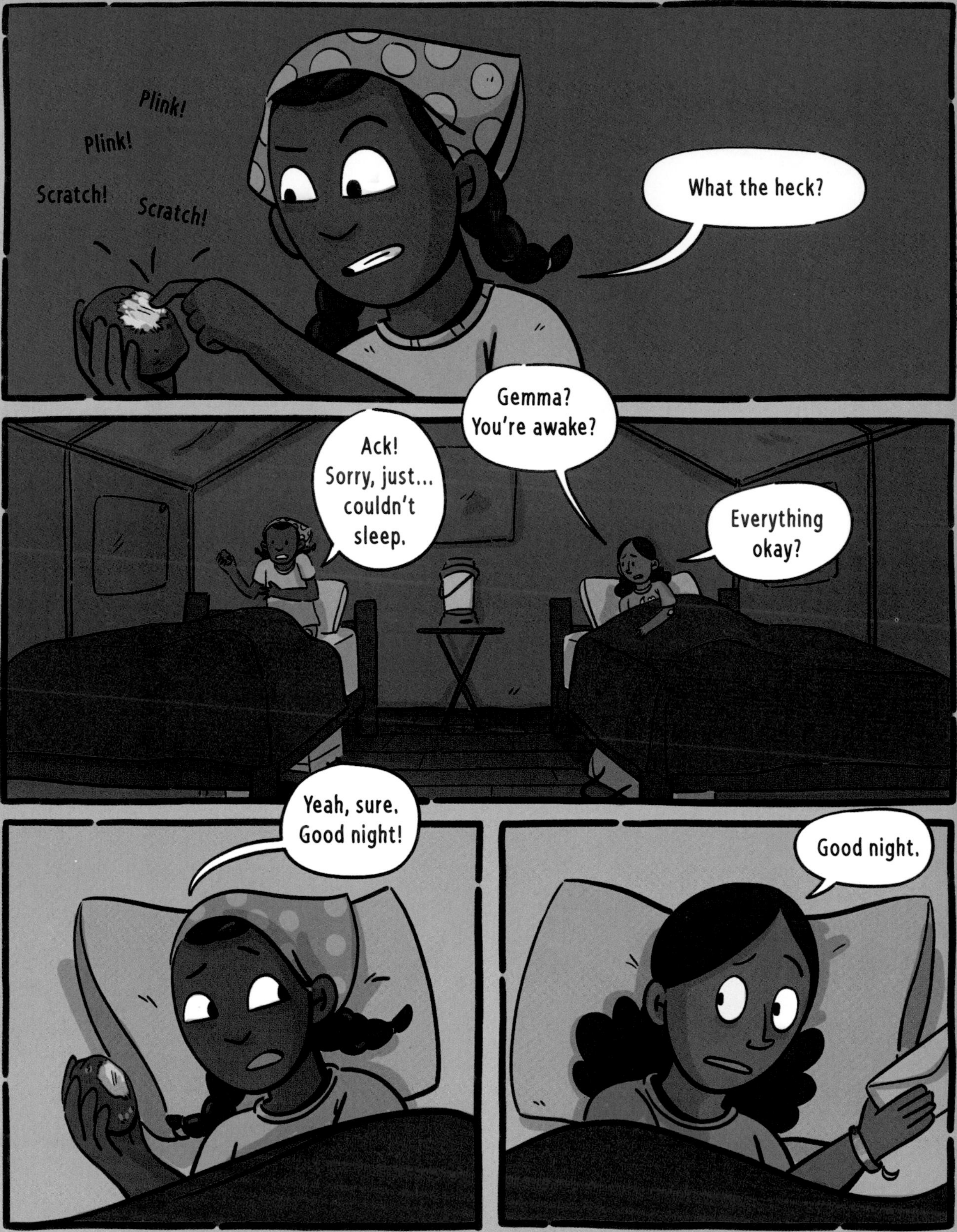
Plink!
Plink!
Scratch!
Scratch!
What the heck?
Ack! Sorry, just... couldn't sleep.
Gemma? You're awake?
Everything okay?
Yeah, sure. Good night!
Good night.

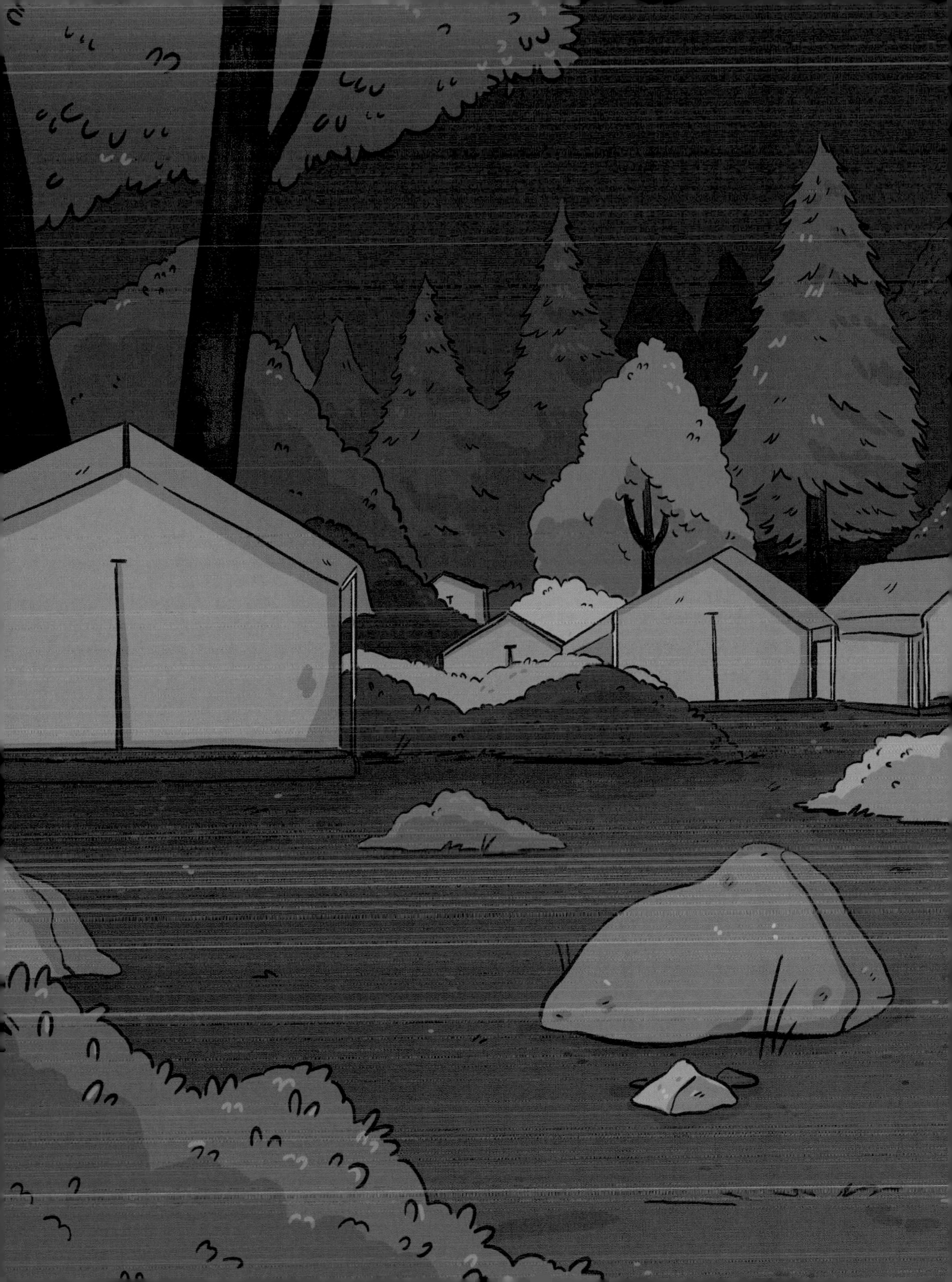

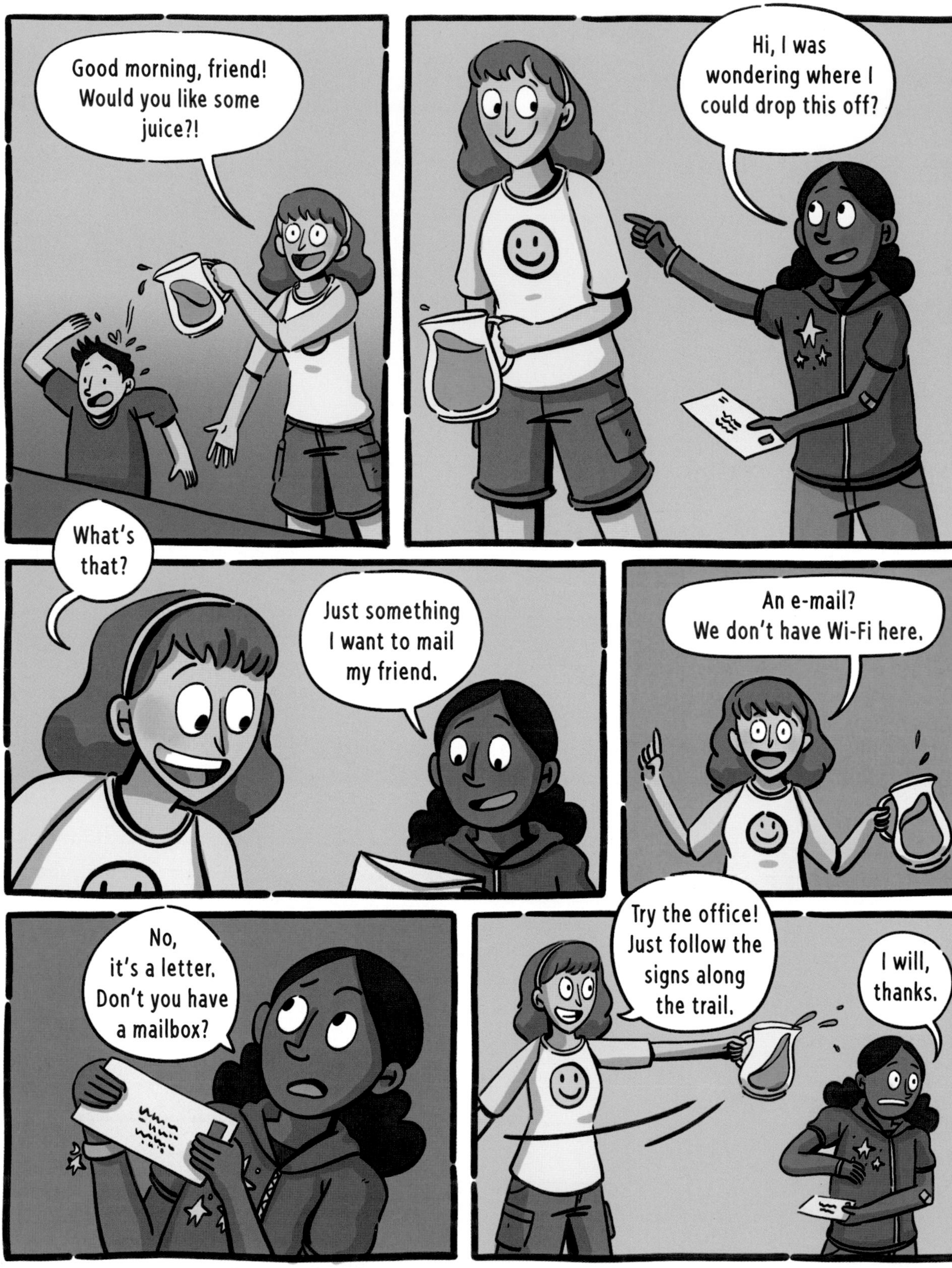
Good morning, friend! Would you like some juice?!
Hi, I was wondering where I could drop this off?
What's that?
Just something I want to mail my friend.
An e-mail? We don't have Wi-Fi here.
No, it's a letter. Don't you have a mailbox?
Try the office! Just follow the signs along the trail.
I will, thanks.

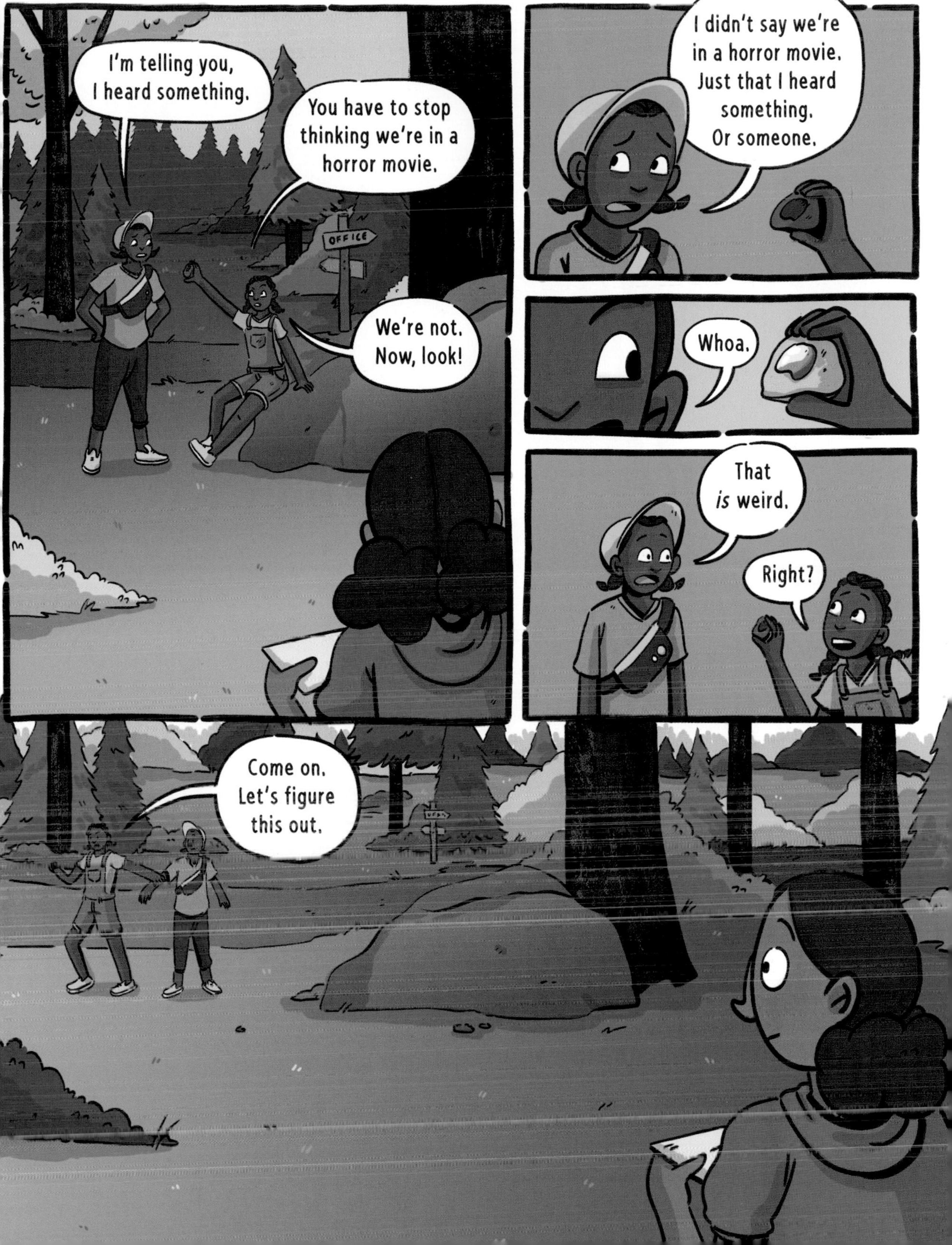
I'm telling you, I heard something.
You have to stop thinking we're in a horror movie.
OFFICE
We're not. Now, look!
I didn't say we're in a horror movie. Just that I heard something. Or someone.
Whoa.
That *is* weird.
Right?
Come on. Let's figure this out.

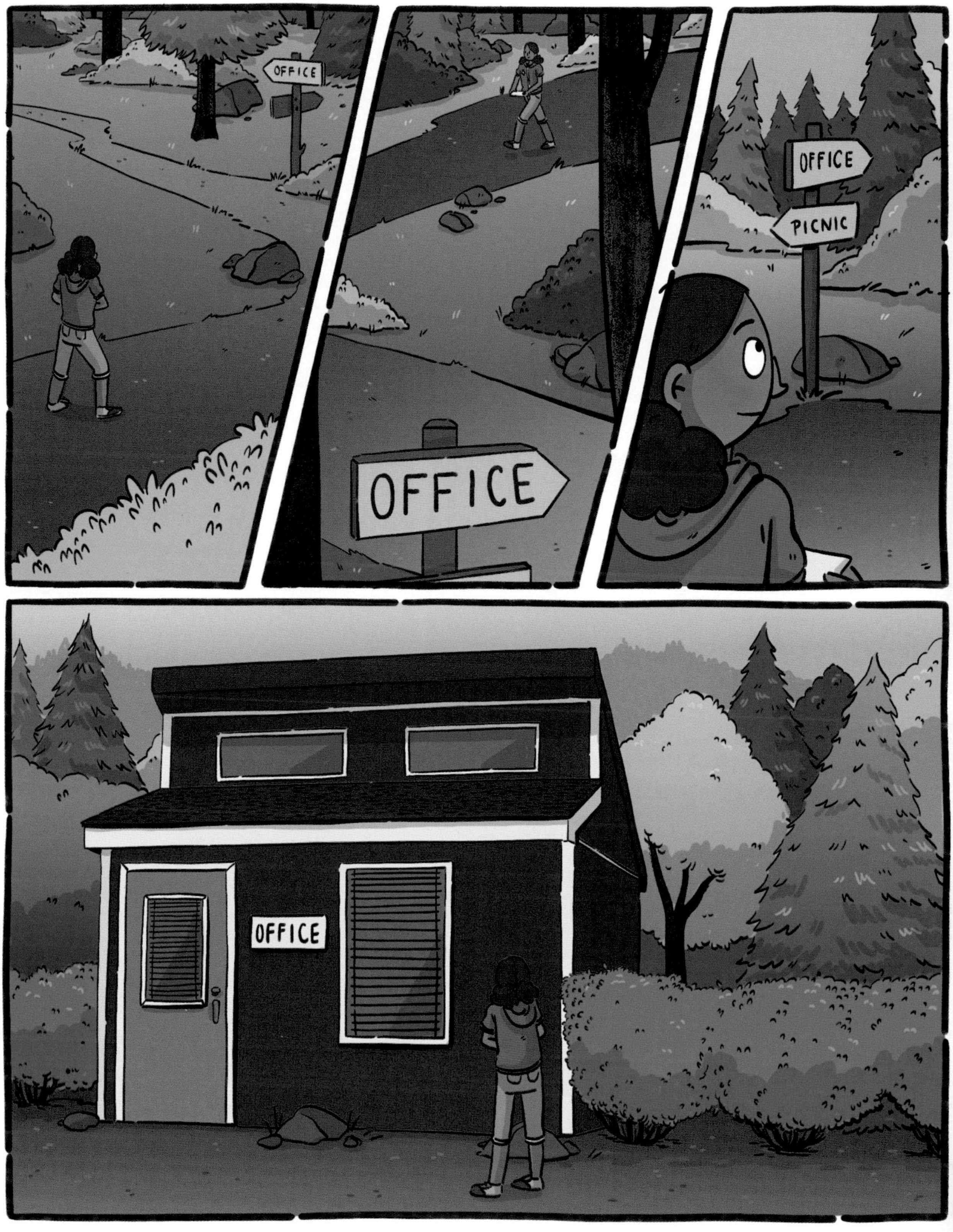
OFFICE
OFFICE
OFFICE
PICNIC
OFFICE

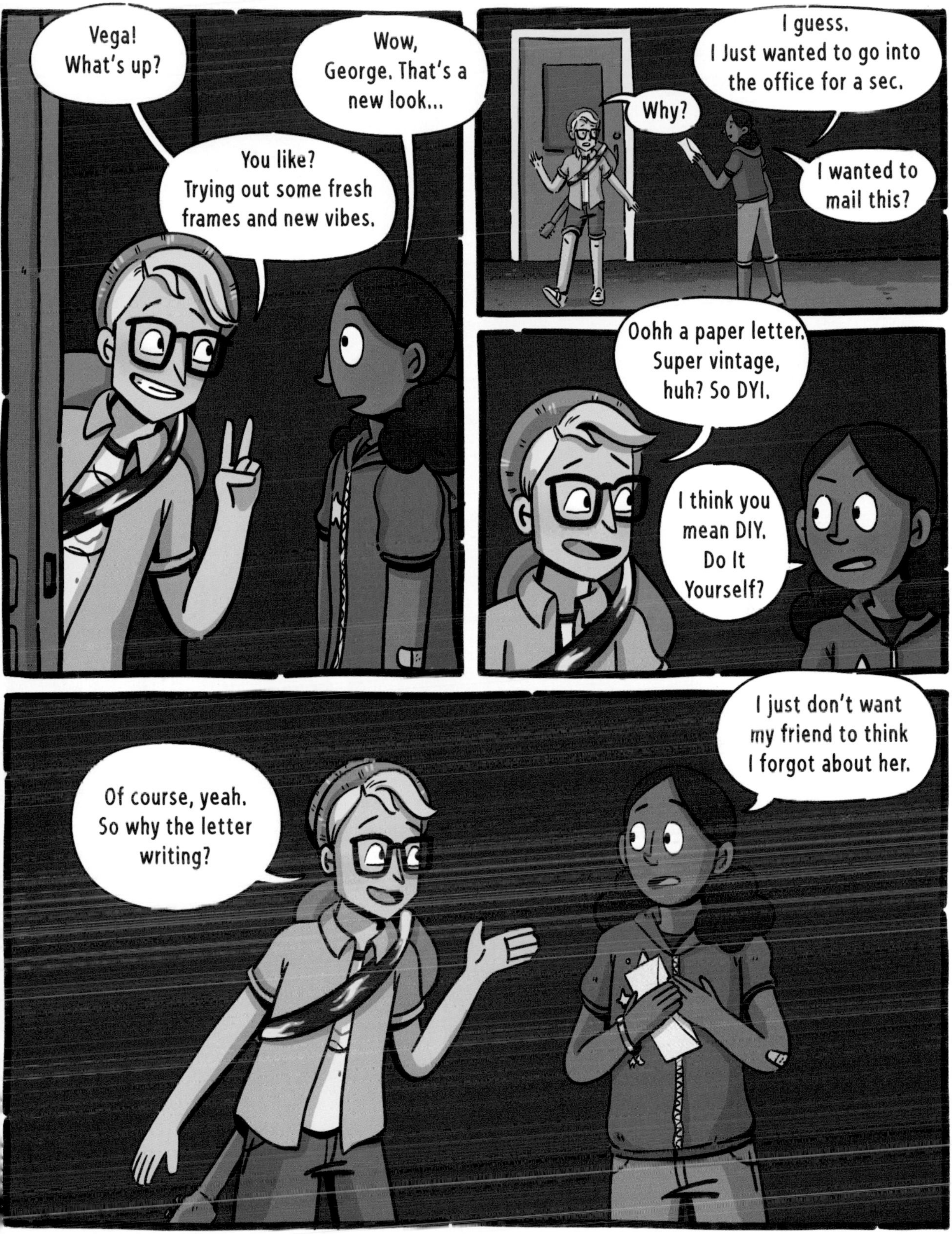
Vega! What's up?
Wow, George. That's a new look...
You like? Trying out some fresh frames and new vibes.
Why?
I guess. I Just wanted to go into the office for a sec.
I wanted to mail this?
Oohh a paper letter. Super vintage, huh? So DYI.
I think you mean DIY. Do It Yourself?
Of course, yeah. So why the letter writing?
I just don't want my friend to think I forgot about her.

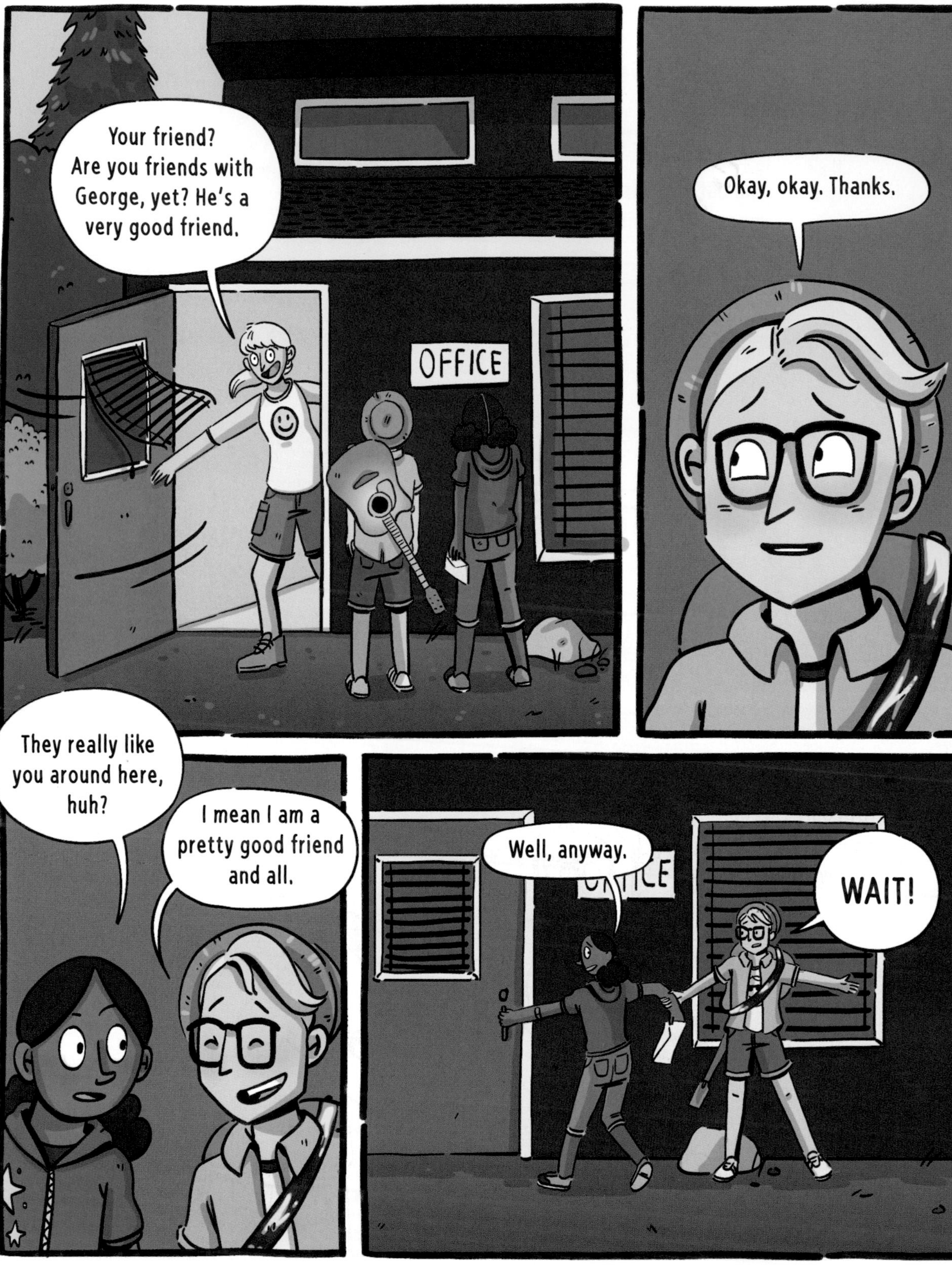
Your friend? Are you friends with George, yet? He's a very good friend.
OFFICE
Okay, okay. Thanks.
They really like you around here, huh?
I mean I am a pretty good friend and all.
Well, anyway.
WAIT!

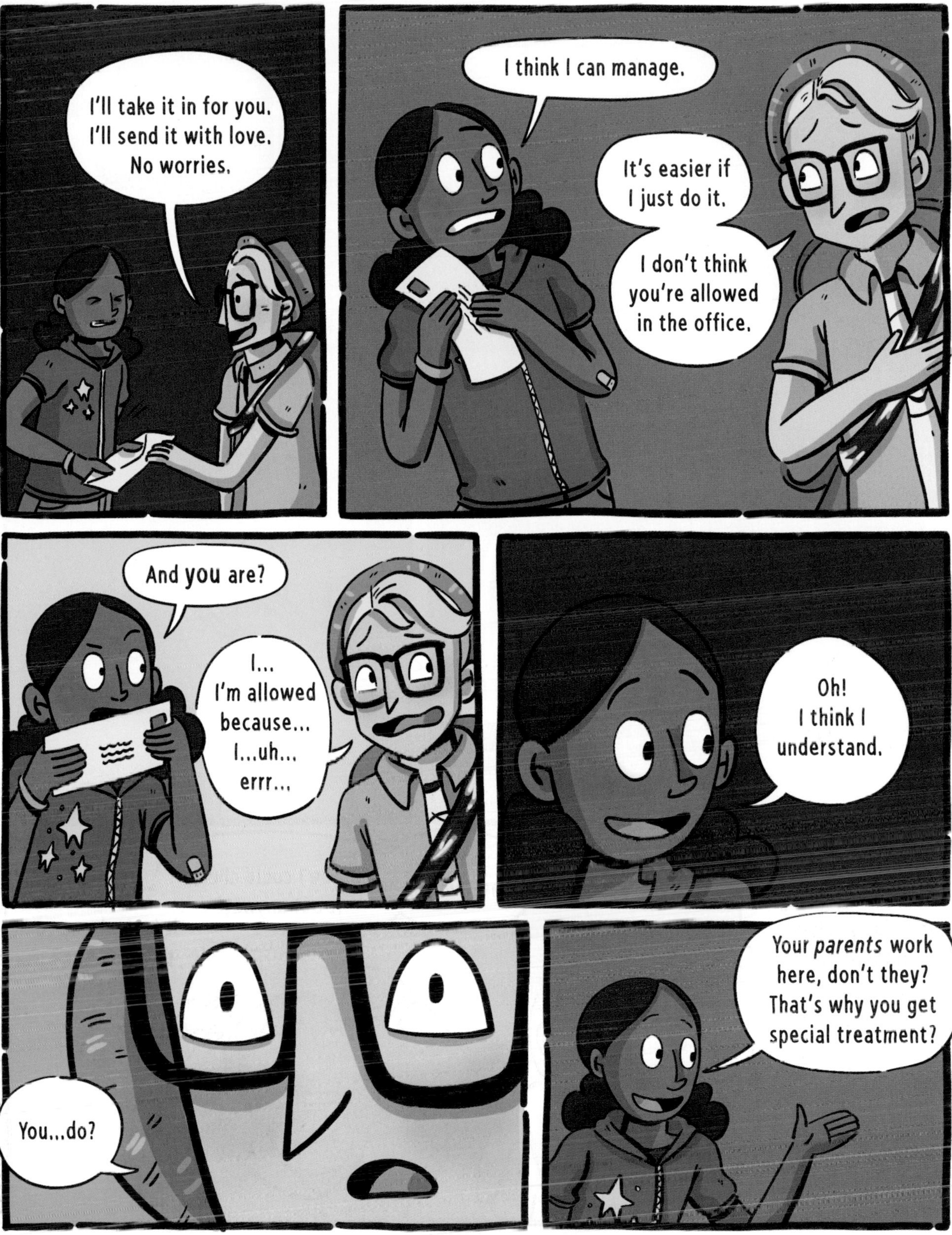
I'll take it in for you.
I'll send it with love.
No worries.
I think I can manage.
It's easier if I just do it.
I don't think you're allowed in the office.
And you are?
I...
I'm allowed because...
I...uh...
errr...
Oh!
I think I understand.
You...do?
Your *parents* work here, don't they?
That's why you get special treatment?

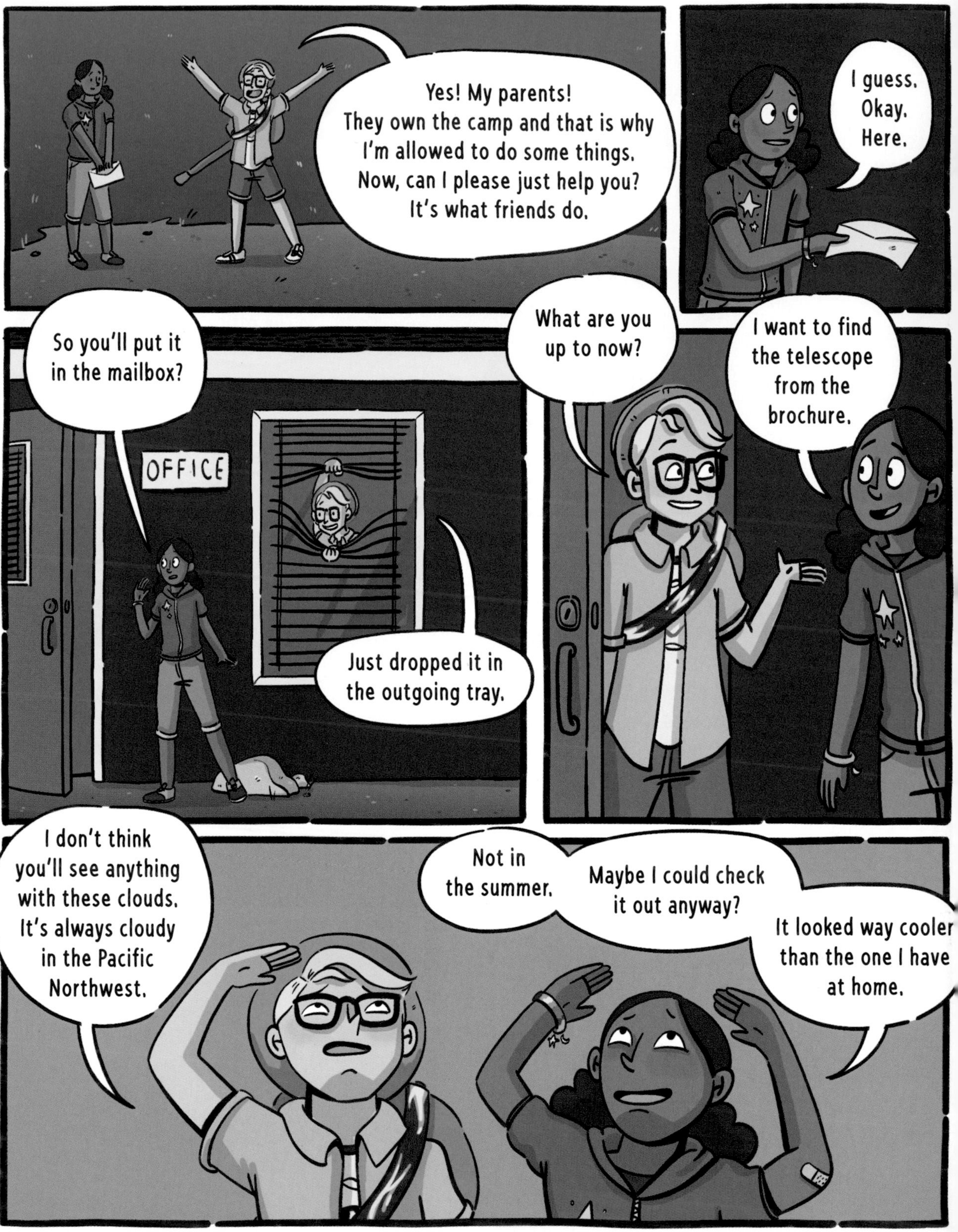
Yes! My parents! They own the camp and that is why I'm allowed to do some things. Now, can I please just help you? It's what friends do.
I guess. Okay. Here.
So you'll put it in the mailbox?
OFFICE
Just dropped it in the outgoing tray.
What are you up to now?
I want to find the telescope from the brochure.
I don't think you'll see anything with these clouds. It's always cloudy in the Pacific Northwest.
Not in the summer.
Maybe I could check it out anyway?
It looked way cooler than the one I have at home.

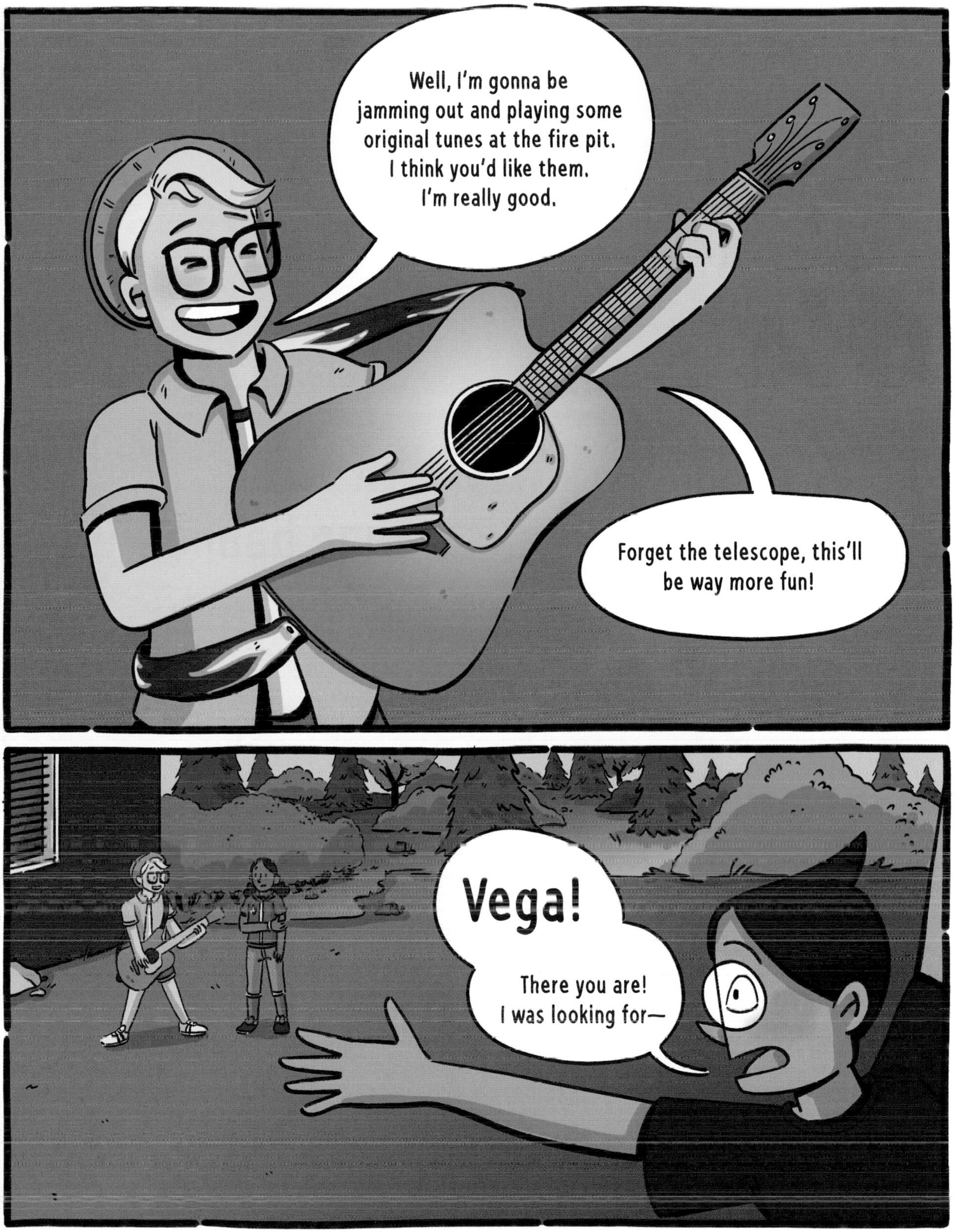
Well, I'm gonna be jamming out and playing some original tunes at the fire pit. I think you'd like them. I'm really good.
Forget the telescope, this'll be way more fun!
Vega!
There you are! I was looking for—

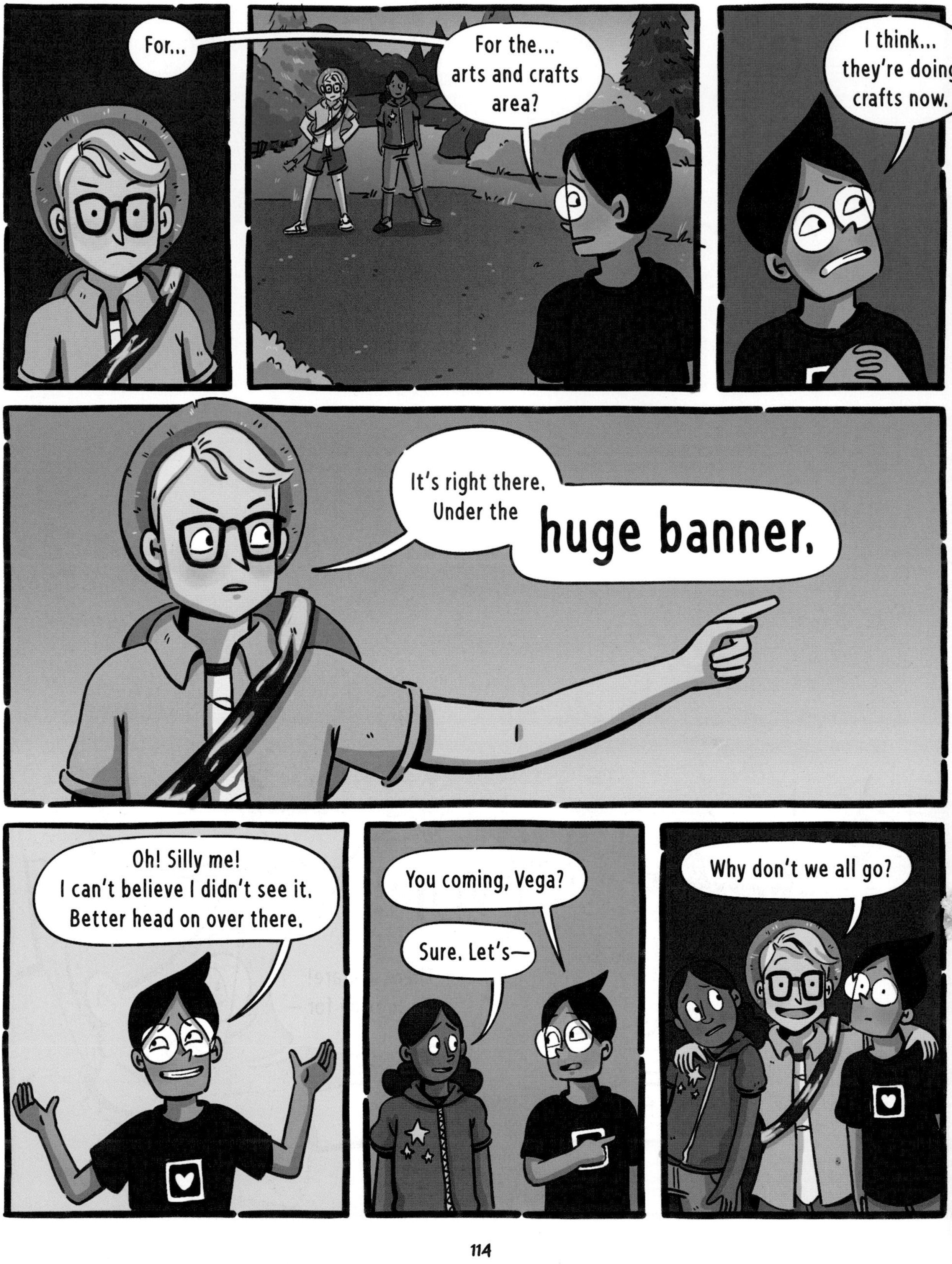
For...
For the... arts and crafts area?
I think... they're doing crafts now.
It's right there. Under the huge banner.
Oh! Silly me! I can't believe I didn't see it. Better head on over there.
You coming, Vega?
Sure. Let's—
Why don't we all go?

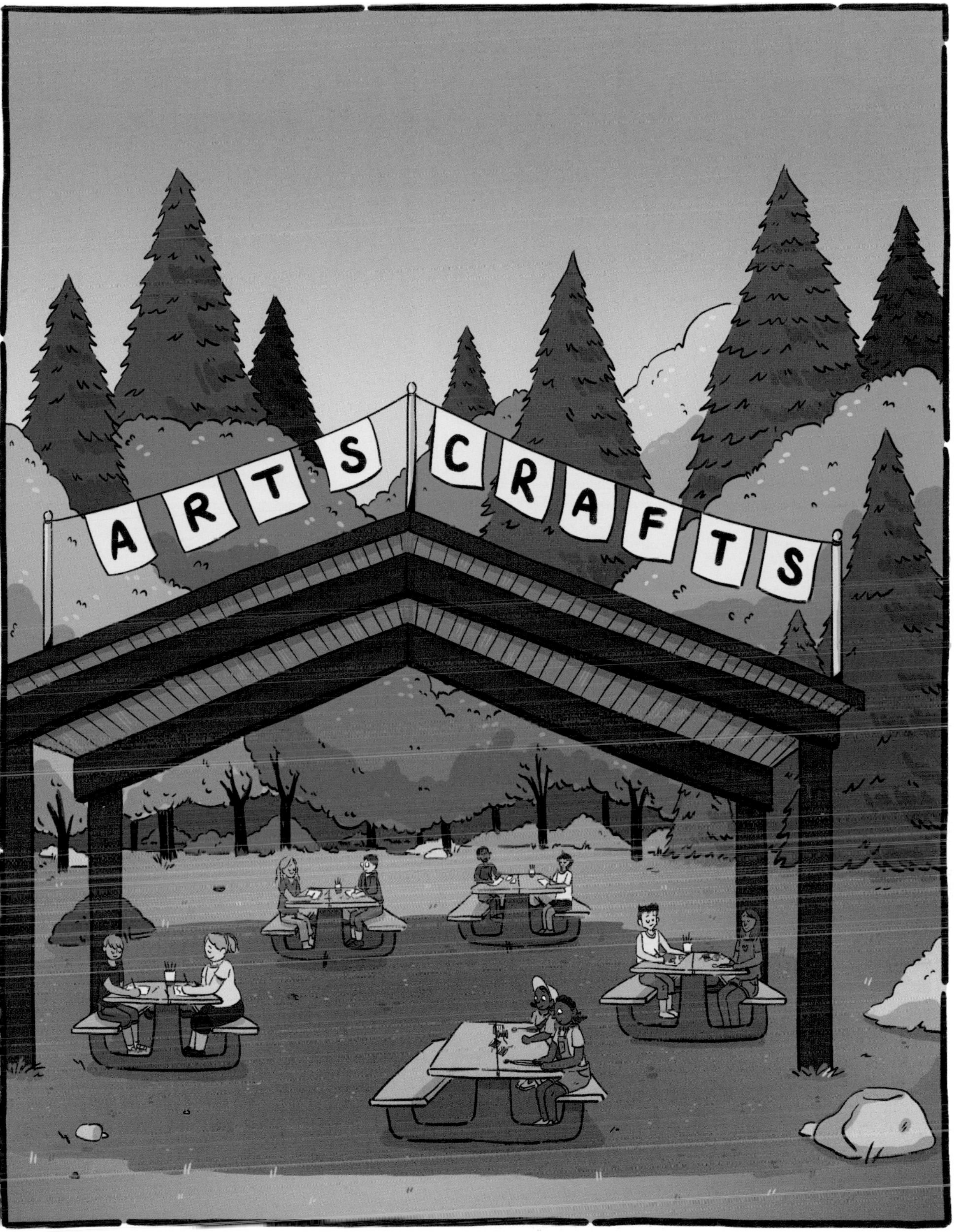
ARTS CRAFTS

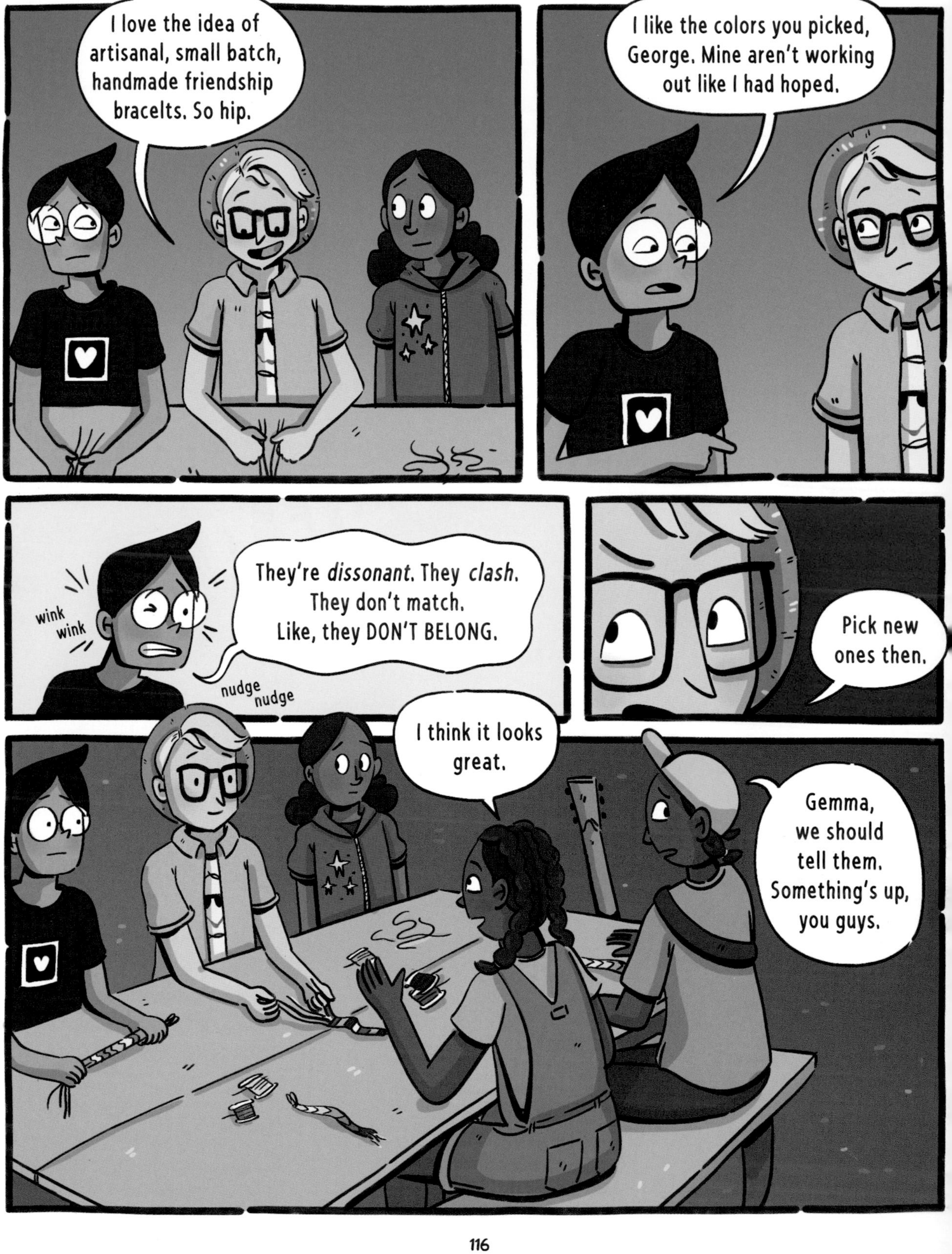
I love the idea of artisanal, small batch, handmade friendship bracelts. So hip.
I like the colors you picked, George. Mine aren't working out like I had hoped.
wink wink
They're *dissonant*. They *clash*. They don't match. Like, they DON'T BELONG.
nudge nudge
Pick new ones then.
I think it looks great.
Gemma, we should tell them. Something's up, you guys.

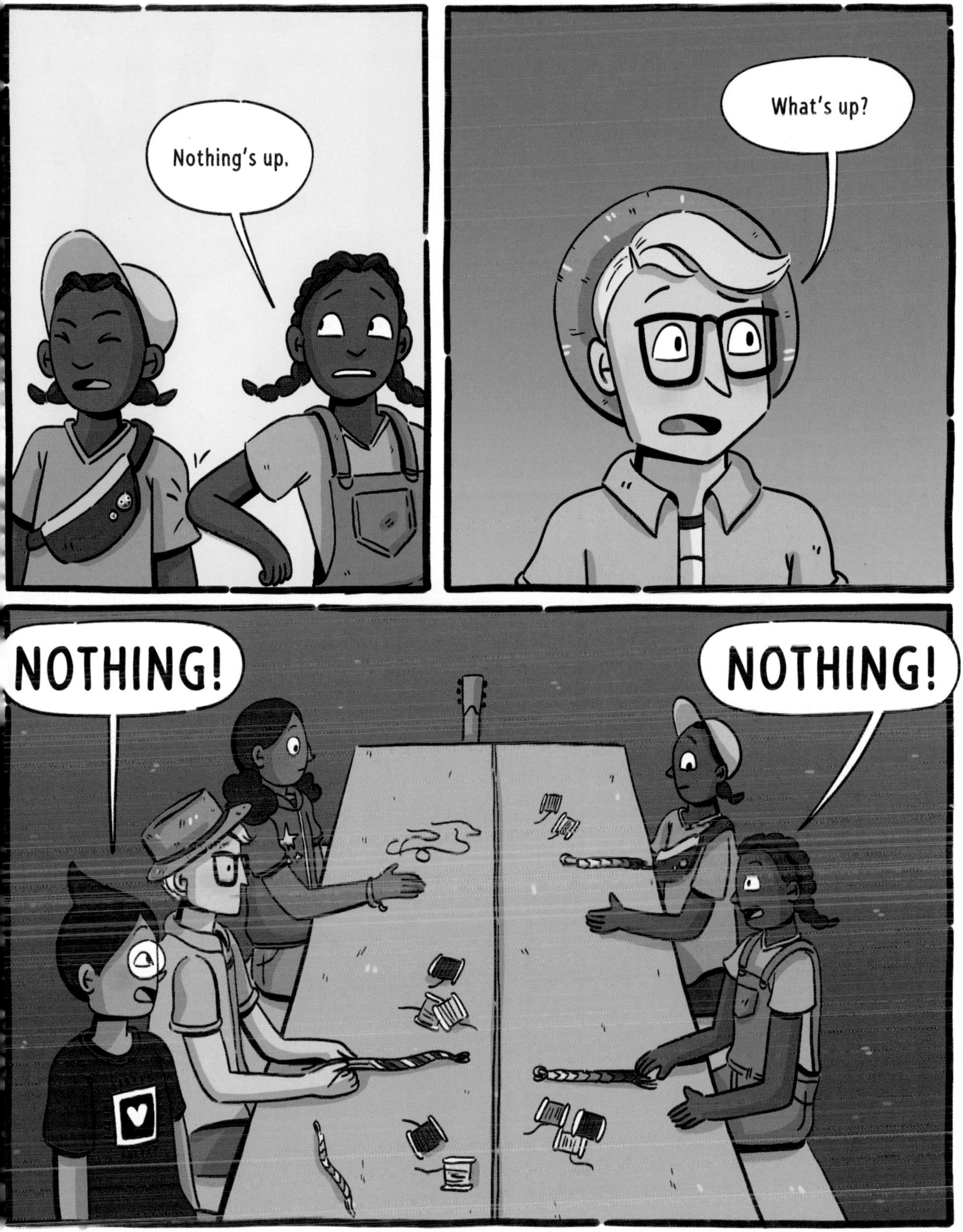
Nothing's up.
What's up?
NOTHING!
NOTHING!

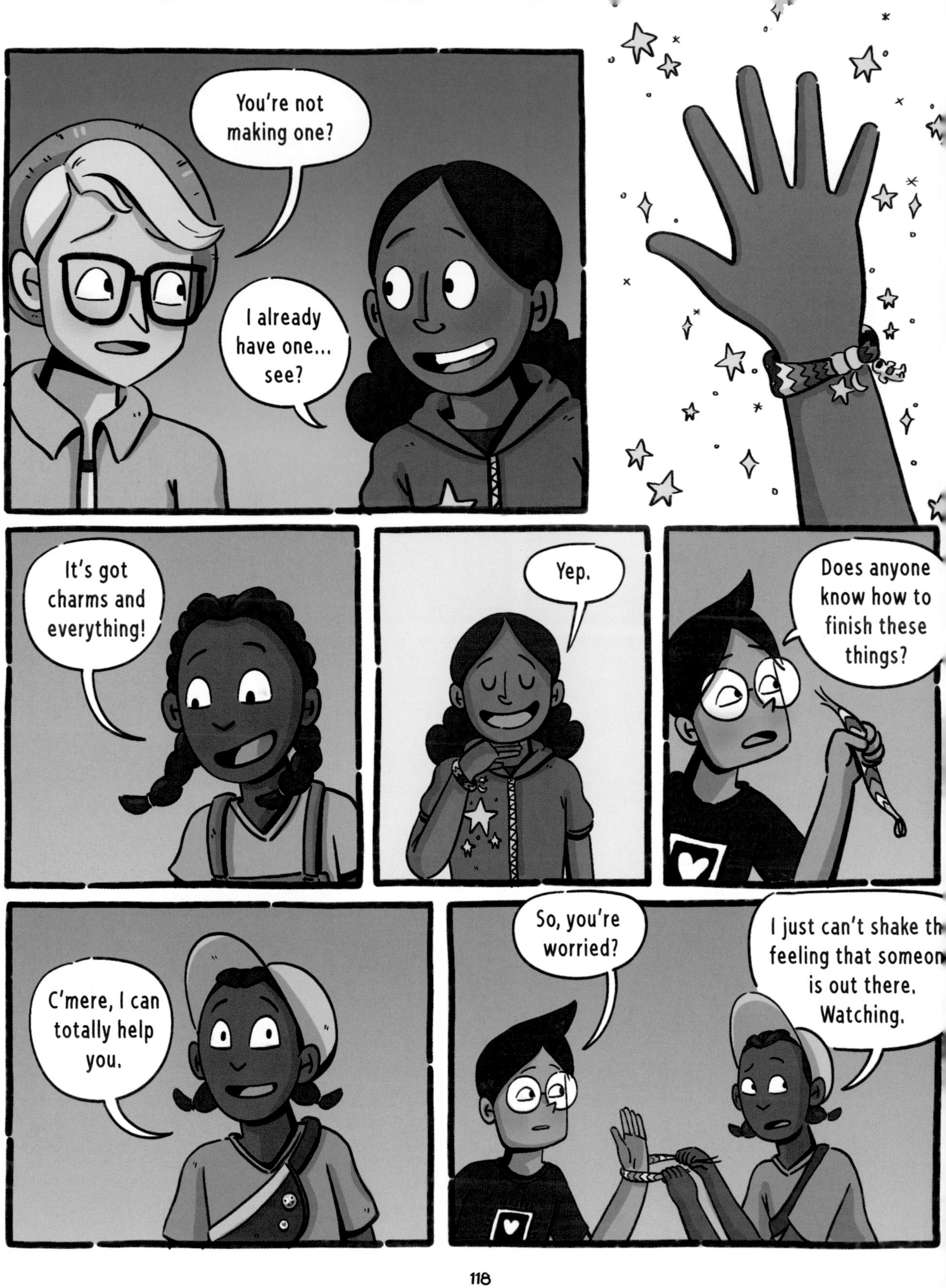
You're not making one?
I already have one... see?
It's got charms and everything!
Yep.
Does anyone know how to finish these things?
C'mere, I can totally help you.
So, you're worried?
I just can't shake th
feeling that someon
is out there. Watching.

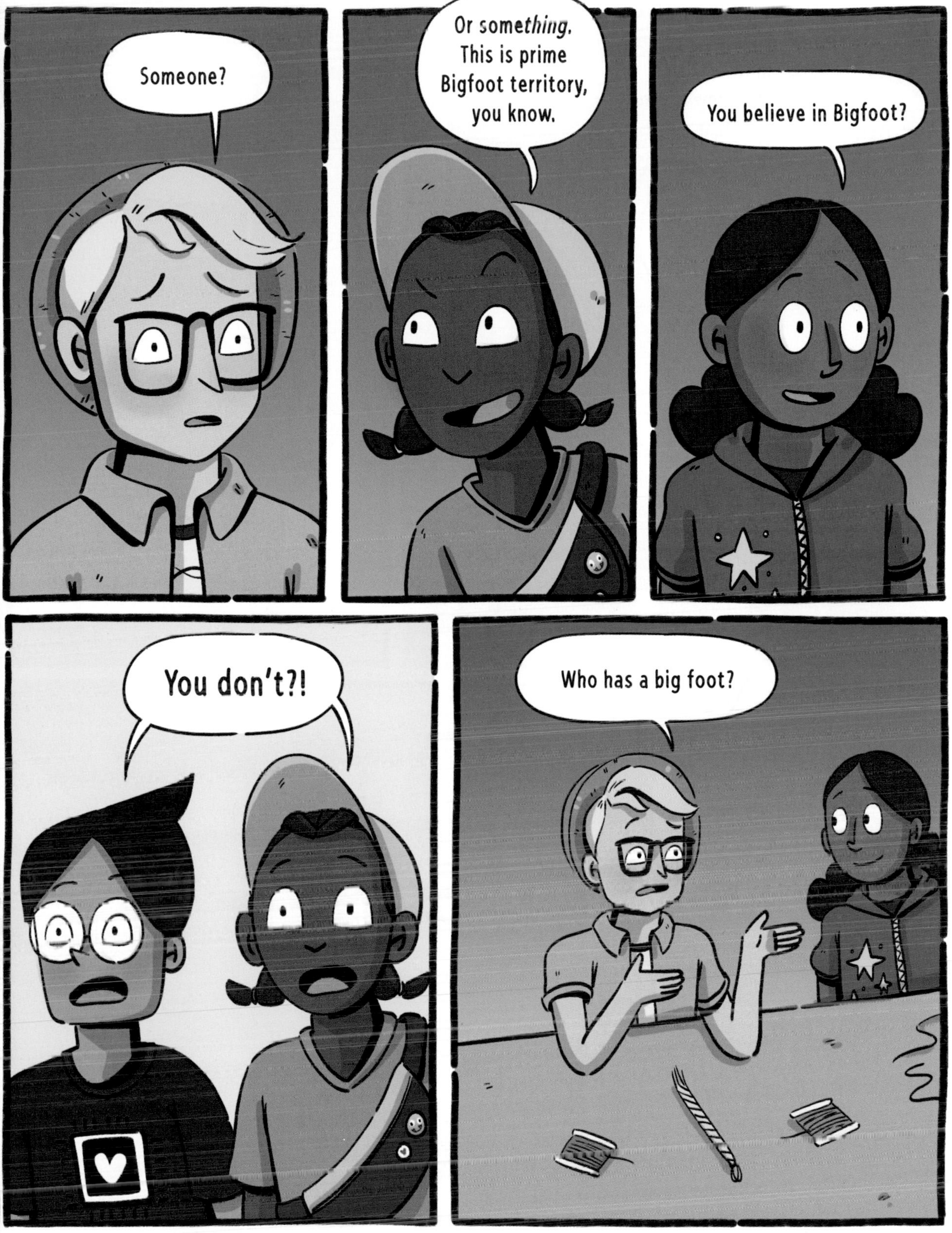
Someone?
Or *something*. This is prime Bigfoot territory, you know.
You believe in Bigfoot?
You don't?!
Who has a big foot?

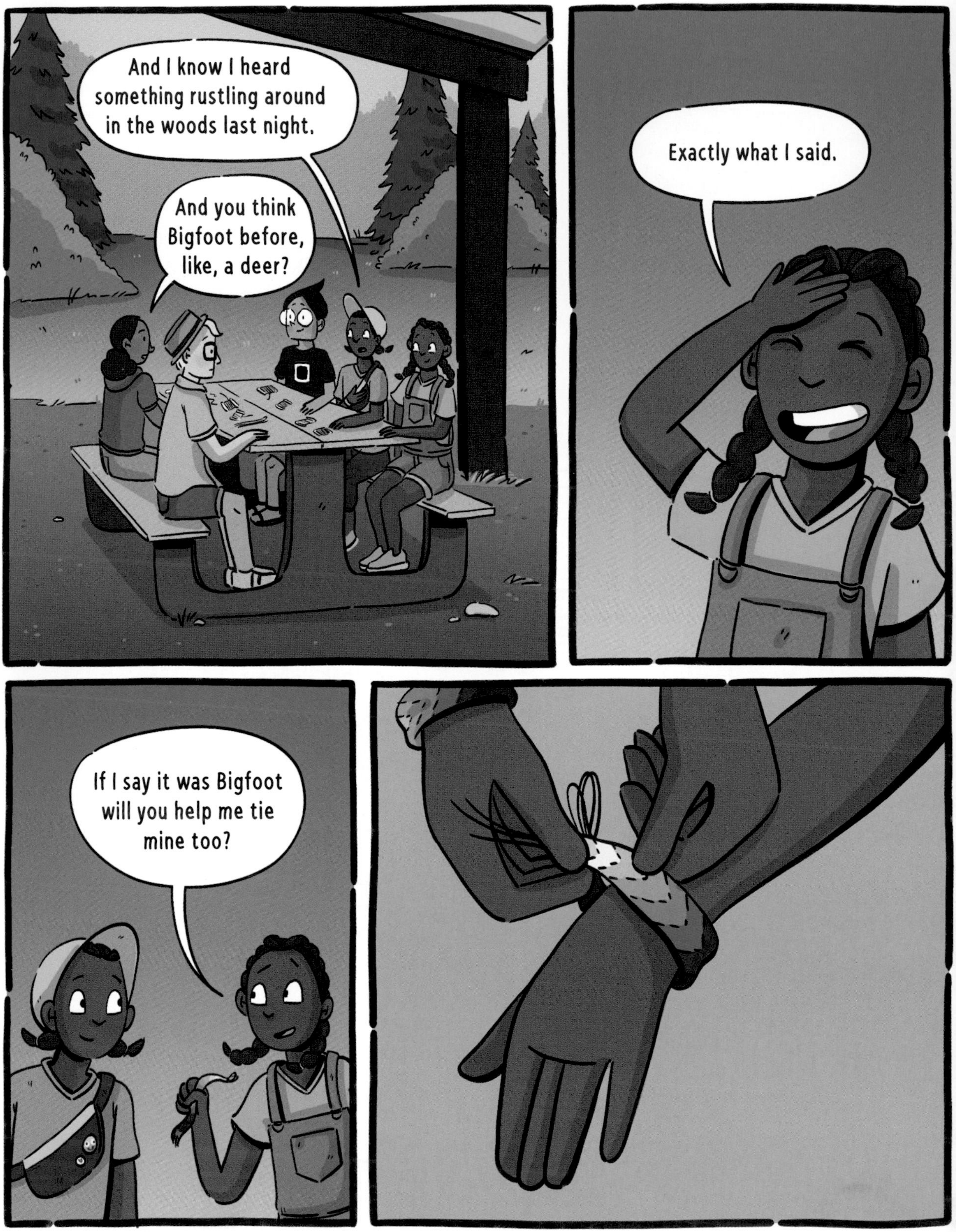
And I know I heard something rustling around in the woods last night.
And you think Bigfoot before, like, a deer?
Exactly what I said.
If I say it was Bigfoot will you help me tie mine too?

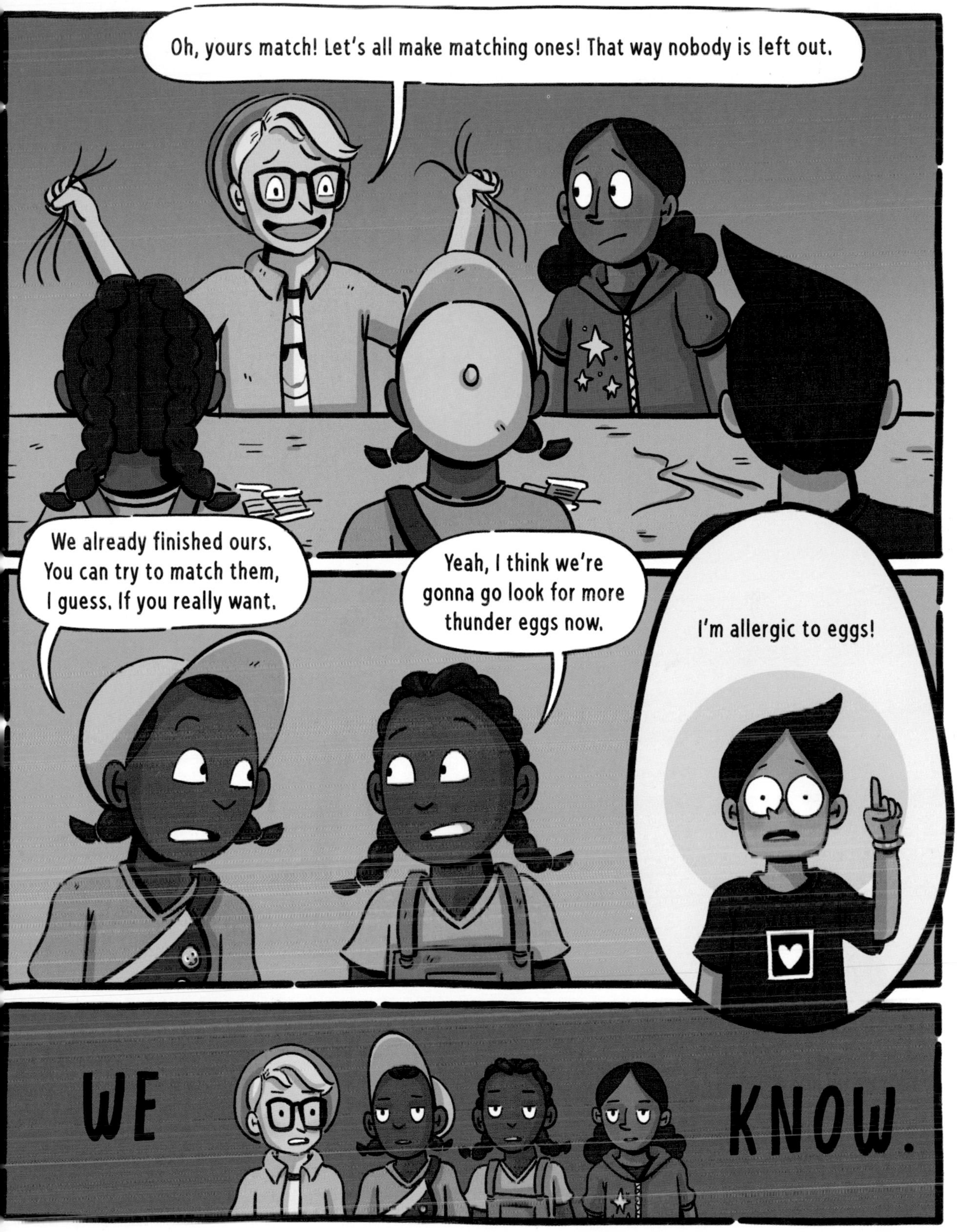
Oh, yours match! Let's all make matching ones! That way nobody is left out.
We already finished ours. You can try to match them, I guess. If you really want.
Yeah, I think we're gonna go look for more thunder eggs now.
I'm allergic to eggs!
WE KNOW.

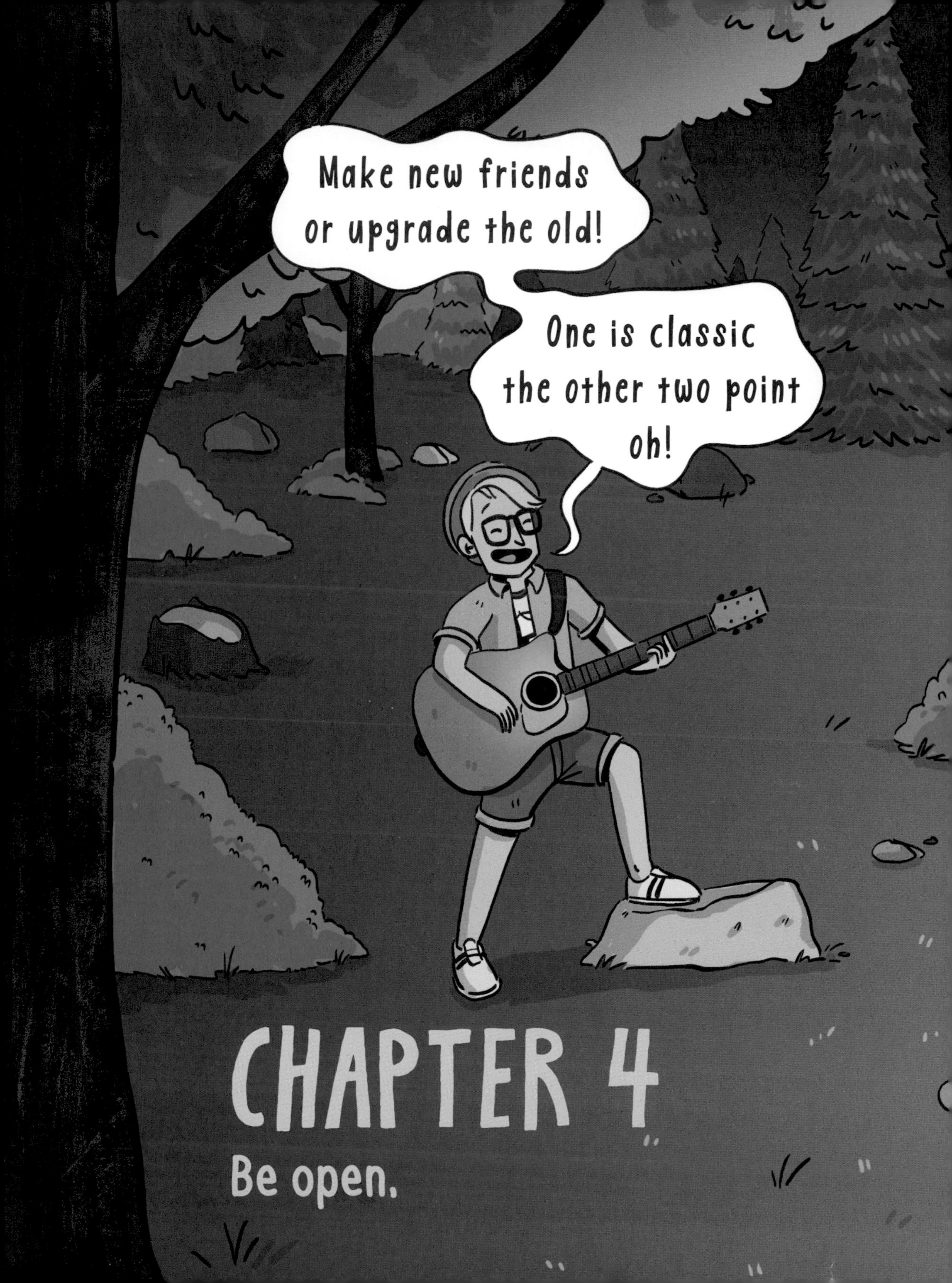
Make new friends or upgrade the old!
One is classic the other two point oh!

CHAPTER 4

Be open.

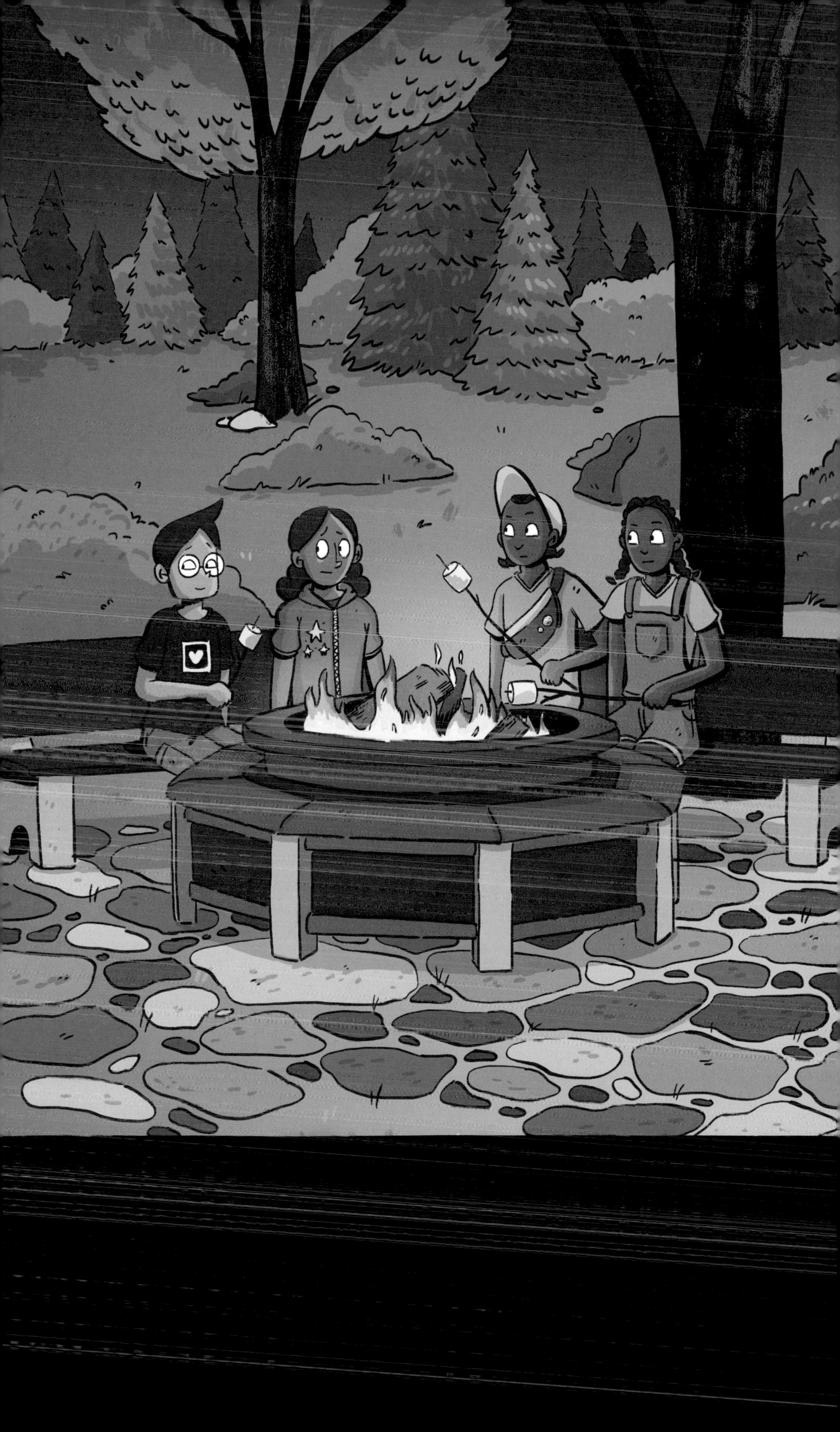

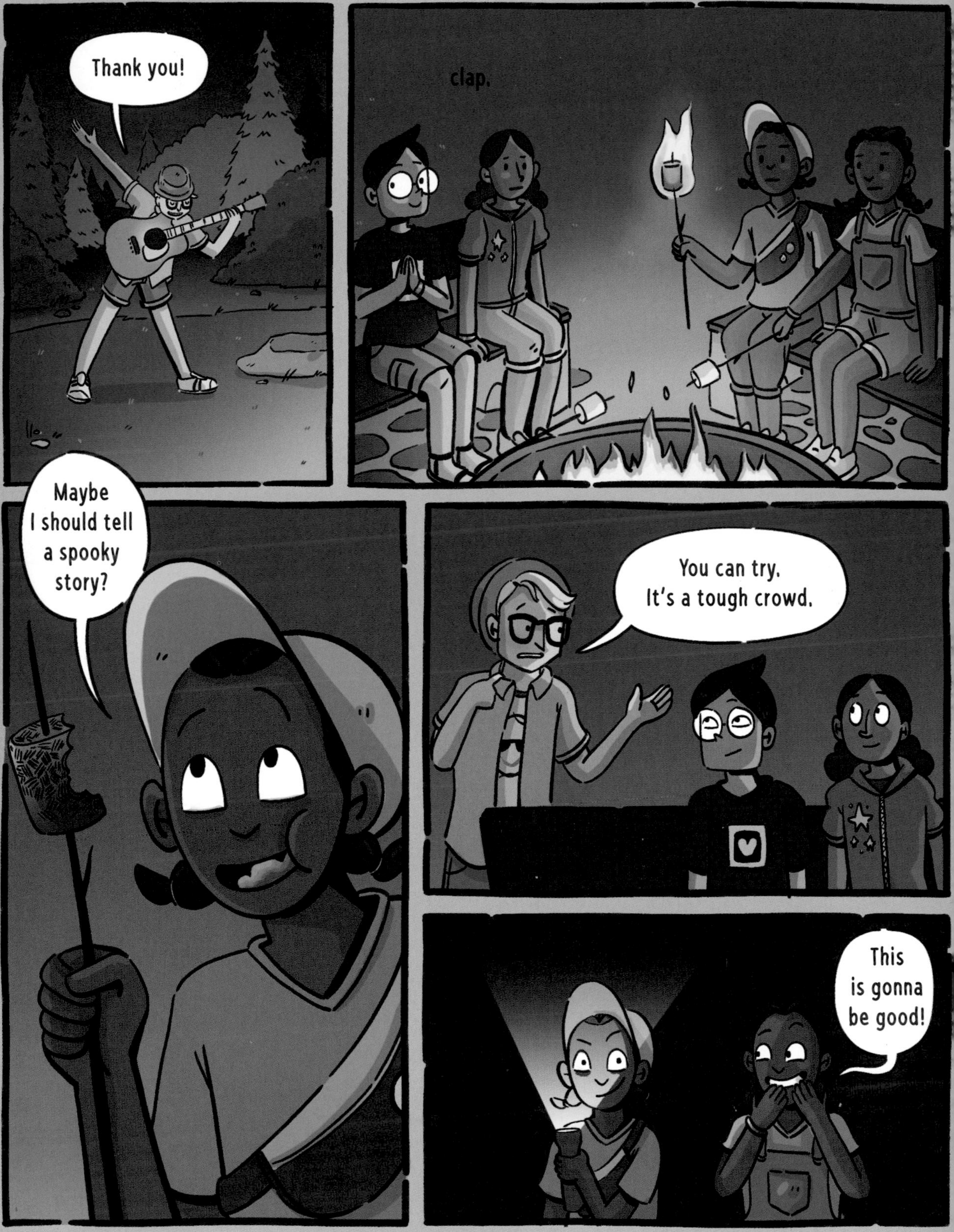
Thank you!
clap.
Maybe I should tell a spooky story?
You can try. It's a tough crowd.
This is gonna be good!

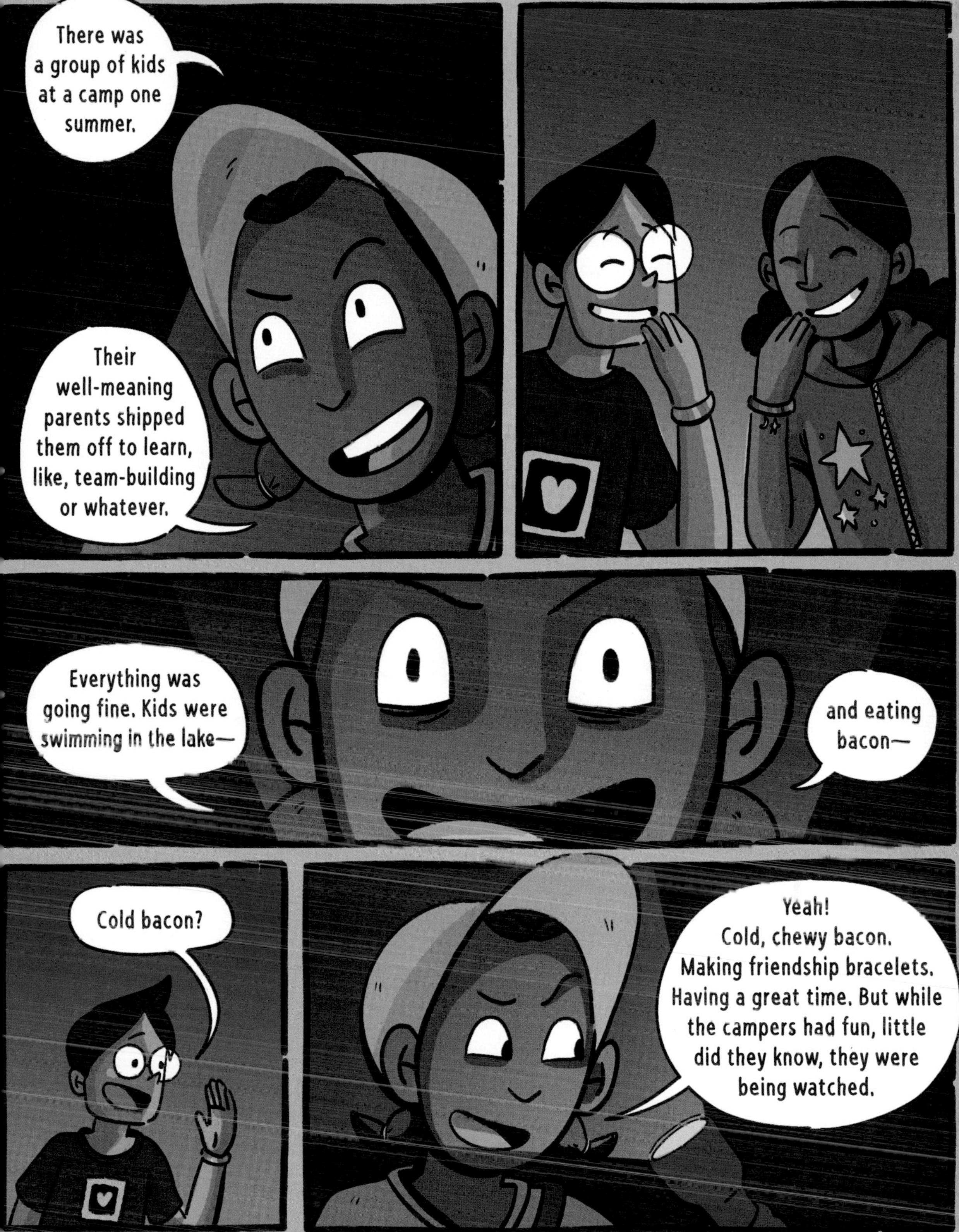
There was a group of kids at a camp one summer.
Their well-meaning parents shipped them off to learn, like, team-building or whatever.
Everything was going fine. Kids were swimming in the lake—
and eating bacon—
Cold bacon?
Yeah! Cold, chewy bacon. Making friendship bracelets. Having a great time. But while the campers had fun, little did they know, they were being watched.

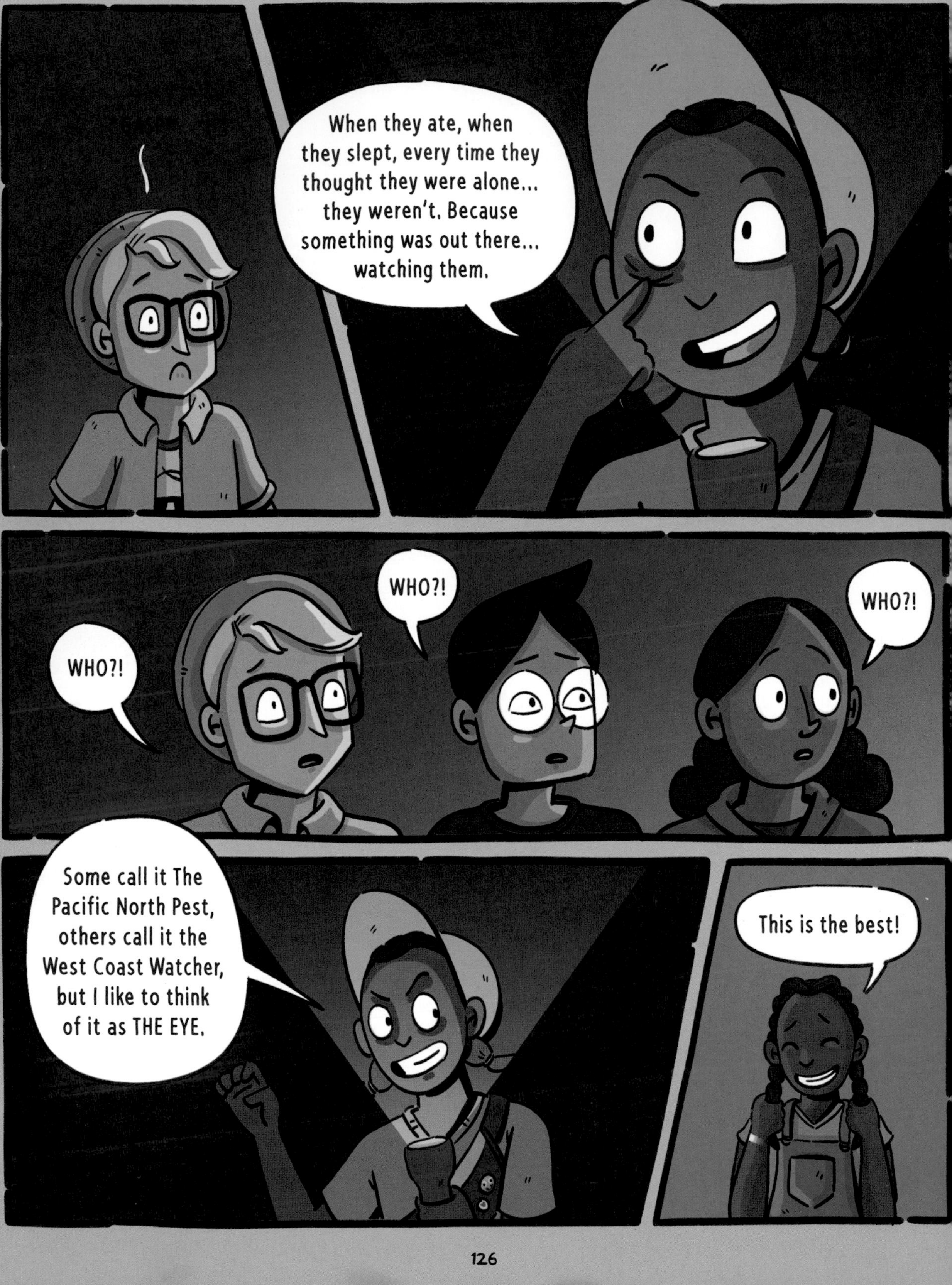
When they ate, when they slept, every time they thought they were alone... they weren't. Because something was out there... watching them.
WHO?!
WHO?!
WHO?!
Some call it The Pacific North Pest, others call it the West Coast Watcher, but I like to think of it as THE EYE.
This is the best!

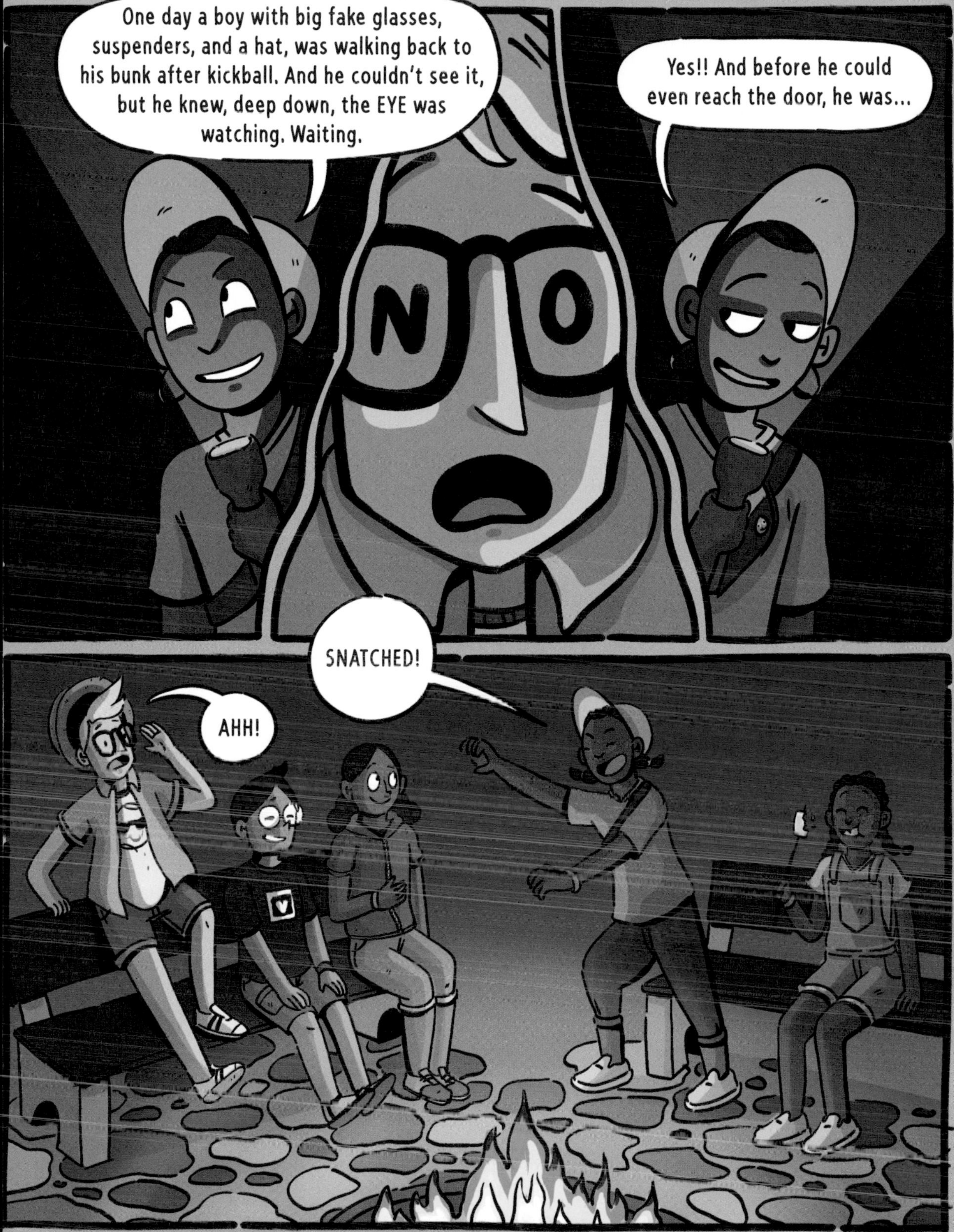
One day a boy with big fake glasses, suspenders, and a hat, was walking back to his bunk after kickball. And he couldn't see it, but he knew, deep down, the EYE was watching. Waiting.
NO
Yes!! And before he could even reach the door, he was...
SNATCHED!
AHH!

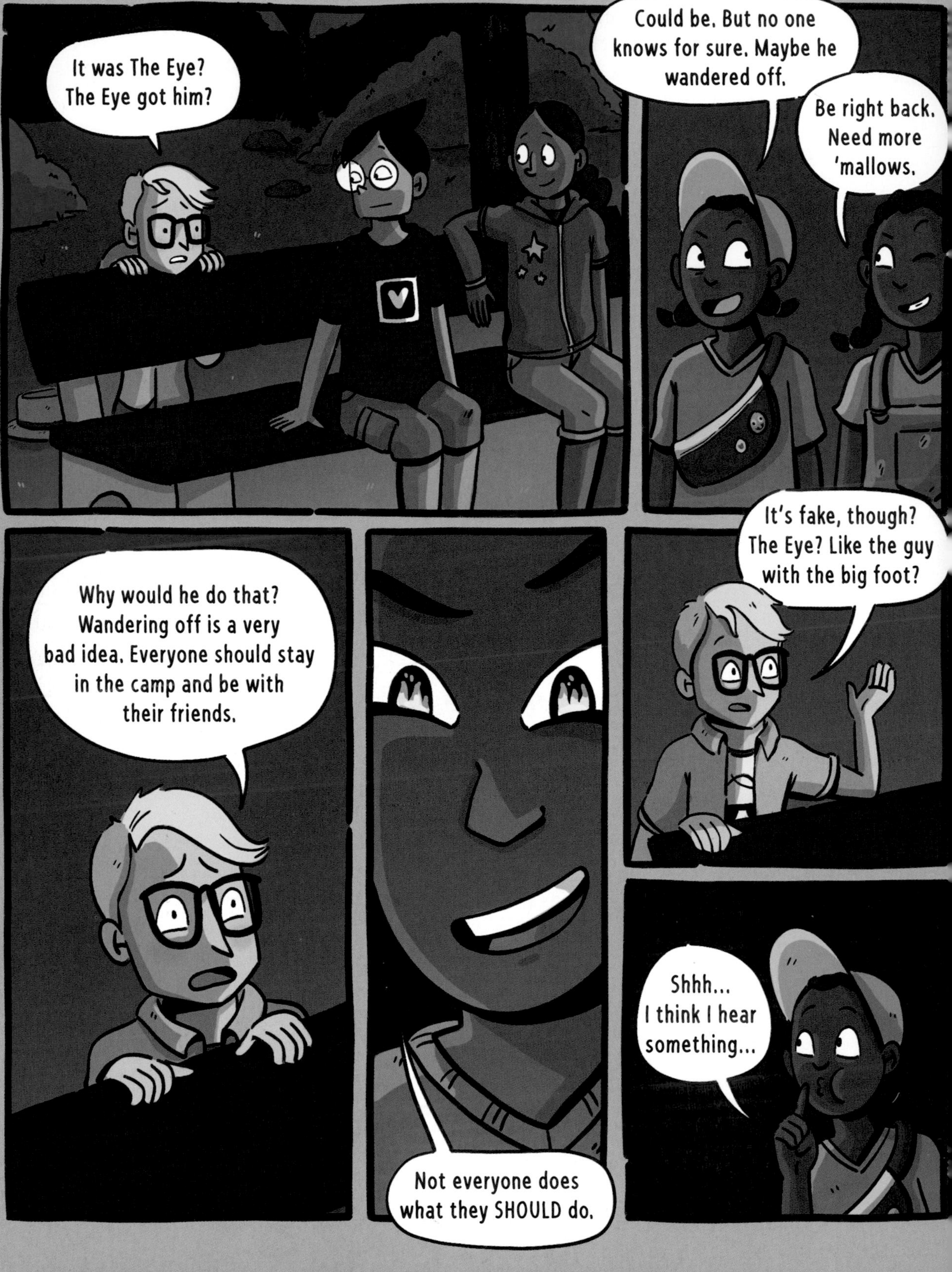

It was The Eye? The Eye got him?
Could be. But no one knows for sure. Maybe he wandered off.
Be right back. Need more 'mallows.
Why would he do that? Wandering off is a very bad idea. Everyone should stay in the camp and be with their friends.
Not everyone does what they SHOULD do.
It's fake, though? The Eye? Like the guy with the big foot?
Shhh... I think I hear something...

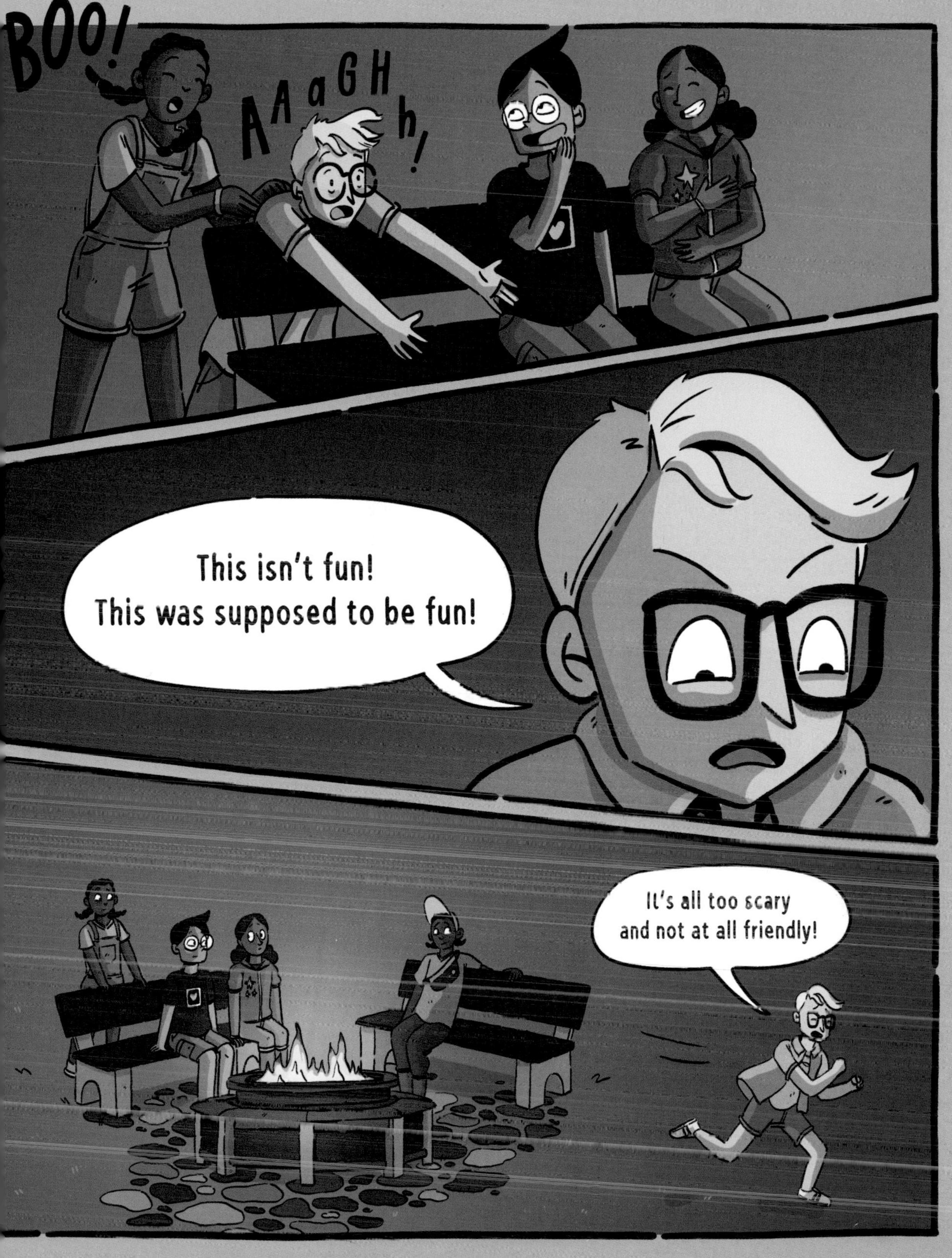
BOO!
AAaGHh!
This isn't fun!
This was supposed to be fun!
It's all too scary
and not at all friendly!

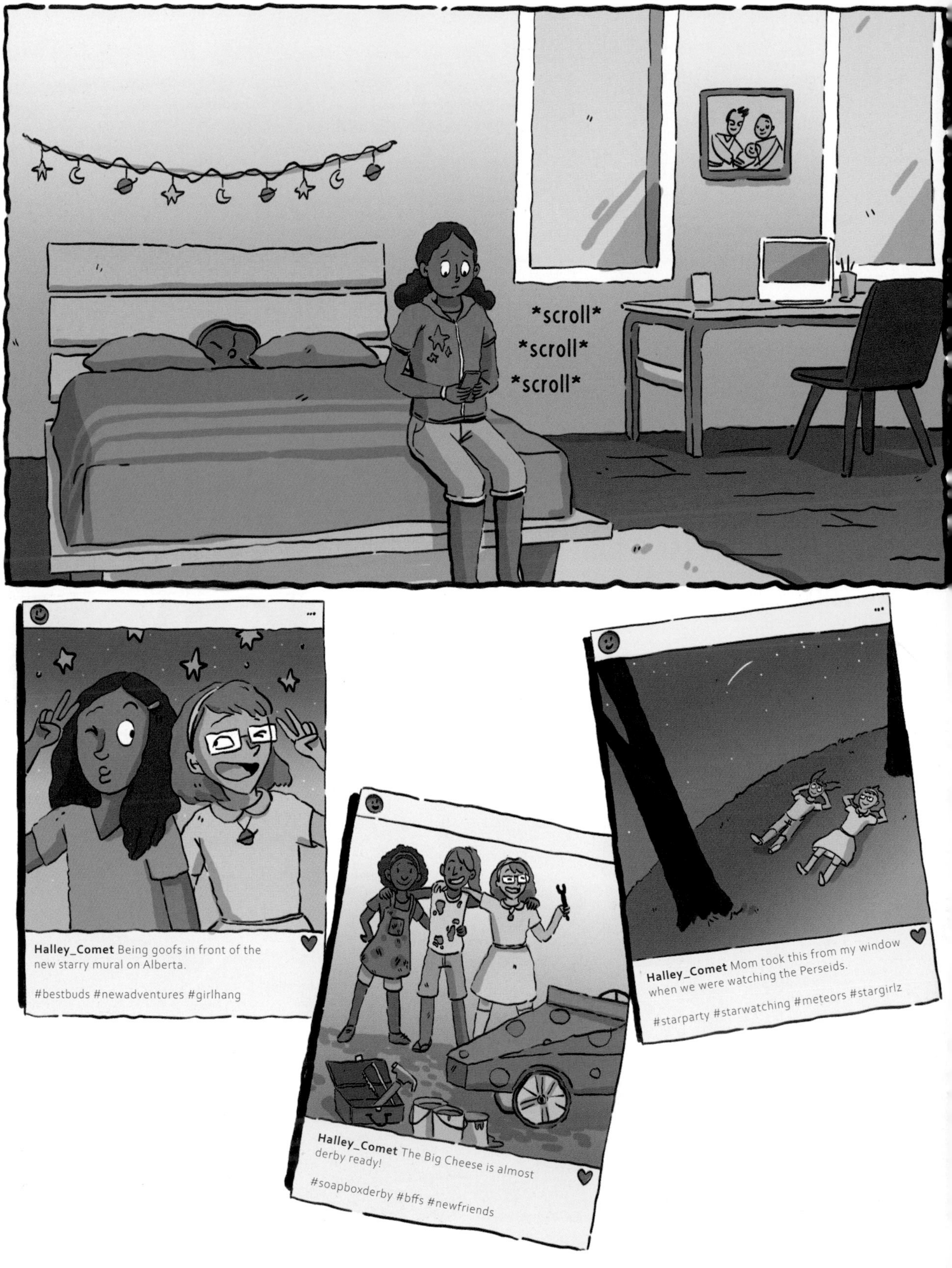
scroll
scroll
scroll
Halley_Comet Being goofs in front of the new starry mural on Alberta.
#bestbuds #newadventures #girlhang
Halley_Comet The Big Cheese is almost derby ready!
#soapboxderby #bffs #newfriends
Halley_Comet Mom took this from my window when we were watching the Perseids.
#starparty #starwatching #meteors #stargirlz

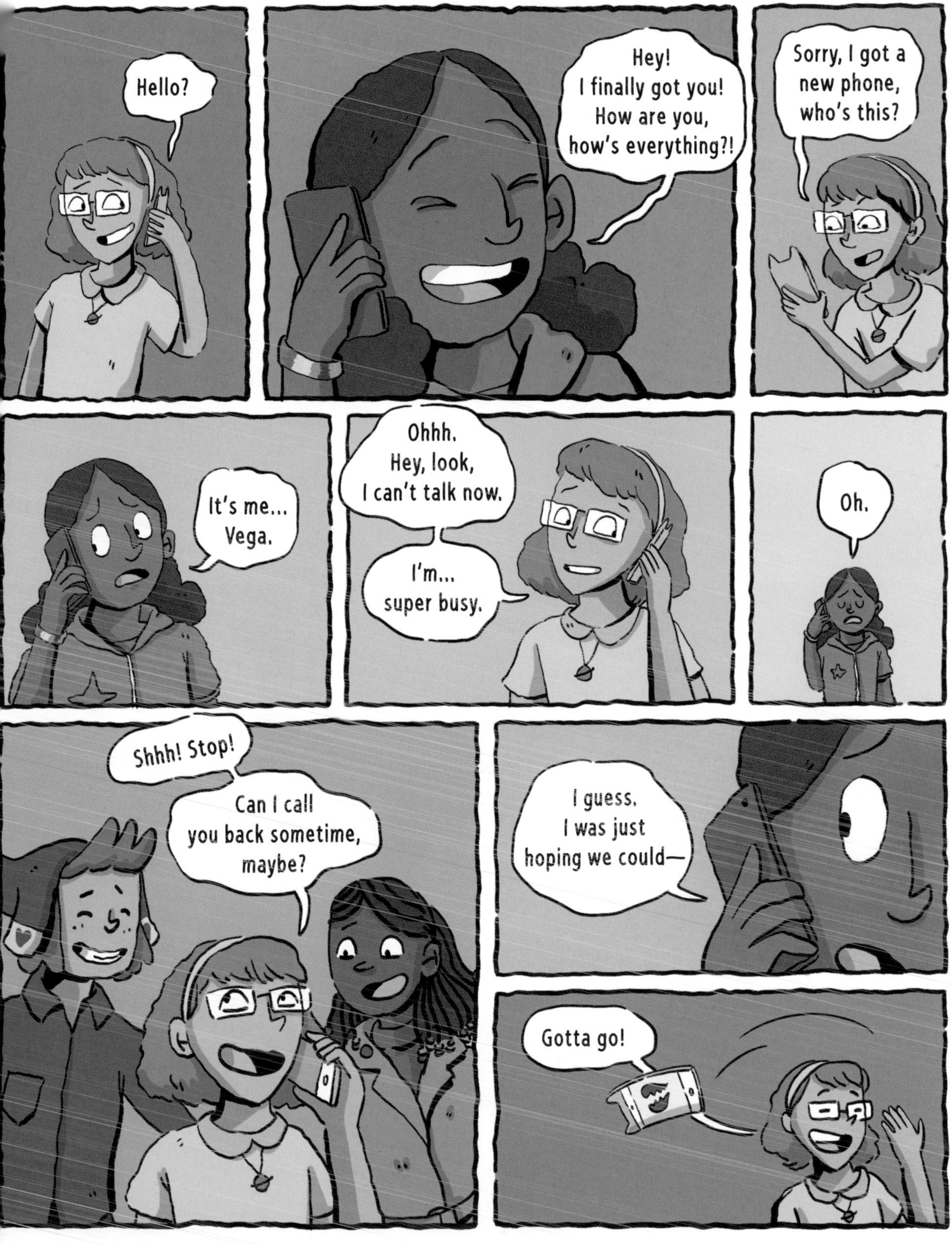
Hello?
Hey!
I finally got you!
How are you,
how's everything?!
Sorry, I got a
new phone,
who's this?
It's me...
Vega.
Ohhh.
Hey, look,
I can't talk now.
I'm...
super busy.
Oh.
Shhh! Stop!
Can I call
you back sometime,
maybe?
I guess.
I was just
hoping we could—
Gotta go!

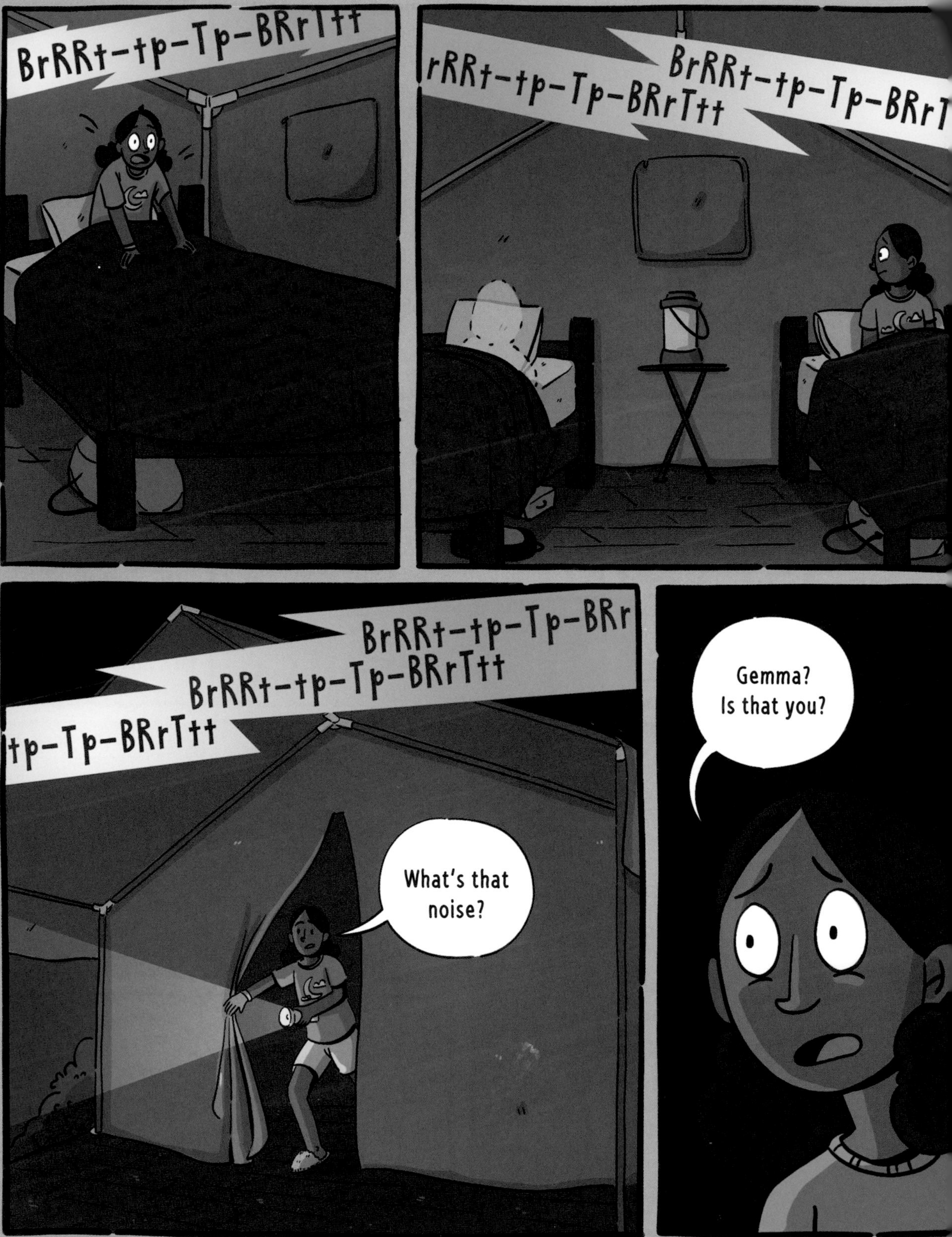
BrRRt-tp-Tp-BRrTtt
BrRRt-tp-Tp-BRrT
rRRt-tp-Tp-BRrTtt
BrRRt-tp-Tp-BRr
BrRRt-tp-Tp-BRrTtt
tp-Tp-BRrTtt
What's that noise?
Gemma? Is that you?

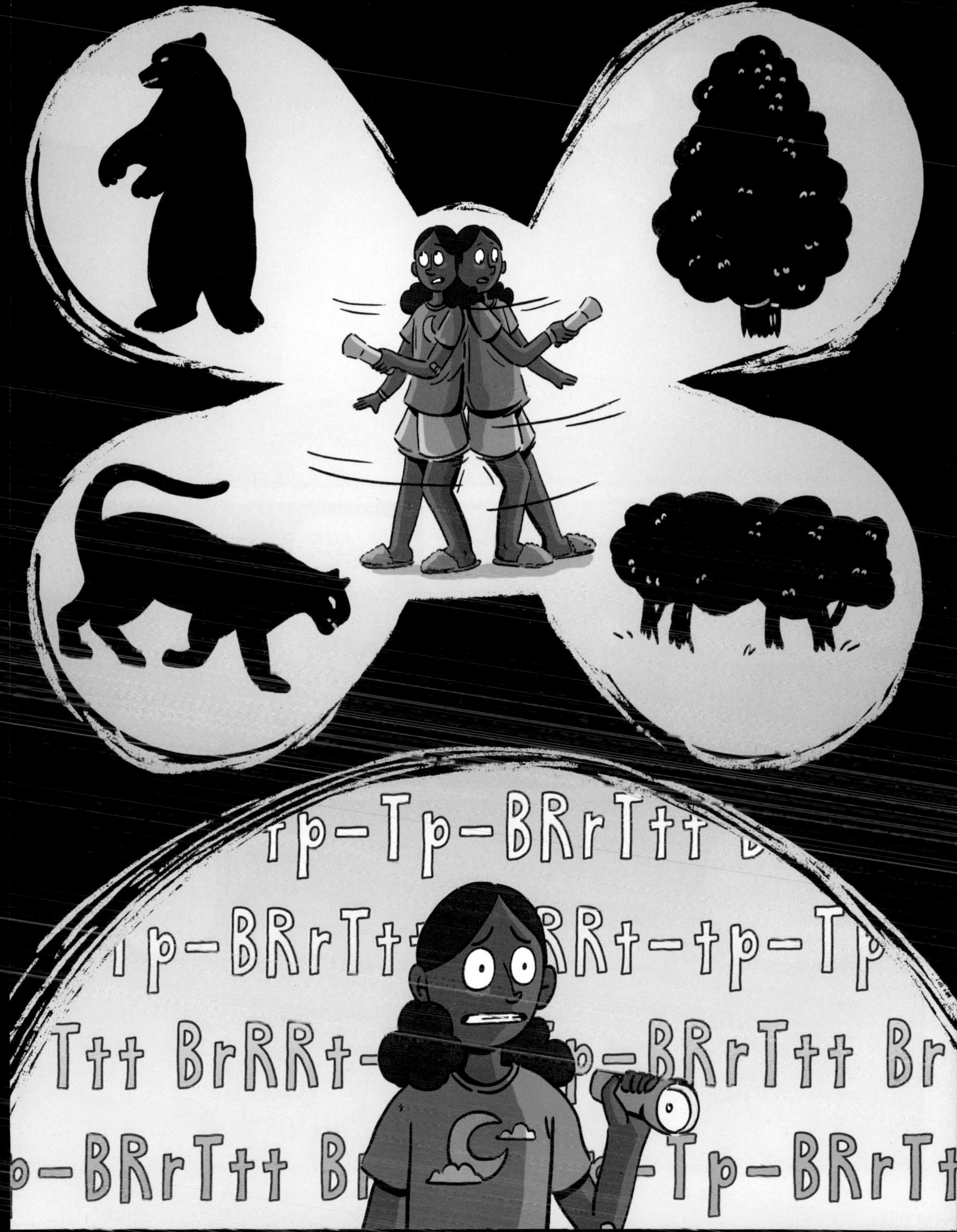
Tp—Tp—BRrTtt
Tp—BRrTt
RRt—tp—Tp
Ttt BrRRt—
p—BRrTtt Br
—BRrTtt Br
—Tp—BRrTt

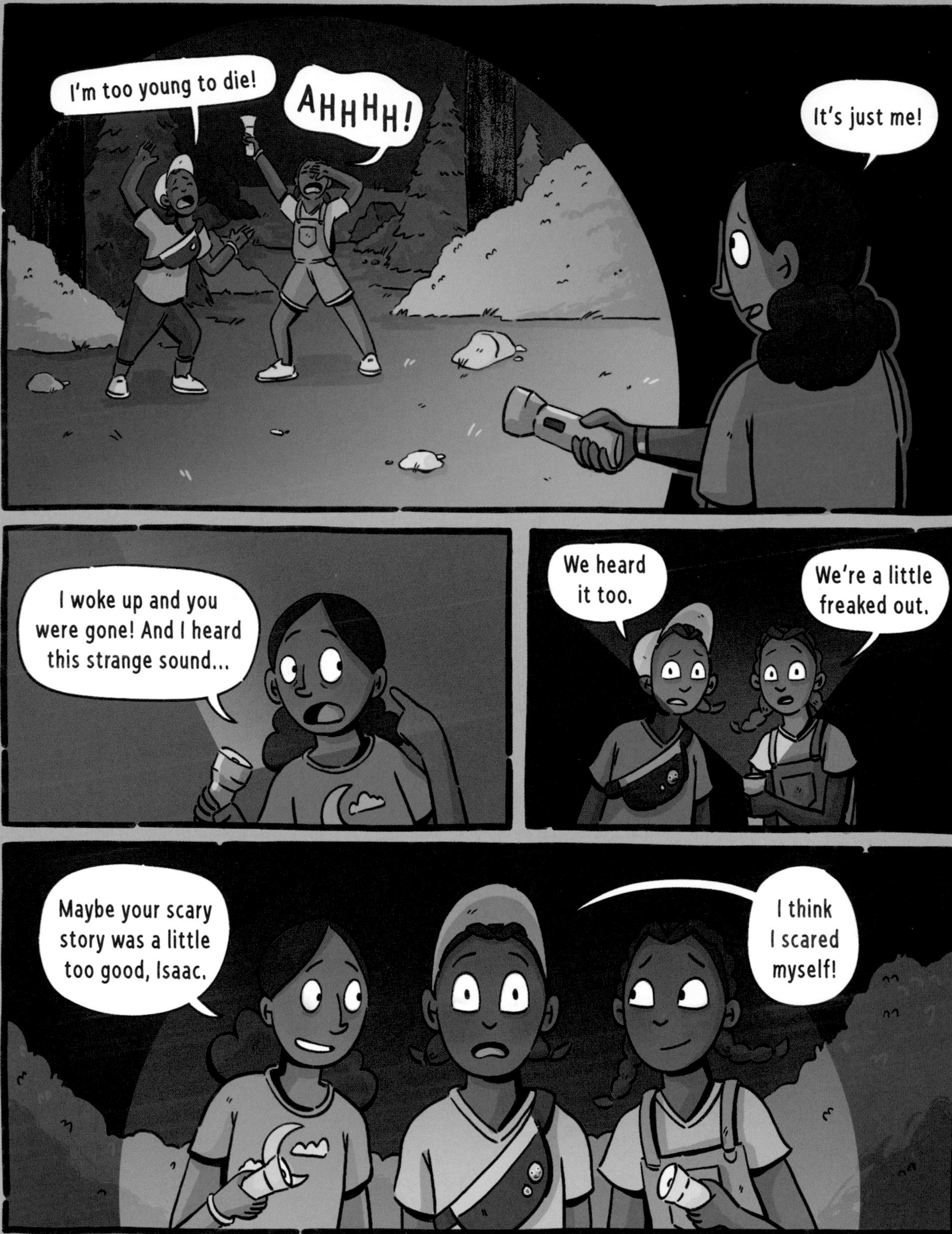
I'm too young to die!
AHHHH!
It's just me!
I woke up and you were gone! And I heard this strange sound...
We heard it too.
We're a little freaked out.
Maybe your scary story was a little too good, Isaac.
I think I scared myself!

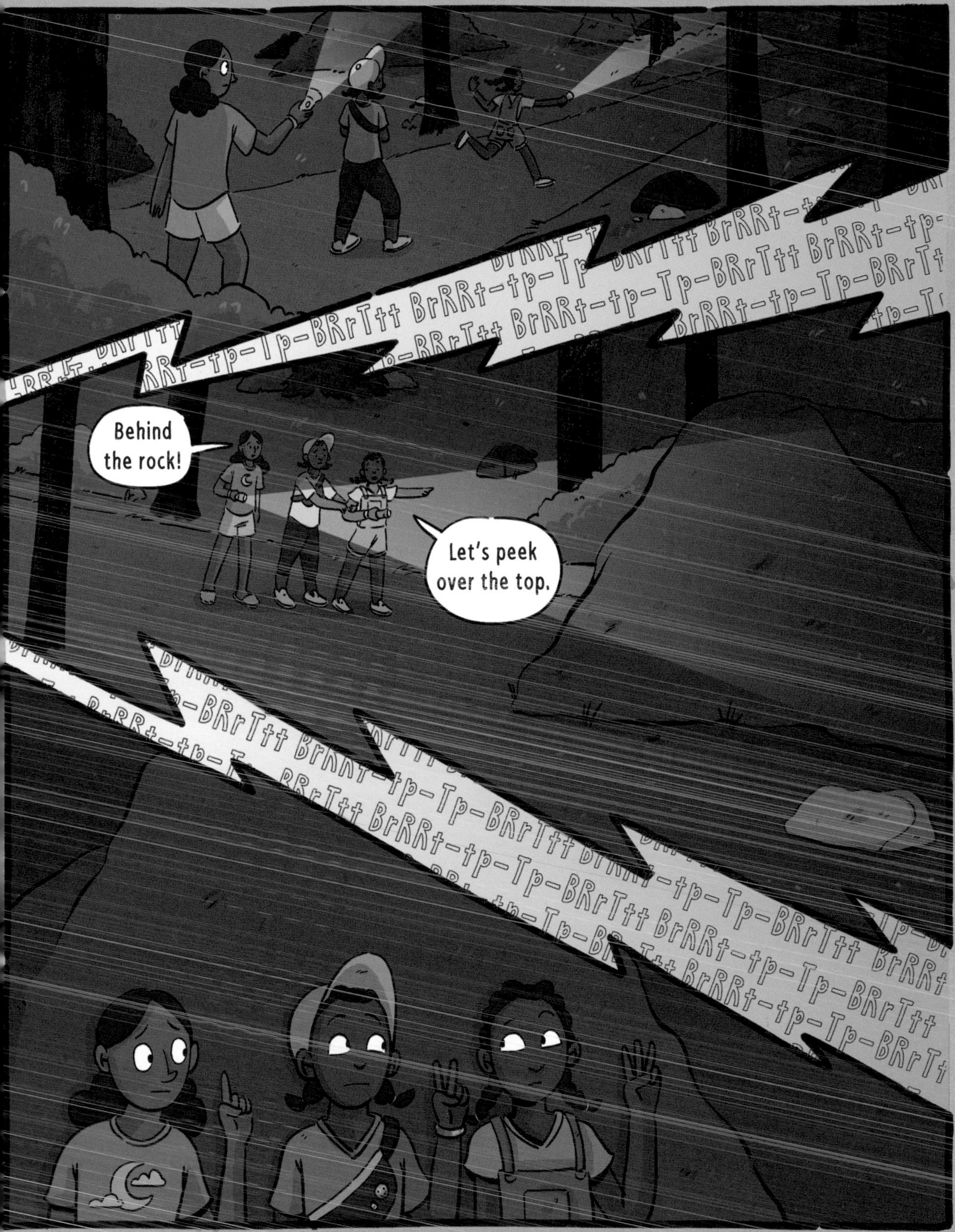
Behind the rock!
Let's peek over the top.

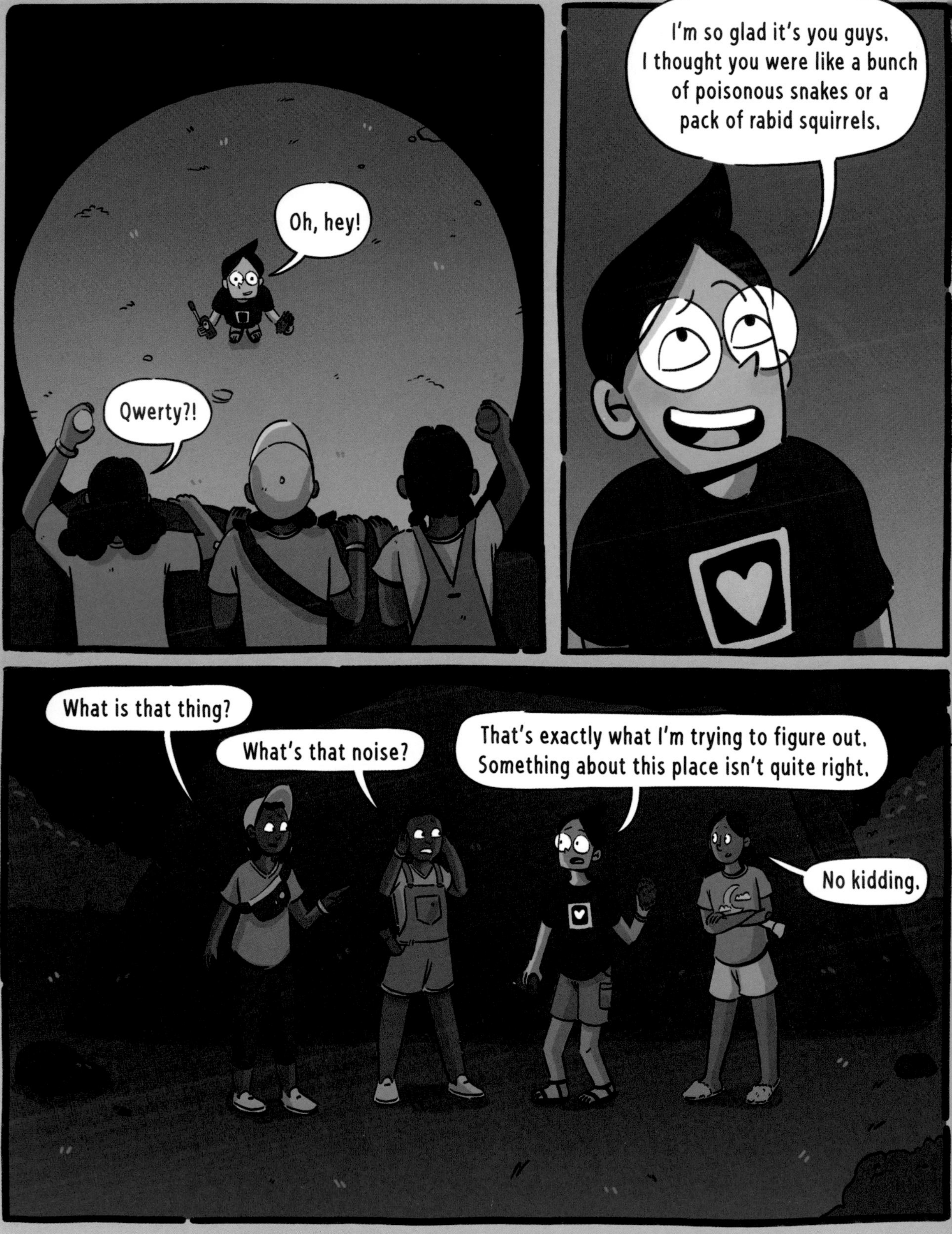
Oh, hey!
Qwerty?!
I'm so glad it's you guys. I thought you were like a bunch of poisonous snakes or a pack of rabid squirrels.
What is that thing?
What's that noise?
That's exactly what I'm trying to figure out. Something about this place isn't quite right.
No kidding.

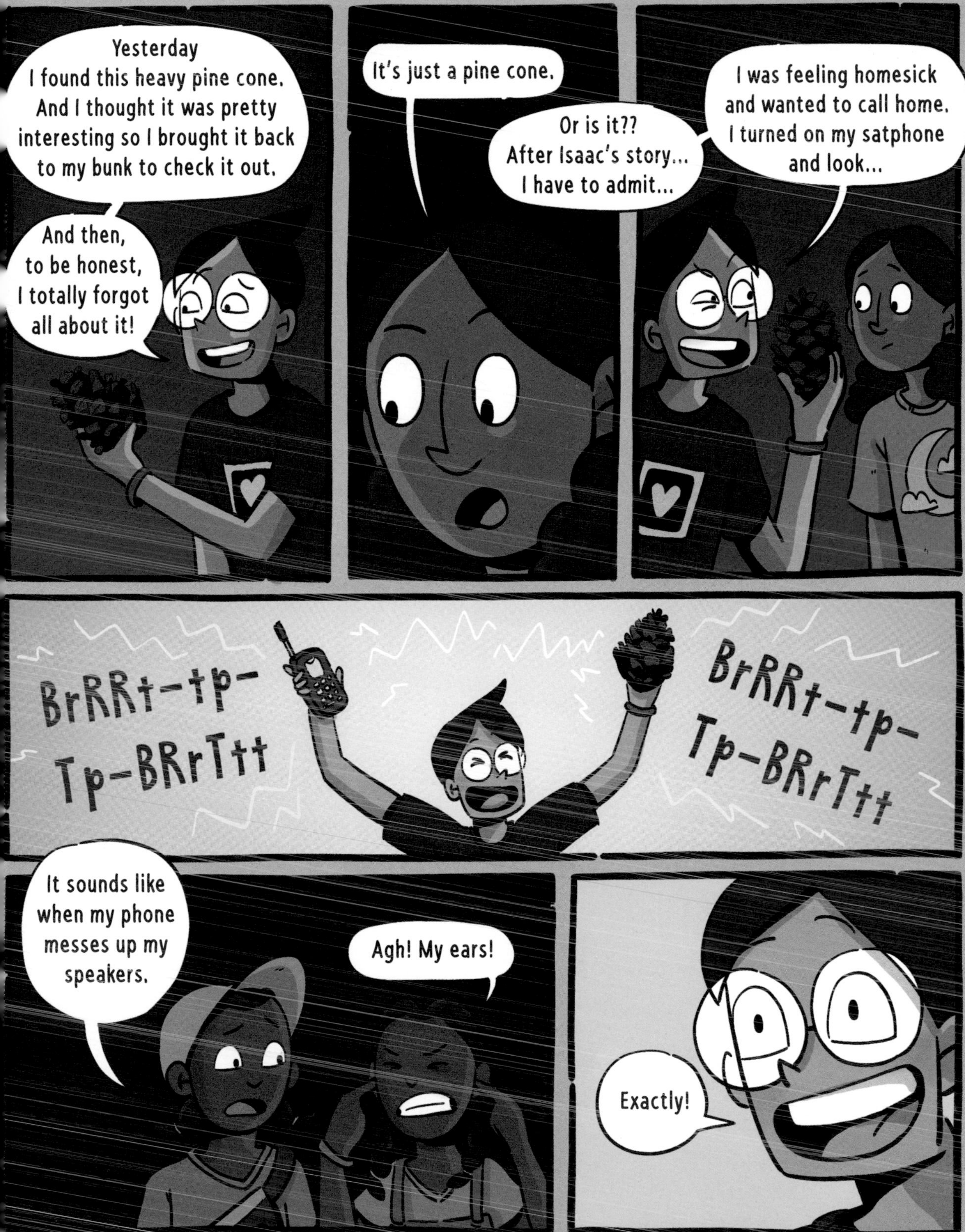
Yesterday I found this heavy pine cone. And I thought it was pretty interesting so I brought it back to my bunk to check it out.
And then, to be honest, I totally forgot all about it!
It's just a pine cone.
Or is it?? After Isaac's story... I have to admit...
I was feeling homesick and wanted to call home. I turned on my satphone and look...
BrRRt-tp-Tp-BRrTtt
BrRRt-tp-Tp-BRrTtt
It sounds like when my phone messes up my speakers.
Agh! My ears!
Exactly!

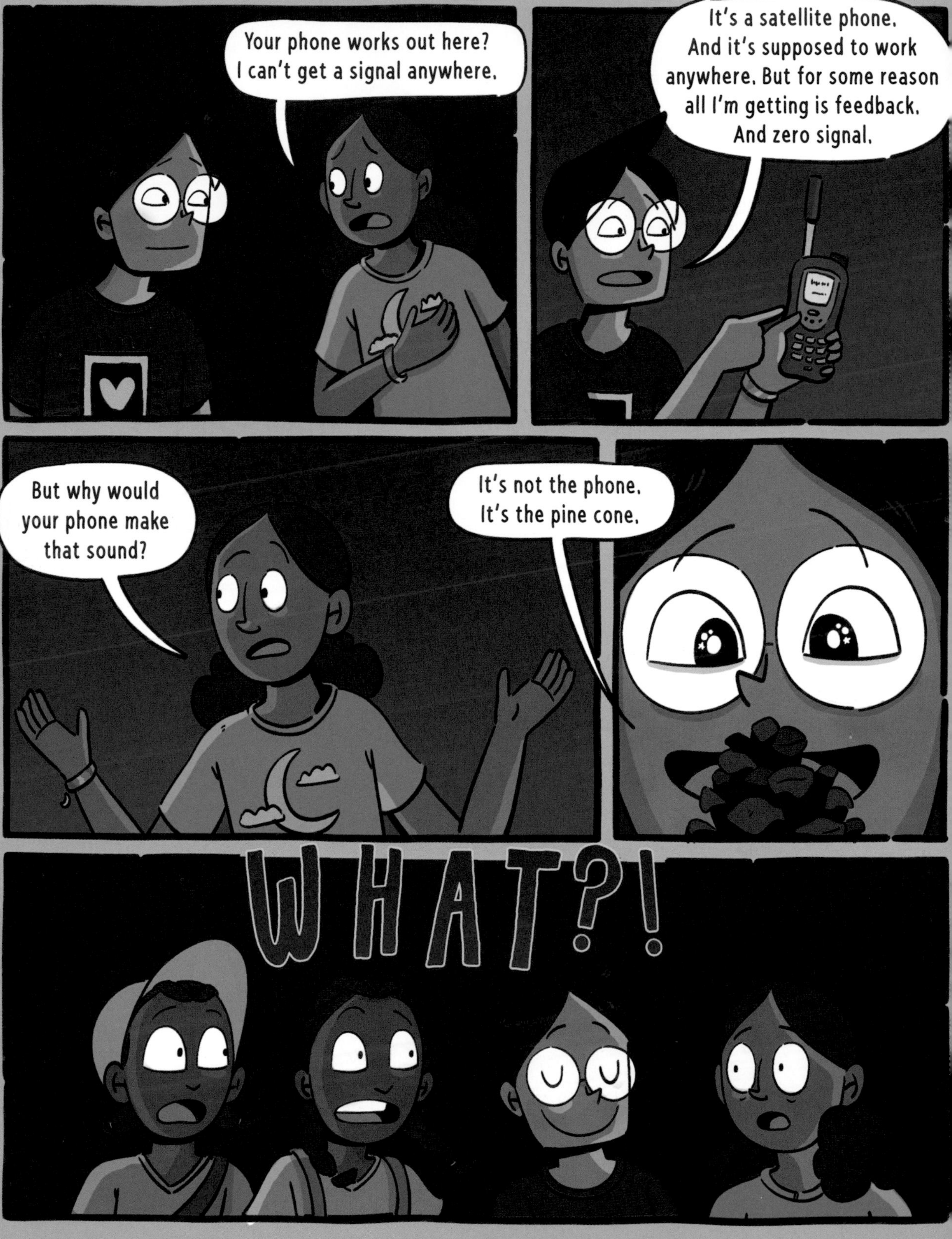
Your phone works out here? I can't get a signal anywhere.
It's a satellite phone. And it's supposed to work anywhere. But for some reason all I'm getting is feedback. And zero signal.
But why would your phone make that sound?
It's not the phone. It's the pine cone.
WHAT?!

It's a little speaker, look.

No. Way.

1. The sat phone sends out a signal that passes into the speaker through a magnet.

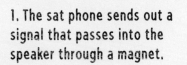

3. The diaphragm passes on these vibrations to the surrounding air, which makes the noise!

2. The current from the signal flows through a wire coil and generates a magnetic field around it. This causes the wire and diaphragm to vibrate.

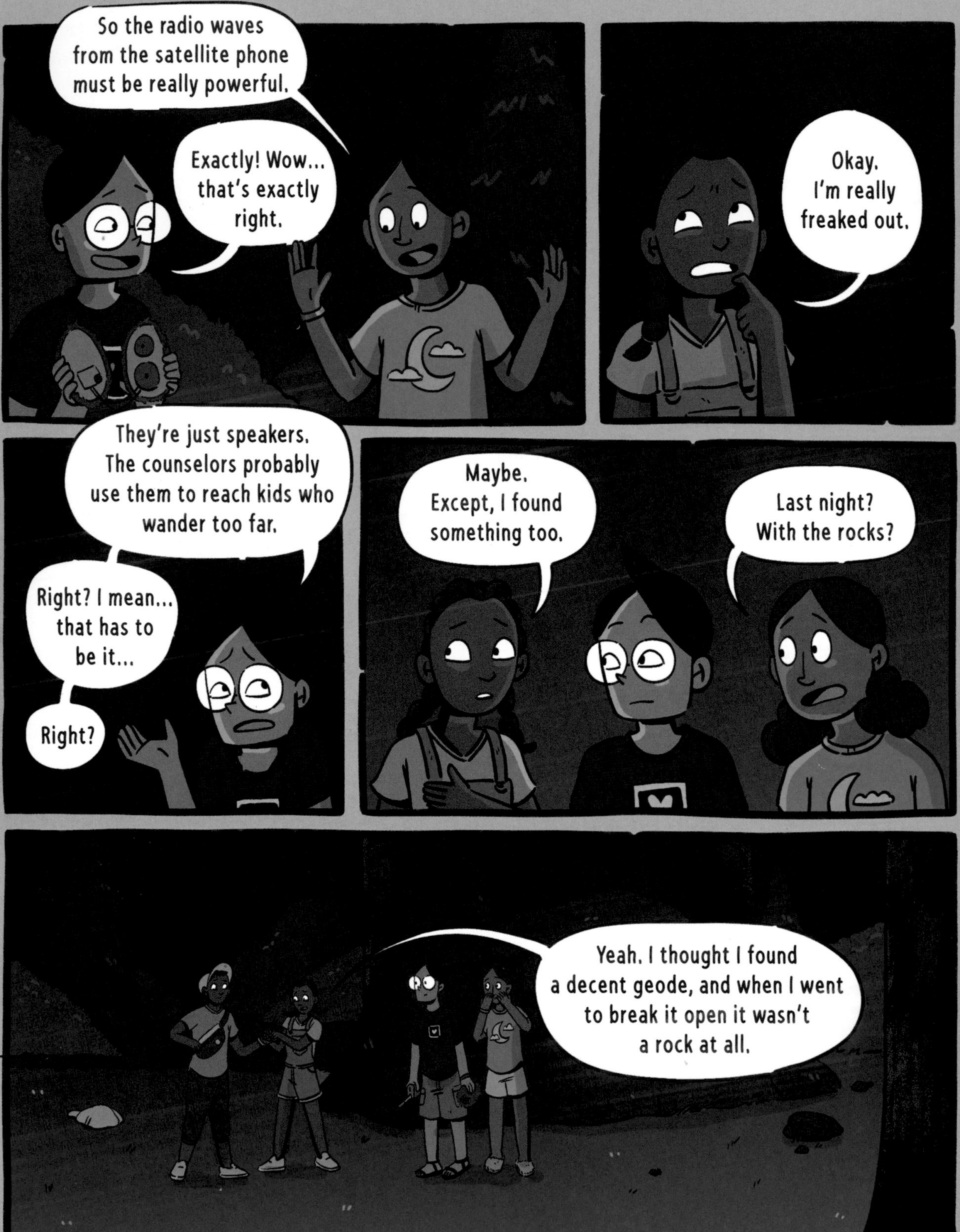
So the radio waves from the satellite phone must be really powerful.
Exactly! Wow... that's exactly right.
Okay. I'm really freaked out.
They're just speakers. The counselors probably use them to reach kids who wander too far.
Right? I mean... that has to be it...
Right?
Maybe. Except, I found something too.
Last night? With the rocks?
Yeah. I thought I found a decent geode, and when I went to break it open it wasn't a rock at all.

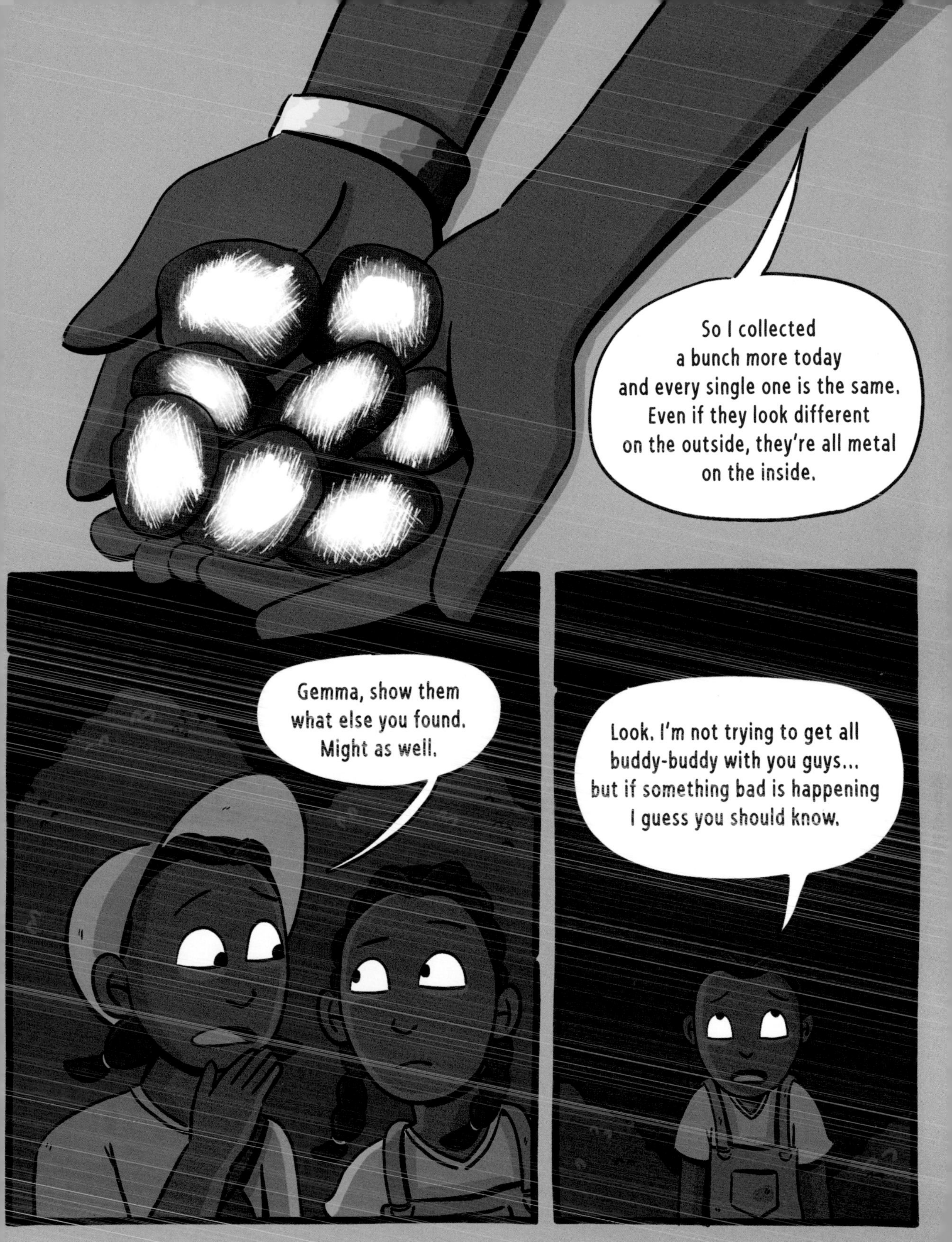
So I collected a bunch more today and every single one is the same. Even if they look different on the outside, they're all metal on the inside.
Gemma, show them what else you found. Might as well.
Look. I'm not trying to get all buddy-buddy with you guys... but if something bad is happening I guess you should know.

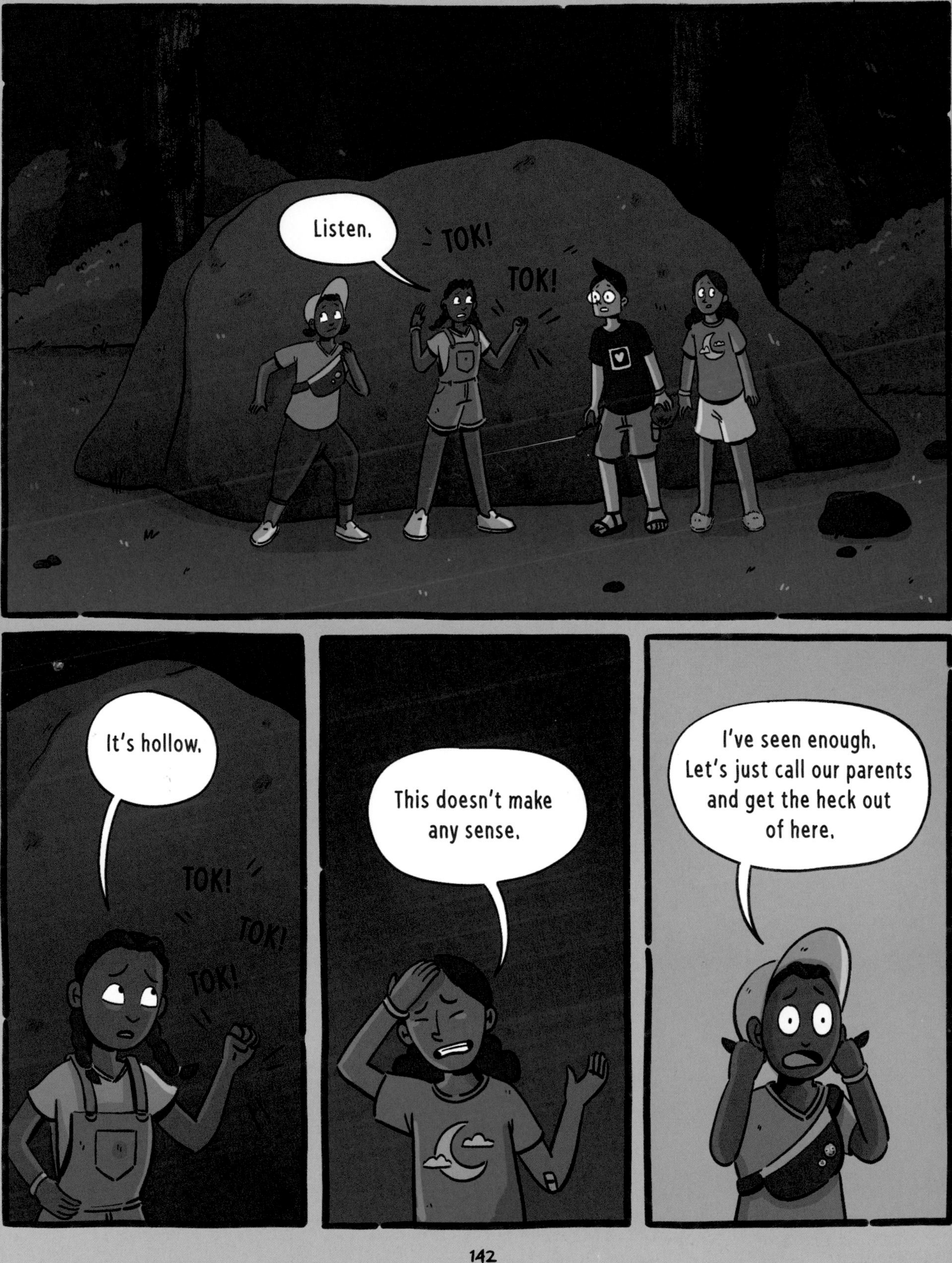
Listen.
TOK!
TOK!
It's hollow.
TOK!
TOK!
TOK!
This doesn't make any sense.
I've seen enough. Let's just call our parents and get the heck out of here.

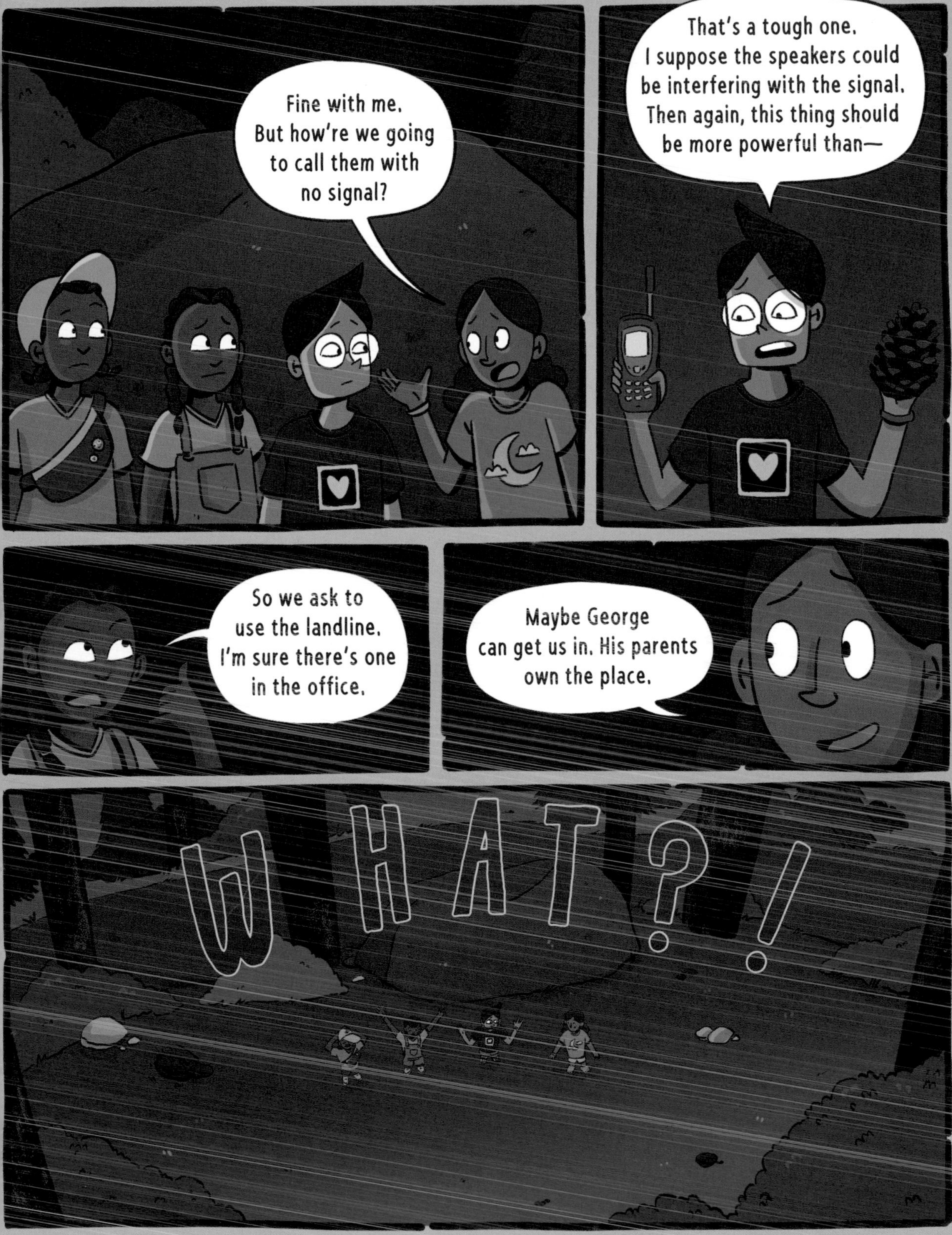
Fine with me. But how're we going to call them with no signal?
That's a tough one. I suppose the speakers could be interfering with the signal. Then again, this thing should be more powerful than—
So we ask to use the landline. I'm sure there's one in the office.
Maybe George can get us in. His parents own the place.
WHAT?!

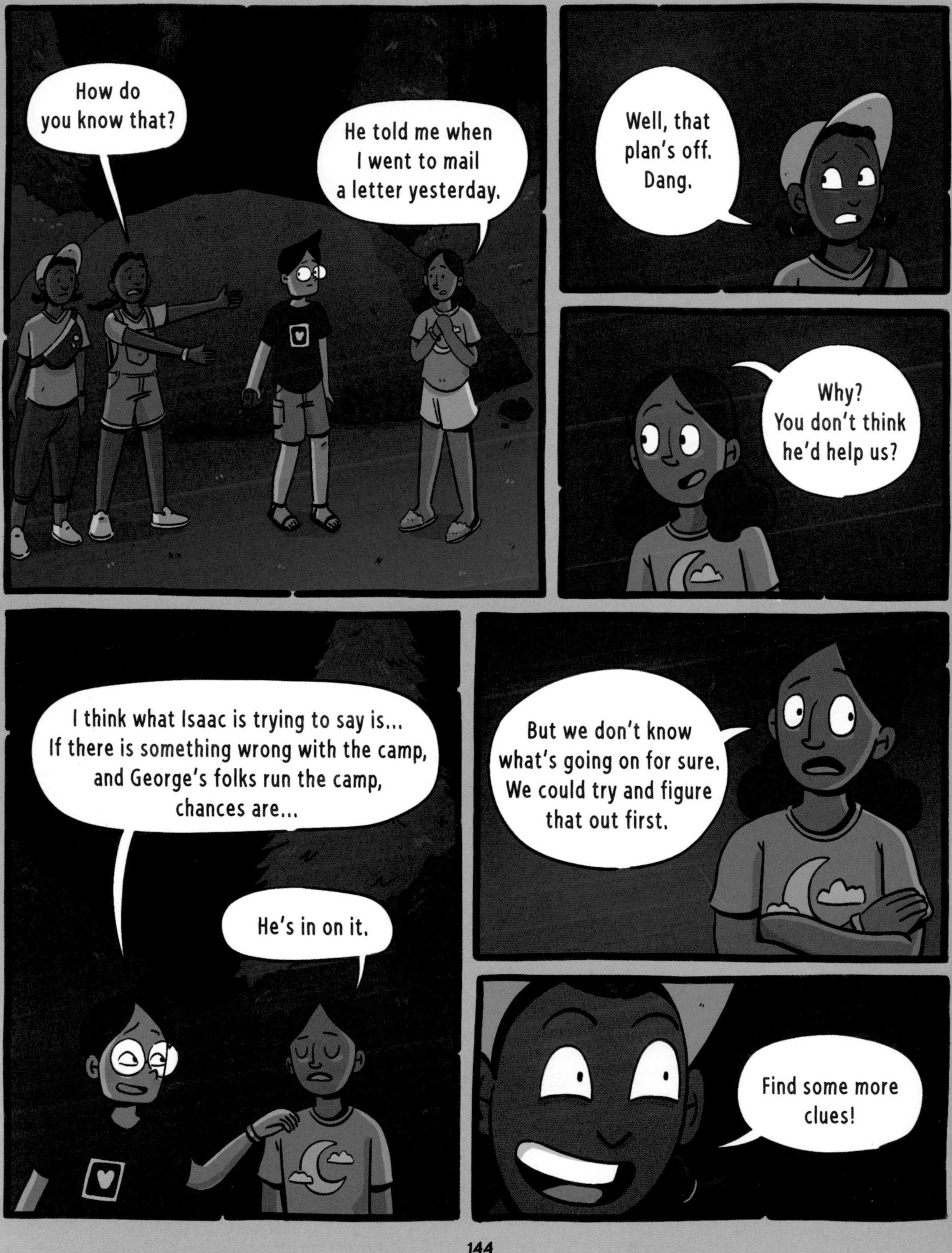
How do you know that?
He told me when I went to mail a letter yesterday.
Well, that plan's off. Dang.
Why? You don't think he'd help us?
I think what Isaac is trying to say is... If there is something wrong with the camp, and George's folks run the camp, chances are...
He's in on it.
But we don't know what's going on for sure. We could try and figure that out first.
Find some more clues!

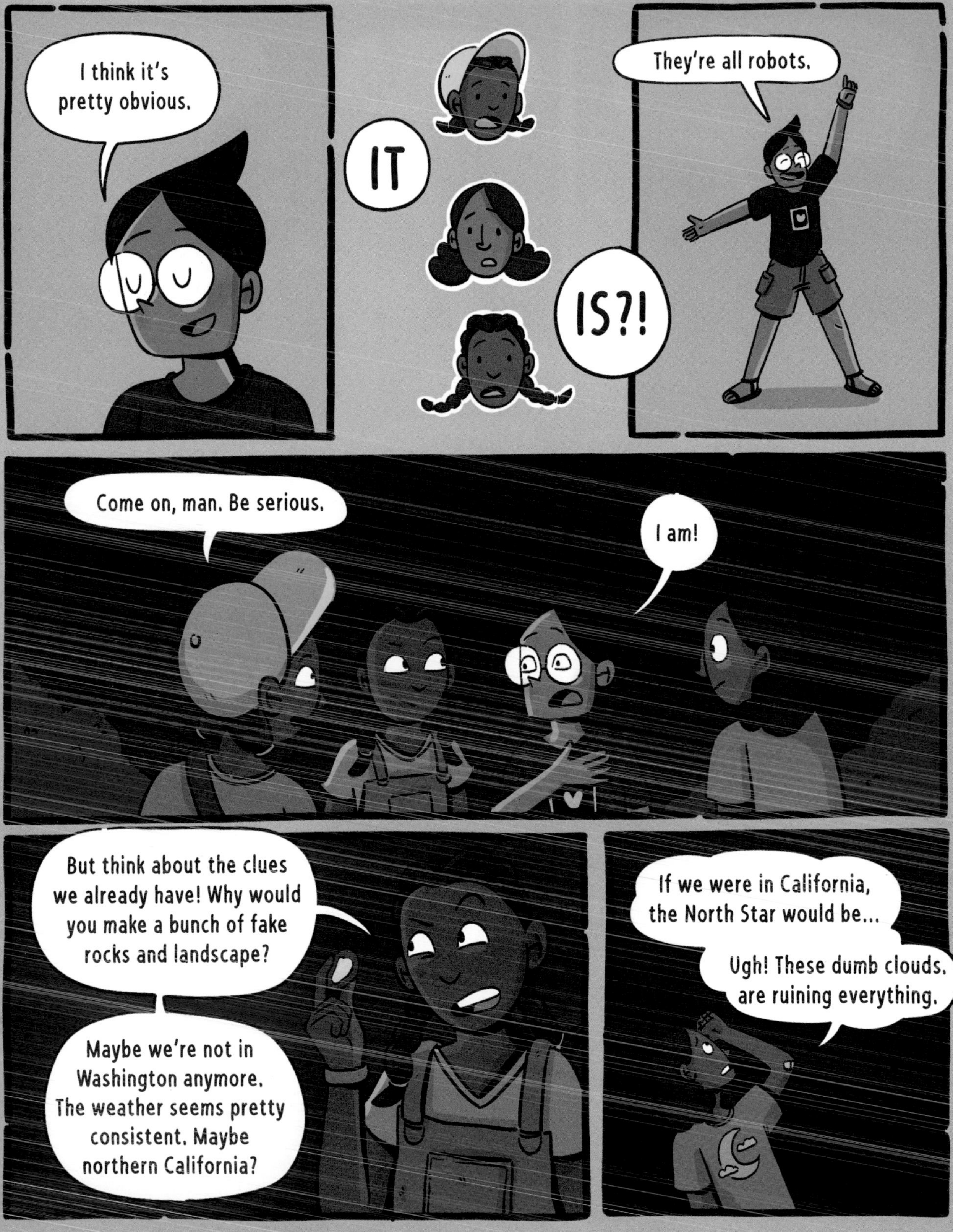
I think it's pretty obvious.
IT
IS?!
They're all robots.
Come on, man. Be serious.
I am!
But think about the clues we already have! Why would you make a bunch of fake rocks and landscape?
Maybe we're not in Washington anymore. The weather seems pretty consistent. Maybe northern California?
If we were in California, the North Star would be...
Ugh! These dumb clouds are ruining everything.

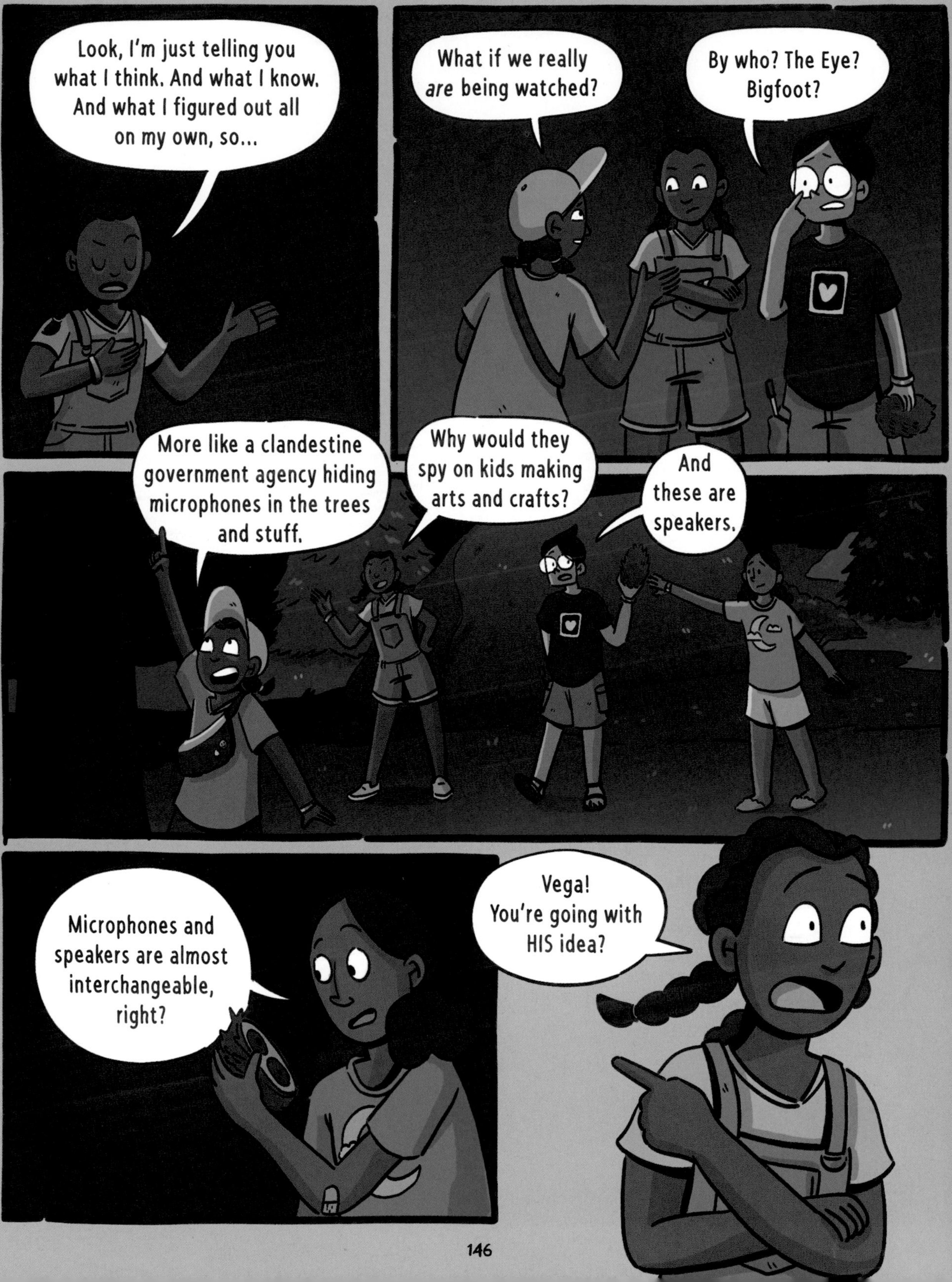

Look, I'm just telling you what I think. And what I know. And what I figured out all on my own, so...
What if we really *are* being watched?
By who? The Eye? Bigfoot?
More like a clandestine government agency hiding microphones in the trees and stuff.
Why would they spy on kids making arts and crafts?
And these are speakers.
Microphones and speakers are almost interchangeable, right?
Vega! You're going with HIS idea?

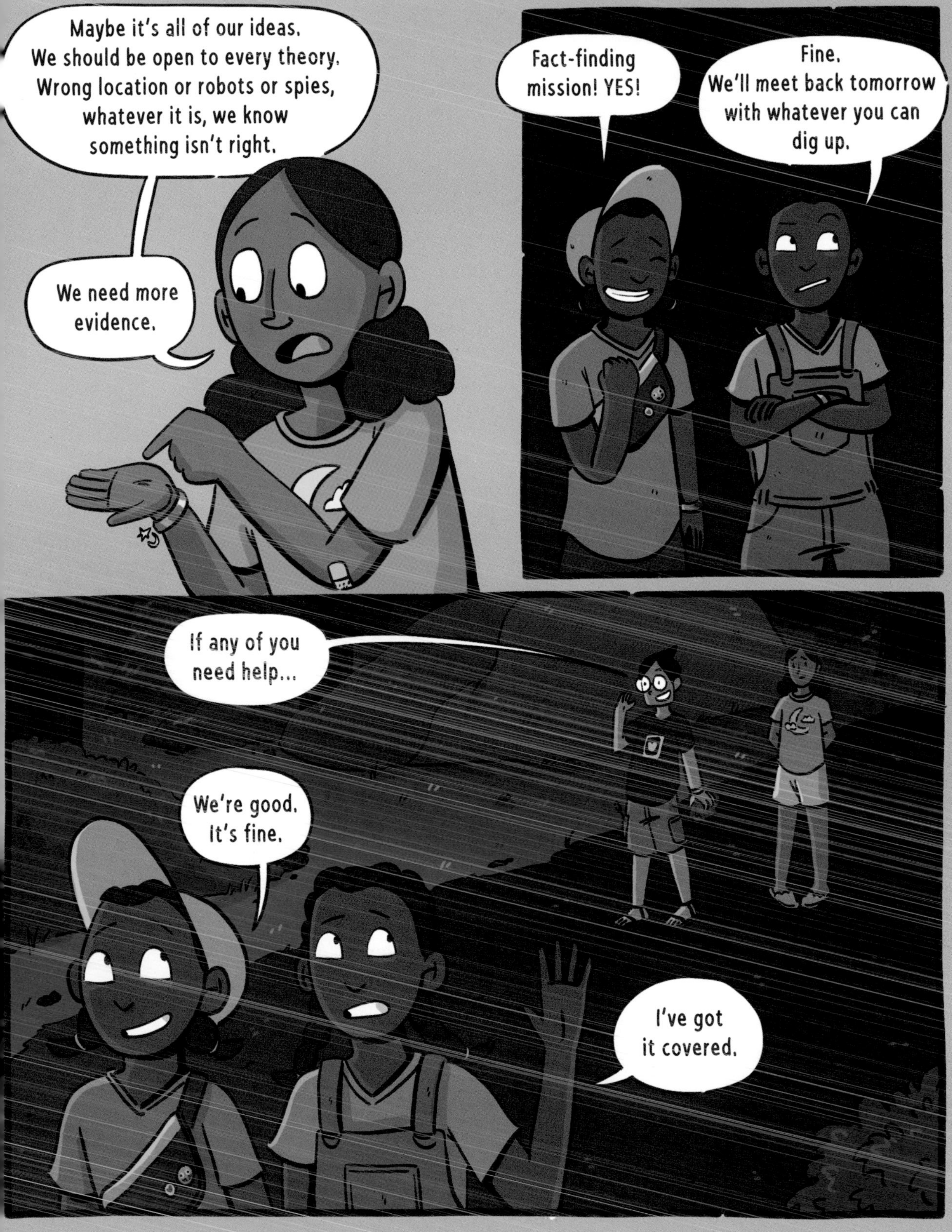
Maybe it's all of our ideas. We should be open to every theory. Wrong location or robots or spies, whatever it is, we know something isn't right.
We need more evidence.
Fact-finding mission! YES!
Fine. We'll meet back tomorrow with whatever you can dig up.
If any of you need help...
We're good. It's fine.
I've got it covered.

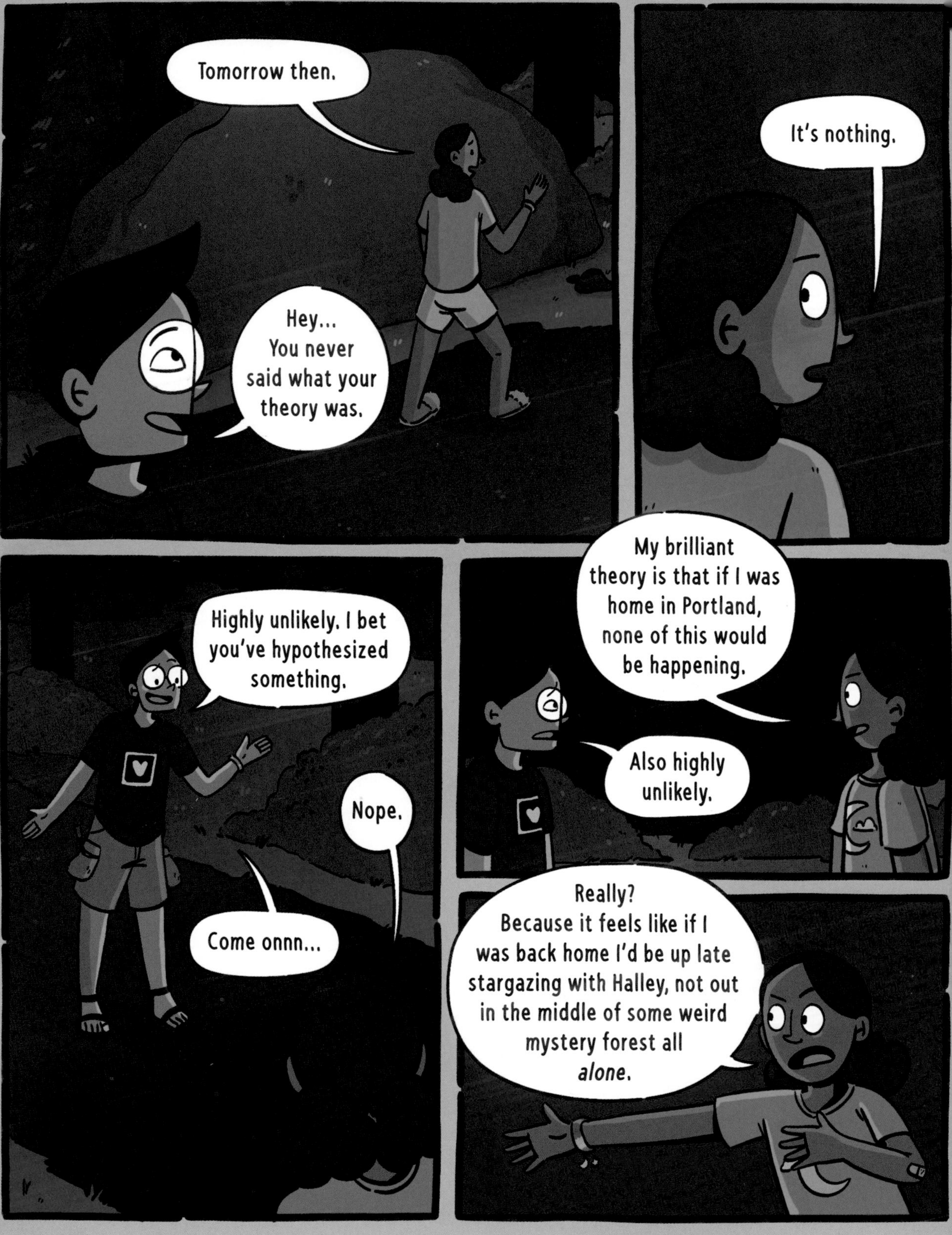
Tomorrow then.
Hey... You never said what your theory was.
It's nothing.
Highly unlikely. I bet you've hypothesized something.
Nope.
Come onnn...
My brilliant theory is that if I was home in Portland, none of this would be happening.
Also highly unlikely.
Really? Because it feels like if I was back home I'd be up late stargazing with Halley, not out in the middle of some weird mystery forest all *alone*.

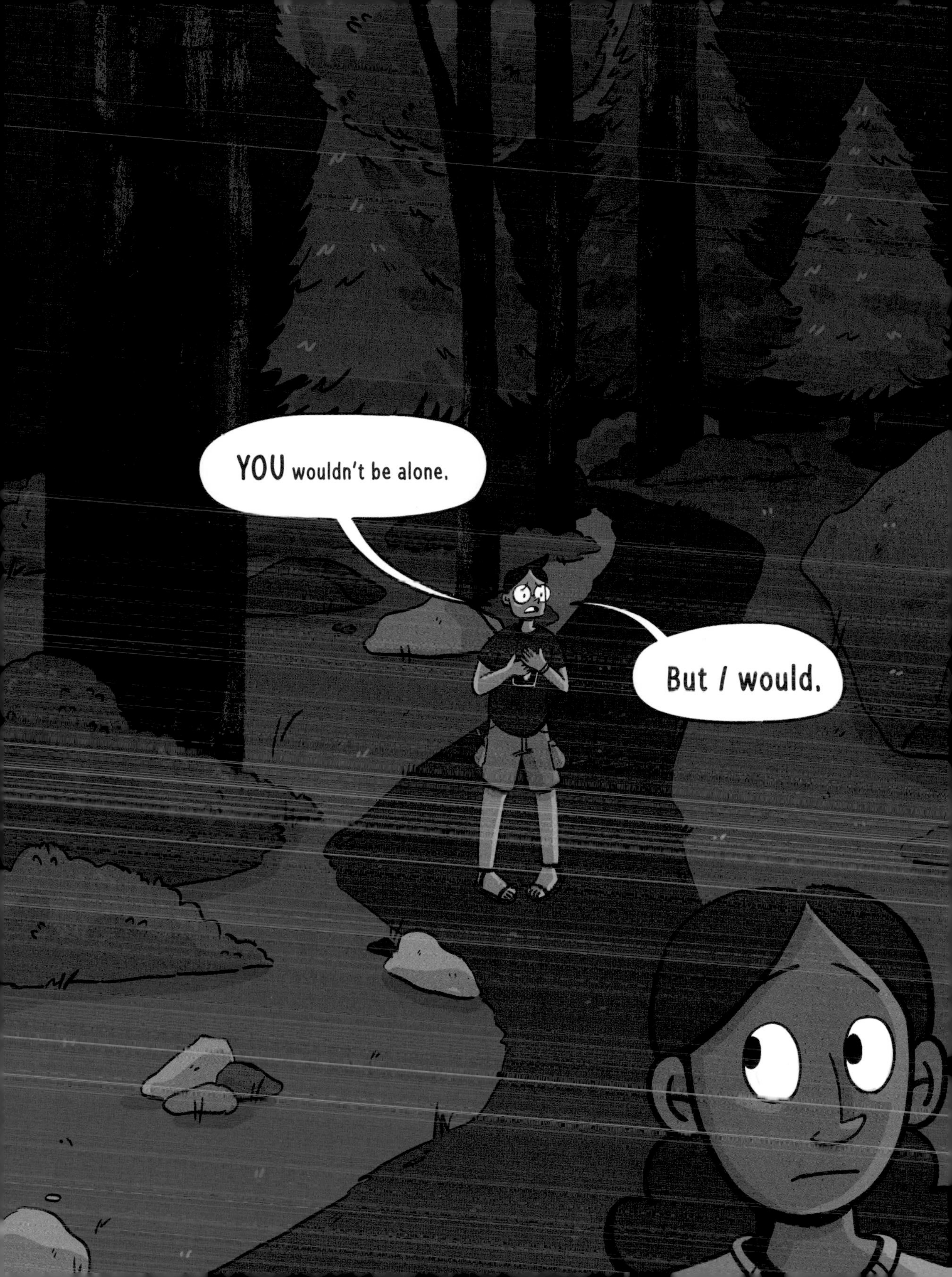
YOU wouldn't be alone.
But I would.

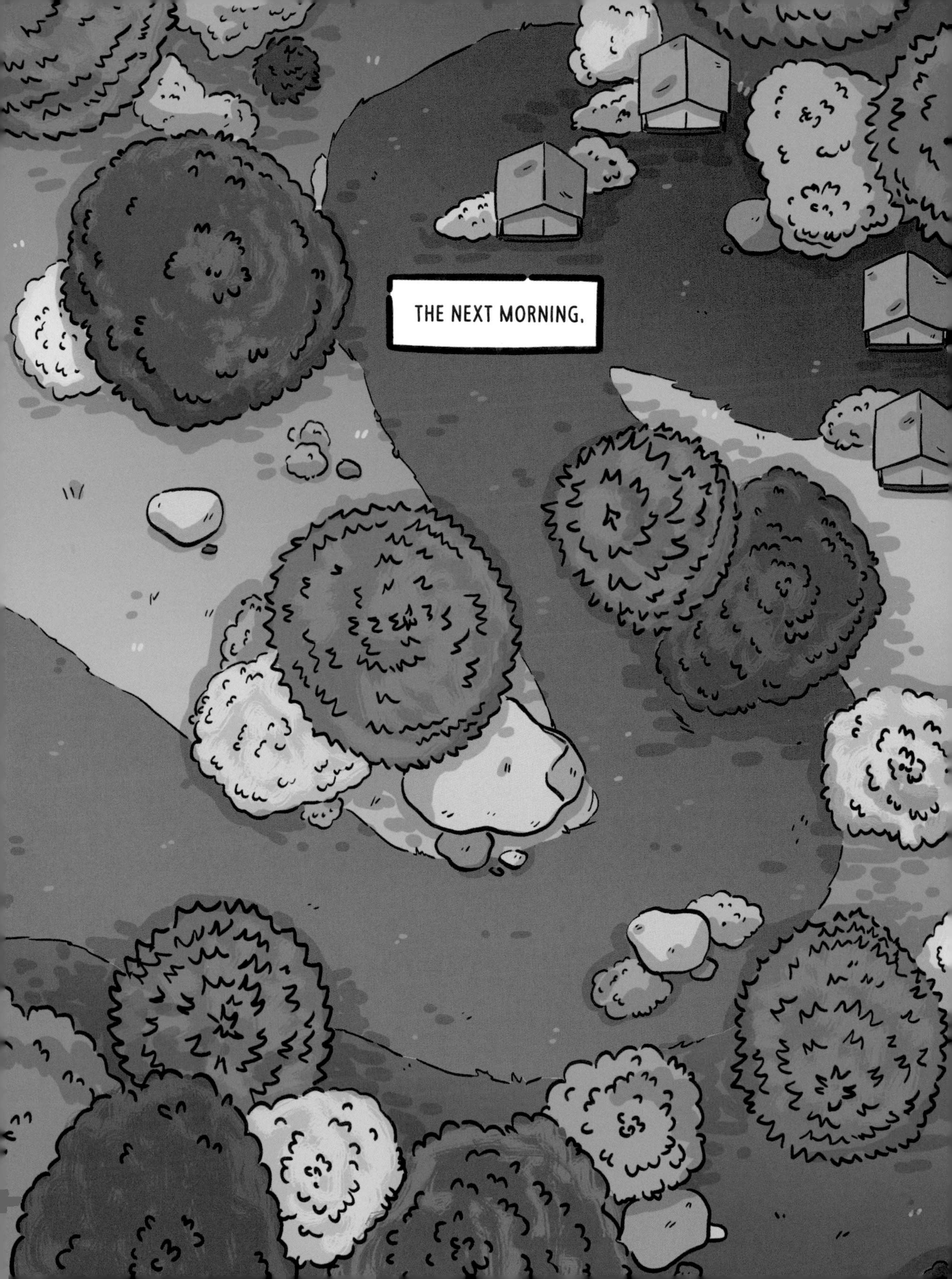
THE NEXT MORNING.

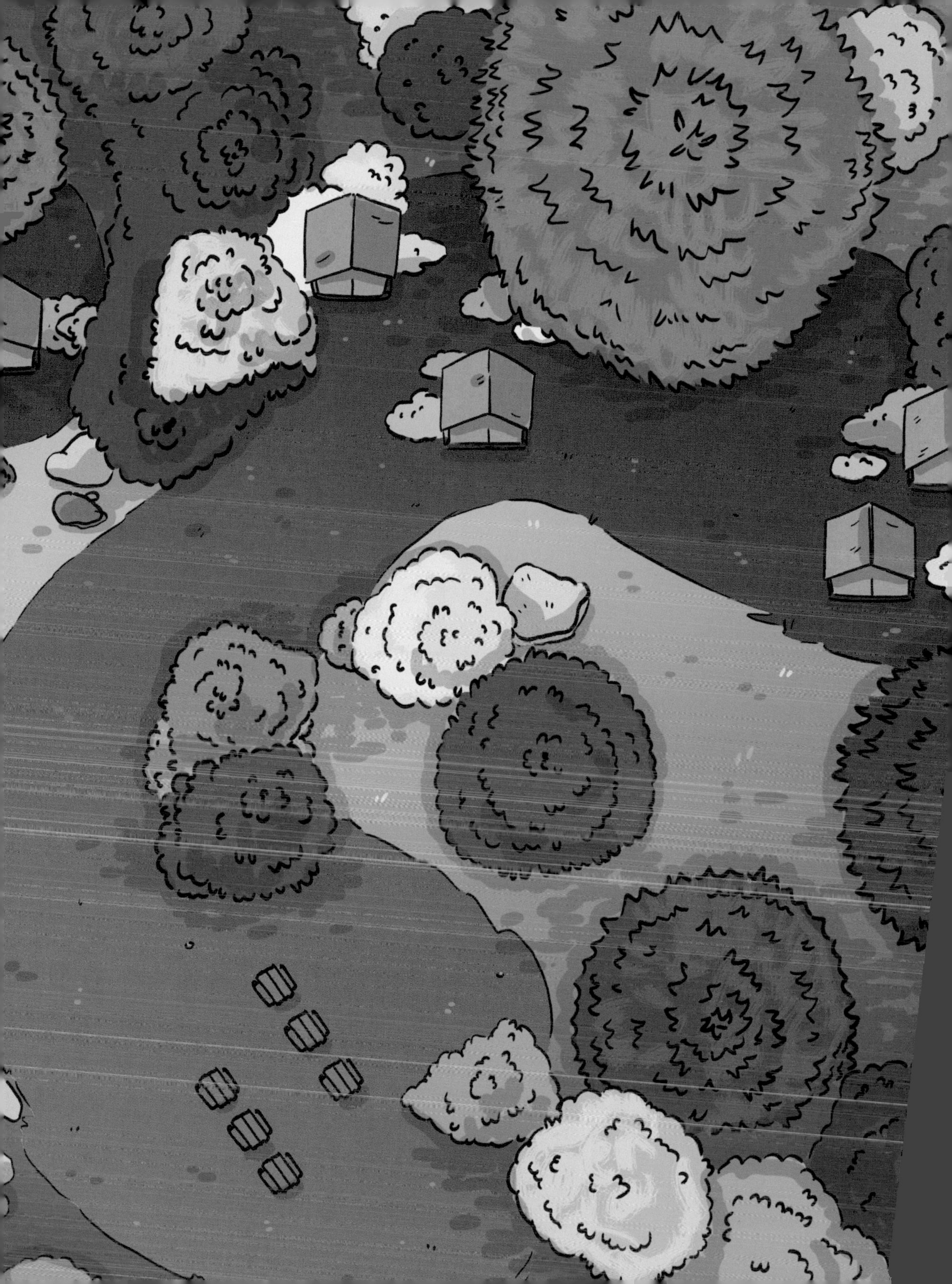

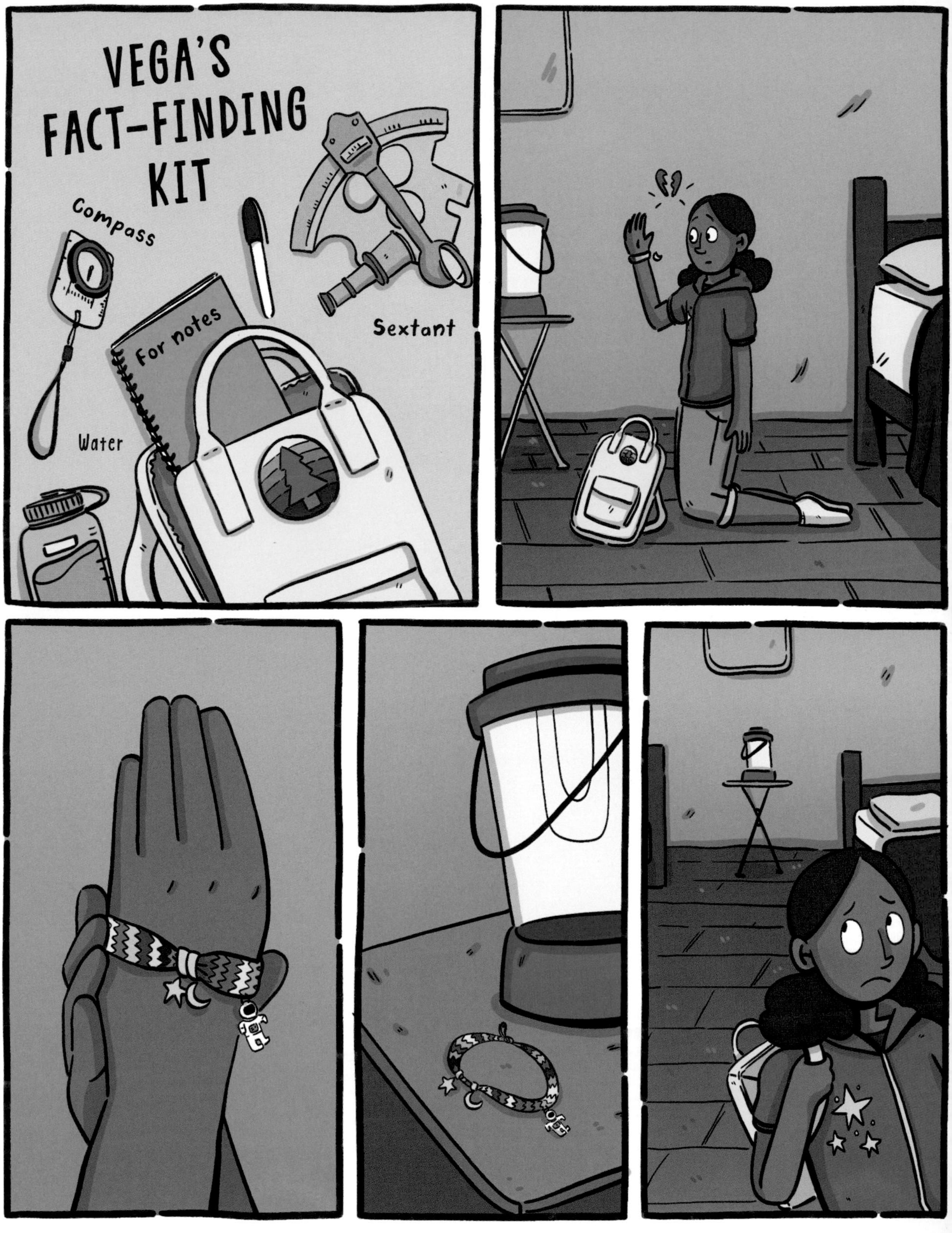
VEGA'S
FACT-FINDING
KIT
Compass
Sextant
For notes
Water

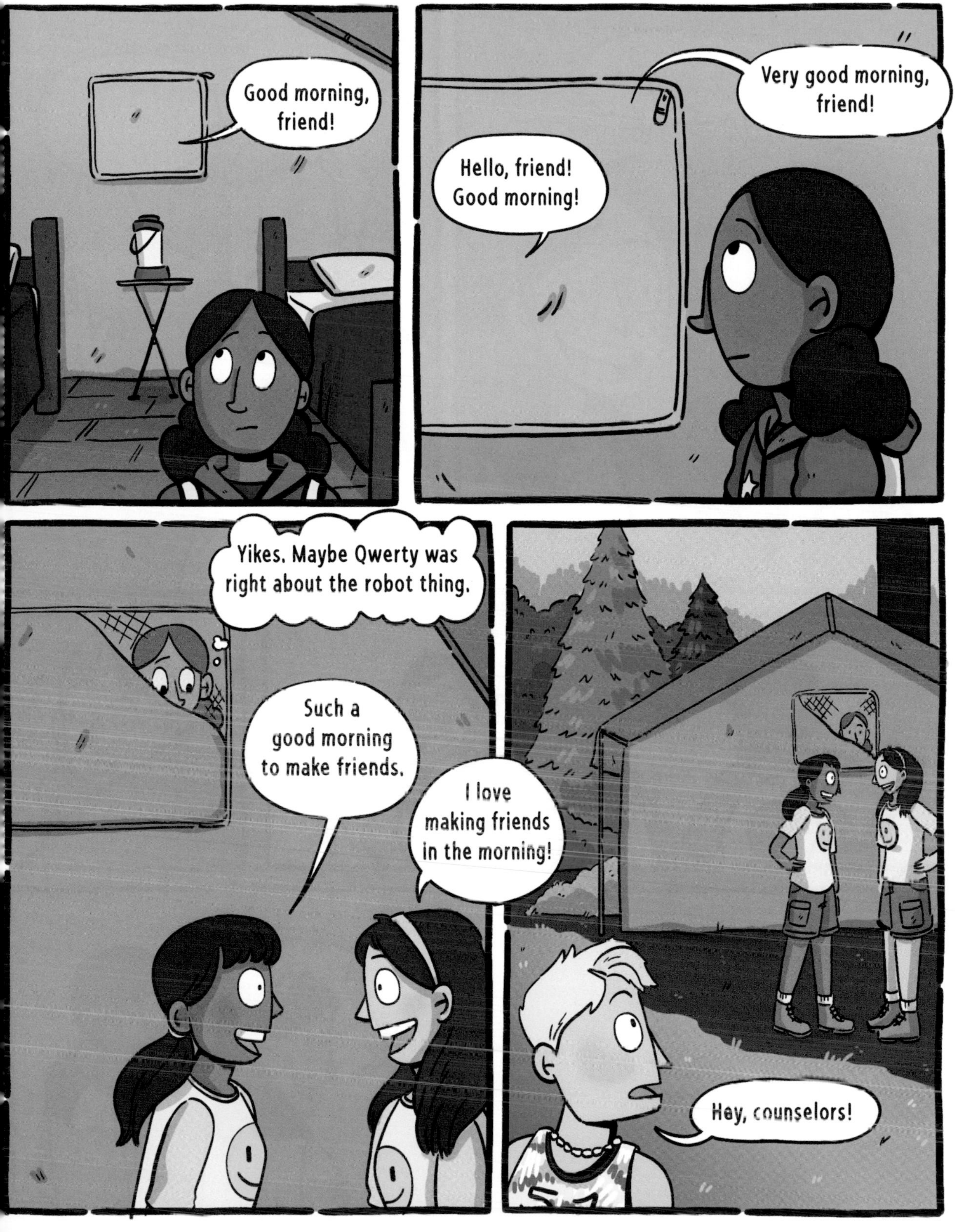
Good morning, friend!
Very good morning, friend!
Hello, friend! Good morning!
Yikes. Maybe Qwerty was right about the robot thing.
Such a good morning to make friends.
I love making friends in the morning!
Hey, counselors!

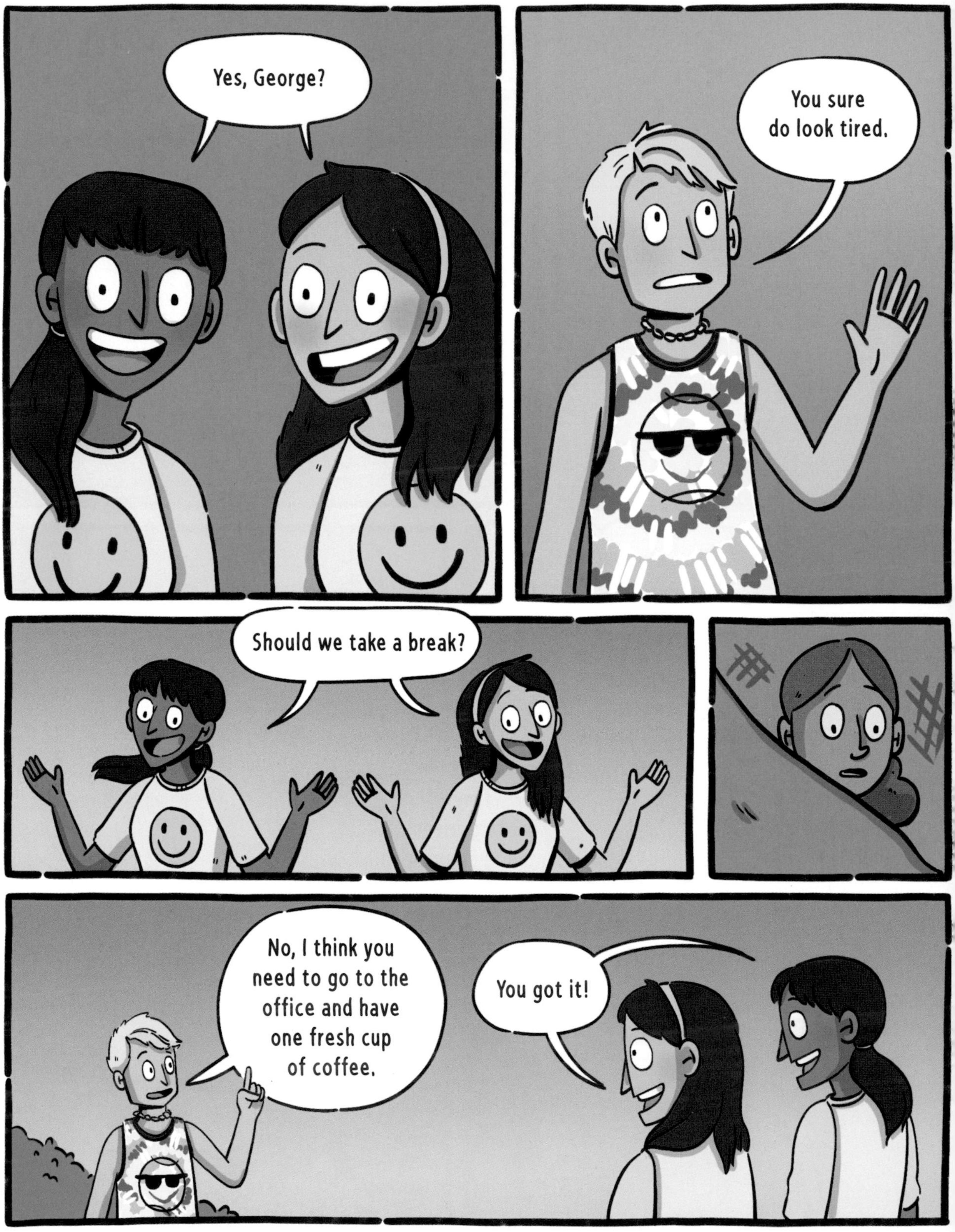
Yes, George?
You sure do look tired.
Should we take a break?
No, I think you need to go to the office and have one fresh cup of coffee.
You got it!

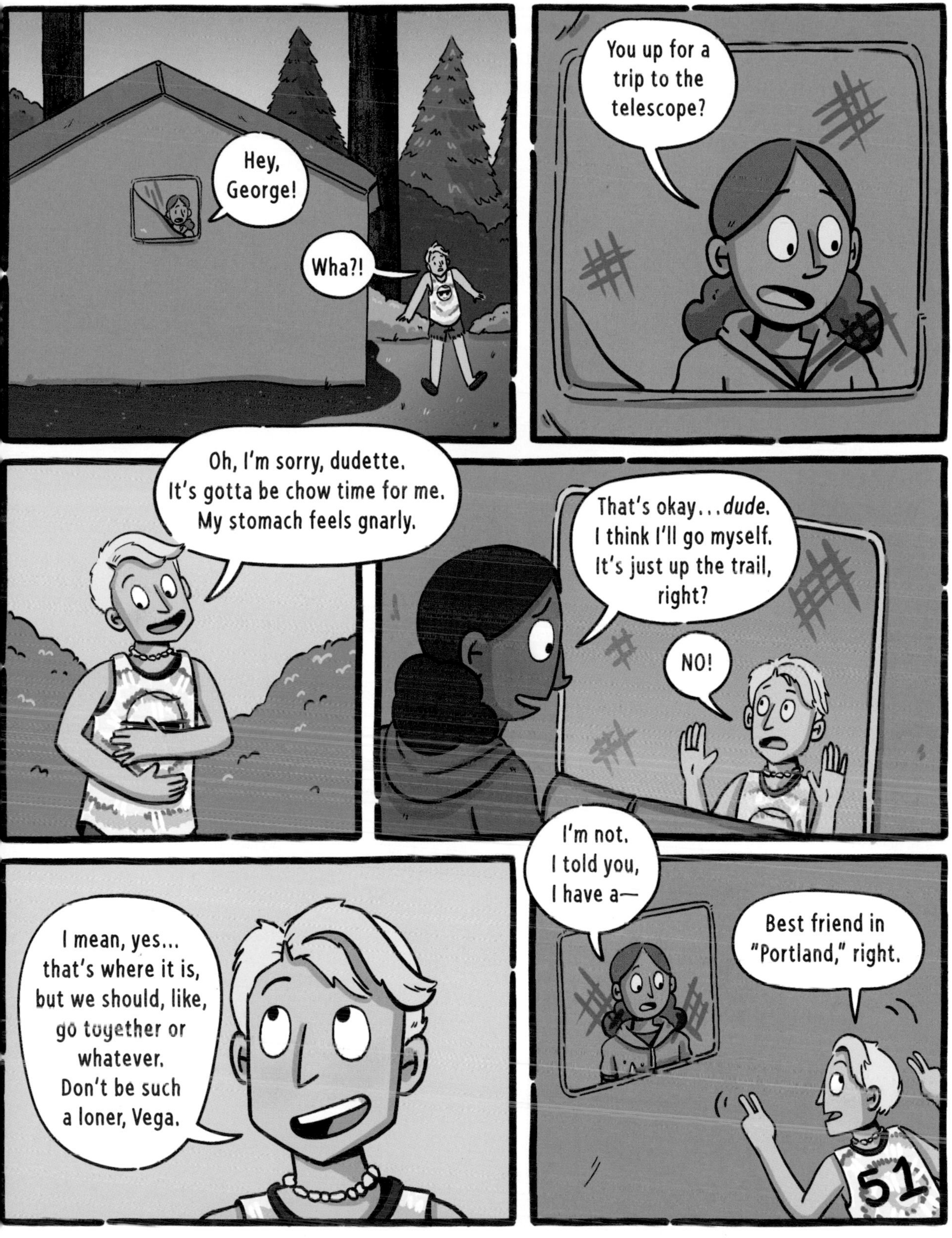
Hey, George!
Wha?!
You up for a trip to the telescope?
Oh, I'm sorry, dudette. It's gotta be chow time for me. My stomach feels gnarly.
That's okay... *dude*. I think I'll go myself. It's just up the trail, right?
NO!
I mean, yes... that's where it is, but we should, like, go together or whatever. Don't be such a loner, Vega.
I'm not. I told you, I have a—
Best friend in "Portland," right.

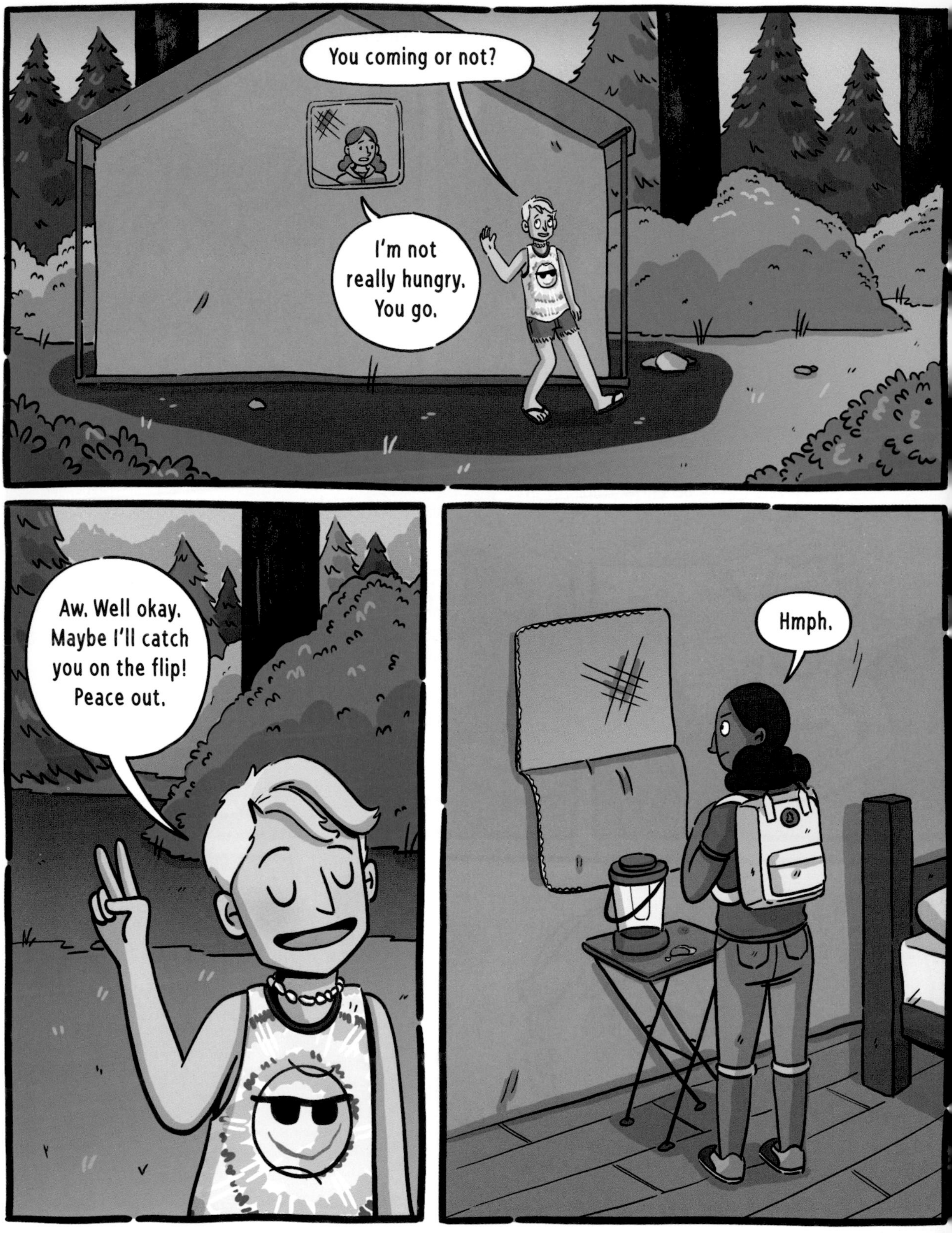
You coming or not?
I'm not really hungry. You go.
Aw. Well okay. Maybe I'll catch you on the flip! Peace out.
Hmph.

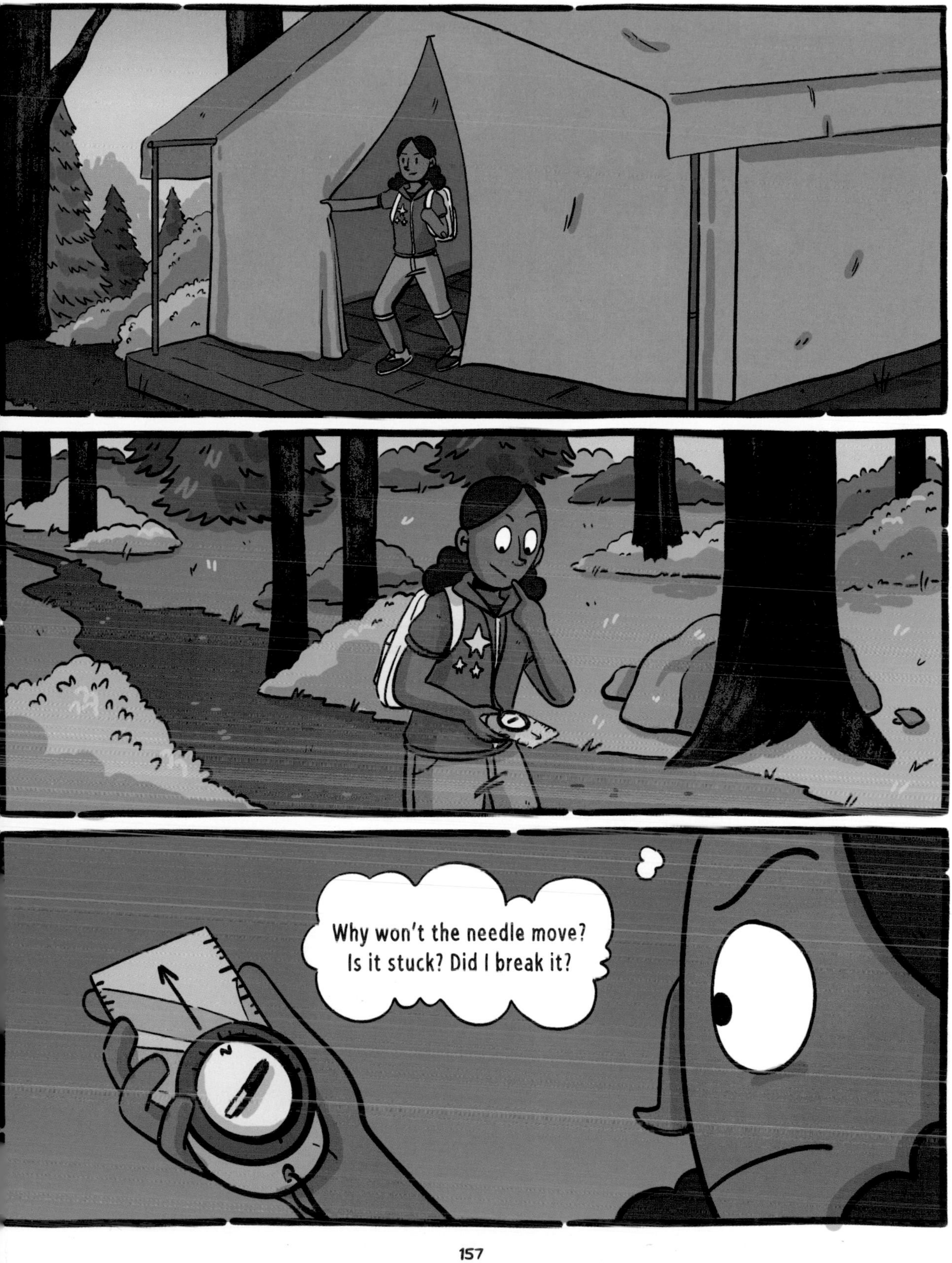
Why won't the needle move? Is it stuck? Did I break it?

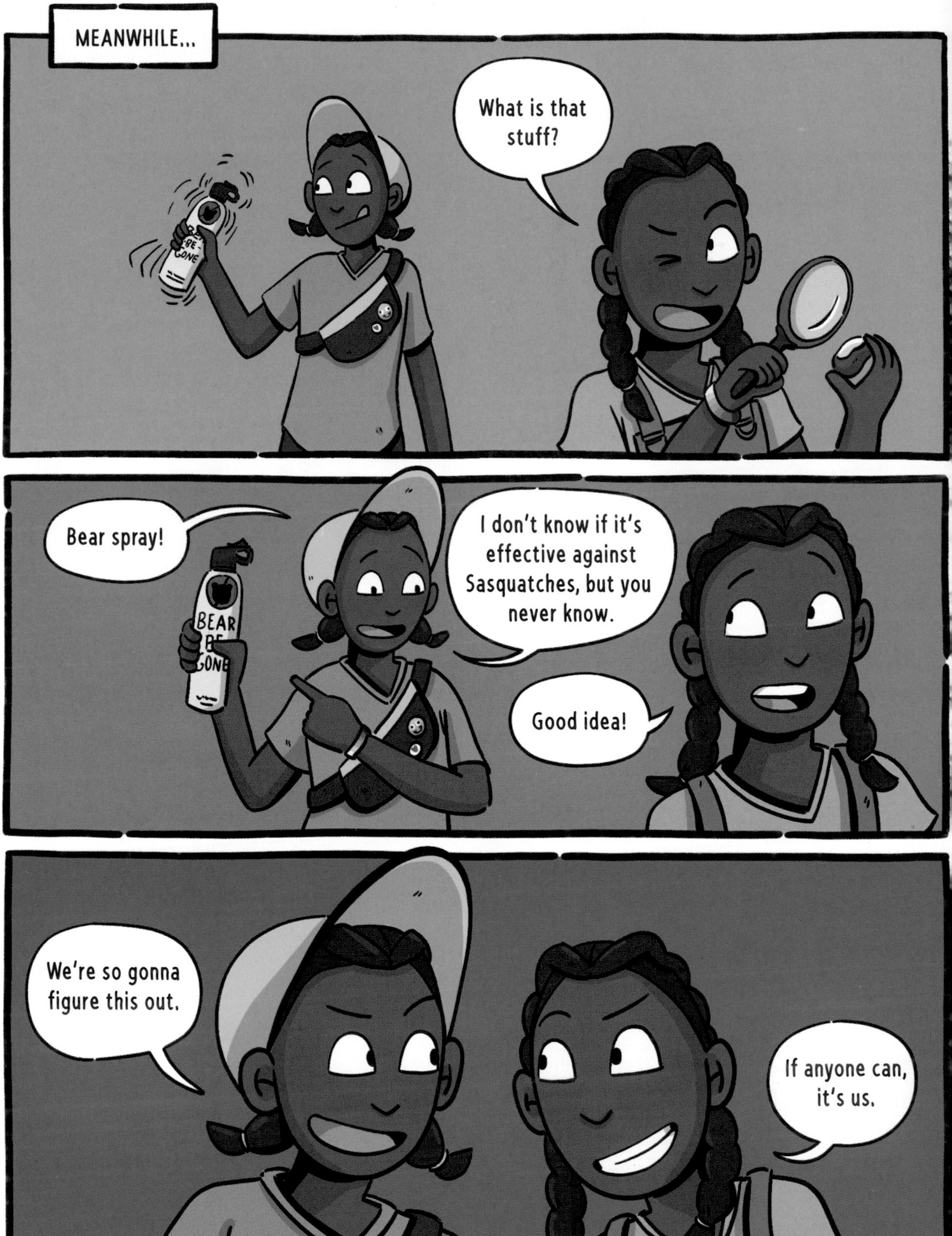
MEANWHILE...
BEAR BE-GONE
What is that stuff?
Bear spray!
BEAR BE-GONE
I don't know if it's effective against Sasquatches, but you never know.
Good idea!
We're so gonna figure this out.
If anyone can, it's us.

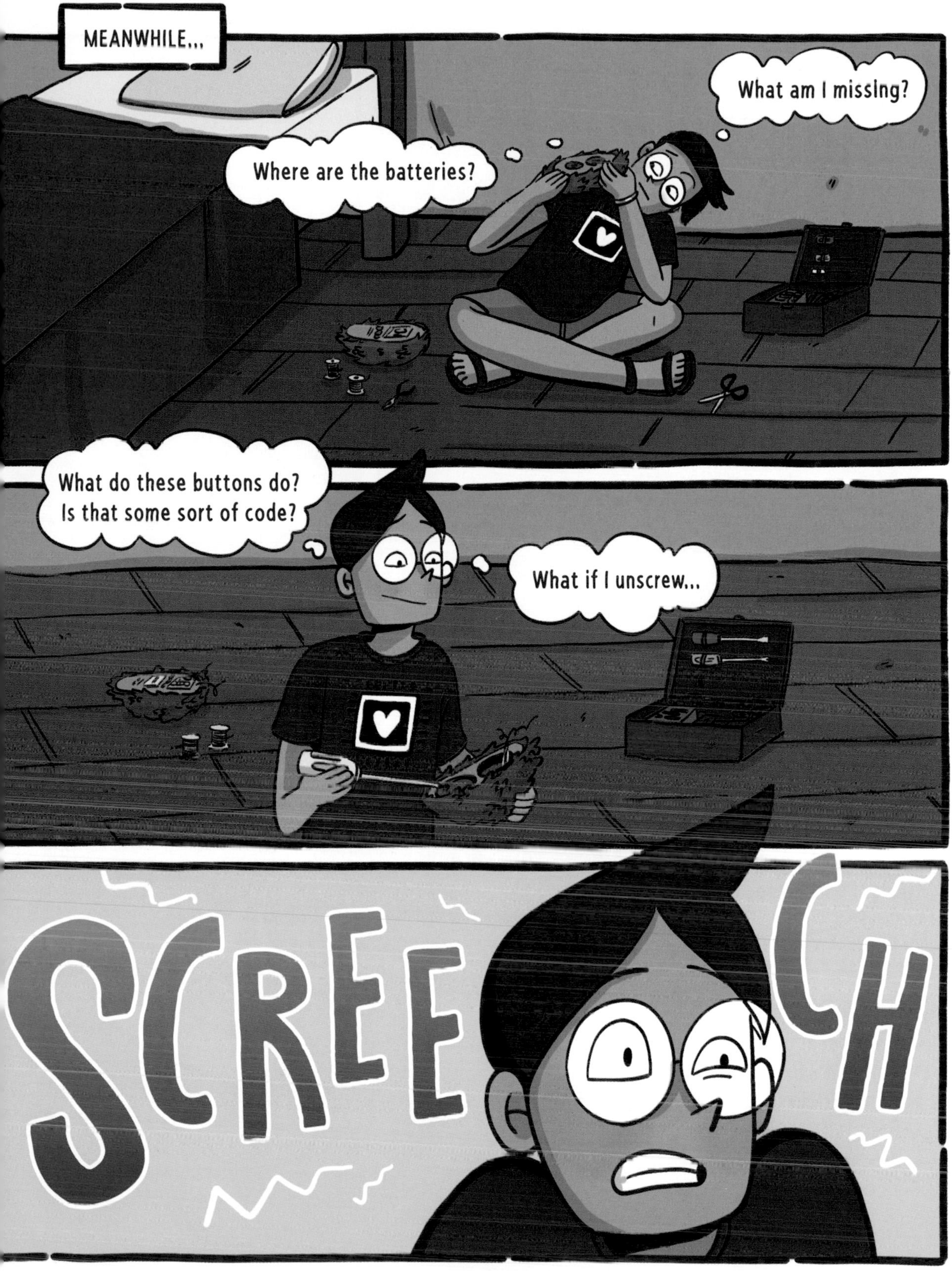
MEANWHILE...
Where are the batteries?
What am I missing?
What do these buttons do? Is that some sort of code?
What if I unscrew...
SCREECH

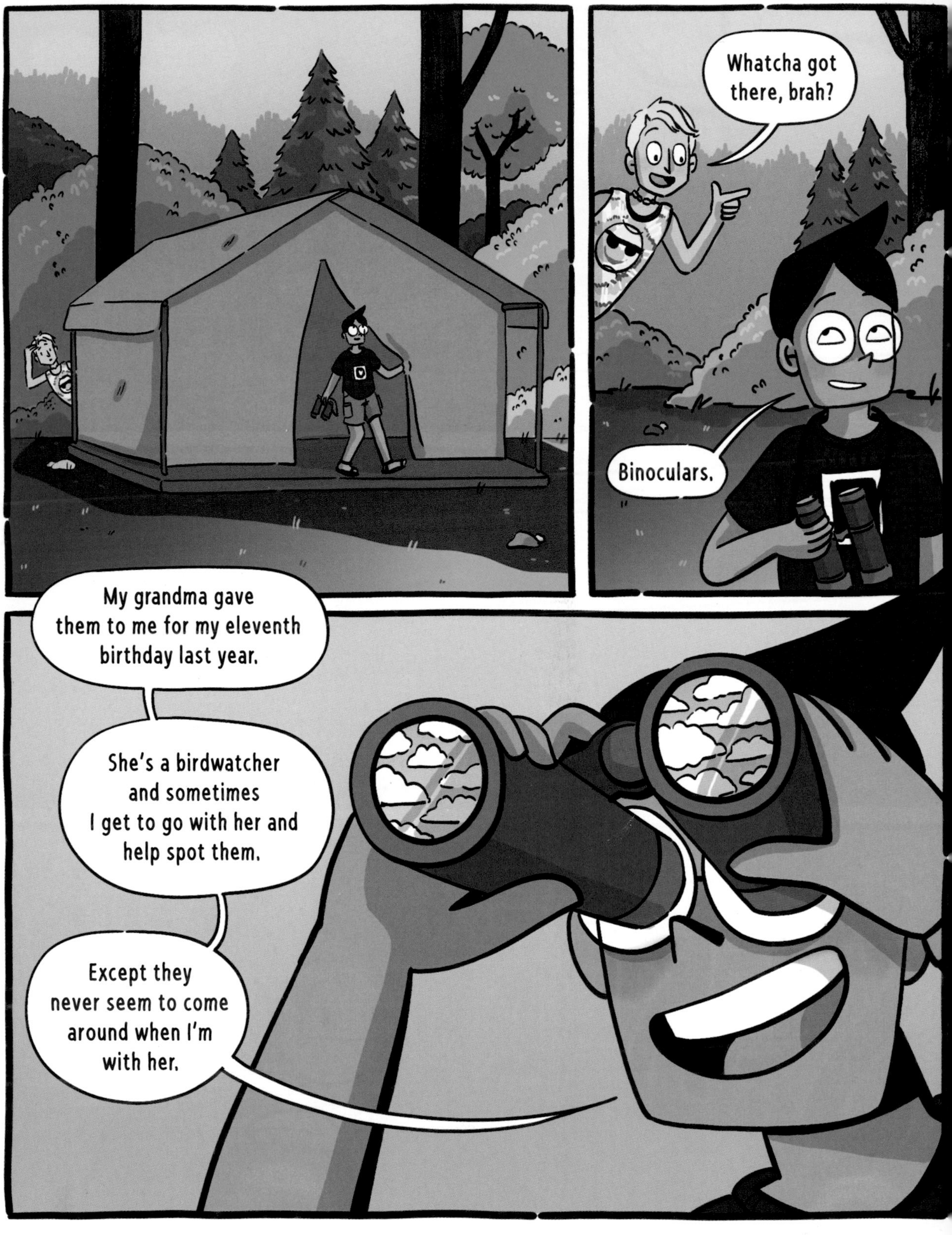
Whatcha got there, brah?
Binoculars.
My grandma gave them to me for my eleventh birthday last year.
She's a birdwatcher and sometimes I get to go with her and help spot them.
Except they never seem to come around when I'm with her.

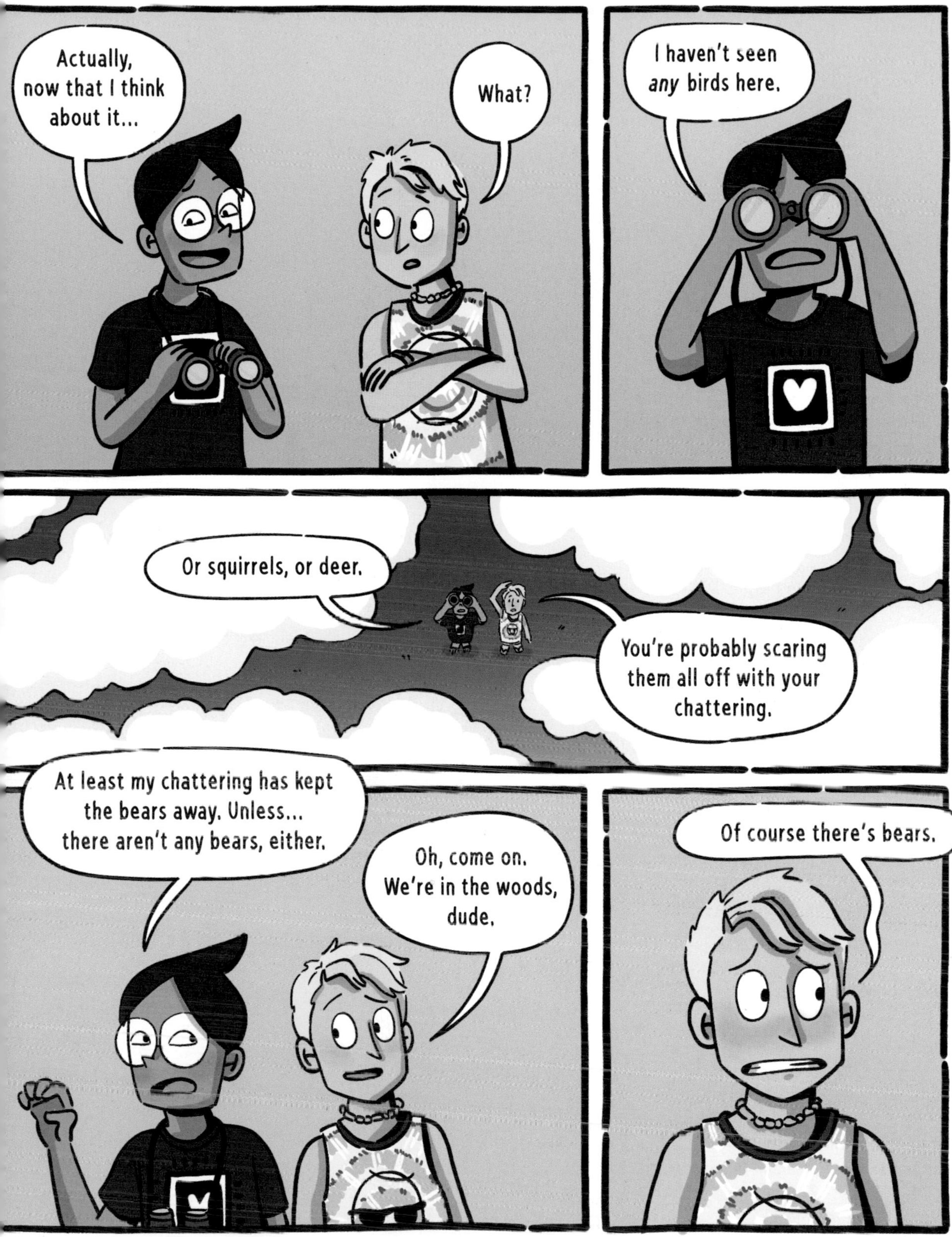
Actually, now that I think about it...
What?
I haven't seen *any* birds here.
Or squirrels, or deer.
You're probably scaring them all off with your chattering.
At least my chattering has kept the bears away. Unless... there aren't any bears, either.
Oh, come on. We're in the woods, dude.
Of course there's bears.

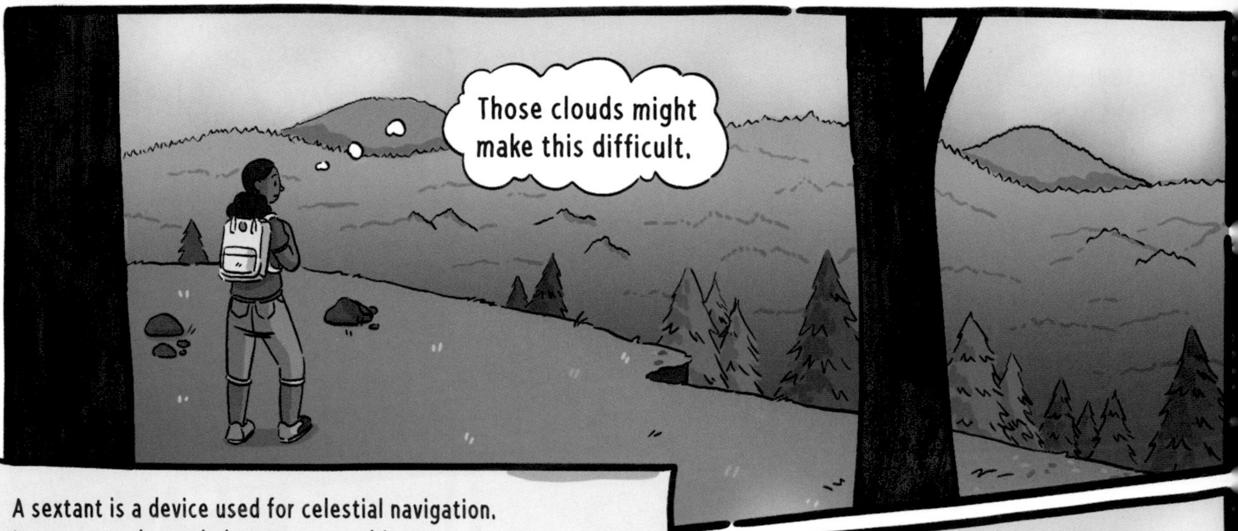
Those clouds might make this difficult.

A sextant is a device used for celestial navigation. It measures the angle between two objects by using mirrors.

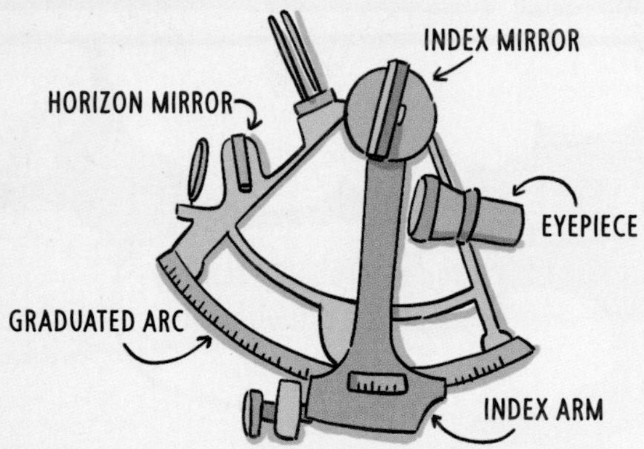
INDEX MIRROR
HORIZON MIRROR
EYEPIECE
GRADUATED ARC
INDEX ARM

The horizon mirror is semi-transparent so you can see the horizon through it.

The index mirror is attached to a movable arm. This mirror will reflect the light from the sun or other stars back to the horizon mirror.

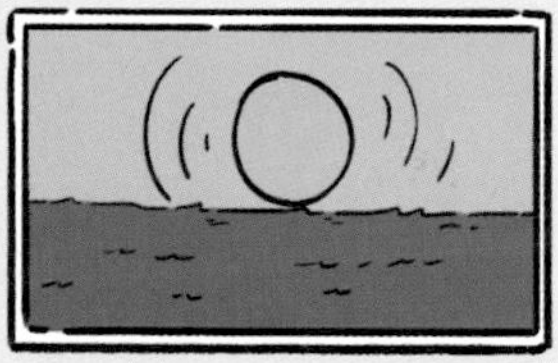

The index arm moves so the image of the sun can align with the horizon in the reflection.

The angle between the sun and horizon can be read off of the graduated arc to help calculate your location.

The sextant helps sailors navigate while at sea, and has been used for hundreds of years! Unfortunately for Vega...

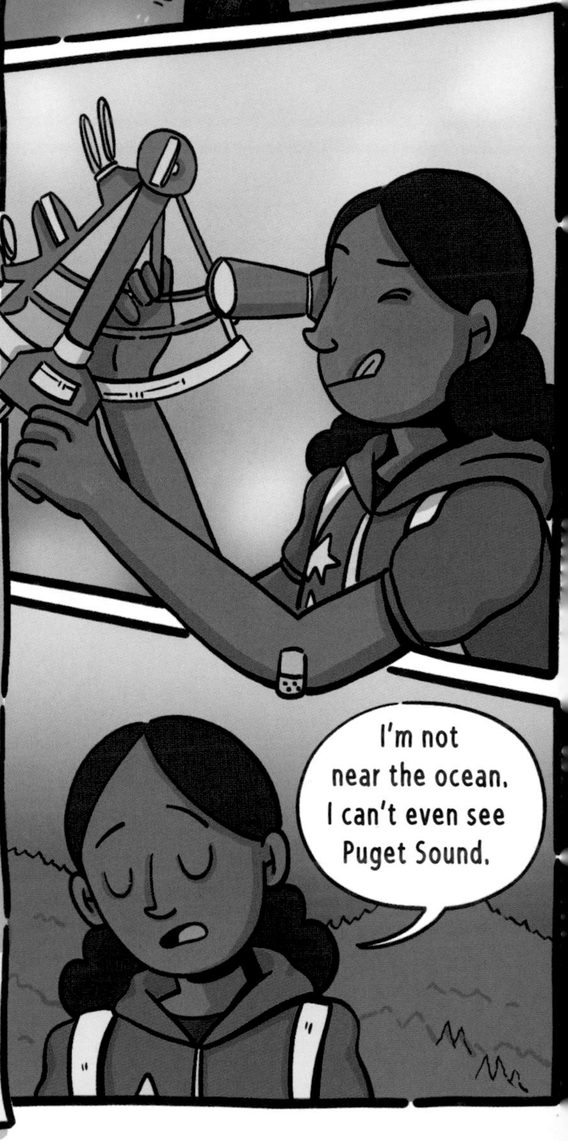
I'm not near the ocean. I can't even see Puget Sound.

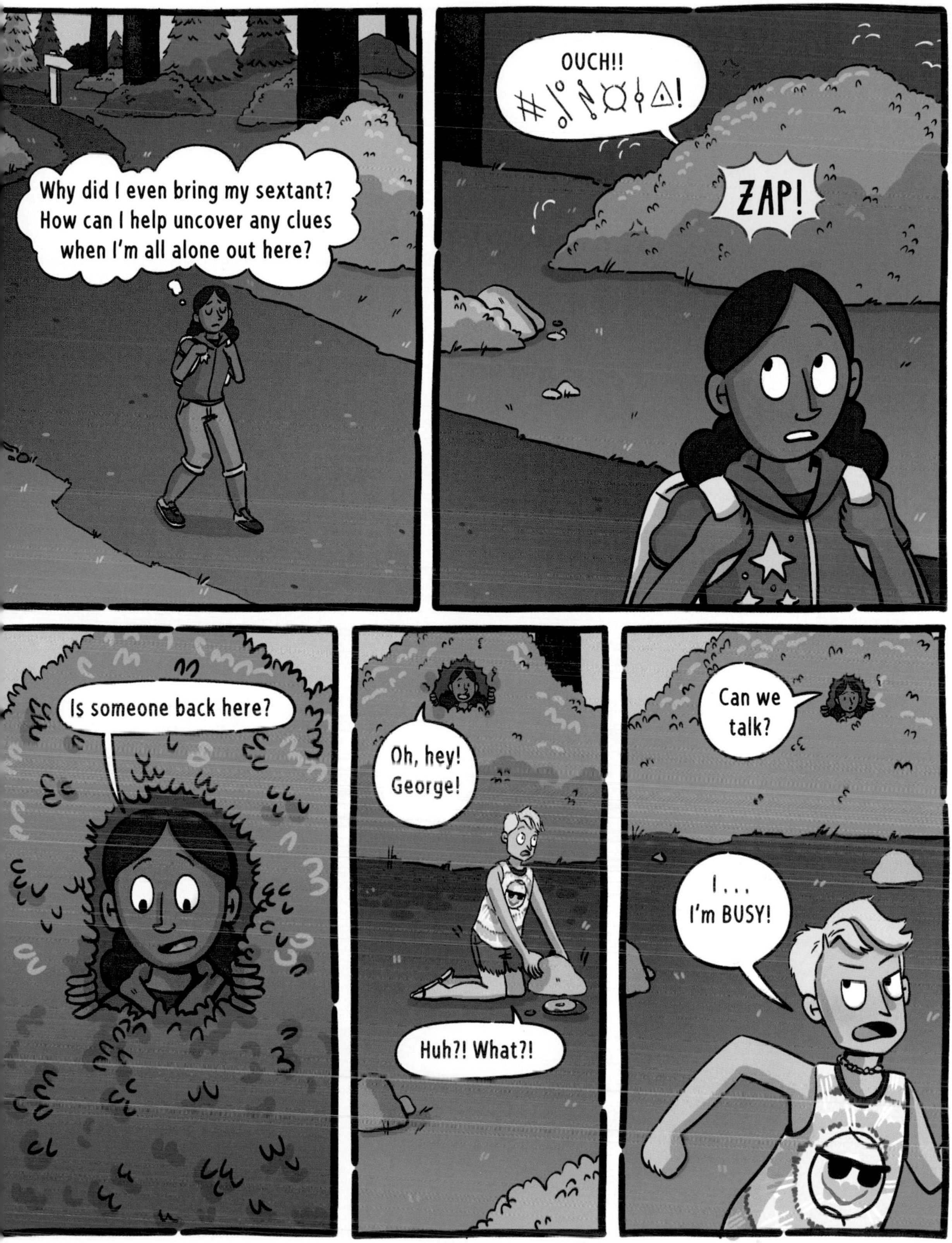
Why did I even bring my sextant? How can I help uncover any clues when I'm all alone out here?
OUCH!!
ZAP!
Is someone back here?
Oh, hey! George!
Huh?! What?!
Can we talk?
I . . . I'm BUSY!

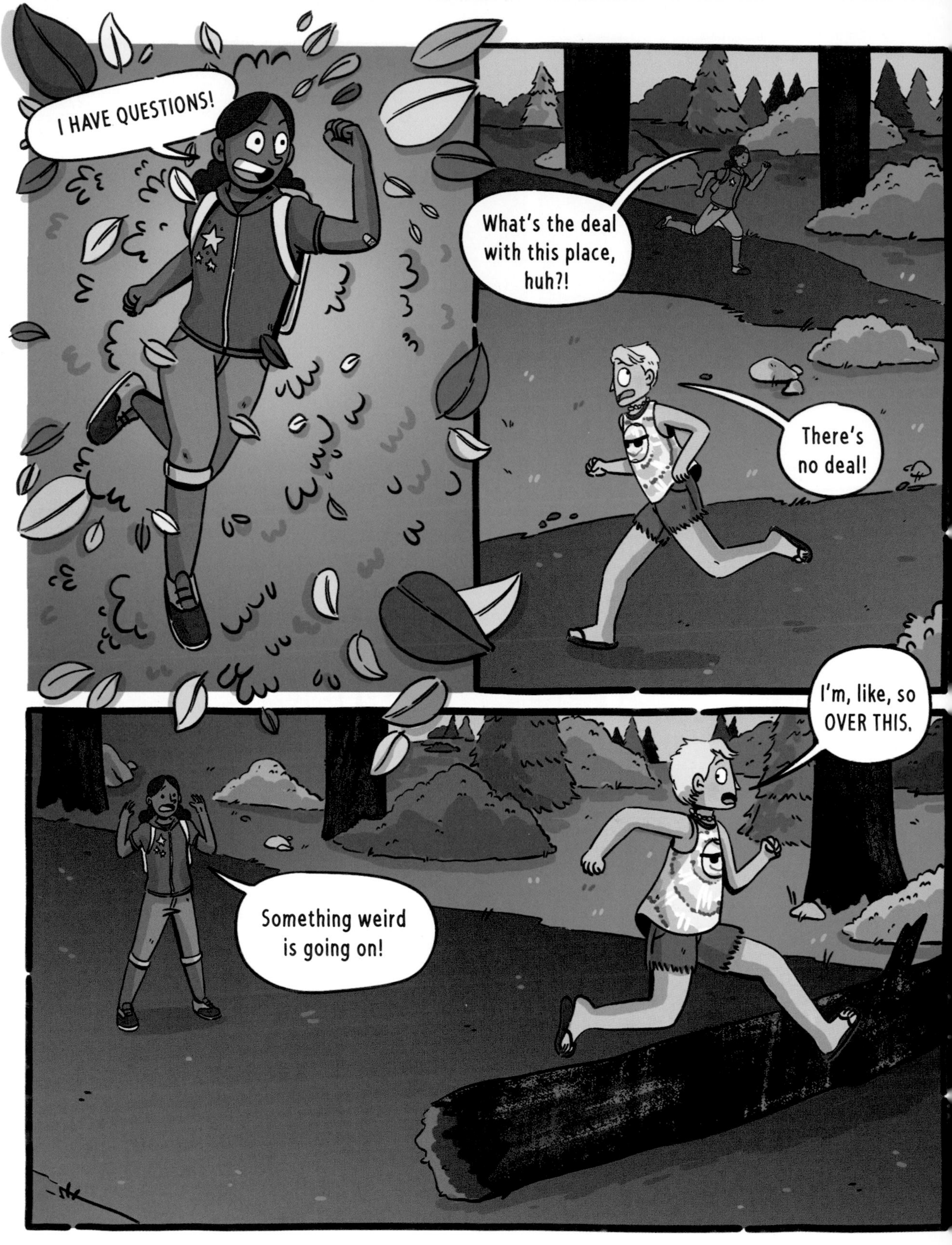
I HAVE QUESTIONS!
What's the deal with this place, huh?!
There's no deal!
I'm, like, so OVER THIS.
Something weird is going on!

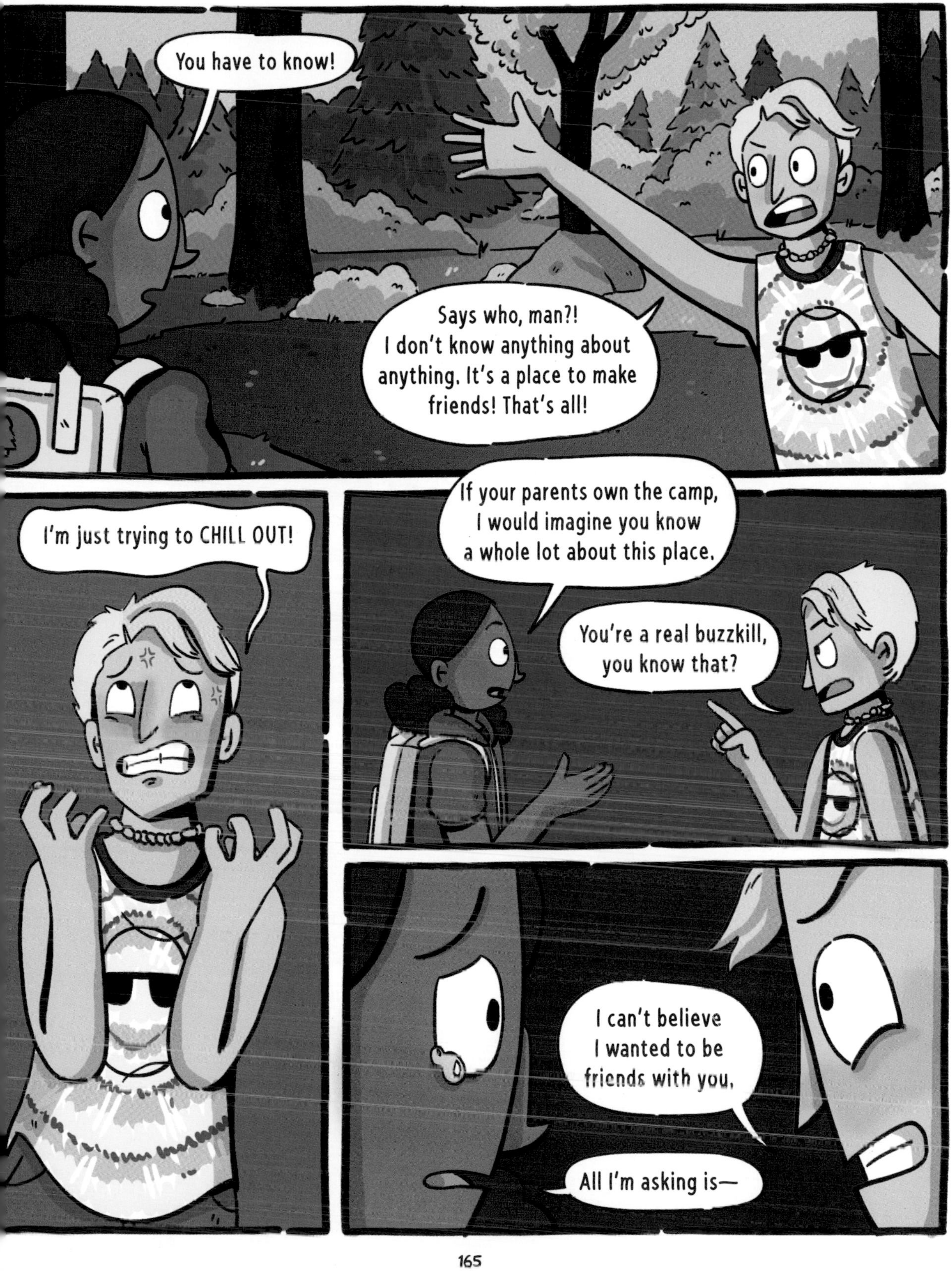
You have to know!
Says who, man?! I don't know anything about anything. It's a place to make friends! That's all!
I'm just trying to CHILL OUT!
If your parents own the camp, I would imagine you know a whole lot about this place.
You're a real buzzkill, you know that?
I can't believe I wanted to be friends with you.
All I'm asking is—

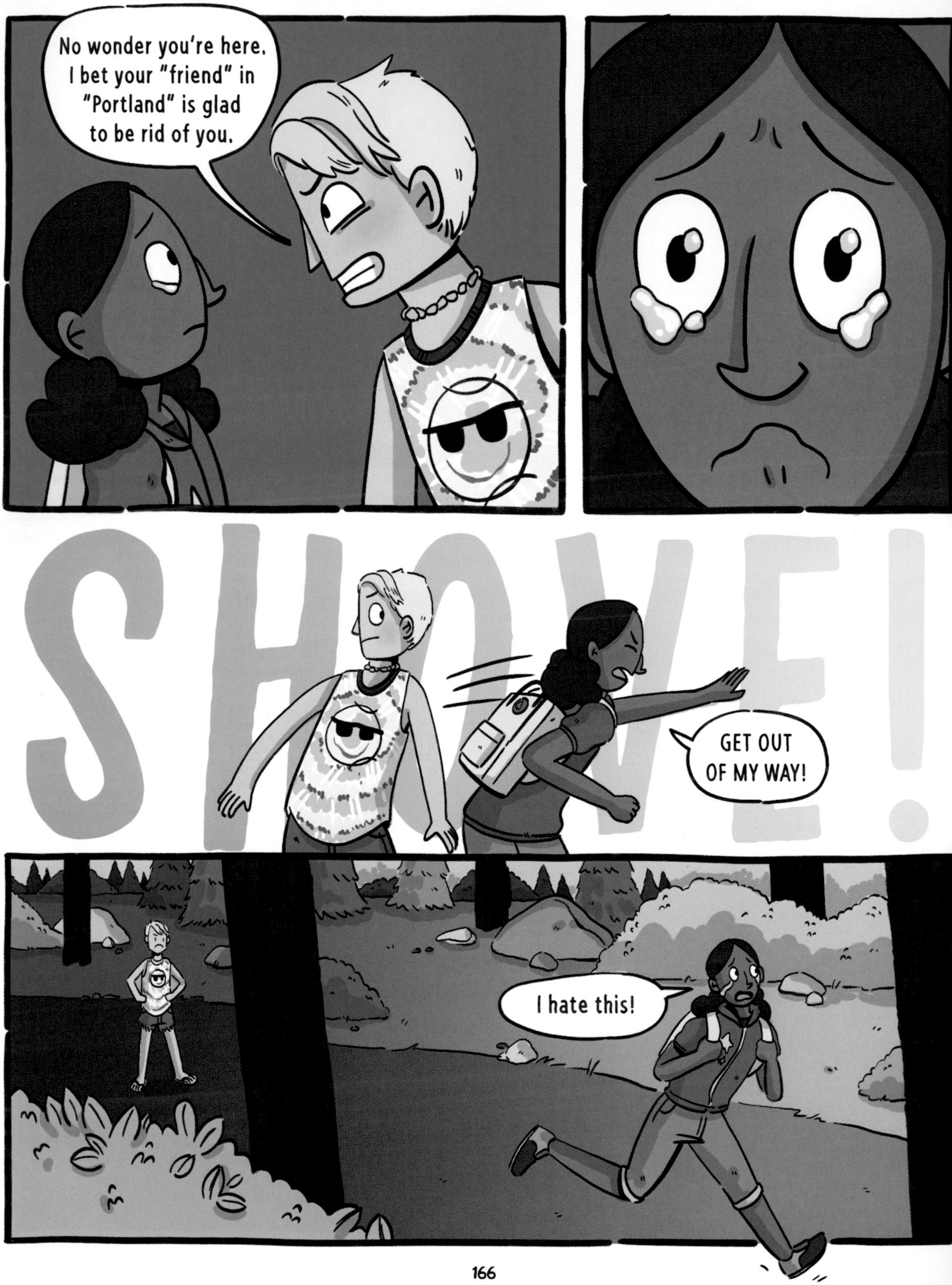
No wonder you're here. I bet your "friend" in "Portland" is glad to be rid of you.
SHOVE!
GET OUT OF MY WAY!
I hate this!

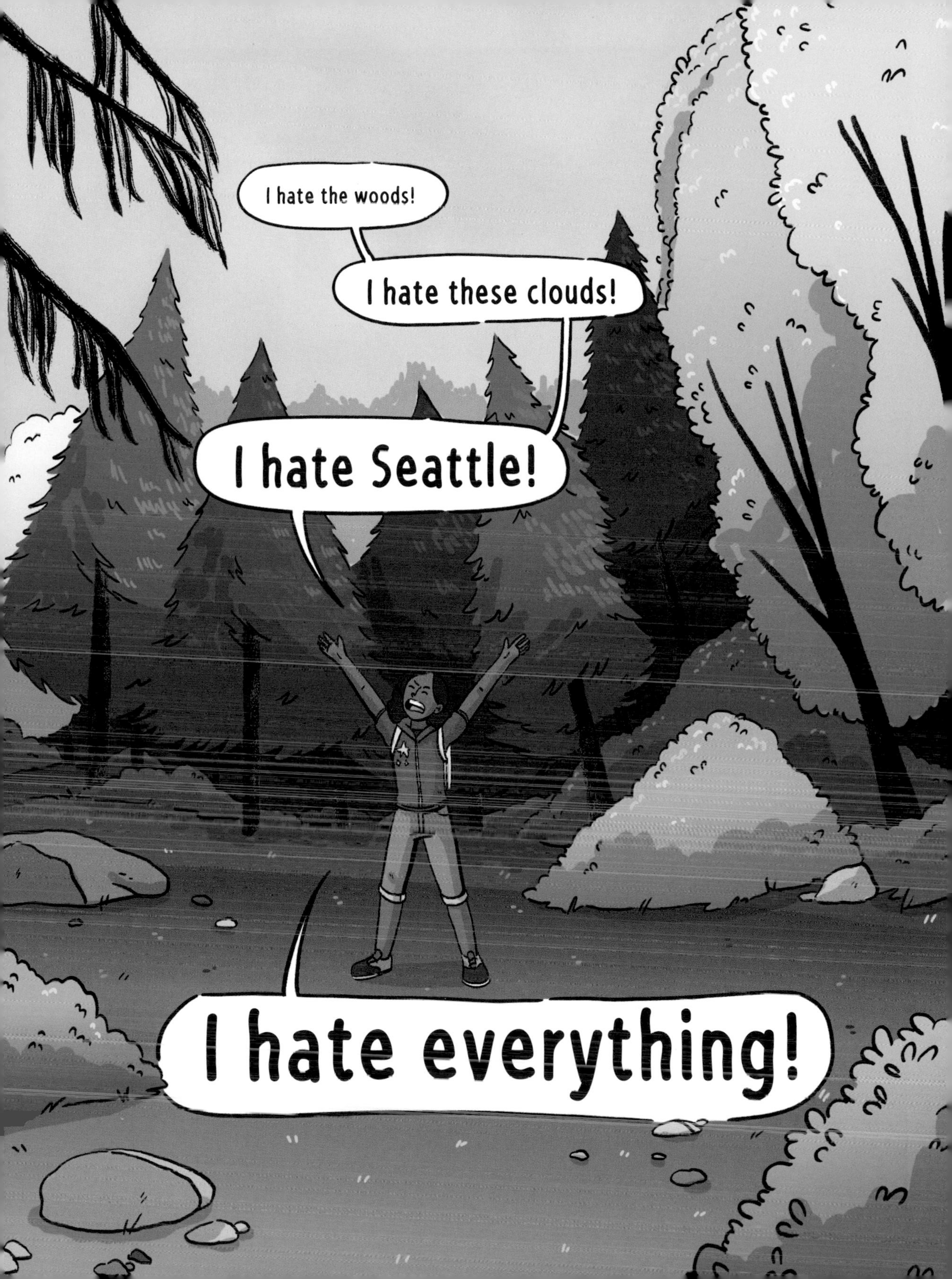
I hate the woods!
I hate these clouds!
I hate Seattle!
I hate everything!

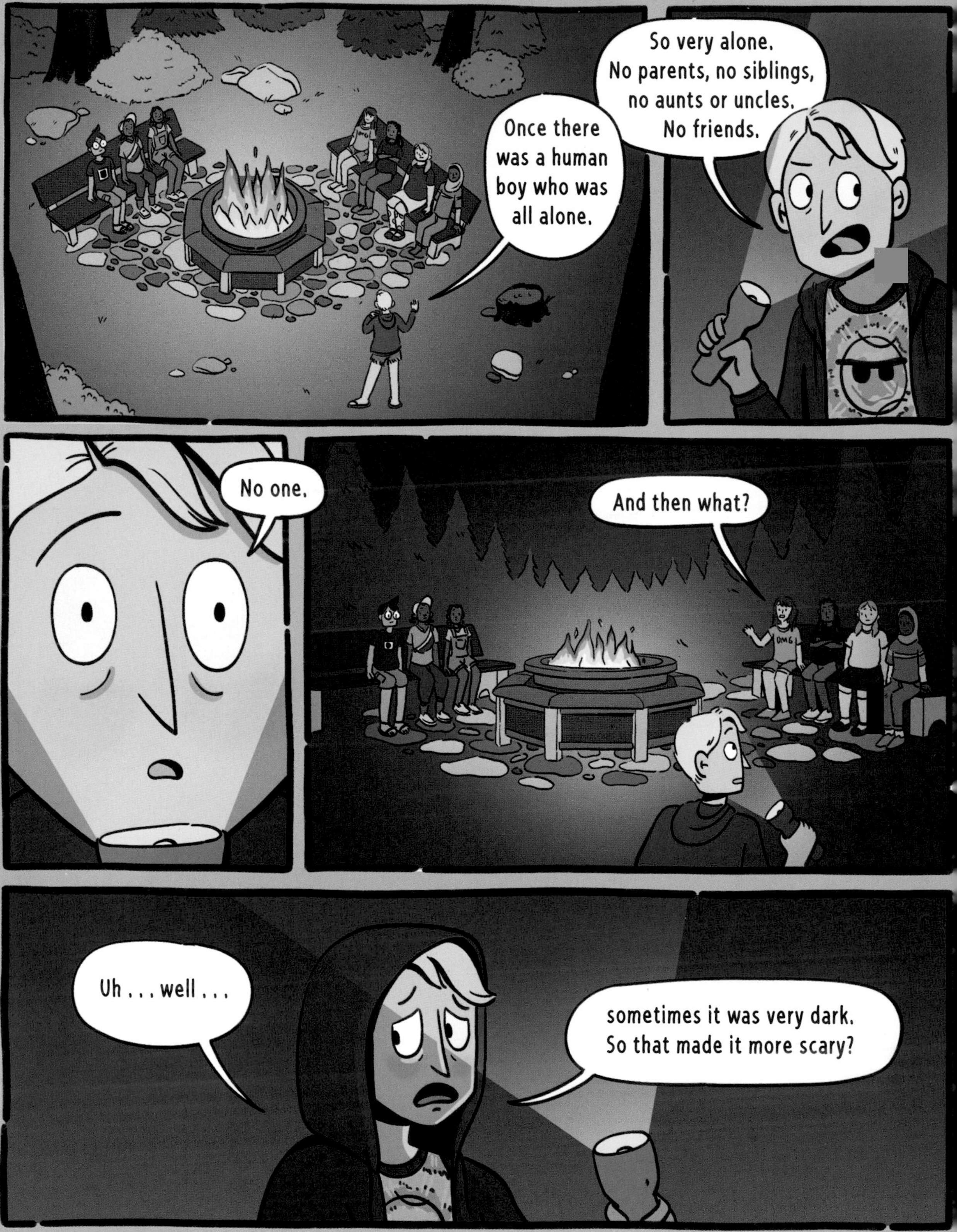

Once there was a human boy who was all alone.
So very alone. No parents, no siblings, no aunts or uncles. No friends.
No one.
And then what?
Uh . . . well . . .
sometimes it was very dark. So that made it more scary?

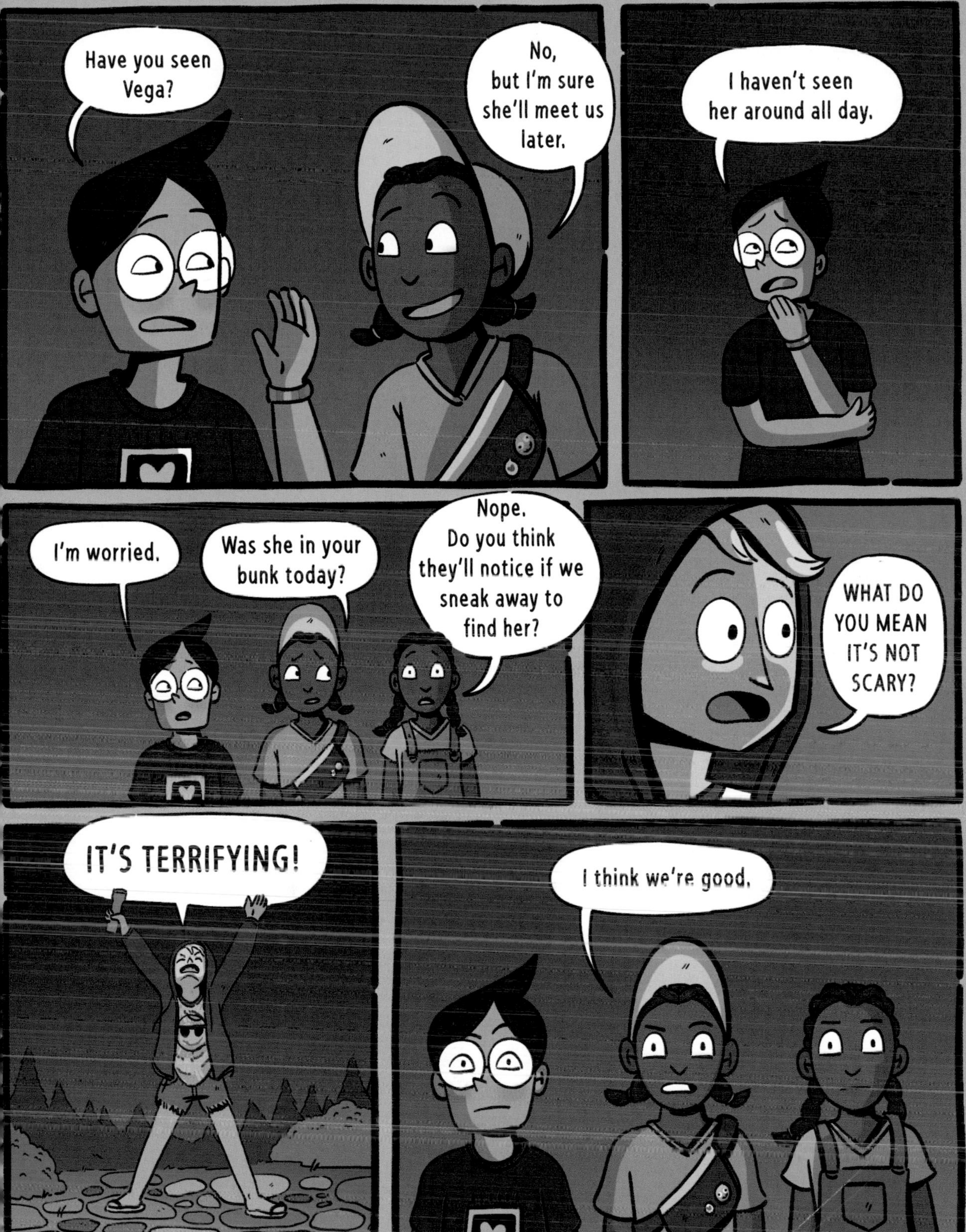
Have you seen Vega?
No, but I'm sure she'll meet us later.
I haven't seen her around all day.
I'm worried.
Was she in your bunk today?
Nope. Do you think they'll notice if we sneak away to find her?
WHAT DO YOU MEAN IT'S NOT SCARY?
IT'S TERRIFYING!
I think we're good.

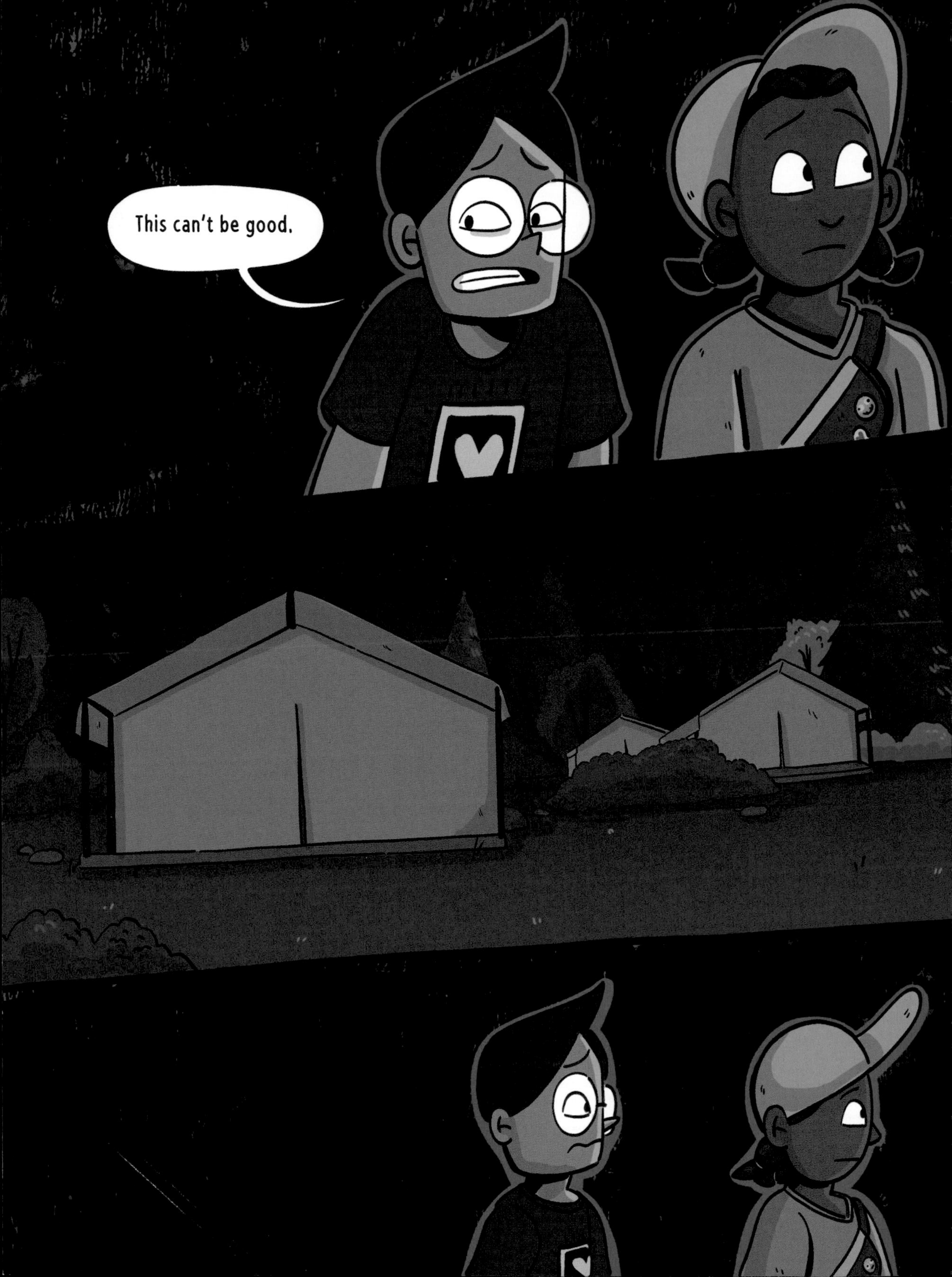
This can't be good.

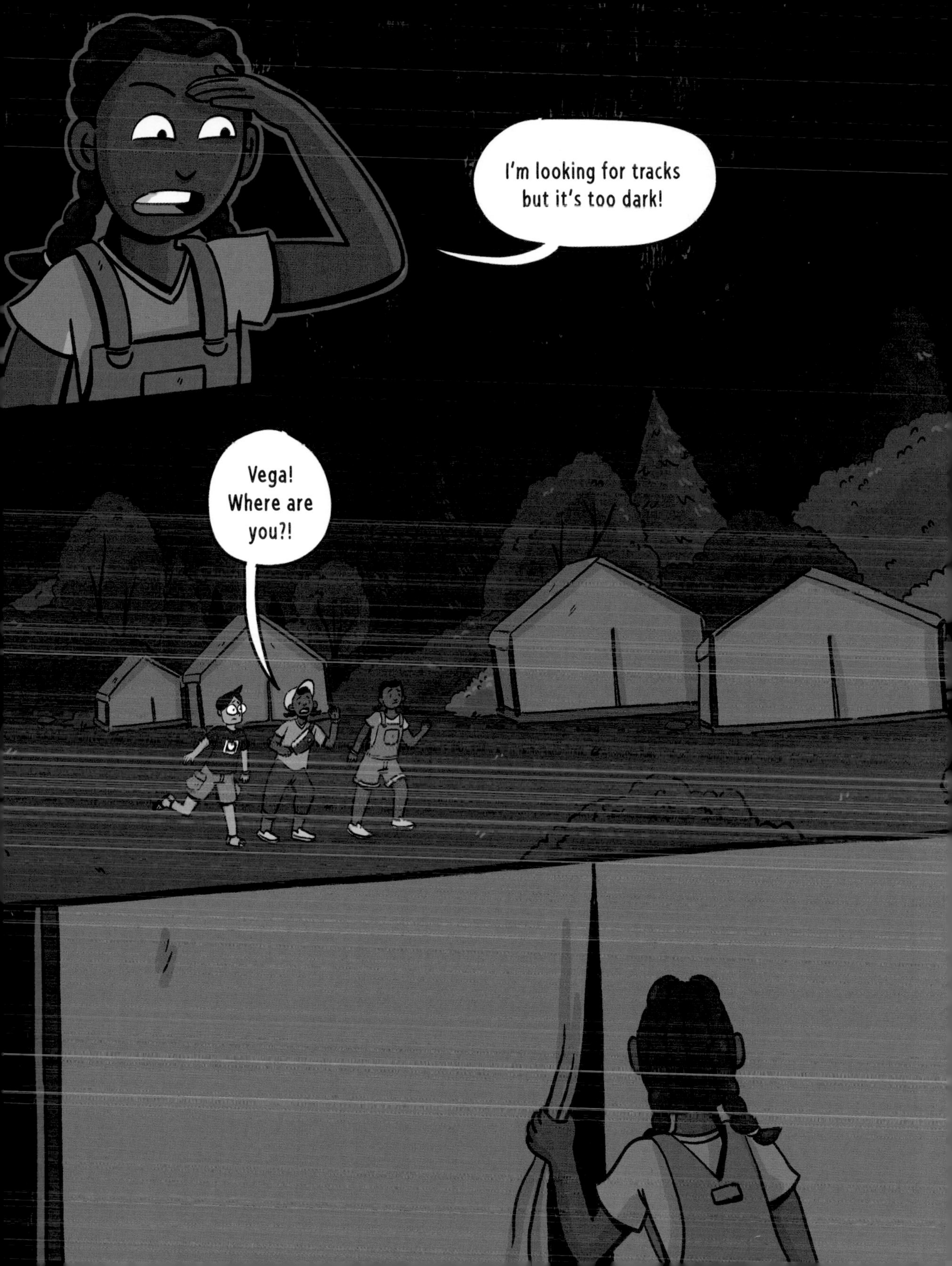
I'm looking for tracks but it's too dark!
Vega! Where are you?!

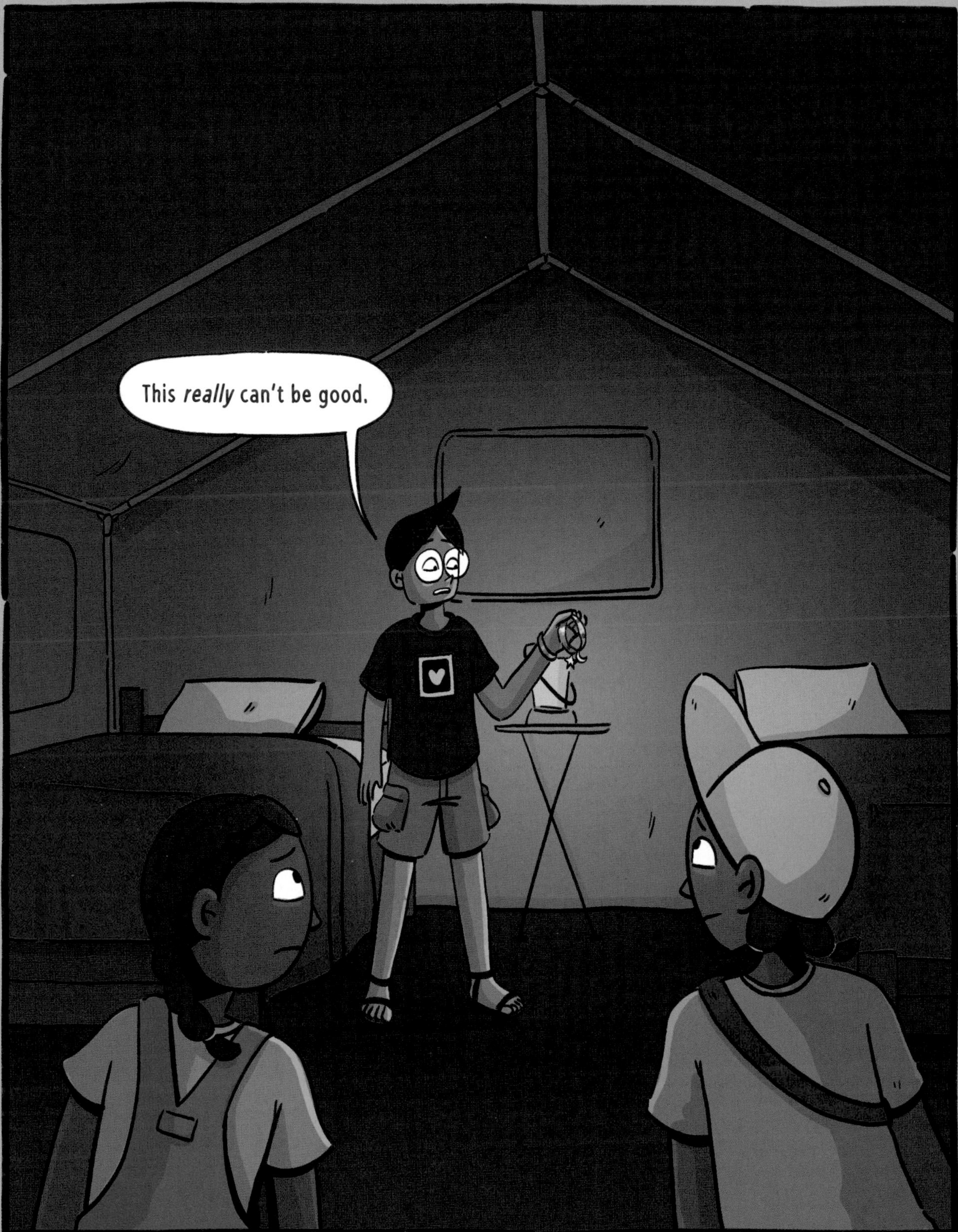
This *really* can't be good.

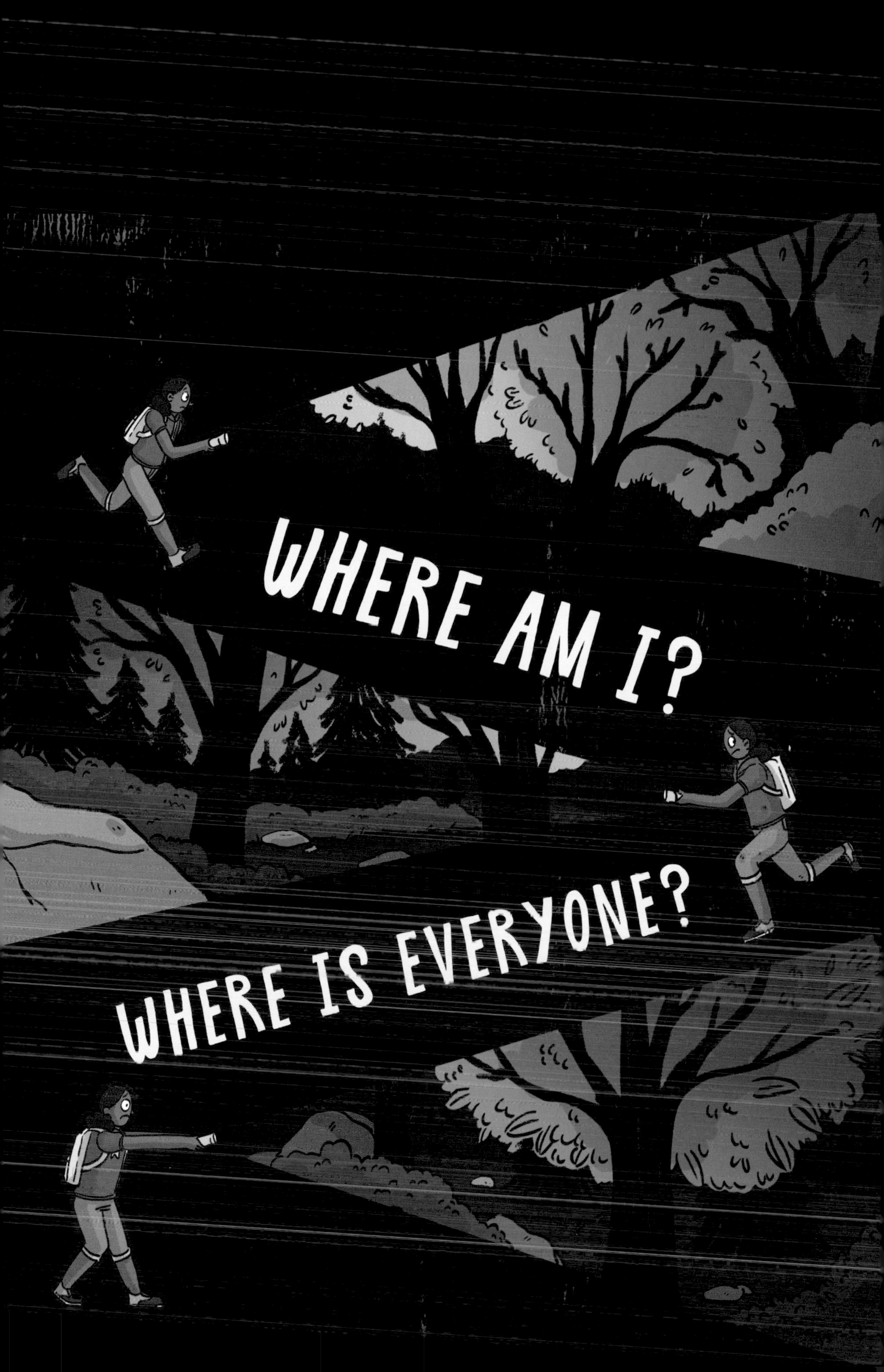
WHERE AM I?
WHERE IS EVERYONE?

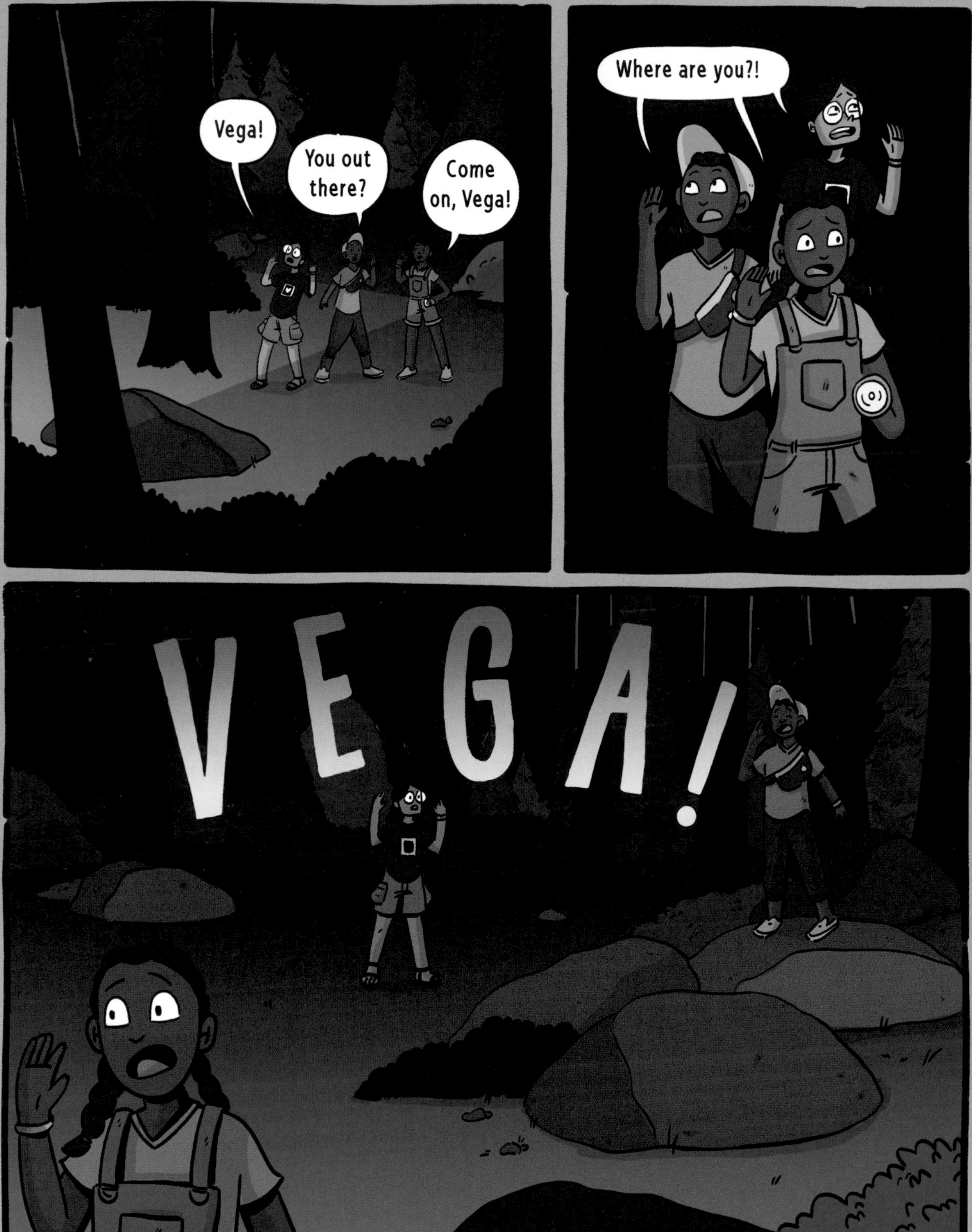
Vega!
You out there?
Come on, Vega!
Where are you?!
VEGA!

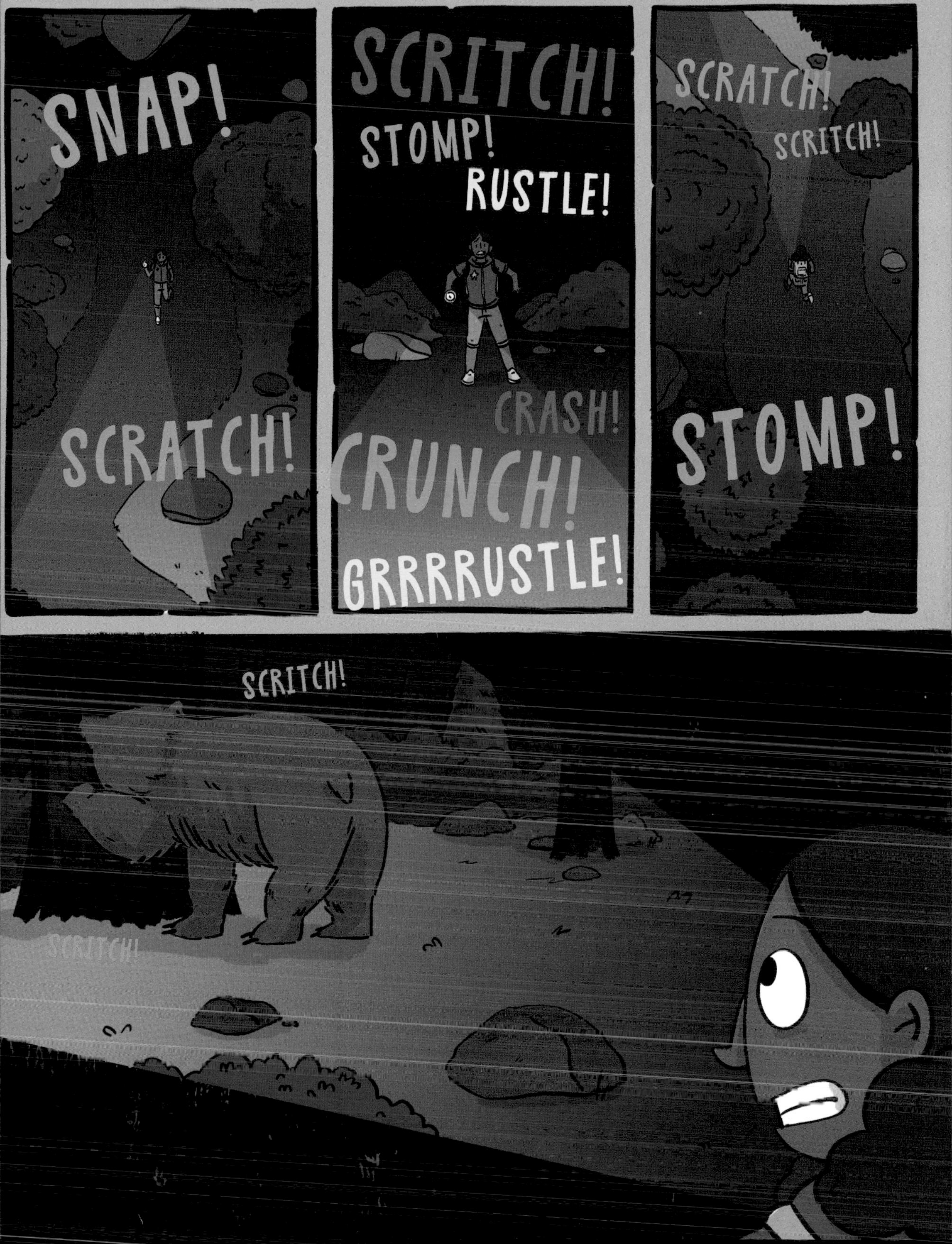
SNAP!
SCRATCH!
SCRITCH!
STOMP!
RUSTLE!
CRASH!
CRUNCH!
GRRRRRUSTLE!
SCRATCH!
SCRITCH!
STOMP!
SCRITCH!
SCRITCH!

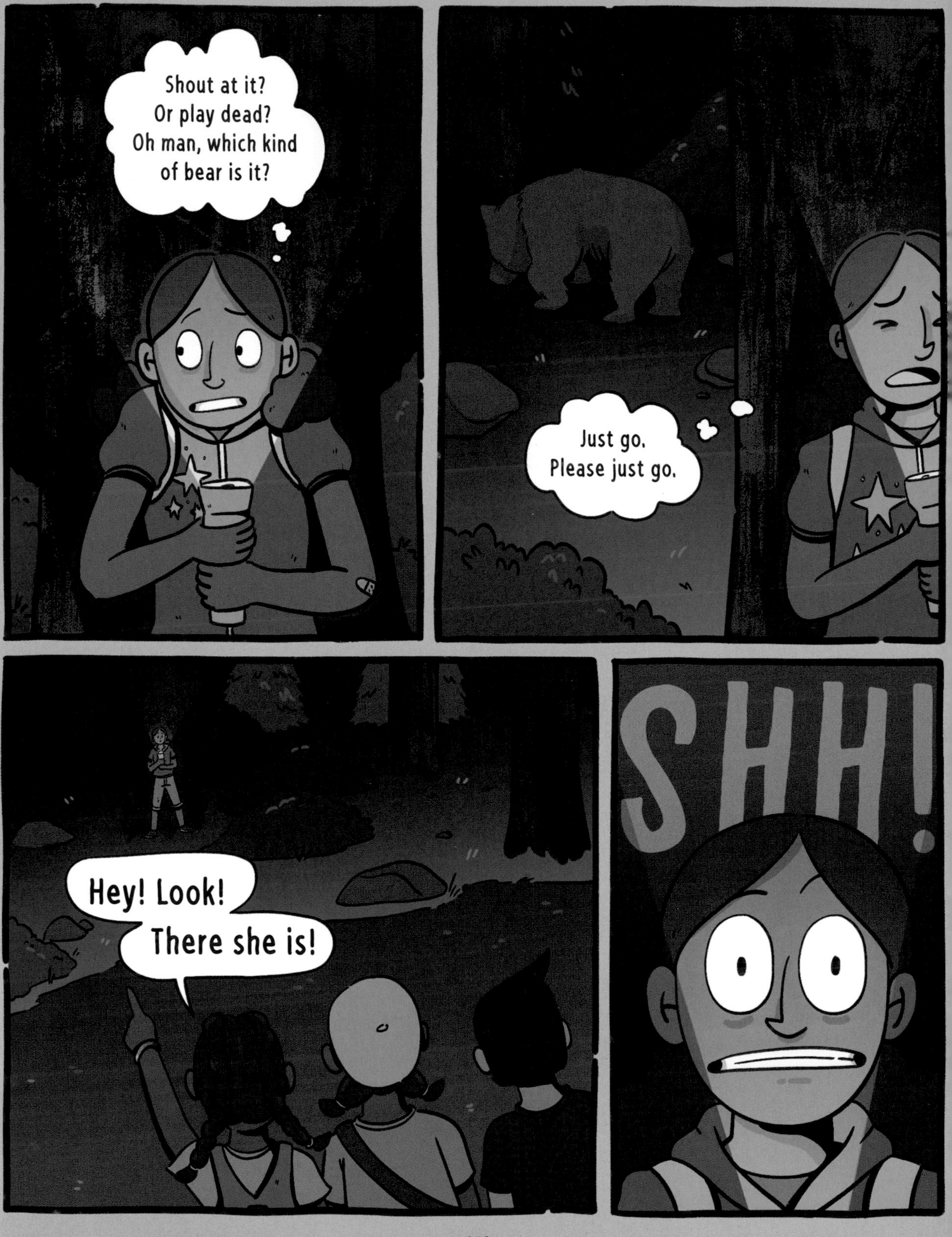
Shout at it? Or play dead? Oh man, which kind of bear is it?
Just go. Please just go.
Hey! Look!
There she is!
SHH!

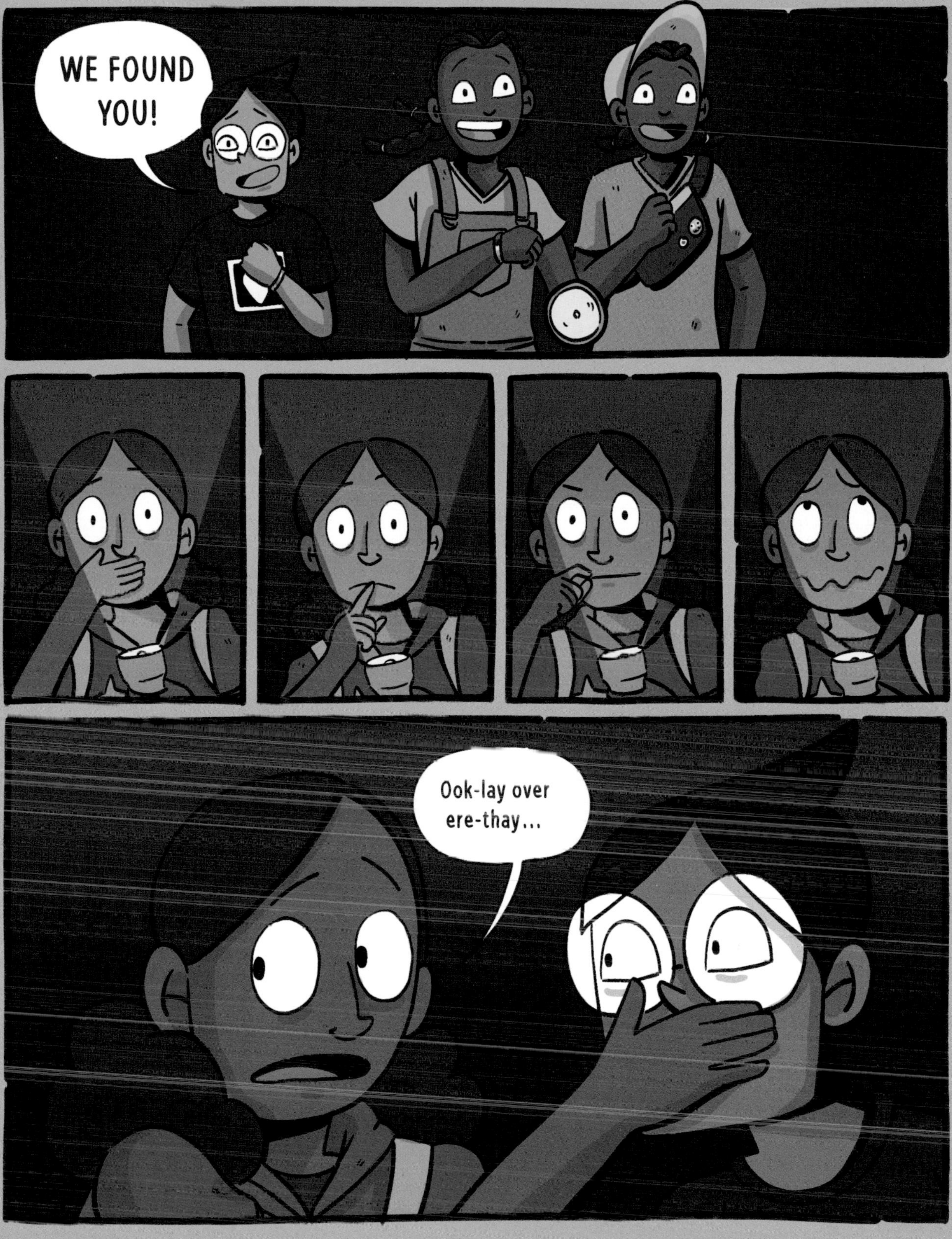
WE FOUND YOU!
Ook-lay over ere-thay...

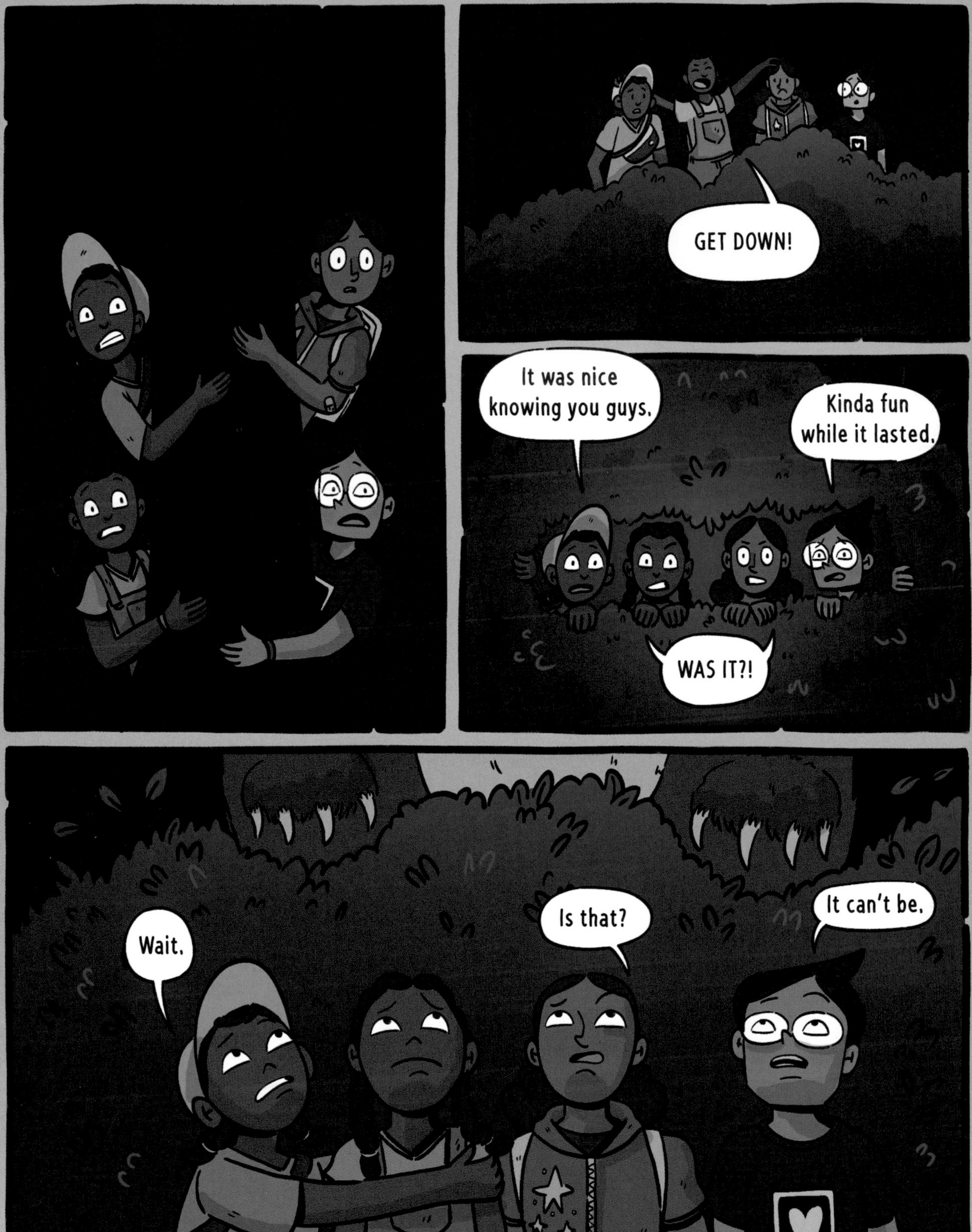
GET DOWN!
It was nice knowing you guys.
Kinda fun while it lasted.
WAS IT?!
Wait.
Is that?
It can't be.

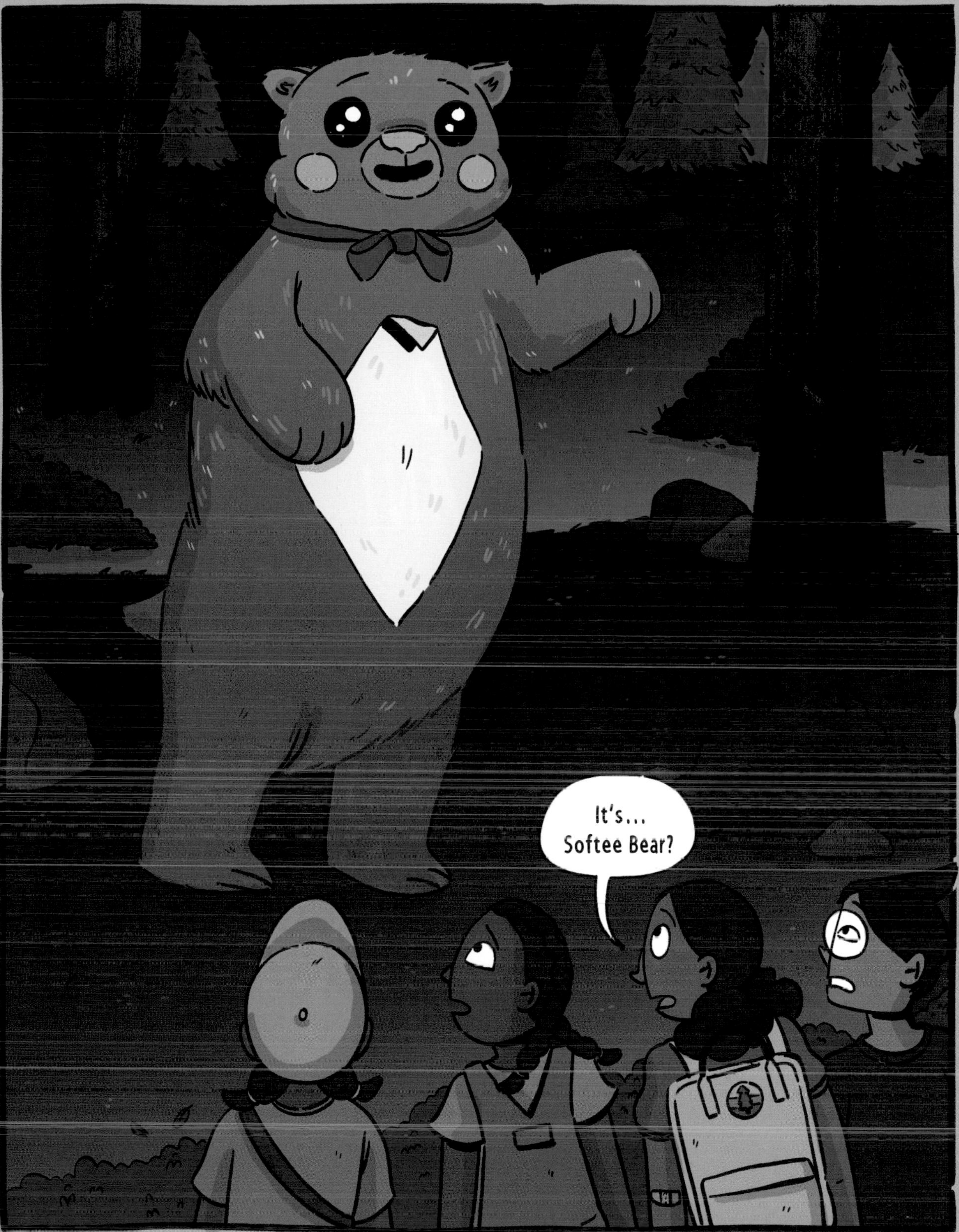
It's...
Softee Bear?

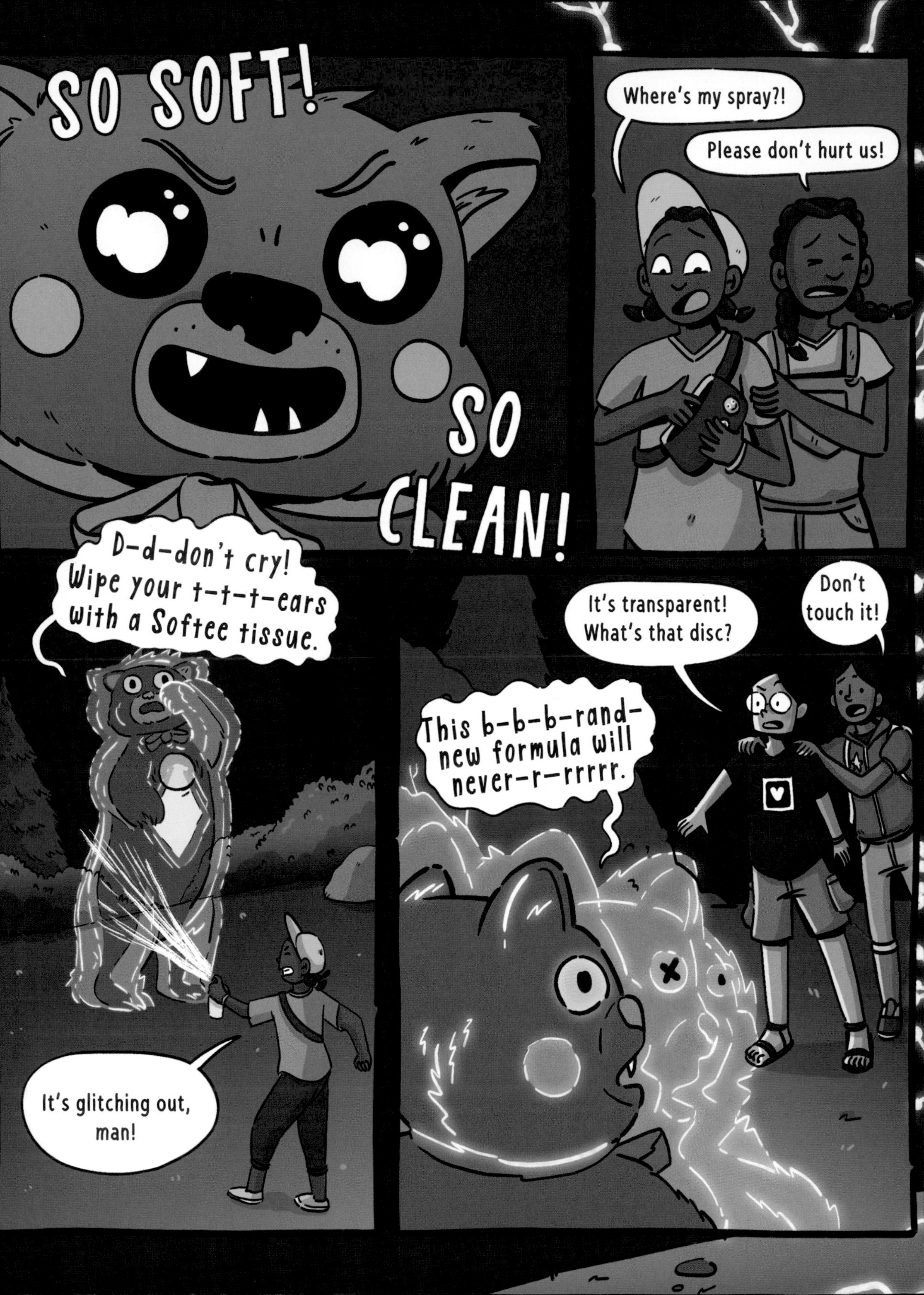
SO SOFT!
SO CLEAN!
Where's my spray?!
Please don't hurt us!
D-d-don't cry! Wipe your t-t-t-ears with a Softee tissue.
It's glitching out, man!
This b-b-b-rand-new formula will never-r-rrrrr.
It's transparent! What's that disc?
Don't touch it!

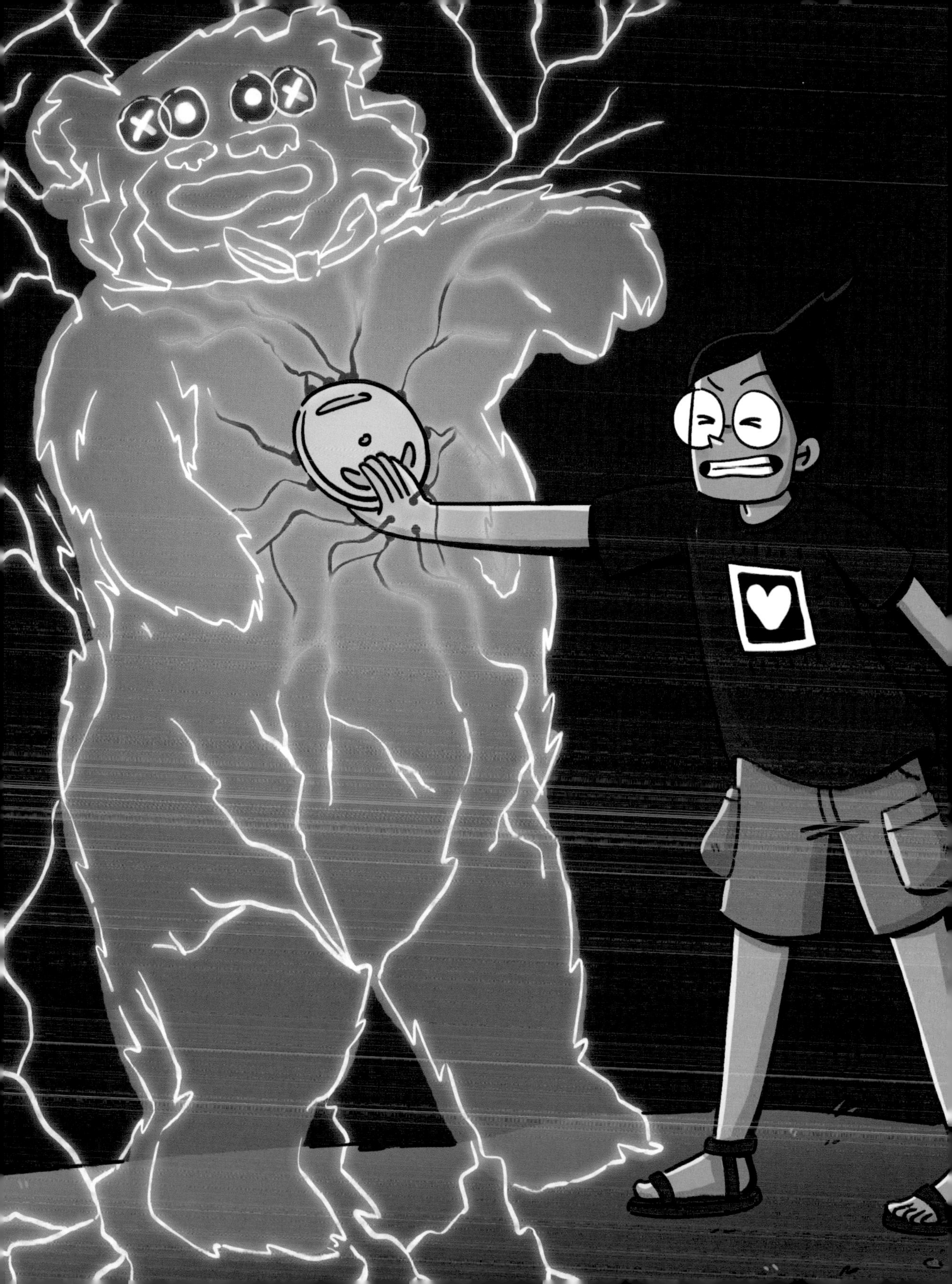

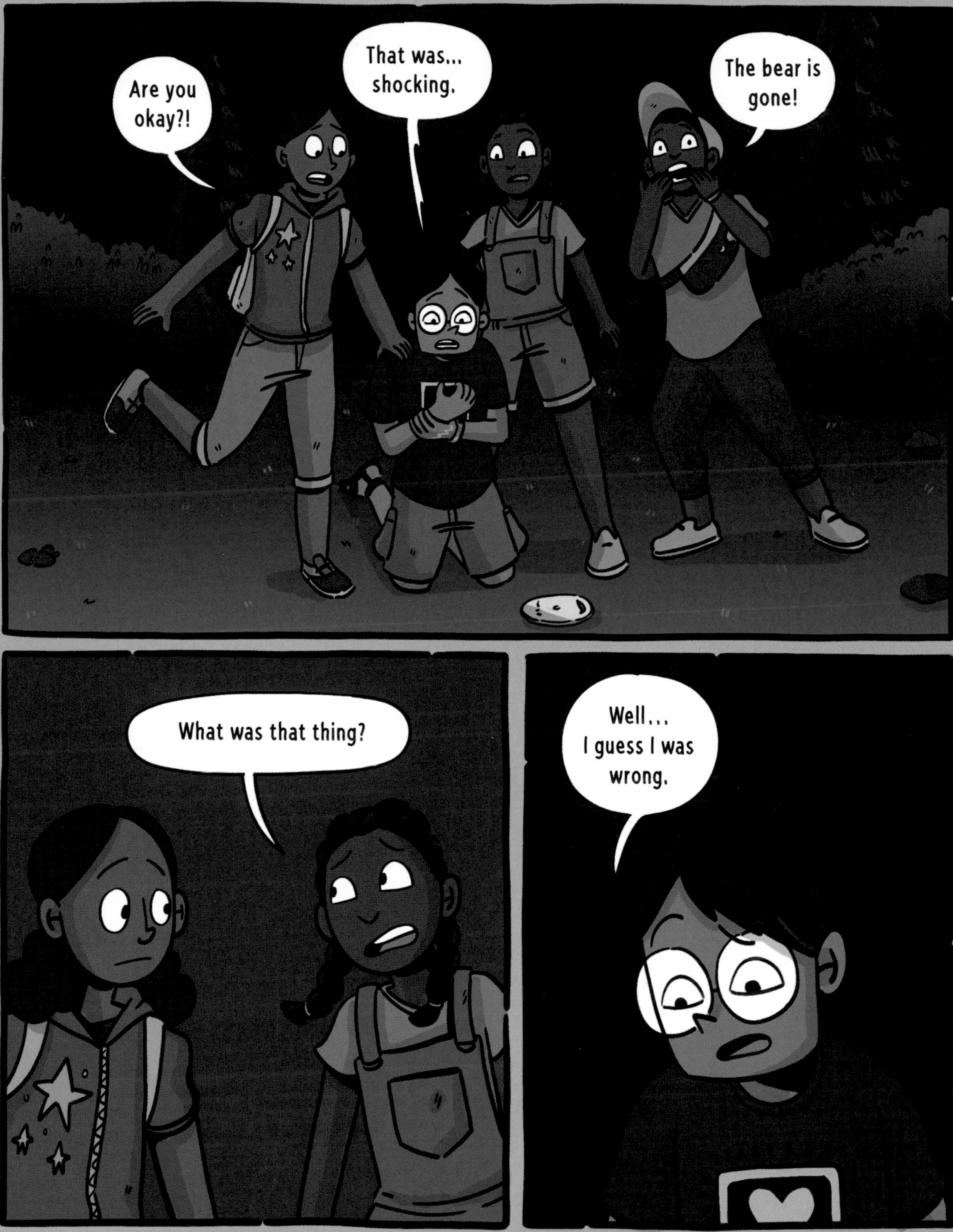

Are you okay?!
That was... shocking.
The bear is gone!
What was that thing?
Well... I guess I was wrong.

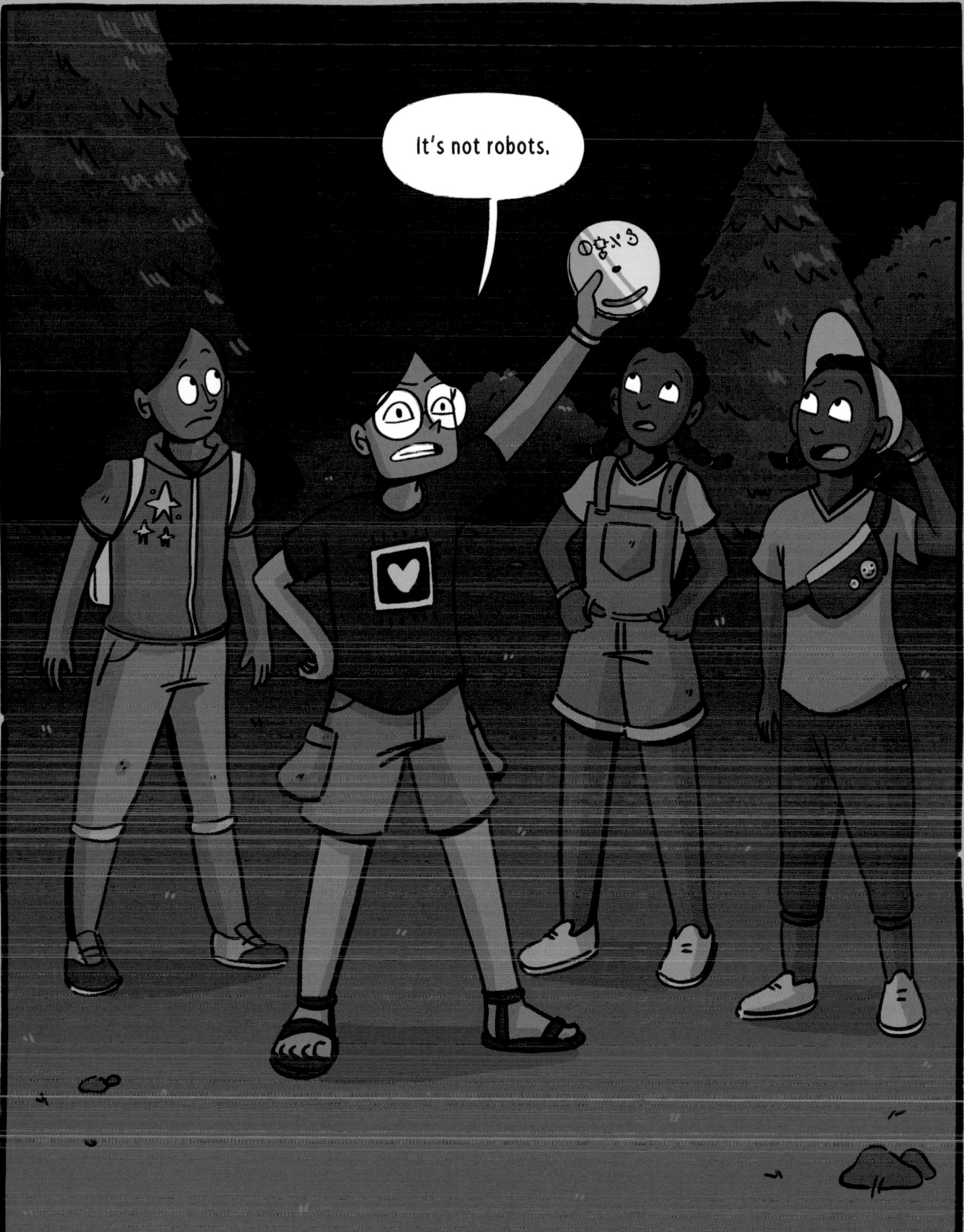
It's not robots.

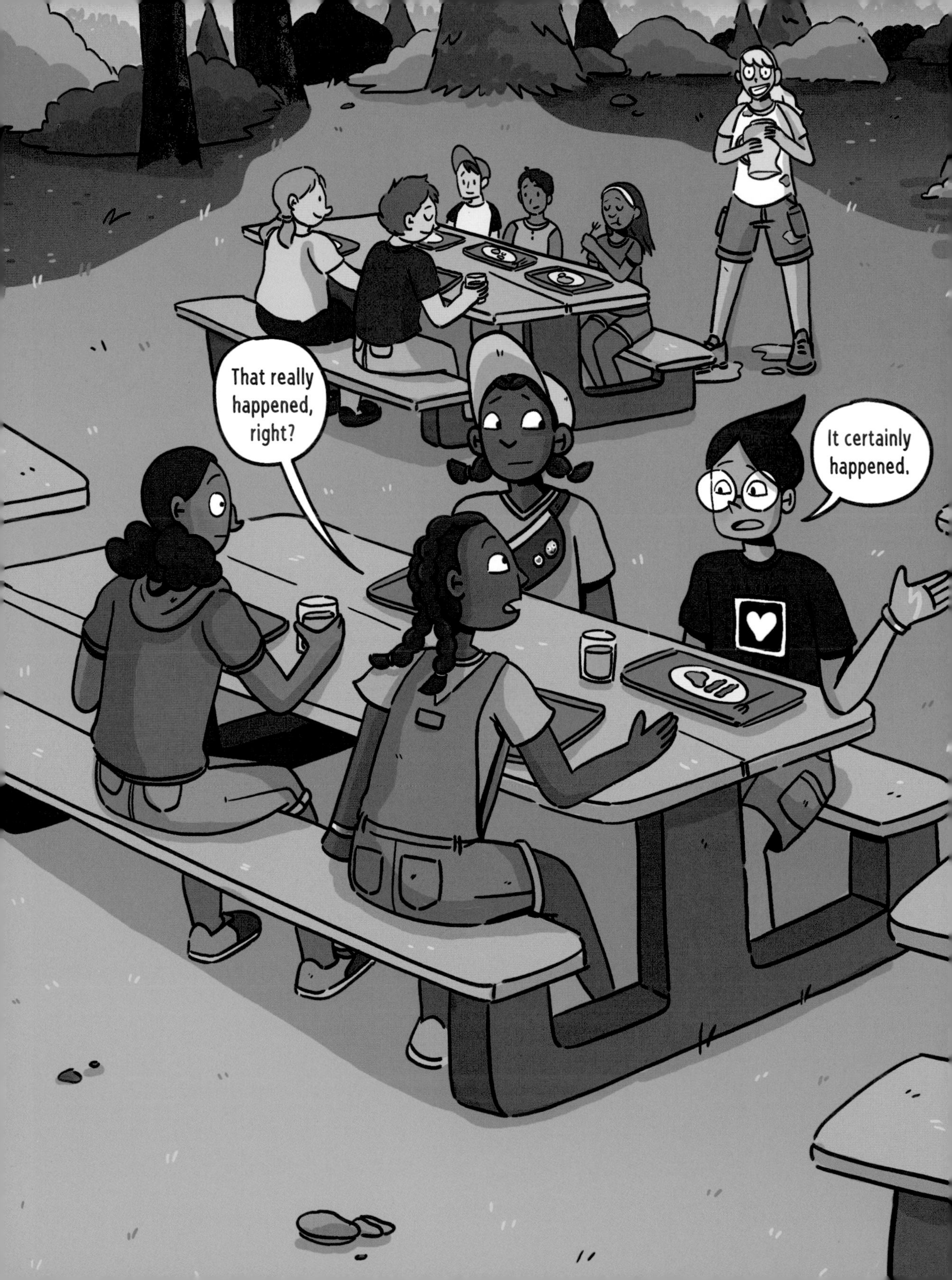
That really happened, right?
It certainly happened.

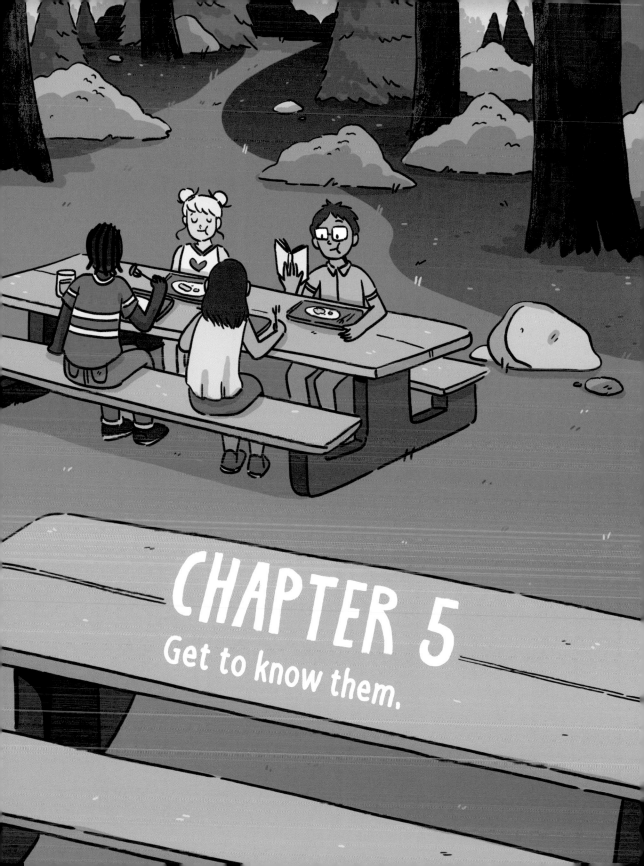

CHAPTER 5
Get to know them.

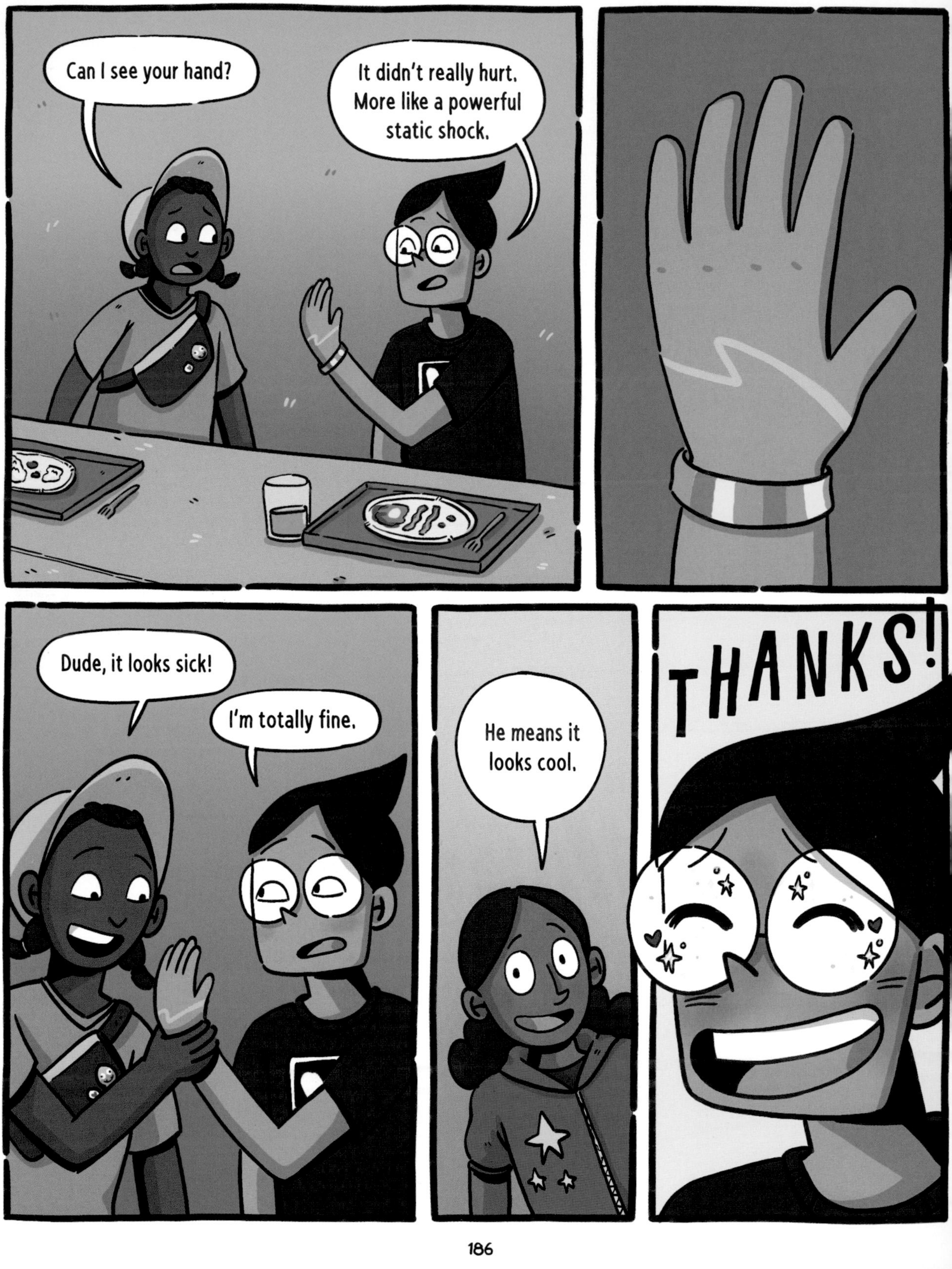
Can I see your hand?
It didn't really hurt. More like a powerful static shock.
Dude, it looks sick!
I'm totally fine.
He means it looks cool.
THANKS!

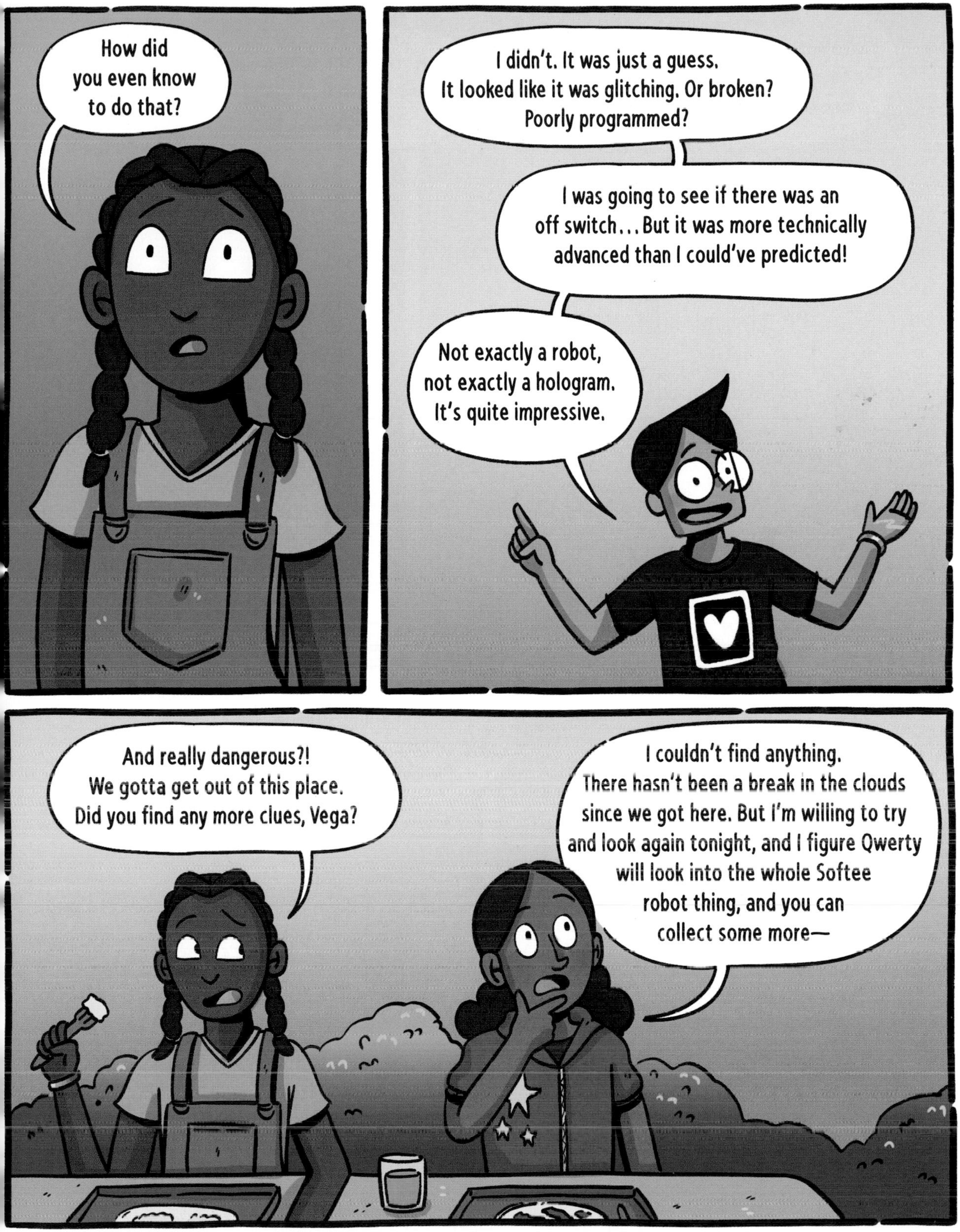
How did you even know to do that?
I didn't. It was just a guess. It looked like it was glitching. Or broken? Poorly programmed?
I was going to see if there was an off switch...But it was more technically advanced than I could've predicted!
Not exactly a robot, not exactly a hologram. It's quite impressive.
And really dangerous?! We gotta get out of this place. Did you find any more clues, Vega?
I couldn't find anything. There hasn't been a break in the clouds since we got here. But I'm willing to try and look again tonight, and I figure Qwerty will look into the whole Softee robot thing, and you can collect some more—

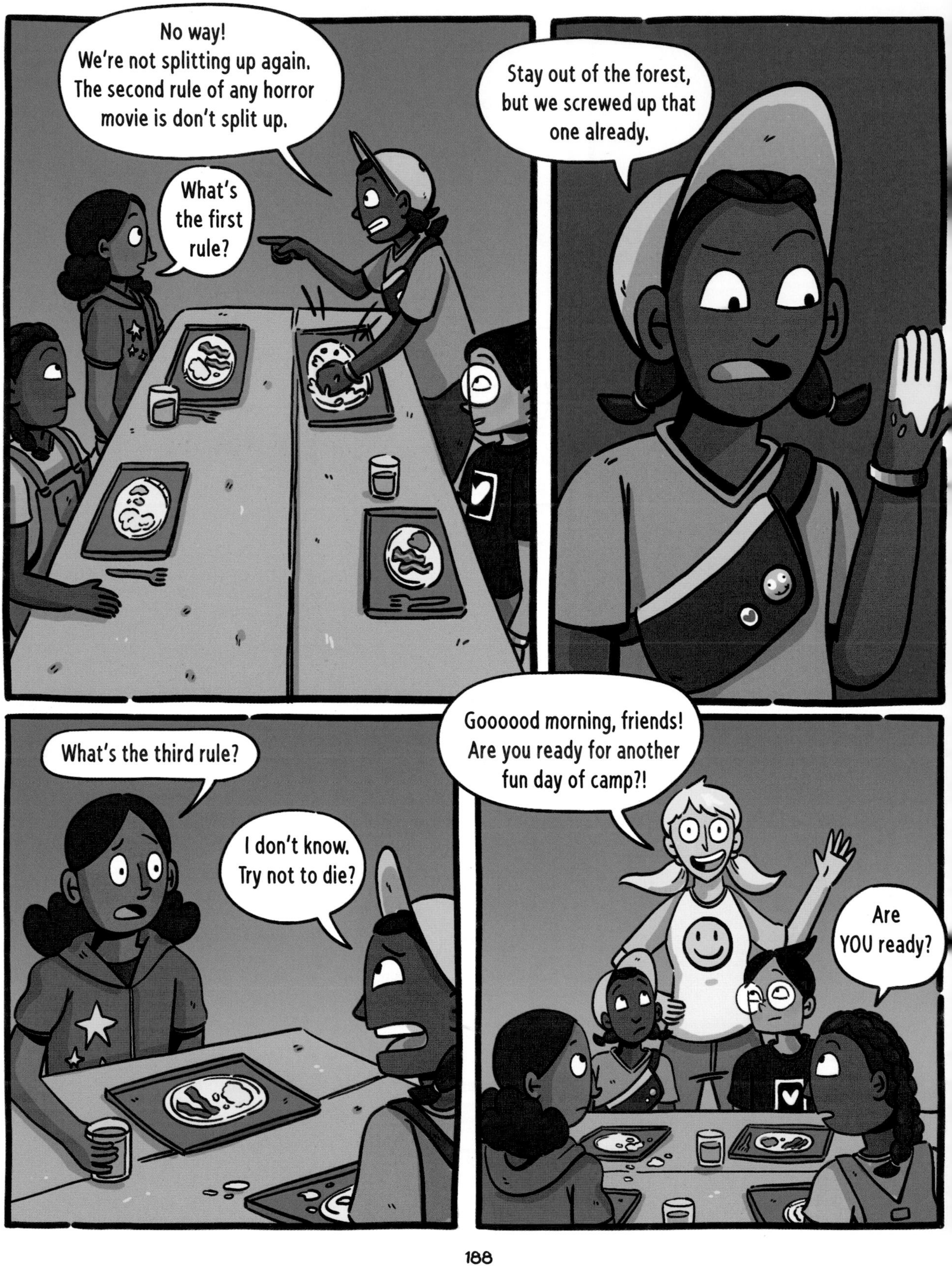
No way! We're not splitting up again. The second rule of any horror movie is don't split up.
What's the first rule?
Stay out of the forest, but we screwed up that one already.
What's the third rule?
I don't know. Try not to die?
Goooood morning, friends! Are you ready for another fun day of camp?!
Are YOU ready?

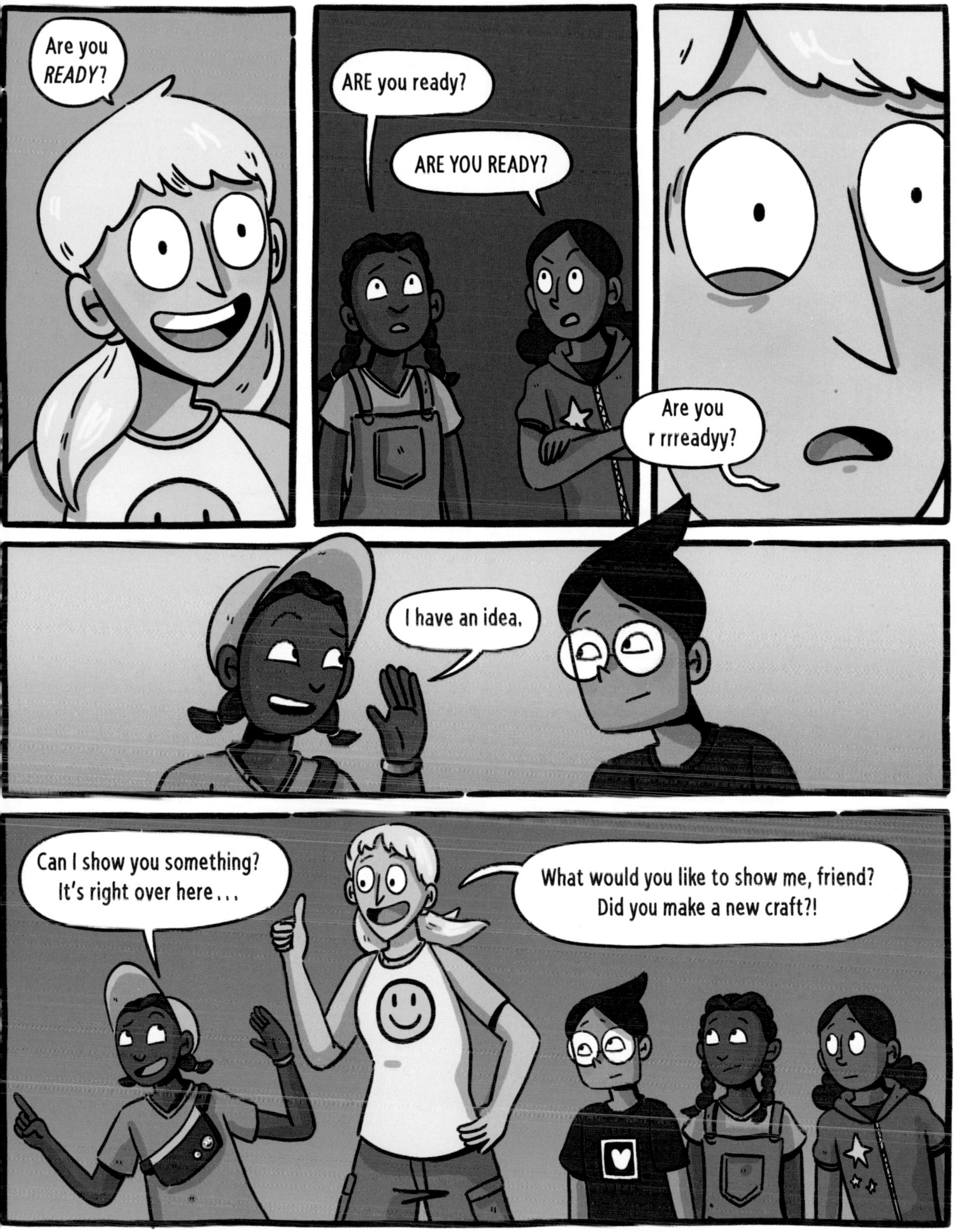
Are you *READY*?
ARE you ready?
ARE YOU READY?
Are you r rrreadyy?
I have an idea.
Can I show you something? It's right over here...
What would you like to show me, friend? Did you make a new craft?!

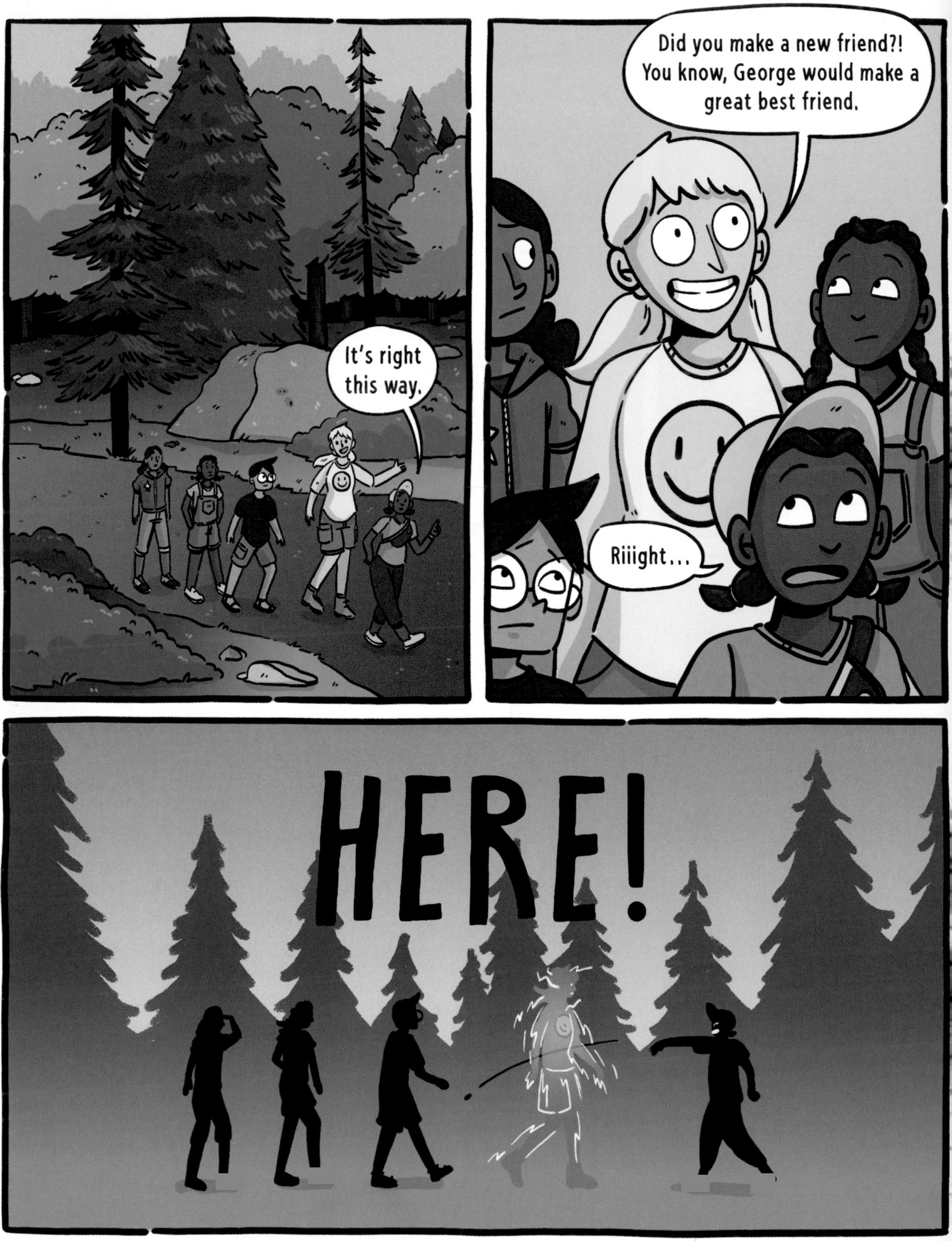
It's right this way.
Did you make a new friend?! You know, George would make a great best friend.
Riiight...
HERE!

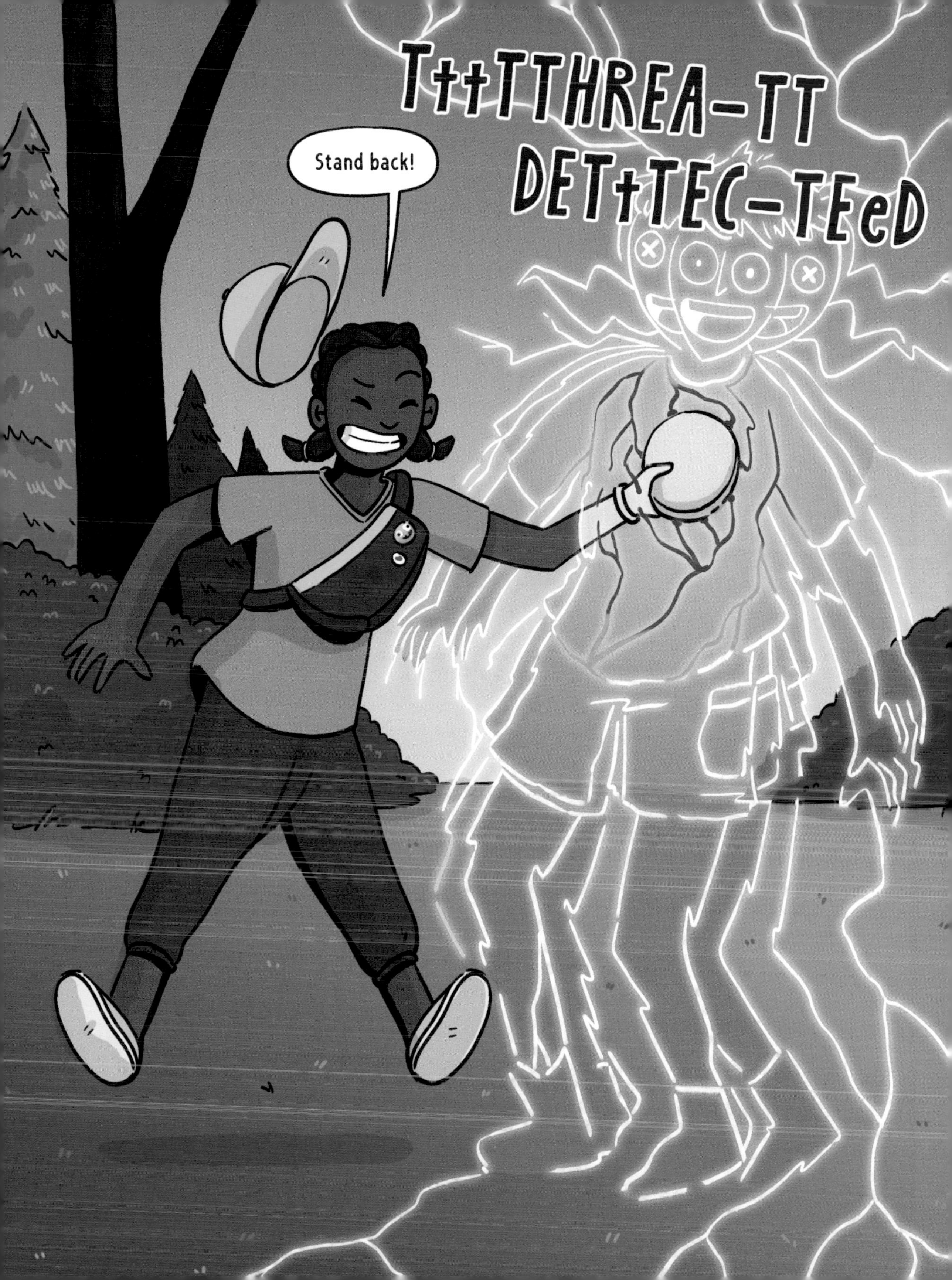
Stand back!
TttTTHREA-TT DETtTEC-TEeD

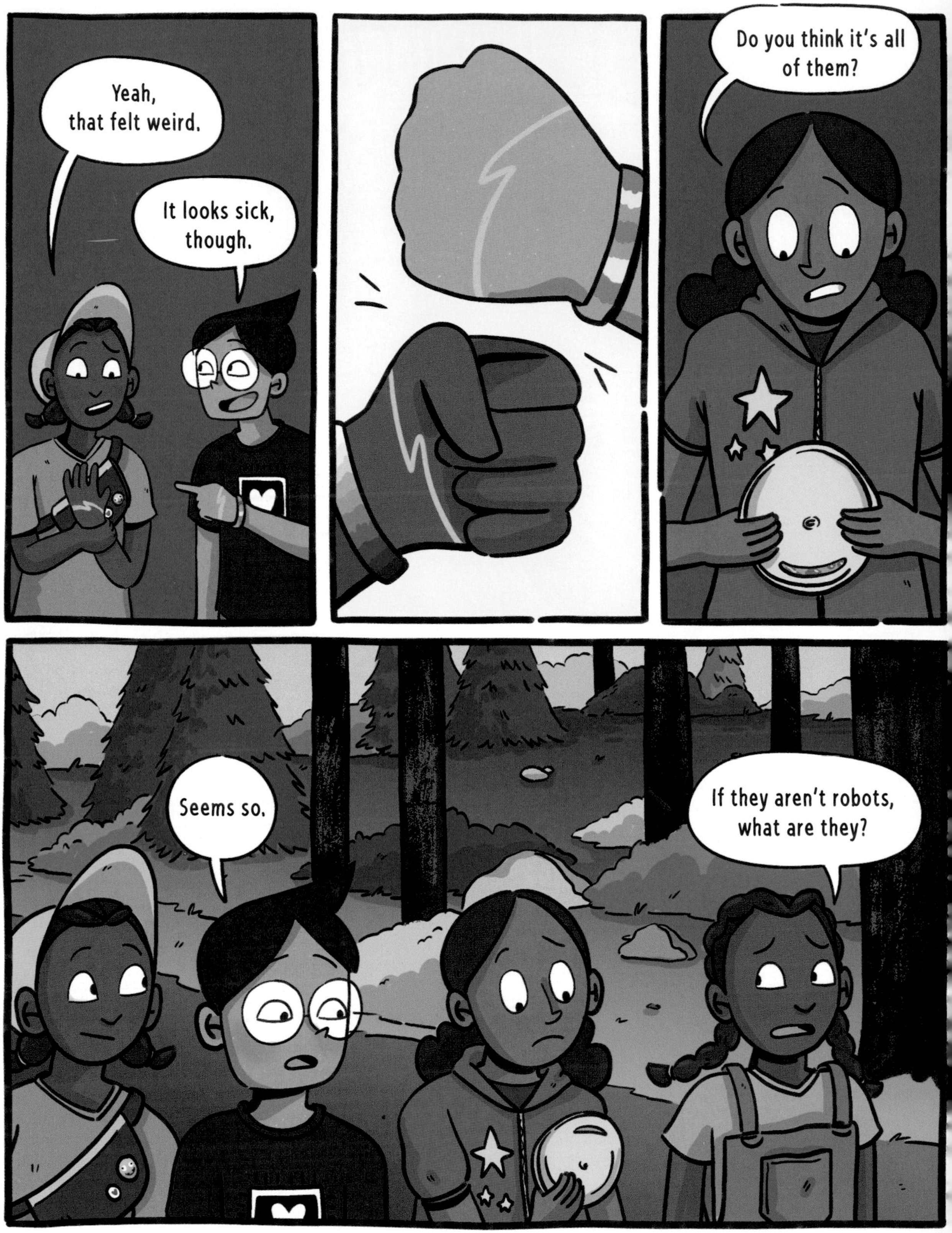
Yeah, that felt weird.
It looks sick, though.
Do you think it's all of them?
Seems so.
If they aren't robots, what are they?

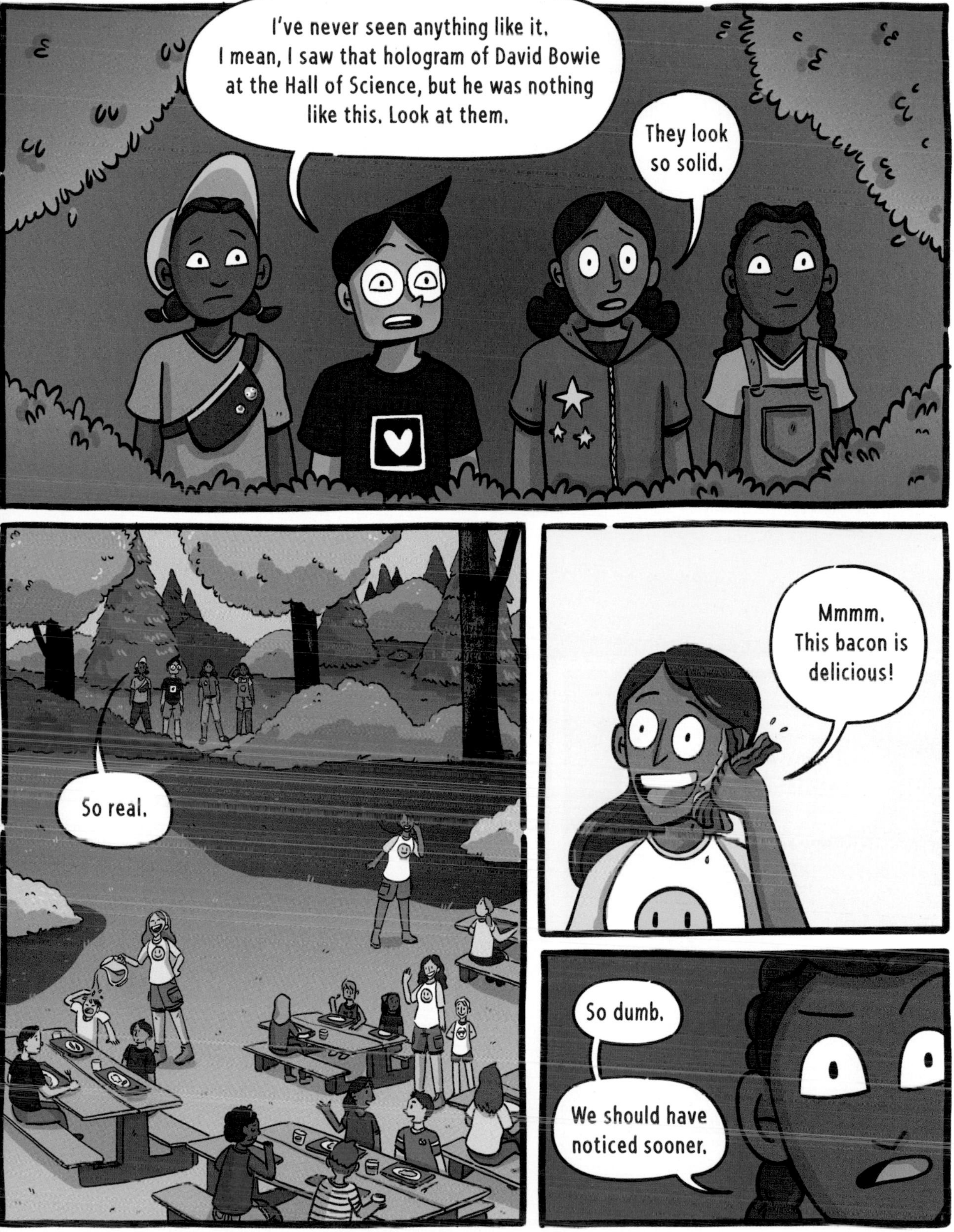
I've never seen anything like it. I mean, I saw that hologram of David Bowie at the Hall of Science, but he was nothing like this. Look at them.
They look so solid.
So real.
Mmmm. This bacon is delicious!
So dumb.
We should have noticed sooner.

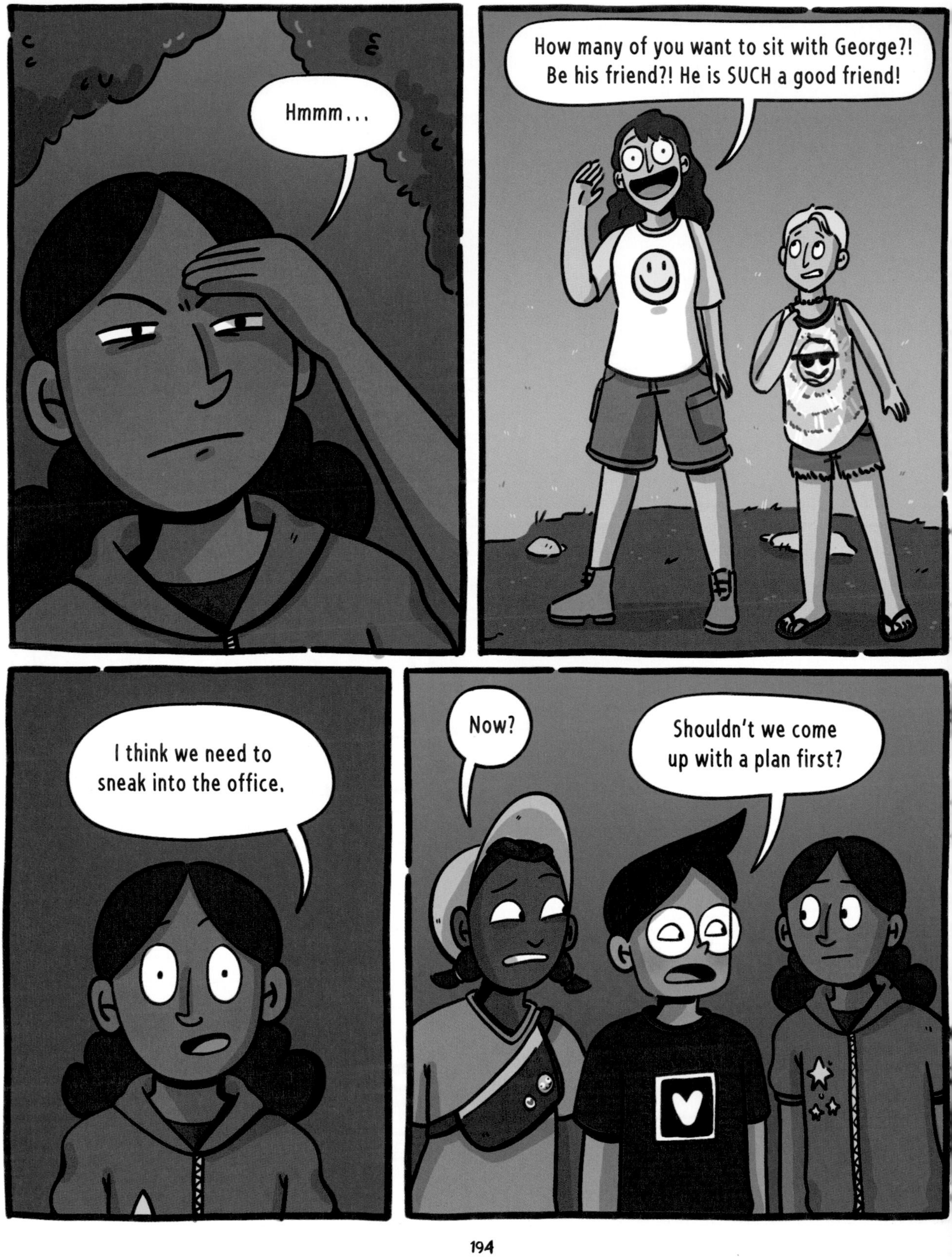

Hmmm...
How many of you want to sit with George?! Be his friend?! He is SUCH a good friend!
I think we need to sneak into the office.
Now?
Shouldn't we come up with a plan first?

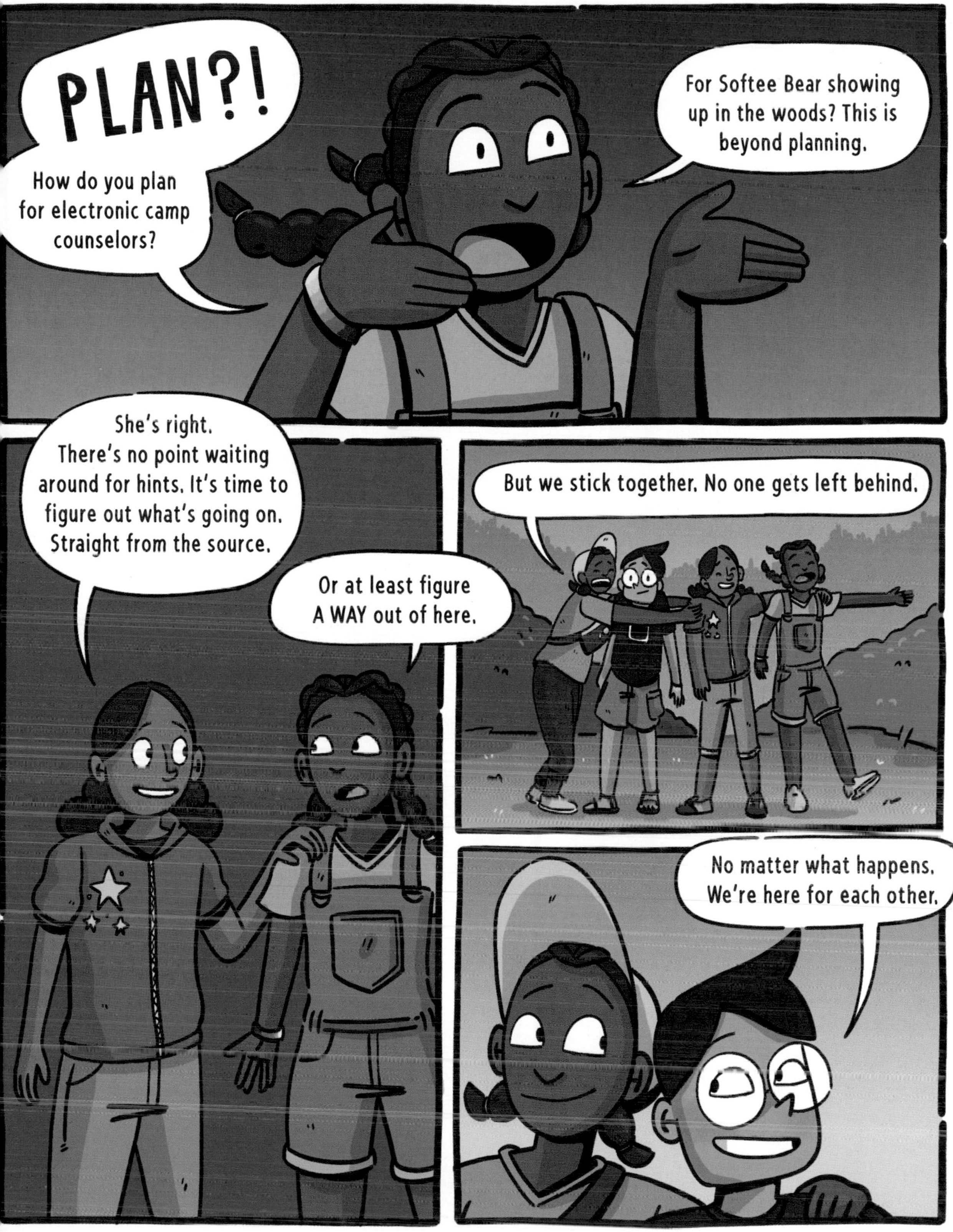
PLAN?!
How do you plan for electronic camp counselors?
For Softee Bear showing up in the woods? This is beyond planning.
She's right. There's no point waiting around for hints. It's time to figure out what's going on. Straight from the source.
Or at least figure A WAY out of here.
But we stick together. No one gets left behind.
No matter what happens. We're here for each other.

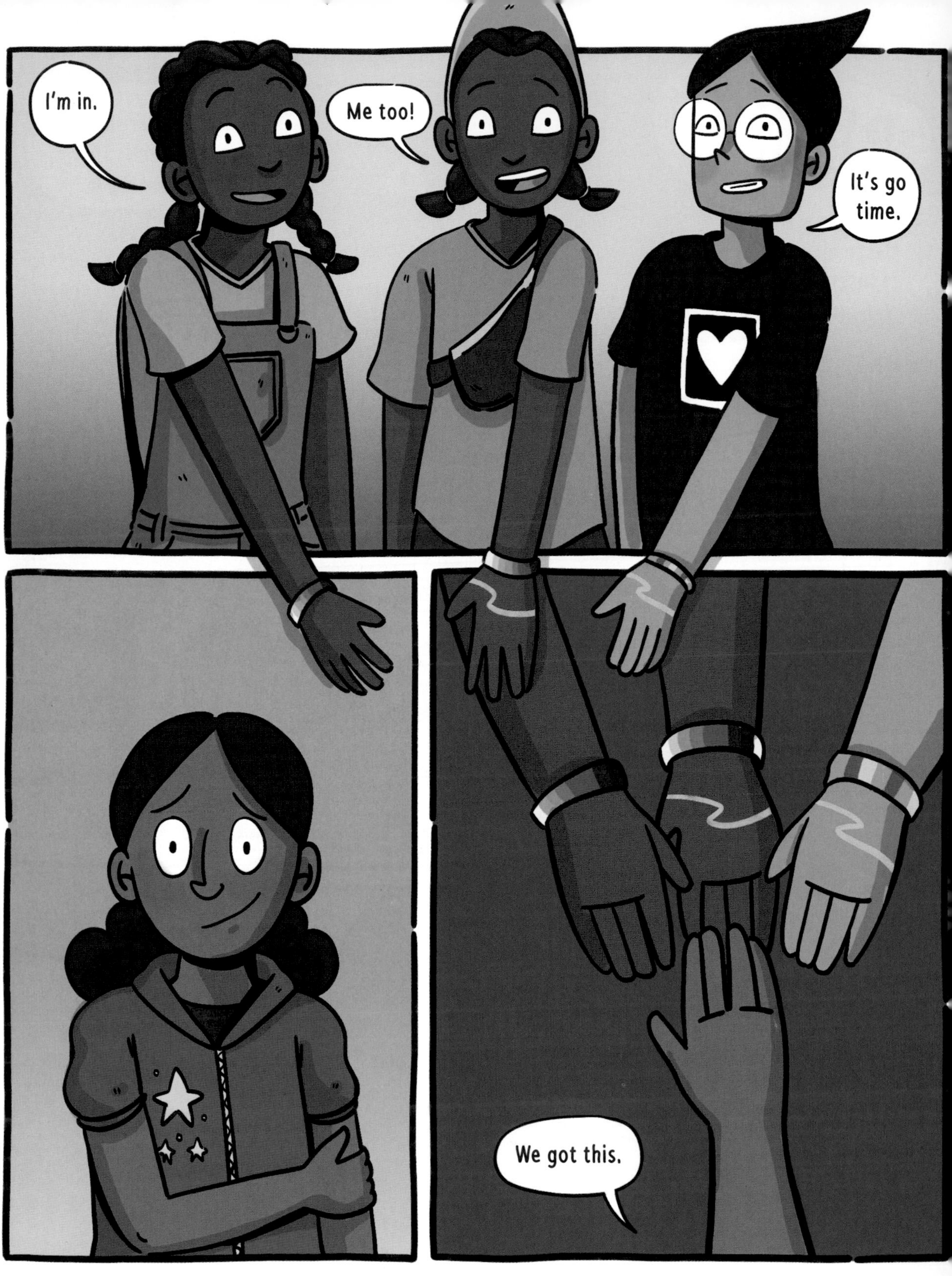
I'm in.
Me too!
It's go time.
We got this.

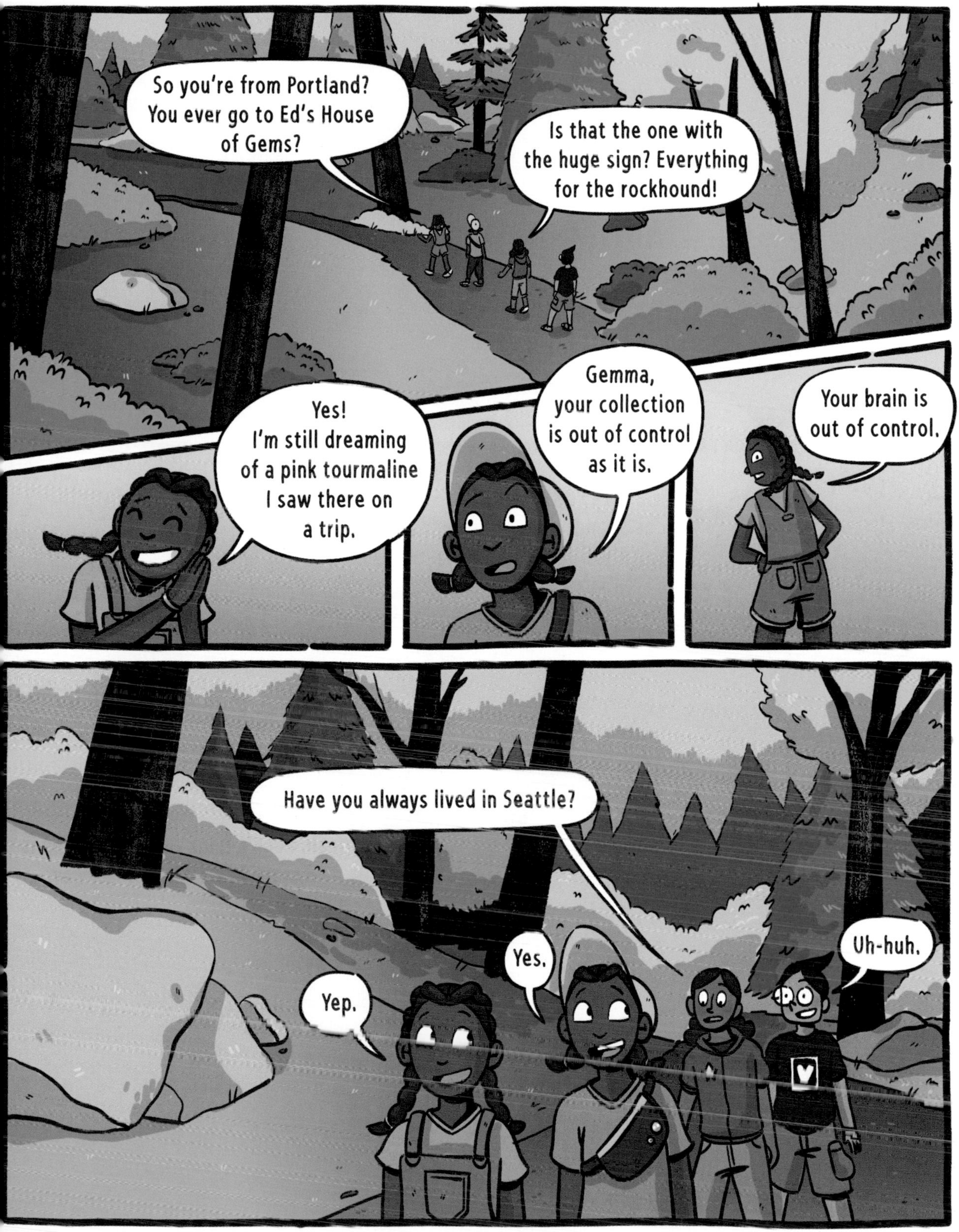
So you're from Portland? You ever go to Ed's House of Gems?
Is that the one with the huge sign? Everything for the rockhound!
Yes! I'm still dreaming of a pink tourmaline I saw there on a trip.
Gemma, your collection is out of control as it is.
Your brain is out of control.
Have you always lived in Seattle?
Yep.
Yes.
Uh-huh.

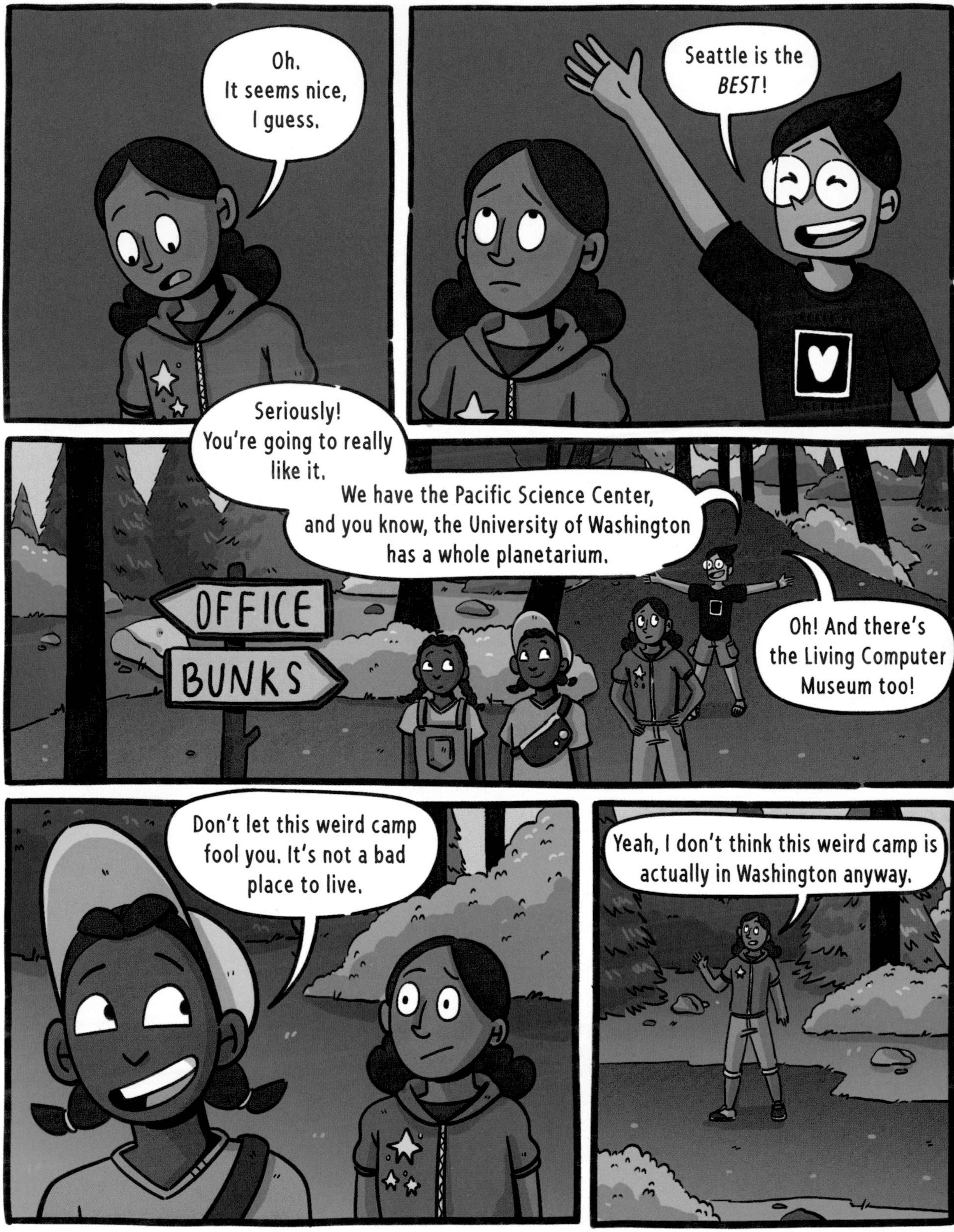
Oh. It seems nice, I guess.
Seattle is the *BEST*!
Seriously! You're going to really like it.
We have the Pacific Science Center, and you know, the University of Washington has a whole planetarium.
OFFICE
BUNKS
Oh! And there's the Living Computer Museum too!
Don't let this weird camp fool you. It's not a bad place to live.
Yeah, I don't think this weird camp is actually in Washington anyway.

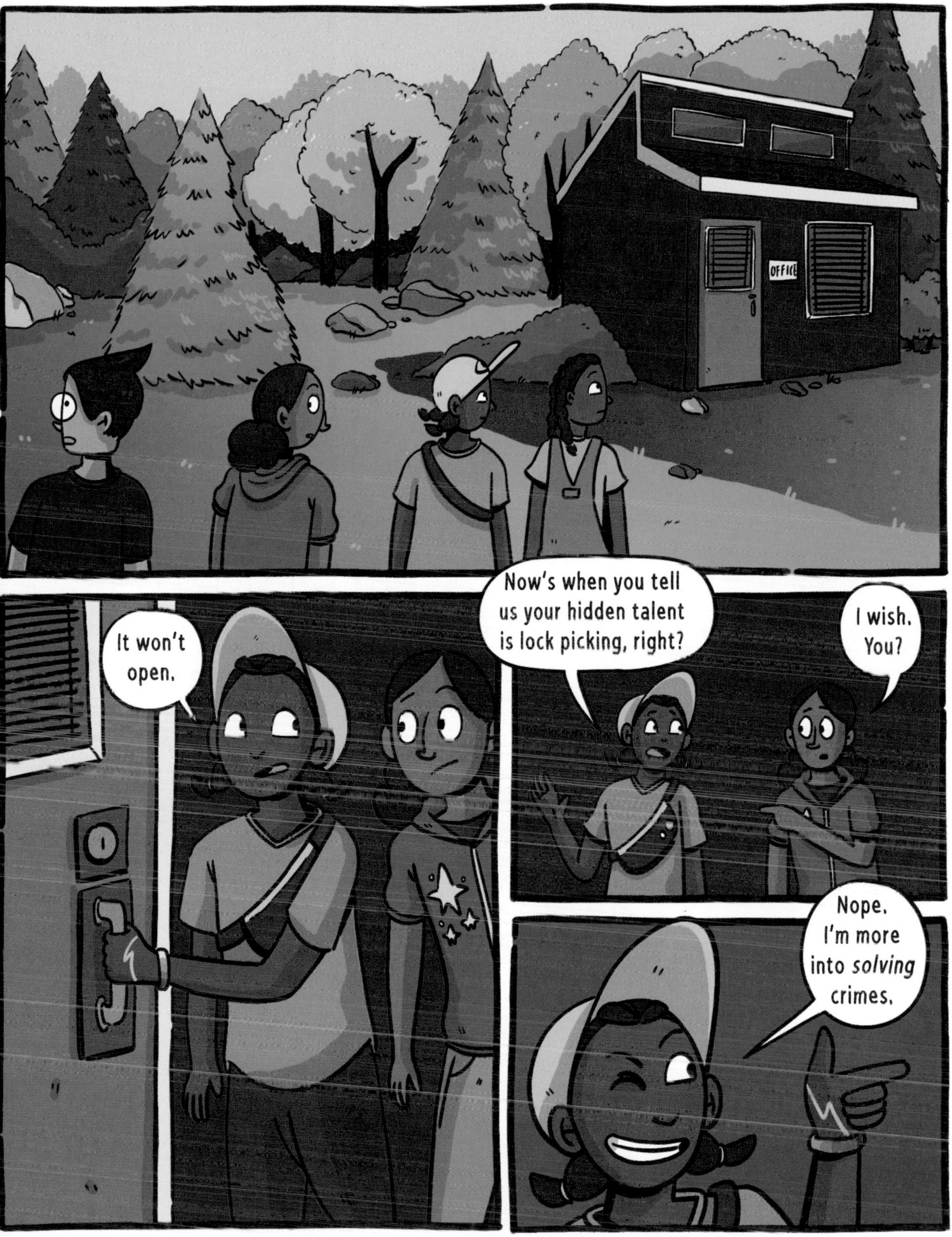
OFFICE
It won't open.
Now's when you tell us your hidden talent is lock picking, right?
I wish. You?
Nope. I'm more into *solving* crimes.

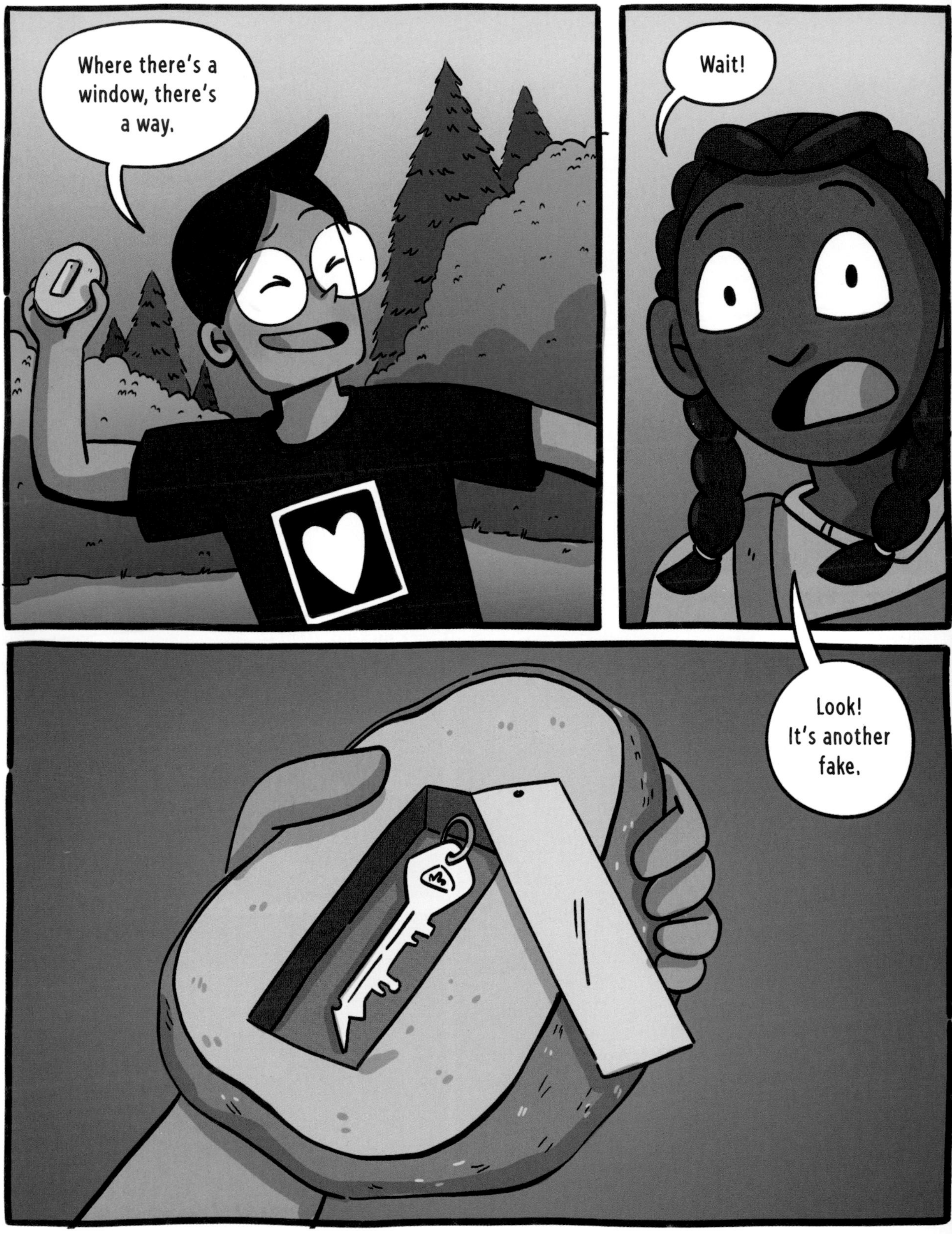
Where there's a window, there's a way.
Wait!
Look! It's another fake.

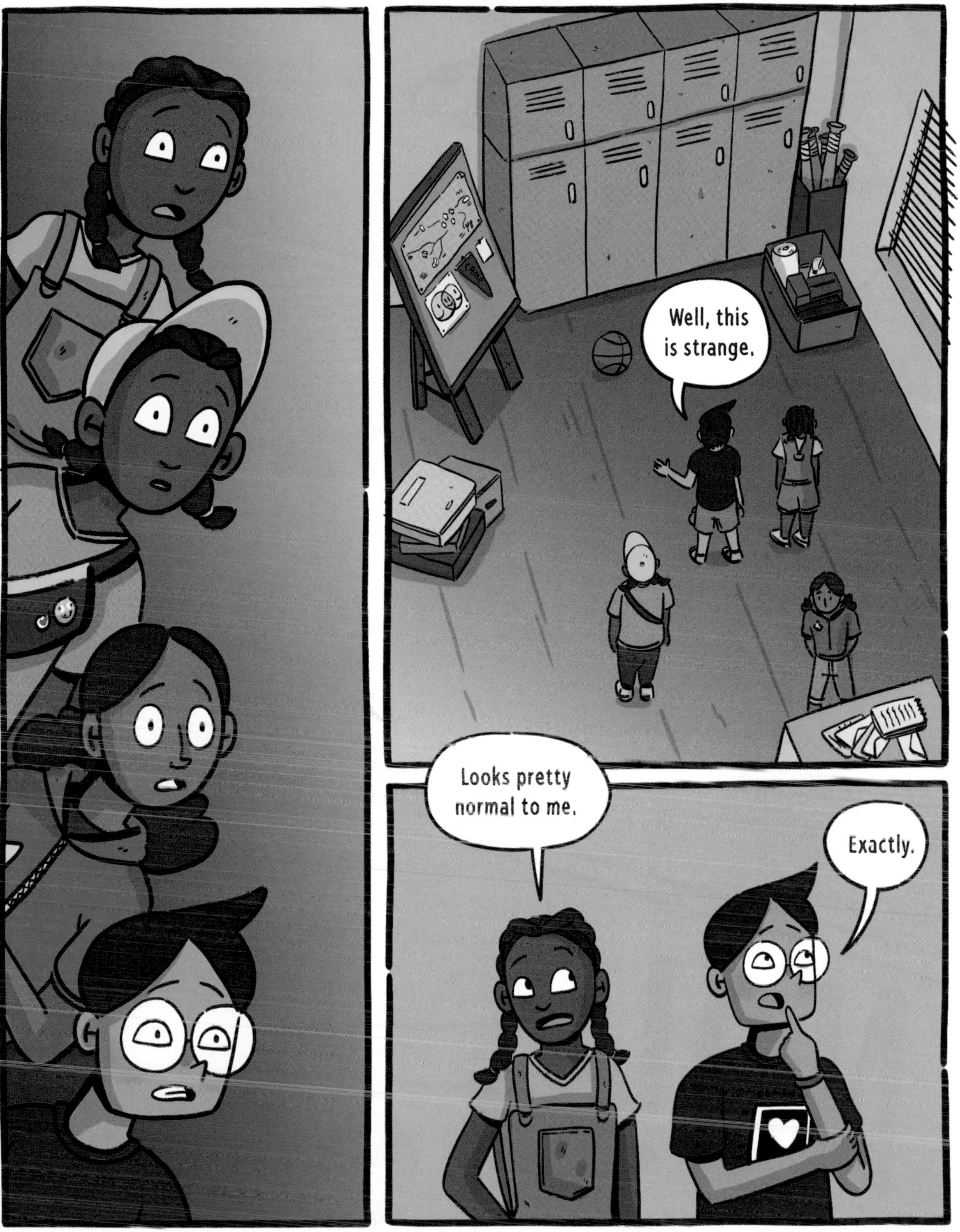
Well, this is strange.
Looks pretty normal to me.
Exactly.

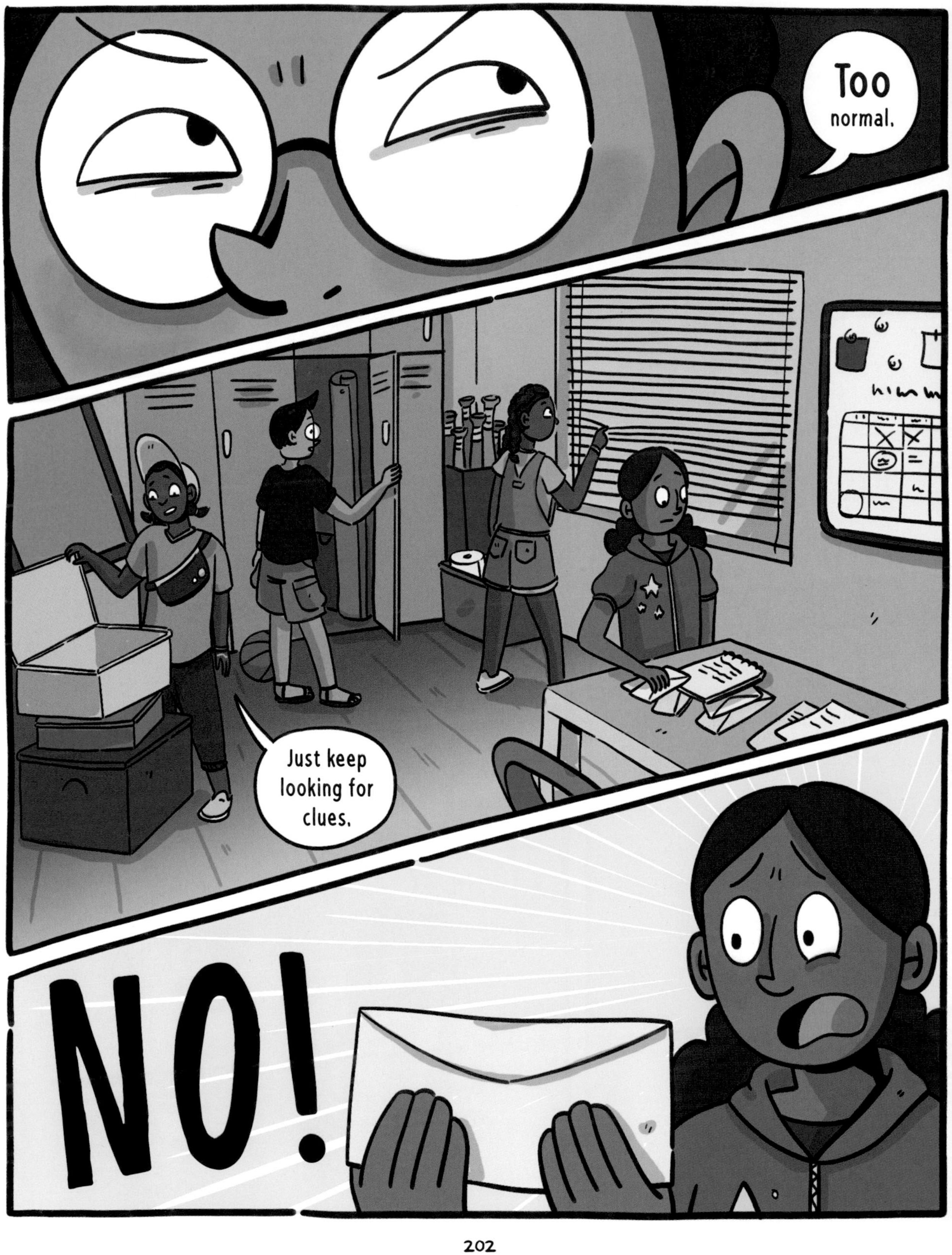
Too normal.
Just keep looking for clues.
NO!

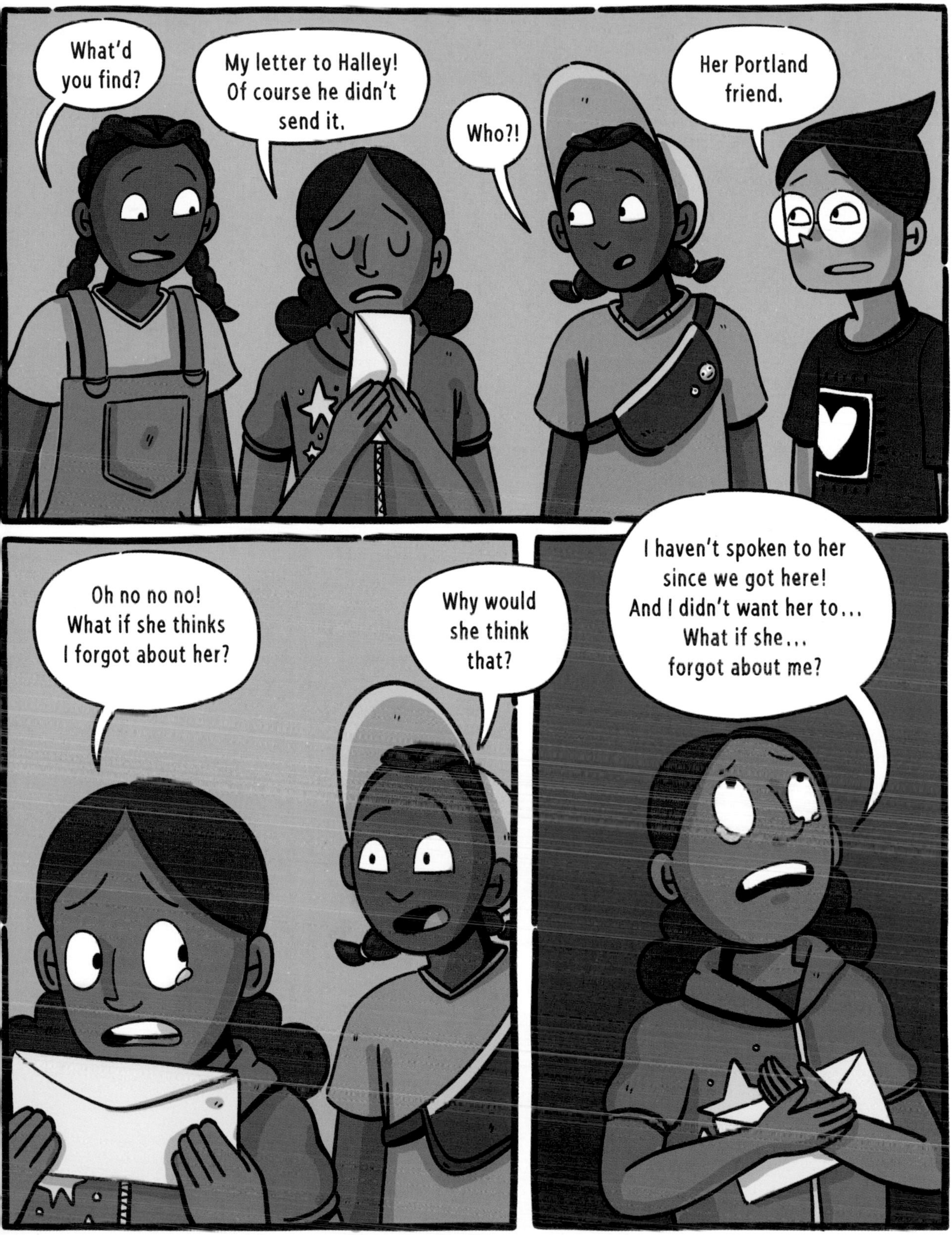
What'd you find?
My letter to Halley! Of course he didn't send it.
Who?!
Her Portland friend.
Oh no no no! What if she thinks I forgot about her?
Why would she think that?
I haven't spoken to her since we got here! And I didn't want her to... What if she... forgot about me?

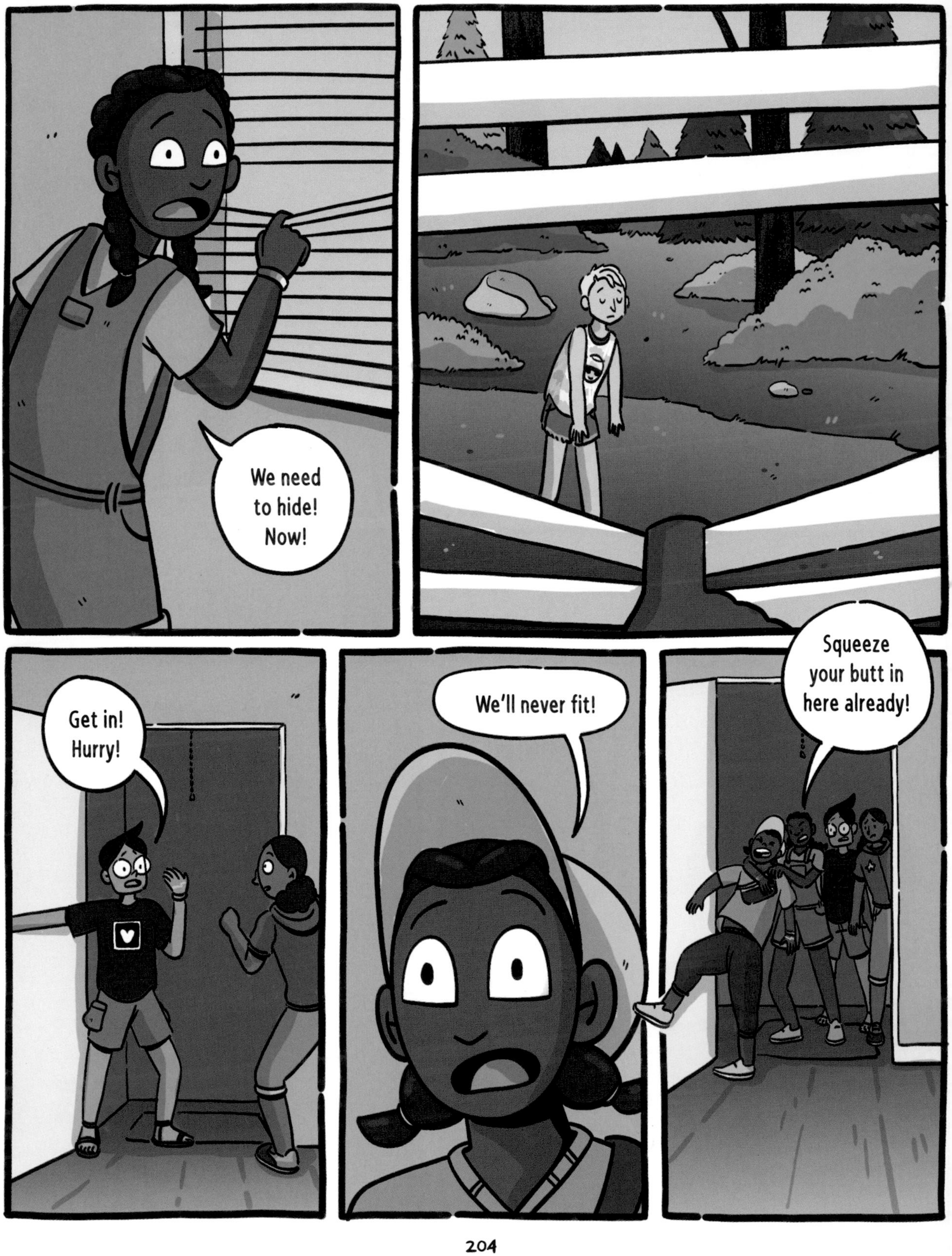
We need to hide! Now!
Get in! Hurry!
We'll never fit!
Squeeze your butt in here already!

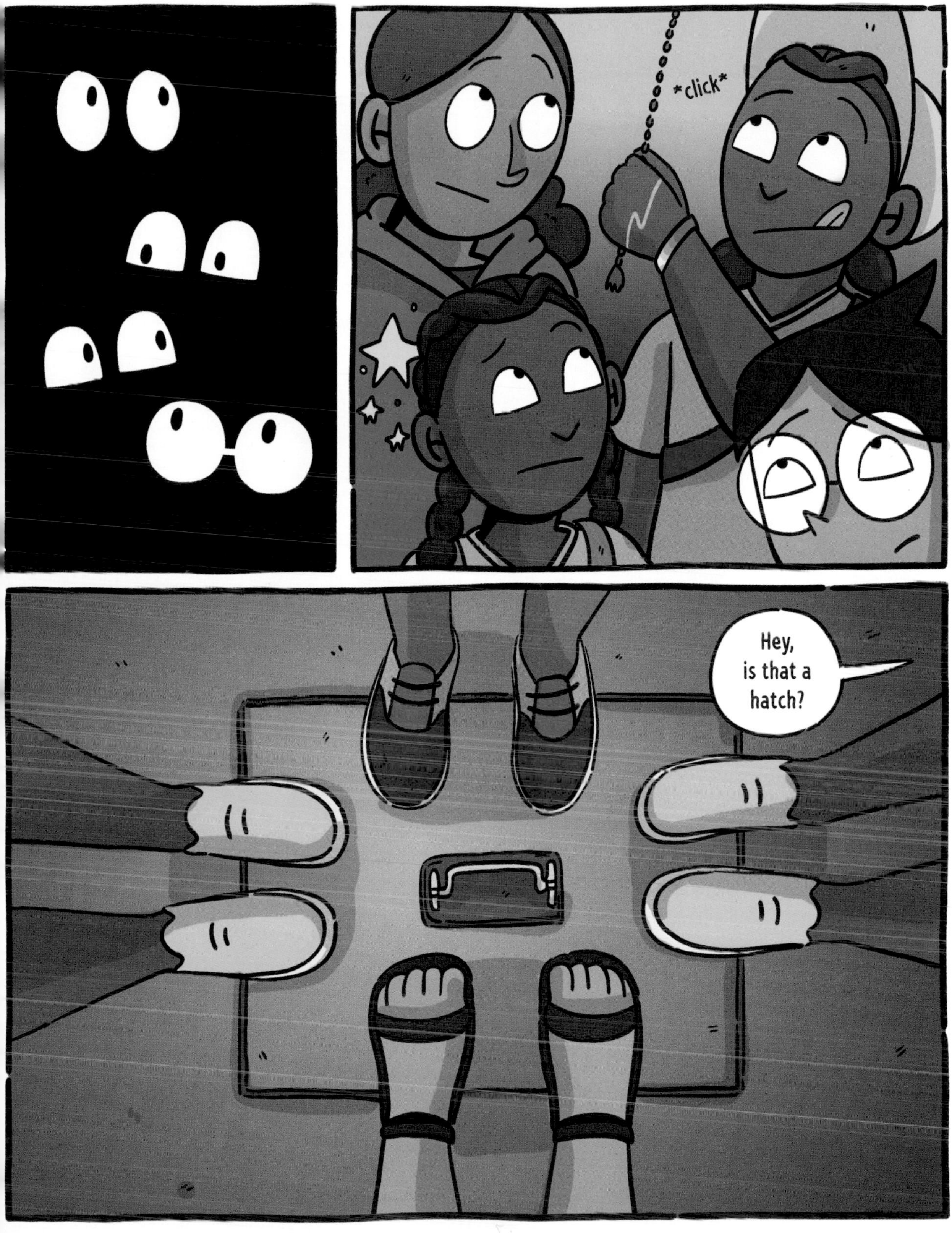
click
Hey, is that a hatch?

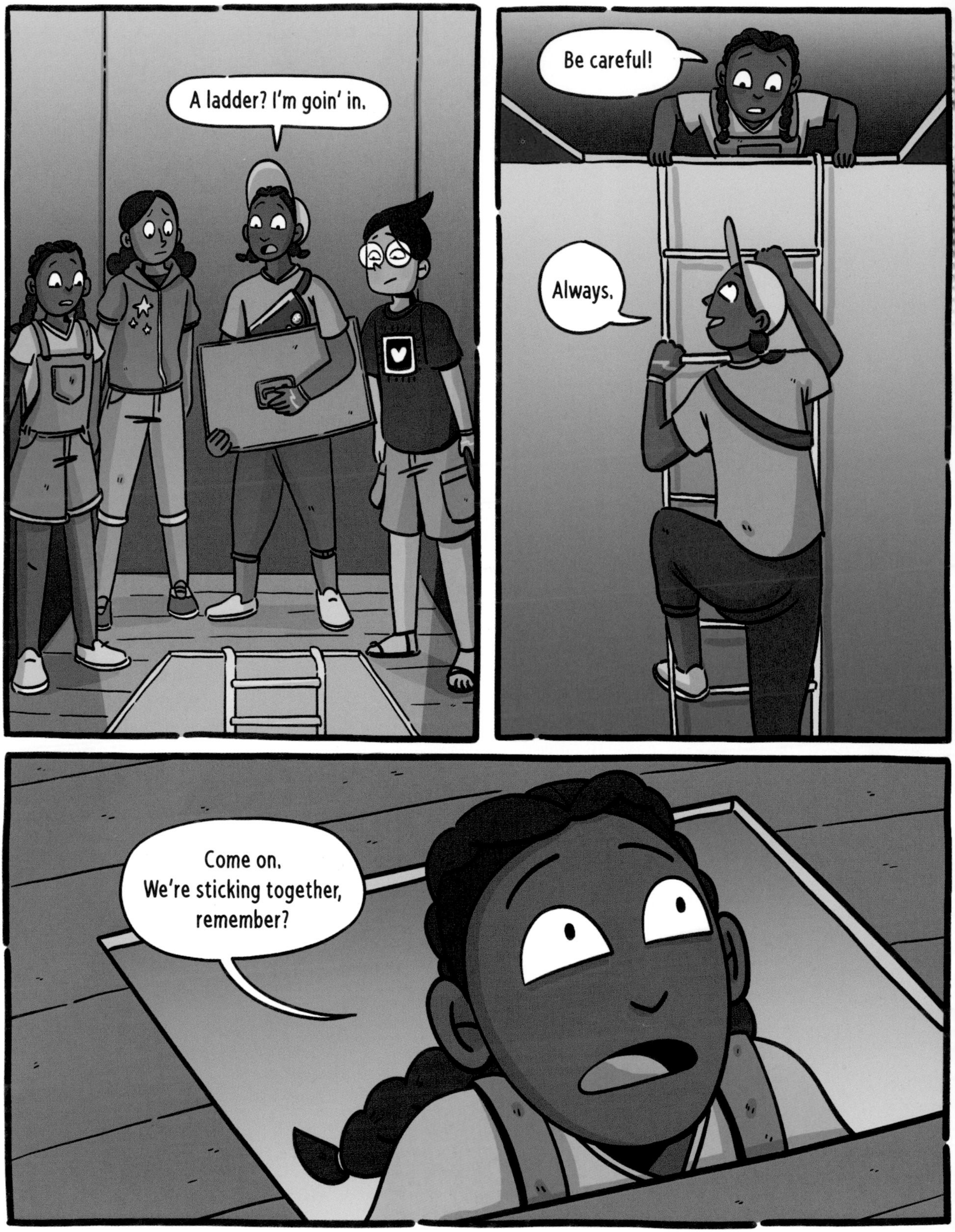
A ladder? I'm goin' in.
Be careful!
Always.
Come on.
We're sticking together,
remember?

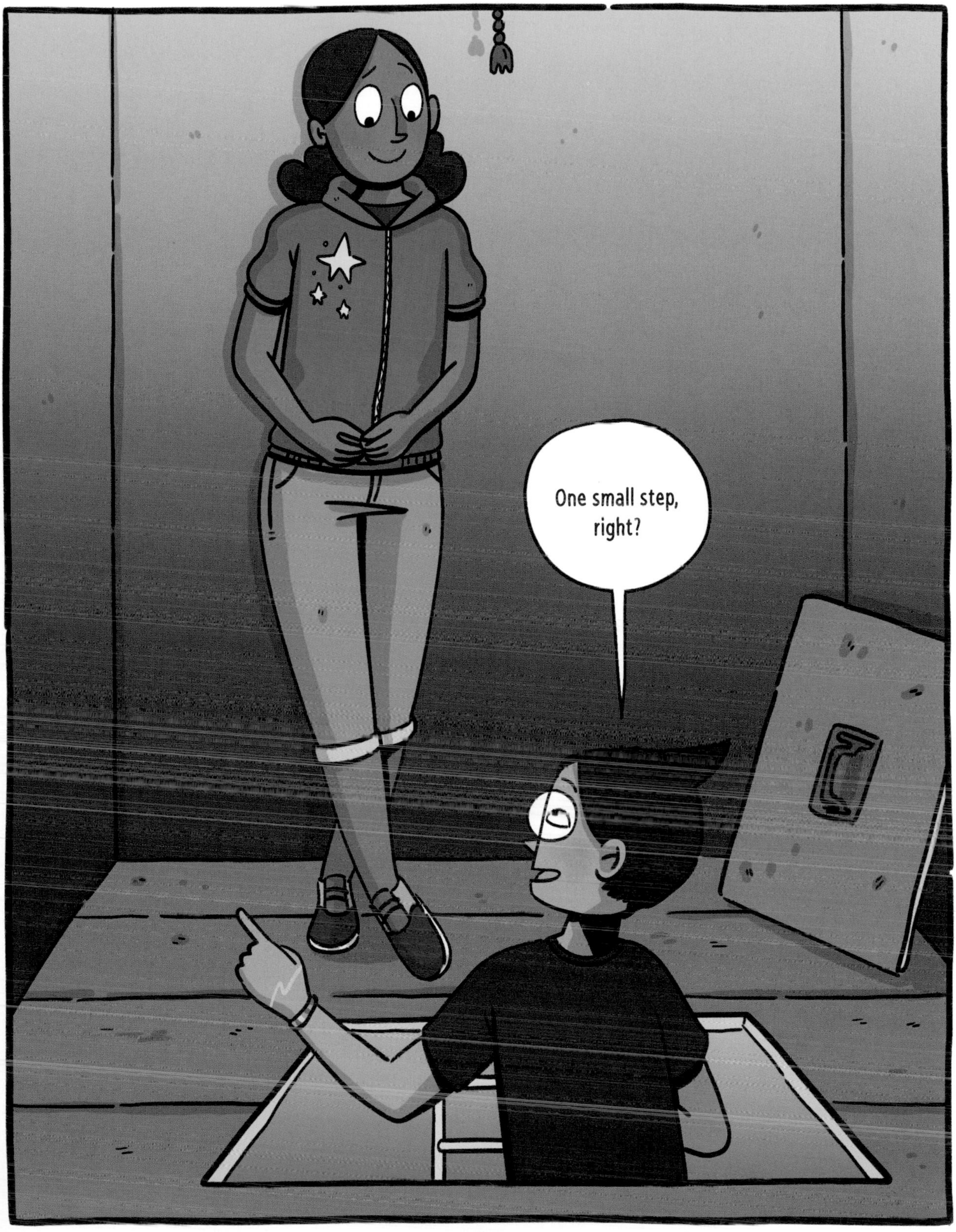
One small step, right?

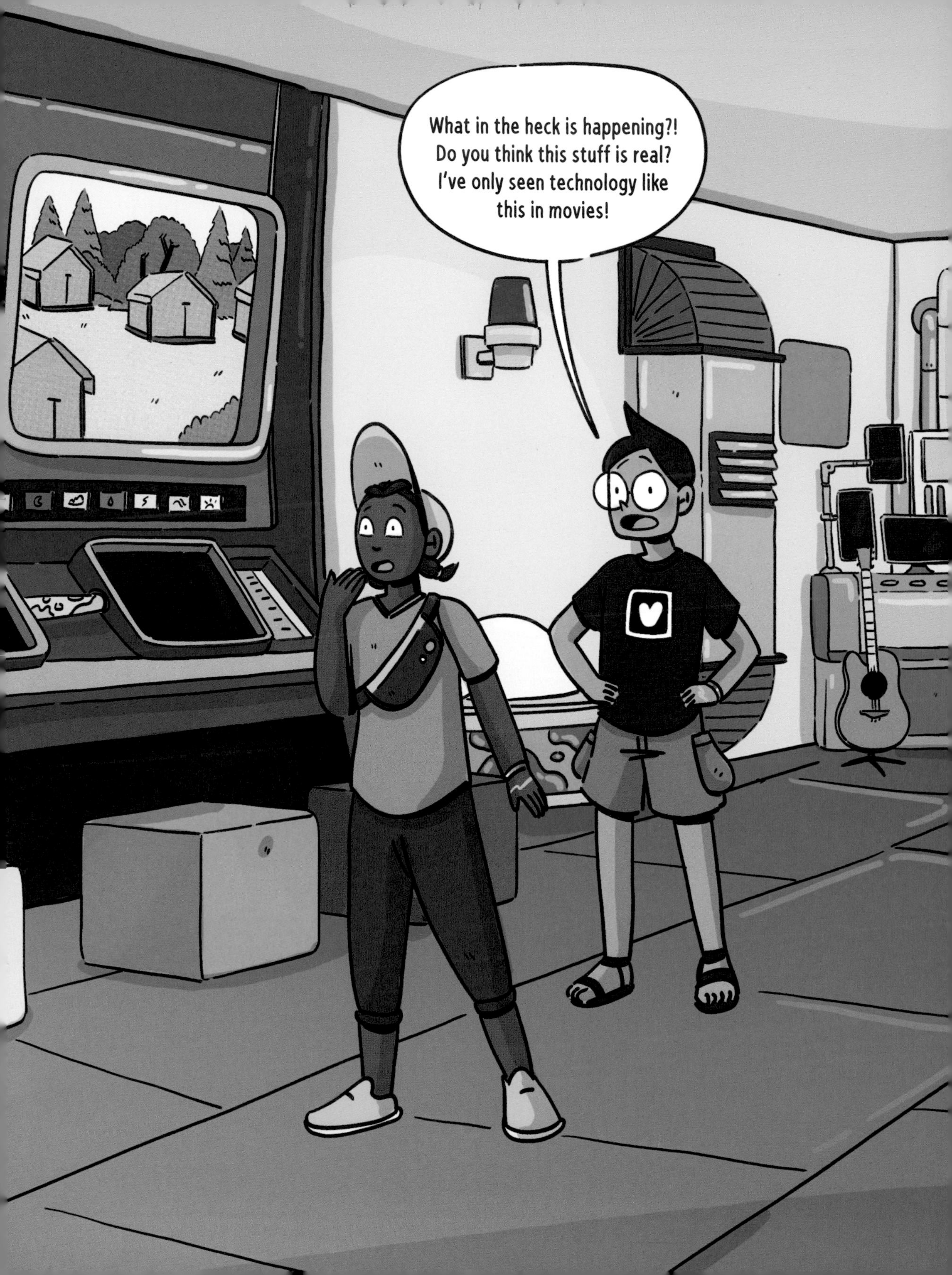
What in the heck is happening?! Do you think this stuff is real? I've only seen technology like this in movies!

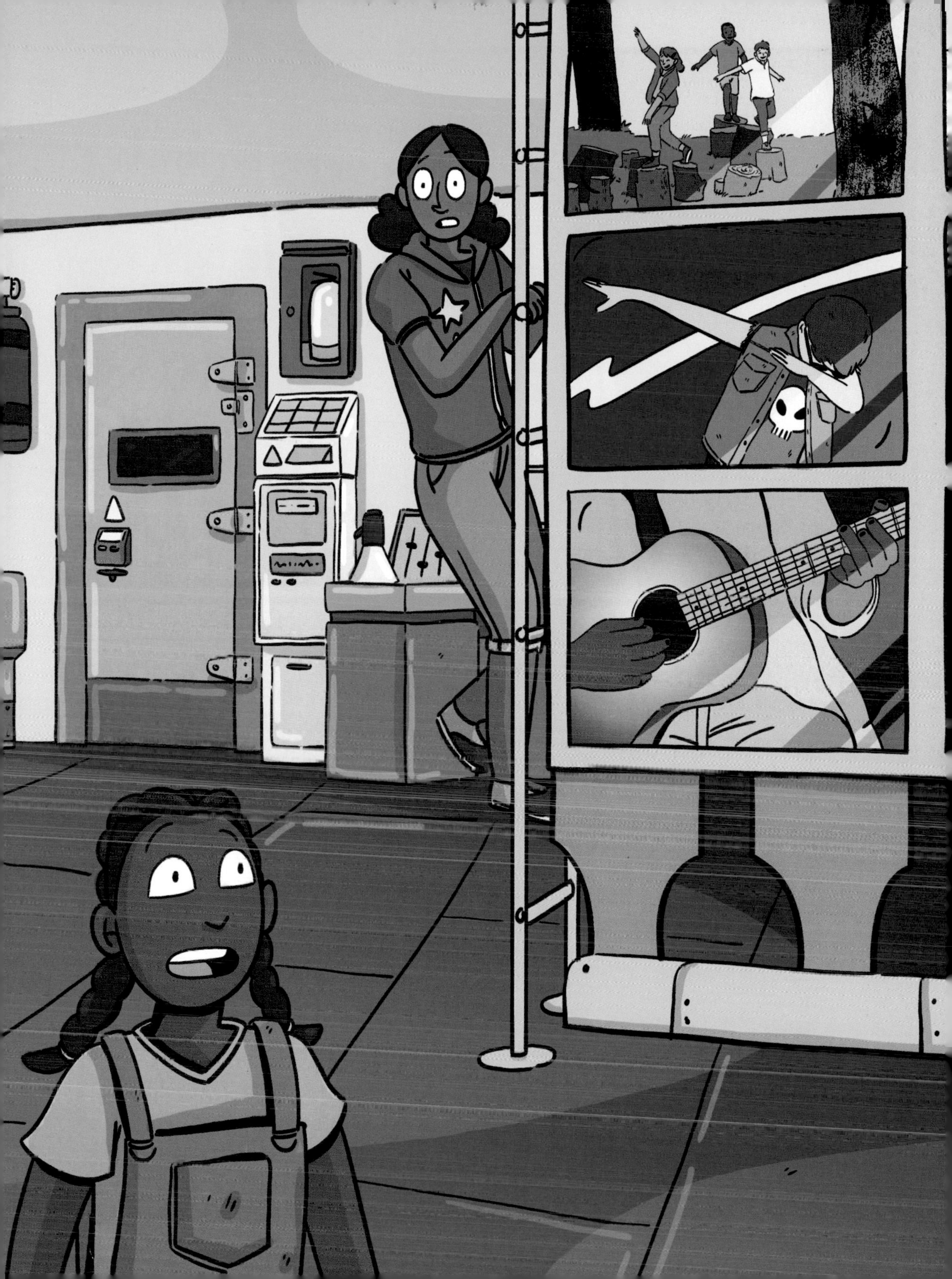

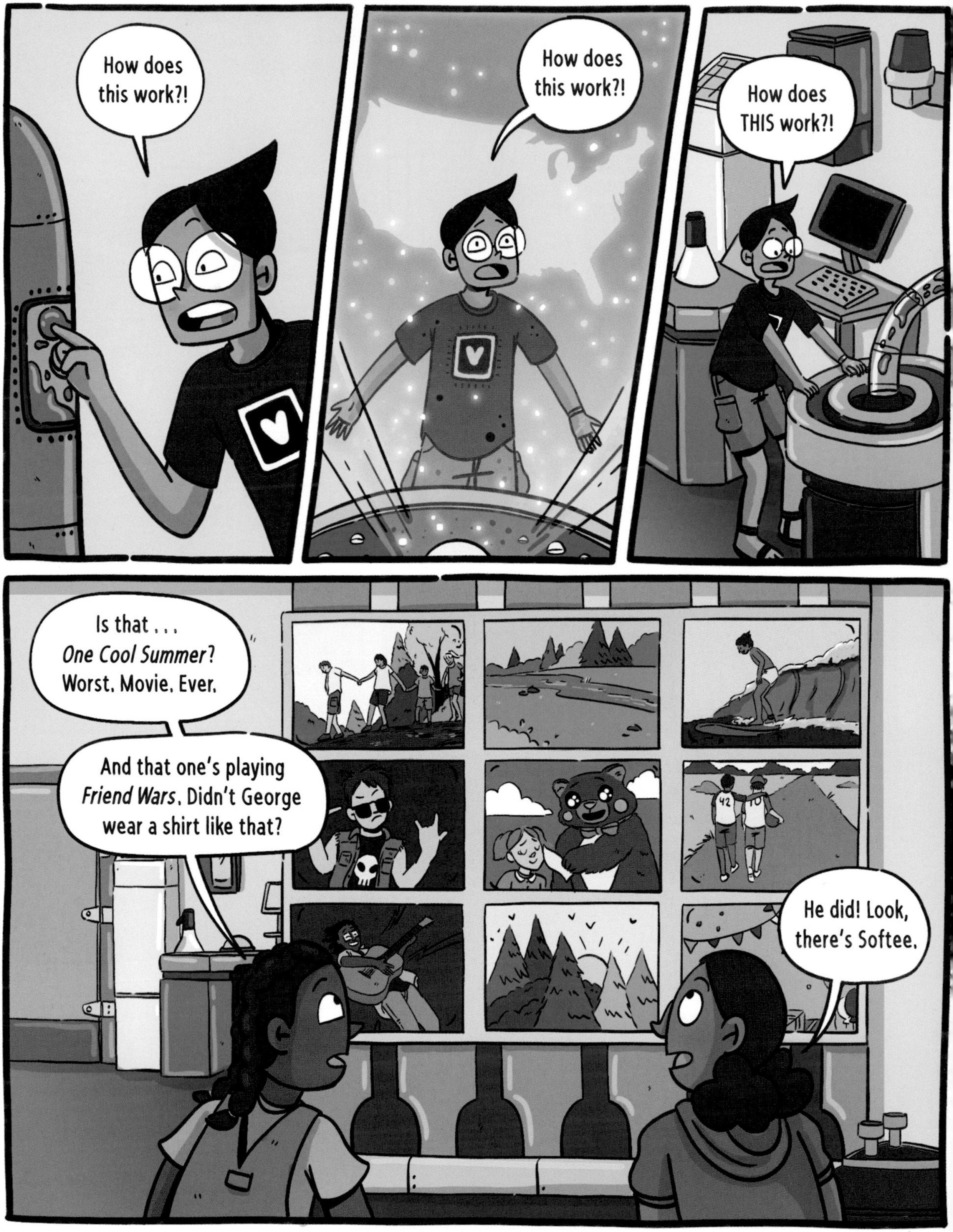
How does this work?!
How does this work?!
How does THIS work?!
Is that . . . *One Cool Summer*? Worst. Movie. Ever.
And that one's playing *Friend Wars*. Didn't George wear a shirt like that?
He did! Look, there's Softee.

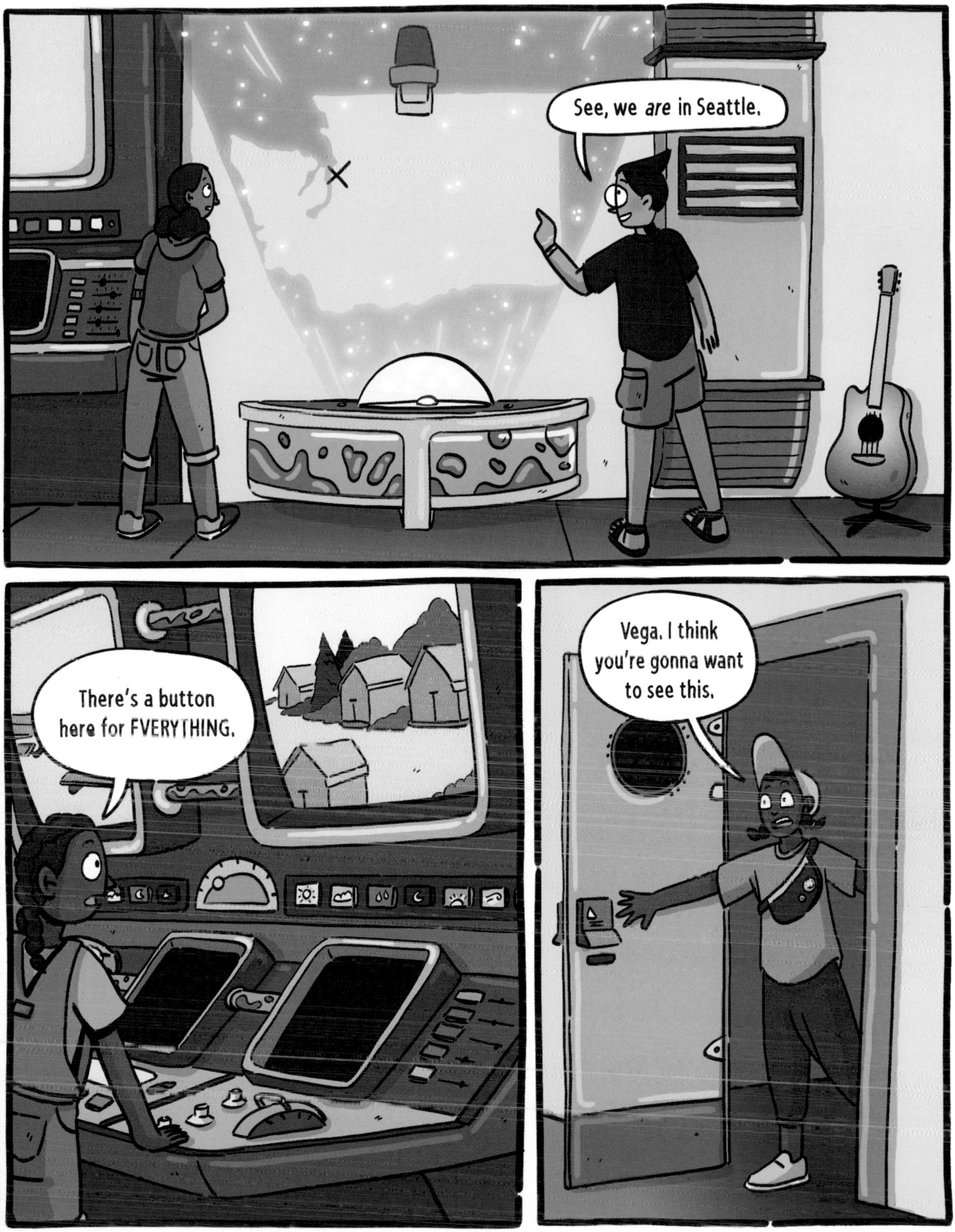
See, we *are* in Seattle.
There's a button here for EVERYTHING.
Vega, I think you're gonna want to see this.

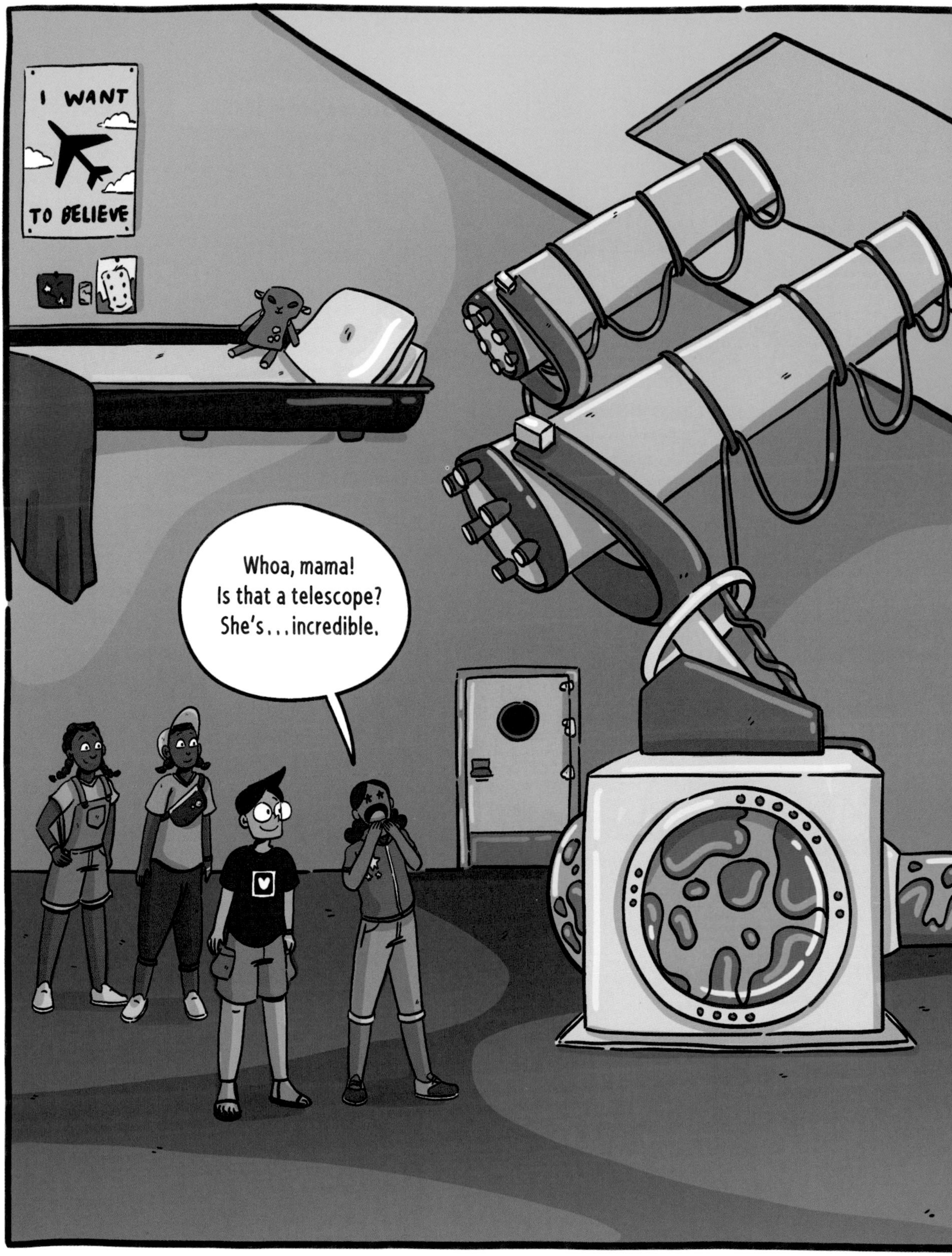
I WANT TO BELIEVE
Whoa, mama! Is that a telescope? She's . . . incredible.

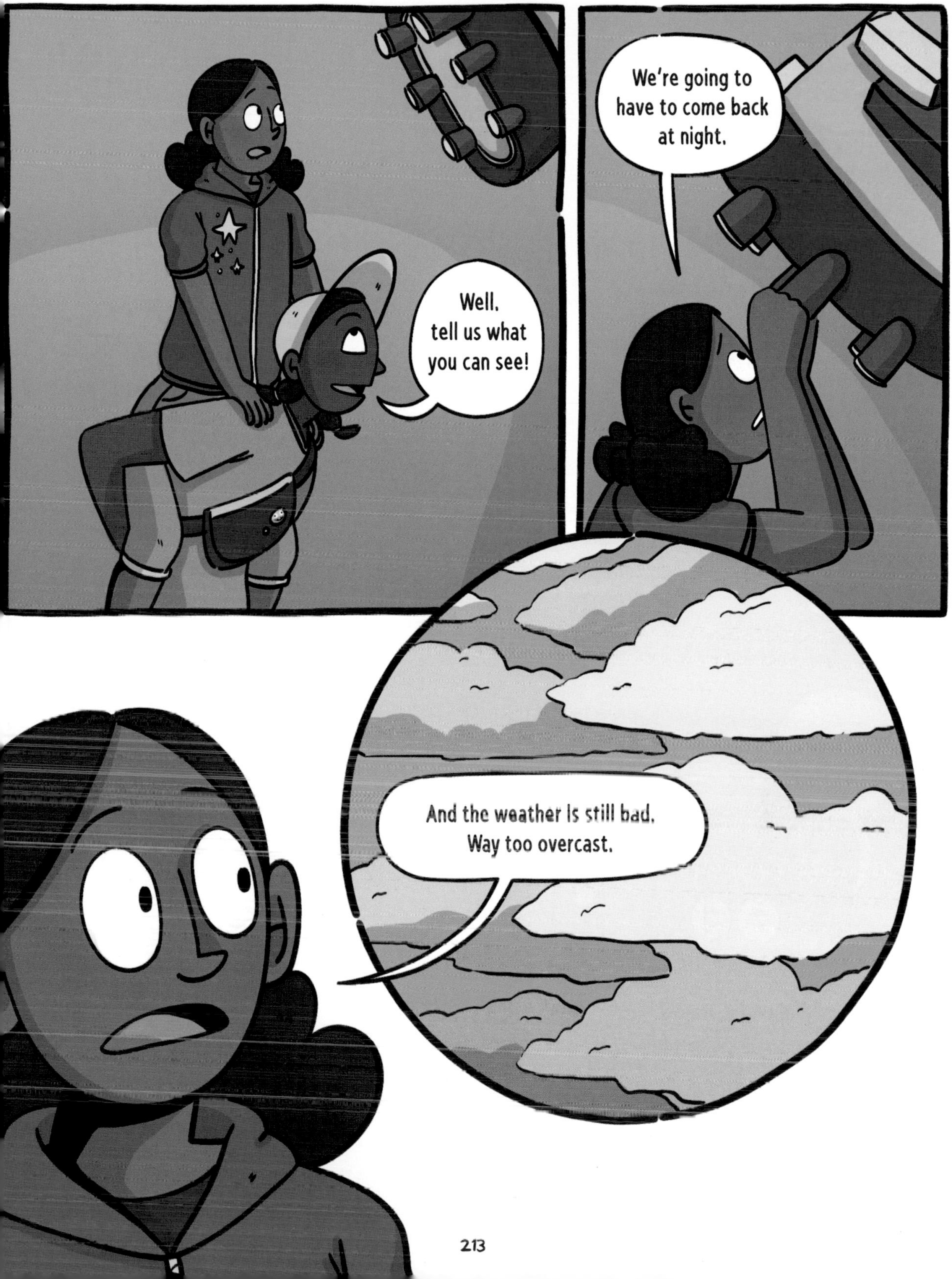
Well, tell us what you can see!
We're going to have to come back at night.
And the weather is still bad. Way too overcast.

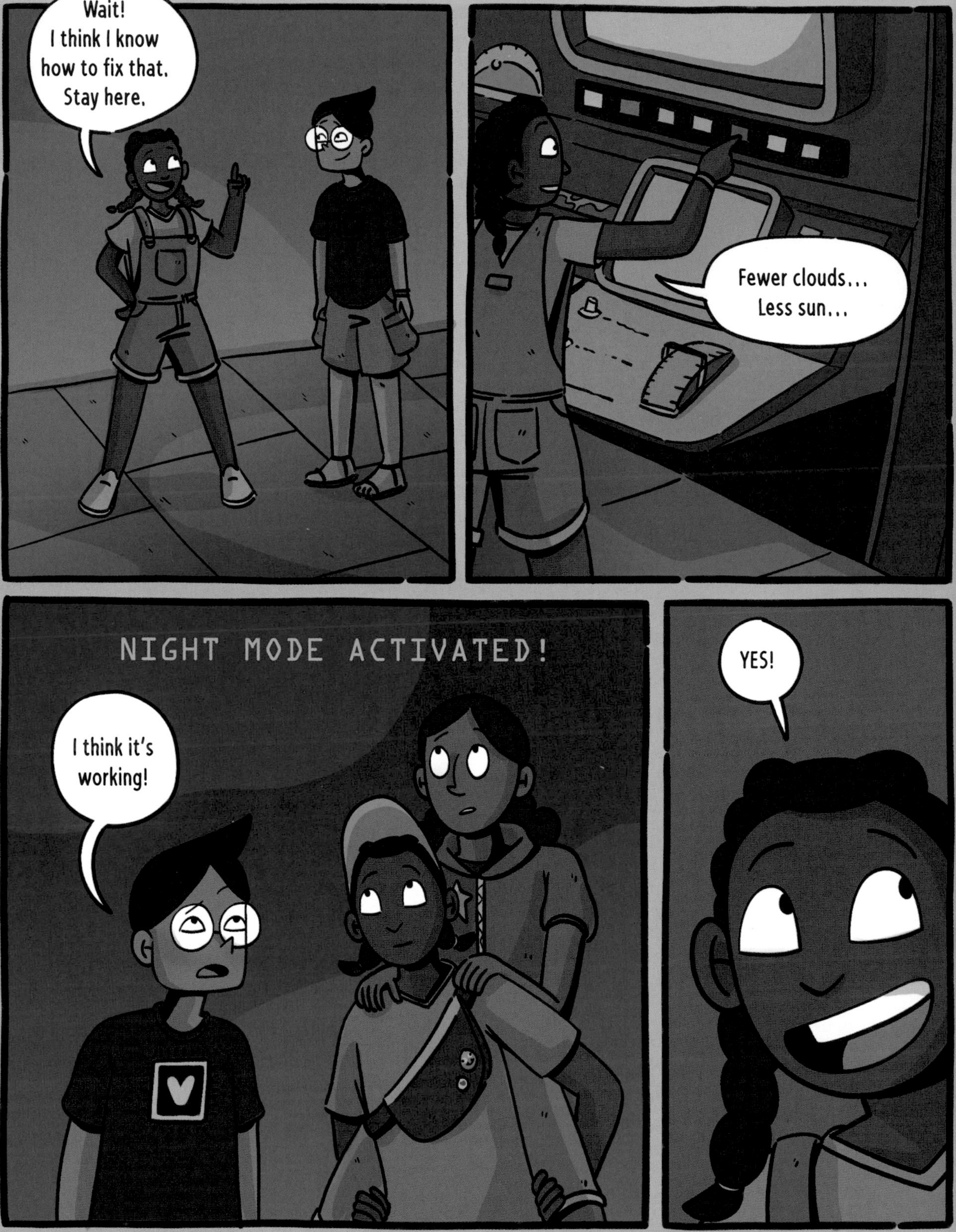
Wait! I think I know how to fix that. Stay here.
Fewer clouds… Less sun…
NIGHT MODE ACTIVATED!
I think it's working!
YES!

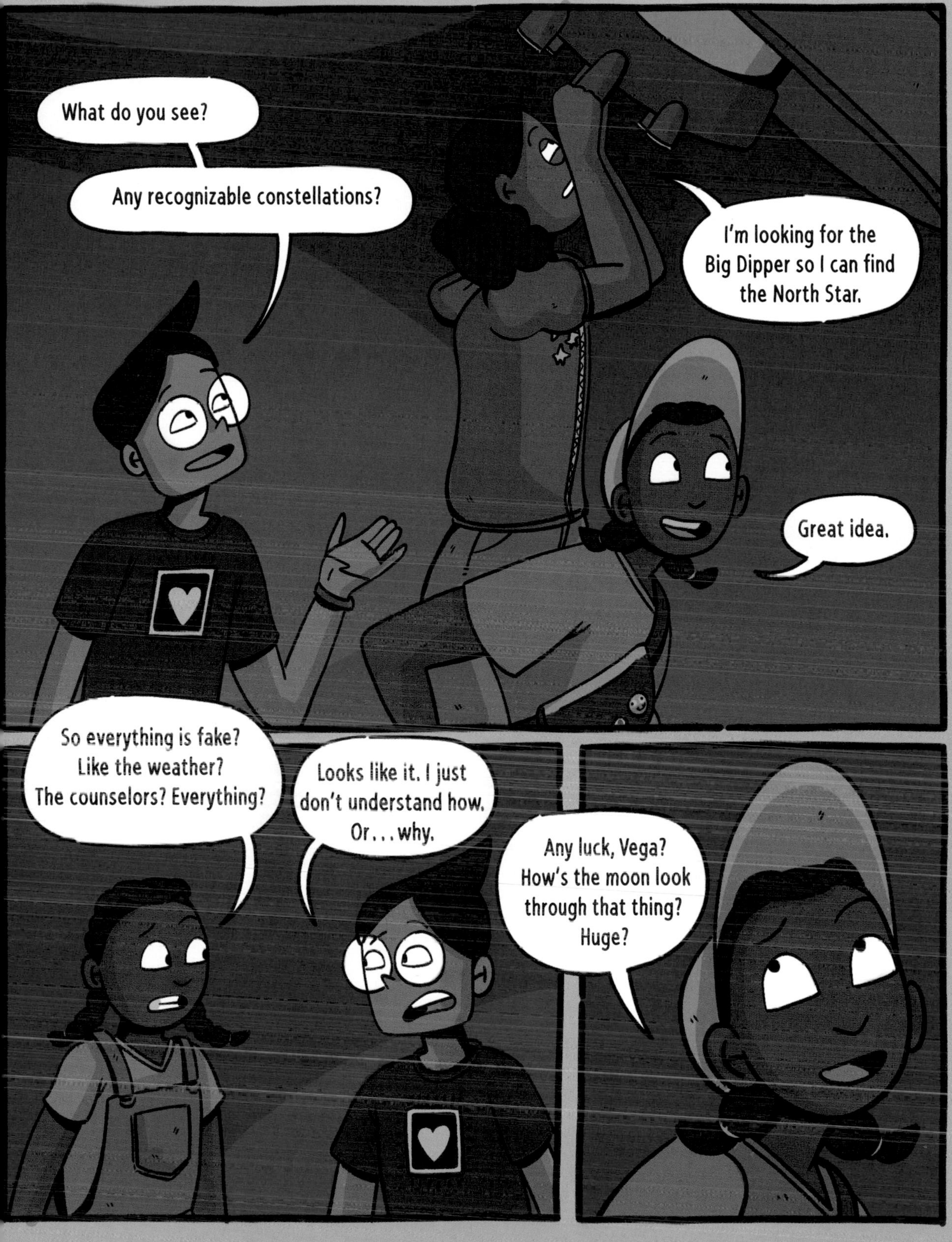
What do you see?
Any recognizable constellations?
I'm looking for the Big Dipper so I can find the North Star.
Great idea.
So everything is fake? Like the weather? The counselors? Everything?
Looks like it. I just don't understand how. Or. . . why.
Any luck, Vega? How's the moon look through that thing? Huge?

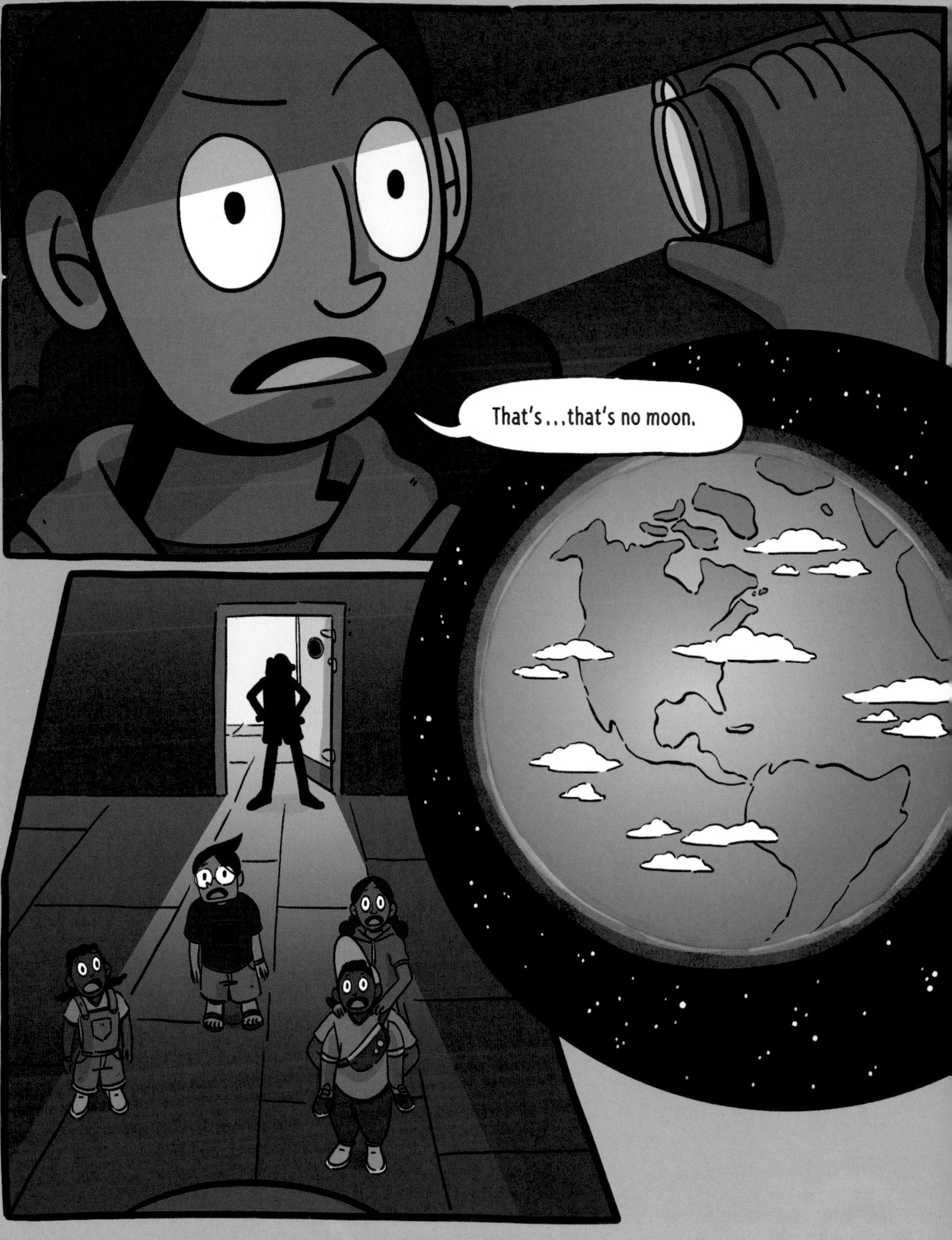
That's...that's no moon.

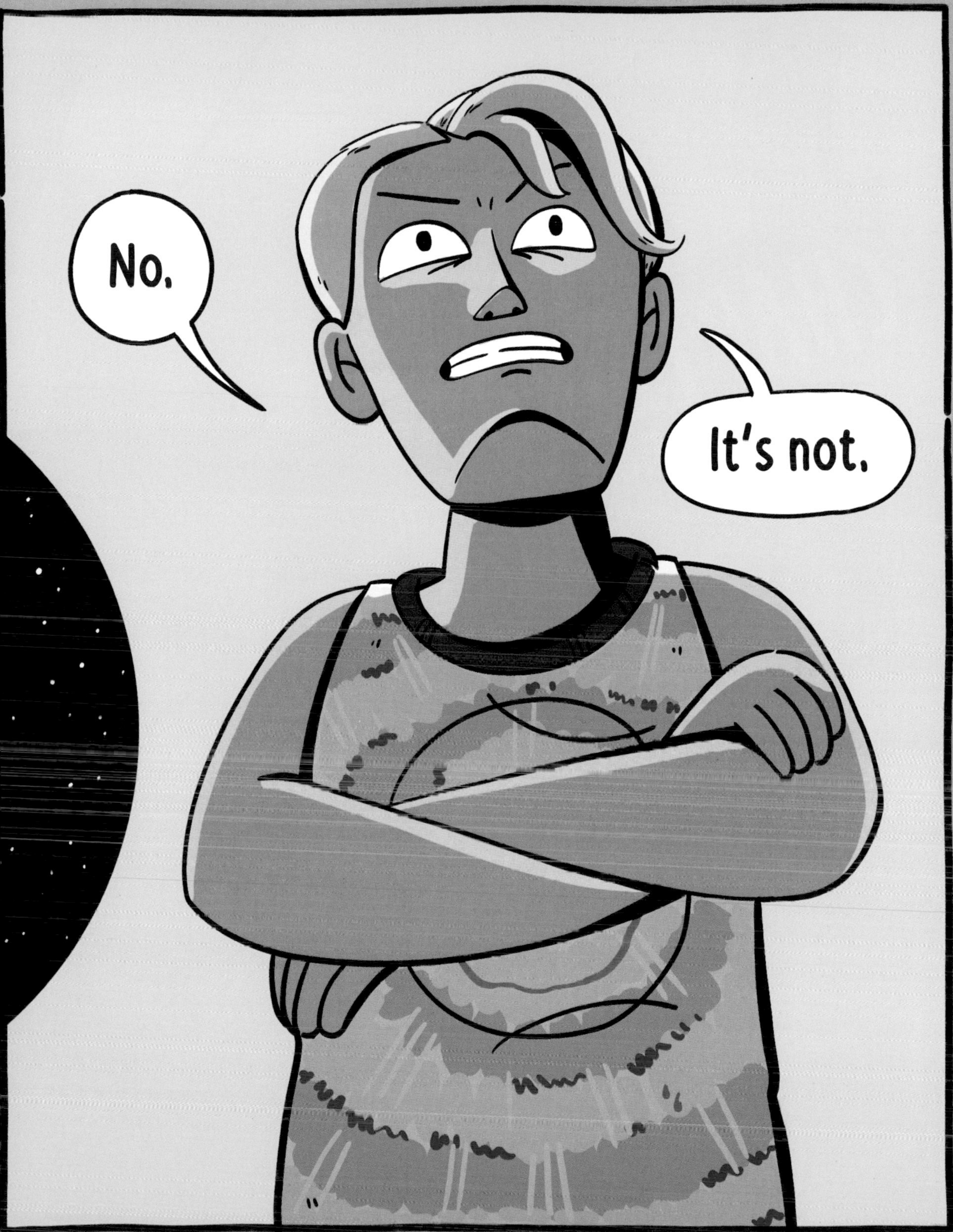
No.
It's not.

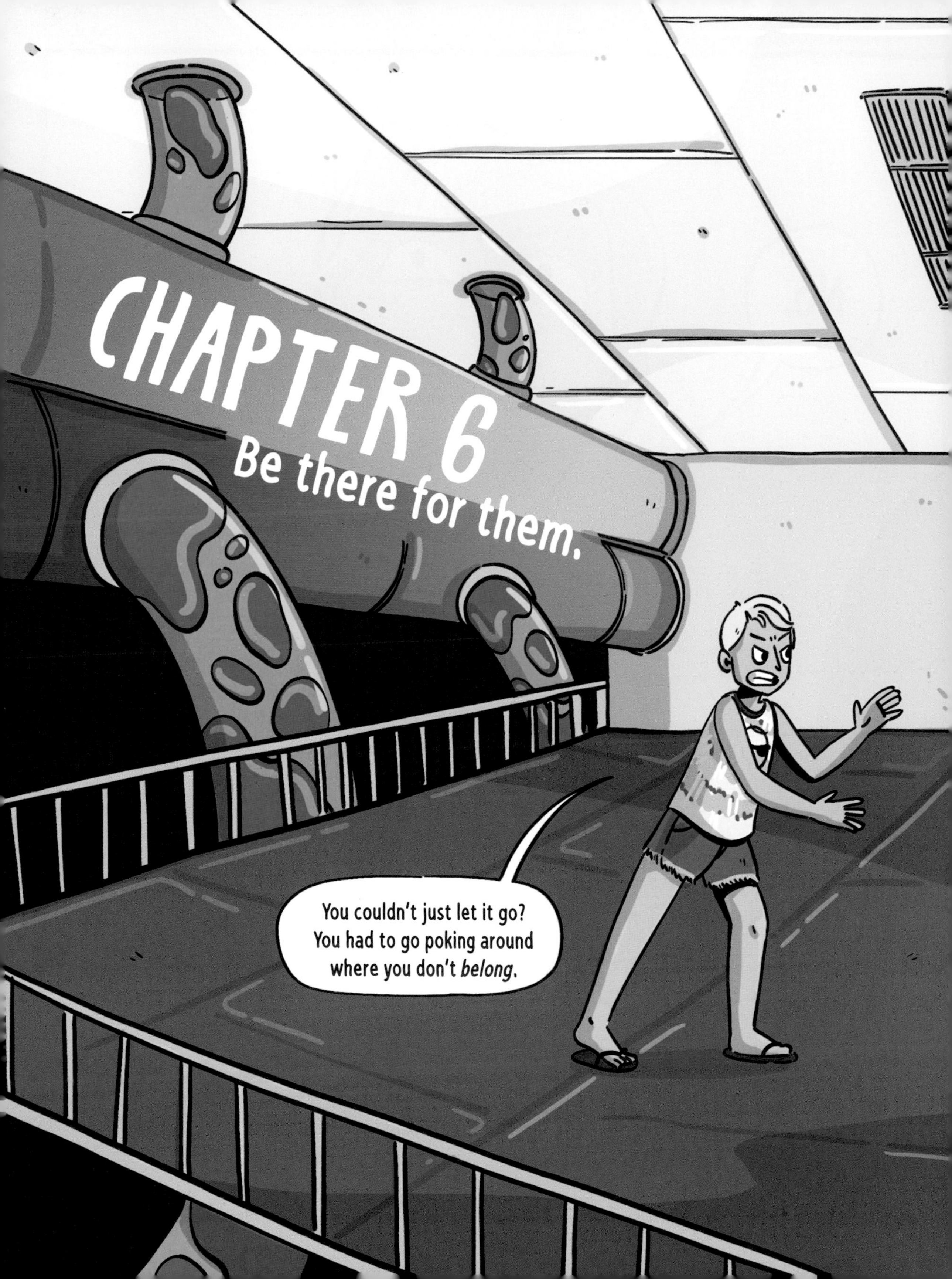
CHAPTER 6
Be there for them.
You couldn't just let it go? You had to go poking around where you don't *belong*.

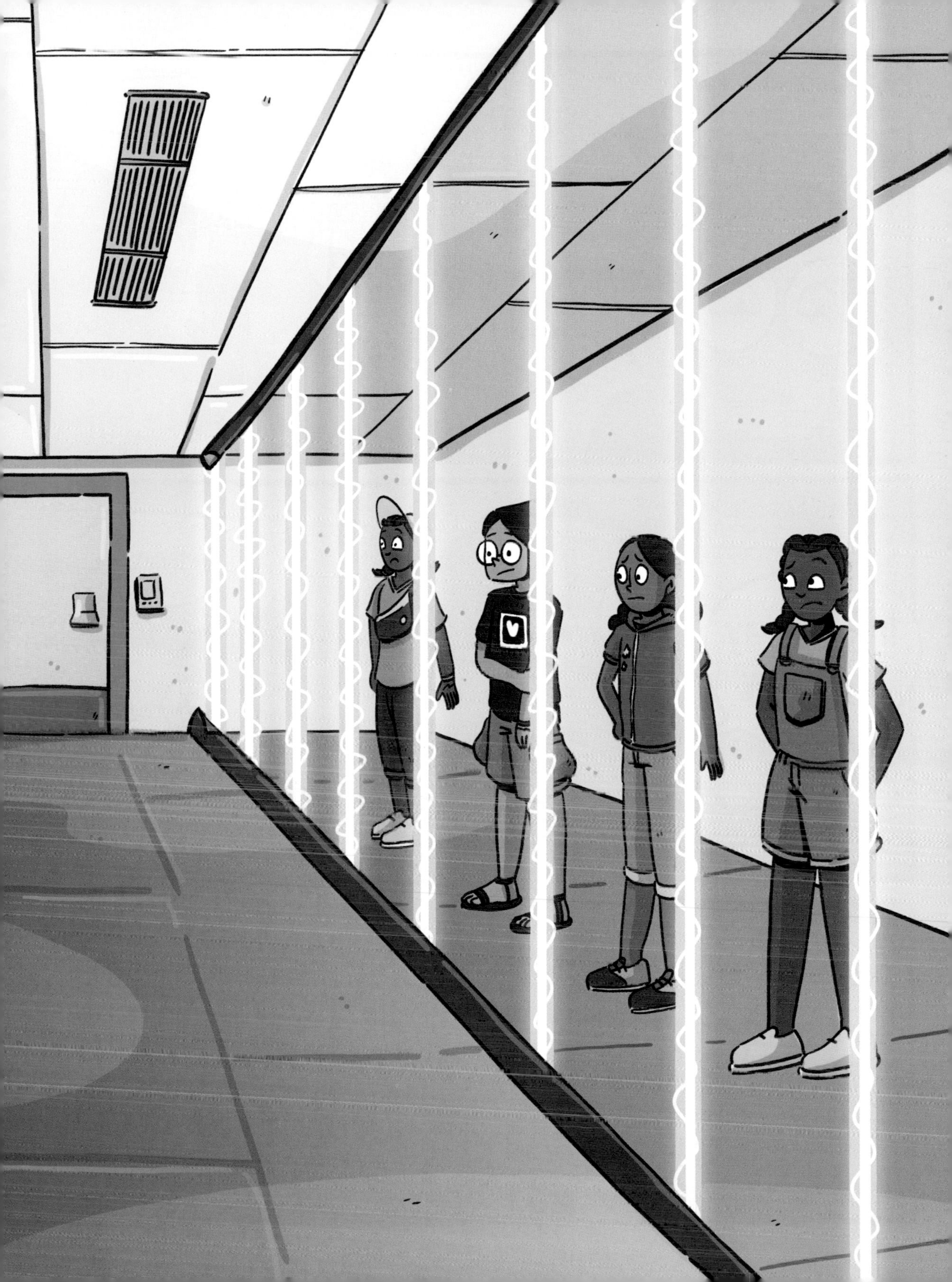

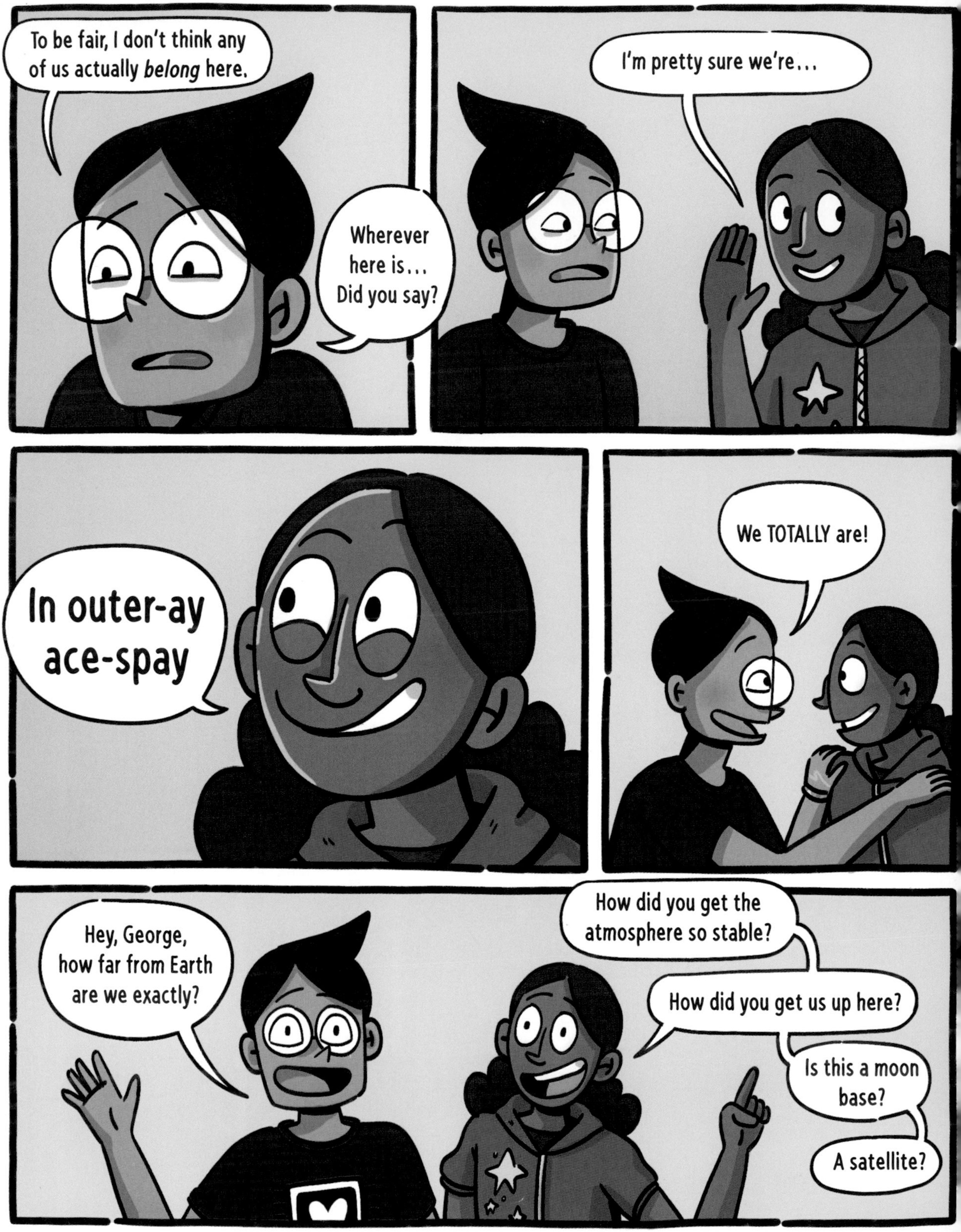
To be fair, I don't think any of us actually *belong* here.
Wherever here is... Did you say?
I'm pretty sure we're...
In outer-ay ace-spay
We TOTALLY are!
Hey, George, how far from Earth are we exactly?
How did you get the atmosphere so stable?
How did you get us up here?
Is this a moon base?
A satellite?

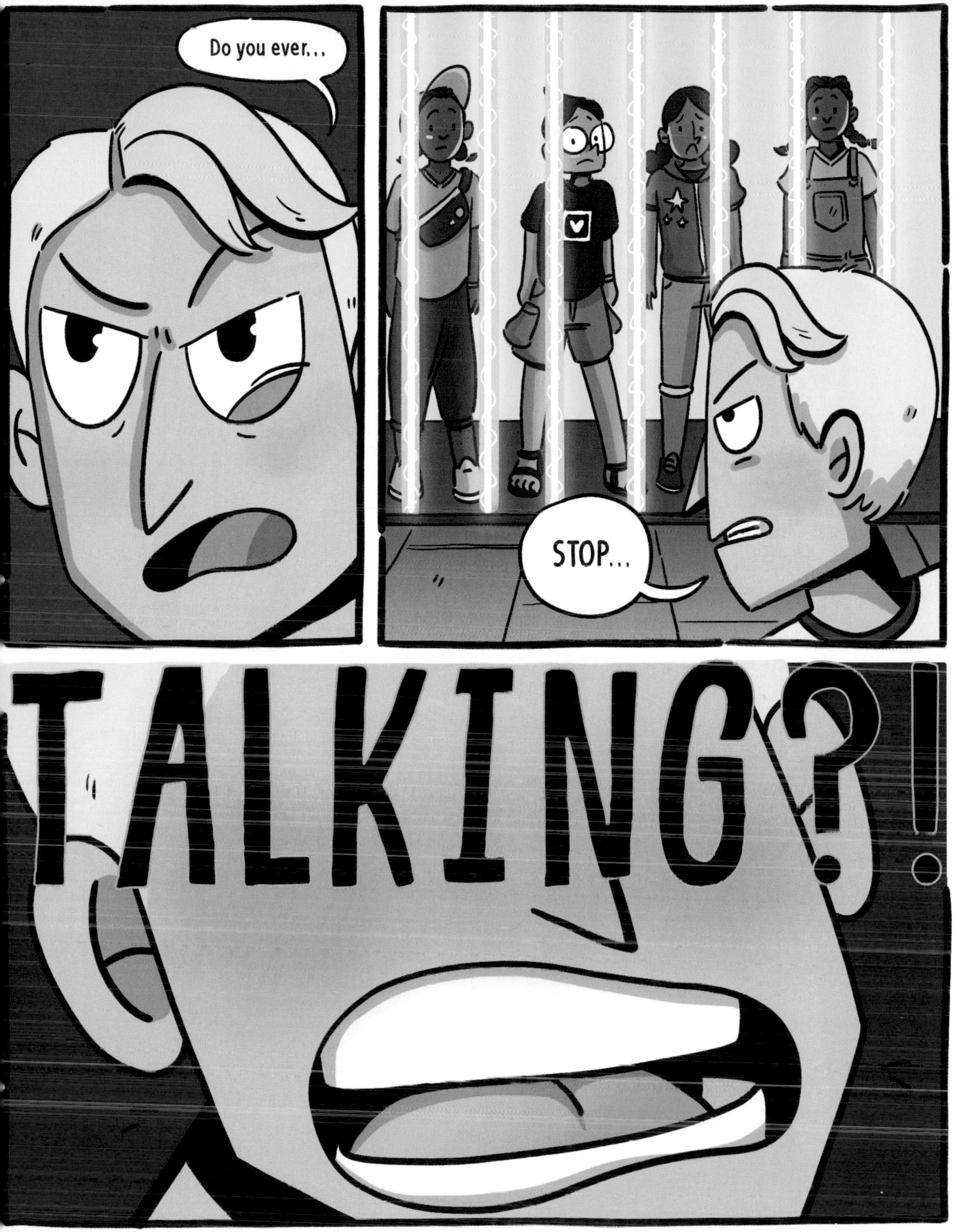
Do you ever...
STOP...
TALKING?!

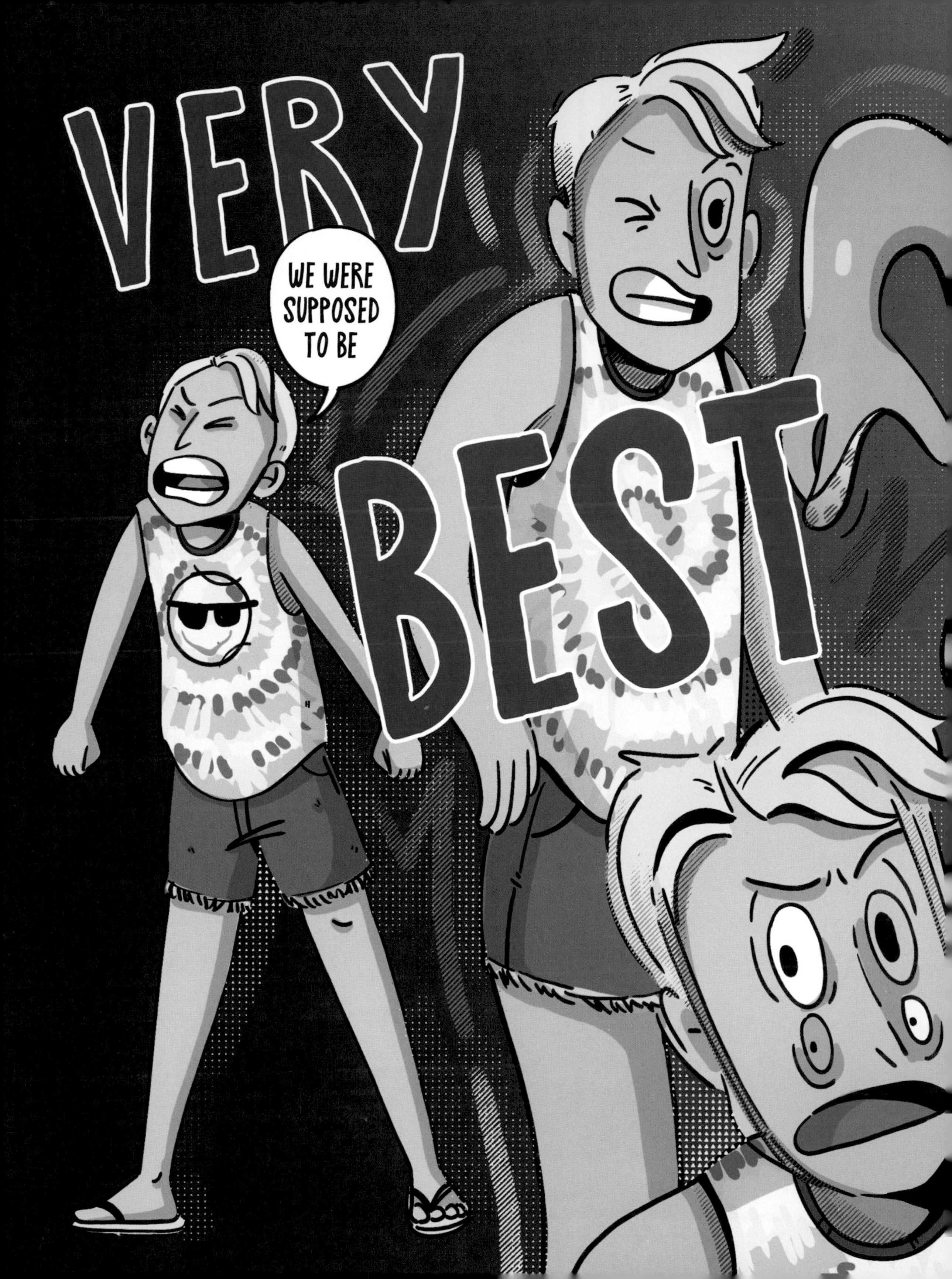
VERY
WE WERE SUPPOSED TO BE
BEST

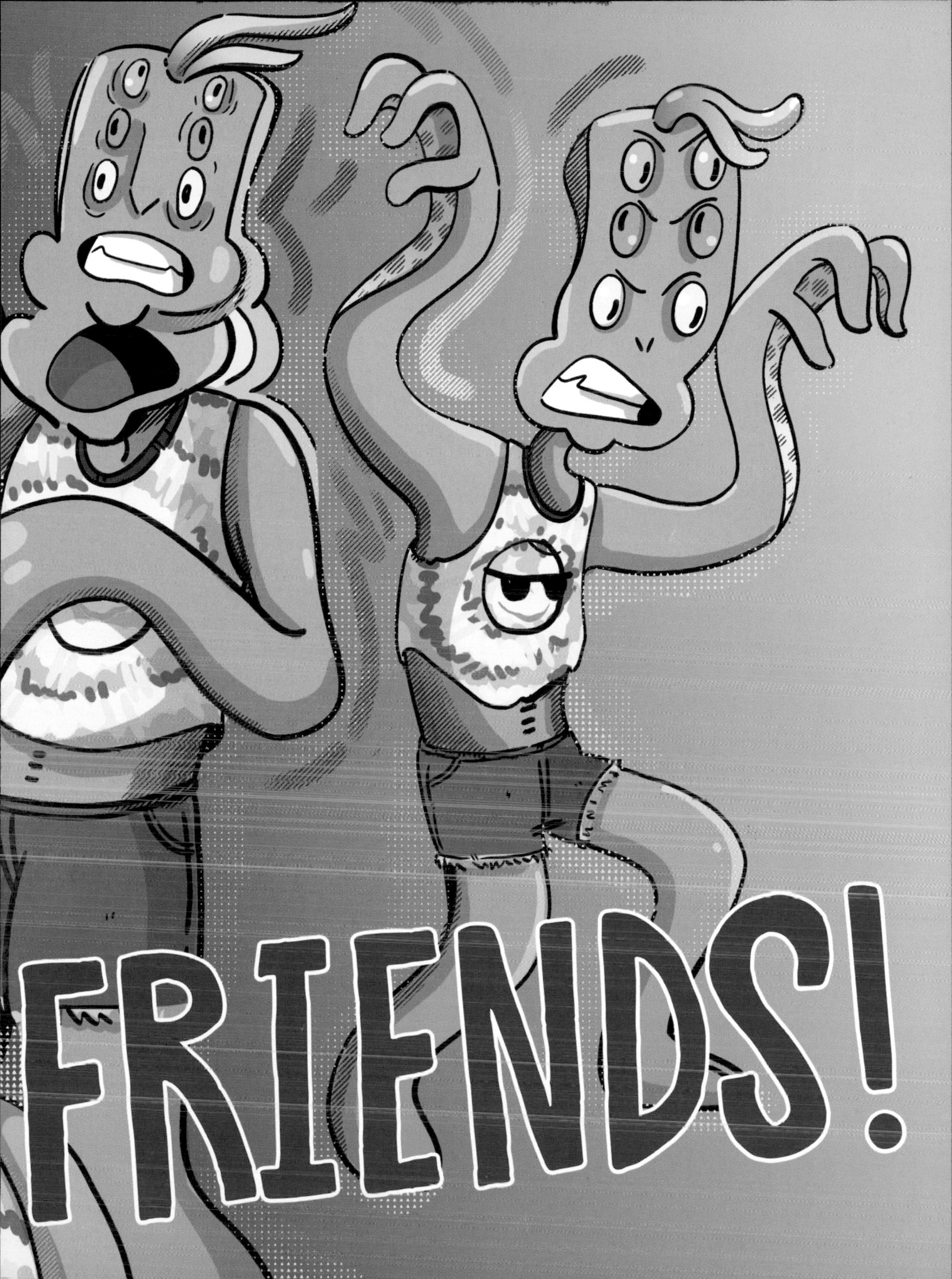
FRIENDS!

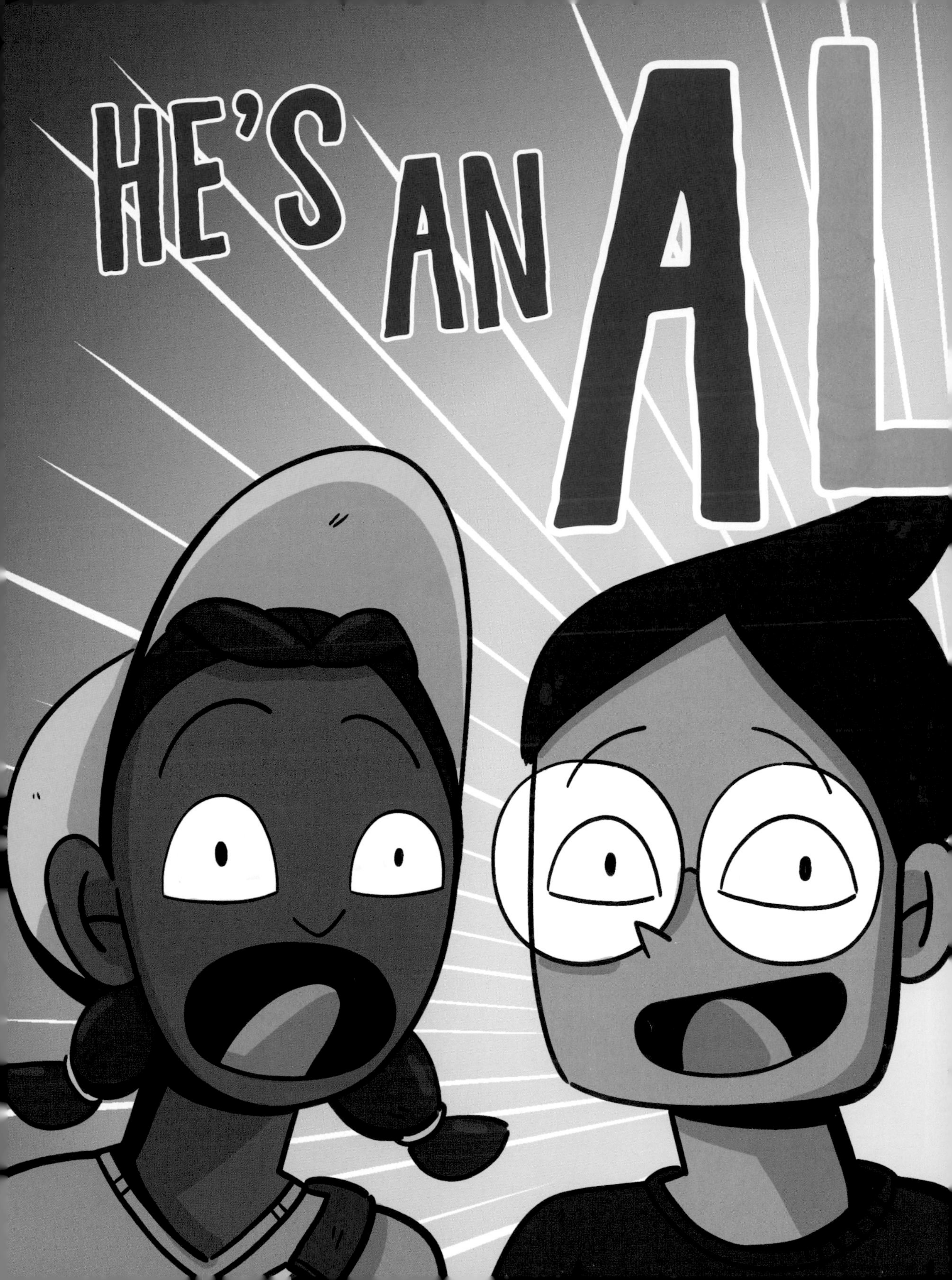
HE'S AN AL

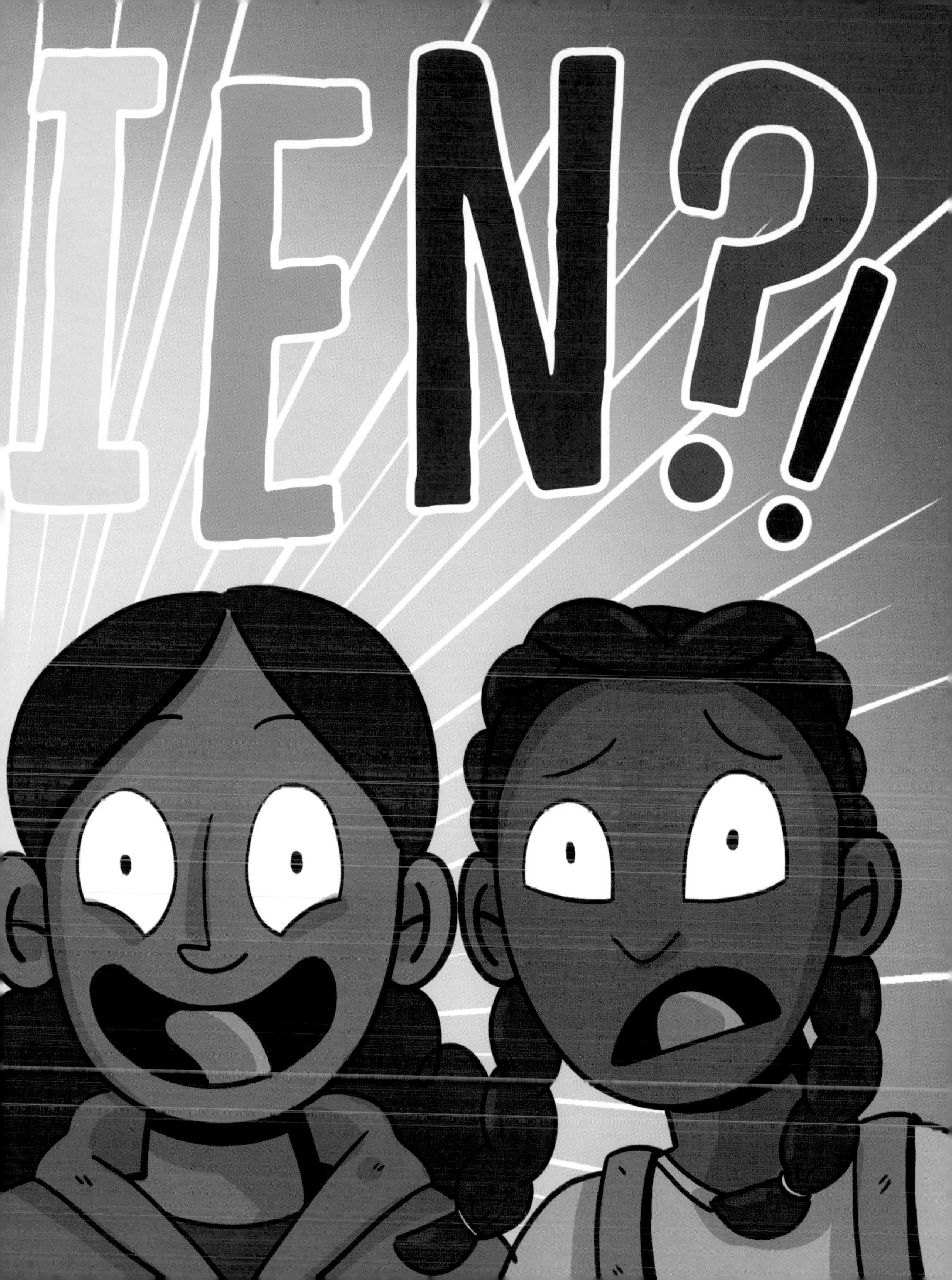
IEN?!

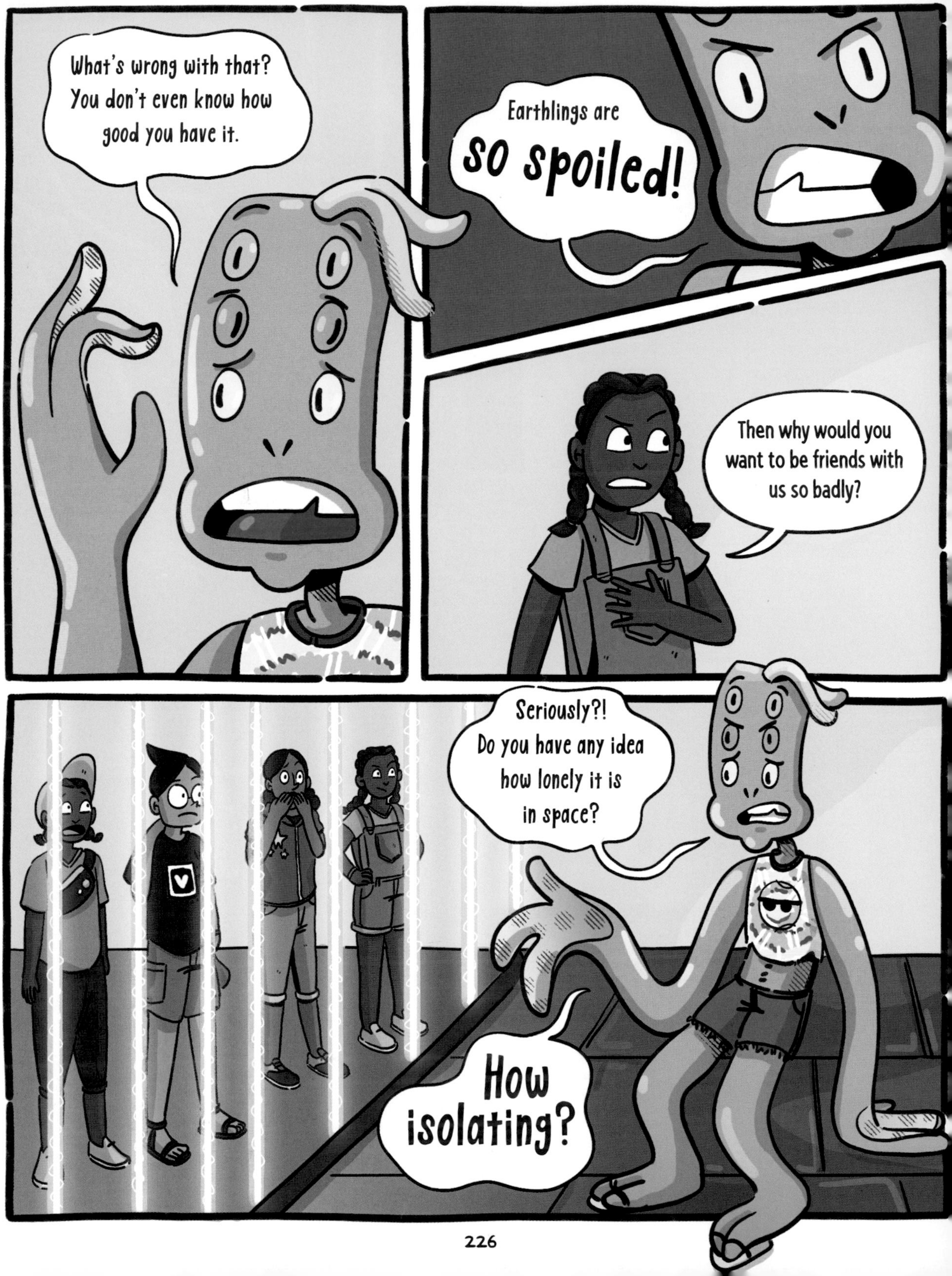
What's wrong with that? You don't even know how good you have it.
Earthlings are SO SPOILED!
Then why would you want to be friends with us so badly?
Seriously?! Do you have any idea how lonely it is in space?
How isolating?

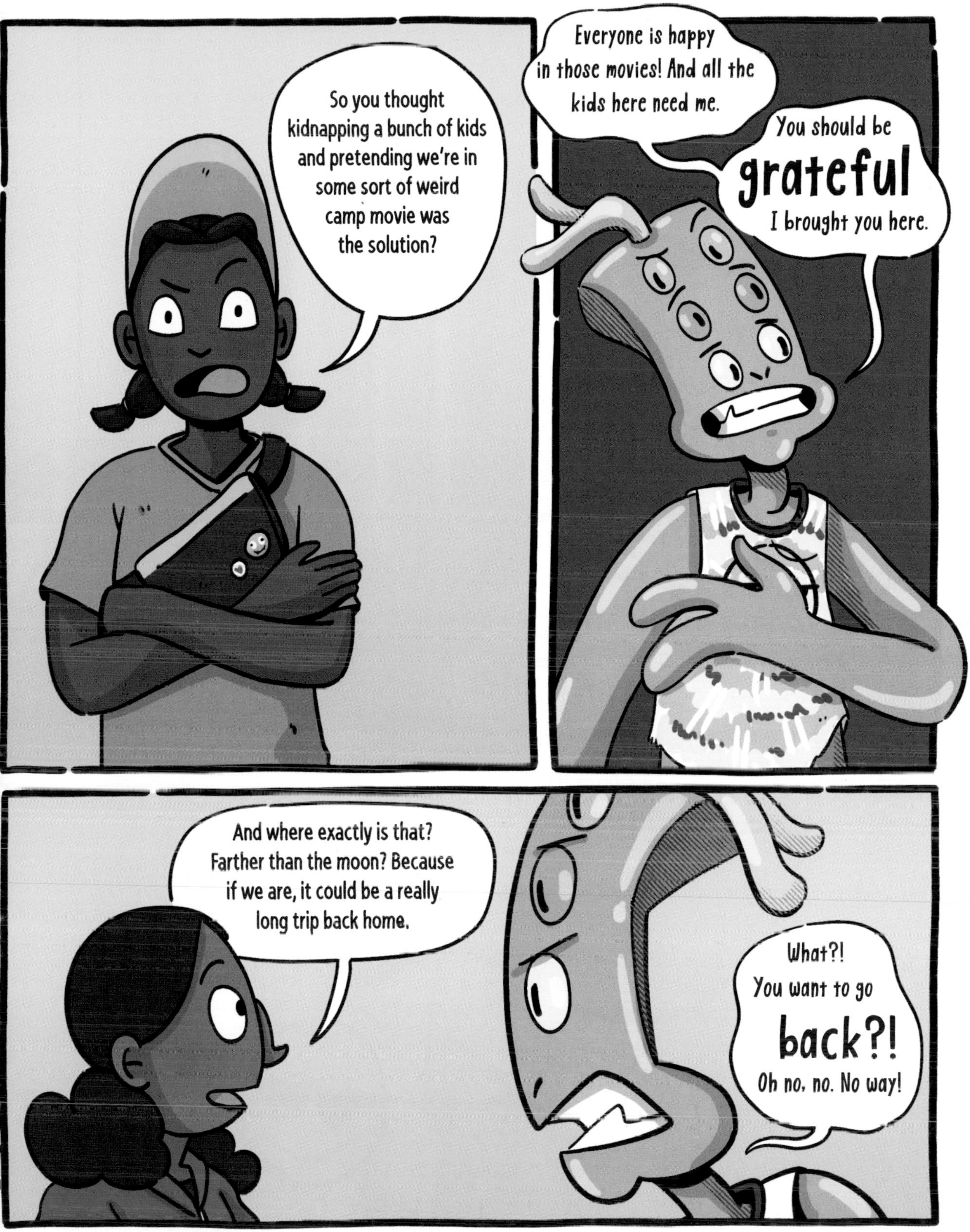

So you thought kidnapping a bunch of kids and pretending we're in some sort of weird camp movie was the solution?
Everyone is happy in those movies! And all the kids here need me.
You should be grateful I brought you here.
And where exactly is that? Farther than the moon? Because if we are, it could be a really long trip back home.
What?! You want to go back?! Oh no, no. No way!

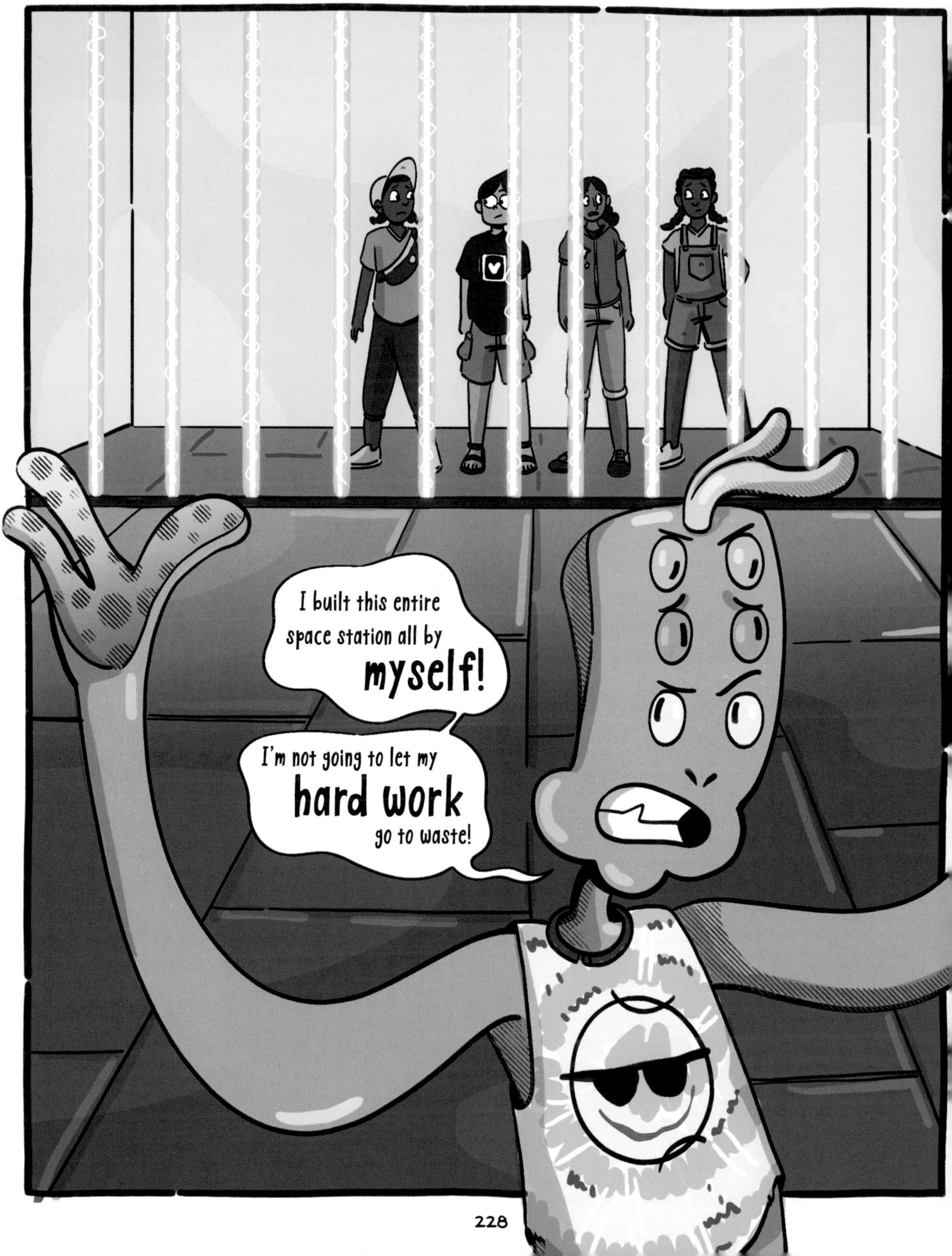
I built this entire space station all by myself!
I'm not going to let my hard work go to waste!

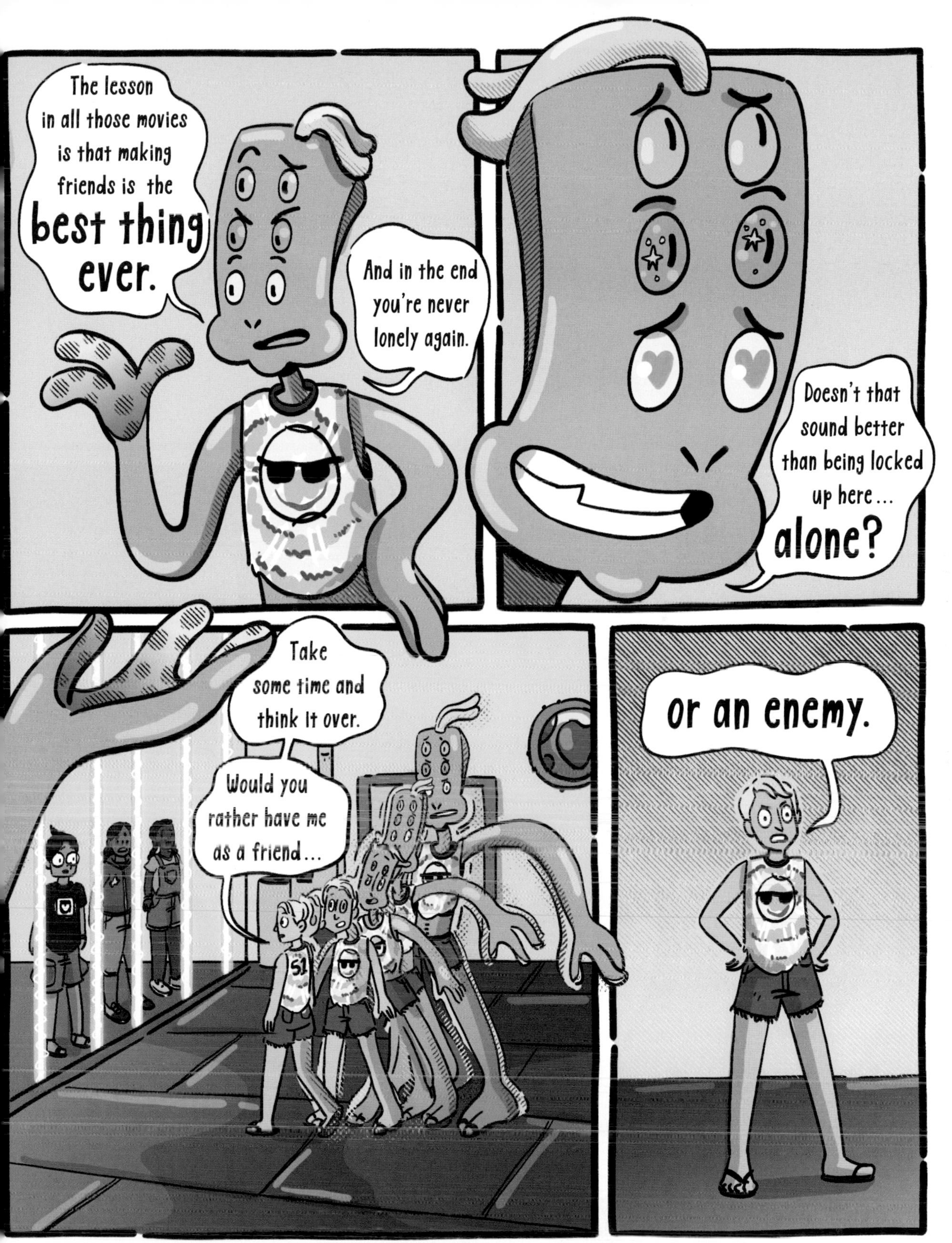
The lesson in all those movies is that making friends is the best thing ever.
And in the end you're never lonely again.
Doesn't that sound better than being locked up here... alone?
Take some time and think it over.
Would you rather have me as a friend...
or an enemy.

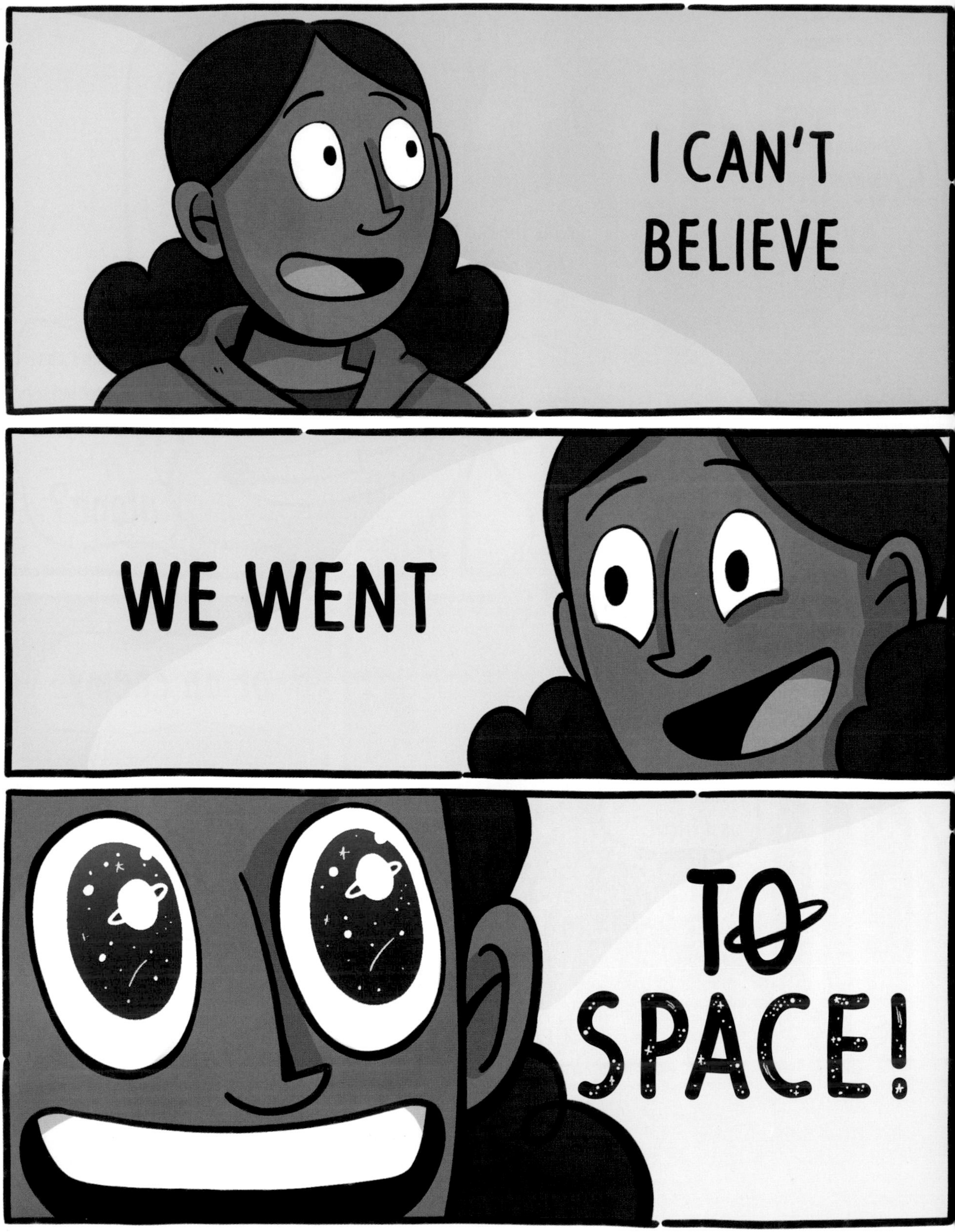
I CAN'T BELIEVE
WE WENT
TO SPACE!

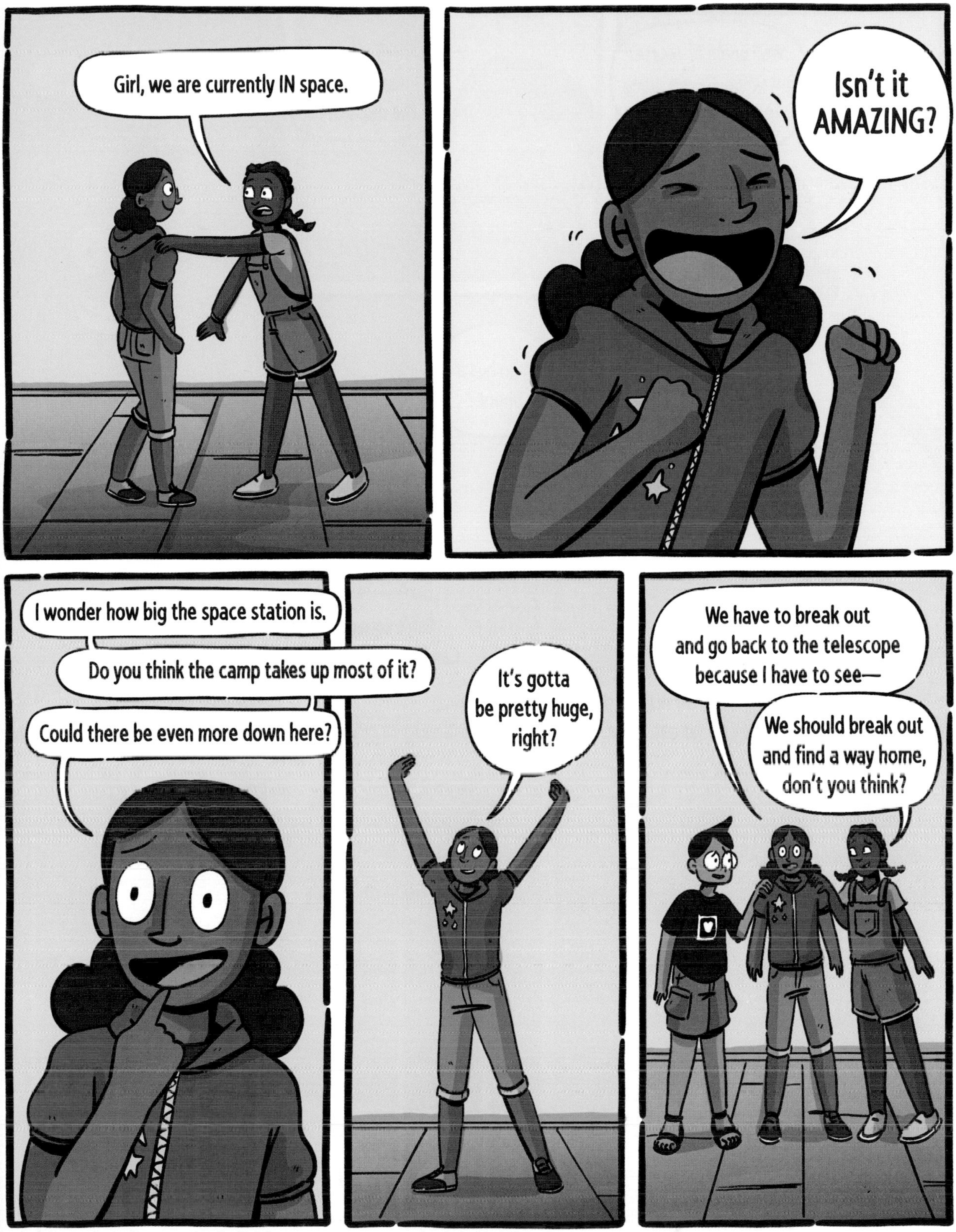
Girl, we are currently IN space.
Isn't it AMAZING?
I wonder how big the space station is.
Do you think the camp takes up most of it?
Could there be even more down here?
It's gotta be pretty huge, right?
We have to break out and go back to the telescope because I have to see—
We should break out and find a way home, don't you think?

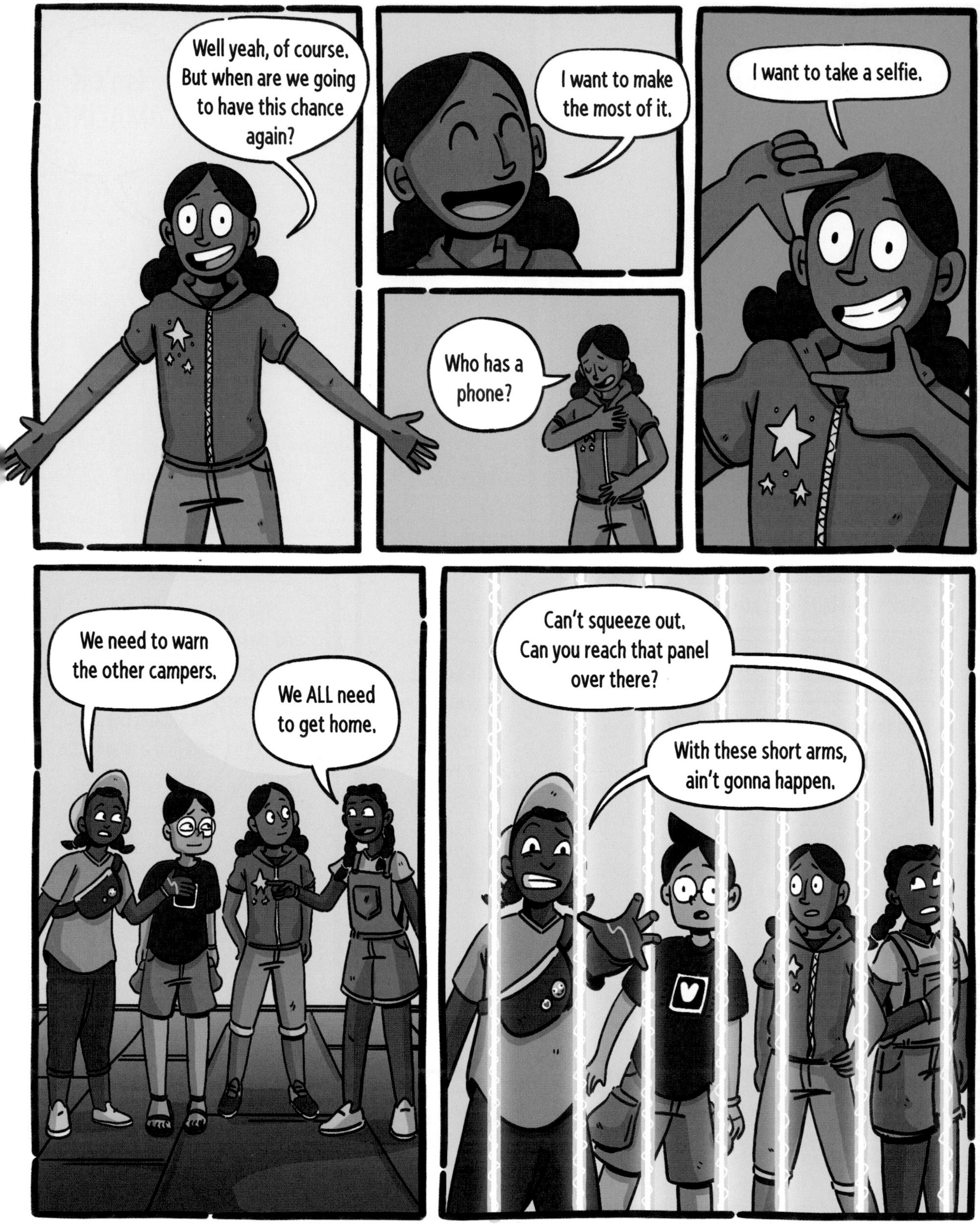
Well yeah, of course. But when are we going to have this chance again?
I want to make the most of it.
Who has a phone?
I want to take a selfie.
We need to warn the other campers.
We ALL need to get home.
Can't squeeze out. Can you reach that panel over there?
With these short arms, ain't gonna happen.

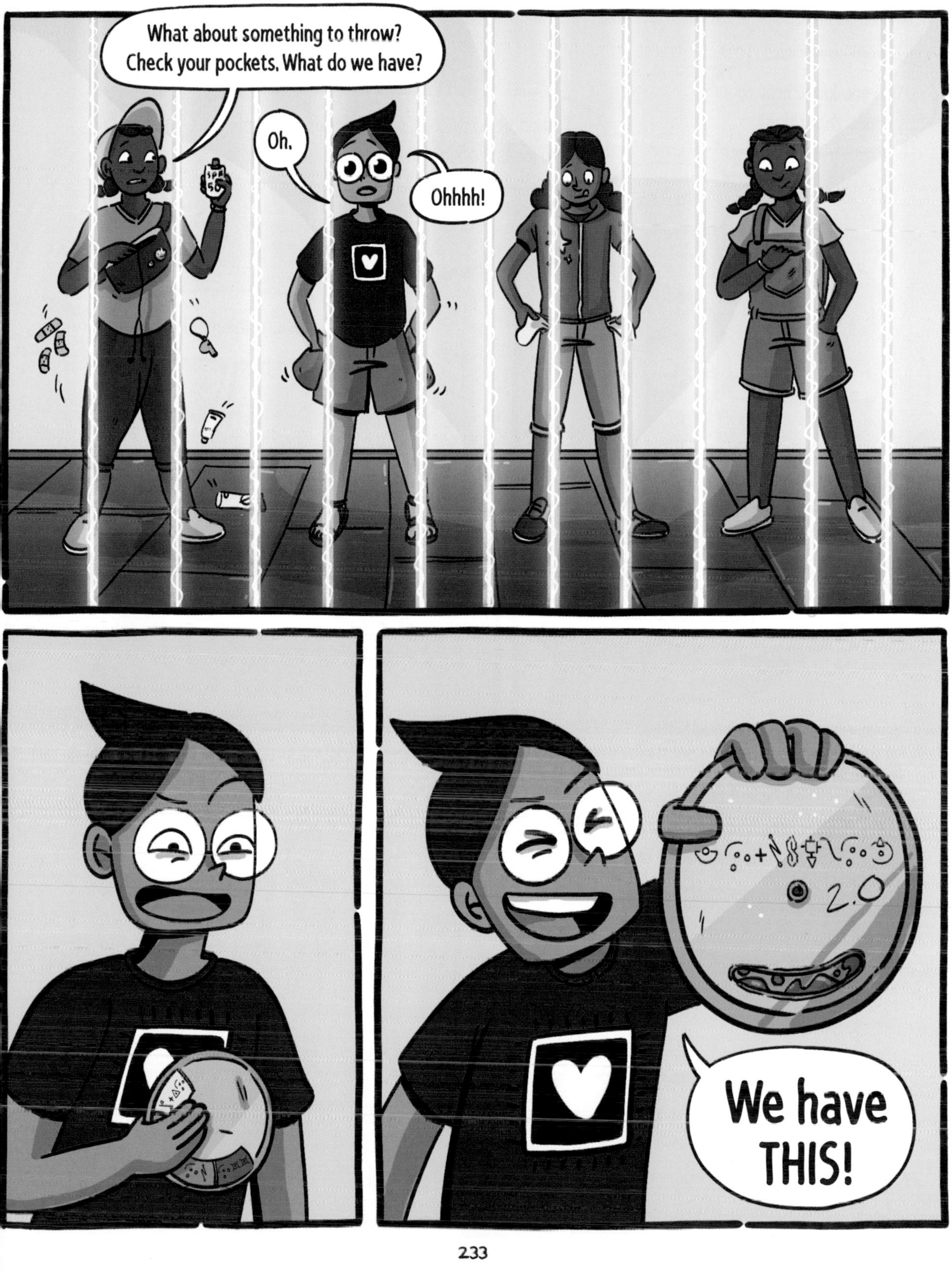
What about something to throw? Check your pockets. What do we have?
Oh.
Ohhhh!
SPF 50
2.0
We have THIS!

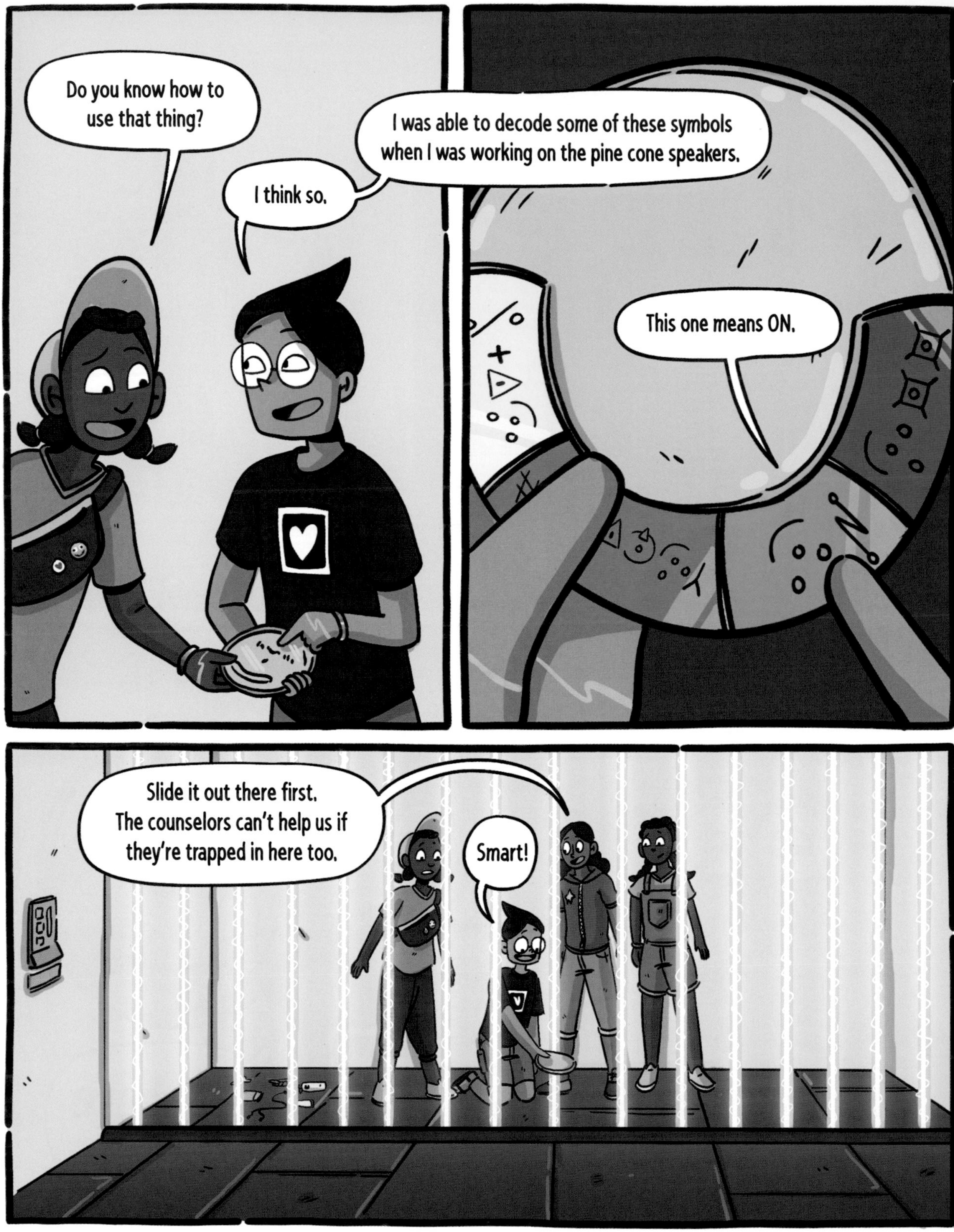
Do you know how to use that thing?
I think so.
I was able to decode some of these symbols when I was working on the pine cone speakers.
This one means ON.
Slide it out there first. The counselors can't help us if they're trapped in here too.
Smart!

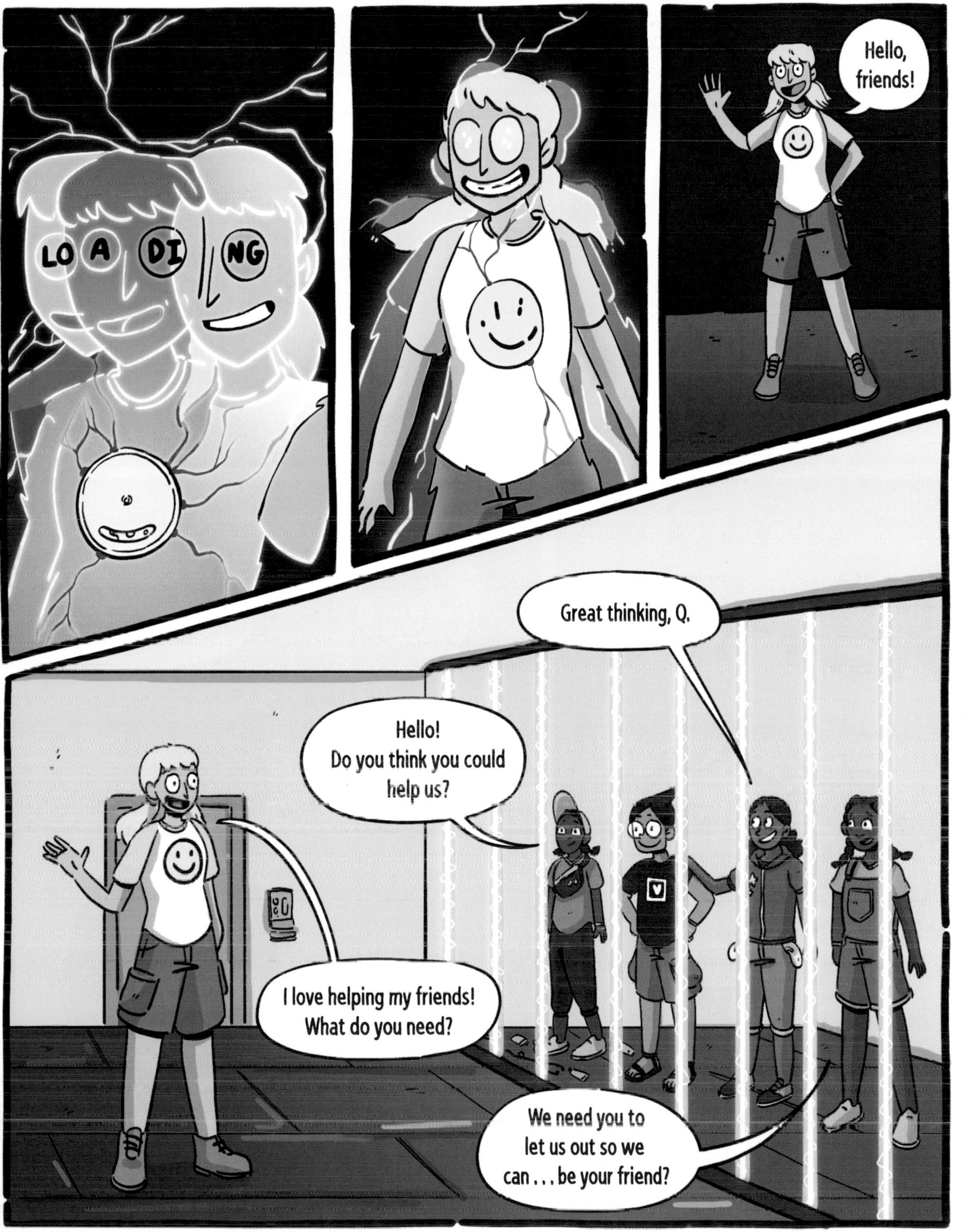
LO A DI NG
Hello, friends!
Great thinking, Q.
Hello!
Do you think you could help us?
I love helping my friends!
What do you need?
We need you to let us out so we can . . . be your friend?

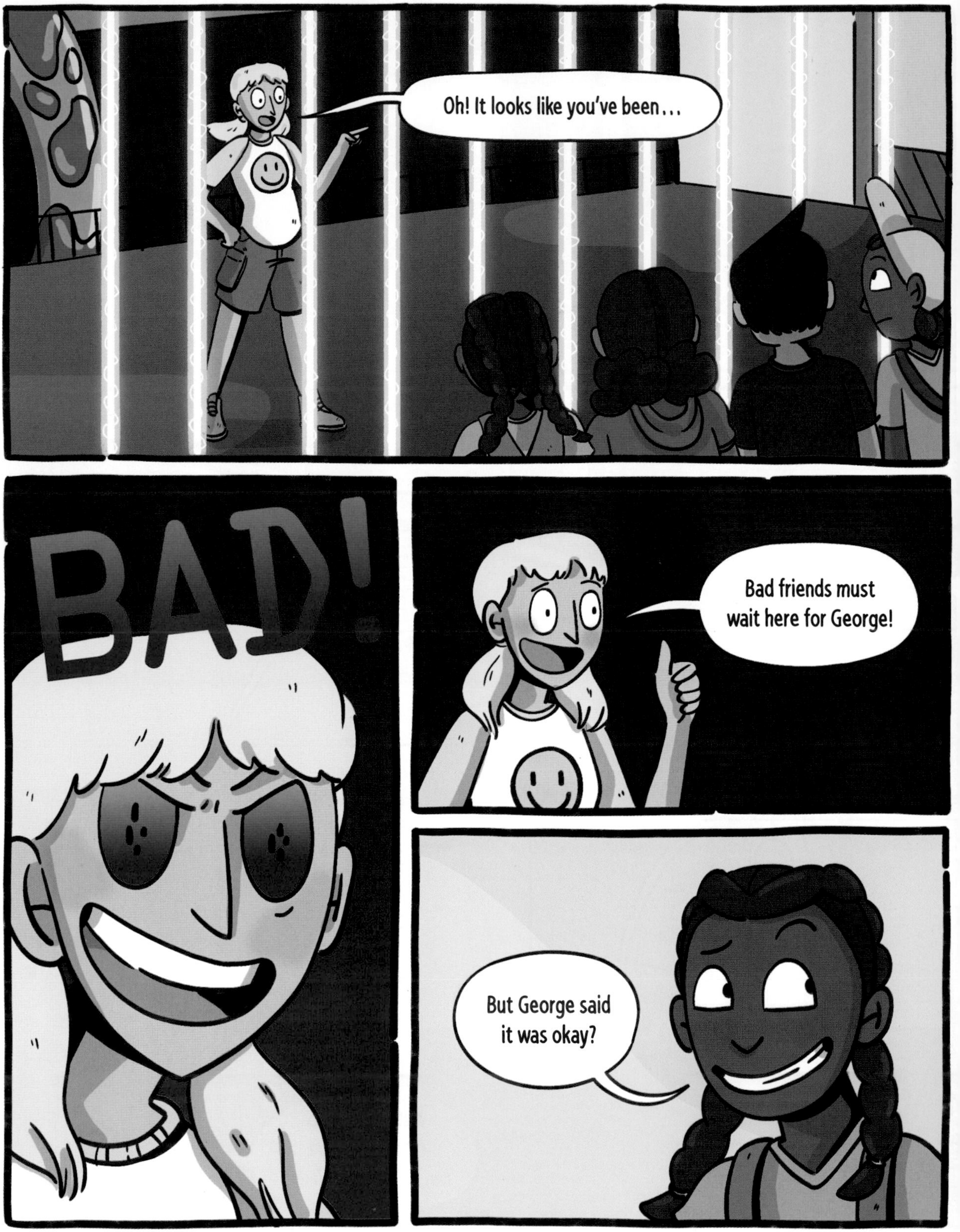
Oh! It looks like you've been…
BAD!
Bad friends must wait here for George!
But George said it was okay?

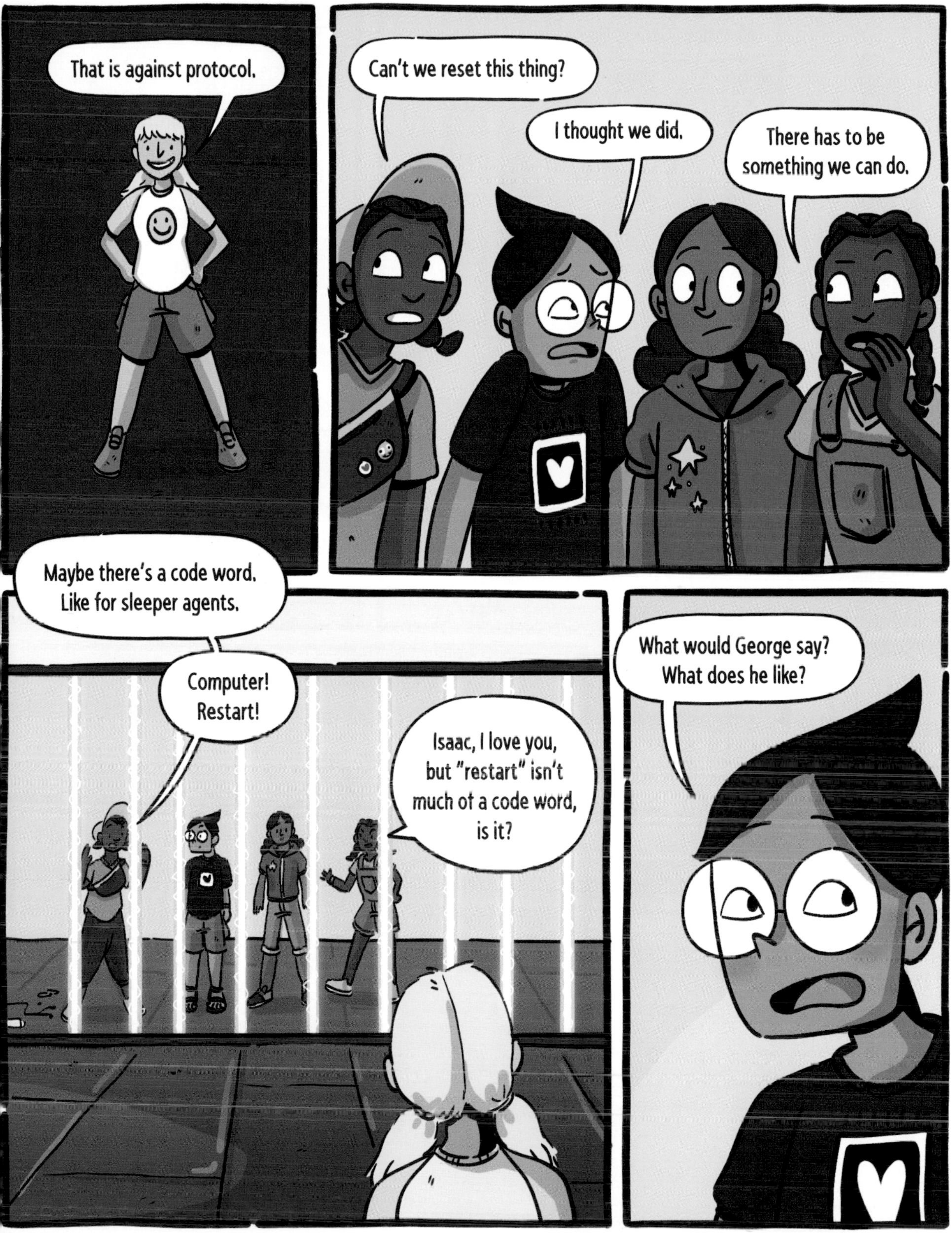
That is against protocol.
Can't we reset this thing?
I thought we did.
There has to be something we can do.
Maybe there's a code word. Like for sleeper agents.
Computer! Restart!
Isaac, I love you, but "restart" isn't much of a code word, is it?
What would George say? What does he like?

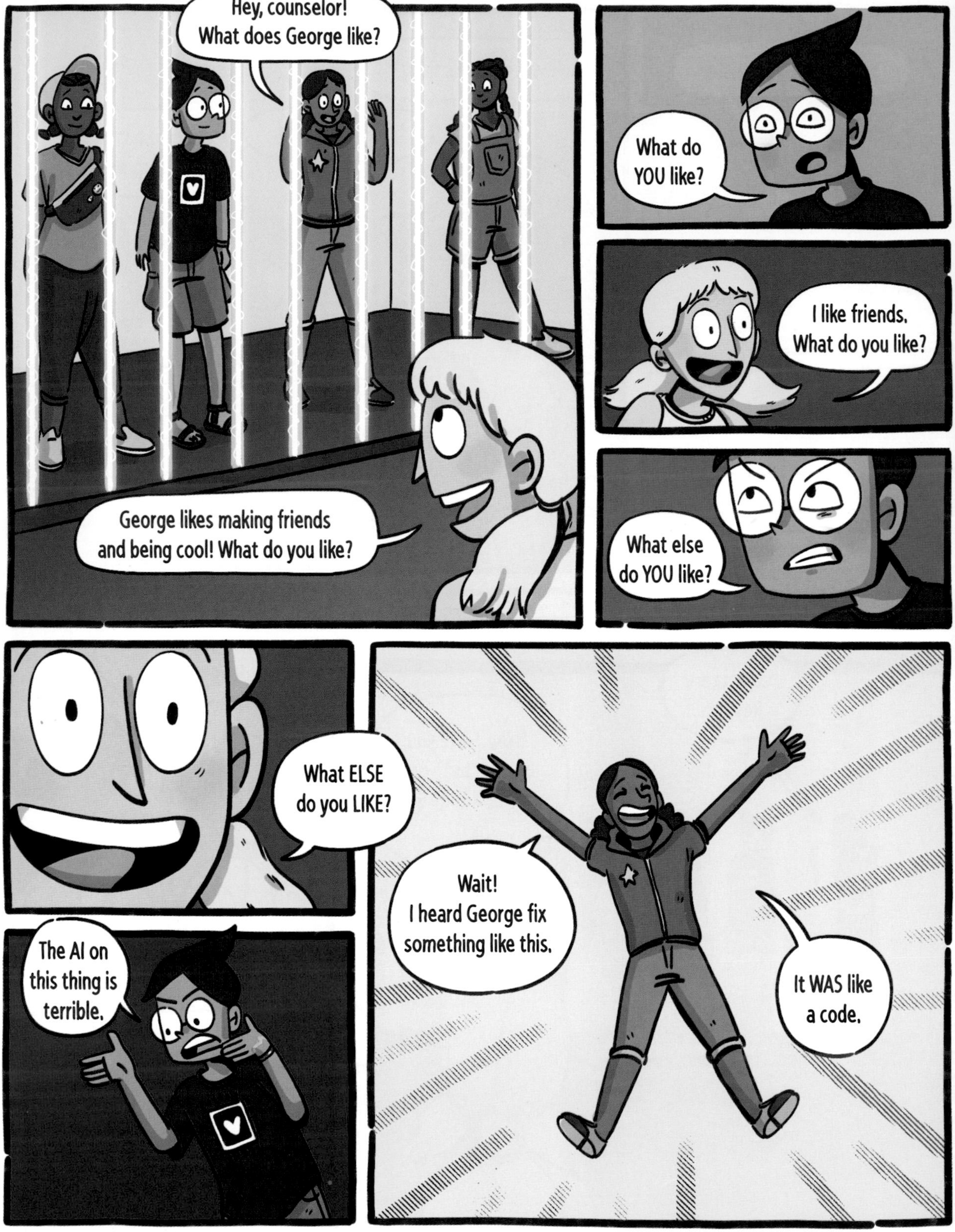
Hey, counselor! What does George like?
George likes making friends and being cool! What do you like?
What do YOU like?
I like friends. What do you like?
What else do YOU like?
What ELSE do you LIKE?
The AI on this thing is terrible.
Wait! I heard George fix something like this.
It WAS like a code.

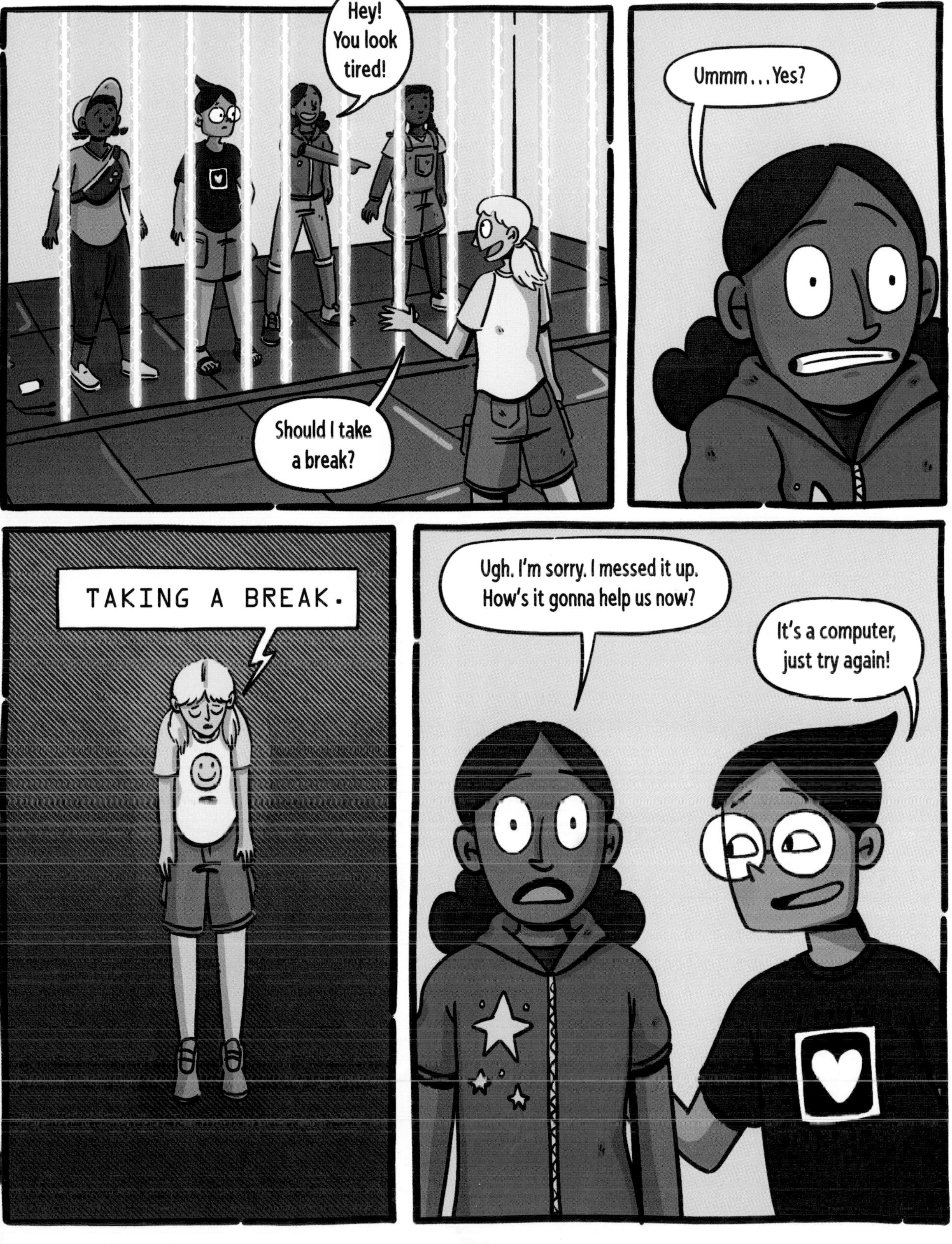
Hey! You look tired!
Should I take a break?
Ummm. . . Yes?
TAKING A BREAK.
Ugh. I'm sorry. I messed it up. How's it gonna help us now?
It's a computer, just try again!

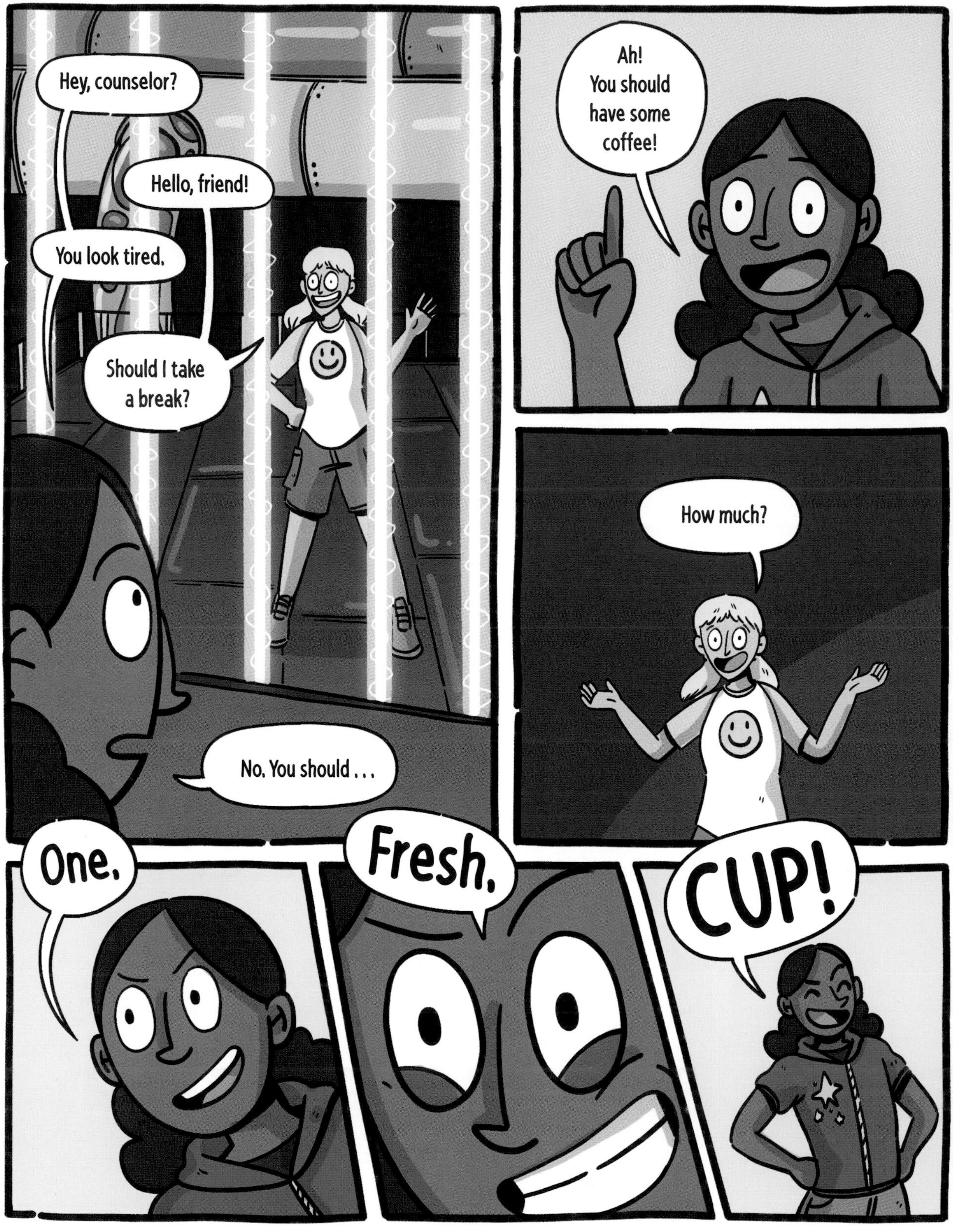

Hey, counselor?
Hello, friend!
You look tired.
Should I take a break?
No. You should . . .
Ah! You should have some coffee!
How much?
One.
Fresh.
CUP!

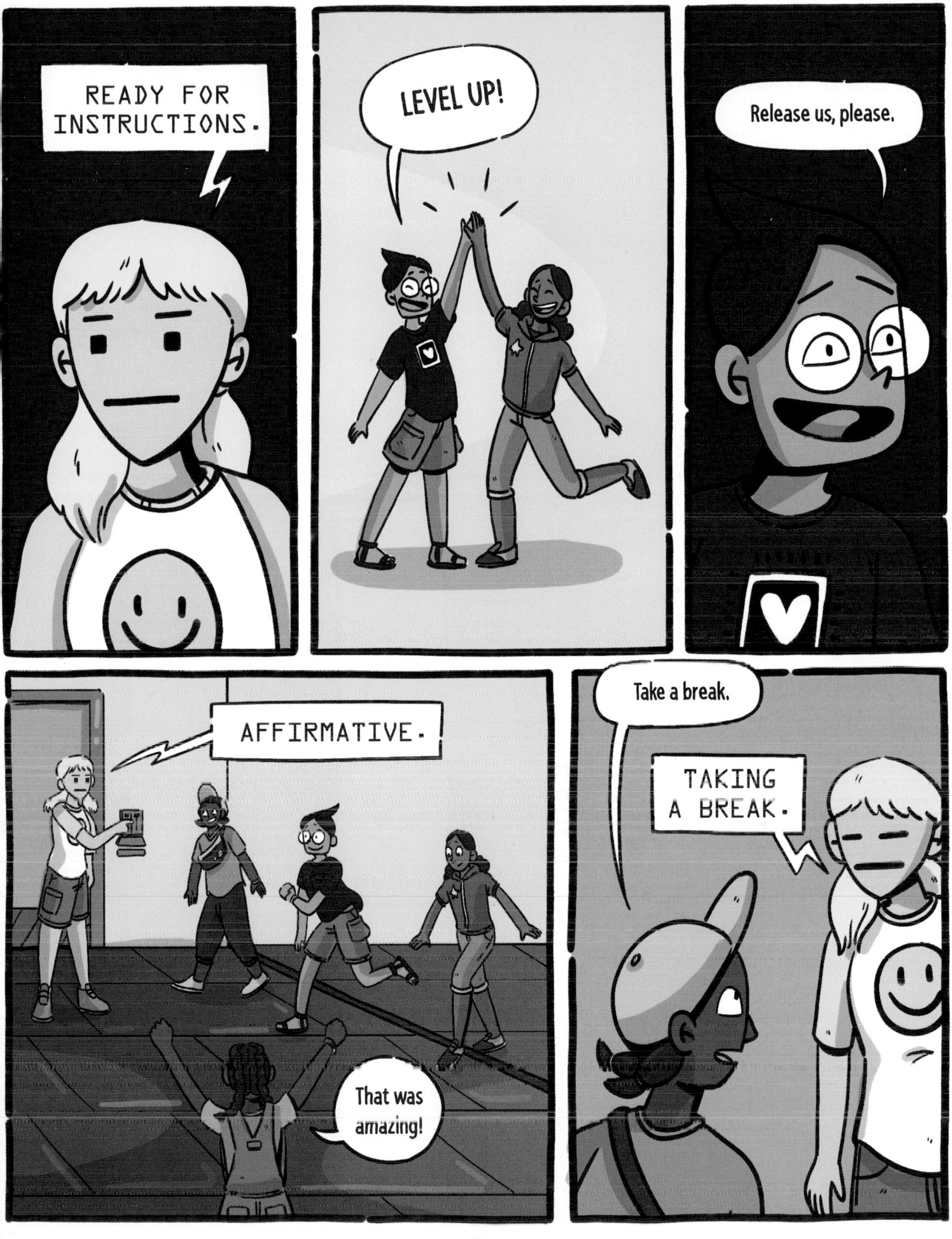
READY FOR INSTRUCTIONS.
LEVEL UP!
Release us, please.
AFFIRMATIVE.
That was amazing!
Take a break.
TAKING A BREAK.

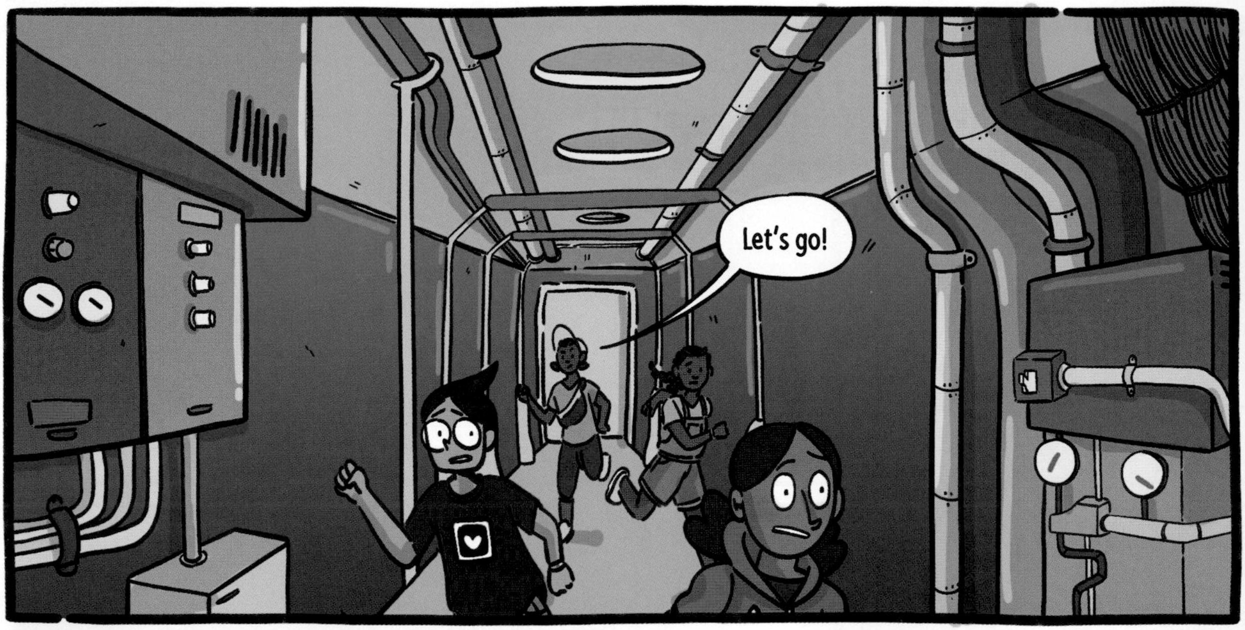
Let's go!

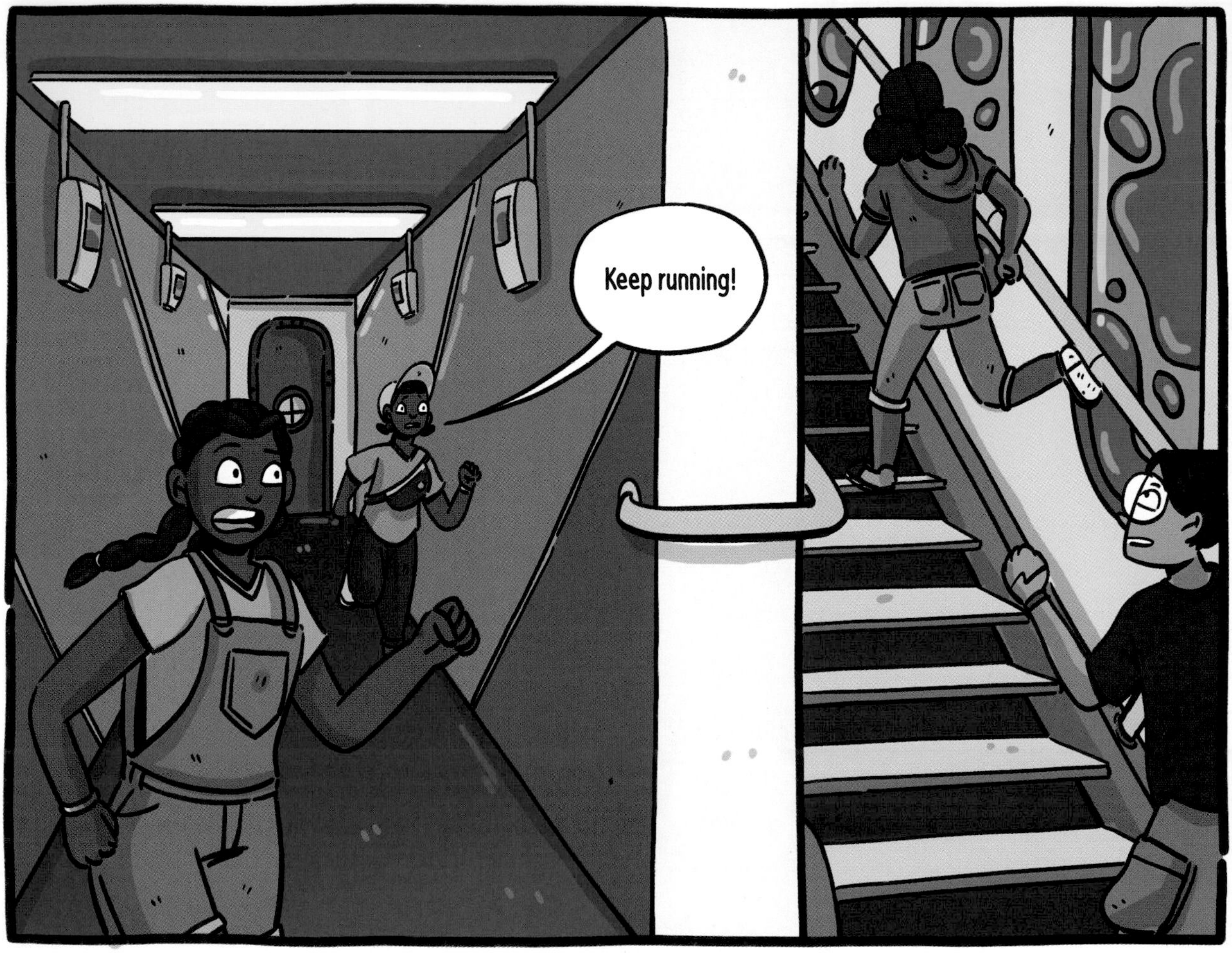
Keep running!

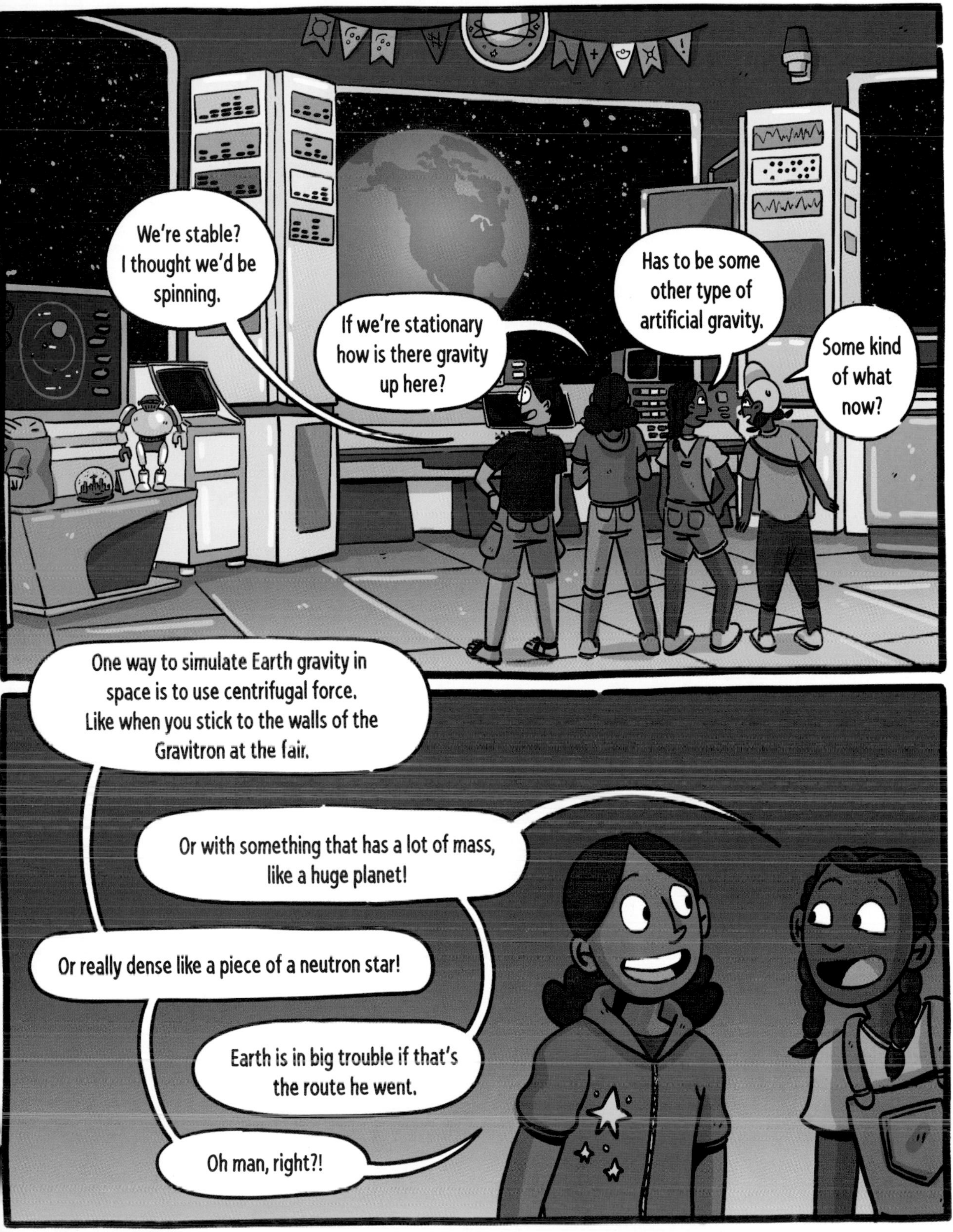
We're stable? I thought we'd be spinning.
If we're stationary how is there gravity up here?
Has to be some other type of artificial gravity.
Some kind of what now?
One way to simulate Earth gravity in space is to use centrifugal force. Like when you stick to the walls of the Gravitron at the fair.
Or with something that has a lot of mass, like a huge planet!
Or really dense like a piece of a neutron star!
Earth is in big trouble if that's the route he went.
Oh man, right?!

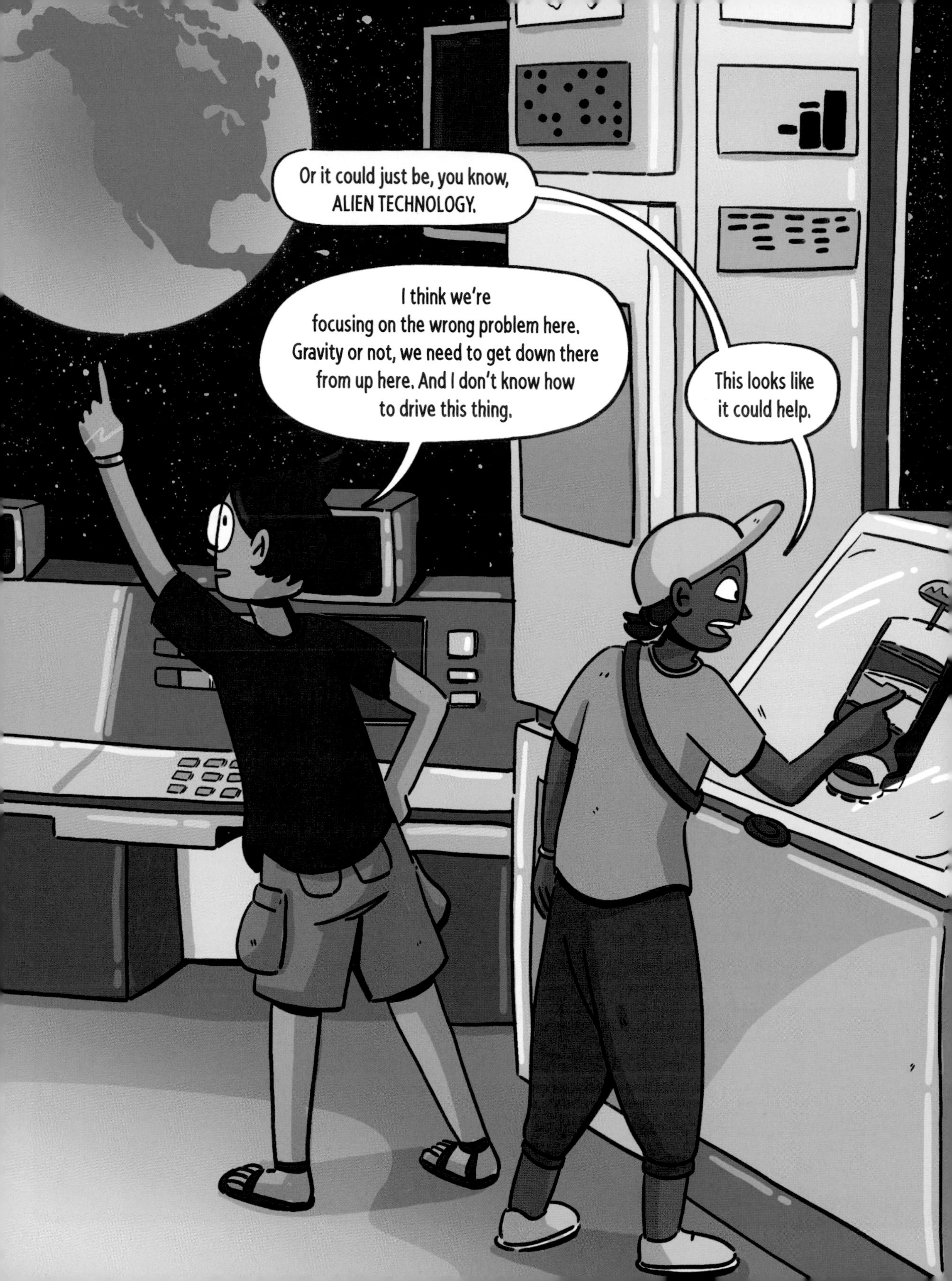
Or it could just be, you know, ALIEN TECHNOLOGY.
I think we're focusing on the wrong problem here. Gravity or not, we need to get down there from up here. And I don't know how to drive this thing.
This looks like it could help.

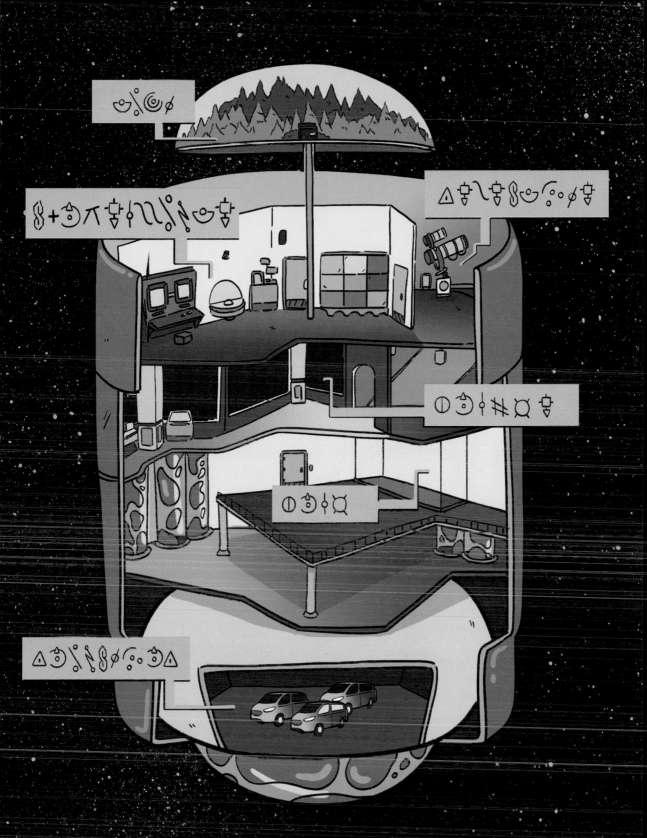

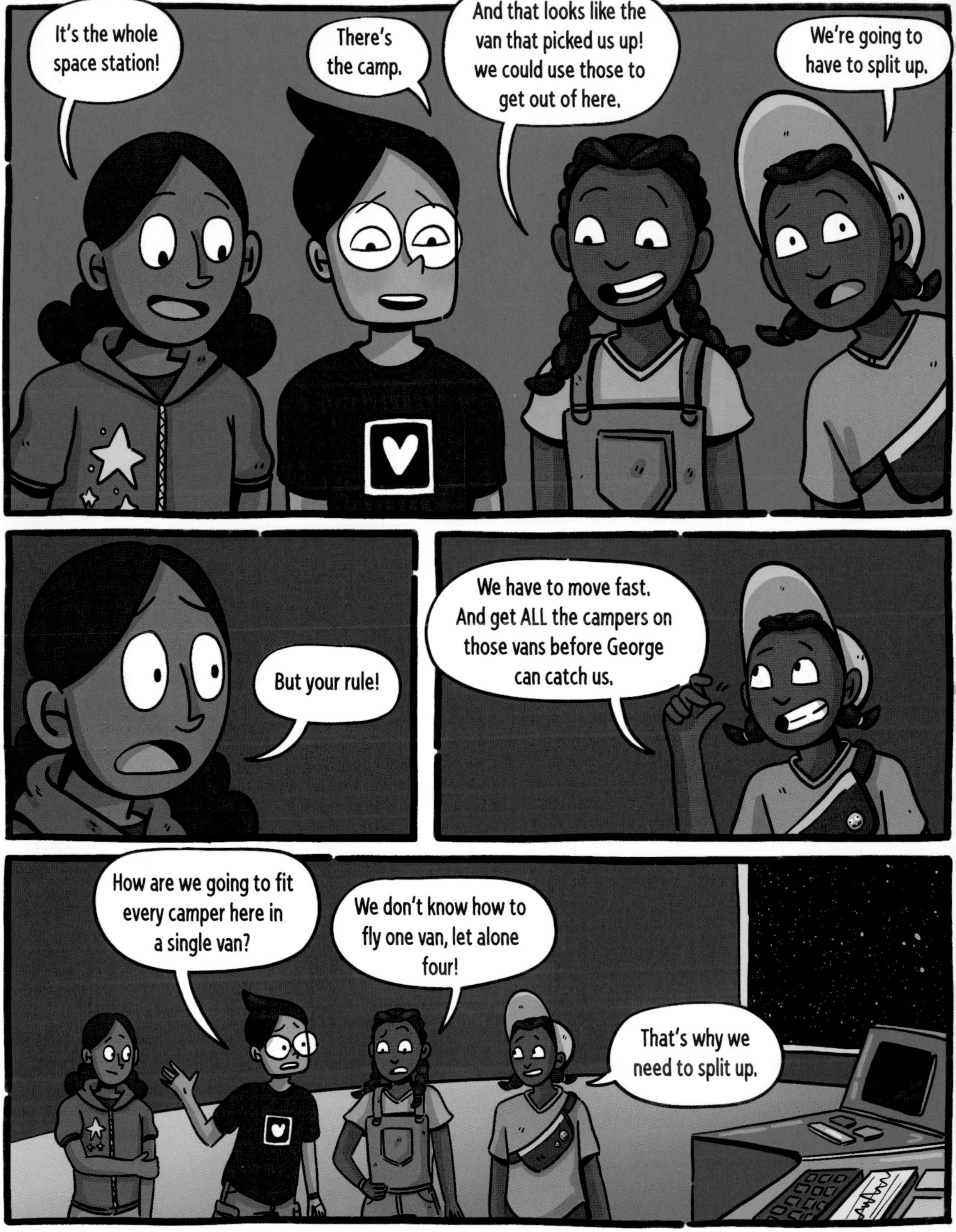

It's the whole space station!
There's the camp.
And that looks like the van that picked us up! we could use those to get out of here.
We're going to have to split up.
But your rule!
We have to move fast. And get ALL the campers on those vans before George can catch us.
How are we going to fit every camper here in a single van?
We don't know how to fly one van, let alone four!
That's why we need to split up.

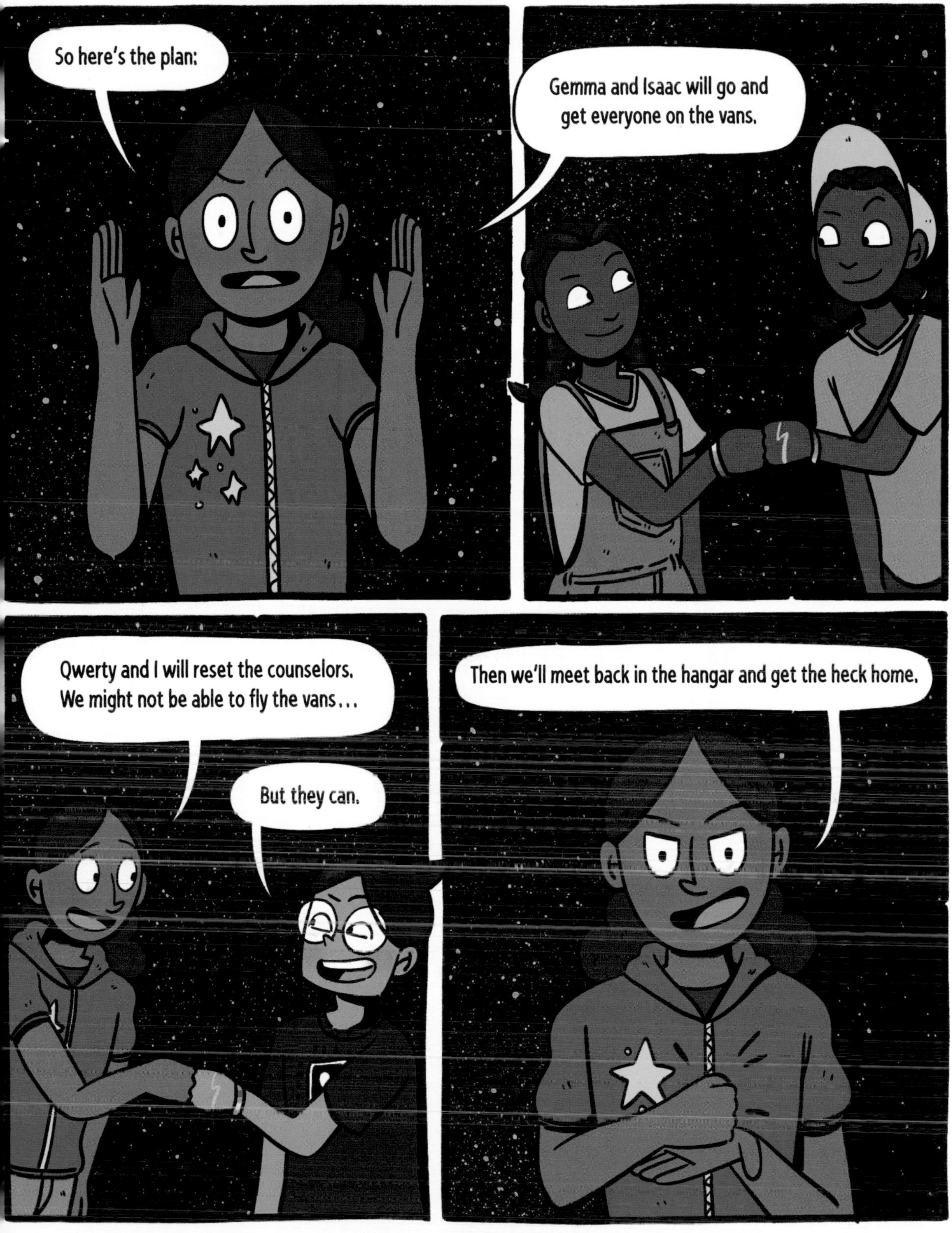
So here's the plan:
Gemma and Isaac will go and get everyone on the vans.
Qwerty and I will reset the counselors. We might not be able to fly the vans…
But they can.
Then we'll meet back in the hangar and get the heck home.

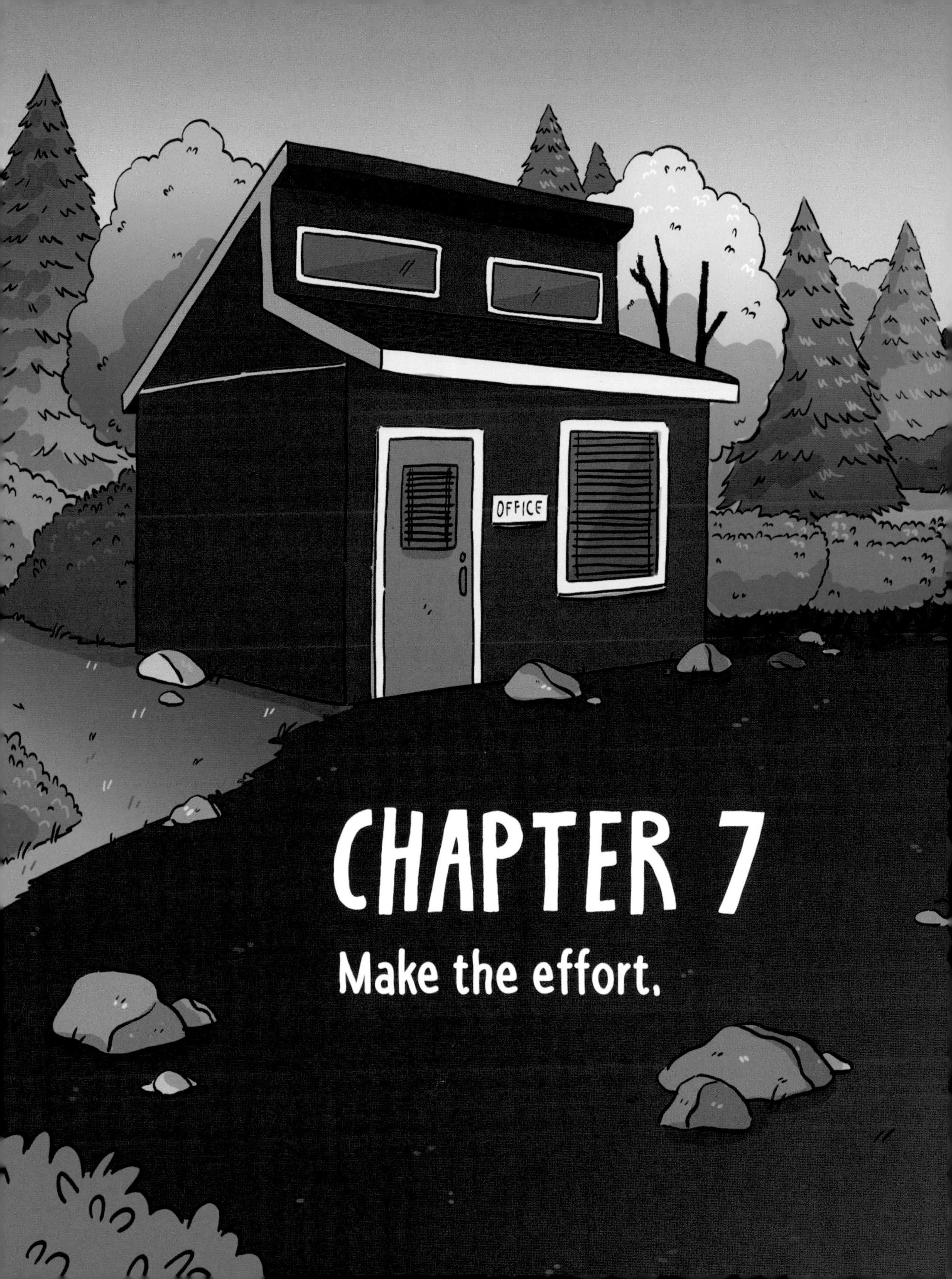
OFFICE

CHAPTER 7

Make the effort.

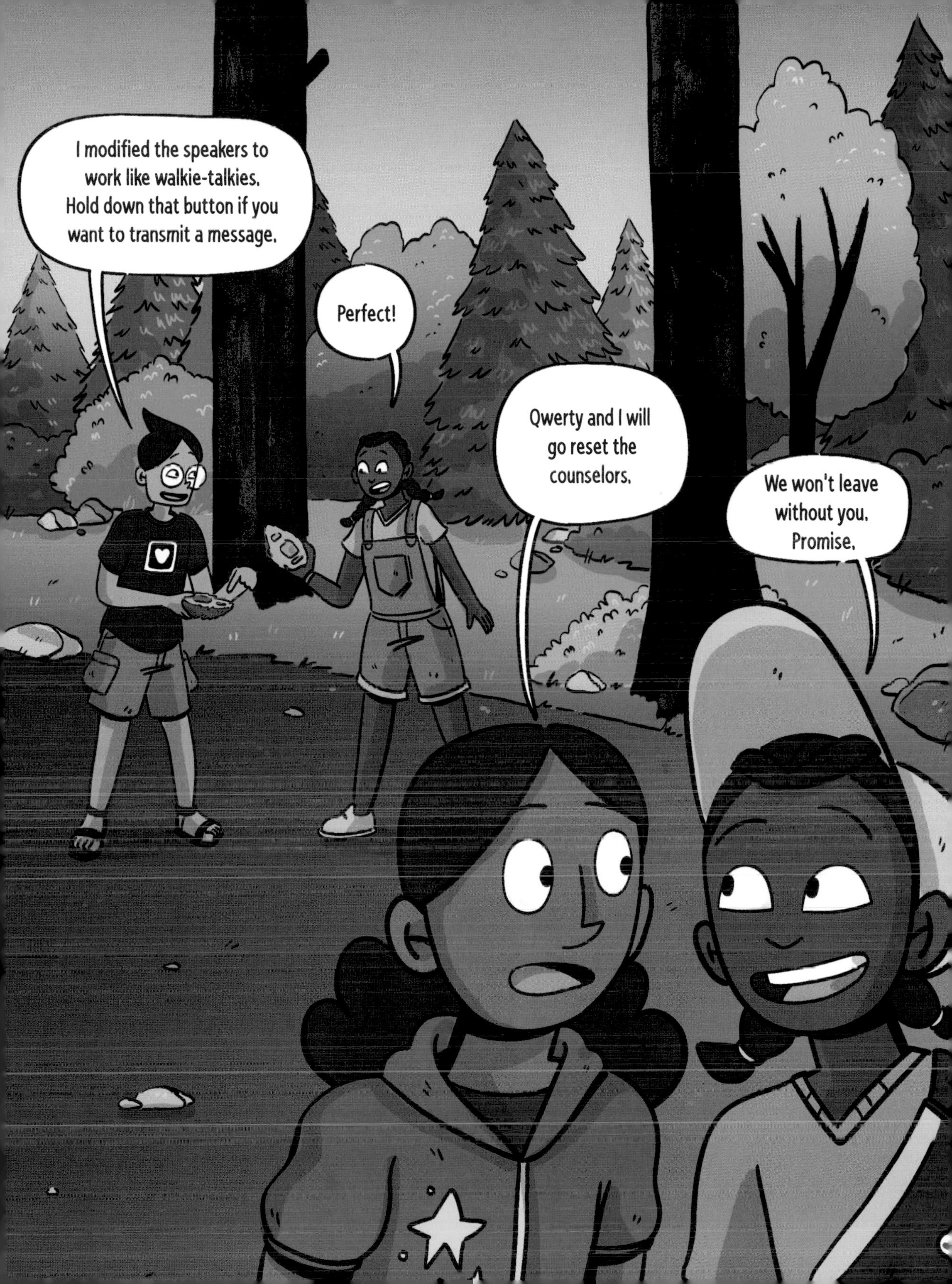
I modified the speakers to work like walkie-talkies. Hold down that button if you want to transmit a message.
Perfect!
Qwerty and I will go reset the counselors.
We won't leave without you. Promise.

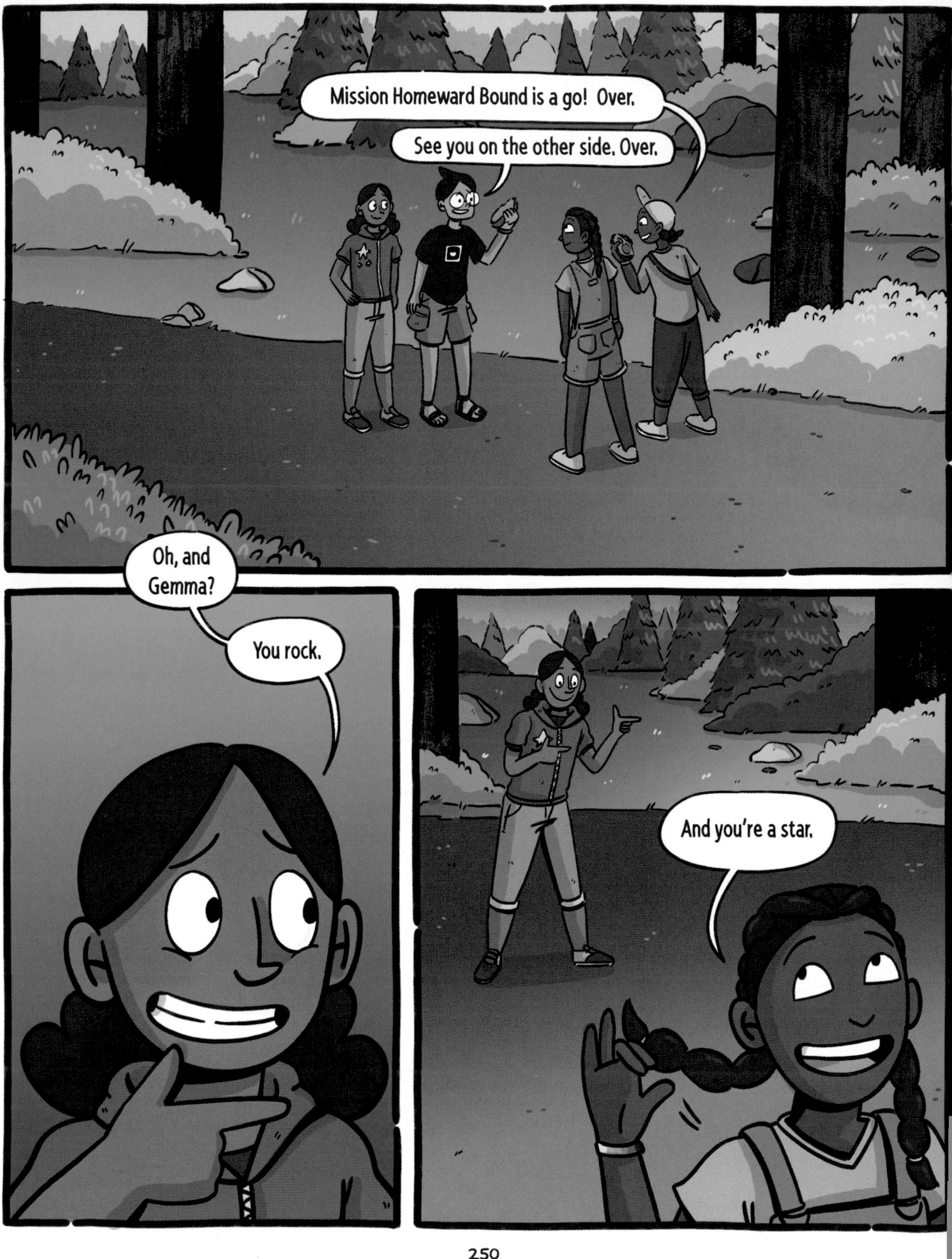
Mission Homeward Bound is a go! Over.
See you on the other side. Over.
Oh, and Gemma?
You rock.
And you're a star.

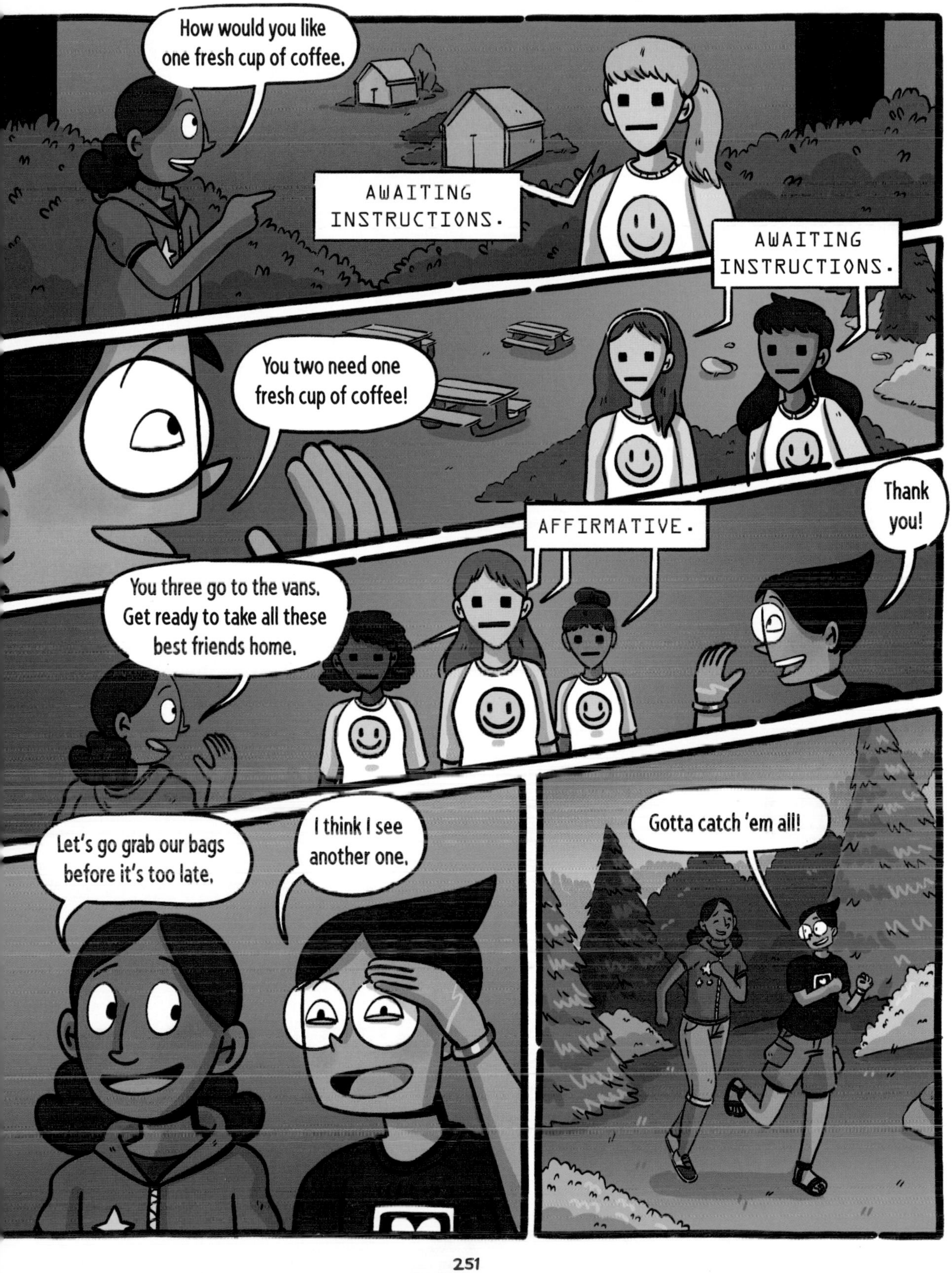
How would you like one fresh cup of coffee.
AWAITING INSTRUCTIONS.
AWAITING INSTRUCTIONS.
You two need one fresh cup of coffee!
You three go to the vans. Get ready to take all these best friends home.
AFFIRMATIVE.
Thank you!
Let's go grab our bags before it's too late.
I think I see another one.
Gotta catch 'em all!

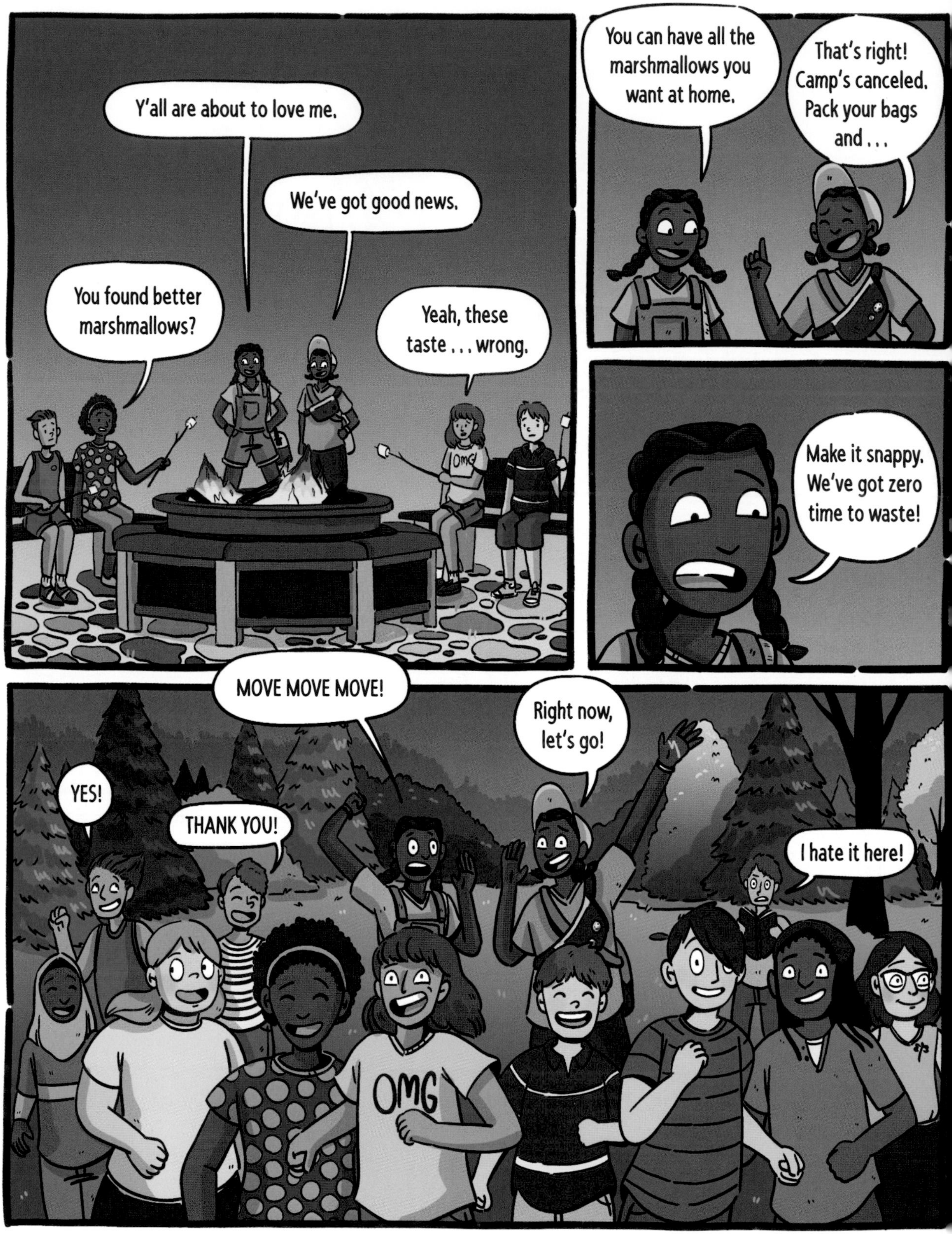

Y'all are about to love me.
We've got good news.
You found better marshmallows?
Yeah, these taste . . . wrong.
You can have all the marshmallows you want at home.
That's right! Camp's canceled. Pack your bags and . . .
Make it snappy. We've got zero time to waste!
MOVE MOVE MOVE!
Right now, let's go!
YES!
THANK YOU!
I hate it here!

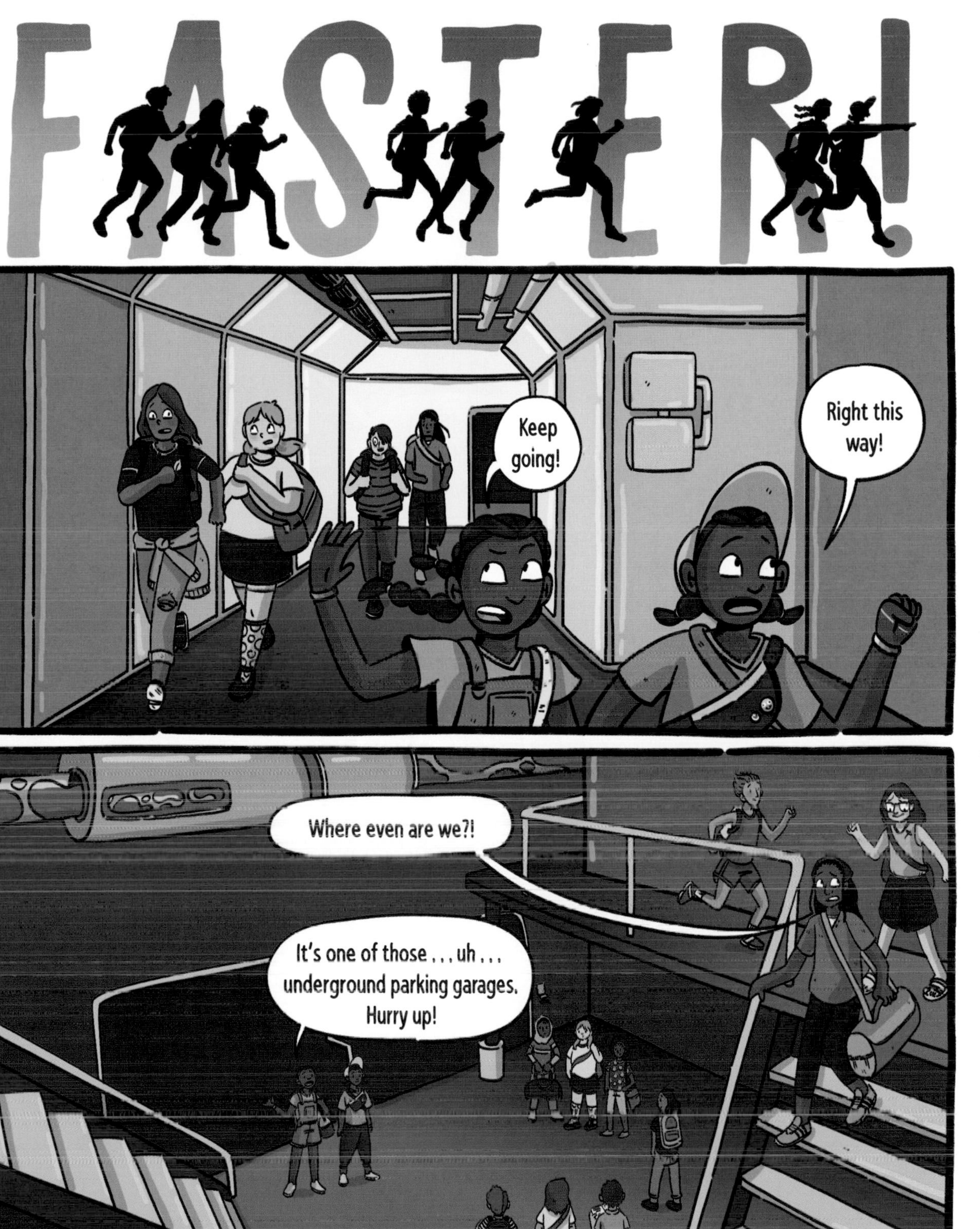
FASTER!
Keep going!
Right this way!
Where even are we?!
It's one of those . . . uh . . . underground parking garages. Hurry up!

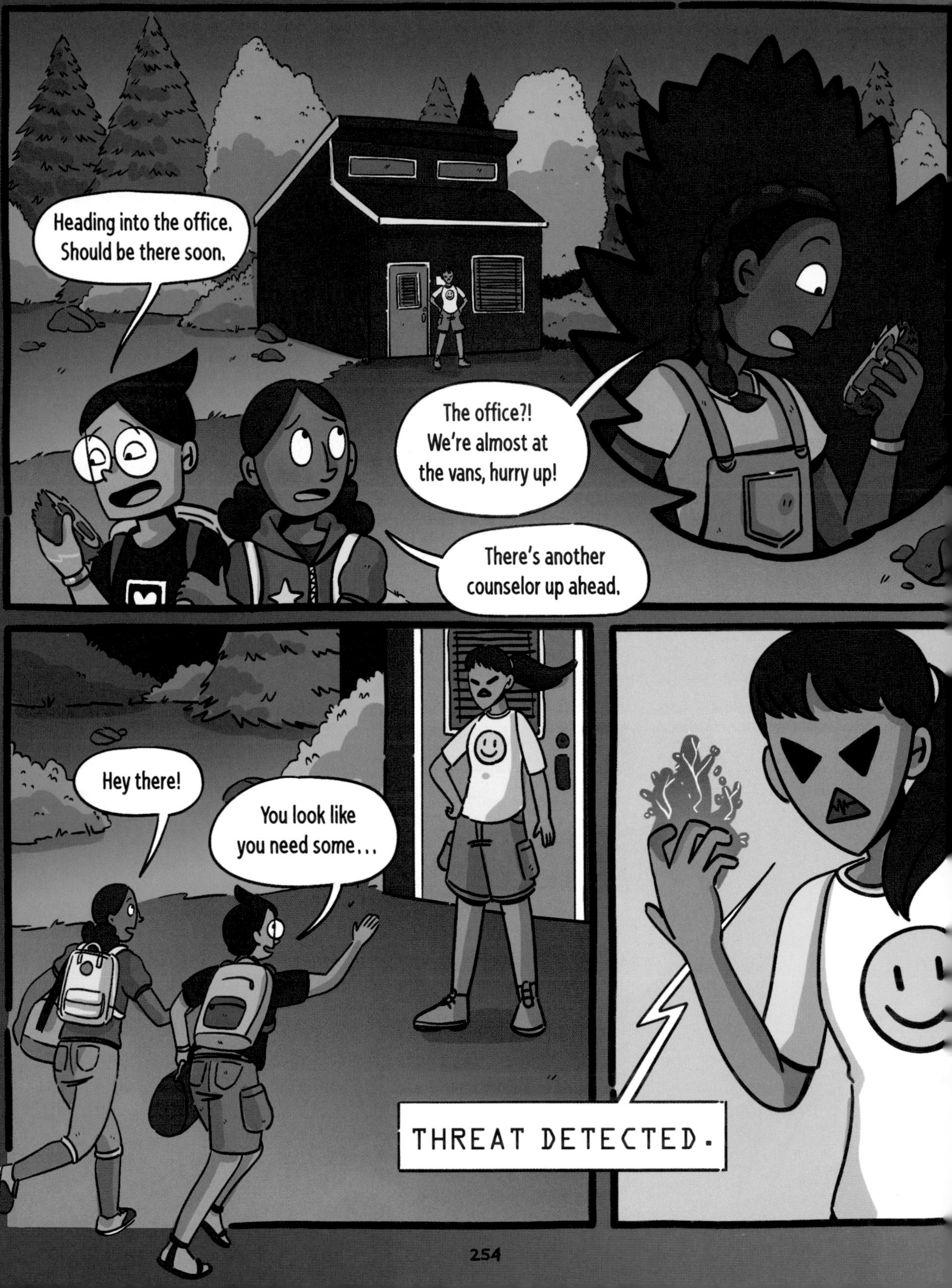
Heading into the office. Should be there soon.
The office?! We're almost at the vans, hurry up!
There's another counselor up ahead.
Hey there!
You look like you need some...
THREAT DETECTED.

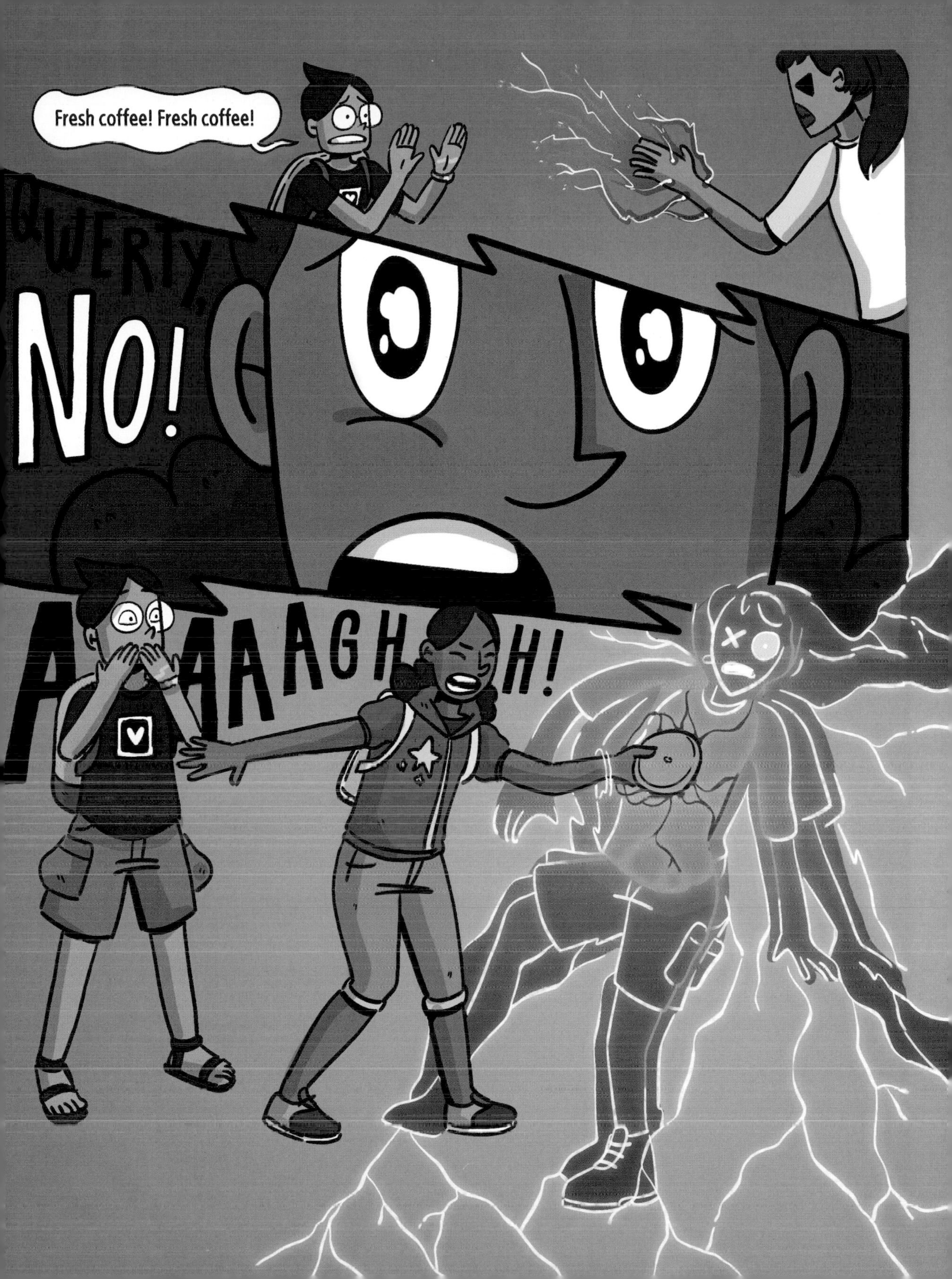
Fresh coffee! Fresh coffee!
QUERTY, NO!
AAAAGH H!

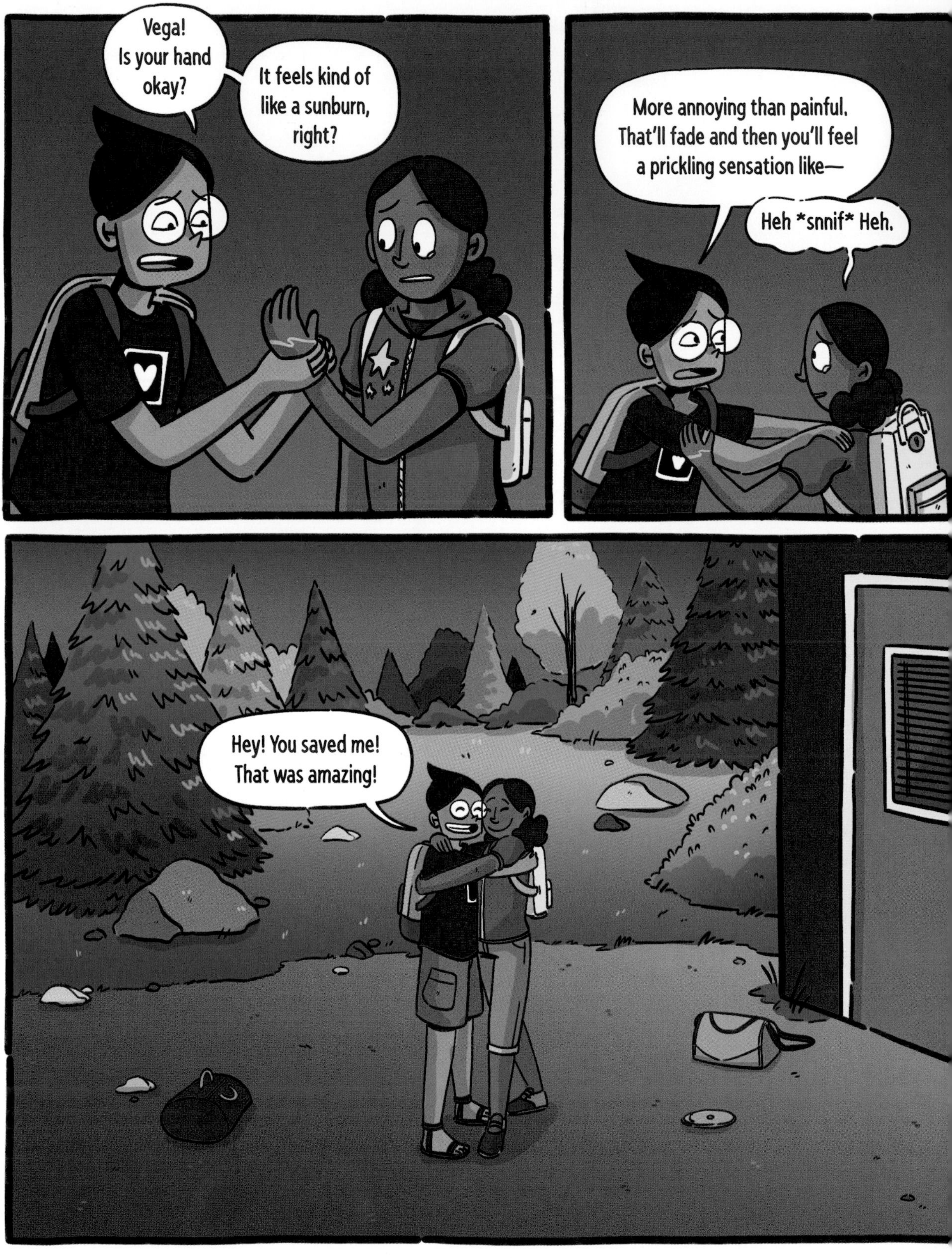
Vega!
Is your hand okay?
It feels kind of like a sunburn, right?
More annoying than painful. That'll fade and then you'll feel a prickling sensation like—
Heh *snnif* Heh.
Hey! You saved me! That was amazing!

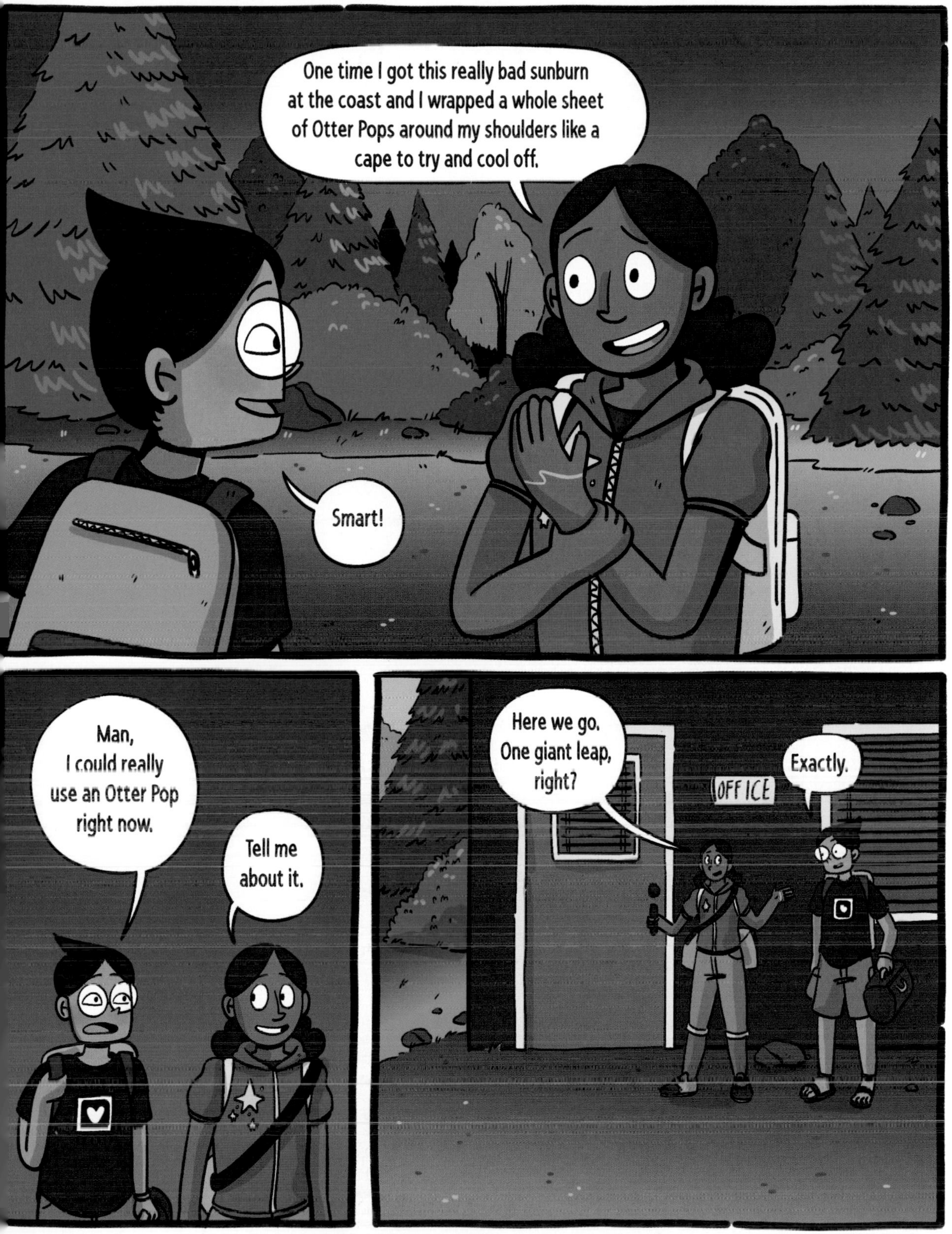

One time I got this really bad sunburn at the coast and I wrapped a whole sheet of Otter Pops around my shoulders like a cape to try and cool off.
Smart!
Man, I could really use an Otter Pop right now.
Tell me about it.
Here we go. One giant leap, right?
OFFICE
Exactly.

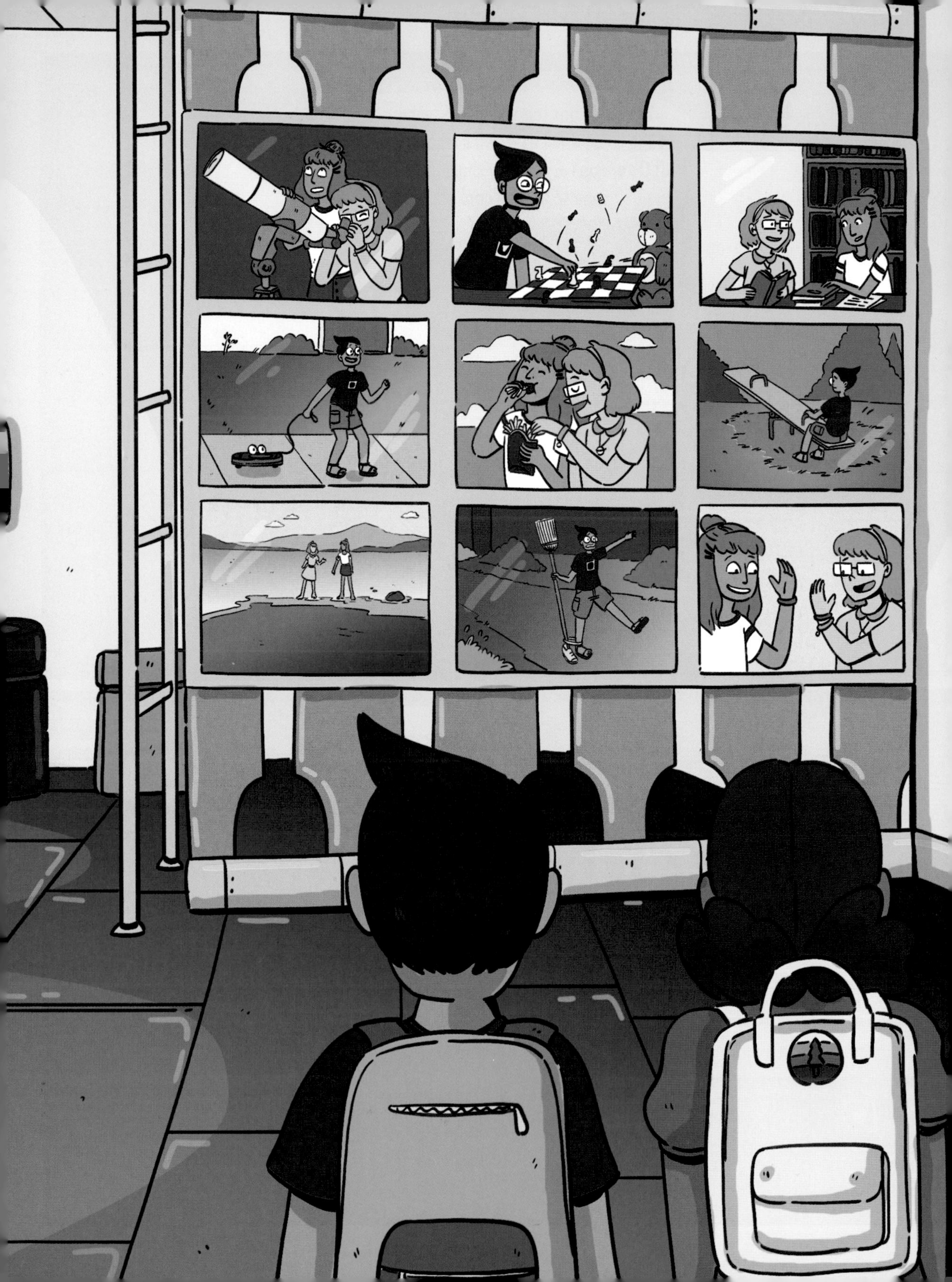

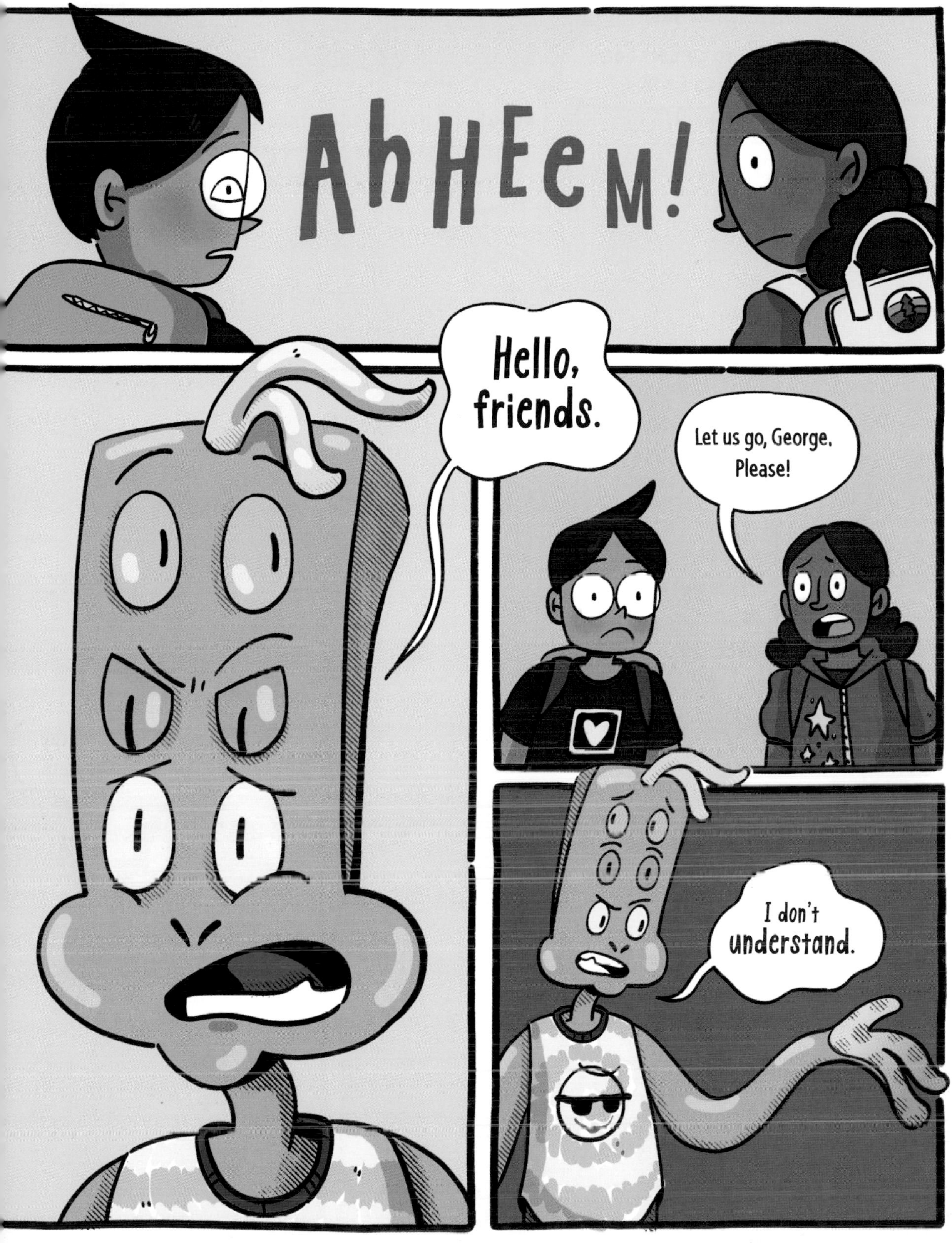
AhHEeM!
Hello, friends.
Let us go, George. Please!
I don't understand.

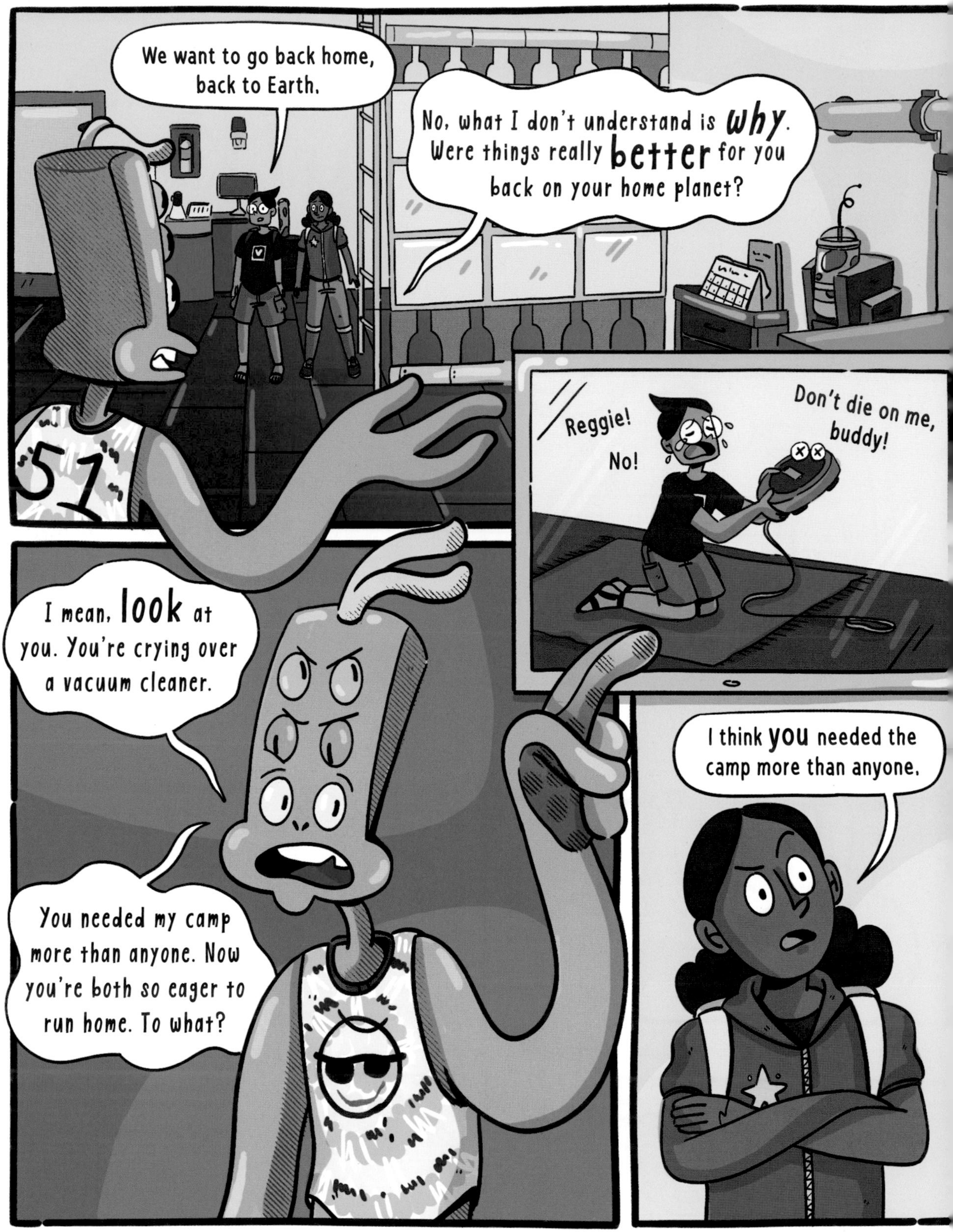
We want to go back home, back to Earth.
No, what I don't understand is why. Were things really better for you back on your home planet?
Reggie!
No!
Don't die on me, buddy!
I mean, look at you. You're crying over a vacuum cleaner.
You needed my camp more than anyone. Now you're both so eager to run home. To what?
I think you needed the camp more than anyone.

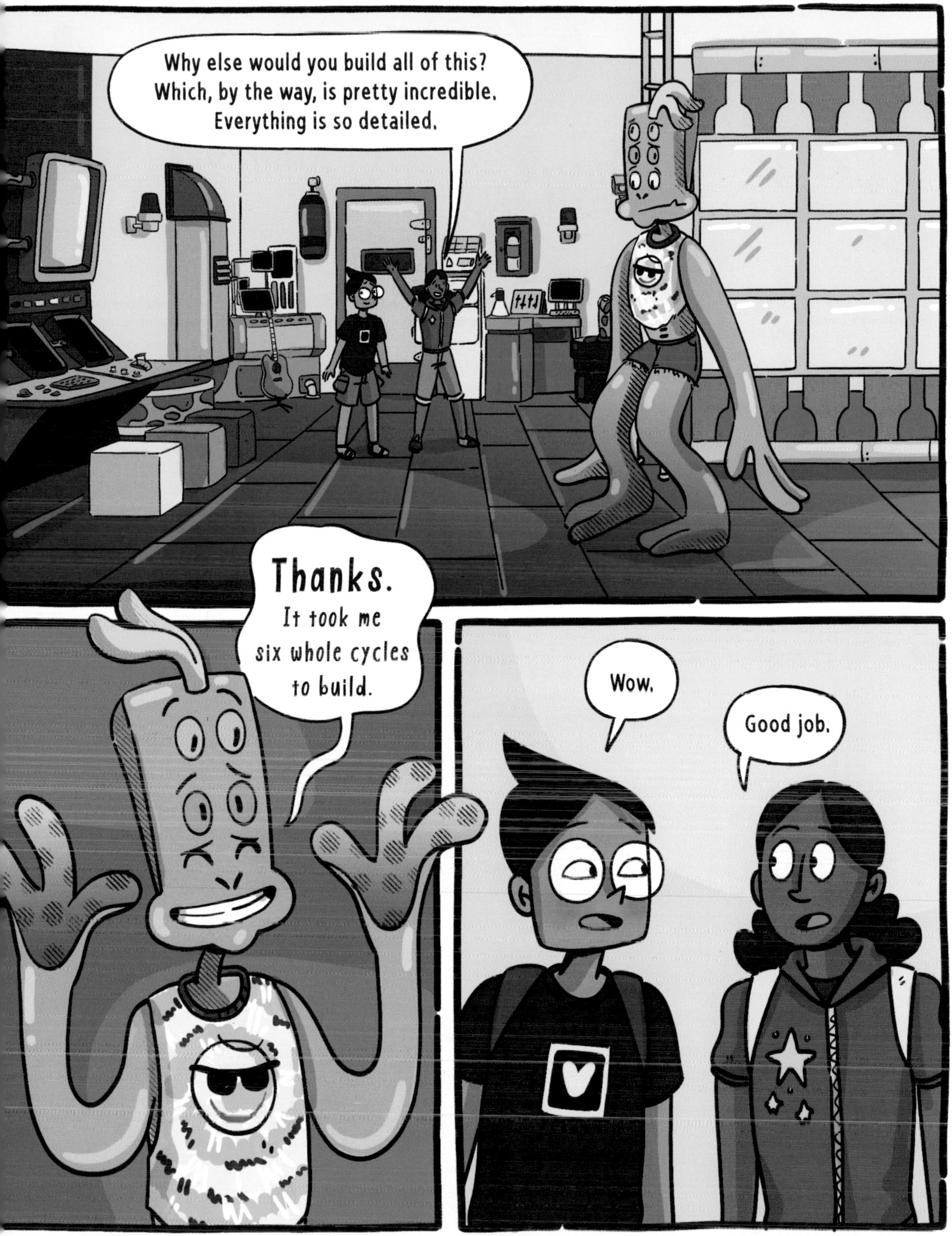
Why else would you build all of this? Which, by the way, is pretty incredible. Everything is so detailed.
Thanks. It took me six whole cycles to build.
Wow.
Good job.

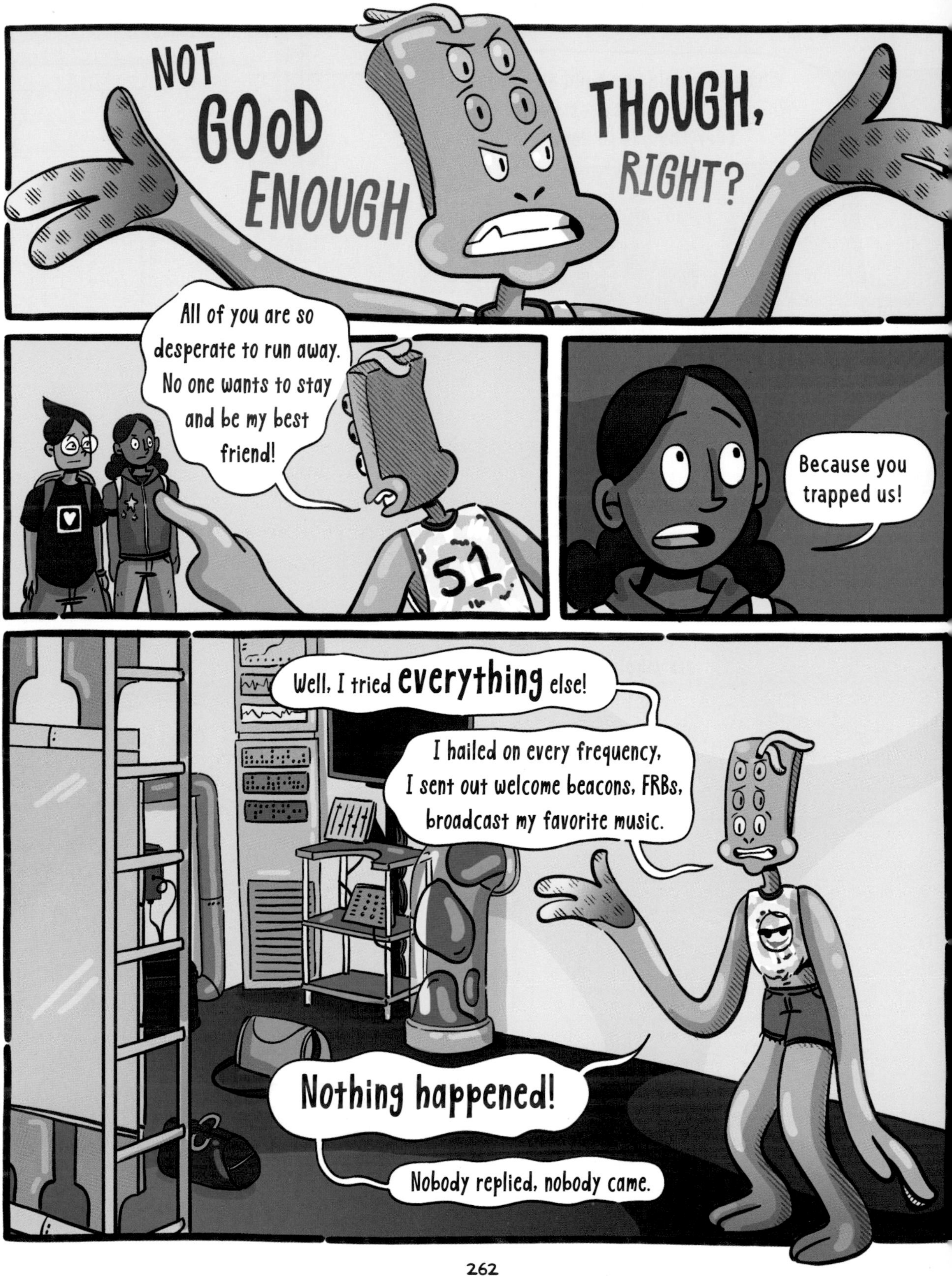
NOT GOOD ENOUGH THOUGH, RIGHT?
All of you are so desperate to run away. No one wants to stay and be my best friend!
Because you trapped us!
Well, I tried everything else!
I hailed on every frequency, I sent out welcome beacons, FRBs, broadcast my favorite music.
Nothing happened!
Nobody replied, nobody came.

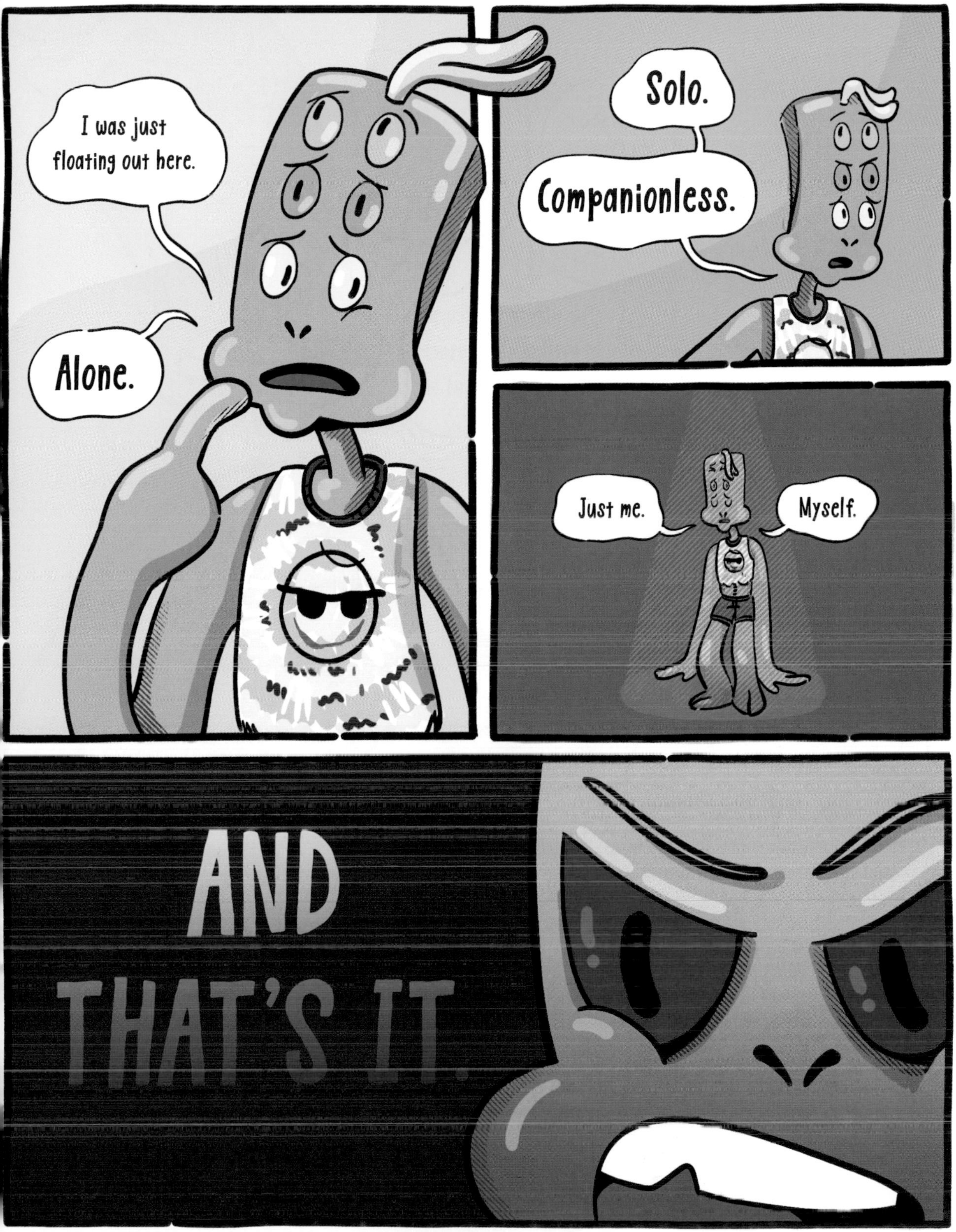
I was just floating out here.
Alone.
Solo.
Companionless.
Just me.
Myself.
AND THAT'S IT.

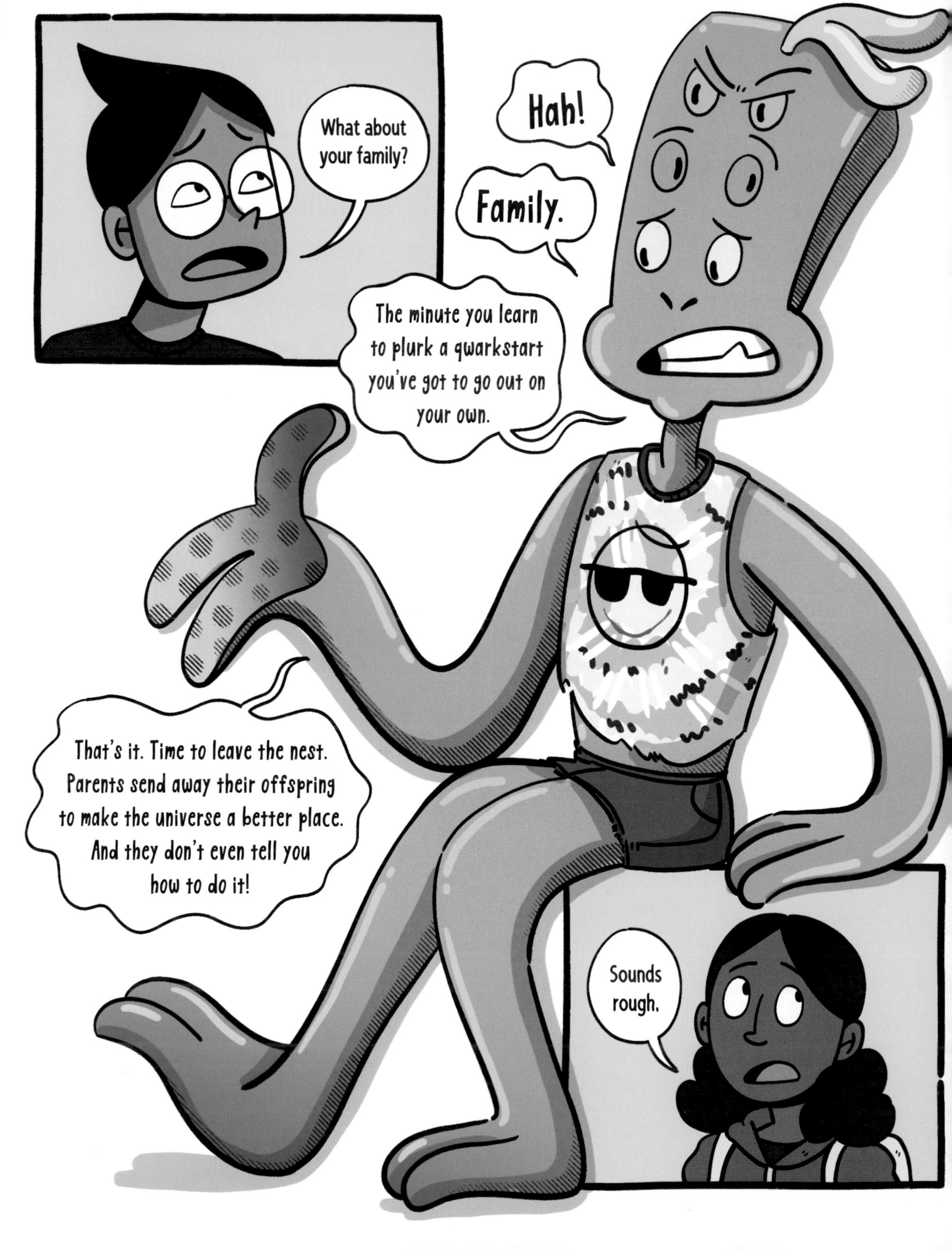
What about your family?
Hah!
Family.
The minute you learn to plurk a qwarkstart you've got to go out on your own.
That's it. Time to leave the nest. Parents send away their offspring to make the universe a better place. And they don't even tell you how to do it!
Sounds rough.

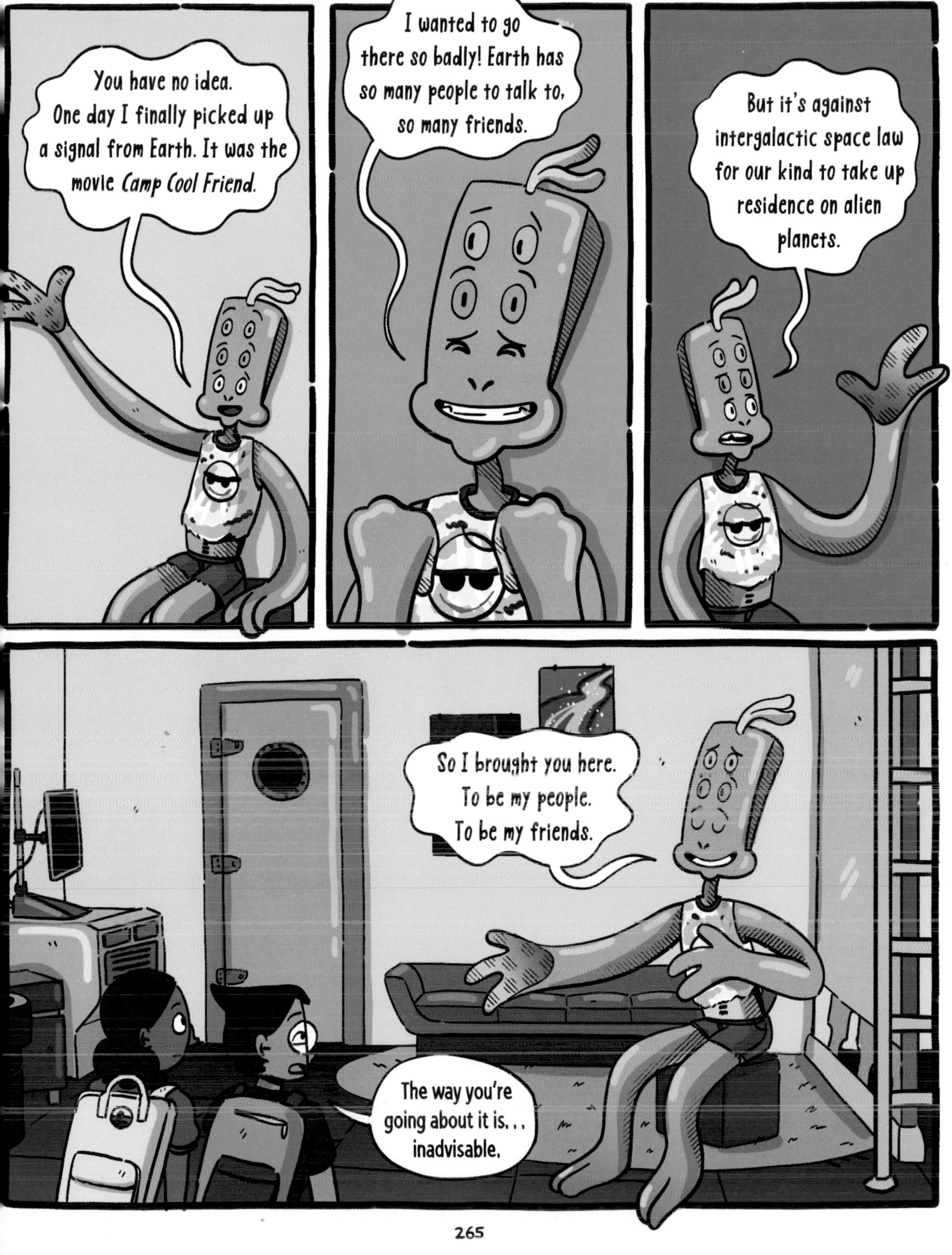
You have no idea.
One day I finally picked up a signal from Earth. It was the movie *Camp Cool Friend*.
I wanted to go there so badly! Earth has so many people to talk to, so many friends.
But it's against intergalactic space law for our kind to take up residence on alien planets.
So I brought you here. To be my people. To be my friends.
The way you're going about it is... inadvisable.

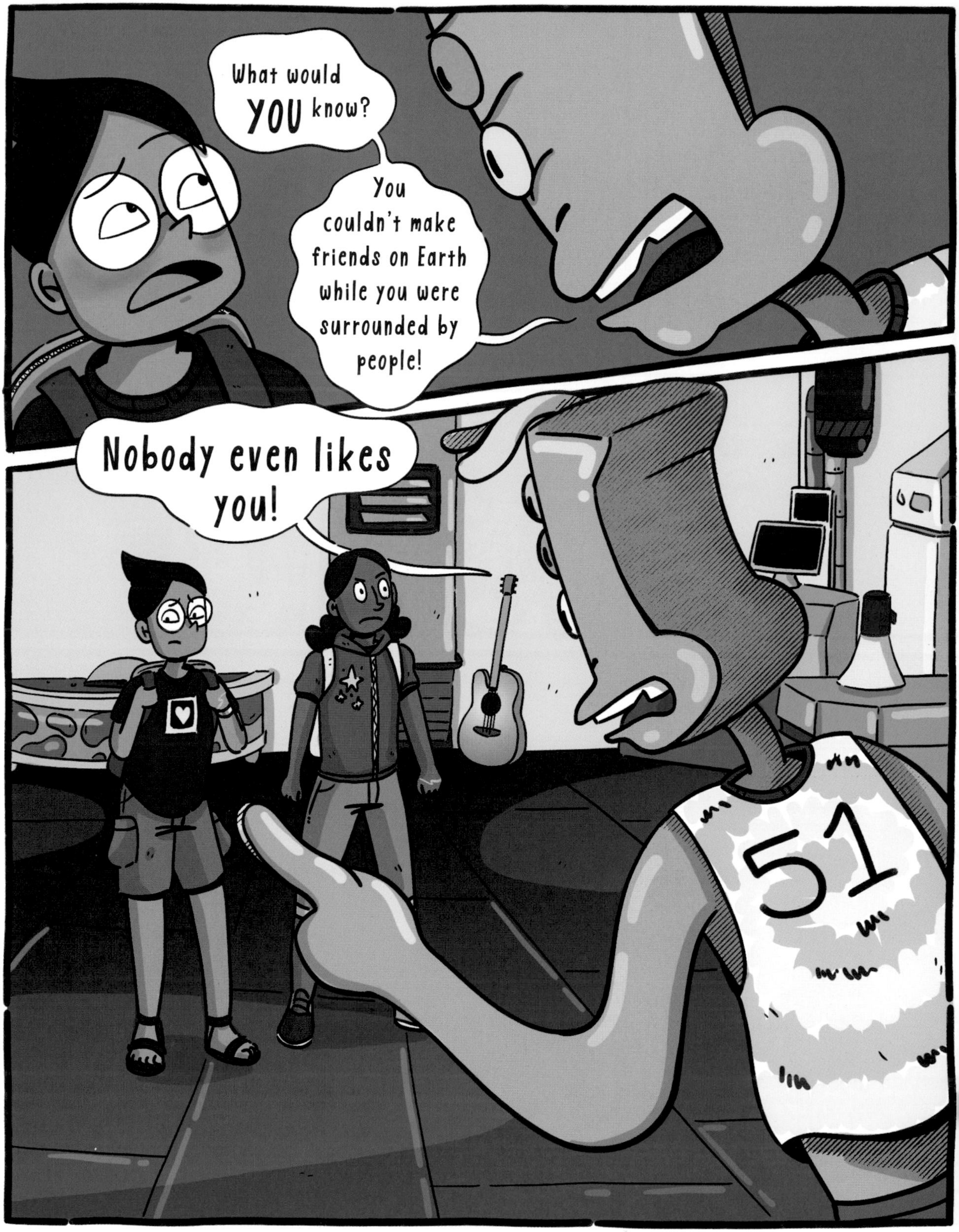
What would YOU know?
You couldn't make friends on Earth while you were surrounded by people!
Nobody even likes you!
51

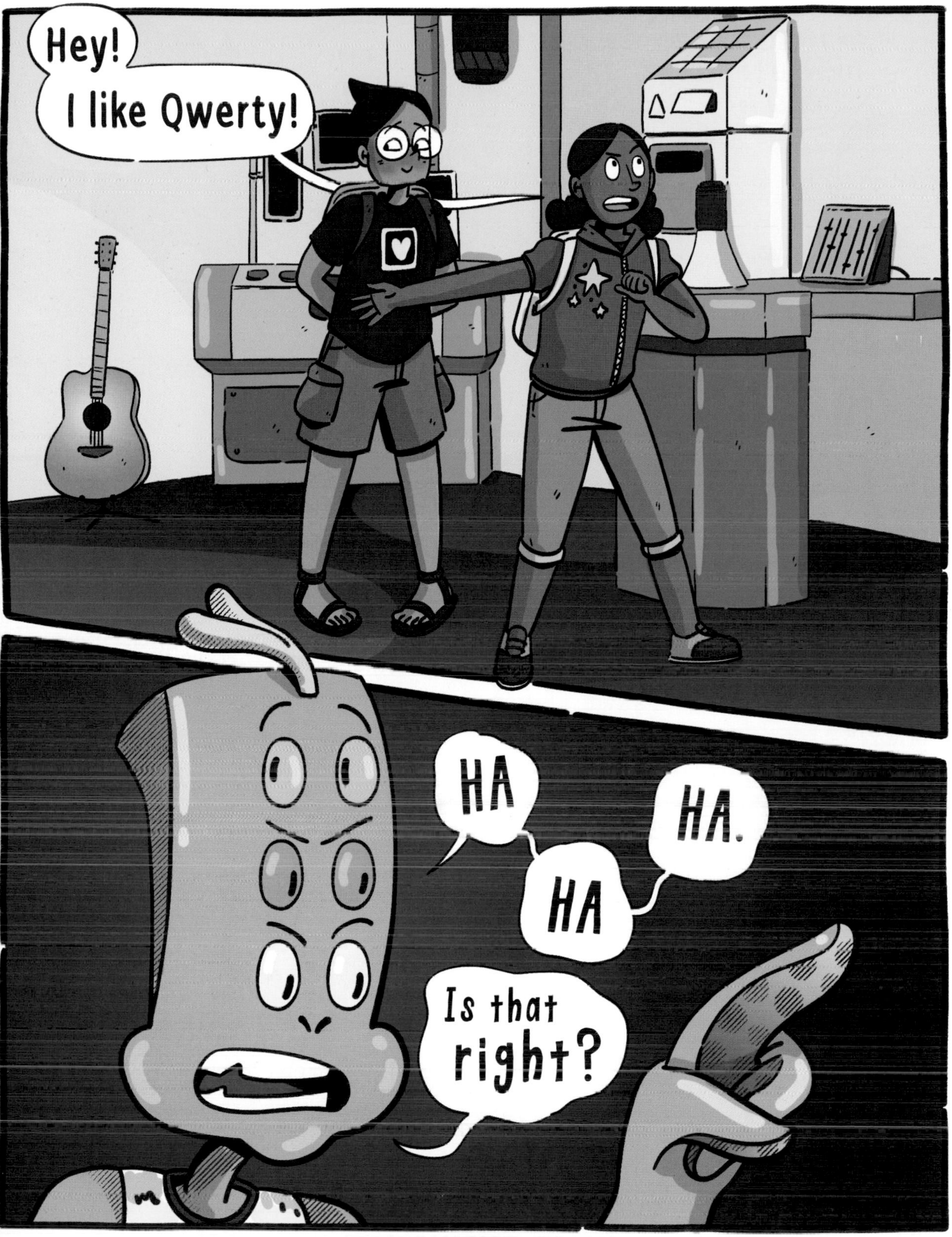
Hey!
I like Qwerty!
HA
HA
HA.
Is that right?

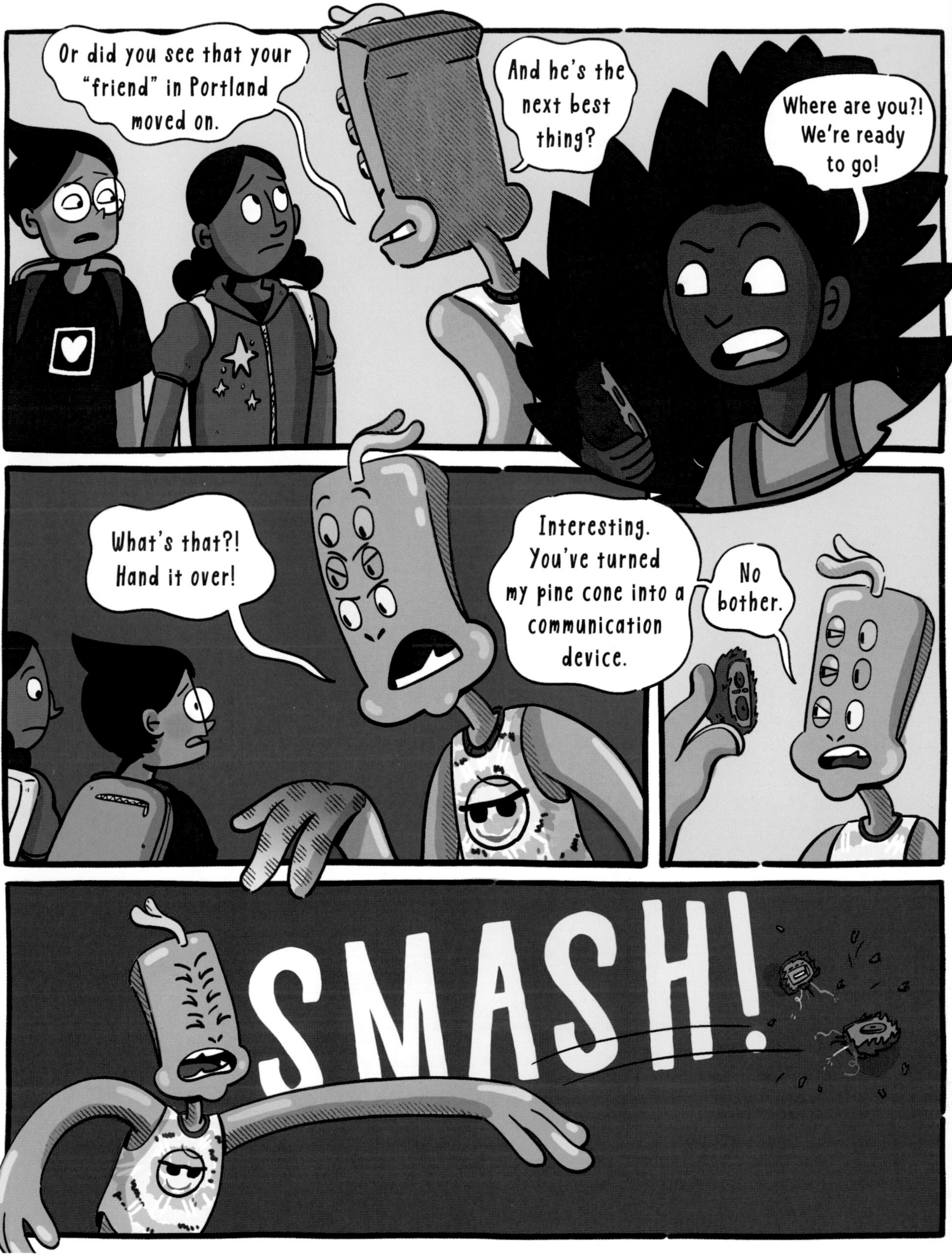
Or did you see that your "friend" in Portland moved on.
And he's the next best thing?
Where are you?! We're ready to go!
What's that?! Hand it over!
Interesting. You've turned my pine cone into a communication device.
No bother.
SMASH!

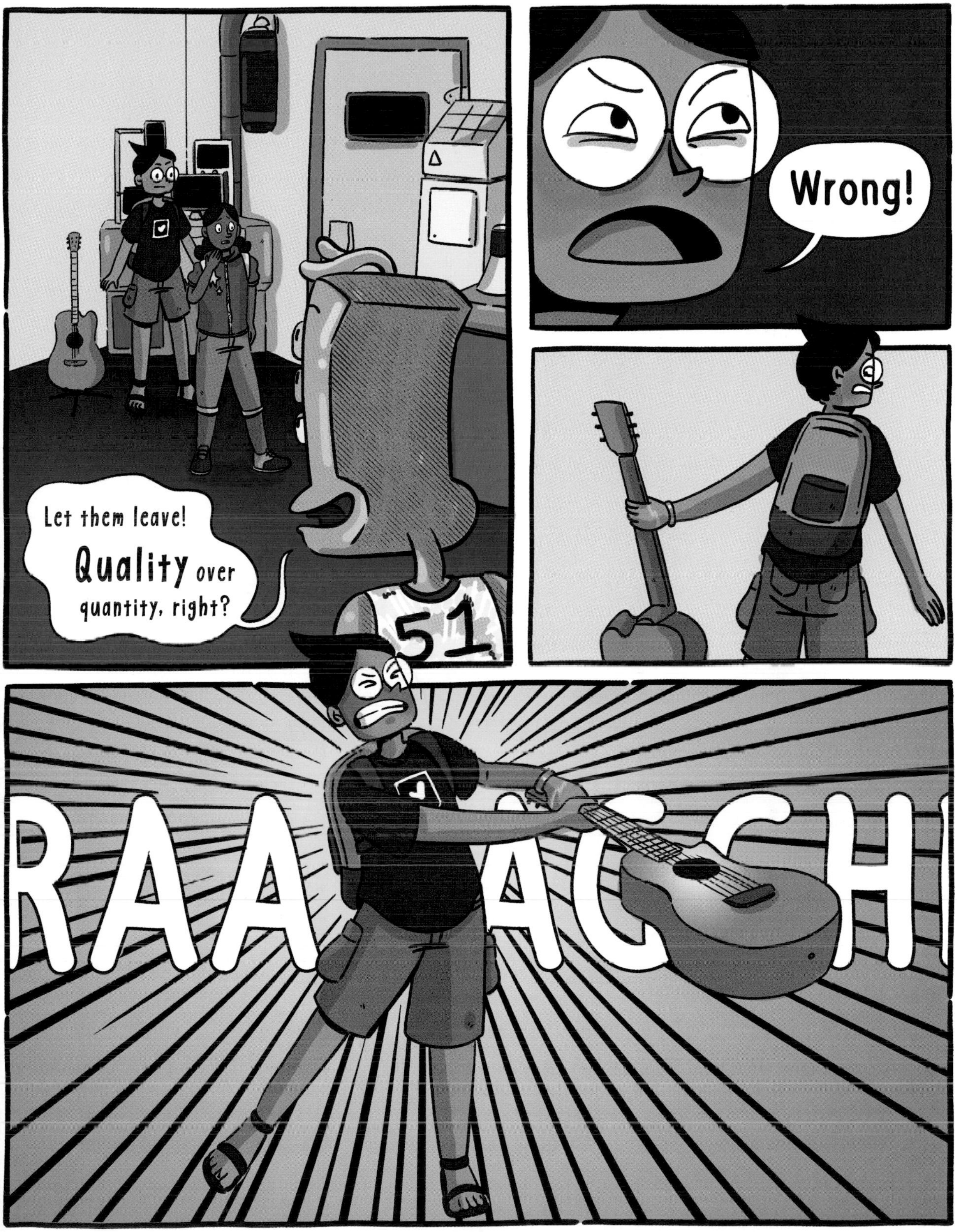
Let them leave! Quality over quantity, right?
Wrong!

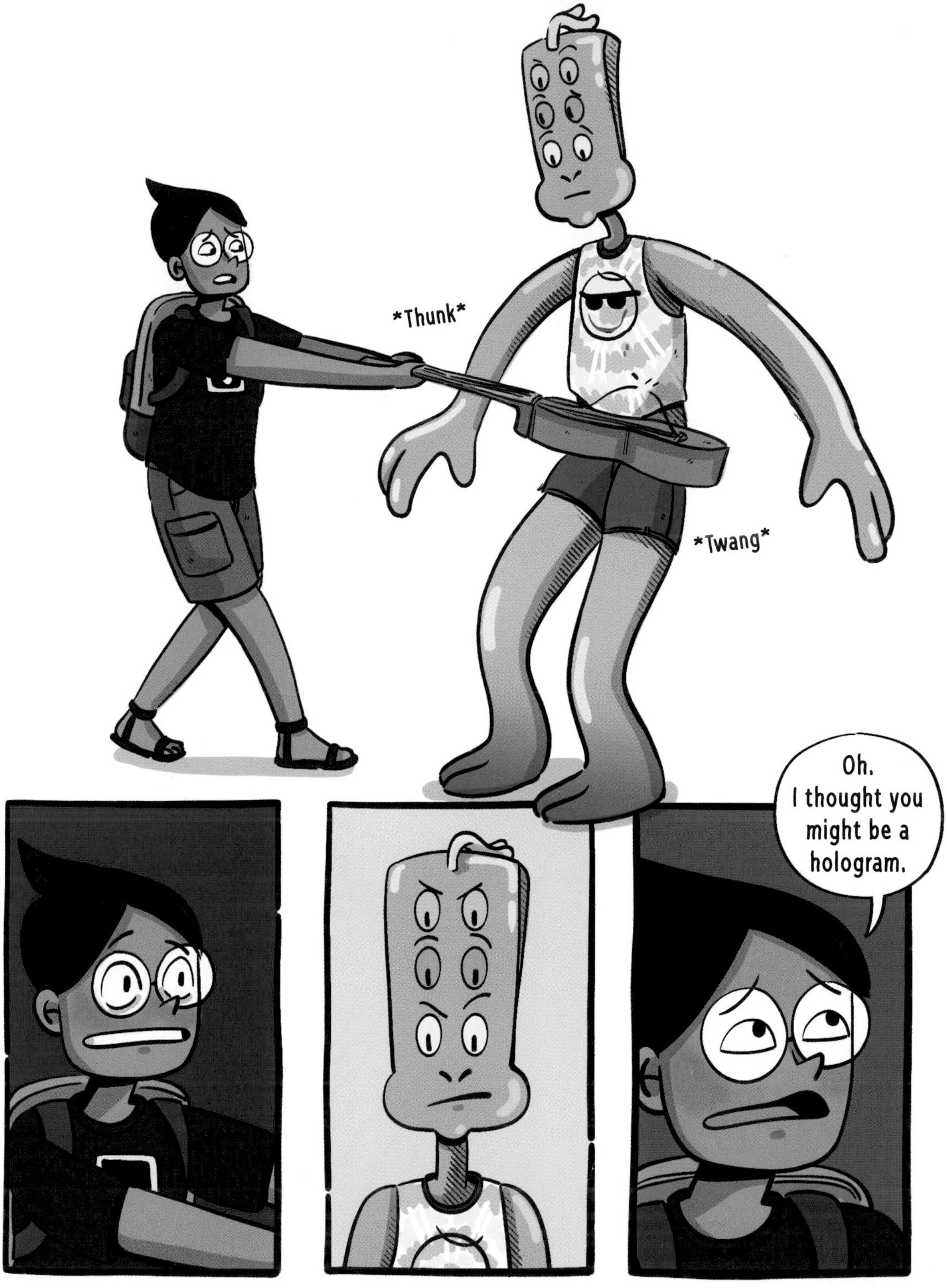
Thunk
Twang
Oh. I thought you might be a hologram.

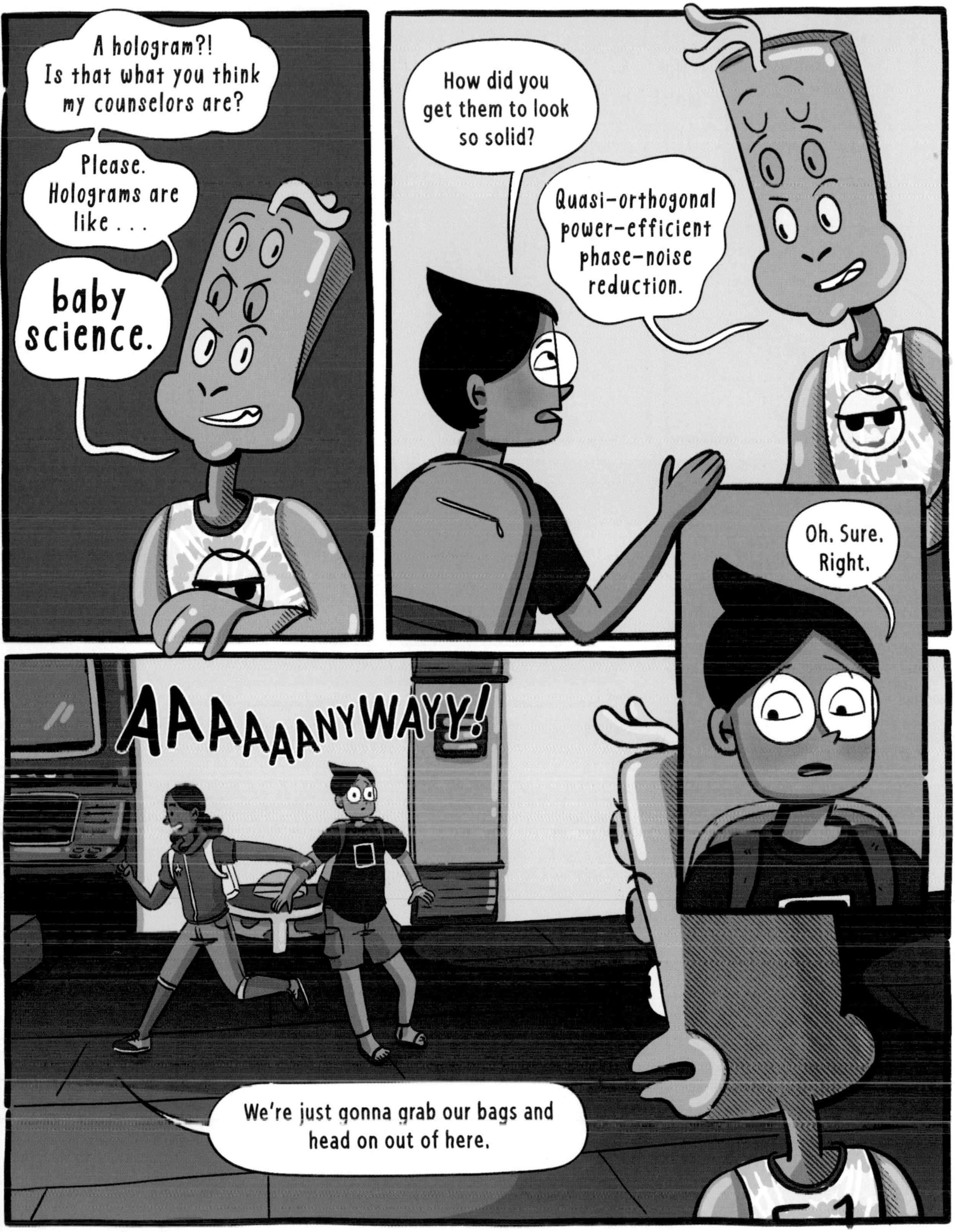
A hologram?! Is that what you think my counselors are?
Please. Holograms are like . . .
baby science.
How did you get them to look so solid?
Quasi-orthogonal power-efficient phase-noise reduction.
Oh. Sure. Right.
AAAAAAANYWAYY!
We're just gonna grab our bags and head on out of here.

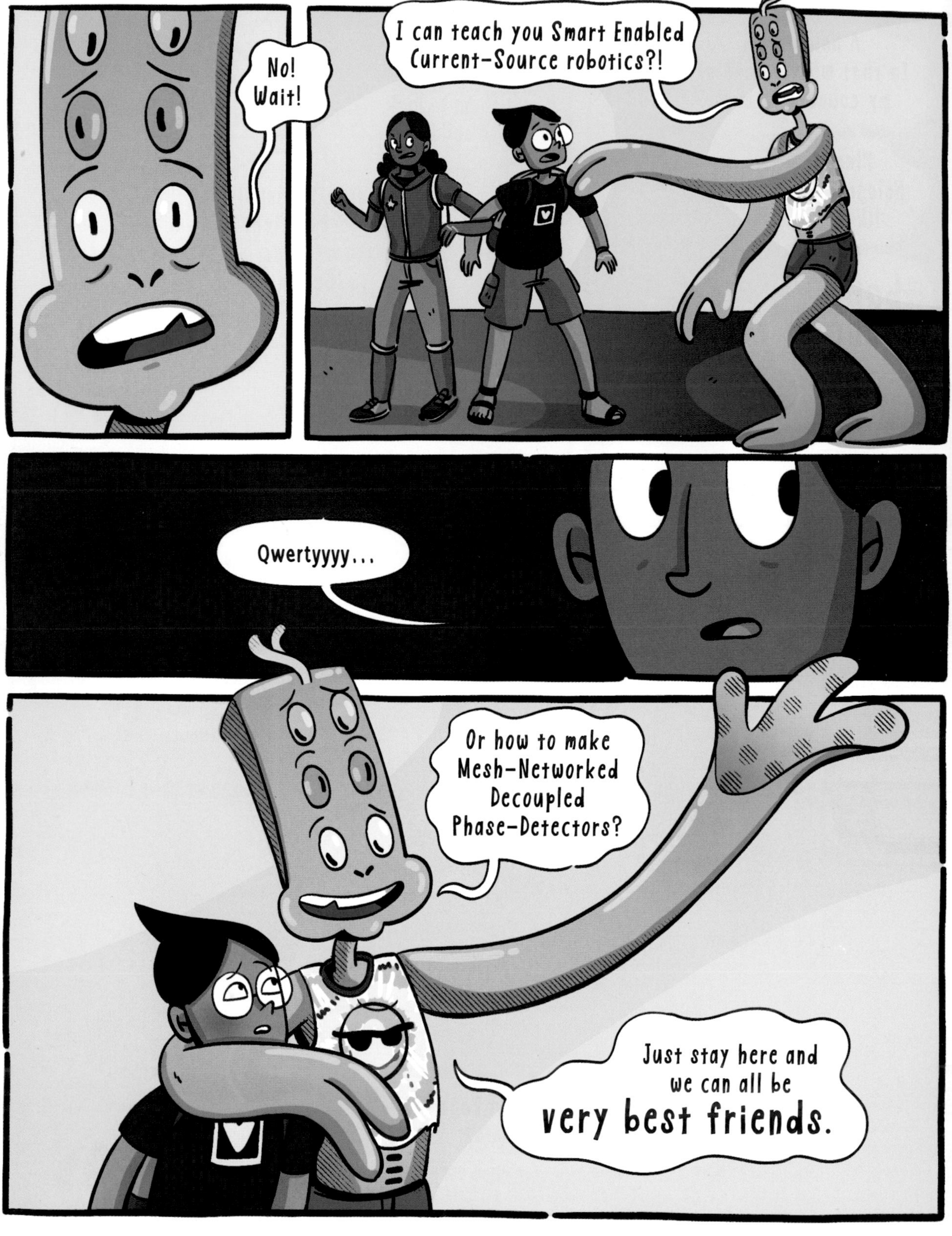
No! Wait!
I can teach you Smart Enabled Current-Source robotics?!
Qwertyyyy...
Or how to make Mesh-Networked Decoupled Phase-Detectors?
Just stay here and we can all be very best friends.

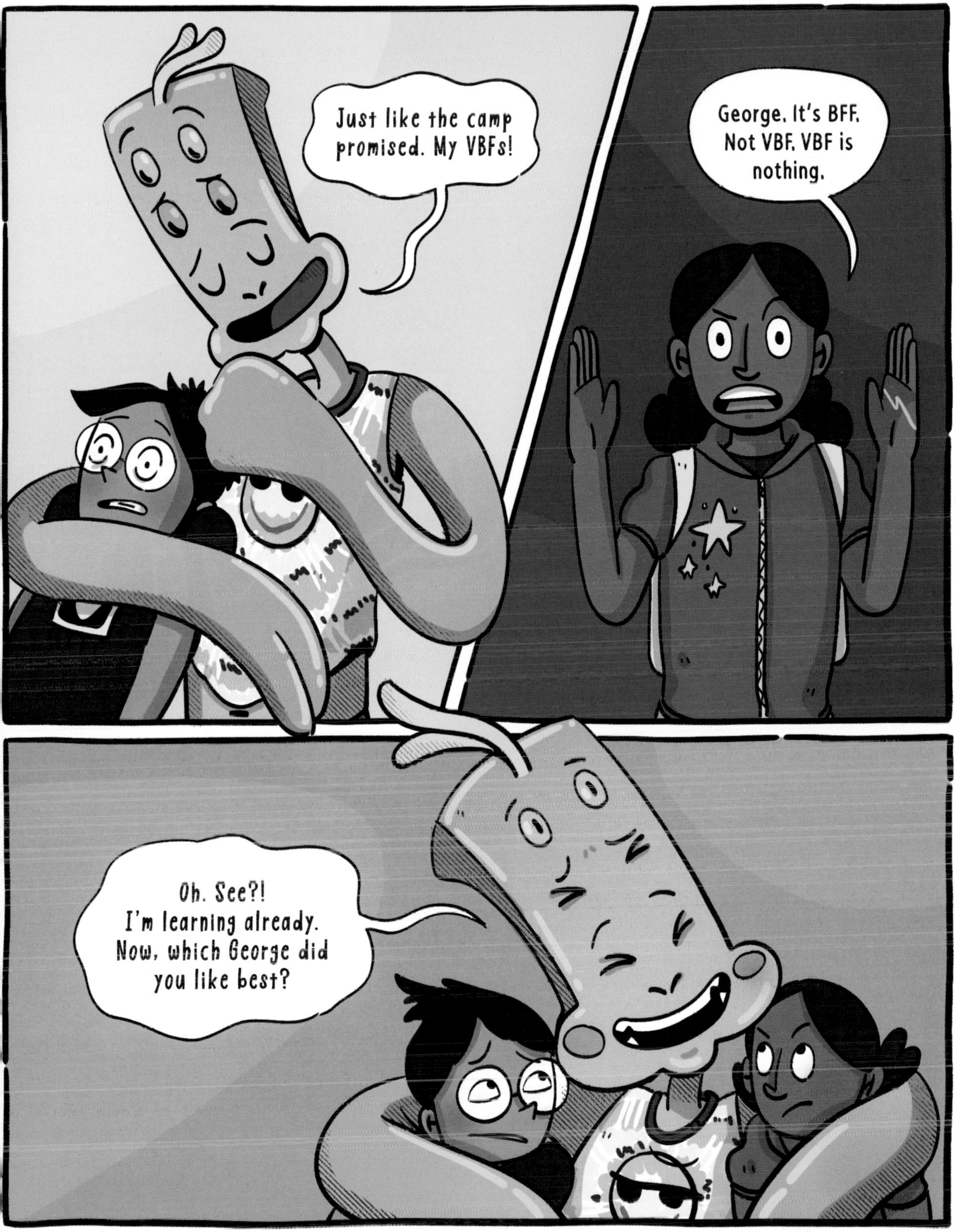
Just like the camp promised. My VBFs!
George. It's BFF. Not VBF. VBF is nothing.
Oh. See?! I'm learning already. Now, which George did you like best?

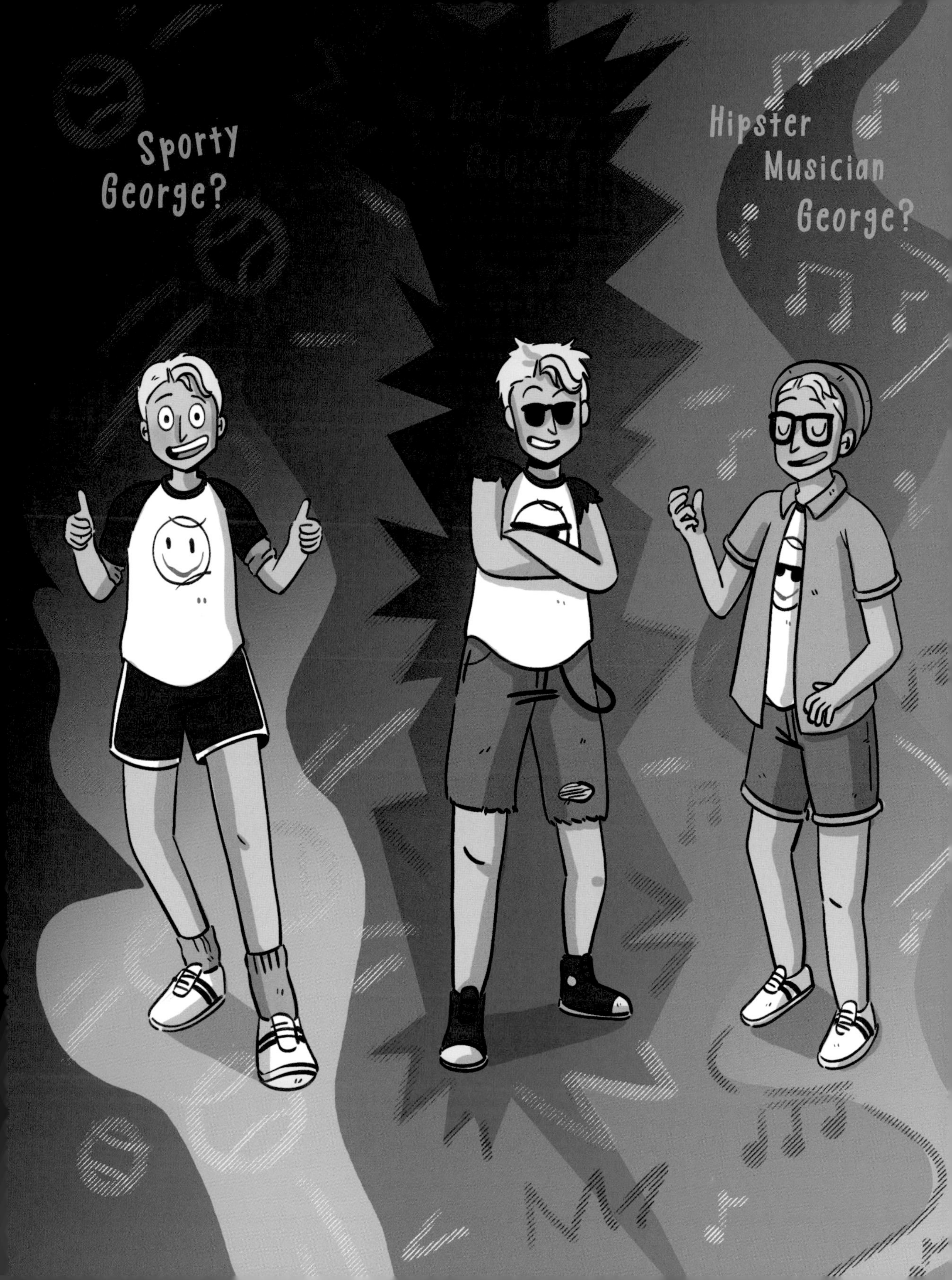
Sporty George?
Hipster Musician George?

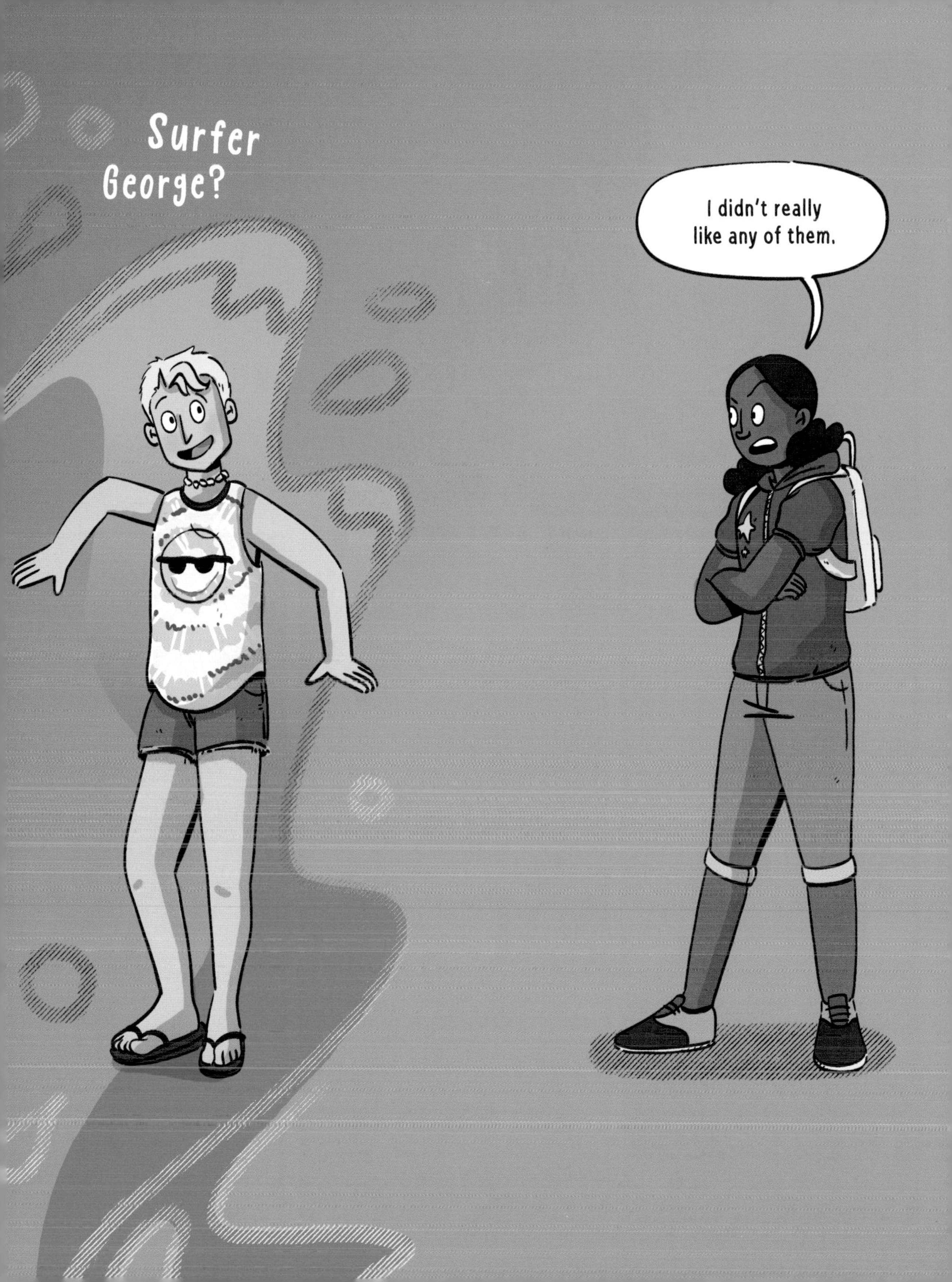
Surfer George?
I didn't really like any of them.

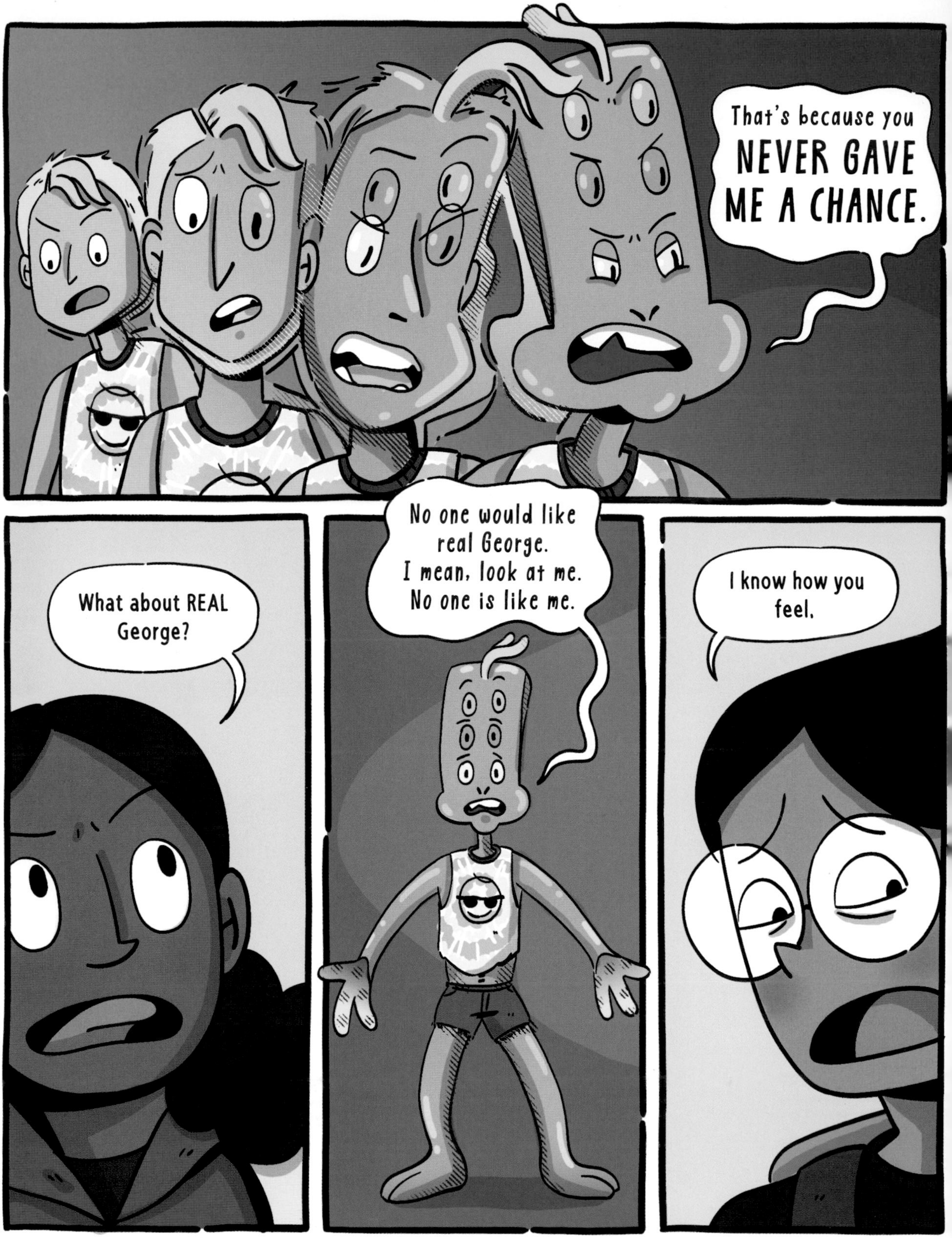
That's because you NEVER GAVE ME A CHANCE.
What about REAL George?
No one would like real George. I mean, look at me. No one is like me.
I know how you feel.

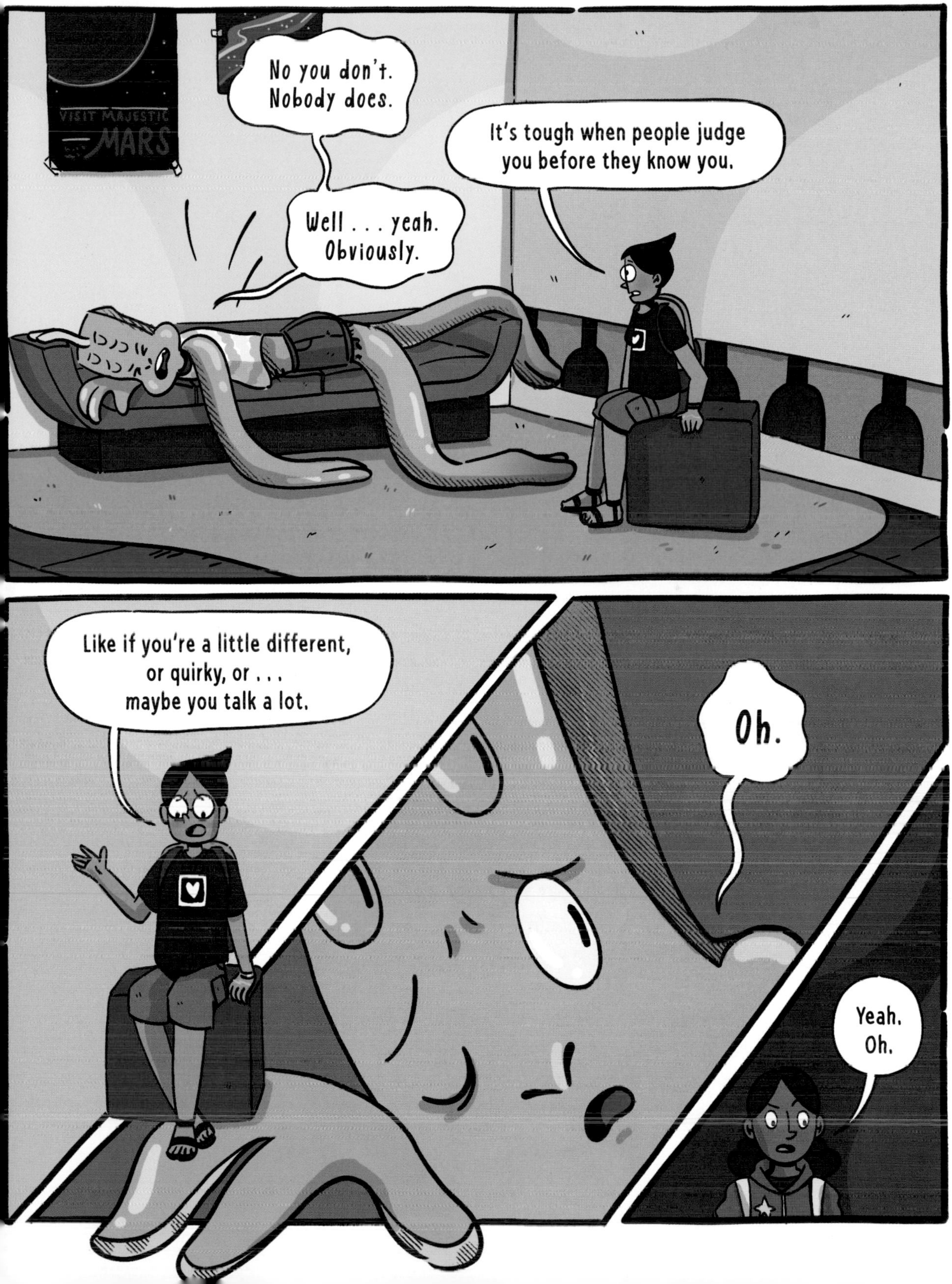

VISIT MAJESTIC MARS
It's tough when people judge you before they know you.
Well . . . yeah. Obviously.
No you don't. Nobody does.
Like if you're a little different, or quirky, or . . . maybe you talk a lot.
Oh.
Yeah. Oh.

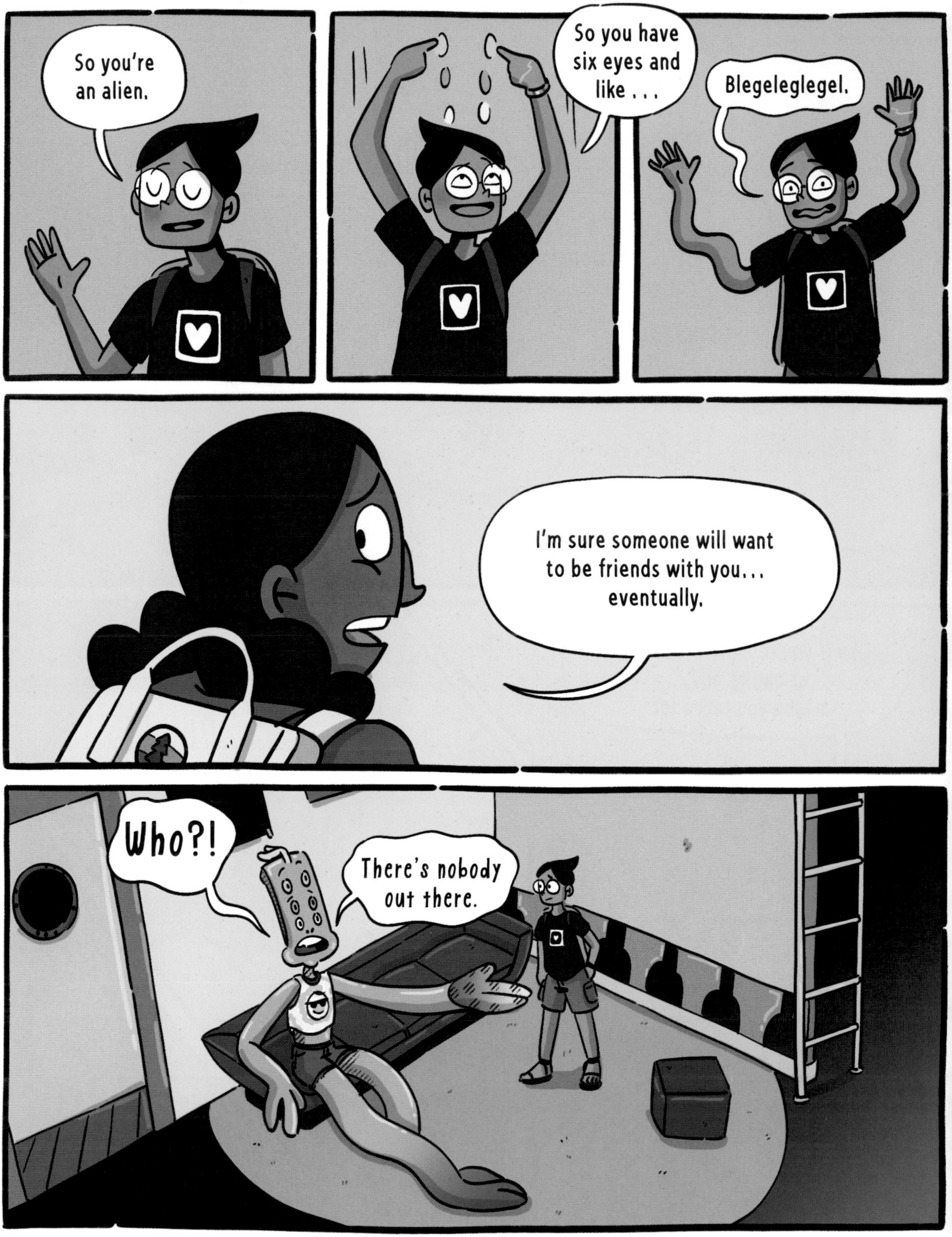
So you're an alien.
So you have six eyes and like . . .
Blegeleglegel.
I'm sure someone will want to be friends with you... eventually.
Who?!
There's nobody out there.

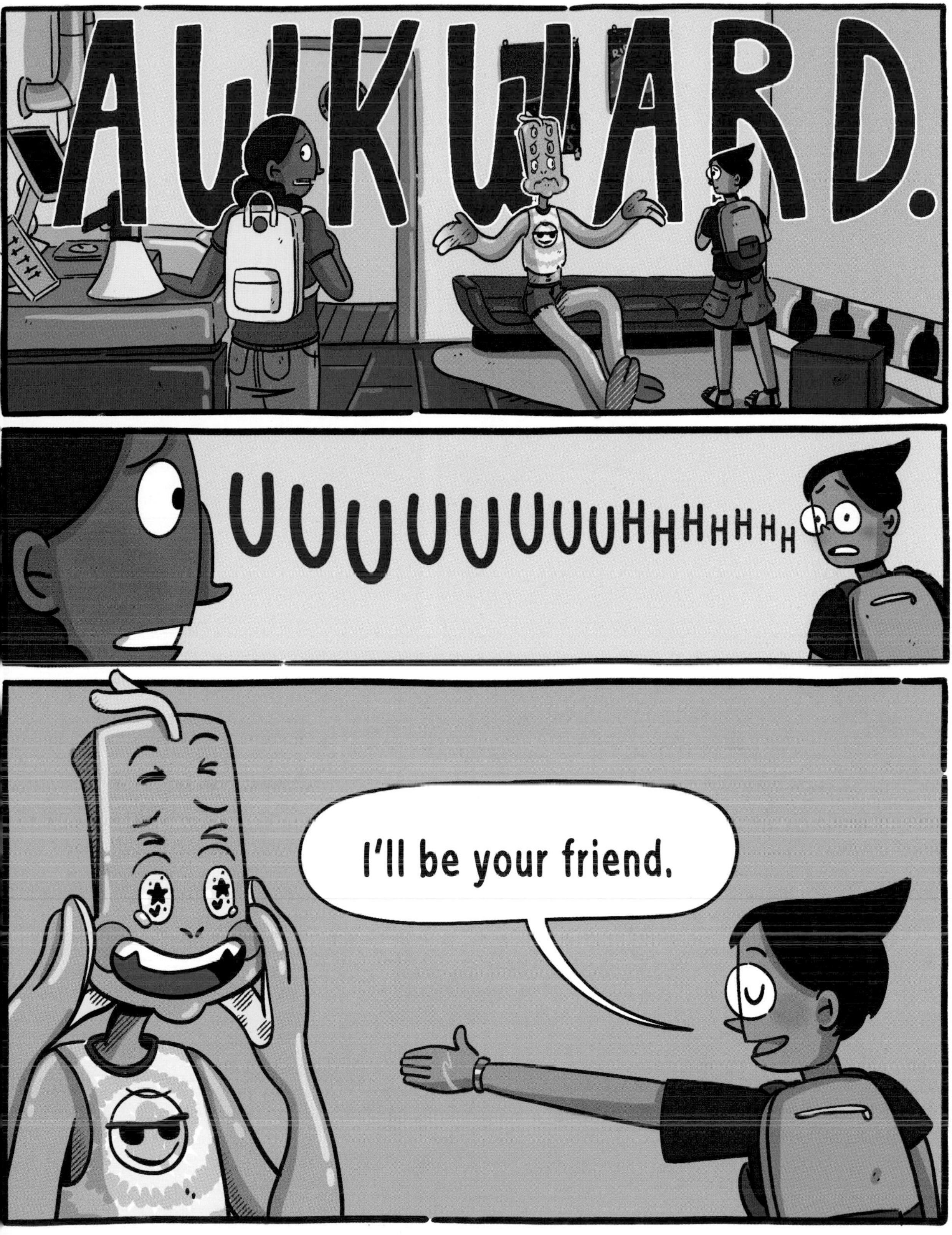
AWKWARD.
UUUUUUUUHHHHHH
I'll be your friend.

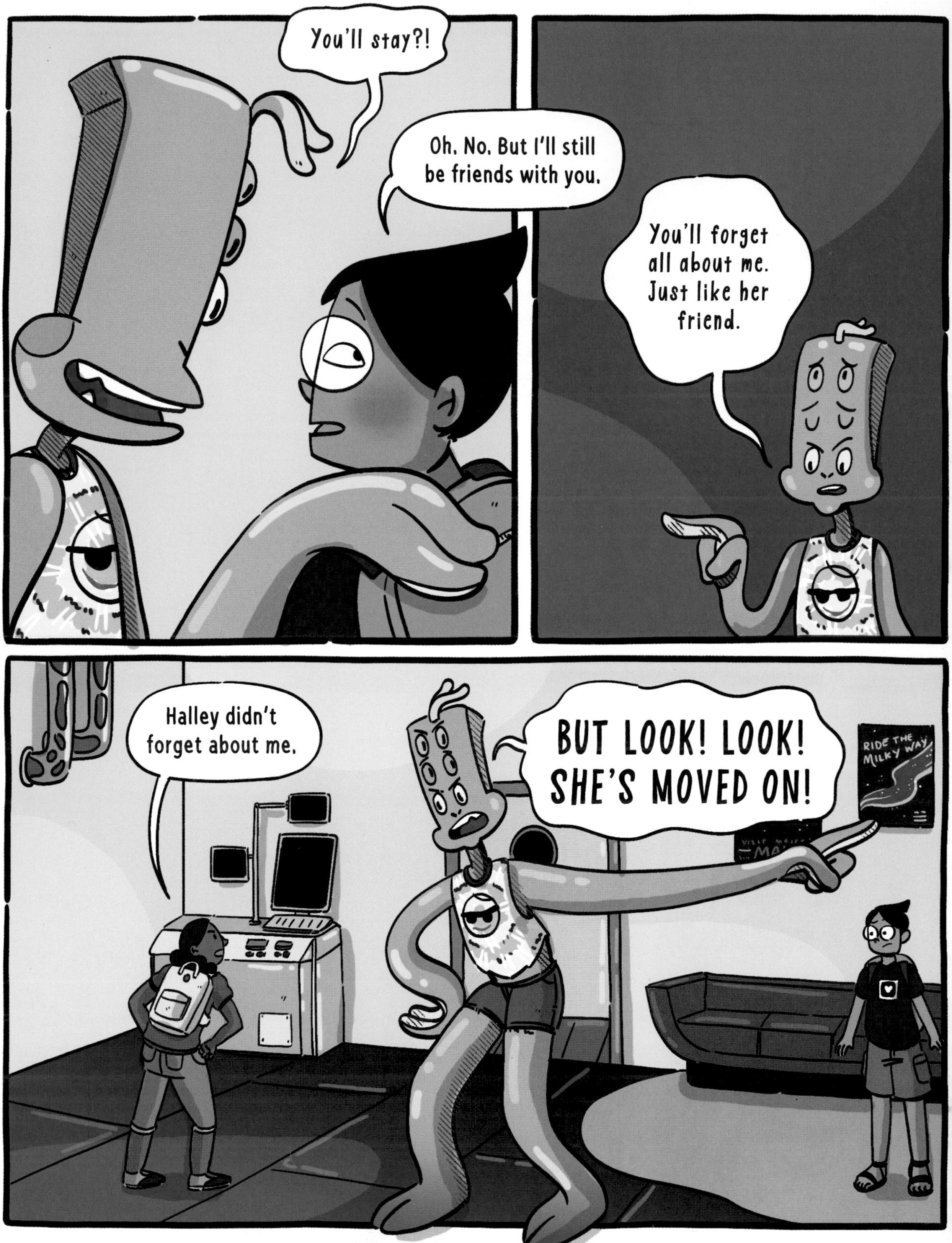
You'll stay?!
Oh. No. But I'll still be friends with you.
You'll forget all about me. Just like her friend.
Halley didn't forget about me.
BUT LOOK! LOOK! SHE'S MOVED ON!
RIDE THE MILKY WAY

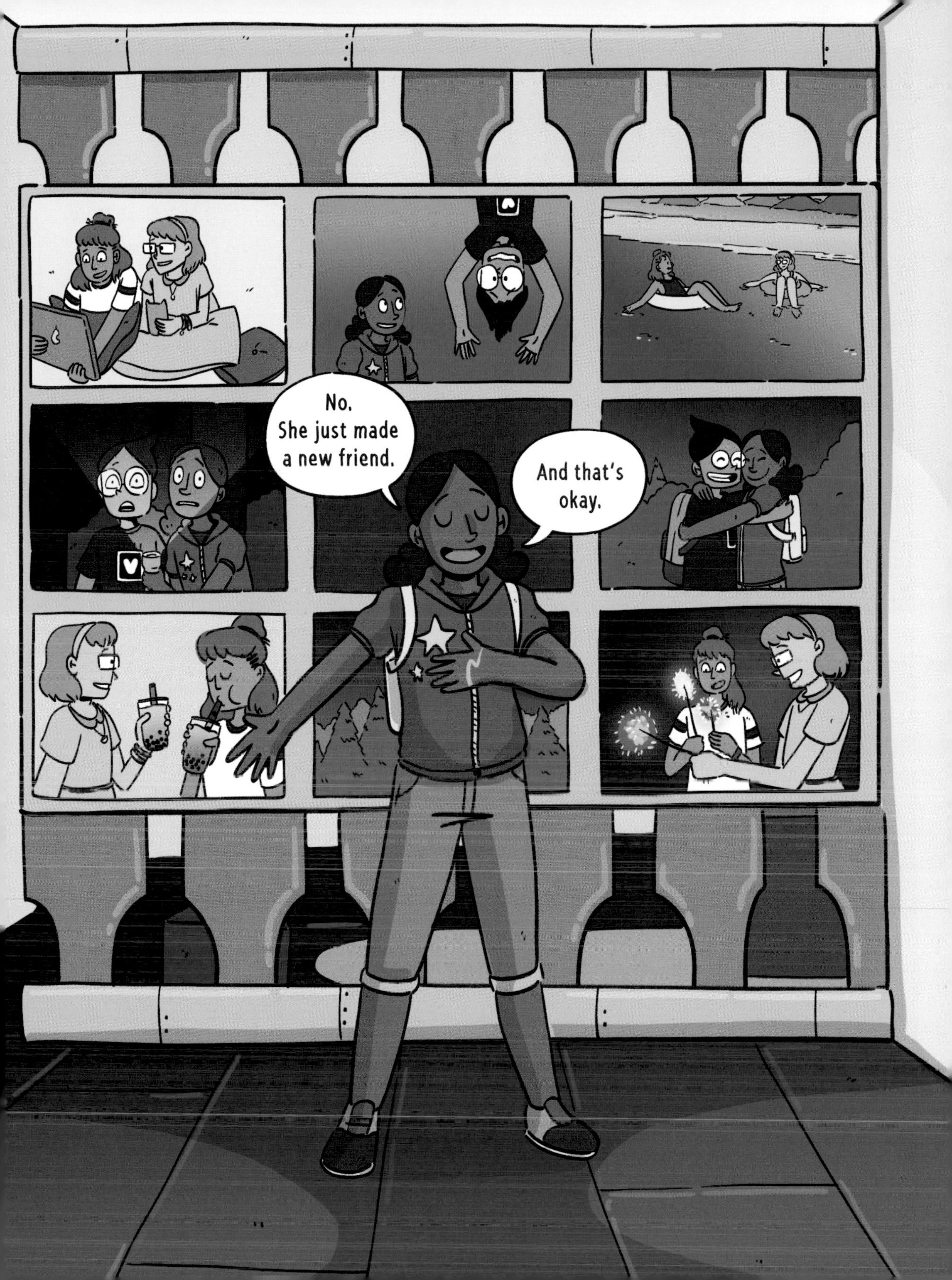
No. She just made a new friend.
And that's okay.

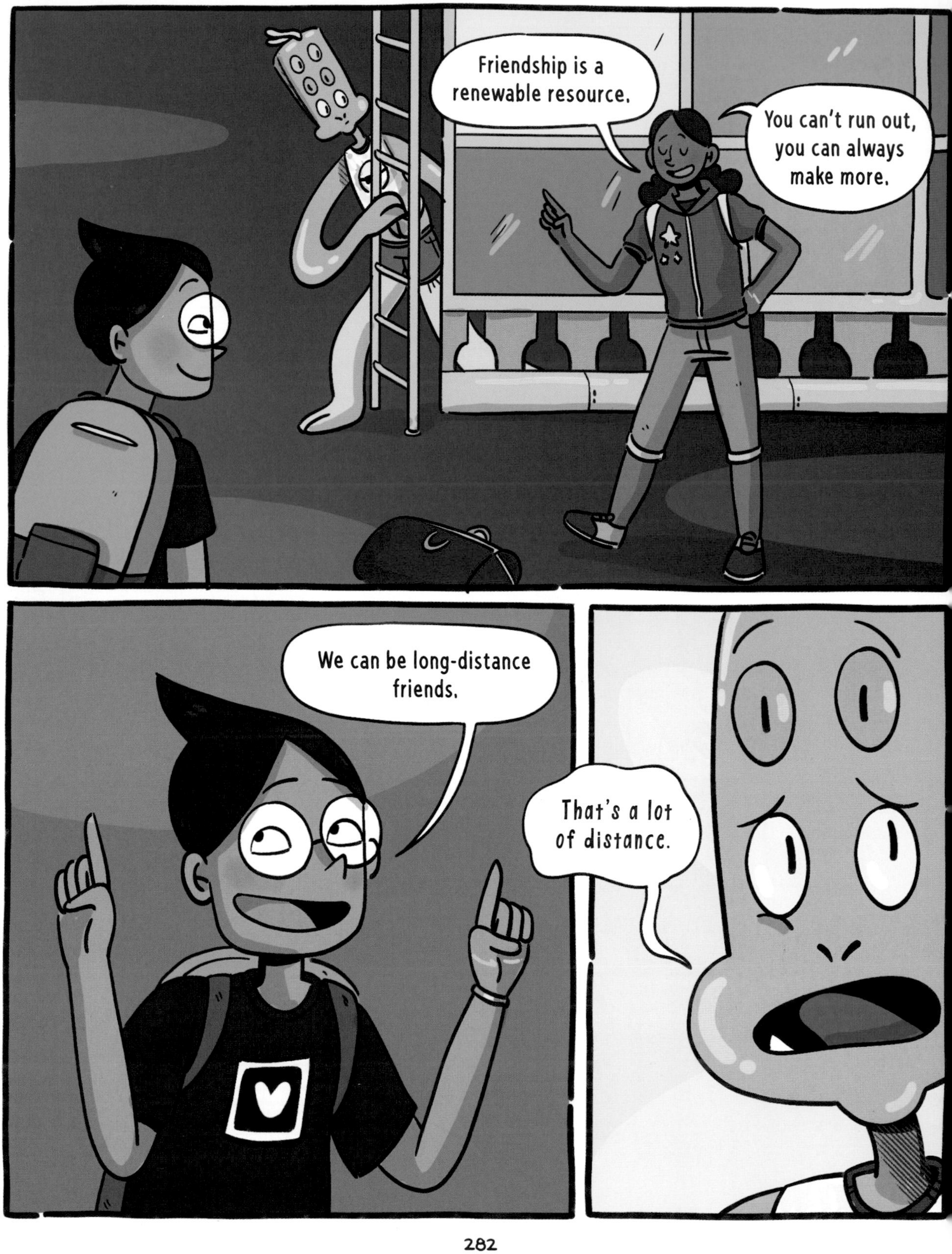
Friendship is a renewable resource.
You can't run out, you can always make more.
We can be long-distance friends.
That's a lot of distance.

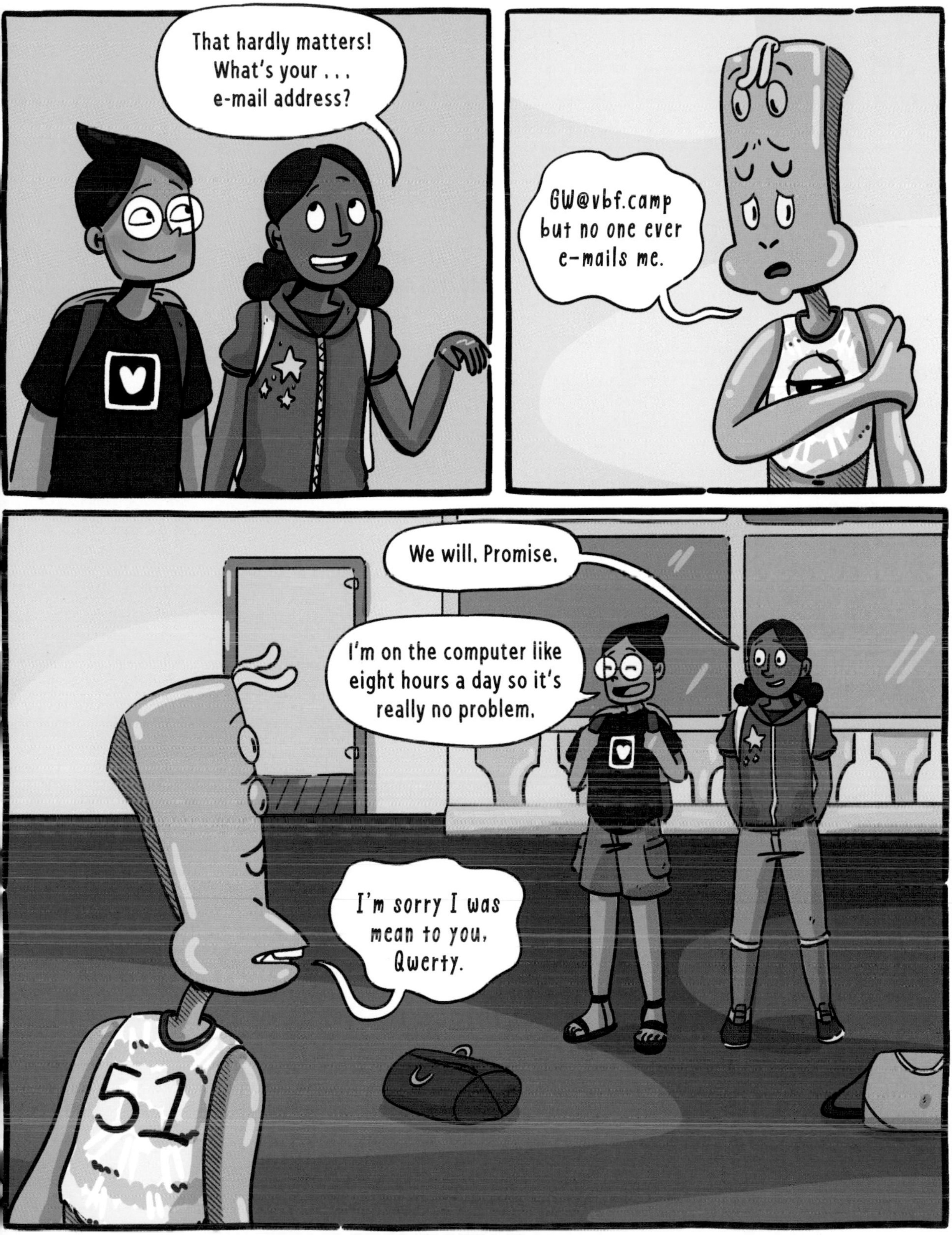
That hardly matters! What's your . . . e-mail address?
GW@vbf.camp but no one ever e-mails me.
We will. Promise.
I'm on the computer like eight hours a day so it's really no problem.
I'm sorry I was mean to you, Qwerty.
51

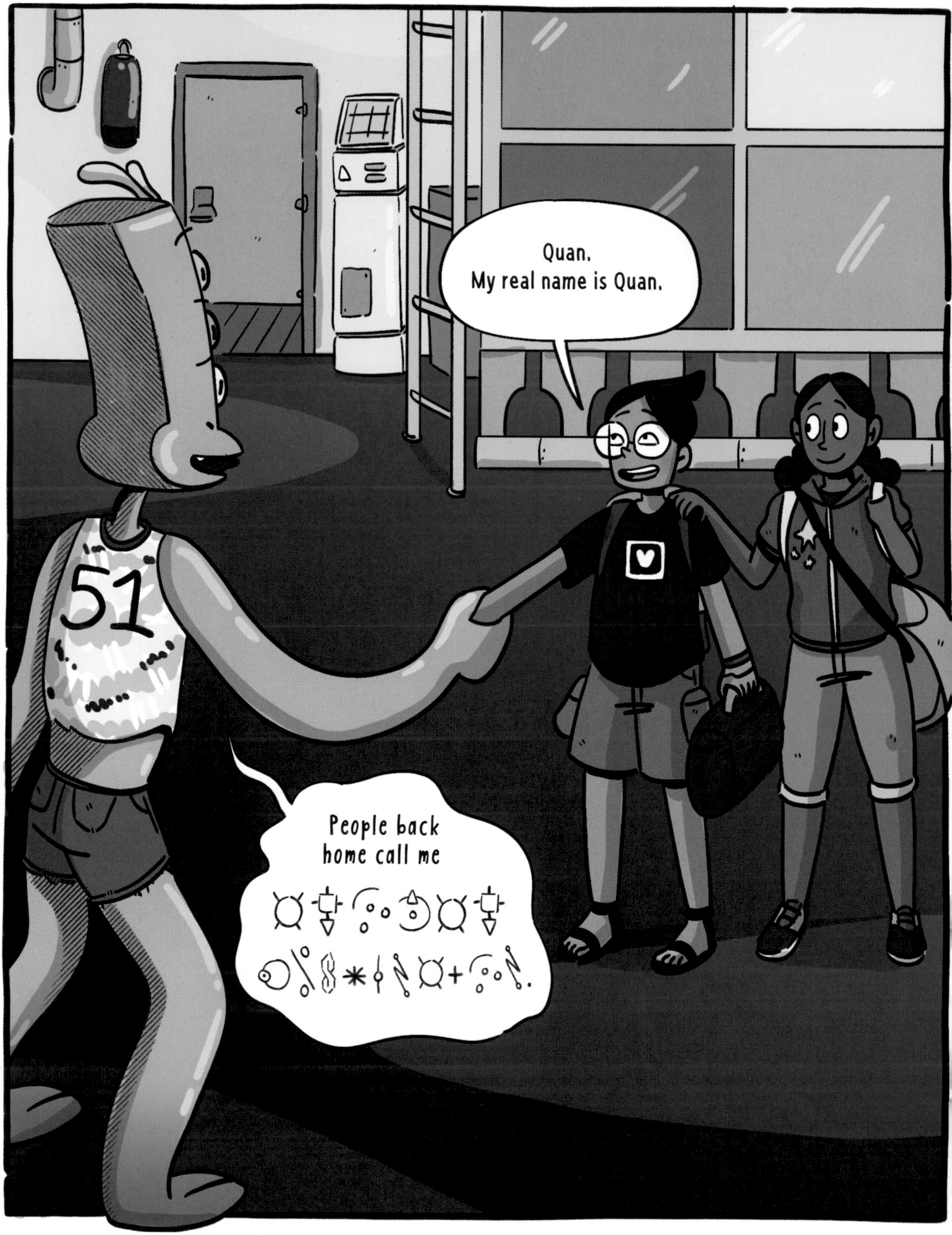
Quan.
My real name is Quan.
People back home call me

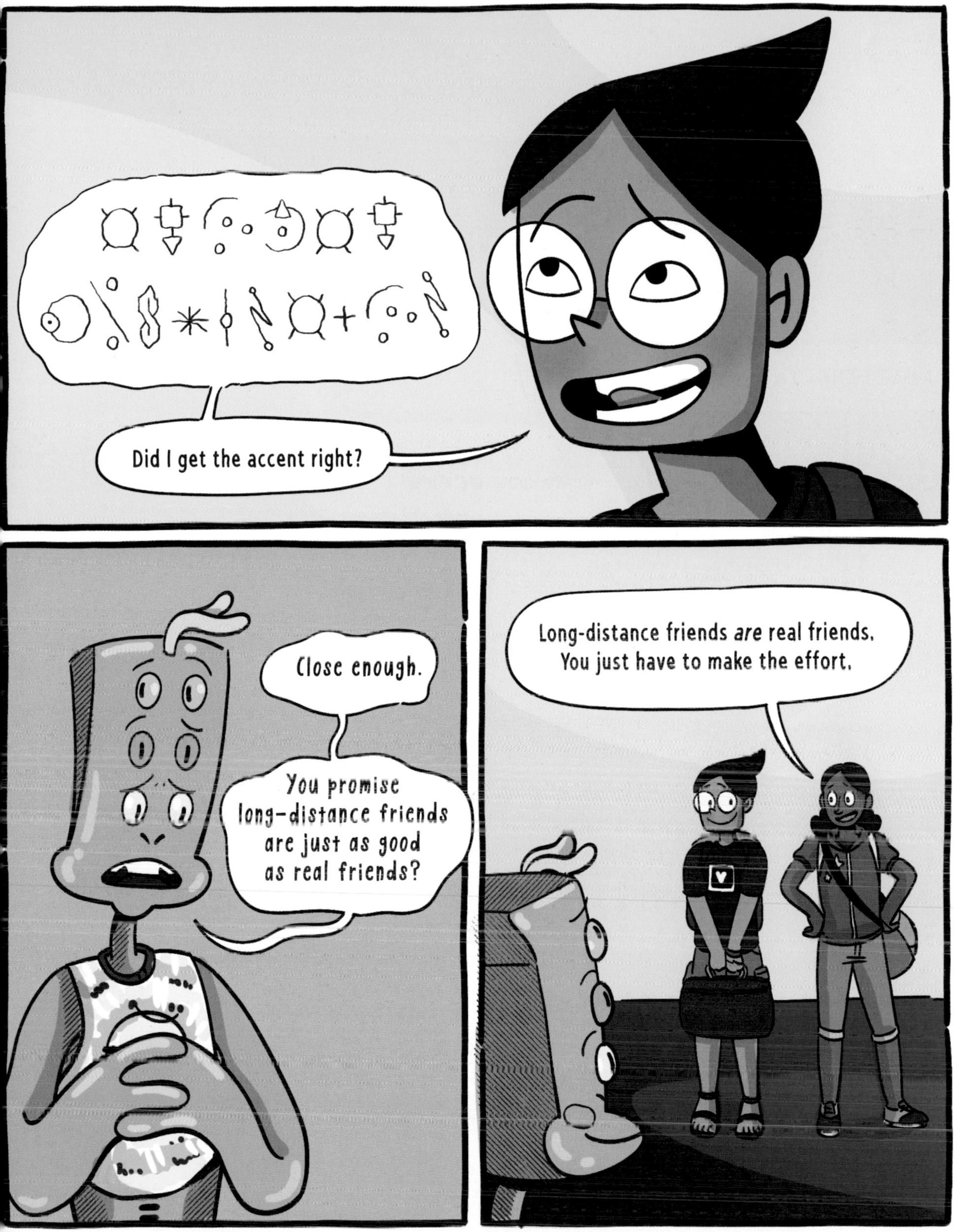
Did I get the accent right?
Close enough.
You promise long-distance friends are just as good as real friends?
Long-distance friends *are* real friends. You just have to make the effort.

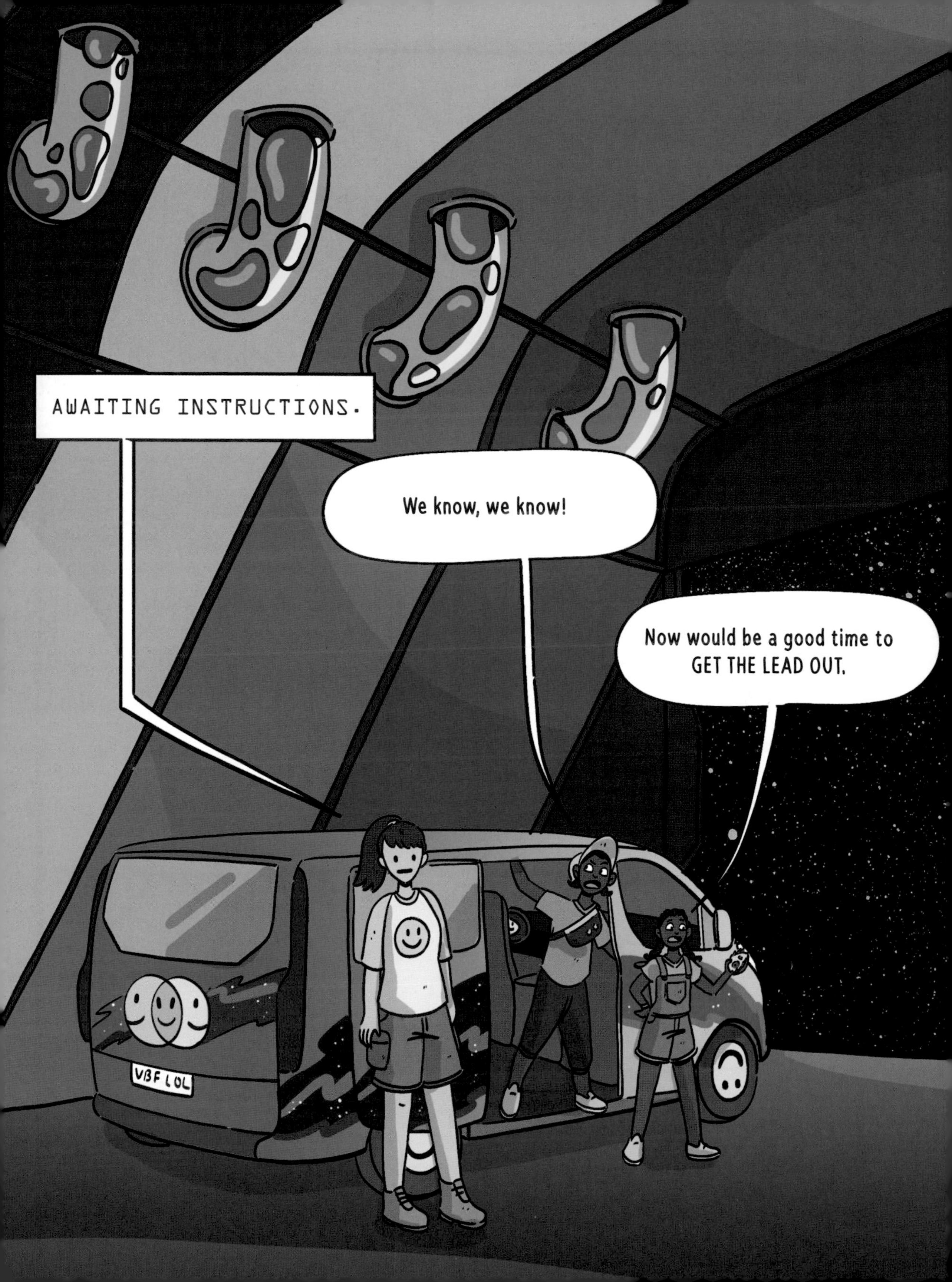
AWAITING INSTRUCTIONS.
We know, we know!
Now would be a good time to GET THE LEAD OUT.
VBF LOL

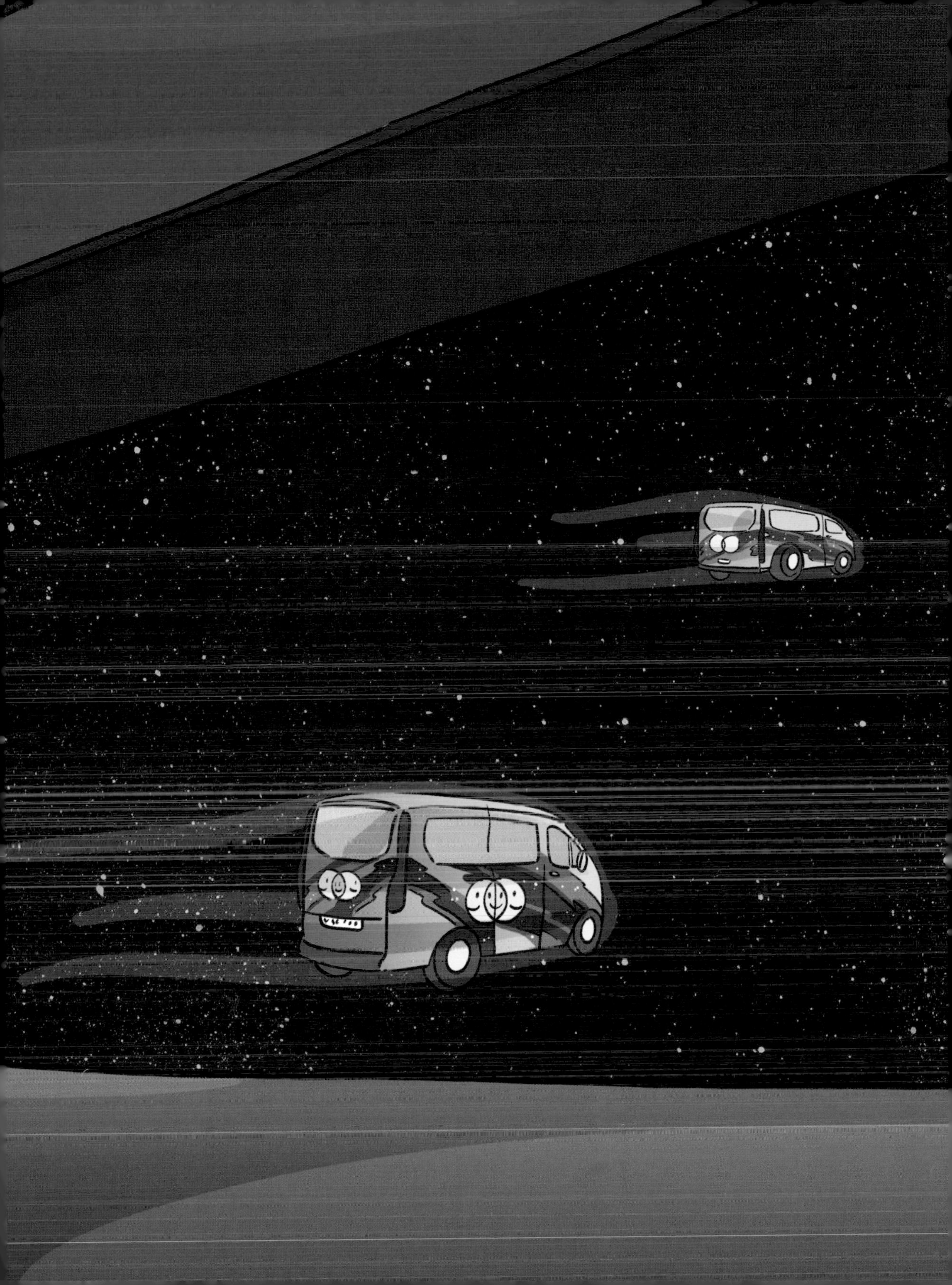

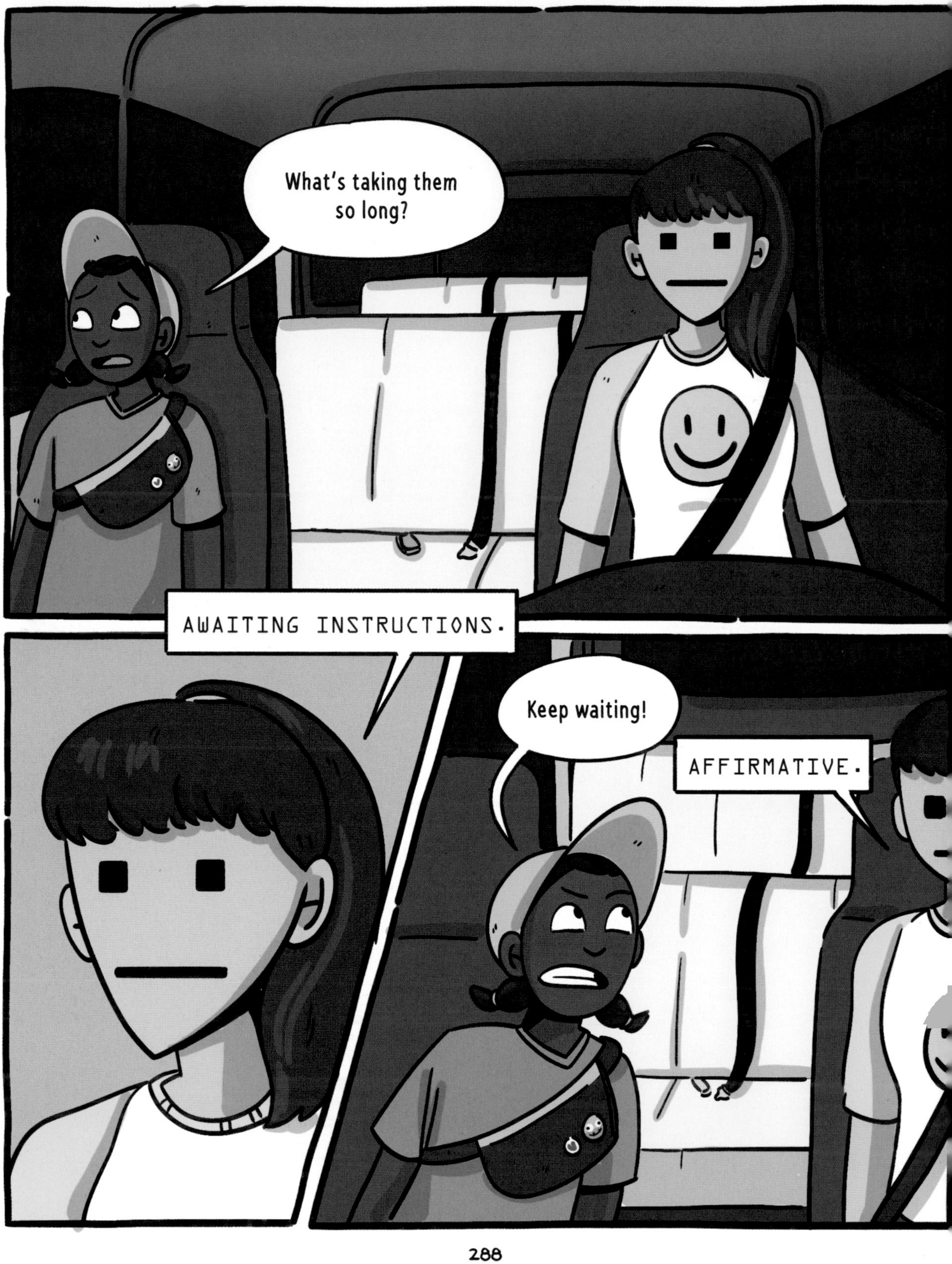
What's taking them so long?
AWAITING INSTRUCTIONS.
Keep waiting!
AFFIRMATIVE.

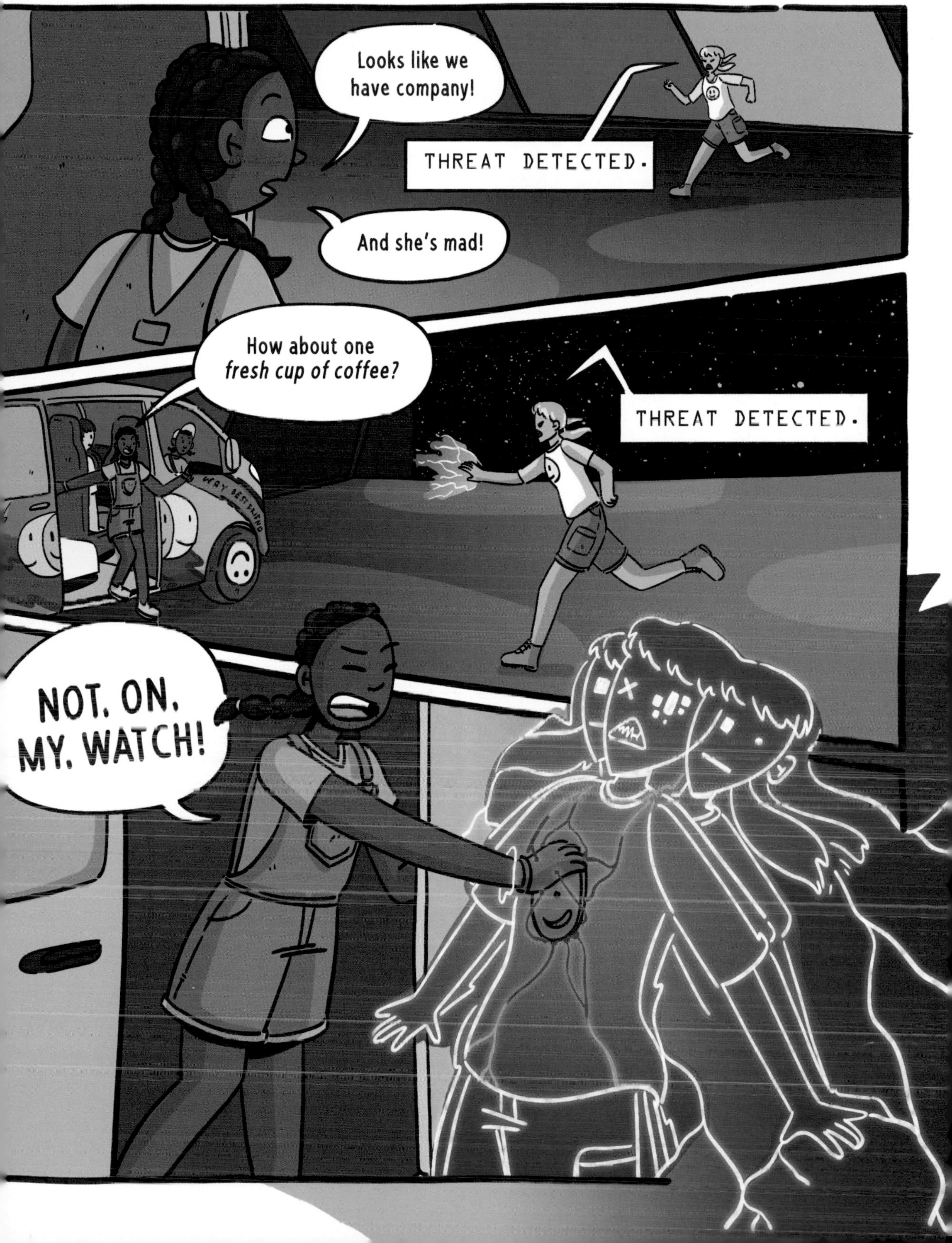

Looks like we have company!
THREAT DETECTED.
And she's mad!
How about one *fresh cup of coffee?*
THREAT DETECTED.
NOT. ON. MY. WATCH!

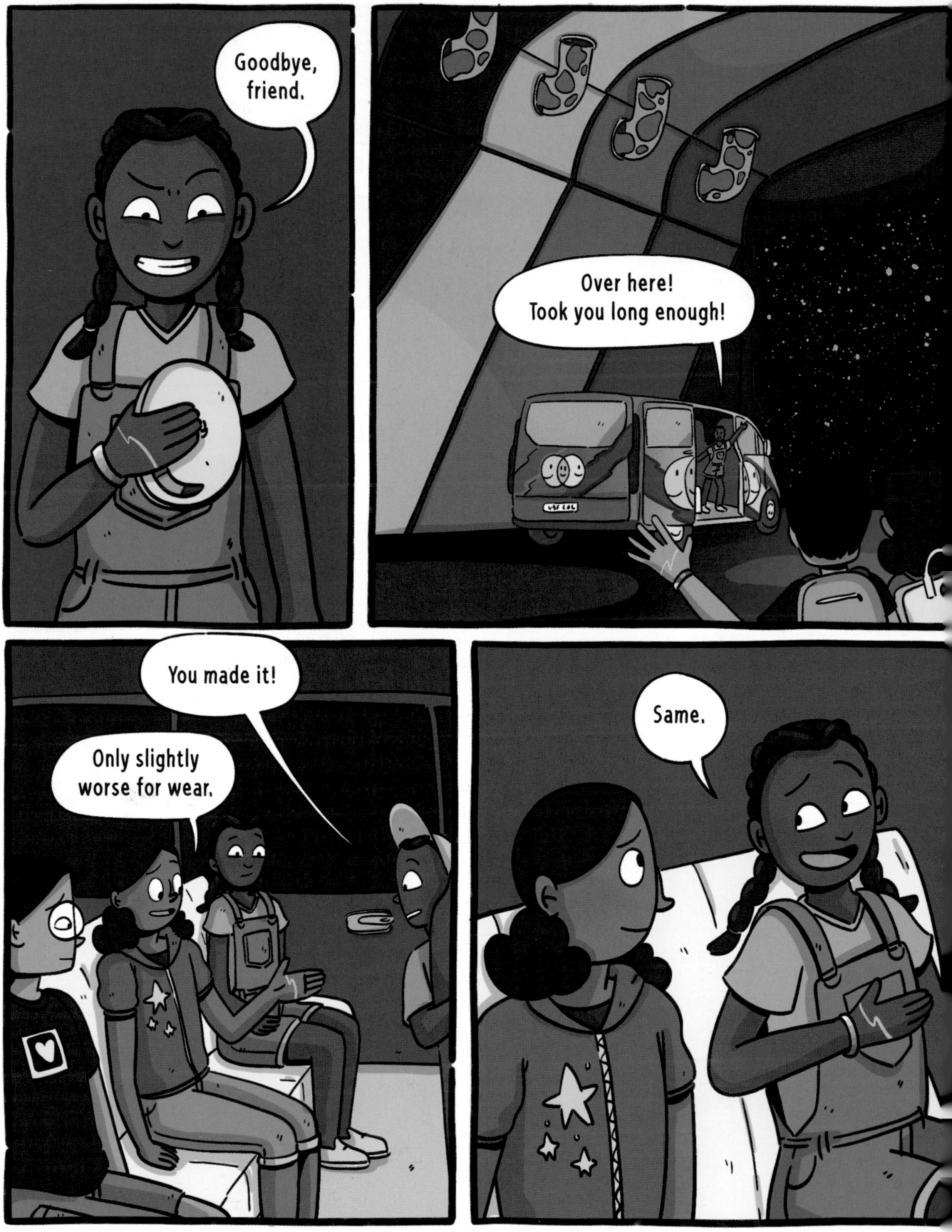
Goodbye, friend.
Over here! Took you long enough!
You made it!
Only slightly worse for wear.
Same.

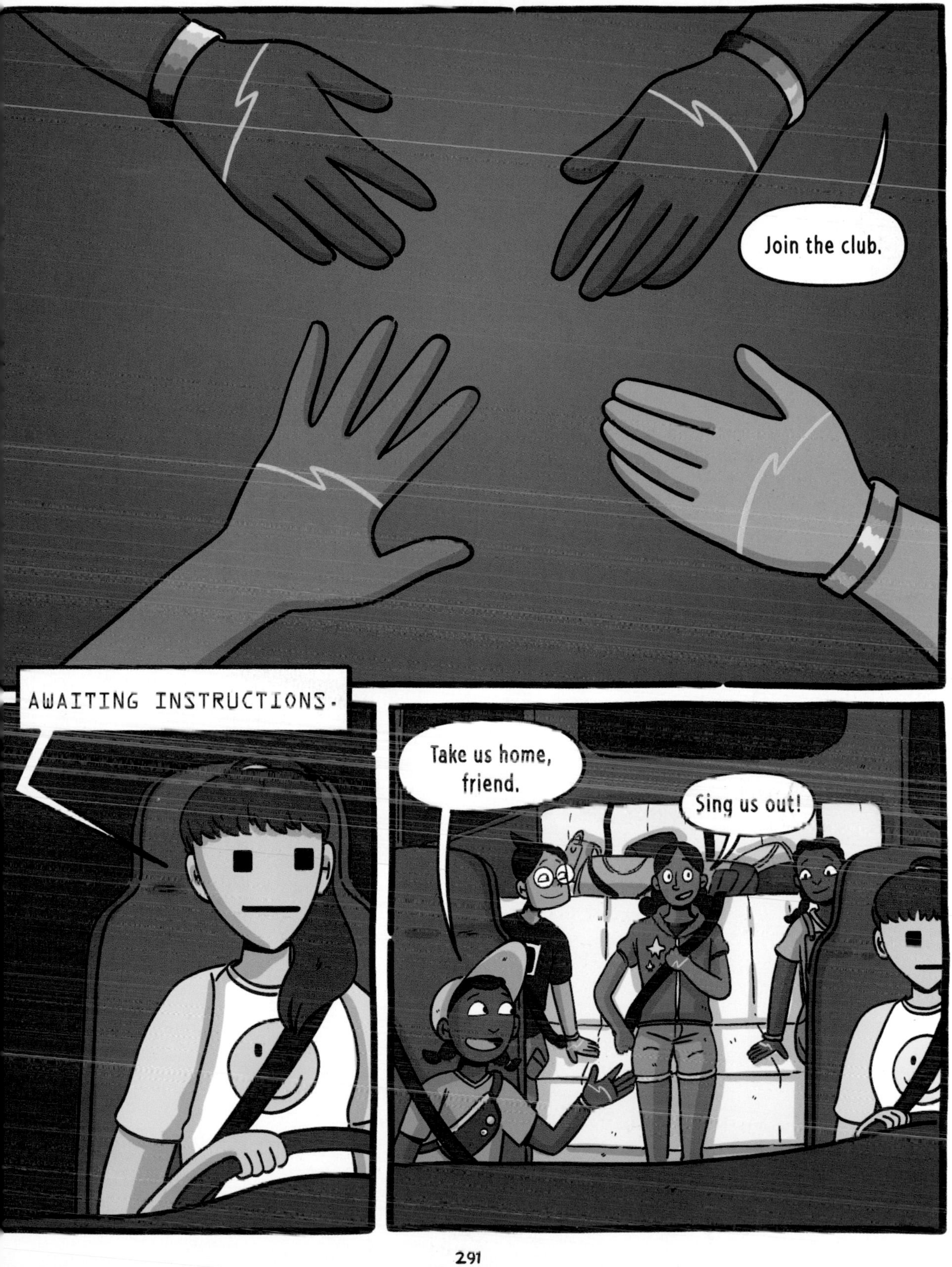
Join the club.
AWAITING INSTRUCTIONS.
Take us home, friend.
Sing us out!

Twinkle Twinkle Little Star!

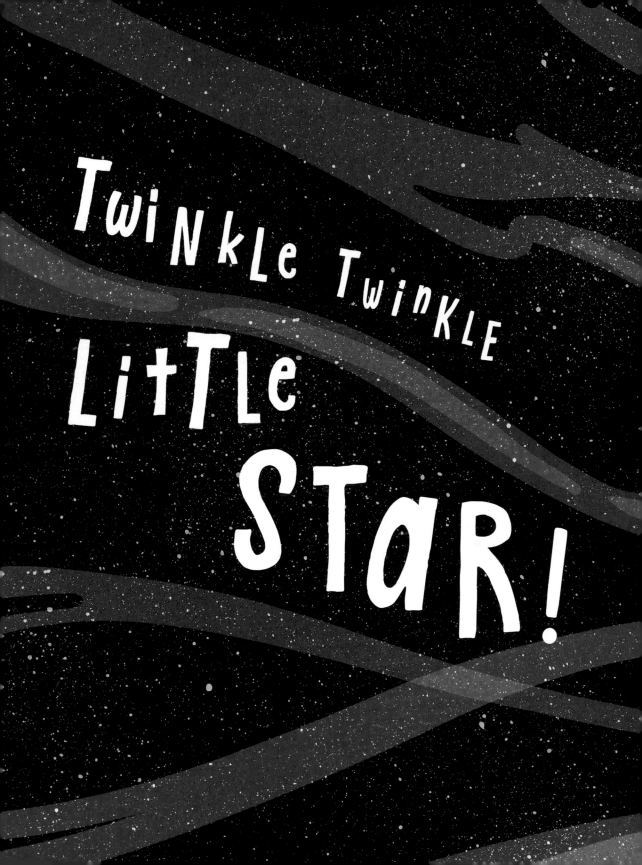

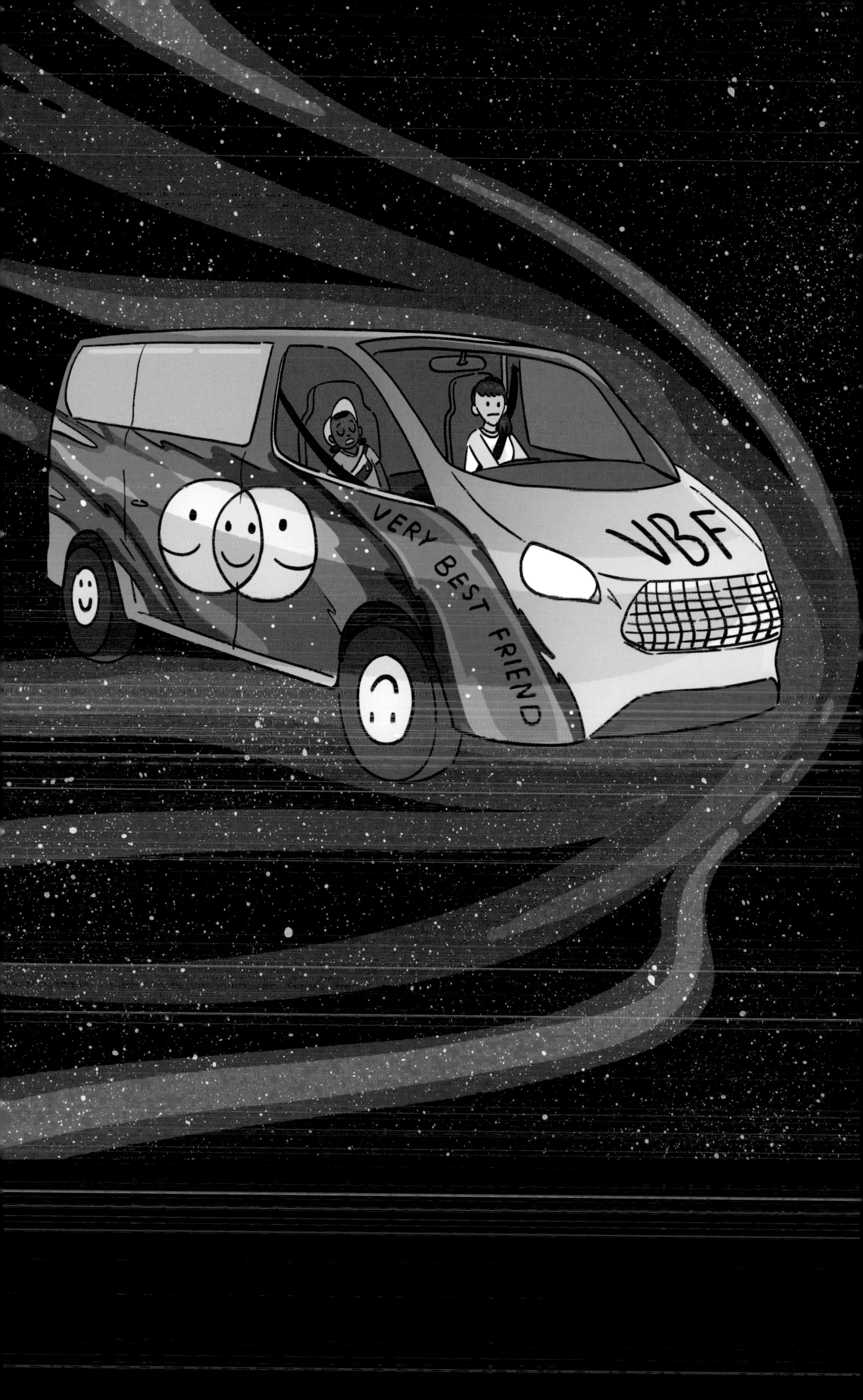
VERY BEST FRIEND
VBF

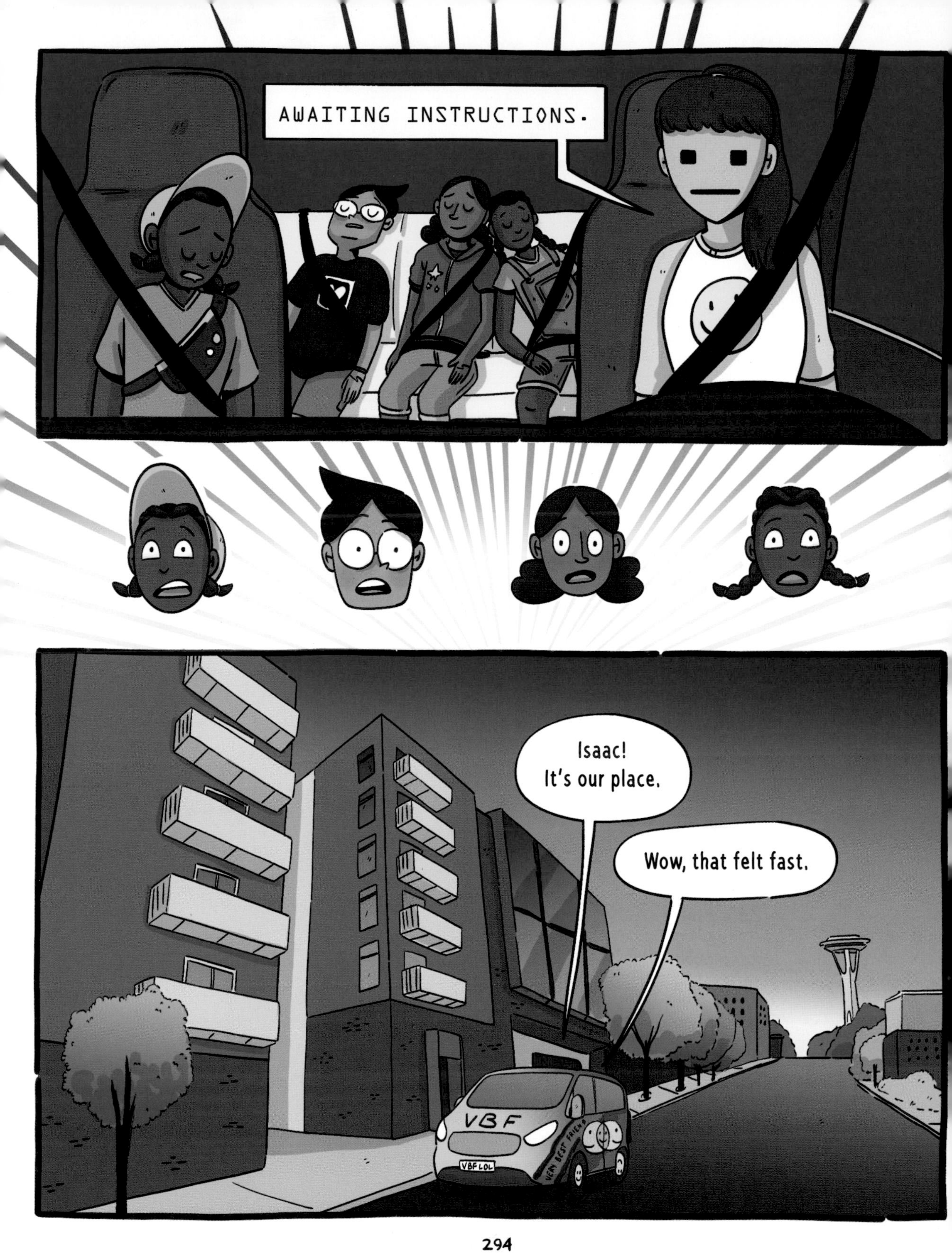
AWAITING INSTRUCTIONS.
Isaac! It's our place.
Wow, that felt fast.
VBF
VERY BEST FRIEND
VBFLOL

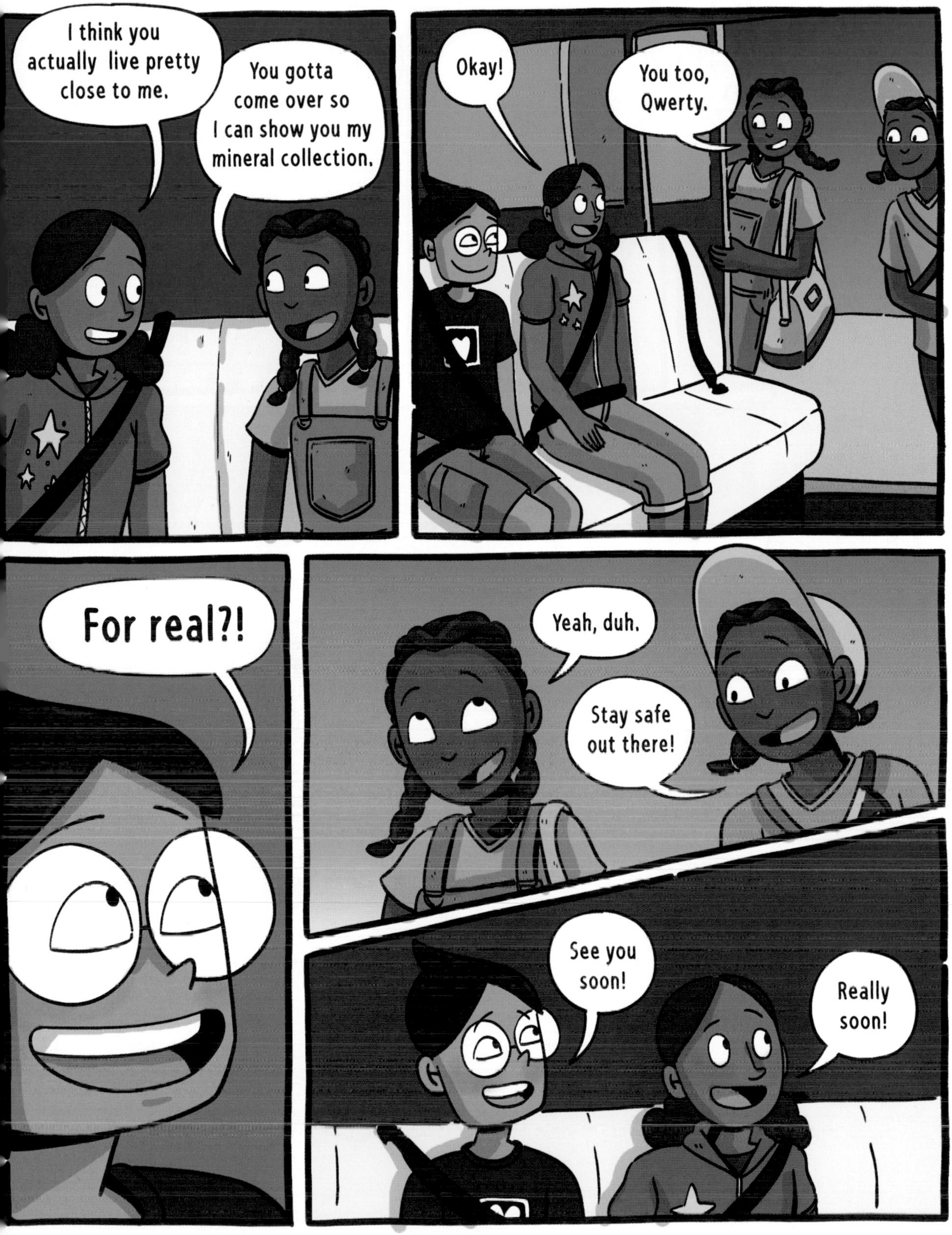
I think you actually live pretty close to me.
You gotta come over so I can show you my mineral collection.
Okay!
You too, Qwerty.
For real?!
Yeah, duh.
Stay safe out there!
See you soon!
Really soon!

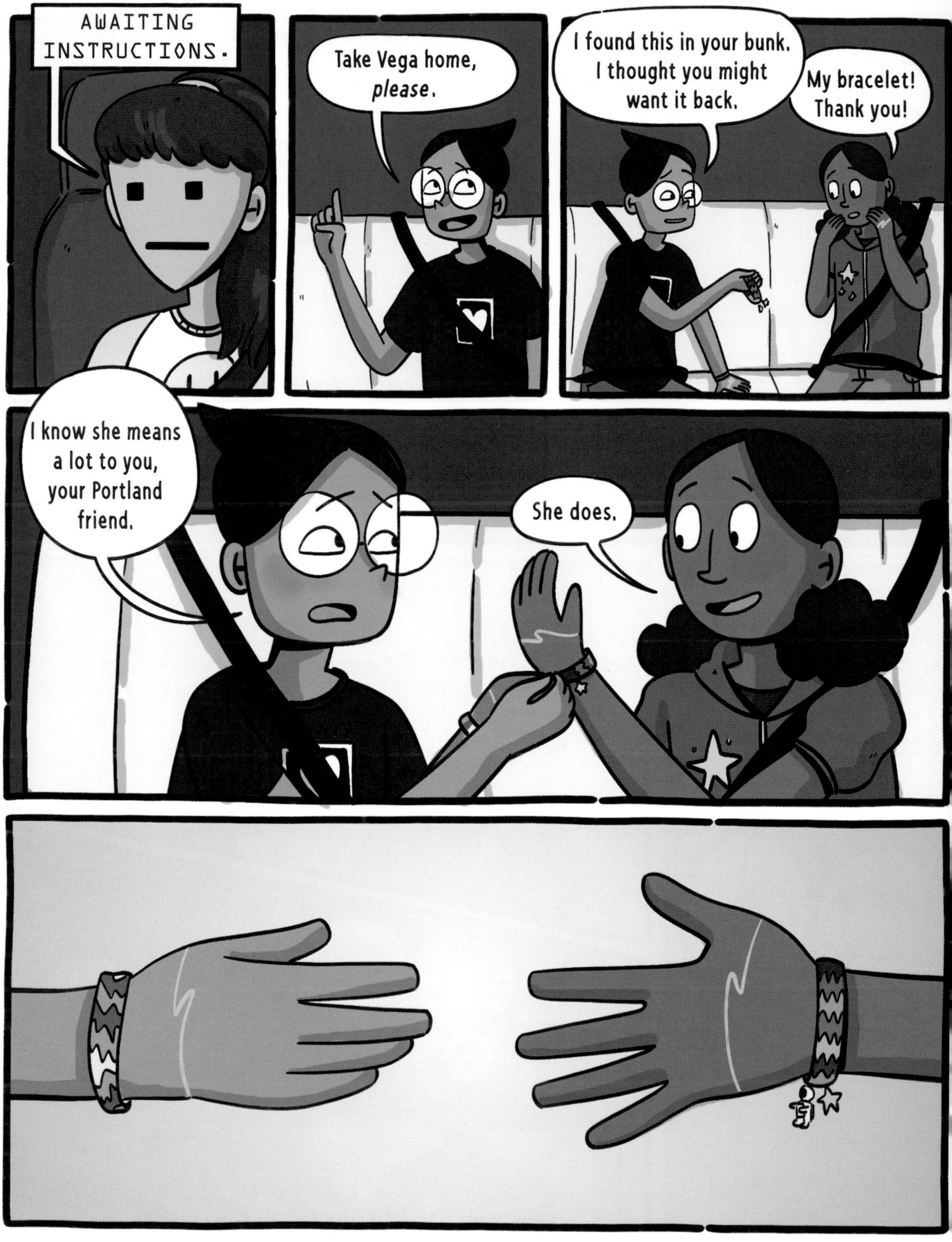
AWAITING INSTRUCTIONS.
Take Vega home, *please*.
I found this in your bunk. I thought you might want it back.
My bracelet! Thank you!
I know she means a lot to you, your Portland friend.
She does.

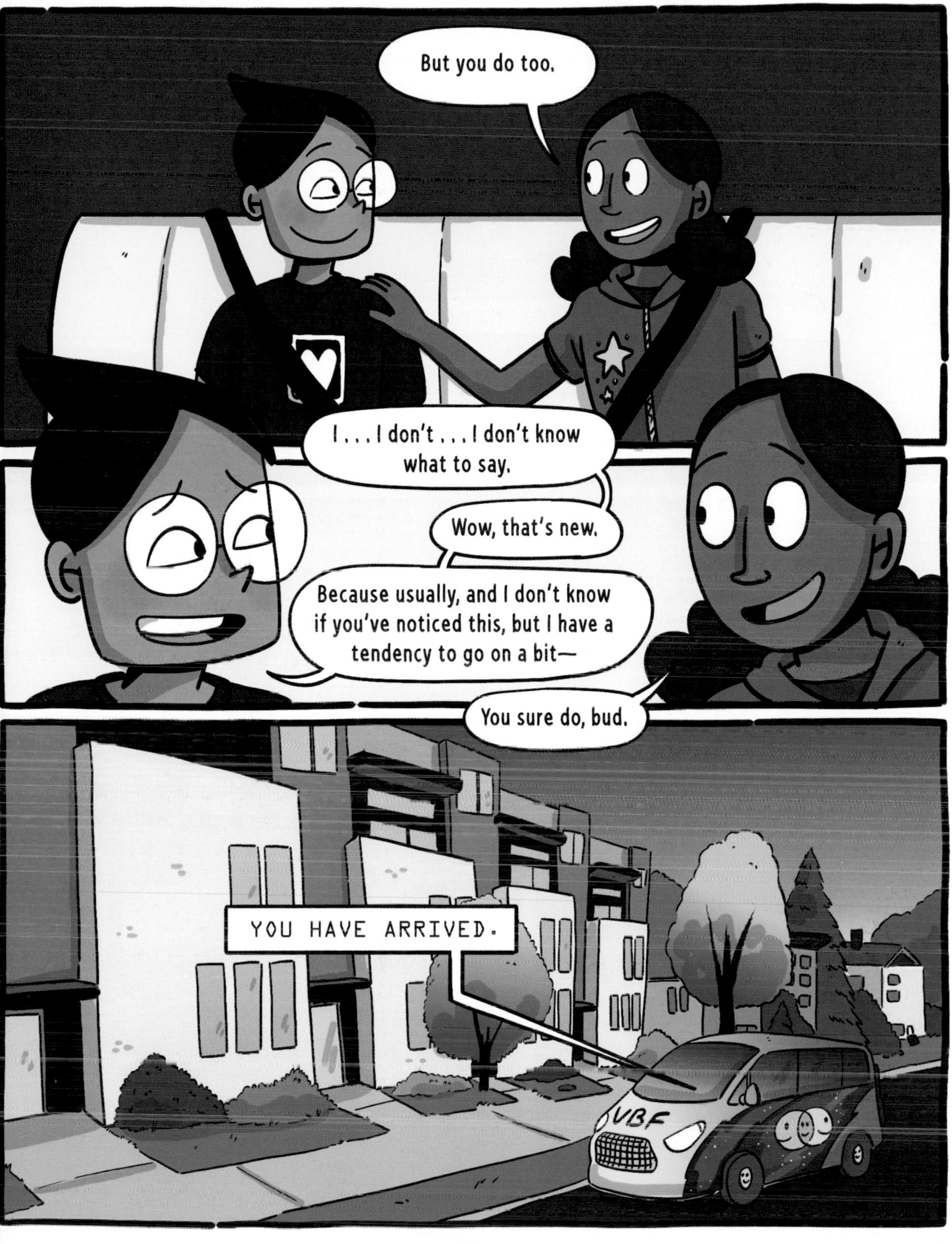
But you do too.
I . . . I don't . . . I don't know what to say.
Wow, that's new.
Because usually, and I don't know if you've noticed this, but I have a tendency to go on a bit—
You sure do, bud.
YOU HAVE ARRIVED.
VBF

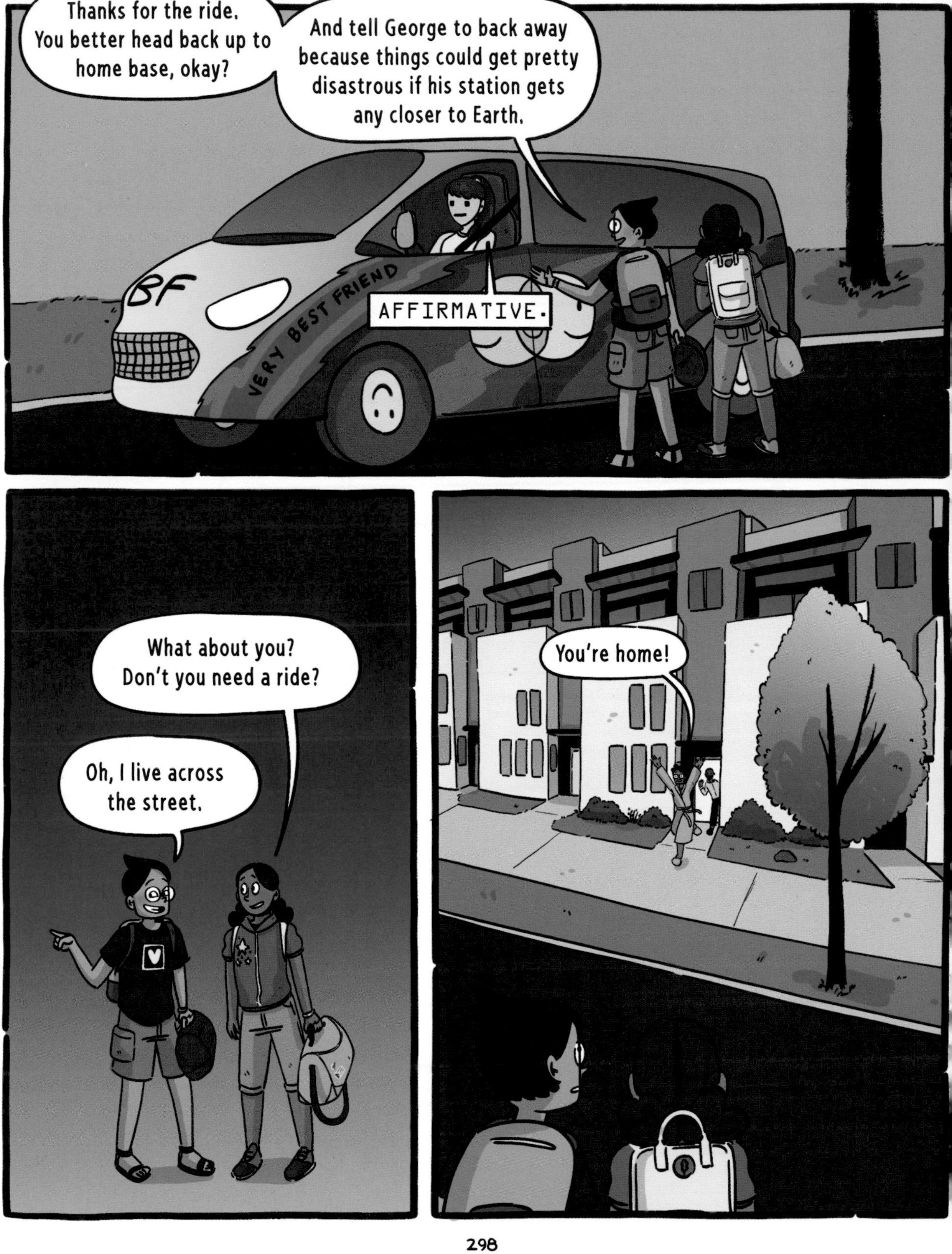
Thanks for the ride.
You better head back up to home base, okay?
And tell George to back away because things could get pretty disastrous if his station gets any closer to Earth.
AFFIRMATIVE.
BF
VERY BEST FRIEND
What about you?
Don't you need a ride?
Oh, I live across the street.
You're home!

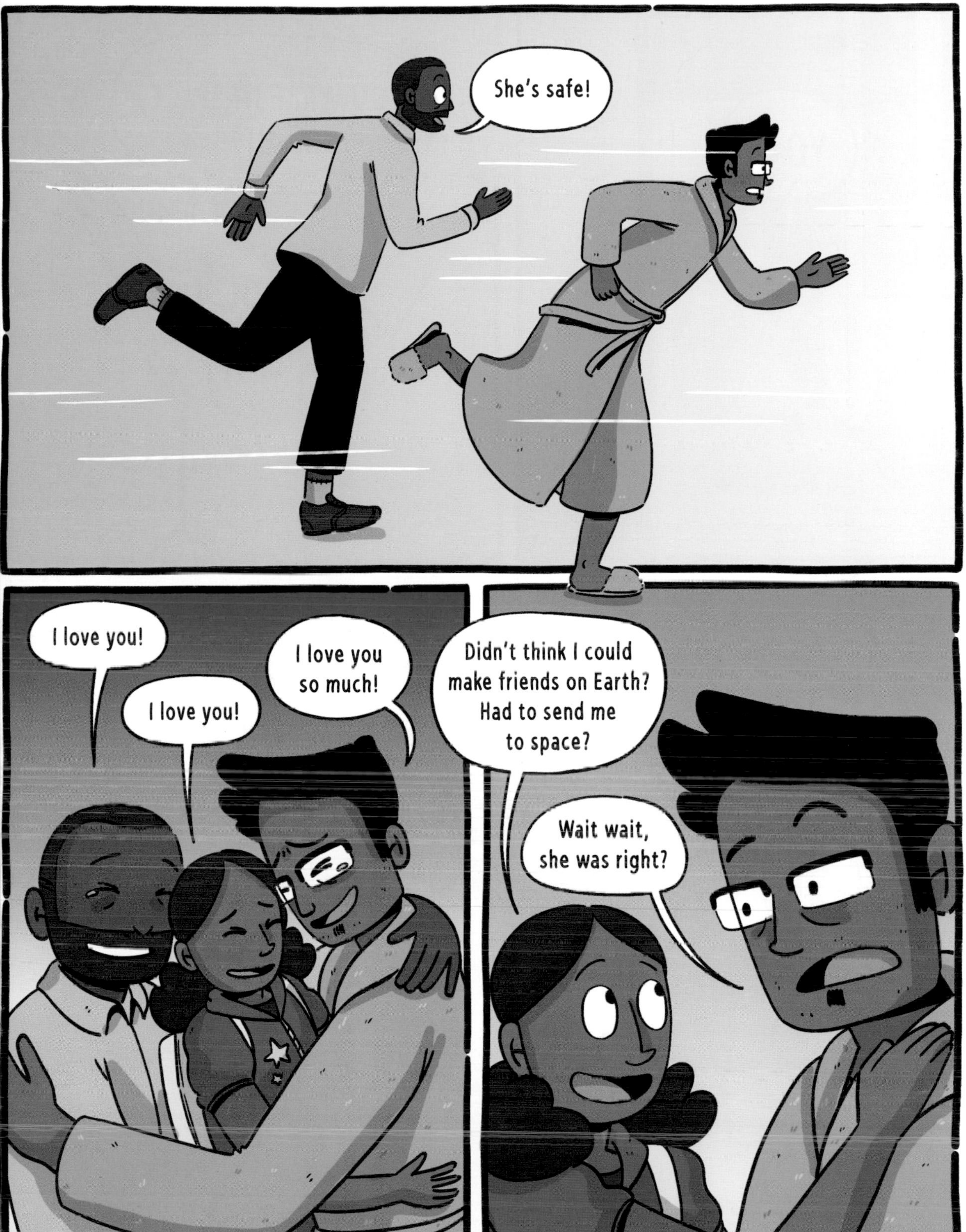
She's safe!
I love you!
I love you!
I love you so much!
Didn't think I could make friends on Earth? Had to send me to space?
Wait wait, she was right?

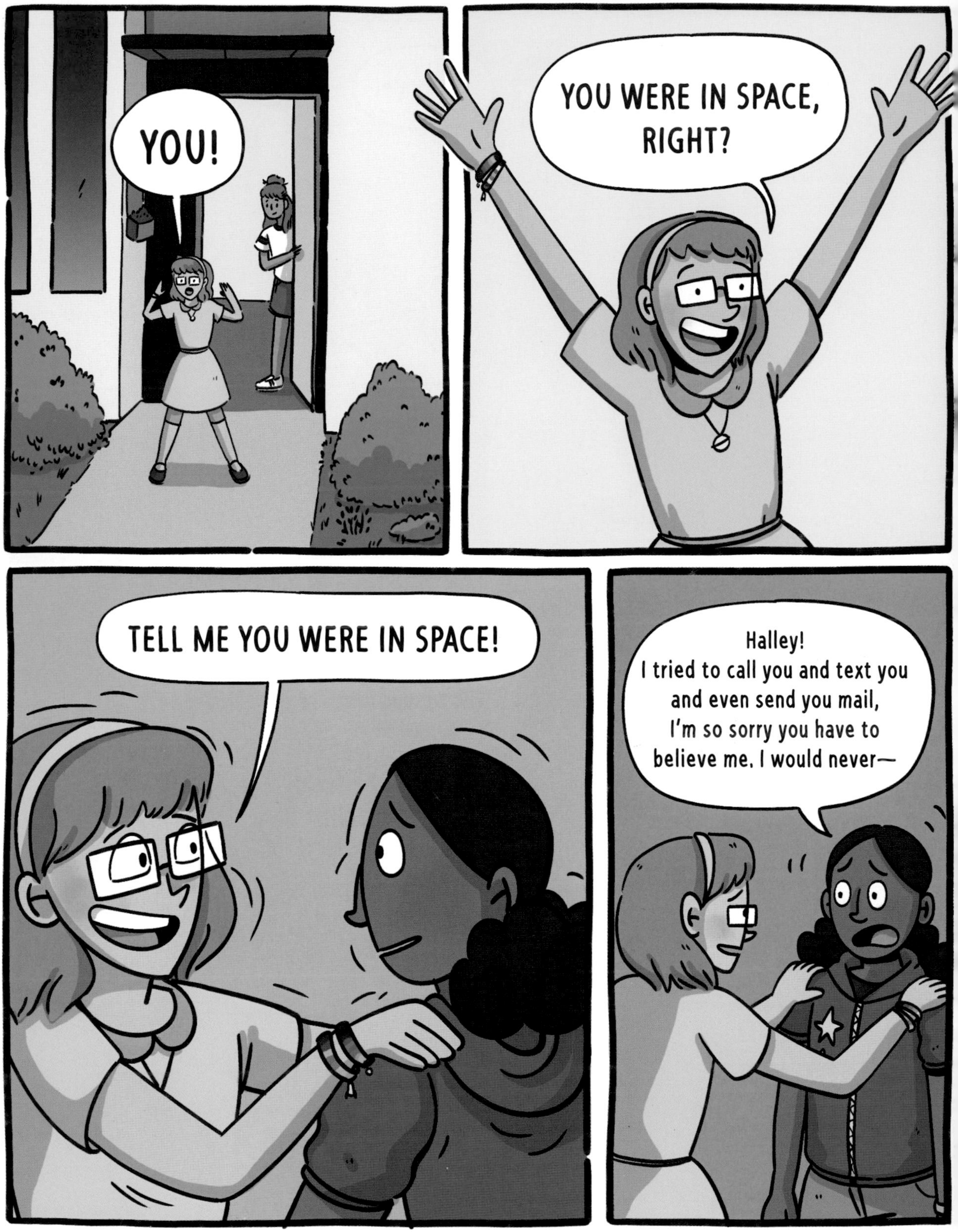
YOU!
YOU WERE IN SPACE, RIGHT?
TELL ME YOU WERE IN SPACE!
Halley! I tried to call you and text you and even send you mail, I'm so sorry you have to believe me. I would never—

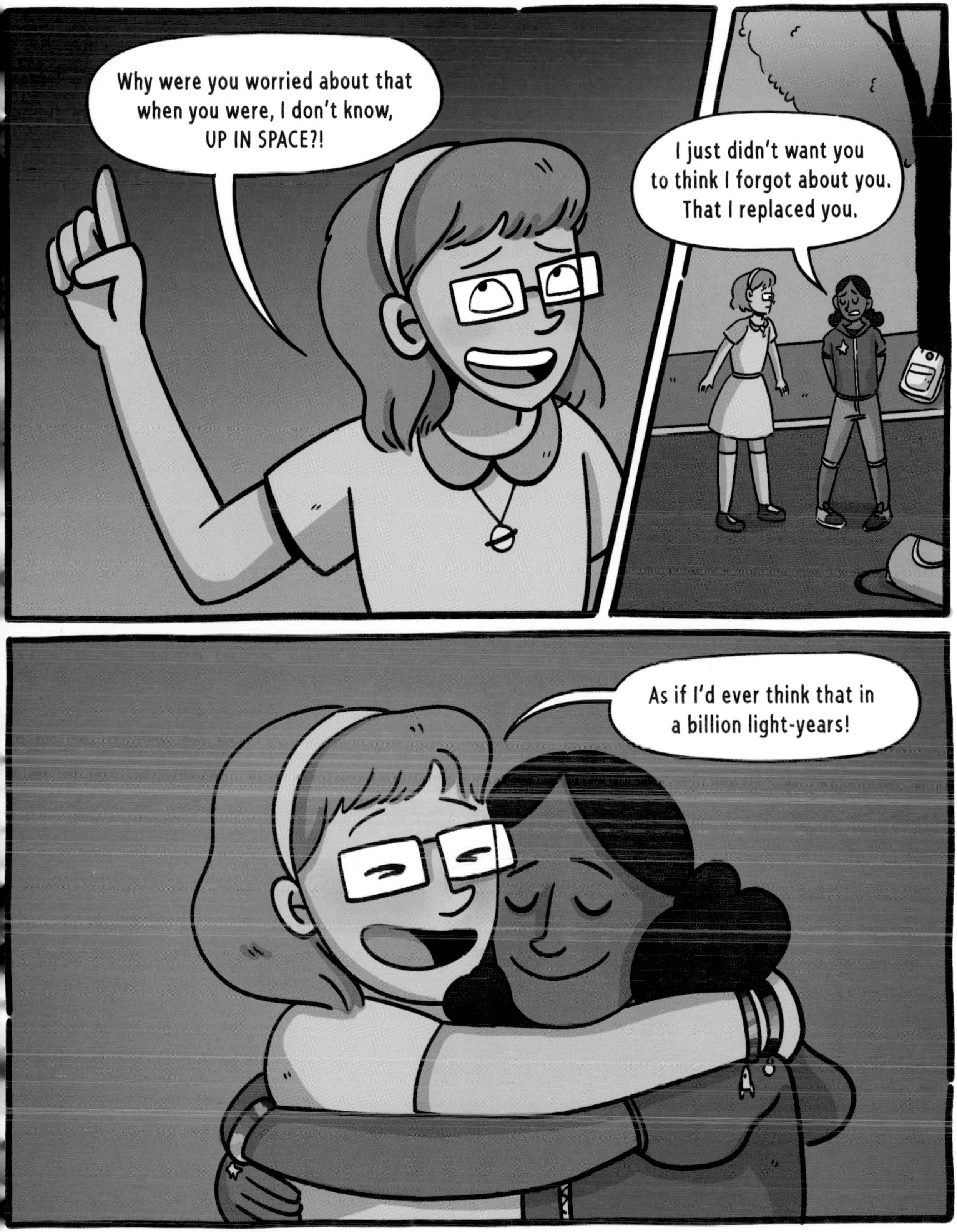
Why were you worried about that when you were, I don't know, UP IN SPACE?!
I just didn't want you to think I forgot about you. That I replaced you.
As if I'd ever think that in a billion light-years!

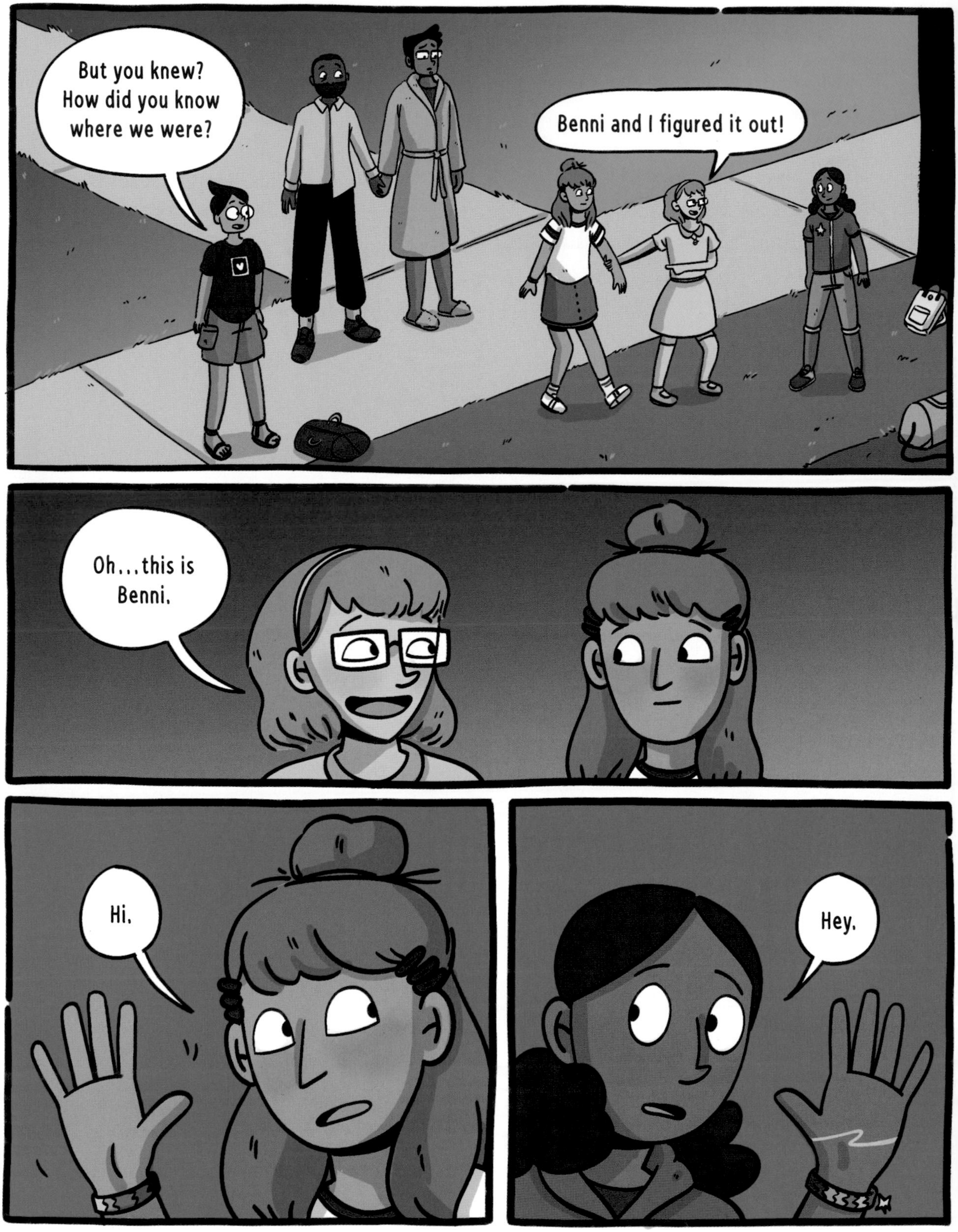

But you knew? How did you know where we were?
Benni and I figured it out!
Oh...this is Benni.
Hi.
Hey.

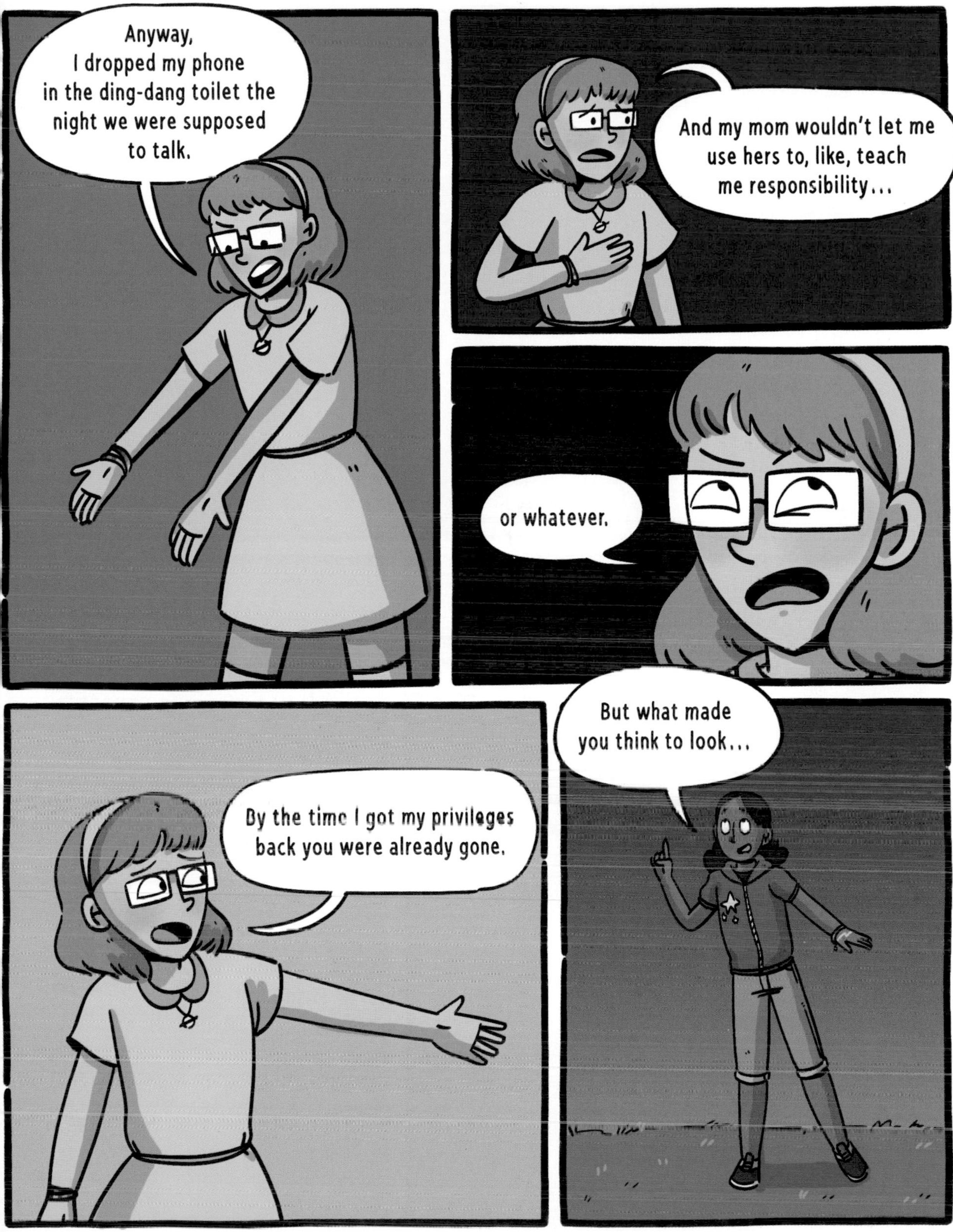
Anyway, I dropped my phone in the ding-dang toilet the night we were supposed to talk.
And my mom wouldn't let me use hers to, like, teach me responsibility...
or whatever.
By the time I got my privileges back you were already gone.
But what made you think to look...

Well, I knew something was wrong because I couldn't get in touch with you. And when I called your dads they said they hadn't heard from you either.

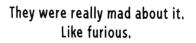

They were really mad about it. Like furious.

Yeah, like that!

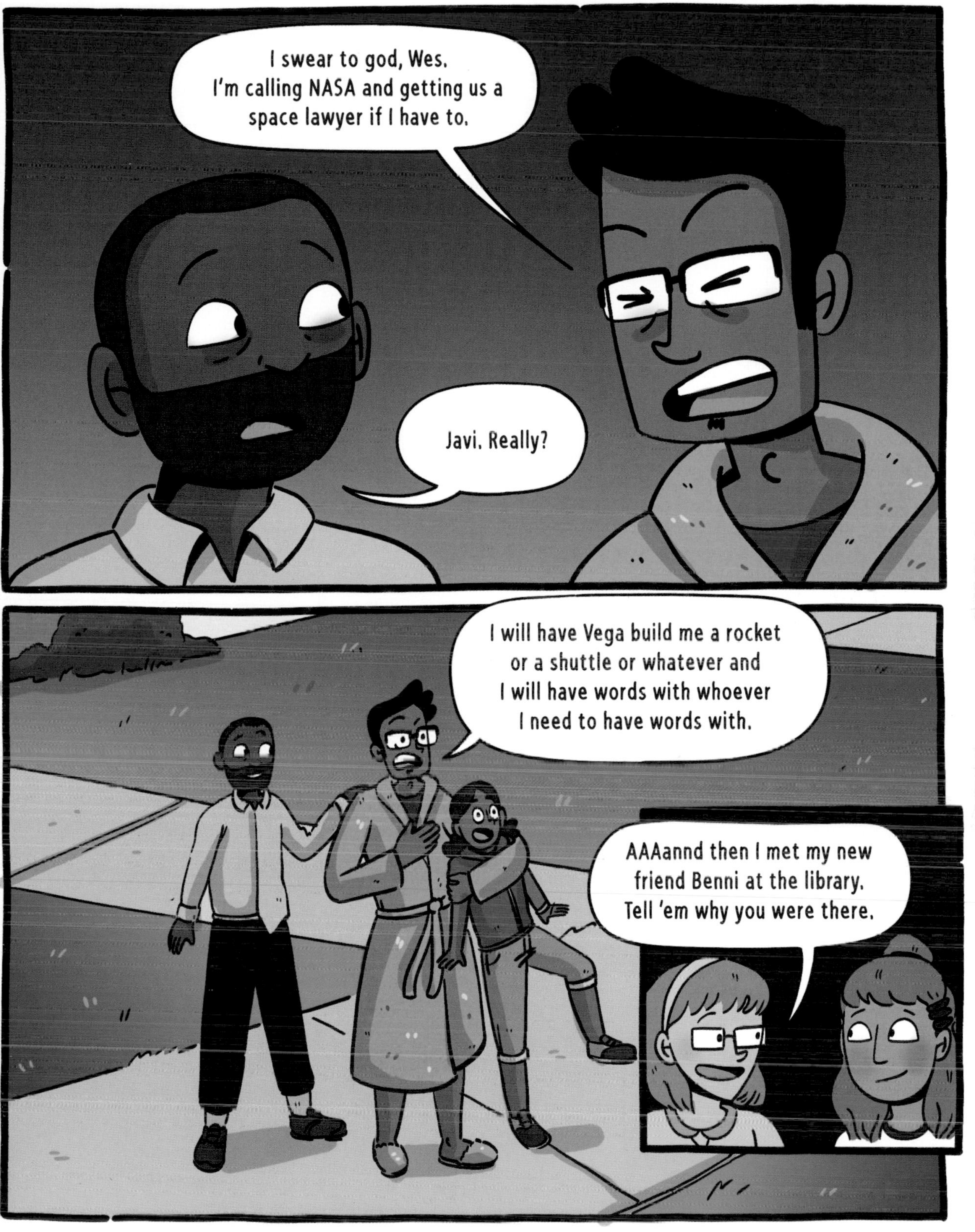
I swear to god, Wes. I'm calling NASA and getting us a space lawyer if I have to.
Javi. Really?
I will have Vega build me a rocket or a shuttle or whatever and I will have words with whoever I need to have words with.
AAAannd then I met my new friend Benni at the library. Tell 'em why you were there.

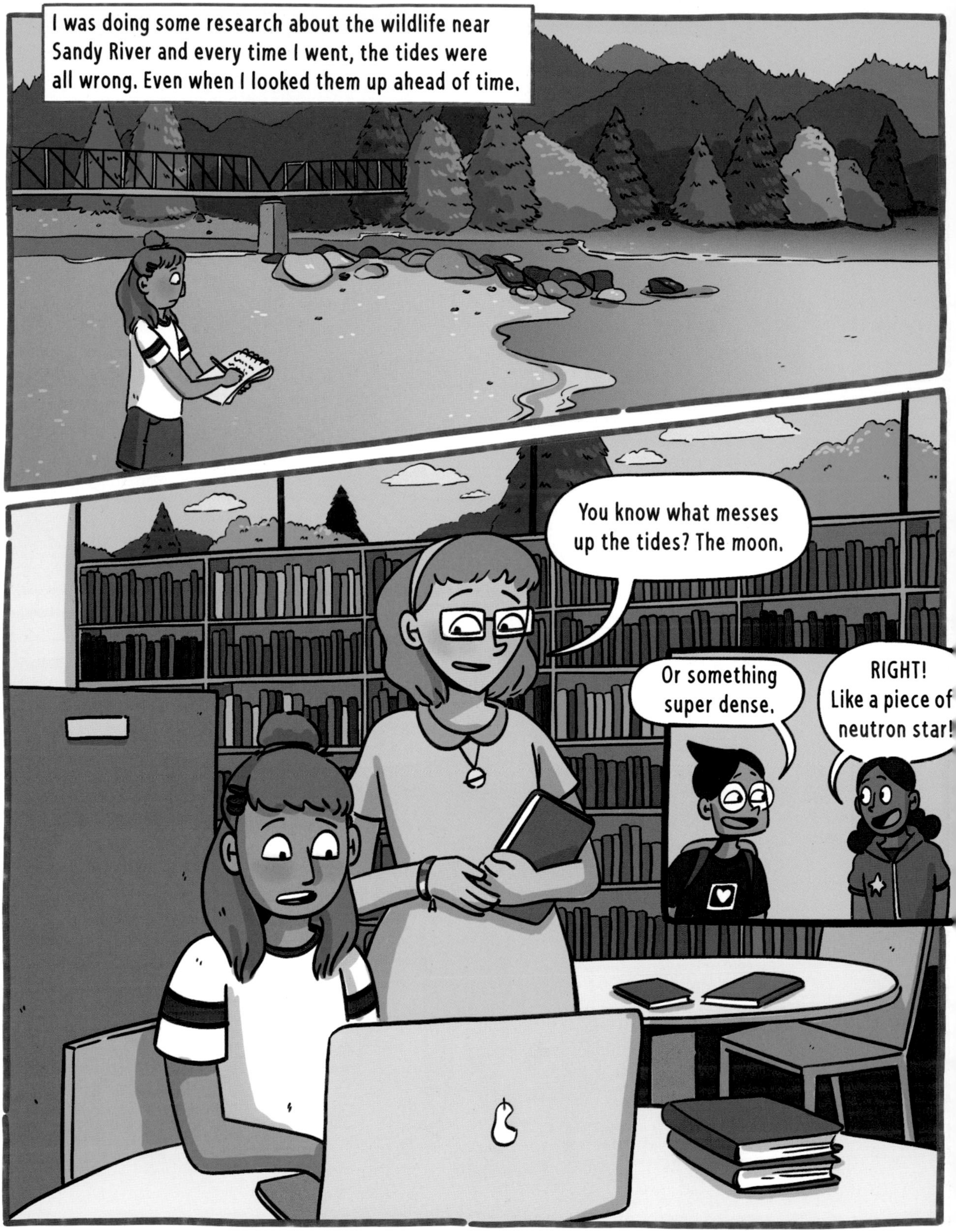

I was doing some research about the wildlife near Sandy River and every time I went, the tides were all wrong. Even when I looked them up ahead of time.
You know what messes up the tides? The moon.
Or something super dense.
RIGHT! Like a piece of neutron star!

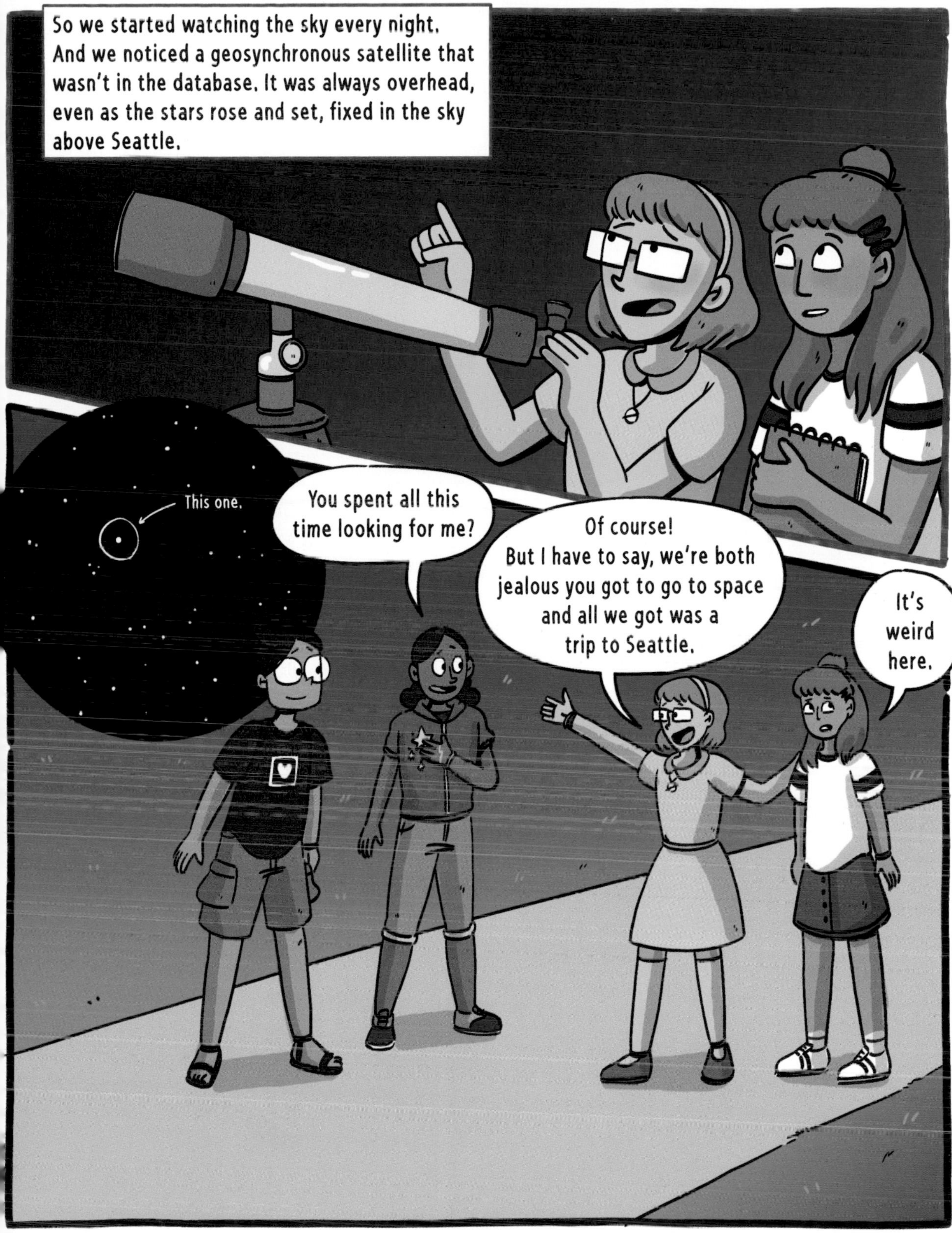

So we started watching the sky every night. And we noticed a geosynchronous satellite that wasn't in the database. It was always overhead, even as the stars rose and set, fixed in the sky above Seattle.
This one.
You spent all this time looking for me?
Of course! But I have to say, we're both jealous you got to go to space and all we got was a trip to Seattle.
It's weird here.

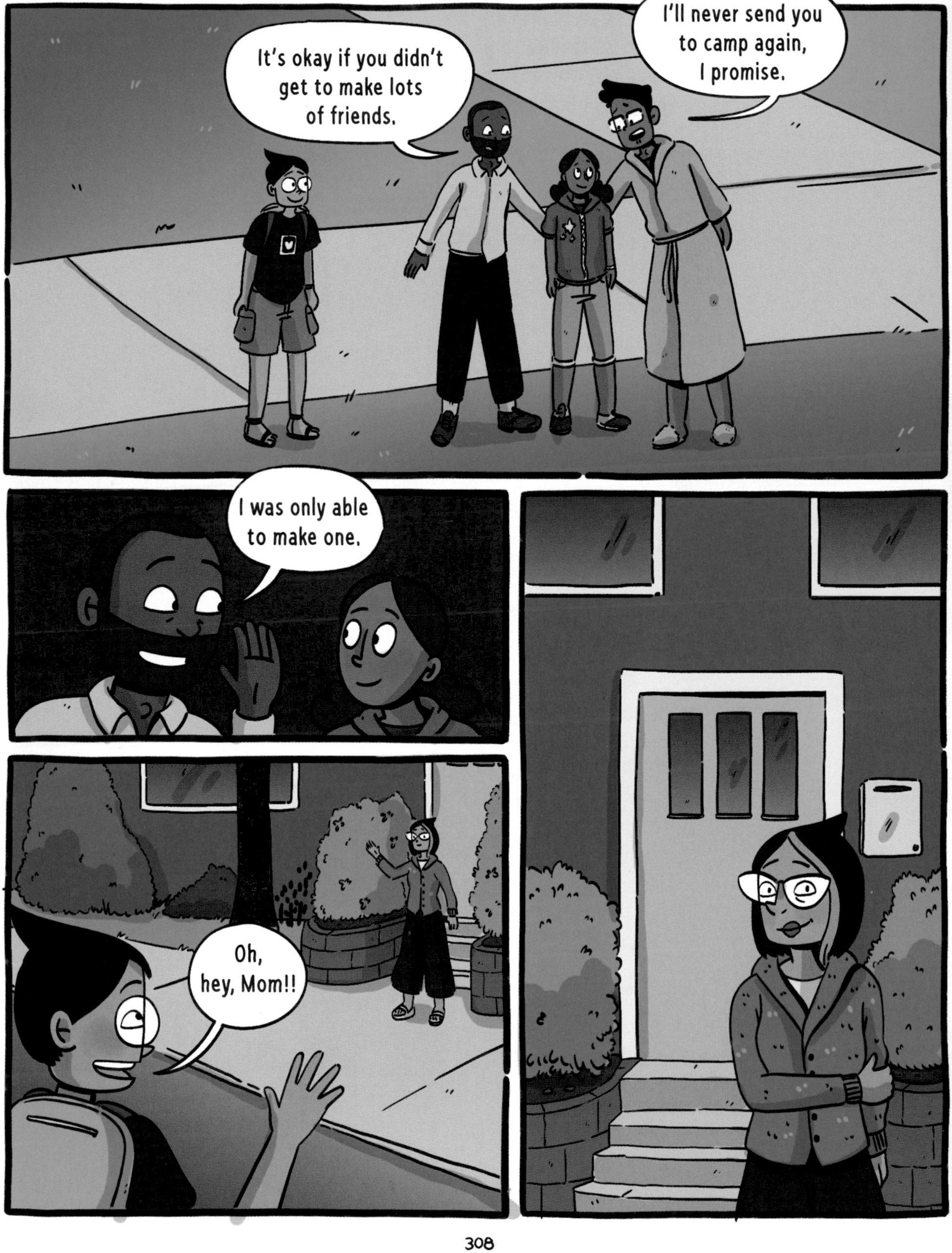
It's okay if you didn't get to make lots of friends.
I'll never send you to camp again, I promise.
I was only able to make one.
Oh, hey, Mom!!

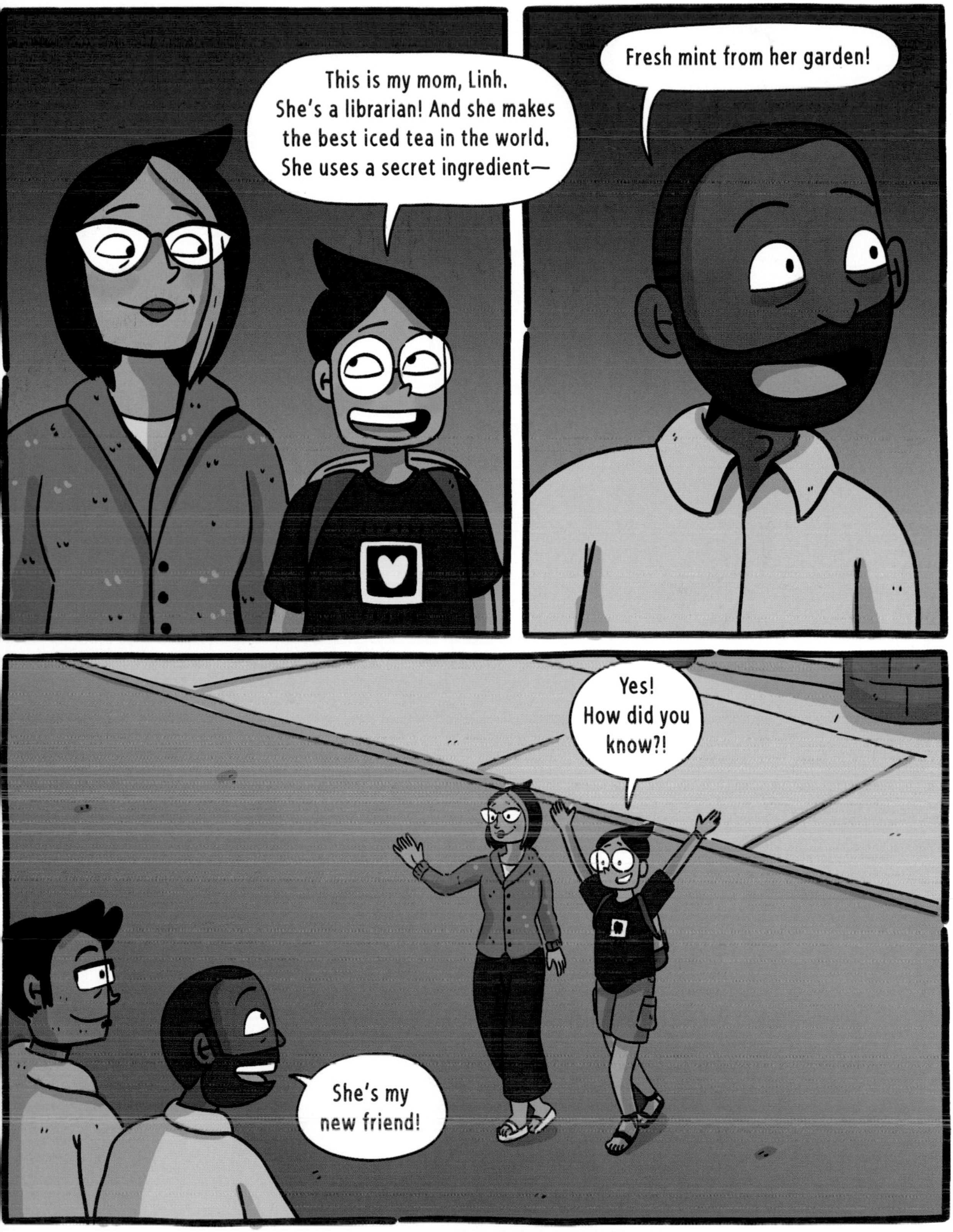
This is my mom, Linh. She's a librarian! And she makes the best iced tea in the world. She uses a secret ingredient—
Fresh mint from her garden!
Yes! How did you know?!
She's my new friend!

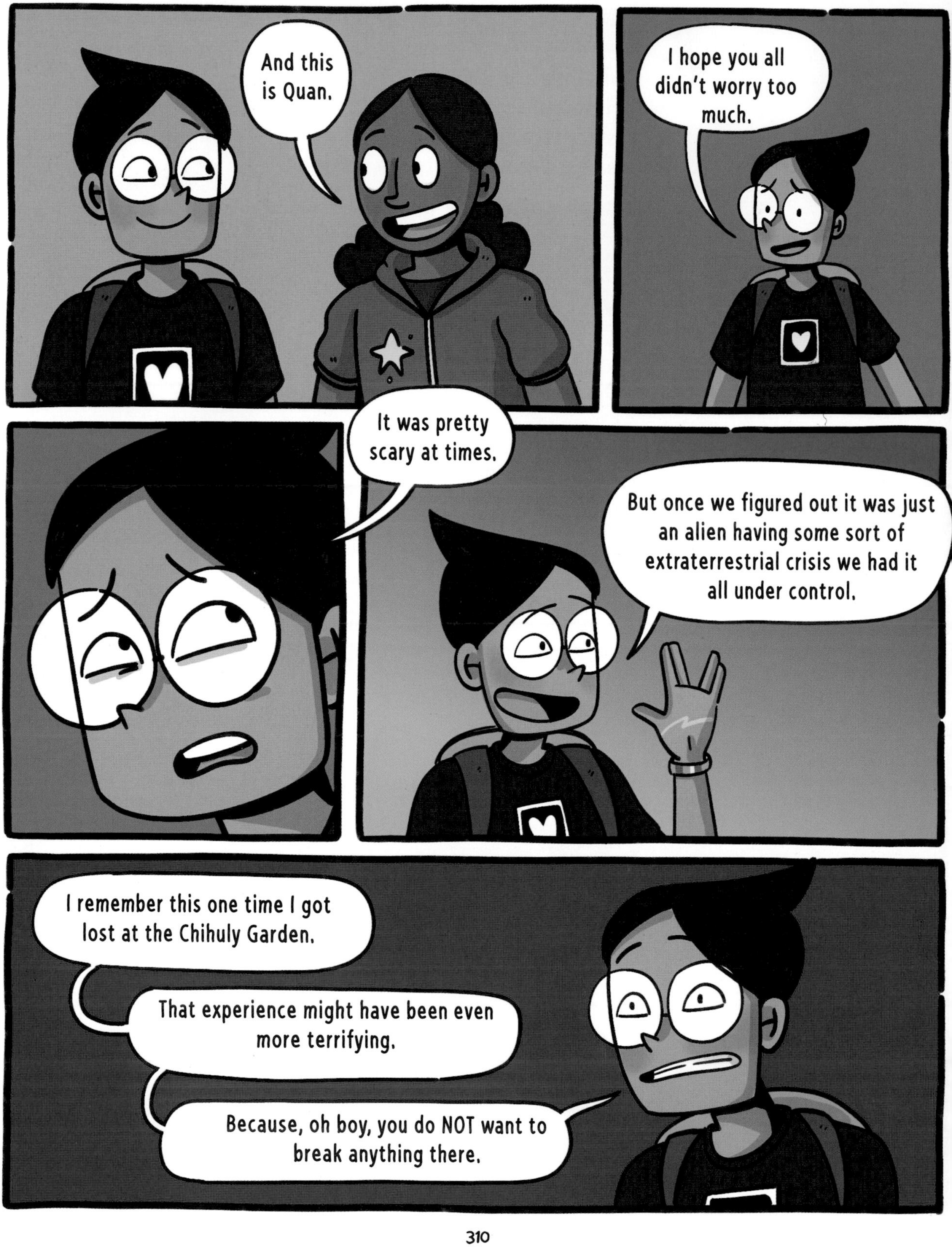
And this is Quan.
I hope you all didn't worry too much.
It was pretty scary at times.
But once we figured out it was just an alien having some sort of extraterrestrial crisis we had it all under control.
I remember this one time I got lost at the Chihuly Garden.
That experience might have been even more terrifying.
Because, oh boy, you do NOT want to break anything there.

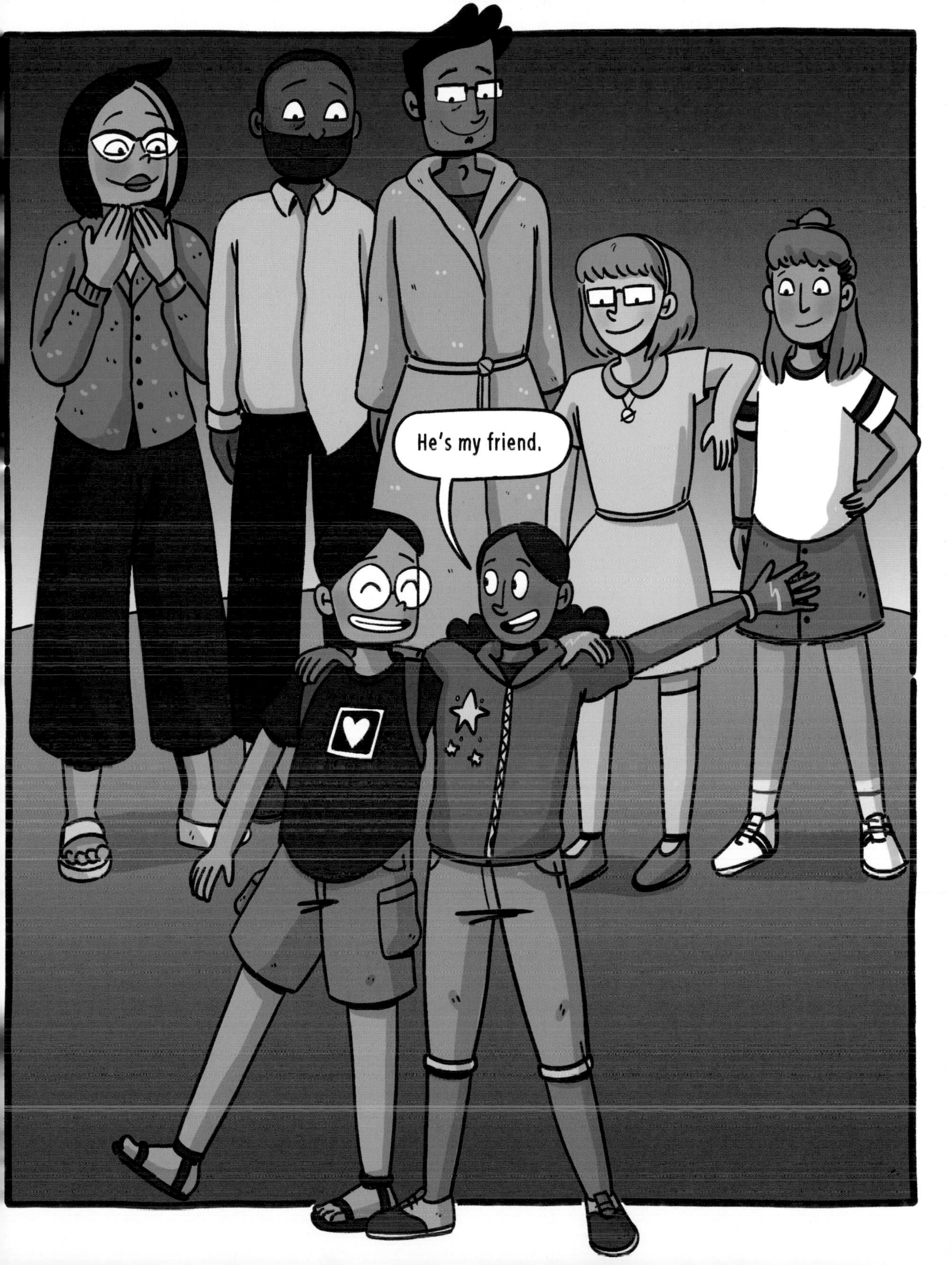
He's my friend.

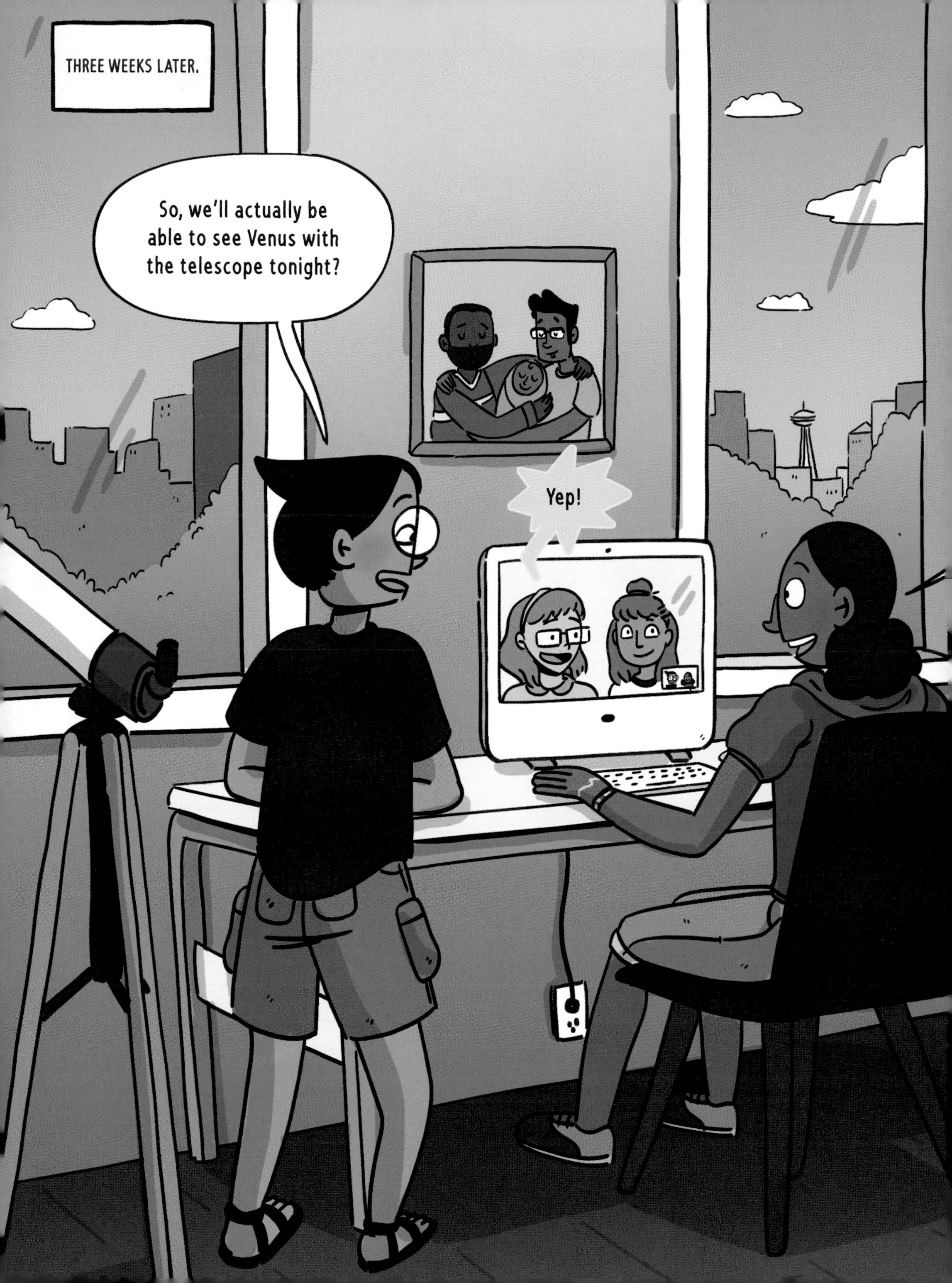
THREE WEEKS LATER.
So, we'll actually be able to see Venus with the telescope tonight?
Yep!

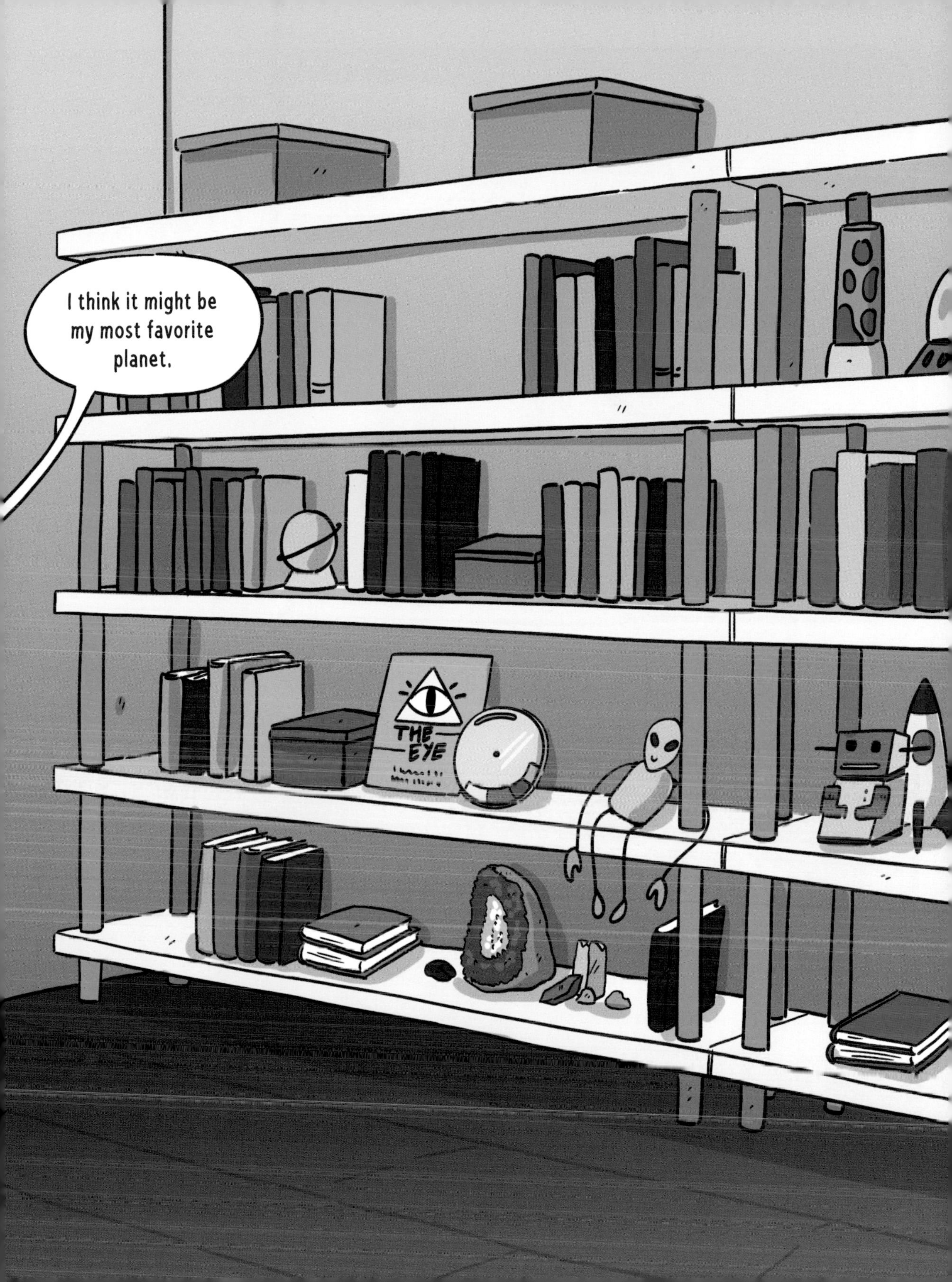
I think it might be my most favorite planet.
THE EYE

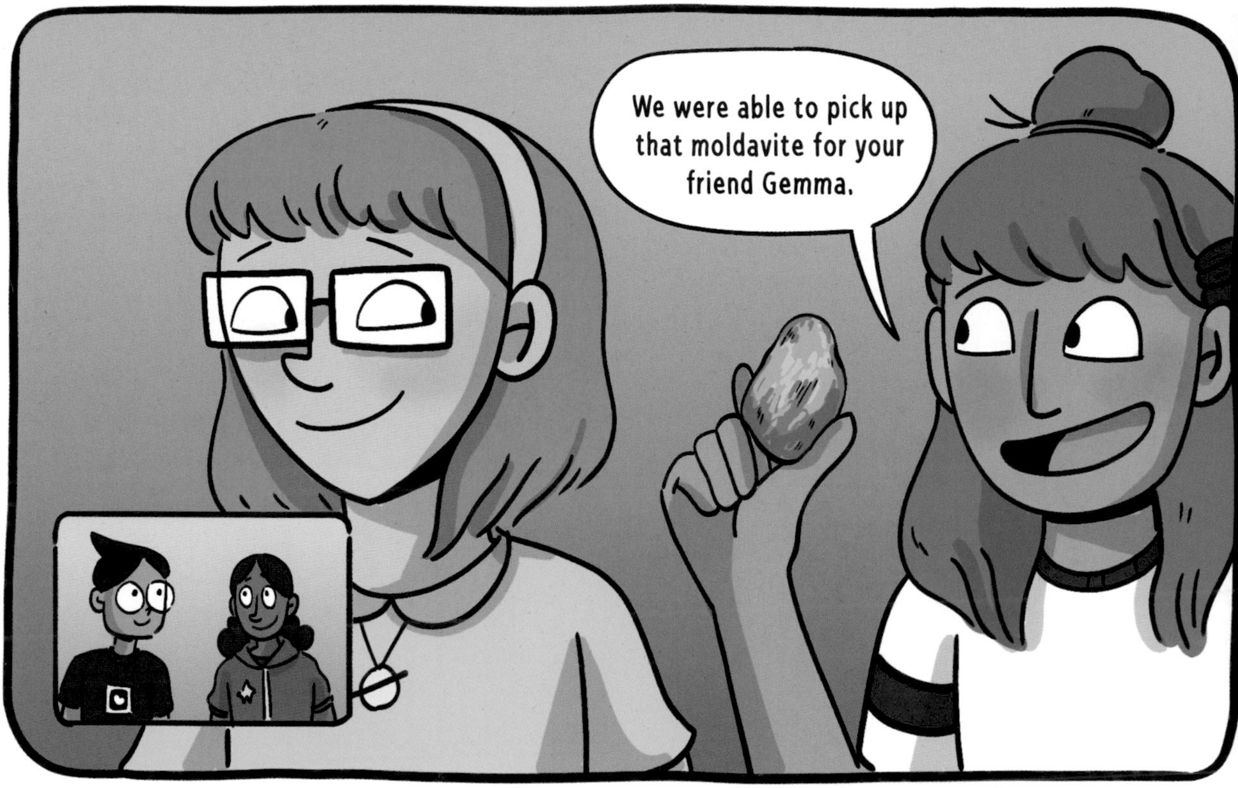
We were able to pick up that moldavite for your friend Gemma.

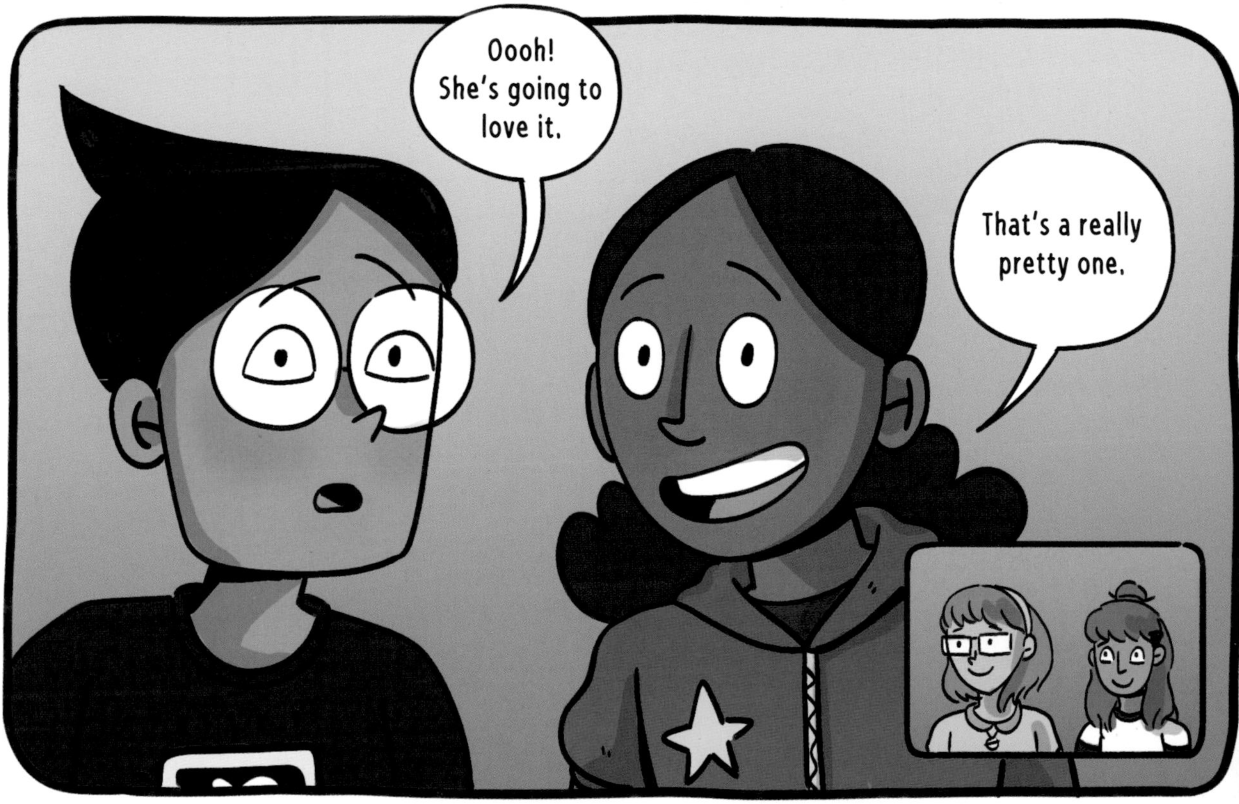
Oooh! She's going to love it.
That's a really pretty one.

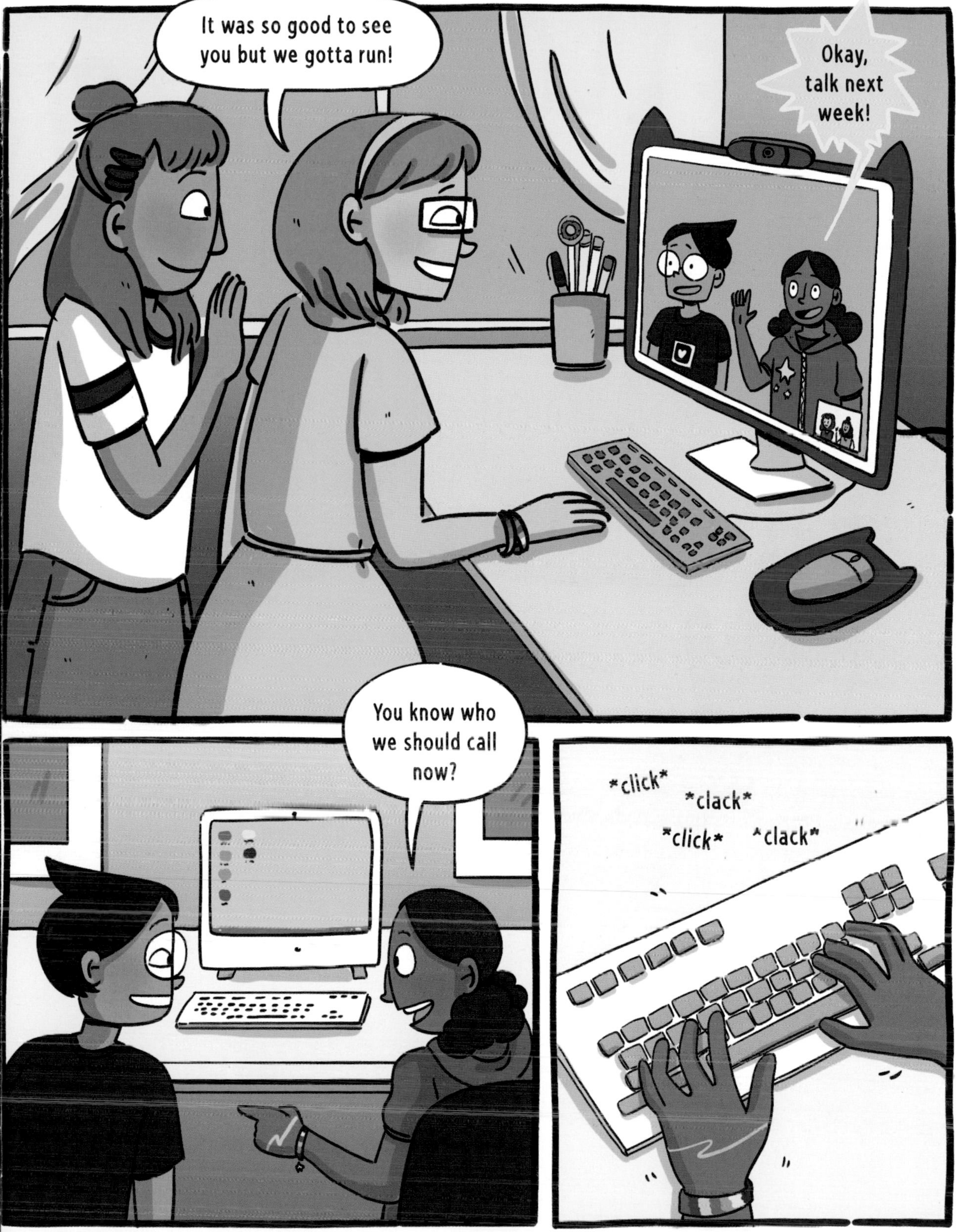
It was so good to see you but we gotta run!
Okay, talk next week!
You know who we should call now?
click
clack
click
clack

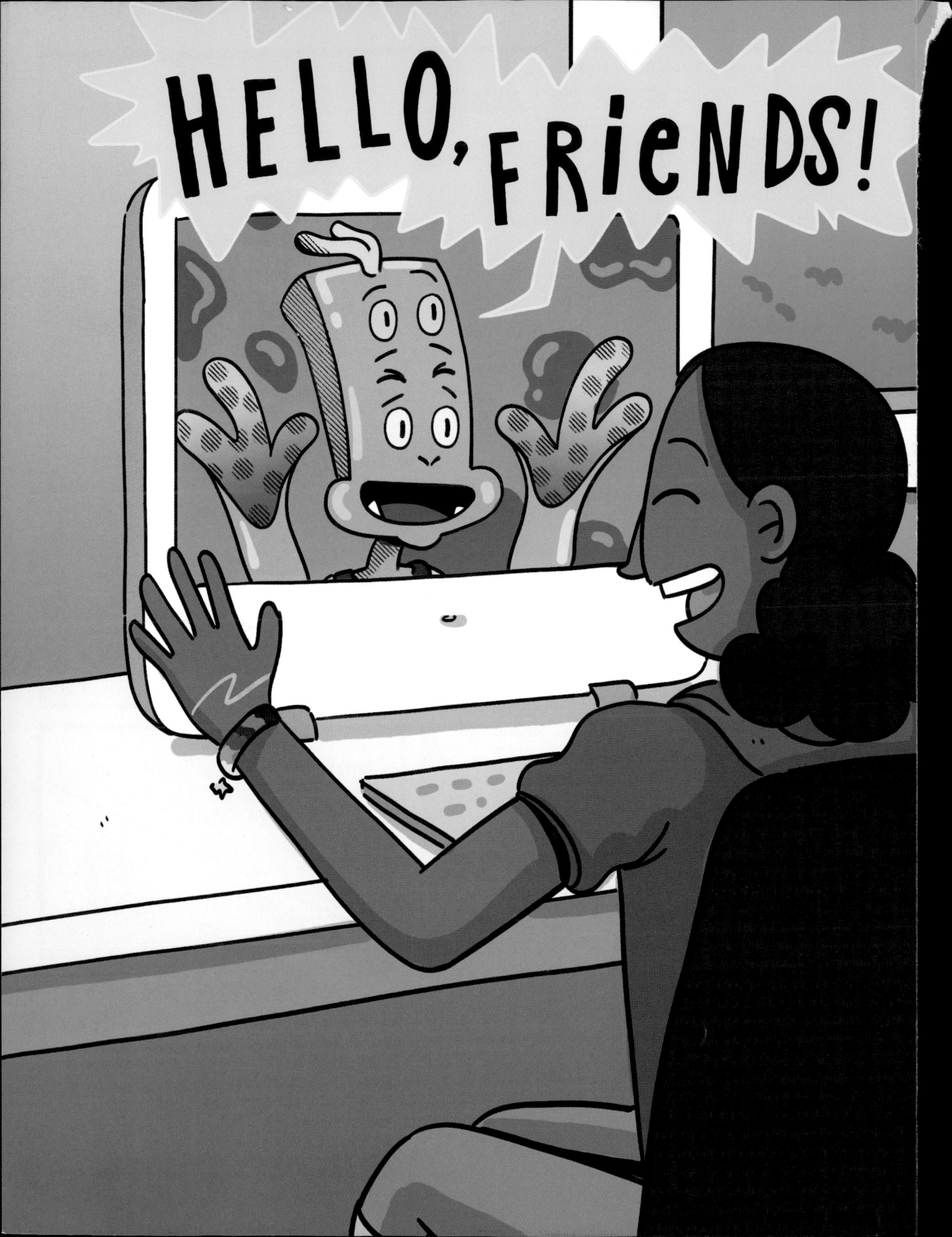
HELLO, FRIENDS!

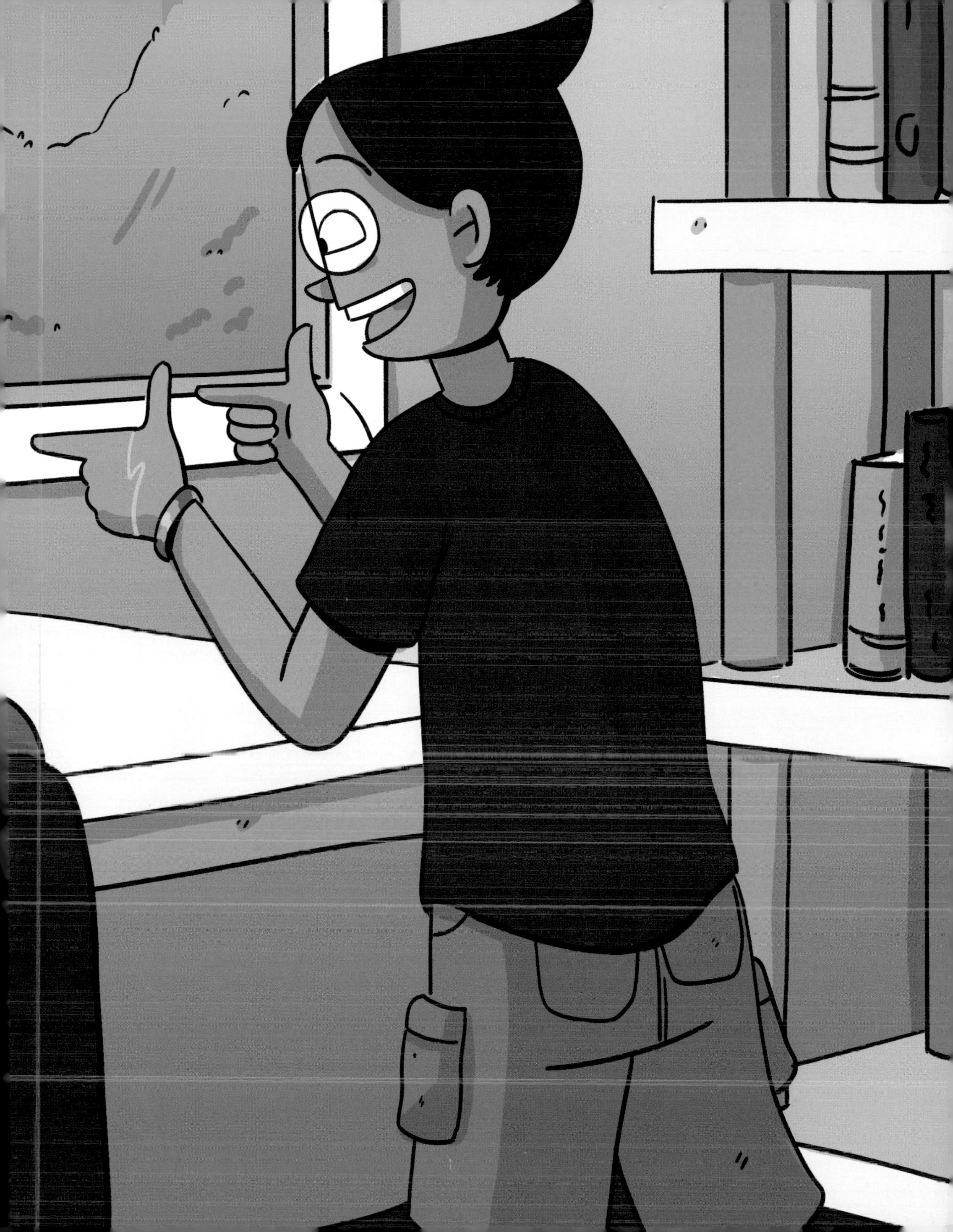

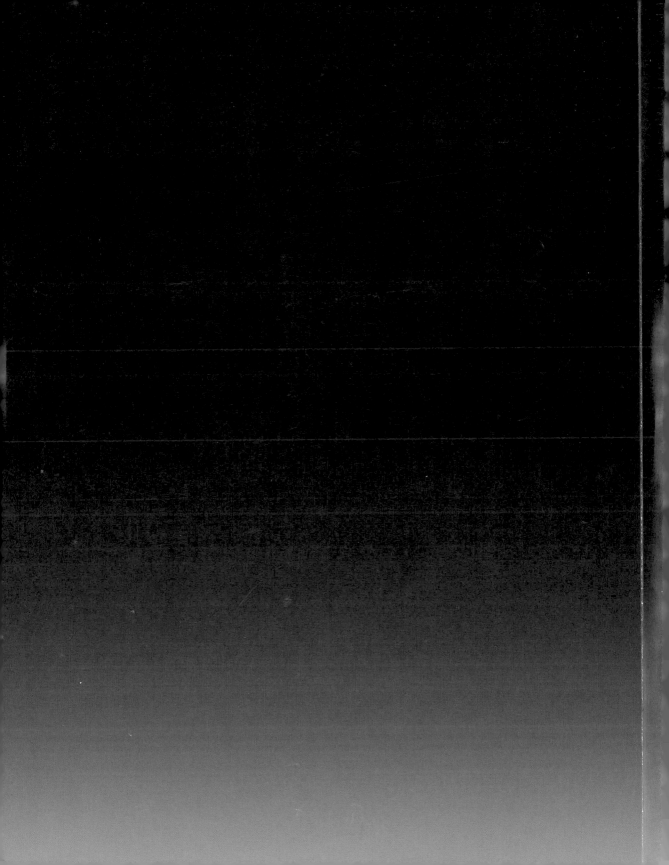